Wolf Blood

Book Two of the Wild Hunt

Tyler W. D. Stewart

Supposed Crimes LLC • Matthews, North Carolina

Published in the United States.

ISBN: 978-1-952150-01-2

www.supposedcrimes.com

This book is typeset in Goudy Old Style.

For Trish Clarke and her sisters, the essence of *Mahihkan*.
May we all face adversity with
such courage and love.

Chris Sawatsky, the bad man. That's the bad man right there.

And Mary and Fern Stewart,
who shone too brightly
for this world.

PART I.
SEWERS (LATE SUMMER)

ONE
Shadow Spawn

SHE WOKE to blinding light.

The mechanical *hiss* was a whisper at first—then it probed her mind for any thought beyond nothingness. She stirred, vision seared a painful white, her body paralyzed as if the air were solid and immovable.

Strange lights flickered and danced through her fogged vision. *Gunfire,* her instincts growled. Her spiking heartrate matched the rapid-fire pace. Her scarred extremities tingled with feeling. Blood flushed her skin with warmth.

She bolted upright.

Wires that were coiled around her wrists and neck tried crushing her to the bedframe like a python squeezing its dinner. She screamed—or tried to, but her throat was clogged with tarred-black hoses, her body snagged in a tangle of wires that slung over her bed like vines in a jungle.

Familiar pain ached like blisters. Blots of crimson dotted her skin when she ripped the dozens of barbs and needles from her veins. Sticky mucus spattered along the hoses as she yanked them from her throat, retching hoarsely, and disregarded the shriek of the machinery alarms. She swung her legs over the edge of the cot.

Where am I?

Her feet slapped cold tile floor. Stark white walls, crinkled curtains drawn across the only window, and a door with no discernable handle—there was no escape. Her breaths grew rapid and uneven, her heart outpaced the beat of a hummingbird's wings.

The door *clicked*, shifting open.

She sprang for the sliver of an opening. Her fingers snagged around someone's collar, smearing black marks across the stiff bleached material. Wide brown eyes stared back at her, bright with the terror of caught prey. A woman she did not recognize. Then a sharp scream pierced the silence.

"Code Seven!"

Celeste swung fast and hard, and connected a fist to the woman's jaw. Her head snapped back and her knees folded under her. Celeste let the groaning woman dangle in her grip, studying the ripple of shadows beyond the door's opening, listening to boots shuffling across the linoleum floor. She glanced over the woman's coat, raking her fingers through the front breast pocket. Crumpled bits of paper. Loose tissue. Then she found something sharp enough to dig for bone marrow if she had to; a ballpoint pen. She pressed its inked tip against the woman's throat like a blade.

"Don't move," she warned. Blood trickled from the tip of the pen.

"P-p-please," the woman gurgled, spitting blood from her busted lips. She was trembling to the point of convulsion. "W-we're here t-to help."

"Shut *up*."

"Dear girl," a mellow voice sang from the doorway. A wolf in disguise, she could sniff him out, luring an injured wolf to be prey. *I won't eat you*, it lied. "She's right. You are in a safe place, there's no need for you to feel alarmed."

She was simmering with fear. "Don't believe you."

"Look." The door, already slightly ajar, creeped open. "There's nobody here who wishes you any harm, dear." The opening revealed a curving corridor and fluorescent light that beamed twice as bright from the alabaster walls and bleached-white tiles. A small crowd was drawn to the commotion, a storm of whispers brewing.

Celeste propped her frightened hostage as a shield between herself and the pack of unwelcome guests. Which, to her, may as well be snarling wolves. But there were no rifles aimed at her, no soldiers armored in shadows—only a flock of women, snugly dressed in the same stiff white outfit. Their gawking faces were powdered and flushed red, their hair curled and sculpted to towering swirling shapes, or trimmed chin-length and layered with colored shades.

They're dolls, not fighters.

Still, her tight grip secured her hostage.

"Ladies," the man whispered. Slowly, he edged through the doorway, both arms raised parallel to his shoulders. His dark, wolfish eyes were fixed on hers, but she saw the color drain from his face. She could smell his fear. "There are no weapons, no restraints, and certainly nobody strong enough to try and hold you down."

Grey stubble furred his cheeks, and his brown-greying hair was unruly and neglected. Slender, almost gaunt, with indented cheeks as if he puckered his lips under his mask. Horned glasses slipped down the bridge of his oily nose. She scanned his attire: identical white scrubs, gloves stretched over his hands like a second skin, facemask tugged tight over his chin. The fluorescent light sheened off his tanned leather shoes as he took another small step towards her.

"Will you allow my nurse Annie to stand?" With a forced chuckle, he added, "Now that the hens have finished clucking?"

"Doctor?" she croaked.

He gave her a small nod. "Yes." Another pace forward. "How about you let Annie go, and you and I have a little chat?"

She shook her head. "No."

He chuckled warily. "It's okay, I'll keep my hands up."

"No," she repeated, jerking her head at Annie. "Save her."

The pen plunged into Annie's neck. Blood squirted through her fingers.

Dropping the bleeding hostage, she dashed for the doorway. The doctor shoved past her and cradled Annie as she choked.

Celeste stumbled. Her guts burned. Her muscles seized like old rusted gears.

The white hallway was a giant glaring light as she sprinted, half-blind and woozy, past a sea of powdered-rouge faces and deer-in-the-headlights expressions. A blood-flecked gown whipped loosely around her waist. Cold air clawed at her exposed thighs. But it was the mechanical ambience that chilled her furless flesh far worse than the sterile air. It was a cage. A treeless forest of metal and glass. No place for a wolf.

Someone reached for her, vials and needles pinched between their fingers. Even through a fog of weakness, her fist found a target. A solid punch struck the soft features of someone's face, staining her bandages bright red.

Perfume hung heavy in the corridor, stinging her eyes and nostrils. *Nothing like the flowers mother used to wear.* She scrunched her nose in disgust. *Pampered princesses–*

"There she is!"

The moment she rounded the hallway corner, she fell under the sweeping aim of a rifle. Her bare feet slid across the cold tile as if the linoleum were ice, then stumbled her to a halt. There were dozens. Fogged goggles and black featureless masks obscured every face like plague doctors, as if the air she breathed out were tainted with the sickness.

Shit!

She spun on her heels and fled the way she came. Heavy boots stomped after her, and her heart synced with the rapid pace. Soldiers rushed through the corridor like a raging river of shadows. Wave after wave of armored men pulled her beneath a violent obsidian surface. Scales gleamed with blood. Crimson eyes rippled fury. She howled her fury, fists swinging.

"Stand down!"

The gravitas in the command forced each weapon to lower. She stared through throngs of soldiers, then glimpsed the steely glare of her uncle. A recently shaved face revealed the set of scars lining his chin like her father once bore, and for a moment, that's who she saw.

"Celeste." An old, familiar smile warmed his glacial expression. "I'm sorry you woke up alone."

Someone behind him squealed with excitement, a cascade of red hair burning bright. Celeste forced a smile in return, then recoiled from the cold draft in her soul. In the shadows, she saw them. Those eyes, a piercing blue blotted by storm clouds, glared at her with creeping malevolence. Patches of scarred skin trickled blood. The monster of her past, her nightmares.

The Blonde Man!

"No!"

Her eyes snapped open.

Sunlight stabbed through the ripped tent-flaps and roused her from a troubled daze. Her eyes flickered, as if she could scrub them clean of what she saw. *It felt so real again.* She groaned and shifted under her blankets. Everything ached and protested existence. Sleep remained elusive. Endless nightmares seemed an appropriate and bitter companion for chronic pain.

I need peace.

Beside her, a warm body stirred.

"Are you okay, Celeste?" A honeyed voice soothed her frayed nerves. "Was it the same nightmare?"

Memory.

"Yes," she replied quietly, "the hospital." Her lips were as rough as sandpaper.

A delicate chortle followed her response. "I'd feel a bit guilty for stabbing that poor nurse as well."

"She didn't die," Celeste countered, a bit defensively. "I just needed out."

"You nicked an artery."

"Nothing serious. Uncle said she was back on duty the next week."

"You know, you probably should have apologized," Melina whispered. "Maybe send some fresh herbs or something."

Although not intended as a rebuke, it made Celeste flinch. *Maybe I am overflowing with guilt. Maybe I should...*

Faces flashed through her mind; bloodstained skin, hollow eyes, mouths twisting into an agony of endless screaming.

She shook her head.

Get it together.

"I wasn't meaning to press."

Her fear simmered. "No," she lied. "Just cold."

"I can fix that," her companion purred.

The cot was a cacophony of squeaky screams as Celeste nestled into her comforting embrace, then buried herself deep in the patchy, wool blanket. Melina's balmy breath tickled the back of her neck. Shivers scurried down her spine.

I want to sleep like this all day.

A frothy tongue slathered her with drool.

"Ugh," she sputtered, wiping her lips. "Good morning, boy."

Aurous pressed his icicle-cold nose against her cheek, then growled and nipped at her blanket. Blackish-grey fur tufted in patchy patterns around his mane. His tawny eyes shone into hers.

"I get it," she said with a long sigh. "Bathroom."

Melina pulled away and giggled a melody. "Like you, he's not one for waiting patiently."

Wishing she had fur to keep her as lovingly warm as her blankets, Celeste groaned and tossed them aside. Pain rocked her abdomen. She stood, one hand clamped around her stomach, cursing the damp that invaded her bones.

"You should rest," Melina began, another gentle reminder.

"I'm okay," Celeste said. She shook her boots to startle any critters that took up residence during the chilly night. Last thing she wanted was her toes nibbled on. "Really."

"You're still recovering from being shot!"

"A few grazes, nothing serious." But a shock of pain quickly countered her assertion. "I barely felt it."

"You almost died," Melina squeaked.

"I'm still here."

"Only because they have excellent doctors."

They. Disgust welled in her heart. *Military. Red Dawn.*

Shadows beneath the cot stirred. Blood-red eyes burned through the veil of black, silently stalking its quarry. Her.

Her cheeks warmed at the foolish thought. *There's no monsters under my bed.* Kinked strands of carmine hair fell over her eyes like spilling blood. *Enough.*

"They left scars," Celeste accused.

"That wasn't from..."

She growled, "Not those. On my stomach."

"It doesn't look as bad as my shoulder," countered Melina. Her brow wrinkled over her green glaring eyes and sharply pursed lips, as if Celeste's presence were something she could no longer tolerate. Her finest scowl. It coaxed a small smile from Celeste.

"I'm taking Aurous outside. I need the fresh air."

"Fine," Melina breathed, defeated. "At least let me check your bandages."

"Later," Celeste promised. She wiggled her chilly toes into scratchy woolen socks, then slipped into her stiff boots. No matter how often, or how hard, she scoured clean the old leather, mud persisted in the ridges. There were also splotches of blood on the tips of her laces. Whose blood from streets that ran crimson from the dead, she would never know.

"Hold on," Melina called out, "I'm coming with you."

"Really, I'll be okay."

Her green eyes twinkled like sunlight over lake water. "You're not exactly a *people* person."

Grey clouds churned along violent wind currents like billowing smoke. Jagged mountains rose over the ruins of the nearby city like fangs ripping into carrion. Tufts of torn up grass clumped to the dirt around her boots; the once-glossy meadow had been trampled into a sinking pit of mud. Rainfall, wash water, and waste coagulated around a sea of forest-green tents pitched along the roadside and field. It reeked of a giant latrine.

Streaks of mud fanned behind Aurous as he gave chase to a chunk of meat she tossed for him. He darted through the soldiers crowding across makeshift walkways and gathering around the simple steaming fires, then disappeared under the green island of tents.

The stench of bodily odors and burning rubber residue strangled the air and coalesced into a fog of fumes. The smog sweltered her lungs, but she was grateful to leave the fusty confines of her tent and grind the aches from her muscles. Refusing any pain medication seemed only to prolong her recovery. Or so Melina gently chastised every night over rationed military gruel, when the stabbing pain of a fully belly meant she ate little at best. She feared dependency. She would *not* make the same mistakes as her father.

Countless bullet wounds, lacerations, broken ribs...infections. She grimaced, then chewed her lip. *Maybe I do need rest...*

Shivers twisted her spine.

"It's getting cold, again," whispered Melina. She pulled the collar of her fur-trimmed coat tightly around her neck. The beige fabric was stained darker brown by the waist, splattering up the backside. The bullet holes left from its previous owner had been stitched closed with bright green thread, the same color as her eyes. Red curls bounced over her rosy cheeks as she tucked her chin into her coat. "Doesn't warm up until the sun rises over the mountain."

Celeste nodded. "The chill makes my wounds ache." *And my bones.*

"Do you want to see how the city is faring?"

"I'm *not* staying here long."

"You said that a few weeks ago."

Mud splattered their tent when a line of marching soldiers treaded across the sinking ground. Boisterous and loud, their cadence call echoed from the far-off mountains. She lowered her eyes and avoided any sideway scrutiny.

"I know," Celeste muttered. She pitched another slab of meat over the tents. Aurous nosed the mud in search of its bloody scent.

"Well?"

"I still want to leave."

Melina said, "I'll go with you, wherever. You know that. But I think you should give your uncle a chance."

Celeste glared from under a bruised brow. "You didn't see what they unleashed in the city."

"Because you *left* me in a building with former prisoners. *In the middle of a warzone!*"

Guilt churned her stomach. She recalled abandoning her wolf and Melina for an impulsive desire for revenge against Vega. She drowned under the bloody waves of her memories, woke feverish from nightmares, and still she craved that jolting fear, the rushing warmth of adrenaline. Melina sensed her unease. She was aware the fight had changed her—Vega had *changed* her—but she'd been trapped in the confines of the hospital, oblivious to the destruction Celeste wilfully treaded. Horror had risen from the spilled blood of men tainted from Vega's touch. *Loosen that thread from the web of deceit and death she wove, and it leads right back to the military.*

My uncle.

She still hadn't informed anybody of the explosives Vega had placed under the city. *In Melina's eyes, I'm callous and cold, with little feelings for anything beyond blood.* Her eyes misted. *Maybe it's true.*

"I'm sorry." She couldn't make it sound sincere enough.

Soft fingers delicately traced the jagged grooves that scarred her hand. Melina squeezed and commented lightly, "You've been avoiding everyone for months. Just give it a chance, that's all I'm asking. Get to know the camp." She shrugged. "It's not that bad, really. And everyone is nicer than the few I met at the hospital."

Her scars tingled. "One chance."

"I'm glad you agreed." Melina raised her voice over the buzzing clamor. "Because I told him you would be ready today."

An engine roared like some territorial beast. Wheels spun into the camp grounds and ripped chunks of dirt into muddy rain. An armored truck slid through the slop that sunk their tents and came to a rumbling stop.

Its patchy-green paintjob replicated the tangled verdure of the woodlands. The windows were unbarred, which she found rather peculiar, until she glimpsed the gouges, chips, and jagging cracks in the bullet-proof glass. The truck was larger than a military Hummer, with an engine loud enough to thunder through the ground as it idled. It wasn't weaponized like a tank but outfitted to transport troops or cargo. *Or beasts.*

The door swung open like a heavy gate.

She swore it was her father who jumped down into the mud

and splattered his pants brown. Thin white scars ran from his neck up to his freshly shaven chin. Tousled black hair, lanky limbs with ropy muscles, the curve in his jaw, and sun-kissed skin all resembled her father. For a heart wrenching moment, she wanted to call for him and fall into his embrace. But his bright eyes were a stark difference to her father's chestnut-dark irises.

Instead, she bit her lip and offered a stiff nod. Her uncle, however, smiled so broadly she thought invisible fingers pinched his cheeks into a clown's expression. He opened his arms and greeted her warmly.

"Celeste! It's good to see you up and about!"

"Be careful," warned Melina, her catty eyes narrowed.

"Ah," her uncle breathed, and clapped Celeste's shoulders. She managed a grin in reply. "You look better than you did trying to flee from the infirmary."

"Sorry. How is Annie?"

Her uncle waved his hand and dismissed her mechanical apology. "She's a tad frightened, but otherwise completely fine. And quite displeased, mind you, but also grateful when I reminded her that you could have chosen to take her head then and there."

"So," Celeste said, "what am I ready for?"

"Oh?" Her uncle threw a smirk to Melina. "The darling little nurse-to-be hasn't informed you yet?"

"Mr. Cavaily," said Melina, giggling. "Learning how to change bandages and clean wounds is a far cry from becoming a nurse."

"Please, call me Jordan."

"Yes, Mr. Ca—Jordan. She needed as much sleep as she could get."

Celeste's anger simmered. "Will somebody please explain what is going on?"

Jordan clapped his hands together. "I knew you'd become restless as you healed, especially if you're anything like my brother."

I've been restless about leaving.

"So," he continued, "I've decided to give you a job if you want it. Responsibility."

"A job?" Her eyebrow raised at the thought of her old mop and bucket, with which she could never scrub the stench of *everything* from, that she had used to clean her old cow's corral. "What kind of job?"

"Something to suit your...special needs, of course." He motioned to the truck behind him. "Hop on up, and I'll show you what I mean."

"Wait!" Melina called out, coaxing Aurous away from the truck with another string of meat. "We have to change your bandages!"

For the first time in ages, Celeste gave her a real smile. "I'll be fine. Something to look forward to when I get back."

She climbed into the truck after her uncle.

They left the campsite and drove to the ruins of the city. The truck crashed through the thicket overgrowing across the edges of the road, snapping branches and brittle leaves under the rigid tread of its wheels. Her head throbbed as the engine roared like extended thunder.

The thick windows blurred outlines of other campsites they rolled past and the mountain silhouettes in the distance. Features, signs, and even the road beyond a few feet were impossible to view. Instead, her uncle kept his gaze fixed on the dashboard console. A small monitor with a split screen displayed the road ahead of them and behind in glass vividly bright detail.

But the shadow in her reflection seized her attention. She tugged at her shirt collar, exposed her neck and shoulder. Black scars dappled her skin like careless strokes of a paintbrush. The fractal patterns consumed the left of her face, dotted her eye like a bruise, then vanished into her hairline. Her minced hands were stained with the same tarry taint.

"Don't worry about it," her uncle shouted over the engine roar, sensing her disgust. "Freckles are more noticeable." The truck lurched when he shifted the gear stick. The engine sputtered, then thundered. "Feel lucky, little niece of mine. Not many people survive a near-death infection like that."

But I still look like a freak.

"I still can't believe Mengele and his team were able to stitch you back together." He shook his head in disbelief. "There you were, full of bullets and bleeding to death. Then we find out you'd been infected, probably for hours. It was a miracle you qualified for the counteragent. I know it's not a cure, but the infection is inert and contagious only by blood transfusion. At first, I'd thought you a lost cause, just a girl caught in the crossfire. Or perhaps a fleeing bandit. Though, you looked far too young and delicate. They only seemed to keep the rough sons of bitches."

"I remember," she replied quietly. Her uncle didn't hear her, and she just stared at her scarred hands instead of repeating herself.

I remember begging for an end to the pain. To let death claim me. But it didn't.

And I remember the repercussions of life at the hands of Mengele. The Blonde man.

"Christ," he spat. "That goddamn map...your father was an asshole, you know that? Big, bleeding heart, but a mean prick. He swore he would never speak to me again and he made damn sure of it. But he was a good man. I'm glad he lost some of his stubbornness with old age."

Celeste snorted, genuinely pleased. "He didn't lose it. Sorry Uncle, but he didn't speak of you until the night he passed." Her eyes flickered. "After months of begging him to leave."

"Right," her uncle replied with a slight chuckle. "Of course, his little princess would be the only exception to his bullheaded stance."

"He told me the military executed those displaying symptoms of infection, whether they were transforming or not."

His jawline creased. "We did."

"Why?"

He hesitated, peering at her from the corner of his eye. "People were panicking. They thought it was a hoax, that we were enforcing martial law on citizens merely to control them. They fought back. But that was when the full effects of the sickness were becoming known. Most people died very quickly. Others...transformed. Even more were caught and torn between both stages. It was pandemonium, and a terrible decision."

"Do you regret giving the orders?"

"I didn't give the orders," he replied defensively. "But I regret taking part in the slaughter."

"What about using those *monsters* on the bandits?"

He almost snarled, "Look, Celeste. We only infected volunteers with a controlled form of the sickness, those too weak or injured to fight otherwise. Our variation does *not* spread the infection. The bandit queen took it too far; she infected all her soldiers, knowing once they were killed, most would likely transform—and spread it further. It was a dirty way to fight, but sometimes you bring fire against fire. It was a desperate act to seize the city with minimum casualties, especially when the *bitch* was conducting experiments and tampering with the sickness to make it more contagious. Your father would never agree, but it had to be done." With a glint of displeasure in his sideways glance, he said,

"You should be thankful we had such a method on hand. We don't experiment nefariously—we're looking for a cure."

She was eager to steer the conversation elsewhere. "Dad stayed mad at you all these years."

He smirked, though his eyes betrayed a shadow of pain. "I bet your mother was all too happy about that."

She shrugged. "I don't remember her hating anybody."

"Oh, she hated me. A demon, I am. Her words, really. Spiteful little minx."

"She was a beautiful woman," growled Celeste. She drummed her fingers with dwindling patience. "I miss her."

"Right, of course. She had a fiery spirit, that's for sure."

Maybe you're the asshole. "So," she said, "what is this job you want me for?"

"The job is a new responsibility and honor."

"Honor?"

"And thanks."

"I don't understand."

"It's a reward for killing the Bandit Queen and releasing the prisoners in the hospital dungeon. Stonem accepted on your behalf." Her uncle winked at her. "He said you'd be more than eager to begin."

She narrowed her eyes. Curiosity percolated. "Eager to begin what?"

"Leading your own squad."

Uncle cut the engine off and the truck rumbled silent.

Stepping into the verdure of the woodlands was like falling into the embrace of an old lover. The rich fragrance of evergreen pines, baking in the sun's midday heat, filled her lungs and cleared her sinuses. Sunlight glittered through boughs with a brilliance that was lost on the sinking mud pits back at camp. Long emerald-green grass rippled with the wind's gentle breath. Roosting robins and sparrows sang through the needled treetops with a rhythm her beating heart echoed.

Her uncle shouldered two black body-length duffel bags retrieved from the backseat of the truck. She reached for the third and dismissed his raised brow. She hauled it out of the backseat and struggled with a shaky grip. Disturbingly, she began to think, it was no different than dragging a dead body. Blood soaking between her fingers, eyes glazing and greying over. She shuddered. The swaying movement agitated her tender belly wounds.

I should be in bed still.

Brown pine needles poked, jabbed, and snagged bloody welts across her skin as they ventured through thick boughs and twisting branches, leaf litter *crunching* under Uncle's heavy tread. After a few minutes they came to a small meadow.

"There you are," her uncle state proudly. "Your very own squad."

Strangers turned to face her.

"This is her," one asked incredulously, "the Queen Slayer?" A young woman scoffed, flicking her fingers across the smooth oak-brown Springfield rifle that extended longer than her arms. A bolt-action relic from the Old West stories her father told around the fire. Glimmering blonde hair was pulled back into a knotted ponytail, revealing a furrowed brow over piercing ice-blue eyes, and a long, slender face like a horse's features. She was tall, a foot more than Celeste, and held herself with a rigidly straight posture, like a soldier standing at attention. Supple and lean like a wolf. Her sun-kissed complexion shone through the gloomy clearing.

The largest of them said, "Small," and his bulbous throat swelled like a bullfrog as he chortled with amusement. His entire body jiggled, but she saw the lumpy definition beneath layers of fat tissue. There was lean muscle deep under that fleshy coat. Each side of his small head was shaved to fuzz, leaving a row of spiked hair down the middle. White scars ran across his head in a spiderwebbed pattern. He squinted his beady eyes to gain a better look. "Real tiny."

"Alright, enough," her uncle barked, bemused. He jerked his thumb toward the light-haired girl. "The blonde one is Snyder, she's a top tier marksman. And that mountain of a man we call Twist."

"Hi," he greeted dully. "Queen Slayer."

"Why do they keep calling me that?"

"Because," he replied with a wink, "you're a legend for killing The Phantom Woman."

Another stranger stepped forward and pushed her stubby-barreled machine pistol to her hip. Her weapon was stockier than Celeste's own revolver, with a clip nearly the length of its own barrel. The woman was short, with black hair kinked around her shoulders, tousled from her stiff stride, and skin the rich colour of ochre like a sunbathed woodland. A heart-shaped face and bronze eyes that shone and brimmed wonder. Cheekbones sharp enough to cut. Perfectly white teeth flashed behind her growing smile. She extended a greeting, and after a moment's hesitation, Celeste took the woman's hand in a firm shake.

"I've been looking forward to meeting you." She said in a husky voice. "You're like, wicked cool. Ma'am."

"Kiss ass," Snyder hissed under a breath.

"Name is Nadie," she said, "engineer by heart, but a survivalist and tracker by family trade. Need anything jerry-rigged and I'm your best bet."

The tubby man proudly blurted out, "Twist."

"Right," Celeste said. "Anyone else feel like sharing?"

"Clark." Small and wiry like a darting field mouse, hair shaved to his pale scalp. His face was craggy with blackheads and pimples from the throes of youth. He was young and held himself as confident as Snyder or any soldier she'd met. "Not sure what my role is yet, but I'd love to stick close to you, beautiful."

Face burning red, Celeste opened her mouth to respond before Snyder sneered, "Really? Look at those ugly black marks on her face."

"What scars?" he countered smugly. "They're freckles, right? Either way, I can dig a tough chick."

Anger percolated. Blood soured her tongue as she gnawed her lip. Uncle's intense gaze burned holes in the back of her skull.

"Haven't you heard the rumors? She's an Inert." Snyder shrugged. "If the sickness is sexy, she's *hot.*"

"They wouldn't let her out if she was contagious," Clark scoffed. Then, stricken, asked, "Would they?"

"Ironic," sneered Snyder, "it took a monster to bring down a monster."

"Are you always this cheery?"

"Only on good days."

Clark gave an obnoxious snort. Snyder idly tapped a finger on the hilt of her oak-brown Springfield.

"Enough!" Celeste snarled like a cornered wolf. Her mind reeled and rage boiled her face red. The primal part of her mind roared for the blonde bitch's blood. For her knife to carve that smug grin into a crimson frown. She steeled herself. Her wounded pride swelled and sharpened her senses with adrenaline.

"All right," she said with a sweeping gaze. She pointed a scarred finger to a hulking man with more muscle stacked on his short and stocky frame than humanly possible, and dark hair longer than hers braided into a thick coiling rope. A polished gold-plated shotgun leaned against his massive shoulders with stubby twin barrels. He grinned through a prickly black beard. "You. Details."

"Name's Harn," he drawled in a thick accent. "Close-quarter combat. Former tanker. I like making things go *boom.* I admire your work, little warrior. I look forward to spilling blood with you." A slight nod out of respect.

She returned the gesture, eyeing his massive height, then turned to the man beside him. Slicked hair, tinged brown like tanned leather, curled around his mousy eyes. Dark stubble speckled his cream-beige skin. The corner of his mouth twitched, almost offering her a smile.

"Colbat," he replied with a voice as smooth as a babbling brook. "Long-range, and a brilliant shot. I'd be more than happy to prove it to you right now."

"Right," replied Celeste, a trickle of blood warming her tongue. "But not necessary right now. We can run some simple drills—"

"Great," muttered the blonde, "I'm stuck taking orders from a *shadow spawn.*"

Celeste hissed through clenched teeth, "And I said *enough.*"

Anger danced in Snyder's striking blue eyes. She set her jaw and pursed her thin, pale lips.

"Drop!" Celeste barked suddenly. Snyder flinched, and the pimple-faced Clark chuckled. To him, she winked and said, "You too, hotshot."

Their unblinking gazes raked her.

"And do what exactly?" Snyder questioned slowly.

"Fifty push-ups," Celeste replied coldly. "Training starts now."

"M-ma'am," Clark stammered, grinning that stupid grin. "We do countless exercises during our morning routines. Wouldn't our time be better spent on shooting or blade dueling? I heard you were an expert with a machete."

"Seventy-five," was her bitter response. Celeste narrowed her eyes until the boy gulped and dropped to his belly. Snyder grumbled and grudgingly followed. The surly blonde held her tongue.

"How many for us?" Twist asked with a dull but innocent tone. He heaved his rear into the dirt and rolled to his belly, kicking up a cloud of dust. "Lots?"

"Until I say stop."

She heard Snyder click her tongue between sharp breaths. "A leader ordering us into the dirt when it looks like she couldn't perform a single push-up to save her life."

Instincts compelled her to reach for the revolver; her fingers slid across its cold steel. Her muscles tensed. *I can't kill her.* Her heart pumped deeper at the thought of it. *But I can break her goddamn skull...*

She relaxed and breathed in the balmy air, shifted her stance, then dropped to her hands and pressed herself flat against the ground. Flames spread from her wounds and lanced through her limbs, shocking her cold, but she pushed up against the dirt, then lowered again. Her arms pumped; the others were quickly outpaced.

Nadie whispered, "Shut you up, blondeie."

"You're just used to the filth," she countered coldly. "Your people scrub it for a living, and pick up candy from the ground."

"Not all brown people are latina, yo. I'm Native, not a stereotype," Nadie shot back. "*Moniyaw.*"

"What the hell did you just call me?"

"If I reach fifty before you," huffed Celeste, face misted with sweat. "You're doing double."

Snyder bit her tongue. Celeste wouldn't tear her gaze away from the irreverent blonde. Her muscles seized solid like rigor mortis. She pushed on, bones creaking in protest. Blood flecked the grass below her. Old wounds ripped open and soaked through her clothes with a creeping warmth. She didn't stop.

When she finally did, pain raked her belly with hot iron claws, and she nearly doubled over as she stood. Her coat was staining dark red. The others slowed and stared with a mix of apprehension and uncertainty. Snyder cringed in disgust.

"Commander," Nadie began.

Celeste cut her off. "Finish, then we test your aim."

She turned her back to them as the warmth drained from her face. The sounds of their grunts and breathless chatter faded, and the landscape twisted into a whirlpool of colors. She staggered back to the truck with the help of her uncle.

"Brilliant," he said, though she barely heard. "You established yourself as a serious commander from the start. They're a promising bunch, but they need discipline. I'm glad we picked the right leader."

He leaned her against the truck. If she'd had any content in her belly, she would have retched over the giant mudded wheels.

"It's in your blood, you know, to lead." He met her weary gaze, beaming pride. "You're going to be great."

"Then I'll need meds," Celeste gasped.

TWO
Paper Tiger

"I KNEW I should have mended your bandages first!"

Celeste winced as the gauze was yanked tight around her waist like she had to suck in her belly to button up her jeans. She bit her tongue. Any half-assed apologies only agitated Melina's patience. Which was proving to be finite.

"I don't even want to know what you were trying to prove."

Celeste overcorrected a smirk into a cartoonish frown. Melina scowled for a moment before she giggled with defeat. She shook her head, and red locks delicately danced against her skin like curling tongues of flame.

Celeste was lost in those glinting emerald eyes; days spent in verdant meadows and rolling mountains, lulled by the warming sun. Lifetimes ago, a long and bloody path to the ruins of civilization. The raucous of men supplanted the symphonies of birdsongs. Their stink overwhelmed. Rainfall congealed the rivers of waste to a fetid swamp. Military life, she had quickly decided, wasn't for her.

She traced Melina's delicate features with a loving gaze. *She's used to living in a community. Having security. I'm used to being alone.*

Mountain whelp. The thought wasn't her own, but it rang like a tolling bell in her mind. *Maybe he was right.*

But he's dead. She bit her lip again. *I'm not.*

"So, were you interested?"

Celeste sighed. "Something to keep me from leaving. For now."

Melina's cheeks burned the same colour of her hair, and Celeste thought she would explode with joy. "Oh! I knew you'd warm up to your uncle!"

Not exactly how I'd put it.

"He speaks quite highly of you," Melina went on, giving the bandages another tight squeeze. Celeste bit her lip against the sharp pain gripping her belly. "Really believes in you, despite knowing you for such a brief time. But then again, everyone seems to be enamored with the girl who brought down a tyrant."

Celeste fidgeted as Melina tugged at her collar. "I hardly thought she was a tyrant."

"You haven't heard the stories they share about her. Mr. Cavarly said she'd been a thorn in the military's side for over a decade."

"That long?" *How did she only capture one city?*

"Apparently," Melina said, "she once led an army from the east and battered the military's defenses while they were busy trying to fortify a scattering of cities."

By killing them to stop the sickness.

"She broke their frontlines, but they decimated her army."

"So, how'd she sink her claws into the city?"

Melina wiggled her brow. "Trojan horse."

"What?"

"Remember the old story of the giant wooden horse?"

"The Greek legend?" Celeste snorted. "Vaguely." Her father once shared the tale over supper, though the details were murky at best, supplemented by her own childish wonder. How long could she have sat inside of that giant wooden horse before she had to relieve her infinitesimal bladder? She had to pee every five seconds as it was.

"Basically, she got herself and a few followers captured. The general wanted her alive."

Celeste mused, "So, she attacked from the inside."

"Started a rebellion with the war prisoners."

Experiments. "Explains why the military took their sweet time to respond," said Celeste. "She seized their largest settlement." *And planned on crippling them permanently—are all their forces gathered here now?*

"Exactly!" Melina squealed her enthusiasm. "She had a walled off city, arsenal and troops to wield. Yet, she let it fall so quickly—what?" Melina arched her brow.

Celeste gently bit her lip. "You seem to have found an interest."

Melina blushed until her freckles vanished. "It's just fascinating, that's all."

"Never guessed you for the battle type."

"Maybe you would have found out beforehand if you hadn't left me out of it."

It was Celeste's turn to blush with creeping embarrassment. "Aurous was there to protect you."

"Speaking of." Melina rose swiftly. "I'll go get him. He's probably chasing the chickens by the trough again. *You*"—she wagged a finger at her—"get some sleep before you leave."

"Okay," she said, defeated. "I will."

Melina slipped her feet into muddy boots. "Are you sure about this afternoon?"

Celeste shrugged. "I won't get a feel for them as a team with routine drills. I need to see them in action."

Worry shadowed Melina's beaming features. "Are you expecting trouble?"

"No." Celeste forced a stiff smile. "Nothing I can't handle."

"Be careful. Now take a nap."

"Yes, Mother."

"Hush," Melina whispered. She unzipped the tent flap. "Don't forget: One pill every six hours. No more. Dr. Andrews said it could be dangerous."

"I'll be fine." Celeste smiled as the pills rattled against the opaque-orange bottle. "I promise."

The woodland was a dizzying blend of greenish brown from the window of their speeding Humvee. Trees closed in overhead. Slow-creeping roots strangled the winding road as if Mother Nature fought to reclaim what man had long ago built and forgotten. A battle which man appeared to be losing.

"So, Commander." Nadie broke the uneasy silence. Her fawn eyes scanned the road and its wooded edges. "Why'd they stick you with Jericho?"

Celeste tore her gaze from the roots that shattered old asphalt. "Jericho?"

"J-Unit. I guess you don't know."

Celeste drummed her gloved fingers along the dash. "Care to explain?"

Nadie grinned as sunlight splashed across her face. "Jericho is the camp on the fringes of this settlement. Basically, the first stop on your way up the ranks."

"Okay." She mulled over the possibilities. "A first defense?"

"More like a distraction while the army can assess the attacking party and counterstrike."

"Jericho is a sacrifice?"

"Everyone knows that," grumbled Snyder from the backseat. Celeste glimpsed the blonde through the window's reflection. Frosty eyes glared back at her. "Joke Unit," she muttered, then clicked her tongue in disgust. "That's what they call us."

"The misfits," Nadie said, then shrugged her shoulders. "Rejects no one else wants."

"Disposables."

"Right," Nadie agreed.

Snyder gave her an inching smirk. "Makes a girl wonder why they put you in charge of the losers, Commander."

"Coming up on the ridge," Nadie stated loudly, driving a wedge between them.

"How far, Snyder?"

"At least half a click," the glowering blonde replied, tracing her finger along the crinkled map. "That's where the smoke was spotted."

Celeste crossed her arms, furrowing her brow. "How did they see it from so far away?"

Nadie bit back a smile. "We have scouts and binoculars, Commander."

"I know *that*." Celeste said dryly. Snyder sniggered from the backseat. "Today is the only clear day in the past few weeks. It's been dreary, dark, overcast. How did they see it the other day?"

"Does it matter?"

Celeste chewed her lip. "Maybe not."

"She's right," whispered Nadie. "Something seems off about sending us so far without backup."

Snyder scoffed, and Celeste almost heard the blonde's eyes rolling around in her skull. "It's a simple scouting mission to keep us busy, nothing more. Given to us because an uncle feels sorry for his niece. We'll find an empty camp, likely from wanderers, then we'll go home, drop off the report, and sink into boredom once more."

"Unless you have something cheerful to say," suggested Celeste, "why don't you shut up?"

"Right away, Commander."

"*Commander,*" a faint voice crackled from the static of their handheld radio. "*I see smoke. Not much, so the fire must have been extinguished this morning.*"

"Right," she barked into the wired mic. "Let's park the vehicles and make our way on foot from here. Clear." The radio clicked with hissing static. She nodded to Nadie.

The wild-eyed woman jerked the steering wheel and slammed into the thicket. Plowing through the coppice, the vehicle bucked beneath them like an untamed stallion, throwing them into the doors and windows. Celeste's seatbelt locked and chafed against her shoulder, pinched and agitated her wounds. The wheels screeched and spun through the leaf litter. The Humvee lurched to a halt.

"Right," Nadie declared with a high-arching grin. "There we are."

Groaning, Celeste rubbed her waist. "Graceful," she muttered, and slammed her shoulder against the door. She forced it open into a tangled nest of branches.

"Sorry, Commander."

"I think I have a concussion," Snyder remarked as she rubbed the back of her skull. She climbed over the front seat muttering yet another grievance.

Celeste stumbled through the twisting low-hanging boughs and away from the Humvee. Teeth clenched, she raked her pockets and snagged the opaque bottle. The lip *snapped* off to another chalky pill.

Pain hasn't stopped. One more. Feeling justified, she slipped the bottle back in her coat as brittle branches *crunched* under the boots of her approaching squad. A whistle pierced the silence of the woods.

"Commander?"

"He's close," she said, sighing. *Hopefully, he kept up...*

Shadows blurred and sprang from the snarled thicket. Aurous yipped and dug his paws into the dirt, bewitched and buzzing with excitement. He cocked his head, ears perked as though awaiting some form of approval at his accomplishment.

"Good boy," she whispered, then offered to scratch behind his ears. He lolled his tongue at her, panting.

"That's a big—erm—dog," whispered Nadie. "*Real* wild looking."

"Part wolf," Celeste said.

"*Mostly* wolf."

"Let the others know to meet us over the hill," she ordered. As Nadie grabbed the radio, Celeste added, "And tell them to hide their Humvee." She edged through the tangled brushwood, with Aurous bounding after her as silent as the wind's breath.

Snyder raised her Springfield rifle to her chest. Oak-brown and gleaming with polish, the wood was grooved and weathered with age. Sunlight scattered from the jutting barrel.

"Seems fairly undisturbed," Snyder commented, idly drumming her finger against the trigger guard of her rifle.

Celeste shook her head and flicked her hair from her eyes. "Not entirely," she whispered, pointing to the impressions in the fallen leaves. "Someone stepped through here. Seems recent."

"Could be an animal," countered Nadie. She peered closer. "A wolf, maybe."

"Just one?" Celeste frowned. "Possibly a bear, but it would have to be small."

"Too narrow. Bears aren't exactly known for walking with elegance."

"No imprints from footwear?"

"Wouldn't have left a mark on this hard ground," Nadie said. "But you're right, Commander. It's definitely someone."

"Man," groaned Snyder, eyes rolling. "Are you two done ogling nature?"

"Let's move," Celeste ordered. Aurous nosed the faint imprint.

They cautiously treaded into the woods, careful to silence their approach. The air was acrid and hot, and a thick haze of smoke greyed the forest. The others, led by the stocky Harn, had circled the road and located the smoke trail, then doubled back to find Celeste.

"The wind is pushing it along the treetops before it begins to rise," Harn relayed, shouldering his - shotgun. "And it's faint like fog." He pointed a log-like finger to the east. "Not far from here."

"Hello, doggy," wheezed Twist. His thick fingers stroked the wolf's black fur. His wagging tail kicked up a swirling dust storm. Aurous was positively pleased at the attention.

"Good work," praised Celeste.

A glint in the far treeline caught her eye. She scanned the wild thicket, but to her eyes the bright green colors bled together like spilling paint. "Okay," she said. "Let's find this campsite."

Silently, they eased through the woods and over the hillside. Everyone except Twist, who seemed intent on stomping in his heavy boots with a wide lumbering stride. Celeste fought a growing smile.

A faint whistle percolated from the deep green depths of the forest. Celeste slowed her pace, cocking her head at the sound. Whispers carried with the breeze. The others stopped and exchanged puzzled glances with each other. Even Aurous wandered away from her, as though he'd heard nothing as well.

"Commander?" Nadie began.

"Did you hear that?" Celeste pressed a finger to her pursed lips.

A breathless silence dominated the forest.

"I'm sure of it," she insisted.

"Birds," Twist pointed out, his simple gaze drawn to the treetops. "They sing." He shifted the strap on his shoulder, rocking the cannonlike machine gun against his equally thick arm. "Fly away, too."

He's right. Chirped melodies were now screeching cacophonies as birds took flight and flitted through the branches.

"Are you okay?" asked Nadie. "You seem spooked."

"Not scared of the woods, are you?" Clark smiled and wiggled his brow. "I'll keep you safe, doll."

"Commander." Celeste snarled the correction, then motioned for them to advance through the woods.

Another few minutes and the whistle sounded again. Her eyes darted through the bowed branches and endless rippling green. She found Twist staring up the wooded swell. She followed his gaze, squinting to see through the thicket.

"Camp," he stated dully, tongue thrusting past his pursed lips, as if deep in thought.

He's right again.

Sheathed inside the thick boughs of needles, about fifty feet through the treeline, she spotted the motley-green material. It was striped brown to expertly blend with the wooded hillside. It took a few seconds of direct observation for it to creep into focus. She motioned for the others to follow. As they neared the bottom of the ridge, she halted. It was only twenty or so paces up a small incline, but steep enough to conceal the camp from below. A perfect vantage point. A quick motion to Colbat and he unstrapped his rifle and retreated for a clear line of sight.

It was sleek, dark blue like a clear evening sky, with an

elongated barrel and a thick, round scope nearly the length of the entire rifle. He peered through the magnifier and swept the barrel across the camouflaged campsite.

"Got one in sight," he hissed.

"What is it?" Celeste asked, hand drawn to her revolver.

Colbat hesitated. "A woman, I think. Bound to a tree, I can just see the ropes." The rifle stilled in his hands. "Older, battered—she doesn't look good, Commander."

"Right," she muttered. "Two teams. One circling the perimeter, the other will venture inside the camp." She eyed Snyder and added, "Carefully. It could be a trap."

At her command, Harn and Twist split from the group and compassed the edge of the hillside. Colbat pressed flat against the grass. Sunlight glinting from his scope followed their ascent.

"What about me?" Snyder asked.

Hesitating, Celeste gripped her holstered revolver. "You and Clark watch our six." She turned on her heels and left the blonde grumbling wordlessly at the bottom of the ridge.

"Commander," whispered Nadie as she approached. "May I?"

"Quickly," Celeste said. Smoke drifted through the branches above.

"Blondeie can take a good shot with that nasty rifle." Nadie glanced over her shoulder. "I wouldn't be so quick to count her out."

Her skin crawled. "Are you saying I should watch my back?" Aurous growled as anger edged her tone.

Nadie's cheeks went scarlet. "No, that's not what I meant." She paused. "She has incredible aim, so she could be useful to the team. It's not wise to alienate potential."

"Keep moving," Celeste said, though her mind wandered to the drills she ran with her team. *Snyder was the only one to get a perfect shot—every time.* She grunted, almost in disbelief. *Maybe she can be useful.*

They reached the edge of concealed camp. Dead foliage littered the barren dirt. The tent was just discarded fabric stitched together and slung over branches. The firepit smoldered behind it. She stopped and carefully peeked past the drawn tent flap. Colbat was right.

An older woman was cruelly bound to a bark-stripped tree with ligatures knotted around neck, midsection, and thighs. Her bare feet dangled off the ground. Toes bloody and bruised black. Her face had been carved into, each cut like a jagged wrinkle across her leathery-tan skin. Grey streaked and spotted her light hair.

She scrunched her nose. *The smell.* Putrefaction.

Then she saw it.

"Damn!"

Nadie asked, "Commander?"

It can't be.

She looked again; the bindings around her midsection flexed every few moments. *She's breathing–barely.*

Aurous growled again, his shadowy fur bristled.

After informing Snyder and Nadie of the captive woman's condition, doubt darkened their eyes.

"So, who left her here?" Snyder wondered. A grim expression crossed her face as if she welcomed a challenge. But her ice-blue eyes nervously flitted to every shadow and faint noise in the trees.

"Better question," countered Nadie. "*Are they still here?*"

"It's definitely a trap..."

"Nadie, Snyder, with me. Clark, six."

The campsite was barren. Dead grass haphazardly had been ripped from the dirt for tinder. Ashes smoldered. Embers littered tufts of browning grass. No ring of rocks enclosed the burning material. *I'm surprised it hasn't spread.* She nudged her weapon at the woman and Nadie kneeled to loosen the binds.

She fell without restraint, as dead weight, and collapsed onto Nadie's shoulder. Nadie grunted and dug in her heels, propping the woman against the base of the bark-stripped tree. For a hazy moment, Celeste wondered why it had been stripped only halfway–

The woman's eyes snapped open.

With a flash of yellow teeth, she let out a ragged scream. She tore from Nadie's grip. Nadie stumbled and drew her machine pistol–the woman clawed through the air for Celeste. Aurous snapped his jaws at her fingers.

"I got this," Snyder began, rifle raised.

"No!" Celeste holstered her weapon and braced for the collision.

There was a loud *crackling* sound, then the woman convulsed and snapped her spine straight with a sudden jerk. She fell back, stiff as a corpse.

The wolf sulked behind Celeste. Wary.

"Stunned," commented Nadie. Clenched in her fist was a black ring that extended over the back of her hand, with two metal prongs for knuckles. She grinned. A loud *crackling* sound startled Celeste and Snyder, and a lightning bolt flashed between the prongs. "Shocker."

"Effective," muttered Celeste. She nudged the limp woman with her foot before rounding on Snyder. "And I didn't give you an order to shoot."

Snyder huffed back, "I was only going to hinder the attacker." She lowered her rifle. "Not kill."

"Wait for my orders next time."

"Hm."

Nadie inspected the woman's facial lacerations. "This seems like the markings of the Disfigured."

She was uncertain about asking. "Disfigured?"

Snyder sneered, "Tales meant to frighten children over the fire."

"They're bandits that were horribly scarred from living in the dead lands, where the bombs fell from the old war," explained Nadie. She muttered something else in a dialect Celeste couldn't understand. "They've been snatching people from camps ever since the Phantom Woman fell. They say she was the one who kept other roving bandit clans from the west."

"Has anyone seen one?"

"No one I know," said Snyder, "and no one admits it without a belly full of whiskey, anyhow. It's bullshit."

"*Commander,*" Colbat's voice crackled with static. "*All clear down here. No further movement.*"

Before she could respond, Harn's voice rumbled through the hissing feed. "*Commander, do you copy? You're going to want to see this. North of camp.*"

She left Nadie and Snyder to bind the woman's wrists. Her mind spun in place, getting nowhere with her hazy thoughts. The tent was just a flap of poorly-stitched material that was barely a shelter from the elements, and the firepit a patch of soil that couldn't contain a flame. Her eyes drifted from Aurous in the bushes to the rustling branches above her. *Surely the birds didn't leave because of the little bit of noise we made...*

She heard it before it blurred into sight; leaves shifted, and branches stirred with a force that wasn't windborne. Through the rippling verdure, a patch of motley-green took human form. She stared, puzzled—then her blood boiled. She launched back into the dirt as the eerily silent woods echoed with a familiar *twang*.

She hit hard, slamming her spine to the ground. The arrow shivered in the ground by her feet, partially buried in the long grass. Her hand fumbled against the holster on her waist—empty.

Crap! The muzzle to her revolver poked out of the dead grass behind her.

Her boots kicked through the dirt as she flung herself backward in a desperate scramble for her fallen weapon. Then she heard the sharp creak of a bowstring as her attacker docked another arrow.

Snyder loomed over Celeste with her Springfield rifle aimed skyward. Her lips thinned, her cold gaze settling on Celeste. The hesitation lasted seconds—

Her scarred fingers closed around the fallen revolver. With a fluid motion, she raised the revolver, took aim, and opened fire on the formless verdure. Leaves blurred. Blood fanned the foliage and turned it scarlet. The attacker plummeted from the branches like a bird shot from the sky.

"Commander!" Nadie called out.

Celeste pushed to her feet with blood boiling in her veins. "Commander," Snyder began, "I was just following your order—"

As soon as Celeste holstered her revolver, she threw a punch at the blonde. Snyder's lip split and spattered blood up Celeste's gloved knuckles, and she stumbled backward, her own hands clenched into trembling fists. Red globs dripped from her chin and dotted her jade-green jacket. Aurous snarled, ears flat against his skull. Anger flashed through those tawny eyes.

"You're starting to be a problem, blondeie," Celeste growled, baring her teeth like wolf fangs. "One I'd like to remedy."

"I don't take orders from a *shadow spawn.*"

Celeste felt her entire body tense and twitch, but Nadie stepped between them. "Whoa!" she exclaimed. "Let's focus on the task at hand, then you can deal with her insubordination."

"Screw you," muttered Snyder, wiping her bloodied lip. When another growl rumbled in the wolf's throat, she shot back, "And why didn't your mutt smell Tarzan over there?"

"Just check the body," ordered Celeste. Her fingers raked her revolver. "Unless you can't understand how to do that either."

"Right away, *Commander.*"

Nadie and Celeste trailed Snyder, their eyes glued to the treetops. *Are there more?* The question gnawed on their minds, flooding them with dread uncertainty. *Where's Harn and Twist?*

Snyder whispered, "Commander."

"What is it?"

"Holy shit."

"Damn it, Snyder." But her stomach lurched violently.

Snyder had removed the attacker's cloak. Boils bulged beneath his skin like fleshy bubbles ready to burst. Pallid as freshly fallen snow, as though sunlight had never caressed his malformed skin. His features were unrecognizable through the fleshy mush. He appeared...

"Disfigured," Nadie gasped. She clutched the machine pistol to her chest. "Holy *shit!*"

"What's that smell?" Snyder masked her nose with the crook of her arm.

Celeste took a whiff of the air. Her nostrils stung. "Disinfectant," she muttered. The man reeked of it. "Explains why Aurous didn't notice."

"So now..."

The man stirred.

A weapon flashed through his hands, an arm quickly extended, and his bloated lips twisted into a sneer—

—but Snyder pulled the trigger first. A single shot rang out from her Springfield rifle, and the man's chest split and fanned the grass with blood. A gurgle escaped his lips, but the weapon in his hands burned bright like fire doused with gasoline. A ball of red flame streaked into the sky like a rocket—then thundered and burst into a flurry of red sparks that flickered brightly against the midday sun.

A flare?

Like wind howling through the forest, branches and leaves stirred in the surrounding trees. A tempest surged toward them.

"Regroup and fall back!" Celeste yelled and drew her revolver.

Then they heard the war cry.

THREE
Bushwhack

SHRILL WHISTLES rang from the sky.

They dropped like stones from the treetops, a blur of motley-green and glinting steel. Her revolver roared with a searing flash of white. The first shrouded figure dropped to the dirt at her feet, lifeless. Another was overhead; she glimpsed the shadows taking human form. She kept squeezing the trigger. Blood spilled like sticky rain. Limp bodies dragged through the branches and plummeted to the ground.

"Nadie!" she yelled. "The trees! Cover fire!"

Nadie took aim at the stirring branches, and her machine pistol sprayed a barrage of bullets. Branches splintered, tree bark stripped, and blood burst; bodies littered the forest floor.

There were even more of them.

She heard the cry before she saw him. The pounding thuds of feet hitting the ground seized her attention, and she reeled to greet the barrel of a rifle with her own revolver. His face was shrouded with motley-green rags. She saw only his eyes, untamed and wild with anger. She was too slow; his finger twitched against the trigger of his pistol.

A terrible blast pressed against her eardrums. Snyder approached on her left, snapping back the bolt to her Springfield rifle. There was a gaping bloody hole where the man's face once was.

"We're surrounded!" Snyder barked over another discharge of her rifle. Bullets *whizzed* past and splintered tree bark behind them. "Who gave these pricks weapons?"

"Snyder, Clark!" Celeste called out. "Cover fire, fall back!"

"Commander!" Nadie began.

"With me!"

Nadie sprang loose her spent clip. "No, it's Clark!"

Celeste glimpsed him through the onslaught, rocking on his knees as wave after wave of shrouded attackers descended from the treetops. She holstered her revolver and sprinted for him. The peal of gunfire was an echo to the thundering of her own heart.

An arrow sliced the air and sank into the soil beside her. Another shrouded figure approached with an axe raised in a final, defiant swing—then staggered with a sudden grunt. Blood spotted his motley-green cloak. Snyder's aim was flawless even at a distance; she'd hit his center mass, inches below his heart. He stood with his hand fishing through his guts, perplexed at the warm slime and wooded surroundings. Those vague, hazy thoughts would be his last. She drew her machete, and its blade gleamed from dappling sunlight—and then from sultry-red blood. Her victim slumped beneath her. She bolted for Clark as the shrouded ones closed in on him.

He had his pistol gripped in both hands, laid in his lap, and sat as petrified as stone. Snot dribbled from his chin. She could smell his sweat and soiled jeans. Fear was pouring out of every orifice. When her grip twisted the collar of his shirt, she startled him into a rocking motion. With tears shimmering his eyes, he begged her for life.

"That depends on you!" she hissed.

Gunfire peppered the thicket with red-hot lead. Bullets splintered branches, kicked up chunks of dirt. She dragged Clark across the abandoned campsite and shoved him behind Snyder and Nadie. "Fall back!" she ordered. Her radio hissed static. "Everyone, it's time to go—Colbat, let's see just how good you are."

Almost on cue, the head of an advancing attacker burst into a slew of chunky, red meat. Celeste almost grinned, shoved Clark ahead of her, and hunched over the prisoner bound by their feet. A warm wave of stink washed over her. As she heaved the unconscious form from the ground, Snyder retreated to reload and allowed Nadie to empty another clip across the campsite, hoping to halt the advancement. Every few seconds there was a sharp *crack* that rang out over the hill, and a body that slammed to the dirt, headless and bloody. A deadly gift from Colbat.

"There's more, Commander!" yelled Nadie, shoving Clark to the edge of the ridge. "Shit! They're flanking!"

"Oh, Christ," Clark murmured and dissolved into tears. "We're going to die!"

"Shut up and keep moving!" Celeste ordered. "Get to the—"

Her words were lost to the eruption of gunfire. A syrupy warmth crept down her spine. Her grip on the prisoner faltered, and they both tumbled into the dead grass. Her face struck the ground first, her mouth shoved full of grassy dirt. Abrasions burned her face raw. She choked. With dreaded certainty she thought she'd been hit. She traced her fingers along her skin and neck but there was no spilling blood.

"Commander!"

She shook her head and cleared her tumultuous thoughts, and found Snyder leaning over the prisoner's body. Bound and gagged, the wild woman's limbs convulsed, her skin ashy and corpse grey. She'd been riddled with bullets.

Celeste lifted herself from the corpse, vision tilted and blurred. Shadows coalesced with the nauseating swirl of light. Something stirred within the darkness, a strange form, a terrible figure. A monster—

"Snyder, behind you!"

It wasn't a monster that descended upon her, but a man with a blade nearly twice the length as her sheathed machete. Snyder, however, weaved under the sudden strike. A split-second later, she opened the man's belly with a stroke of her knife. Blood darkened the patchy-green of his shroud. He fell with a sharp yelp—then gurgled when her knife blade ripped in-and-out of his throat. Before the body was still, she dove for the next attacker.

"Get up, *moniyaw!*"

While Celeste fought her disorientation, Nadie gave her a sharp nod and descended the ridge with a firm grasp around Clark's collar. The boy was basically deadweight.

"Move!"

Celeste turned, reaching for her revolver—but fell into the grip of something far stronger than she could have anticipated. Hands as cold and strong as steel wrenched around her neck and crushed her airway shut. Her heartbeat *thumped* like thunder strikes in her ears.

Her vision spotted. Her legs buckled under his spine-crushing force. The back of her head rocked off the compacted dirt. Her lips parted in a wordless gape. The overhead forest dimmed and tumbled into the ravening jaws of darkness.

Then the force lifted from her neck, her lungs nearly burst with rushing air. She coughed and spewed into the dirt, staggering to her feet. She saw her attacker writhe and flail his bandaged fists, pinned beneath a shadow with flashing bloodstained fangs.

The man screamed as the wolf tore at his shroud, fangs pressed against his neck. There was a sharp *hiss* of ripping fabric. Before the wolf snapped his jaws around bulgy, swollen flesh, Celeste called out through the clamor.

"Aurous, enough!"

Fur bristled, the wolf halted his onslaught, but his amber eyes bore into the man trembling under his paws. Muddy saliva frothed across the wolf's lips.

More shrouded attackers charged out from treeline. Celeste braced for the imminent volley, revolver drawn and raised. But then it was as if the forest shook under an earth-splitting force. Bodies were shredded, blood fountained and flooded the campsite red. A massive machine gun thundered from an even more massive grip. "Boom," said Twist with a jutted tongue.

Celeste acknowledged him with a slight nod. "Boom," she repeated. "Time to retreat."

The large man nodded, throat rippling. As Celeste reeled, pinpoints twinkled across her slanted vision. Twist lumbered past her, leaned over Aurous and the shrouded man. The barrel of his machine gun—which was more like a cannon, even in a giant's grip—jabbed into the man's throat and branded a smoldering crease. Celeste ordered the man to his feet, then quickly bound his arms with the torn sleeve of her muddy coat. Was that her blood or theirs? The shrouded man hissed at them, warming the air with rancorous breath.

"You're going to die here for what you've done."

The man's eyes were shadowed by his cowl, but hatred radiated from his harsh words. She struck his jaw until her knuckles stained red. His knees buckled.

"Twist, get him to the vehicle," she spat. Twist gave her a simple nod, and hauled the dazed prisoner to his feet. Aurous growled and flicked his ears toward the abandoned camp.

There were others.

Candlelight flickered from the unseen regions of the forest. She stood still, perplexed, then opened her mouth to warn Twist and the others—but her words were lost to a ravenous roar overhead.

Crimson spilled across the sky in bright streaks like meteors, then faded to a pulsing glow below the ridge of the hill. Heat rippled the air into sweltering waves. A thick plume of smoke expanded and curled over the edge like drawn curtains, veiling the surrounding landscape.

"Commander?"

The voice was muffled, panicked; Celeste squinted into the haze, eyes bleary, searching for the others. A figure blurred against the smoke. Stalking her movements. She reached for her revolver.

"Commander!"

Halfmoon eyes as red as fresh blood glared back at her, narrowing at the scent of meat. The shadow crept toward her, claws ripping through the air—

—a deafening *blast* thundered against her chest, and she was splattered with sticky red. An attacker crashed into the dirt at her feet. Blood pooled beneath a shuddering form. She lowered her weapon. Ice spread through her lungs with shallow, rapid breaths. Then she glimpsed an arrogant sneer through the grey haze.

Bright blue eyes pierced through like a glimmer of sky. Blood speckled her smooth glowing skin like swelling pimples.

"Second time I've saved your ass, Commander," Snyder remarked with a curling lip that was both a smirk and a snarl. "You owe me."

Celeste nodded—grudgingly. The sultry smoke seared her vision to pinpoints. "Where's Twist?" she asked. For all she knew, the man had no concept of fear and would wander toward the flame with little thought of the scorching consequence.

Besides, I want that prisoner.

"They were trailing Nadie and Clark before the fire started burning the hill," Snyder said. "And we need to do the same if we want to live—I'm not burning alive on your order!"

Celeste almost snarled back at her. "No, we move. Go!"

But when they stumbled through the smoke, they found the inferno had devoured the hillside. Thick smoke beat them back with blistering winds.

"Shit," cursed Snyder, reeling toward the forest. "We're trapped."

Her lungs broiled. Celeste nudged Snyder to the ridge and

stumbled alongside ravaging grip of fire. As the inferno raged and rose around them as a rippling wall of flames, she heard the howl through the trees, the echo of a joyous hunt. Then there was a bloodcurdling scream, like the fearful, desperate cry for help as death loomed.

Aurous was hunting.

She heard the wolf scramble through the thicket, panting heavily and nipping at his blood-soaked fur. With her attention diverted, another attacker lunged through the grey haze at her. She heard the small grunt and the ruffle of clothing, then reeled into a piercing blade.

The impact rocked her off balance and she crashed into the dirt with her attacker. Their limbs entangled, she felt her coat rip and cold steel press against her abdomen. His grip faltered. She yelled for Snyder, but the blonde was taking aim at another. The blade snagged and twisted in the fabric of her coat. She bashed in his nose and crunched cartilage, but with one forceful strike and infuriated roar, he slammed her into the dirt. Her lungs were painfully robbed of air. She was certain the next blow would be the last moment of pain she would ever endure again—

—until a slight *pop* echoed through the ringing in her ears. She could breathe again. Her eyes snapped open. Her attacker's hand was firmly pressed against his neck. Blood seeped from his fingers. Snyder snapped the bolt and reloaded the Springfield. She was thrown to the ground as bladed blows rained down on her from another shrouded figure.

A shadow blurred between them. The wolf collided with her attacker, and the knife was torn from his grasp. His wail carried over the roaring inferno. He fell in a flurry of fangs and claws. Blood streaked his motley cloak and pumped into the charred earth. Snyder snatched her rifle as the second figure attempted to flee in terror at the sight of the wolf's fangs. She trailed his movement, exhaled sharply—a single shot rang out. The man slid face-first through the dirt.

The wolf's fangs ripped into the man's cowl, snapping for his neck. Celeste had to shout three times for him to stop. His ears perked. His snout was crimsoned with blood.

"Let's go!"

The greying air strangled her lungs with heat. She leapt to her feet and staggered alongside her wolf and the blonde. They were outnumbered and flanked. Countless shadows took shape in the smog.

"Commander," Snyder began, shaken.

But Celeste reached for the radio strapped to her shoulder. "Colbat, get everyone in that goddamn vehicle and move north. Slowly!"

A faint voice broke through the hiss of static. "*Roger.*"

"Great plan," Snyder drawled, "going out in a literal blaze of glory."

"To hell with that," Celeste hissed. *I have someone I need to see again.*

Snyder grinned and turned a shoulder to her, exposing webbed patches of scarred skin stretched across her trap muscle. She raised her Springfield. The barrel trembled. Her finger slipped through the trigger guard—

Celeste careened into her like a runaway truck. Both women had the air painfully thumped from their lungs. Whipping flames flickered and reached up like thousands of hands from the depths of some hell. They both plunged into the fiery glow below the ridge.

Pain seized Celeste's guts and shocked her limbs numb when she hit the ground—twice. She clawed at embers and charred brush and staggered to a stop. Her clothes were singed black and smoldering. She could only wonder with dismay at how charred and frizzy black her hair was. Her lungs were broiling hot. She choked, sputtered, coughed up bloody mucus. But her heart was racing at a marathon pace. She was alive—for now.

There was a playful nudge at her heel, and a low throaty whine. Aurous limped against her, nuzzling her legs into small, awkward motions. She stumbled, slowly, from the rippling wall of flame. The wolf trotted at her side, panting, his fur dappled red and steamy.

"Snyder?"

"Alive, mostly. Thanks to you."

Celeste gazed over her shoulder to find the cheeky blonde hunched against a tree. Her bangs were singed black with grey streaks of ash through her hair. Her jacket was torn and smoldering, one boot charred and misshapen like a clubbed foot.

"Our ride's here."

Celeste staggered after her. The fire was a bright blazing sun spreading through the campsite along the ridge, belching storm clouds of black smoke into the sky. They sprinted for the clearing to the north.

"So," huffed Celeste, "is that the infamous Disfigured you were so eager to dismiss?"

Snyder rolled her eyes and pursed her lips into a thin line. "Tall tales, Commander. They're not the revenants of the bandits we've killed. They're all that's left of those savages."

"They seem organized to me, and willing to sacrifice plenty." Celeste spotted the Humvee through a scattering of trees.

"Desperation."

"Get in." Celeste reached for the door, noting the blemish of red against the splatter of shaded green.

"Trouble's coming," said Colbat from the front seat. "Nadie regrouped at the second transport."

"Hell of a fight you put up, Miss." Harn chuckled and flared his nostrils at the scent of smoke. "Bet those fools are burnin' alive."

"What did these assholes even want?" Snyder asked as she climbed across the seat and latched the door. "Did they plan on just burning us?"

Celeste hissed, "They were *blocking* our escape."

Snyder scoffed. "Then why not do that from the start? This makes little—"

The windshield spiderwebbed when what sounded like hail peppered the glass. Celeste yelled for them to get down—glass exploded and whipped around her like thousands of tiny needles.

There was a deep grunt to her left, followed by a horrified sputter of blood. Colbat gasped for air. Crimson fountained from a gaping hole in his sternum. His eyes found hers, wide and brimming fear. His mouth gaped, but his scream was stuck gurgling in his throat. An arrow had impaled his chest, shattered his ribs, and ran through his heart. Flames scattered across his clothes, and the burning oil filled the Humvee with strangling smoke. His skin blackened like roasting meat, then rippled and dripped like slime from glistening bones. Teeth gnashed and misted the air with rot. Bony fingers raked and clawed the steering wheel, setting off the horn with intermittent blasts. Crimson eyes flashed malice.

Colbat was infected.

"Get out!"

The confines of the Humvee made it difficult to reach for her revolver or her machete. When she pushed away from the ravening jaws of Colbat, she tumbled over Snyder and into the opening door.

She hit solid metal, fell over backwards, and slammed her spine against the ground. Snyder entangled with her. The loose Springfield drove into her belly, rocking her guts with waves of crippling pain. She nearly retched—then panic wrenched her back into focus. The mutating Colbat snapped against his seatbelt like a barking dog at the end of its leash. His claws minced the steering wheel to rubbery ribbons.

"Colbat!" howled Harn from the backseat. "My friend, no!"

Snyder leapt to her feet and ignored Celeste's protests to fall back.

"Come on, Harn!" the blonde snarled. "He's dead, time to face facts—"

The door swung open. Scabrous bone ripped through the last remnants of Colbat's flesh and crawled across the seat. Talonlike claws raked deep gashes into the upholstery. Harn squeezed through the opening, screaming his disbelief. He raised his shotgun on his former friend. His hands trembled, as did his voice when he spoke.

"What happened to you?" he whispered.

Perched against the dash of the vehicle, the creature sputtered and flashed its gnarled fangs. Its flesh was charred black, weeping from the bone. Blood streaked across its alabaster skull. Ragged strands of black hair clung to the exposed scalp. Its eyes burned like the deep glow of a distant wildfire, searching their horrified gazes. It gnashed its fangs.

Splat-splat-splat.

Celeste studied its twitching movements, her fingertips inches from her holstered revolver. The creature focused on her with scorching crimson eyes. Twisted fangs gnashed. Saliva splattered its bony chin. It hissed at her like a feral cat, but she swore she heard words awkwardly form along its long wiggling tongue.

"*Kill...her!*"

Claws scythed for her drawn revolver and glanced off the barrel like a sparking ricochet. She retreated a step as it lunged from the burning vehicle and flailed with gangly limbs. It crashed into the ground, writhing madly, and its dark flesh slopped to the dirt, the melted remains of its former human shell. Celeste turned to the others with a warning caught in her throat—

Snyder stepped forward, Springfield rifle raised, and the sky filled with another terrible blast. Murky blood streaked the Humvee's paint. But the creature only spun to face her charge, fangs *snapping* for her sun-kissed skin. Snyder staggered from its reach—her hand slipped from the bolt and failed to reload her weapon.

Celeste *never* ignored instinct; her fleshed prickled, the hair on the back of her neck raised. She jammed her revolver between its jaws, and its snapping fangs scraped steel and spat sparks. She threw her weight into it, hurling them both back into the confines of the vehicle.

White-hot pain crushed her arm, thundered through her bones. A flooding warmth soaked through her jacket. The creature nearly ripped her entire arm off at the shoulder as it wrenched its jaws above her clavicle and viciously sawed through skin with fangs like serrated blades. It whipped its head back-and-forth, and tossed her away like an old carcass.

She slammed into solid metal. Glass exploded outwards, and the Humvee door wrenched open in the opposite direction than it was manufactured to function. The ground came punching upwards, driving the air from her lungs. The creature roared and rained frothy warm saliva, its breath a bitter wind of rot.

Shadows formed beneath the creature. Amber eyes flickered with hunger. Aurous snarled, fangs gleaming bright red. His jaws ripped upwards, pinning the creature against the Humvee.

A threatening growl rumbled her throat, and Celeste clawed to her feet, teeth bared as fangs. She was all but howling for the creature's head. She lunged for it—but Snyder locked an arm around her waist and clenched tight like a shackle, dragging her into the densely tangled brush.

The road curved and sloped into the forest, vanishing below the wooded horizon. The trees themselves were looming sentinels, swaying with the wind and creaking an eerie melody. To the north, the sky was a shimmering blue, a deep contrast to the black carnage that billowed across the southern horizon.

The Humvee crashed through the coppice. Its speckled-green paint blended it with the wooded landscape. It towered like a tank, lifted far enough from the ground that Celeste thought she could almost stand and remain unharmed as the vehicle drove over her. The wheels seized and rutted the grassy dirt, sliding to a halt near them. A heart-shaped face stared back at her through the stained glass, bronze eyes wide with silent understanding. There were only three when there should have been four...

The door swung open. Harn grimaced at her, beard dappled with blood, and looked as if he desired nothing more than to throttle her with his ham-sized fists. He lifted himself into the Humvee without breaking his venomous gaze.

A feral and ferocious howl broke through the hum of the idling engine. There was a sharp, distressing yelp, then a low throaty whine.

Aurous!

Anger was a scorching release from pain. It numbed her to it. She fed her revolver a fistful of bullets. Excitement kindled in her narrowing gaze. The hunt was on. She gave Snyder a disturbing look of excitement.

The blonde's smooth and glowing skin was smeared with soot, her clothes charred and crisped by the blistering heat. Sweat greased her furrowing brow.

"Get on the other side," Celeste ordered. "And make sure that rifle is loaded."

"Right away," Snyder said, "Commander."

"With all due respect—" Harn began.

Celeste hissed through clenched teeth. "With all due respect, shut up and follow my orders. *Move* over."

Anger blazed in those beady eyes. "Oh, I *will.*"

She crawled in and slammed the door shut as the sky filled with a terrible cacophony. Her stiff fingers barely curled over the roof the vehicle, but she hauled herself up through the open window and wedged her hip against the pane and her shoulder against the roof. A tingling pain in her arm sapped the strength to properly hold herself steady, but she whipped her revolver out of the window and flicked its hammer back. Snyder planted herself in a similar position on the opposite door, crooking her legs around the pane and practically hanging out of the window. Every muscle in her body tightened and held her in place like a statue. Shouldering her Springfield rifle, Snyder gave a sharp nod—Celeste yelled for them to go.

The engine roared, revving as loud as thunder. Wheels spun and ripped into the road, accelerating the vehicle into a sharp swerve, jerking her grip loose from the metal frame. Pain coiled around her belly and crushed her of air like toothpaste squeezed from a tube. She fought to steady her aim.

A moment later she saw it—the wolf bounded from the thicket, bloody tongue lolling past his fangs in a triumphant display. His sharp ears perked at the sound of a piercing *screech.* Crimson burned through the darkness of the woods. The creature lunged after Aurous.

But the wolf was far more agile.

It was their all too familiar game, their thrilling chase, the wild hunt. Aurous caught sight of her hanging from the Humvee window, and he raised his snout in a long resonating howl.

Her heart thumped into her throat. The creature's bony claws gutted the dirt where Aurous stood a fraction of a second before. The wolf snapped from its reach, and his bounding stride shot him down the road as a shadowy blur. Gurgling on its own ribboning throat, the creature sputtered its fury and thrashed after him.

Aurous was leading the monster right to them.

The Humvee fishtailed through the rutted road. Celeste fought against the slewing motion, and took aim down a wavering barrel. Her jaw clenched tight enough to crack teeth. She squeezed the trigger—her aim faltered at the last millisecond, and the bullet blasted the road far from the creature's charge. The next shot missed as well, and soon Aurous weaved past the vehicle, legs pumping frantically as the black creature slashed through the road after him.

With her grip firmly wrenched around the doorframe, she leaned away from the vehicle as the creature neared. She crooked her legs around the door as Snyder had, and leaned out of the window—and quickly found she wasn't nearly as in shape as she thought she was. Her calves scorched. Joints painfully popped. Pain gripped her belly. She yelled wordlessly, whipped her arm at the skeletal blur, and squeezed until her revolver was empty. Shrapnel scattered from its bony skull. Claws cleaved through the dirt, and the creature flung its momentum at the passing Humvee—twisted jaws snapped open with a rippling scream.

Aurous collided with the creature's mindless charge. Dust clouded the road as they skidded across the dirt. Celeste yelled to turn around—and slammed the butt of her revolver against the roof. She feared, with dreaded certainty, the creature was going to kill Aurous. The proud wolf clambered atop the creature, his jaws wrenching through the clumpy flesh and jutting bone.

The Humvee veered left, and her hip slammed into solid metal. Wheels spun into the dirt, whipping the backend across the road. The sharp motion jarred her grip loose and her fingers slipped from the window. She fell backwards, flailing her arms like a bird taking flight, and came inches from the rear-wheel's crushing spin.

A viselike grip pinned her legs to the door with so much force she thought her bones would shatter like glass. She curled her stomach like a sit-up—pain exploded through her guts with the tingling warmth of blood—and managed to lift herself upright. She gave Harn a small nod, but caught a glimmer of regret deep in his eyes. She half-expected him to drop her.

She caught sight of her wolf and his final desperate dash toward the creature. Swallowing her pride, which felt like razors in her throat, she ordered Snyder to take the bastard out.

Icy eyes flicked down the sight of her rifle, and the barrel gently bobbed against the Humvee's jarring motion. Barely a moment crawled by before the rifle erupted in a blinding flash.

Blood fanned the road in murky splotches. A crooked limb bowed inward and *snapped* from the bullet tear. The creature stumbled and wheezed from its rotting throat. Its narrowed eyes darkened like pooling blood when its feral gaze found Celeste's. Its jaws snapped wide—

The Humvee slammed into the creature. Black smoldering flesh burst apart, splattering the grill and hood with clouded ooze. Its mangled form dragged beneath the Humvee's enormous wheels, crushed and shredded to a fine mist of blood and pulverized bone. A dark trail of guts streaked across the lightly tanned dirt. Its detached skull rolled away with heavy thuds.

The brakes seized loudly, jarring the vehicle to a halt. Snyder dropped from her perch and dissolved into a fit of breathless laughter. Nadie leaned back in her seat, hands trembling from taut nerves. The prisoner writhed, waking from a daze, and Harn drove the shotgun barrel into his guts. Twist and all his enormity took up half of the front seat, wedging Clark between himself and Nadie. The big man was clapping with excitement. Clark had the pallor of a ghost. Celeste could barely stand the sight of him.

Bloody paw prints marked the wolf's trail. He limped along, tongue lolling and frothing blood. Celeste greeted him with a long and stiff scratch behind his perked ears. "Stay back, boy," she said.

"So, Commander." Nadie's voice nearly broke. "What now?"

Celeste caught her breath and prayed no one spotted the slight tremble in her lip. The momentary slip of façade, the fear clawing to the surface of her mind. Ice crept into her lungs again. Her body ached with a terrible agony that seemed cruel and unending, yet familiar, welcoming. She felt alive and vibrant.

"Now," she finally said, brow wrinkled. "We put some distance between ourselves and that camp—then we get some information from this asshole."

Tattered rags clung to his bulgy features. The prisoner, the disfigured man, glowered back with hatred blazing in his eyes.

FOUR
Crow Bait

THE FIRST few minutes were unnerving. The salty-sweet scent of sweat and blood permeated the vehicle while a dread silence crept between them. Their gazes searched the green-spotted landscape endlessly, nerves frayed at every darting shadow or shimmering leaf. The prisoner kept his eyes to the trees as if awaiting the perfect moment to escape...or for the cavalry To descend. Either way, Celeste bided her time until she was certain nothing stalked them through the depths of darkness, unseen. Then with a quick motion of her hand, Nadie eased the vehicle to a rocky halt.

"Commander?" began Snyder—but a sickening sound of *crunching* cartilage shocked her silent.

The Humvee door slammed open.

Celeste, startled by the commotion, pensively watched Harn haul the prisoner from the backseat. His thick tree-trunk arms flexed and curled around the shrouded man's neck, then squeezed— his pockmarked face turned a deep shade of scarlet. Eyes bulged from sockets like overblown balloons. She imagined them bursting with a moist *pop-splat* sound, grinning at the macabre desire.

Harn released his strangling grip on the prisoner, and the man fell to the dirt, winded and gasping for air that wouldn't come. He propped his head up, squinting against the glare of sunlight, then dug his elbows into the dirt in a feeble attempt to crab-crawl backwards for safety. Harn drove his heavy-treaded boot into the man's chest, *cracking* multiple ribs.

"You'll all die," the prisoner gasped. "You broke the deal, you suffer!" He held Harn's threatening glare. "You'll die just like your pathetic friend."

A vengeful roar erupted from Harn like the blast of a rifle, and he brought his boot down on the prisoner's face with a heavy stomp. A sudden scream trailed into a gurgling sputter. Patches of the man's flesh peeled like soggy paper when Harn lifted his boot. The man's cowl was soaked crimson.

Reality set in like a cold blade to her throat. Her words were an incoherent slur as she scrambled out of her seat. Another meaty *thud* echoed. She circled the Humvee, revolver drawn.

"Harn!" she called out. Her voice nearly broke. "Stand down!"

Pearly teeth gleamed through a blood-spattered beard. Slowly, he lowered his boot into the blood weeping from the man's face. His beady eyes narrowed and grew dangerously dark.

"You saw what they did to my friend," he snarled at her, barely containing his explosive temper. "He cannot live!"

"Stand down."

The wolf growled at her side, and Harn stepped away from the fallen man. Celeste holstered her revolver, then called for Nadie. The man below her wheezed and coughed through the blood flooding his throat. His face was a mangled mess, and trembled to the point of convulsions.

"He's bad, Commander," Nadie replied grimly. Her fingers palpated the sharp depression around his collapsing sockets. She relented a sigh. "He won't make it."

Damn it. "How quickly?"

"I'm surprised he's holding on."

Celeste eased down and crouched over him. She felt her joints pop and groan in protest, and the familiar scorching pain in her gut returned with vehemence. A fuel for her determination. For now.

She stared into his mangled face, and caught sight of what remained of his eye still rolling in its socket. There was a glimmer of coherence in his flitting gaze. If she commanded, she ensured torture and the worst pain imaginable for the few moments he dared cling to life. That is what the military would do, and she knew it. Felt it churn within the pit of her stomach.

Is this what Vega foresaw? The malicious thought probed her mind. *Nothing but savagery in my path?*

"All right," she whispered, "mercy of a quick death if you give me the reason behind the ambush."

The convulsing movement of his head spattered her with blood and torn bits of flesh. "Y-you're...dead."

"Yeah," she replied solemnly, "I've known that for a while. Tell me about the ambush or I'll make certain you beg for the offer."

Memories surfaced in blips of vivid flashes; crimson dappled the snow around her lap, hands throbbing with warmth and stained red. The body beneath finally stopped convulsing, face pulverized into hamburger meat.

A piercing pain in her head brought reality shifting into focus. The shrouded man stammered, mumbling into his cowl, and flecked her with blood. "Supposed to die," he wheezed repeatedly.

"Why?" A sinister chill crawled along her skin.

"That...w-was the...deal."

She wrinkled her nose as the stench of death began to settle. "Well," she replied, "the deal's off."

"Die," the man rasped, shuddering. "D-die...die...die!"

He was sputtering nonsense, but the gleam in his eye forced her to understand he would say no more. Death was not to be feared. She recognized that fiery gaze, even through a puddle of torn flesh. She gritted her teeth and retreated from the fallen man.

"Harn," she whispered. Her eyes fluttered shut. "Have your vengeance."

Another hefty stomp and the man's skull shattered like thin glass.

"Commander, what about this?"

Celeste, vision spotting, tore her gaze from scattered mess of brains and blood. Snyder leaned against the mottled paint of the vehicle, skin still smeared black with ash and crusted blood. She eyed a ragged lock of black hair poking out of Colbat's severed head. Or at least, the creature's head that was sculpted from Colbat's flesh.

Celeste almost grinned again, caught in a maddening grip of adrenaline. She had neglected to inform her team of her intentions when she had seized the head from the roadside. To them, it was an infectious hazard, one drop into an open wound away from contracting an unknown strain of sickness. However, she did have the decency to bind it with bloody rags. And strap it to the roof of the Humvee.

"We're taking that as proof of betrayal," she declared.

Unease spread through them as silence. Snyder sneered at her. "Betrayal?"

"Someone wants me dead, and I want to know *who*."

The metal gates loomed against the skyline like impervious mountains. Rain had pummeled the winding road through camp into a rutted pit of mud. Sprawling tents, decrepit latrines, and military vehicles littered the mudded outskirts of Fort Thompson, and slowly sunk into the forming bog. But the fetid grounds teemed with faceless uniforms and bodies she already smelled through the closed window. Nadie eased off the gas pedal, slowing the Humvee near their camp—but Celeste motioned for her to drive through the city.

When they reached the gate, Nadie pulled the Humvee to the shoulder of the road, and chewed through the grassy hillside. Someone stirred near the entrance. She wondered if they'd grant her access to the city; it had been off limits since the liberation. She peered through the clouded glass, fingers stiff against her revolver, lungs heavy and restricting air. The soldier approached with his rifle shouldered but slanted down. He gave them one sweeping glance, hesitated for a split-second, then gestured for them to proceed.

The metal gate rifted from the wall with a slow, grinding wail. Celeste peered through the fogged glass. Sweat beaded her clammy skin. She jumped down from the Humvee and unstrapped the severed head from the roof. Viscous blood dripped in strings from the sullied rags. But it was the fetid stench of man she choked on. Smog permeated the air as a thick haze of stink. With her trepid gaze stuck to the guard's weapon, she waded through the muck, splattered her pants with thick slime.

Every pair of eyes from camp burned into the back of her skull. Beyond the gate was a sea of black, a blur of inquisitive gazes, all curiously drawn to her arrival—or, more than likely, the bloody rags dangling from her grip.

"Celeste!" Uncle greeted her, chuckling at the sight of her. "All in one piece, I see, which is fantastic news! I gather your first mission was a success—"

"I need to speak with whoever is in charge. *Now*."

"What, why?" His brow sloped and narrowed his bright eyes. "What is going on, Celeste?"

"I need to speak to the asshole in charge!" Her sudden

outburst echoed off the barren city walls and carried across the valley. Clenching her jaw tight, she let out a shaky breath and lowered her voice. "I need to speak to the *one* in charge."

Worry wrinkled Uncle's face and lined his cheeks and brow like rigid scars, exactly like her father. "You're not making any sense, Celeste." His gaze wandered past her. "What happened out there?"

"The blonde..." She bit her lip, silently cursing. "Mengele?"

"He's not in charge, and he's not here, but he is the one who cured—" Uncle began.

"Then *who?*"

She was stunned to silence by a voice like a thunderclap. "I'm in charge of this organization!"

Her heart lurched up into her throat.

The man was old. Older than anyone she had ever seen. He walked with a short but powerful stride, his left arm swinging, but his right anchored firmly to his hip—inches above his holstered pistol. He was no taller than her, but his commanding presence lifted him the height of giants. Spine arched forward but shoulders rigidly straight. His vest was a motley of forest green, sleeves torn and frayed. His skin sun-crisped and as leathery as a dinosaur. Stubby arms with loose hanging skin but muscle as thick as her thighs. The colors etched into his arms had long faded like old peeling paint, but the flaming skull still blazed bright and silently screamed from his skin. His hair was a glinting grey, like dirty snow, and his facial hair was trimmed to curl down his lips and past his chin in thick bushy strips. Her own shadow-marked sneer reflected from his glasses.

He grinned as he drew in a deep breath of his cigarette. Smoke curled from his flared nostrils. His eyes flicked to the muddy blood that dripped from the rags in her grip like a slow leak from a faucet.

"Celeste, I presume, the one and only Queen Slayer!"

His voice was hoarse and crackling. Smoke rolled over his lips as he spoke and beamed at her like he had never laid eyes on a killer with such delicate features.

"Yes," she managed to say, tongue unbearably dry.

"General Blackwell," he greeted with a snorting chuckle. "What seems to be the cause of commotion then, Celeste? Is that perhaps a gift you have for me?"

The soiled rags unfurled like a scroll, and the severed head landed with a squishy thud. Bone gleamed through the oozing flesh.

Its features scrambled like broken eggs. Predator's fangs jutted through the human remnants of its lips. Blackwell nudged the fleshy stump and shifted the creature's jaw. Its unhuman tongue slapped the dirt.

"What is this?" he asked with a heavy grunt. "You bring the infected here?"

She spoke carefully. "It's been here all along."

His face was as rigid and still as stone. No flinch, no twitch of the eye or pupil dilation. Tang-scented smoke wisped from his nostrils.

"I'm not certain what you speak of, Miss."

Her uncle motioned he was about to speak, but a snapping gesture from Blackwell commanded silence. His cold, colorless eyes remained on her, unblinking.

"The girl can speak for herself." Another sharp grin. "She *is* a hero, after all."

Dread coiled around her belly. If there was a line to cross, she had plummeted clear over its edge. "I was informed," she spat, "that the sickness was controlled and weaponized *only* to retake the city. Yet, here we have someone who suffered from a controlled infection."

"Celeste." Her uncle's tone was flat and stern as if addressing a child during a tantrum. "We explained to you in the hospital after you awoke. Those were volunteers, who had little life left and believed in the war we continue to fight. They gave their lives to ensure our victory. There is no experimentation here."

"He's right," agreed Blackwell. "And a victory is a victory—but it was an abhorrent way to win, nonetheless."

But she only heard echoes of Vega's brutality. "Then it seems you are no better than the bandits you eliminated."

Her uncle was stunned and stammering. She heard Snyder snort in disbelief. Nadie whispered in her tangled dialect. Tension hung heavy in the air like rot. General Blackwell's lips thinned and pursed around a brightly burning stub, burly chest swelling with smoke. A deep-rooted anger crimsoned his cheeks, and his colourless eyes narrowed to match her intensity.

"How old are you, Celeste?" he asked. "Hit your twenties yet? Almost? See, I was around *long* before the world fell to this, as some call it, disaster. So, I learned a lot in my time, especially combat."

His voice pitched high as he baked his lungs with smoke. "Plenty of wars to keep a soldier busy before our mighty society collapsed to absolute shit"—smoke jetted from his flared nostrils— "but the greatest knowledge I have ever acquired, by far, was from a goddamn book. I kid you not, girl, education is crucial."

"I agree," she said through the lump forming in her throat. She almost saw a glimmer of her father behind those soulless eyes.

"There was once a man brought into the world that changed the course of history more than any before him. A terrifyingly brilliant leader, a man of true military convictions—Napoleon Bonaparte, the French conqueror. More than eight countries were controlled by his military rule, and no army could withstand his onslaught. Men would tremble at the mere mention of his name— fleeing the battlefield when they saw his flag hoisted high over his approach. Soldiers would die for him, and that is what you learn as a soldier—how to die and how to be proud doing it. But he was smarter; and learning that he was smarter made *me* smarter.

"You see, I had zero intentions on dying as a goddamn soldier. I wanted to be Napoleon—waves of soldiers at my command, throwing themselves against the perils of death for *my* convictions. I, alone, foresaw what was best for this world, just as Napoleon had all those years before. I wanted to conquer evil and restore tranquility— so I did. I became the very thing that had inspired me not to die." Smoke crawled between his scummy, crooked teeth. "I became *that* man, feared by my enemies, revered by my people. Those under my command willing to sacrifice for what I have envisioned for the world."

Her tongue unraveled. "Bonaparte sentenced his men to freeze to death during a failed expedition. Half a million. Many of those *loyal* to him wound up stranded or hunted down like rabid dogs. Bonaparte retreated safely—days before his army." Her father's smirk crawled across her cheek. "Not exactly a decision to revere."

"Oh." A glimmer of admiration in his drab eyes. "It is pleasant to come across someone with a cultured childhood, and the intelligence to match such piquant wit." Before Celeste responded, the glimmer faded to a clouded grey. "But on the contrary," he countered coldly, "he made the necessary call, the cruel and difficult decision most leaders tend to shy away from. *That* makes *them* weak. They are nothing if they can rush to battle, yet lack the heart to command others to die for the same cause. *I* know that sacrifice, *I* embrace the darkness of this world. Yes, girl, infected soldiers were weaponized to retake my stronghold and end the Bandit Queen's tremulous rule over this land. But that is because I knew that sacrifice meant victory, and that victory ensured the lives of all you see before you in this camp—including your own."

"It was your men who shot me," she began. Even to her ears the outburst was juvenile.

"Perhaps. But from what I gather, you would have died of the infection during your battle with the Bandit Queen—freezing to death in the bitter cold of the mountains as a malformed beast with an unending ache for blood." Wisps of discolored smoke drifted toward her, stinging her eyes. "Just as those who had once followed the mighty Napoleon, correct?"

"I'm certain those who froze to death would disagree with such high regard for a monster." Her voice crackled like burning wood.

"I'm certain they would not! In fact, so enamored with their charismatic and invincible leader, I'm sure their beacon of hope burned bright into the dark, unforgiving grip of inevitability. Because they *believed* in his cause—just as my soldiers believe in mine."

Celeste froze—Blackwell's right arm tensed, inching to his holstered pistol—her own extremities tingled against the cold steel of her revolver.

His cold eyes flicked past her.

"*Down!*"

His voice exploded across the sky like thunder, *booming* through camp like a shockwave. His chest swelled with smoke as silence spread through them like some terrible affliction. Slowly, one by one, they struck their knees to the mud, fists clenched tightly over their chests and pounding with a steady rhythm like a beating heart. Even her team kneeled in muck with their heads bowed. Not a single word uttered amongst them. Even Uncle lowered to the rushing rivers of mud.

She heard and felt nothing but the thundering of her heart. Adrenaline electrified every muscle in her body. Instincts raged at her to fight before she was cornered. Her fingers quivered against her revolver. He held her uncertain gaze.

"That is why I, alone, am the Napoleon of this era," he praised, "the conqueror of lands and bringer of new worlds."

He leaned in, flicking his eyes up at her, and his breath flung ashes against her cheek.

"That is why *I* lead," he whispered through a rising cloud of smoke, "and that is why *you* kneel."

Her lungs refused air even as a fierce ache developed in her chest. Her propensity for violence resonated. *Survive!* the thought screamed, rooted from the anger in her heart.

"*Kneel.*"

The command iced the blood in her veins. Her fingers drummed against the smooth metal of her gun—her mind raced unending circles, soaked in the frenzy of bloodlust. She felt the wolf stir against her leg, his throat rumbling with a deep growl—

But a flash of red crossed her mind and chilled her rising temper. *Melina.* A flicker of green in the darkness shifted her thoughts to order. Her pride sank like a stone into the pit of her stomach—as she slowly sank into the mud. She bowed her head.

"Well!" Blackwell exclaimed. Aurous flinched and bared his bloodstained fangs at his abrupt motion. "That was rather simple, now, wasn't it? My, oh my, what a big *dog* you have." He winked at the wolf.

There was no sound other than the *hiss* of a striking match. Crimson flared along the thin splinter of wood and burned deep into the stub of another cigarette. Smoke curled from his nostrils in faint wisps.

"Now that we have a better understanding of ourselves and my operation, we can continue to build. And you will continue fighting for my cause."

She made a subtle movement with her head, but refused to meet his commanding glare. He chuckled at her intractability.

"Was there anything else, *soldier?*"

She couldn't even bring herself to answer no.

"I'm sure a thorough investigation is warranted, and we have a means of detecting the sickness. Your team will be evaluated, and if anyone else is infected, there is quarantine. We'll trace this outbreak." His narrow eyes wandered over her swirling scars. "Though, if this proves Mengele's little *experiment* failed—well, I'm sure you'll find out for yourself soon enough."

With another bellow, everyone around her pushed to their feet and retrieved their fallen gear. She remained in the muck, unable to tear her gaze from the severed head. Strands of Colbat's hair still poked through the mangled flesh.

Mud splattered up her coat as the general stomped away from her and barked his commands at the others. She drew in a shaky breath and a foul taste adhered to her tongue. It nearly choked her.

"Get a sample from that head!" the general called back over his shoulder. To her, he sneered, "Try not to lose any more members of your team."

The murky land stirred as the crowd scattered like cockroaches when the lights flipped on. She sat there for a moment, disillusioned, her temper simmering. Guilt seeped through her mind like sickness. Her throat tightened.

"Commander?"

She blinked her eyes into focus. Nadie offered her a hand, her eyes glittering like a wooded hillside.

"I'm fi—" Celeste croaked. She cleared her throat. "I'm fine."

"I didn't understand the soldier life once, I was an outcast," Nadie said. "Come have some tea, Commander."

Sweet-smelling steam warmed her cheeks. She inhaled slowly, clearing her lungs of the fetid air of camp. Her lips still tingled from an eager sip of the boiling hot tea. An earthy rich flavor nearly masked by a thick serving of honey. Her father would have loved it. *Without so much honey.*

"It's delicious."

Nadie glanced over her shoulder. "It's nothing," she said. "Simple herbs that grow around here. Mostly dandelion. Honey is from last year's mishap with a bee's nest."

"Worth the trouble."

Her tent was mostly bare, with moss-colored walls and a solitary cot placed across from the sealed entrance. Clothes were haphazardly tossed over the tucked sheets of her cot, and an assortment of dismantled weapon parts and screwdrivers of various sizes littered her pillow. There was a small knee-high tabletop that looked meticulously carved by hand adjacent to the entrance, but no chairs, cushions, or other amenities. Celeste perched herself against the table, her fingers curled around a chipped mug of tea. Nadie leaned next to her, nose drawn to the steam rising from her own cup.

"You haven't been here long, have you, Commander?"

Celeste paused and struggled to piece the foggy puzzle together. "Only a few months, I believe."

"Before that, I mean."

Another pause. "I was only with the bandits for a few weeks, if that's what you're getting at." She slowly sipped her boiling-hot tea.

"No," said Nadie, "where did you grow up?"

"To the north in the mountains."

"Parents?"

"My dad."

"I lost my mom before the world fell, too," Nadie said with a shaky sigh. "It's been so long since I've even seen a picture of her, I can't remember what she looks like."

Celeste shivered as the memories haunted the edges of her thoughts like old ghosts. All she remembered was the blood. So much blood.

"But I remember my dad."

Celeste clenched her jaw and listened.

"He raised us, alone," she said with a hint of pride. "Mom died giving birth to me. I guess I was stubborn. The fifth child. He did it *alone*." She was grinning madly. "I don't remember much of the old world, before the sickness, but I remember his face when he got home from work, dirty black, and how his eyes would light up at the sight of all of us. He never complained—even when the world fell."

"I don't remember those times."

Nadie shrugged. "I remember the house I lived in, with blue siding and a slanted porch. I remember my sister...getting sick in her room, and our father, who had been glued to the TV set for weeks, rushed her to the hospital. She never made it."

"I'm sorry."

"My brother was next, and he was only eight. I think it was his birthday, or it was coming up. Something like that. By then, the panic was spreading, and my dad had enough of the hospitals and brought us to the Elders. When my brother passed, h-he turned, badly, and killed so many of the them. There were more of them, too, turning and killing. Some were creeps, half-dead and transformed, but many of them fully mutated—what did you call them, Commander? Hunters?"

Celeste shrugged. "Yes, my dad did. They never stop. Everyone seems to classify them differently." She thought for a moment. "I've seen some that looked like dogs with rabies."

"Right. Hellhounds." She almost laughed. "My dad called your hunters, 'windigos.' After the Elders were killed by one my dad got us into the car, the three of us left, and drove into the woods." She paused to take a sip of her steaming mug. "You grew up in the mountains, you said?"

"Yeah," Celeste replied, "my dad brought me there after my mom and brother died. The world was ash, he used to say, nothing to rebuild."

A smile touched the corners of Nadie's mouth. "My dad said

that too, whenever my older siblings would talk about exploring towns and finding survivors. My dad was adamant there was nothing left. And if there was"—she gestured around her—"it was this. He hunted for us. Clothed us. We were fine until he was injured with his own bear trap. He needed antibiotics, badly, and he refused. So, he got worse. And worse, and worse. Finally, my older brother went out and"—her voice broke slightly—"never came back. He was just gone."

"Shit," Celeste breathed.

"Gone," Nadie repeated the finality of it. "My dad pulled through, and when he did, he tried to find him. He tried. That was the end of my dad as I knew him. He became withdrawn, surly, paranoid that we were being watched and hunted like deer. The food supply dwindled. It was a rough winter, Commander, I won't lie. I was young and I wanted to die. I remember the cold, the goddamn cold. It's still in my bones. One morning...I remember so clearly. One morning, when we woke up, my sister wouldn't. She wouldn't wake up. I didn't understand as I do now, how much she loved me. I thought she wanted to leave us. She saved my life, Commander, giving me her rations of food.

"After she passed, my father nearly went mad with grief. There was nothing left of him. We found ourselves burning our home, all of it, and her body with it. It wasn't long before a Red Dawn patrol found us, and forced my dad to bow to their regime, or side with the dead. For me, he chose life, but I never saw him again. Died on the frontlines, they said. Died with honors."

Unease gnawed at Celeste's heart. "And you believe that?"

"I don't know what I believe anymore." Nadie sighed, her lips circled over the brim of her cup. She waited another moment to cool her tea, then took a long drink. "You must think I'm crazy. It's been years, but I miss him. I miss them all. I miss our life before the sickness."

"Not at all." Thoughts of her own father spilled through her mind like pooling blood. "I miss the hell out of music."

Nadie's tense but bubbly laugh broke the bitterness between them. "A beautiful aspect of life taken for granted until the world fell." She nudged her head toward her bed and Celeste glimpsed the tangled mess of wires and gutted components to several pieces of machinery. "We get special privileges when we succeed. Downgraded for failures. Me, I just scavenge for parts until I can fix what I already have. It's a Walkman, an old device for listening to cassette tapes."

Even gazing at the splayed array of components, she couldn't imagine their final constructed state. It felt like a lifetime since she'd lived with such luxuries. The records her father once possessed were rather too large to fit in such a small device. With a creeping smile, she recalled stumbling upon his collection, and one album in particular; tucked into a sleeve of the record was a note with her father's name scrawled in looping hearts across the cover. A gift from her mother. Her father, when he had found it in her hands, played her favorite song for the first time.

"We had a record player," Celeste said, voice cracking. "A few albums, but never lived close to any electricity. But on the odd occasion we had fuel for our generator, he would bring it out by the fire and play his favorite band. Well," she added with a wide grin. "My favorite, too."

"Dad music, huh," Nadie said. She snapped her fingers. "Jazz, right?"

"Not a chance. Rock, all the way."

"You must hate hip-hop music, then," Nadie said, playfully mocking her with a sigh. "I'm all about the party and the good times. Plus, I don't let anyone step."

Celeste grinned. "I was taught that everything has its place...but all I need are killer riffs and solos, with hard-hitting drums." She shrugged slightly. "Rush. Can't be beat."

"I can dig it."

"It's funny," said Celeste. "The similarities between our lives when my dad thought we were the only ones." Tears stung her eyes. "I appreciate the sentiment, Nadie, showing me I'm not alone in camp. There are others with my pain. But I don't care about fitting in."

Nadie clenched her jaw. "That's not it, Commander. Yes, I was like you, lost in this ferocious cycle, but I'm not telling you to fall in line and accept fate as I did. I'm telling you to get *out* before Blackwell breaks you...like he breaks everyone."

The cold, rancid mud that had soaked into her jeans was a direct and chilling reminder of her forced subservience. Bound to the Napoleon of this era, the fierce and unstoppable conqueror. His victories bathed in the blood of his own people—was it still considered a victory if so many innocents were caught in death's grip as well?

Vega's disembodied voice resounded through her mind. *It was *necessary, as you will understand one day when you are leading your own people in battle.*

"I can show you a way to escape the city undetected, at least until roll call," continued Nadie, apprehensively quiet. "If I can sneak enough provisions, I may be able to guide you through the woods and out of their reach—"

"No." Celeste abruptly shook her head, her carmine hair whipped against her cheeks.

"Commander?"

"What if I said there was another way." Her mind flashed toward the dam and the device buried in a sweater soaked in her own blood. "Something that can end this madness."

Nadie's dark, brown eyes radiated. "Tell me more."

FIVE
With Wild Abandon

"STEADY YOUR aim."

Melina's brow smoothed when she drew in a sharp breath. Her fingers slid down the dappled-red metal, tracing arches along the worn paint. She clenched her jaw; her finger twitched against the trigger. A resounding *blast* tore through the ink-blotted target across the valley.

"Not bad," Celeste praised, grinning. "You hit all three."

There was a small huff of disappointment. "My aim was still off."

"You haven't had a chance to practice in *weeks*," Celeste said with an arm slipped around Melina's hunched shoulders. "I'd say you did pretty well, considering." Her fingers tangled in twisting, red ringlets of hair—like ribbons of silk curling in her hands. Chills prickled her.

Another huff. "You're trying to make me feel better."

"You did great, really."

"Not so well with the other techniques."

Celeste frowned. It was their third hour of shooting drills down in the valley that carved through the mountains below the campgrounds. A sprawling meadow littered with targets in its narrow expanse, with fragmented metal glinting across the shimmering green. Even the thought of direct conflict frayed Melina's nerves. She had slashed the practice blade wildly, with her eyes clenched shut—and left her vital areas wide open for fatal counters. A pistol brought more hesitance. Celeste knew the weight of the weapon was a gut-wrenching reminder of her confinement within the hospital. Her first kill. But the moment she found a firm grip on a sniper that Celeste had lifted from her uncle's personal collection, dappled-red like spots of blood, on a glinting silver polish and chestnut stock, Melina heard her true calling. She had loaded that sniper as if on muscle memory alone, raised it, flared her nostrils—and blasted each target apart.

Even if Colbat was here, Melina would need to learn how to fight. If Blackwell caught wind of anything—

"Celeste, are you okay?"

The melody of Melina's voice reeled in her spiraling thoughts. Celeste looked down into the bright bursting green of her eyes. Freckles dotted her porcelain-white skin. *Like stars dotting a bright sky—*

She jumped from Melina's touch like it was a jolt of electricity. A creeping warmth seemed to spread between her fingers, like blood gushed from an open wound. She recoiled, cursing, hands clasped over her aching guts. There was no blood, no splitting scars—just tender flesh and rigid black blemishes.

She struggled to meet Melina's despondent gaze.

"Seriously, what's been on your mind?"

Each breath was heavy like the air was made of lead. She struggled to unravel her tongue, bound by the uncertain pursuit of victory. That word cleaved her mind with unending torment. *A victory is a victory.*

Right?

"Celeste?" Worry squeezed Melina's voice to a squeak.

"Do you trust me?"

"Yes." Melina flicked her fingers against hers. "Of course, I do."

Celeste clenched her jaw as if cold. "Do you *trust* me?" she asked again, swimming through the sea-green of Melina's eyes.

"Yes."

"There might be trouble ahead, Melina, and I'm not sure if I can control the outcome."

"What is this about?" Melina's eyes flicked past her. "Did you invite him?"

Celeste froze. "Who?"

Uncle. A soldier's gait carried him through the grassy stalks with commanding presence, like a stranger in military garb approaching civilians. He held his arms behind him as he loomed, with an air of command—no longer an uncle calling on his dear niece.

"Melina," he greeted. But to Celeste, his voice tightened. "Celeste," he said formally, "a word in private, please?"

"Sir," she replied coldly.

His lips thinned as he searched her narrowing eyes, and for a moment, his cheeks creased, brow knitted—exactly like her father when he was frustrated. The resemblance at times could be staggering. Particularly his cold, almond-brown eyes. Then, just as her father had, he commanded her to follow with a glowering look. Celeste gave Melina's hand a gentle squeeze, and the redhead gently warned her to play nice.

Sunlight scattered through white dappling clouds and tinted the meadow a motley shade of green that reminded her of military camouflage. Even the land was with them. Babbling brooks meandered down from the mountains and snaked through the deep-green meadow, strangled by weeds and runoff. Few trees rooted in the damp soil, remaining stunted and irregular like twigs, but lilacs were bursting with prismatic colours, blossoming in billowing clusters. The wind was perfumed with gunpowder and pollen.

"Amazing view, is it not?"

Uncle positioned near the opposite hillside, a silhouette with his back to the sun. She squinted at him, unease gnawing at her belly. She had to wonder if he positioned himself in a blinding advantage. Or was it to gain a proper look up at the ruins of Fort Thompson?

Beyond the steel wall, buildings were gutted, crumbled, or crushed like discarded toys, the streets buried in debris that resembled a rockslide. Few structures along the city border remained intact, while other sections of the ruins were fenced and barricaded completely.

"A bit tarnished," she replied with a shrug. It was a blemish, an ugly scar against the emerald landscape. But there was a glimmer of hope in the wild, untamed expanse beyond the city. "But I'll take it."

"If only you could have seen what it was like, Celeste," Uncle said. "Before the end of the world, I mean. The city...what it used to be. It was gorgeous..."

"I can't remember much of before."

He chortled and swayed on his feet. "I don't expect you to." His finger traced the jagged, mountainous skyline. "We grew up not far from this city, your father and me. He was much older than I was, so we never connected as friends. I was just joining the army when the world fell, and he was the first person I tried to get through the quarantine. He came with our mom, your grandmother, but he never went in with them." His smile grew. "He left, looking for your mother."

Her heart stirred. Never had her father spoken of losing her mother during the outbreak. Curiosity fluttered through her chest like a swarm of butterflies.

"Where was she?" Celeste found herself asking with a quiet, raspy whisper. Apprehension gnawed on her nerves.

There was a slight chuckle in response. "She was gone, as always, running from the love your father had." His almond-brown eyes melted. "Not that it was a bad thing. It seemed to be almost be a game between them. He chased her since the moment he had met her. Did you know that he was with someone else when he met her? Swear to God, first time they get introduced, they're young and dumb, looking at each other like fire scorched both their asses! They were friends that couldn't help but fall for each other. Years apart, it didn't matter. It was always her." He laughed, a sort of uncontrollable bark, and then said, "He told everyone that goddamn story."

Tears crawled down her cheeks like icicles as she recalled his last moments, her mother's name touching his lips with his final breath.

"He crossed the goddamn province to find her," he went on, a hint of pride to his voice. "Defied every military sanction or border on his way. But he found her, and that meant he found you. Through impossible odds." He shook his head, amused. "Star-crossed lovers, they were. He always wrote about her."

"Wrote?" she asked, wiping the snot from her nose.

His stubbly cheeks wrinkled with a smile. Pressed between his hands was a small book. The edges were crinkled, cracked, and peeling, pages stained yellow like bad teeth, loosely taped together with a tattered crimson leaflet. Etched into the cover was the unmistakeable scrawl of her father. Blotchy curves and loops she had not seen since the map he had charted for them.

"Daddy…"

"He kept meticulous notes on his journey from the outbreak until the—our falling out." Another shake of his head. "I've had it ever since. Truly, the last thing I have of him. Now, there's you as well."

The craving to peer through the pages of her father's written heart burned as fiercely as the need to kill the pain in her guts. Grinding her teeth, she stared at the crimson cover, watching blood drip from the pages of her father's open wounds…

She blinked, and reality unblurred.

"I wanted to give you this when you woke up," he admitted quietly. He tucked his chin to his chest, carefully considering his words. "I just wasn't sure how you would react. When we found out you had killed the Bandit Queen, we knew you had to be a fighter. Melina was very vocal about seeing that you were safe. But one of our own had shot you—nearly killed you. We had our best minds save you, and it could have been worse. I know those scars are a burden, Niece, a reminder of what you almost became. But that's just it—what you *almost* became."

The deep, black scars in her neck tingled. She had never given it much thought until now.

"I thought you might hold it against us," he continued, "the way we seized the city, the staggering amount of lives that were lost—but I saw you with your team, and it was like you were one of us your entire life. You were fitting in! Until you drove through camp like a madwoman, tossed one of your own, transformed and *dead*, at our feet, and then called down the general for his tactics—which, I may remind you, saved not only *your* life, but the lives of your friends."

She was stunned silent. It was a cold assessment of her erratic and foolish behavior—but entirely truthful. Her cheeks burned against the chilly breeze sweeping across the hillside.

"In your report, you claimed it was the Disfigured who attacked you, that there was a trap awaiting your team at the source of all that smoke." His voice tensed and cracked. "That you were lured there to be ambushed—but you do not know these 'Disfigured' individuals. They are not boogeymen snatching children from campsites. They are bandits, and they are the last of the army we decimated. They live in the Exclusion Zone, like savages, with disease and radiation. They don't operate this far out, so there was no reason to believe you would face any immediate danger. But your discovery and sacrifice will allow us to strengthen our defenses."

There was a bitter silence between them while Celeste mulled over her thoughts. Was there truly a price on her head? Or had she finally cracked and tumbled into the feverish grip of lunacy?

"You're a lot like your father, you know. Strong, ridiculously stubborn—and morals too high for a world long fallen to hell."

She glared up at him under a deeply furrowed brow. He laughed heartily in return.

"You even have his charming, sullen look! Truly is a wonder." He paused for a moment. "You're probably more like him than you realize. He, too, had trouble yielding to authority. His morals clashed with our tactics. But Blackwell is on a mission to fix this world, and he has liberated many places from uncivilized rule or complete and utter ruin. His methods may seem brutal, but I'm sure you could attest to the world's savagery, Celeste. I've seen the scars—and the dangerous look in your eye when you want to kill. Yes, Niece, don't think I haven't noticed your bloodlust."

"It's not—" she began.

He spoke over her. "I've seen what you can do, how well you can lead. So, I want you to remember that you don't have to like Blackwell, but you *will* obey his command. I had to learn as well, and I'll help you along the way."

"Yes, Uncle," she muttered, masking her disdain. "I'll follow orders."

"I need you to prove this, Celeste," he said. "That you can be a soldier like your uncle—and like your father should have been. If you can prove that to me, I'll hand over his journal so you can learn everything there is to know about the man your father once was."

It was not a subtle temptation. Part of her recoiled at the prospect of bowing to a despot for her father's belongings, an item that was rightfully *hers.* Yet, rationale reined in her wild thoughts. Perhaps her uncle only watched over his only remaining relative, hoping she would find a place in the new world as he had. For a moment, she felt the warmth of his generosity thaw her heart.

"Alright," she said with a small sigh. "I'll be a good soldier."

"That's my girl," he said, chuckling. Her eyes grew wide as the crimson-laced journal slipped back into his jacket. "Because there's grunt duty to make up for your brash display earlier. A lot of footwork."

She groaned at the burden of more chores. Just like her father had doled out punishment. "What now?"

"Fence patrol." He whistled in mock-envy. "You get the walk the perimeter of the border and keep an eye out for any peculiarities or trouble."

Her mouth gaped in disbelief. "This city is *huge!*"

"So was your outburst."

Stunned silent again, she bit her tongue and sulked.

"Get your team together," he said, hand clasped against her shoulder. "You move out immediately."

"Yes, sir."

"Niece."

She didn't look back.

"A good soldier."

Right. A furtive glance over her shoulder revealed the blot of bouncing red amidst the wavering sea of green. *Too soon for Melina to be on a mission, yet not enough time to train her.*

She nearly scented the tangy odor of spilled blood.

The pulse in her head had dramatically increased to a hot, hammering pain. Her guts rotted from the overindulgence of meds. To hell with the doctors, she had thought, they weren't the ones who had been shot multiple times. Regardless of her silent justifications, she kept it hidden from Melina and the others. Especially Melina.

Pain *thudded* inside her skull after every beat of her heart. Still, her hands drifted against the bobbing handle of her revolver, bleary eyes peeled and lost in the wooded landscape, a deep and shadowed maze of trees and bursting greenery. Her footsteps were muffled by slick grass and clinging moss, her breaths small and unsteady, lungs gripped by fire.

It was a struggle to piece together the puzzle of how quickly their deployment fell into chaos. They had trekked along the fenced borders almost an hour into their patrol when they were drawn forward by the faint sound of gunfire. Then it was a blur of green-dappled woods and incomprehensible orders, and an uncaring uncertainty if the others followed or not. She was a drone, on autopilot, responding monotonously and only reveling in the sense of apparent danger. They fanned out through the woods, creeping with their guns drawn and eyes peeled for movement.

"Commander?"

Nadie snapped away her autopilot. Celeste turned her head, a strained effort through the throbbing pain . The doe-eyed woman clutched her weapon at her hip, slender fingers pressed against the trigger guard.

"Did you get your girlfriend on board with the plan?"

"Melina?" Celeste asked stupidly, then shook her head. "No, at least not really. But don't worry, she'll follow me wherever we need to go."

"I'm worried more about firepower—you know, just in case," whispered Nadie, crouching below thick, twining branches.

"She's a great shot."

"I hope so, Commander."

"What about Snyder? You vouched for her before."

"As part of a sanctioned team," countered Nadie. "Not a covert operation. She's a military brat, born and raised into this way of life. Her loyalties may lie with them."

"She has a problem with authority." Celeste bit her lip, cheeks warming.

"Her older brother was killed on-duty, and she's always spoken highly of him—she wants to die a soldier as well. She's made no secret of it. It's in her blood. Depressing, really."

"Alright." A sigh escaped Celeste. Her eyes wandered past Nadie. A few dozen meters through the trees was a slight shadow, a blemish against the rippling brown thicket. Snyder flanked them, cutting through the green as silently as a ghost. "She's off the list."

"Got anyone else in mind?"

"Clark?"

Nadie swore in her own tongue.

"I know what you're going to say—"

A scoff. "Damn right," said Nadie, nudging her head forward. Clark stumbled over a protruding root, scraping his pistol against the cragged bark of a tree as he fought for balance. "He's a pussy."

"Yeah, he is."

"He looks like Mr. Bean," Nadie said, eyes rolling.

"Mr. Bean?"

"It's a show about an oblivious dude—I'll show you some night when I get a DVD player fixed." A broad smile lit up her creamy-brown features. "I still have the movies."

"Deal." Celeste was more interested in the opportunity for more honey drowning in that earthy tea.

"So, what about Harn?" suggested Nadie.

Harn tromped through the thicket like an ambling bear, gold-plated shotgun bobbing in his heavy hands. His form was nearly too stout for the Kevlar vest stretched around his military attire. He was apparently taking little chance since the appearance of the Disfigured. Celeste chewed the inside of her cheek.

"No," she finally said. Her boots sunk into the soft soil of the unlit forest. Cragged branches thickened and twisted skyward like bony fingers reaching for the sun. "I couldn't account for his whereabouts during the camp raid, and Twist seemingly came out of nowhere—I doubt he was even paying attention."

Twist lumbered into view, his portly belly rippling like waves crashing against the shore. His shirt had frayed and curled up his rounded gut. Still, his tongue pushed past his pursed lips, and his beady eyes glimmered like a child in wonder. He hurried after Harn, his own massive cannon of a weapon shouldered and tightly gripped.

"We need others, Commander."

It was like a rockslide in her stomach when her eyes drifted ahead of her.

"Clark," she said quietly. Regret festered as her prime candidate stumbled in his awkward advancement. His knees buckled, and another glance over his shoulder revealed the ghostly complexion. He was in fear's grip, forced along the frontlines as reprimand for his cowardice during the camp raid. Gone were the moments of immodesty; now he was trembling deadweight, a fearful rat draped in wolf's fur. But that emanation of fear could be controlled, loyalties divided. She could drive a wedge between him and his military service, dangle him from her own strings with the promise of survival.

"You can't be serious."

"He's malleable," Celeste declared, with a mischievous grin. "He'll do what I want."

Nadie grudgingly agreed.

"Shall we make our impression on him?" began Celeste—then a terrified shrill pierced her ears. Ice clung to her throat. Her lips parted, a soundless scream, her revolver drawn and *cocked* in one swift, deadly movement. She heard the apprehensive huff from Nadie, then silence cleaved through her with uncertainty. She knew the source of the scream.

Melina!

"Commander!"

The forest was a nauseous blur of green and muddy brown.

Panic fueled her erratic charge back to the fence. Her legs pumped with vigor she thought long drained, muscles flexed with strength long atrophied. Nadie was a pace behind her and steadily losing ground to such an abrupt burst of speed. The others straggled behind, perplexed at the lack of command. She didn't care. She would *kill* whoever dared hurt her tempered rose.

A sudden wave of regret as she selfishly wished her wolf were here with her. Her senses were dulled without his vigilant presence.

"Melina!" Celeste hissed. She slowed to a cautious creep and stabbed the glinting barrel through the thicket. When she finally spotted her redhead, her blood boiled and heated her skin.

Melina was caught in the crushing grip of a toothpick-thin man, her head forced back with the milky flesh of her throat fully exposed. There was a blade pressed firmly against the carotid artery. A slight jerk and nick and the life-giving blood would drain in seconds.

Her captor had his long, lanky arm around her waist like a jealous lover, his eyes peeled with desperation. Filth dripped from his face like sweat, staining his light skin with muddy streaks. His cheeks were sunken and sallow, teeth carious and broken. Unkempt facial hair curled from his lips and chin in ratty clumps. He was hunched over with like a spider spinning prey into a webbed coffin. Melina's rifle was in the dirt under the toothpick man's boot.

"Melina," Celeste whispered soothingly, "are you okay?"

"Y-yes," she squeaked in response, overwhelmed by an icy rush of fear. She quivered in her captor's deadly hold. Freckles faded with her pallid complexion.

"You talk to me now," the toothpick man snarled. "Do as I say, and we can all walk away with our lives."

Celeste flicked her eyes to him. Her forced smile was a cold shark's expression. "If you so much as spill a drop of her blood, I'll kill you."

He glowered through the ragged strands of his hair like a stalking beast. "You're not in the position to make demands."

"I'm a hell of a shot," she countered.

"I'm sure you are," another voice sneered, hidden within the tangle of trees. A sharp *click* echoed. "But I am, too."

"Shit," cursed Nadie, lowering her machine pistol.

Another man stepped out from behind the cragged trees, blonde hair matted to the mud crusted on his forehead. He was thin, too, but rigid with muscle that flexed through his tattered military garb. A small, black barrel trembled only inches from her face, burning a metallic scent into her nostrils. Recently fired.

Still, she kept her revolver drawn to Melina's captor. "If I die, none of you make it out of here alive."

"Snarky *bitch*," another muttered from the forest clearing, with an accent so thick she dreaded the presence to be Caden. The approaching man was of smaller stature, pudgy and tanned with filth. His hair was a bright clownish red. A steel machete, blade curved near the tip, waved in his hand as he skulked into view. Against his hip, nestled securely in his other hand, was Snyder's oak-brown Springfield.

Damn it. "Where's my team?"

"Dealt with," the toothpick man sneered. His eyes narrowed at her gun's vicious glare. "Lower you weapon."

"Not a chance," she began, hissing.

"We just want your guns!" he interjected with a hoarse bellow. "You give us those and directions into the base, and we'll let you live."

Nadie's fingers drummed nervously against her weapon. "There's room enough for everyone—"

"Not a chance in hell I'm falling in line with that tyrannical *prick*, Blackwell."

Clown-hair mumbled, "Damn right."

"We have your other companions by now," the toothpick man went on, tongue flicking over his chapped lips. "Bound and secured. Like we said, we just want your goddamn weapons. We have no trouble with you—only the general."

Too convenient. The thought was an anchor for her fleeting rationale.

"You hand over everything you got, show us the quickest way in, and we'll let you get far from here before shit hits the fan."

"How do I know my team isn't dead?"

"I would have brought you their heads before I took *hers*." The blade nicked Melina's throat and a thin rivulet of red trickled down her skin.

Grinding her teeth, she replied, "You made a mistake not killing us from the start."

There was a glimmer of green; Celeste caught the subtle flicker of Melina's gaze, so she hesitantly lowered her revolver. Her ears tingled with the quick, ruffled sounds of Clown-hair approaching her with Snyder's weapon drawn.

"You don't need to be caught up in this," the toothpick man said. "You look like good people, not soldiers, so I'll let you go. Like I said, Blackwell is our only target." He quickly nodded to his cohort. "Take their gear, too, so we look like one of 'em."

"Aye," said Clown-hair, grunting slowly. "Ya heard him, miss, take yer damn clothes off."

The toothpick man called out, "Oliver!"

"Got 'em tied!" Another disembodied voice hollered from the forest depths. "The fat one was hard to wrestle down!"

"Well, now that we have—"

There was a sudden commotion ahead of her. The toothpick man was silenced when Melina drove her elbow into his belly, wrenching her head from his rigid grip. Bloody welts formed where her hair ripped and peeled from her scalp. Still, she tumbled to the dirt in a desperate scramble from death.

The next moment, Celeste reeled with the ferocity of a starving predator. She whipped her arm, revolver almost weightless, and grazed the trigger as she swung. The barrel erupted in a blinding streak of light and Clown-hair fell with his neck hollowed from the blast, shock peeling his eyes wide. Before his body even hit the ground, Nadie snatched her machine pistol and aimed through the tangled thicket. She heard the loud, disgruntled curse, followed by the *snap-snap-snap* of brittle branches beneath every careless step. Then there was a blur through the trees, and Nadie's gun opened fire in short, but calculated bursts. The fleeing figure rolled into the dirt with sputtering grunts and wordless moans.

Celeste adjusted her aim again, but found the toothpick man over Melina, her own sniper rifle jabbed into the back of her neck. Melina was forced to the ground, her ragged, fearful sobs muffled by soggy grass.

"Don't!" the toothpick man roared, but desperation broke his voice. "I'll shoot the bitch!"

Celeste grimaced, but steadied the revolver. "I'm going to kill you!"

The toothpick man shook his head. "You're a goddamn psycho! This isn't what I signed up for!"

"What?"

"Stand down!"

The stern command was abrupt, short, but the toothpick man and Nadie both froze as if ice seized their limbs. Celeste felt her heart painfully lurch. The deep bellow was familiar, hauntingly so, and now she knew it was no coincidence she found herself embroiled within chaos once more.

General Blackwell.

He strolled through the trees, a smirk ruffling the silvery wisps of his mustache. Short, with a commanding presence, he paced between her and the toothpick man, his lips curled around the stub of a burning cigarette. With a quick nod of his head, the amorphous shadows scurried from the forest depths and blurred into view. Waves of soldiers crashed in through the trees, the *thudding* of their boots sounding like the rolling thunder of a storm in the distant skies. She was surrounded by rows of faceless soldiers and long rifles, each barrel level with her center mass.

"I said stand down, Kurt," Blackwell urged with a gentle, but firm voice. "This went as far as it could."

"My friends are dead," the toothpick man, Kurt, sniveled back. The sniper rifle trembled in his unsteady grip. "That wasn't the deal!"

"Unfortunately, it was," the general stated briefly, before addressing his armed men. "If he doesn't lower his weapon by the time I am finished speaking, you may open fire on him—and *him* alone."

Just before the last word fell from the general's wicked tongue, the ragged man Kurt dropped the rifle to the dirt by his boots.

"What the hell is this?" Celeste demanded with her revolver still raised. "Where is my team?"

Blackwell cocked a brow at her, almost as a dare. When silence gripped her wildling tongue, he chuckled to himself, visibly pleased with her inaction.

"They're fine," he informed her, a quick nod to the soldiers surrounding them. "Took their weapons for show—they are being briefed of the situation now."

Celeste gathered her few remaining nerves, demanding, "And what situation was that?" The next word rolled in her mouth with a foul taste. "*Sir.*"

"A test of loyalties."

Behind the advancing throng of soldiers was her uncle, pace slow and gaze sheepish and flitting. His refusal to greet her curious expression only solidified her belief of his warning in the valley earlier that day. He had begged her to fall in line, to put the military before her own desires—had she? She had nearly sacrificed—no, she *did* sacrifice them for Melina's safety. There was barely a second thought spared for any of them.

Shame burned through her.

Melina slowly rose to her feet, trembling, complexion ghostly pale. Her cheek crimsoned against the faint chill of the flickering shadows. Blood gently smeared between her fingers. The cut was superficial, a small, red blot against the milky skin of her throat. But it was her wide, wondering eyes, a fading green, that said more than words ever could. A shimmering betrayal. She was hurt, and not just physically—Celeste had needlessly risked her life.

General Blackwell's hoarse, booming voice snapped the world into focus around her. "I must say, Celeste, I'm impressed with your tenacity to survive! I mean, by God, you had two people gunned down who had already secured the weapons of your comrade! Yet you *still* took them on..." Smoke slithered up his silvered cheek. "I don't know whether to commend you for your bravery or your terribly impulsive luck."

"Sir," started Nadie, "what is happening to us?"

"Nothing!" he barked. "You succeeded. Or rather, I should say your *commander* succeeded in keeping your team alive."

"I don't understand..."

"You bastard," Kurt snarled. His hands balled into trembling fists. "You set us up to be killed by a mad *bitch!*"

Impatience came from the general as a loud *click* of his tongue and a sharp inhale of smoke. "I gave a choice: Life or death. You live with the consequences."

"I was told I would get my freedom!"

"No," Blackwell said flatly. The corners of his mouth twitched in a small, predatory smirk. "I told you to get an admission of treachery, and I gave you the means to separate her from the rest of her team. Which was done quite admirably, I must say!" His smile abruptly sank into a deep, dismal frown. "But you failed to produce any evidence of wrongdoing. That means your guilt is no longer forgiven. The deal is finished—you have sealed the fates of your men."

An alarming blast carried through the trees and silenced the dying man's low, gurgling groans. Behind her, one of the soldiers stood over the man Nadie had injured, his rifle smoking over a pool of crimson. The man was motionless, now dead.

"No!" Kurt cried out. His gangly limbs dropped like anchors to his sides. His filthy features sagged. "You promised—"

"I promised your life in return, regardless of the outcome."

"My brother..."

Celeste fidgeted uncomfortably, revolver trembling in her grip. She had been played.

"Commander Celeste," the general greeted. Brightly stained teeth gleamed through a vicious smile. "Our earlier encounter left a foul perception of your loyalties and where they may lie. Your uncle stated that you will stand under my command, but I had to see for myself. An opportunity for assassination—perfection for a brash, power-seeking *rat*. But not only did you refuse to stand down, you had them *killed*."

A fierce gaze was her only response.

"Even at the expense of your team."

Her jaw shifted, teeth grinding.

"This was a setup."

Blackwell mimicked her impetuous glare. "You're goddamn right it was."

Her heart *thumped* into her throat.

"But I no longer doubt your loyalty," Blackwell continued. "Your strength is to be commended. Your impulsivity, well, I'm sure we'll make a *leader* out of you yet."

Disappointment welled. Celeste turned to Melina, but the redhead avoided her gaze.

"I—I am free?" Kurt wept. "I can claim my brother's body?"

The general stiffened, his chest rising with a deep breath of smoke. "Indeed. I do keep my word"—his cruel glare flickered to Celeste—"But that also depends if *she* keeps hers."

Celeste had never lowered her revolver. "I said spill one drop of her blood and I would kill you."

Kurt stumbled. There was a slight twitch of his eye, a partial gape of his thin, filthy lips. Then realization lit up his face the very moment her revolver erupted in a blinding flash. A ruby gleam fanned the grass before his body slammed against it, motionless.

A disgusted sound escaped Melina, but there was a deep guffaw from the general as the revolver blast ripped through the sky. The wiry old man slapped her shoulder and nearly knocked her off balance.

"Welcome to Red Dawn," he said coldly. Smoke burned against her nostrils. "Now finish your patrol."

Her team emerged through the retreating soldiers. None met her despondent stare. Melina shoved past her, sniper rifle dangling in her listless grip. They fell back into formation, grudgingly awaiting her order. There were no words she could muster; Melina's avoidance was a cleaver through her heart.

They're always one step ahead, she thought. *I need to be two ahead of them.*"

Commander, what now?"

The silence was almost deafening; her thoughts were a cascade of bloodlust, her skin crawling at the bittersweet scent of spilled life. It was a maddening irresistibility, a swirling mess of greying morality.

"Now," she said quietly, so only Nadie heard the poison to her words. "We dig up the detonator and find the bombs."

SIX
King of the Hill

THE MUD between buildings was an unyielding swamp, a flood of rancid runoff from the city above. It crept down the hills in boggy streams and sank the derelict structures in deep muck, oozed through the rifts and cracks of the wreckage scattered through the steep, winding streets. They hid within the shadows between slanted columns of evening light, knee-deep in waste, and at least a dozen blocks deeper into the siege than she had ever fought to. Only a portion of the streets had been cleared of mud and debris, an operational lane for vehicles and troops passing through into General Blackwell's camp in the heart of the city.

Again, they heard the rising pitch of voices, and the rumbling *hum* of an engine as faint light flickered across the wall. Through the opening ahead, she spotted the slow-rolling advance of a rusted lime-green truck, with wheels that chewed and ripped the street to mudded ruts. They took another shuddery plunge into the muck, and chills constricted her to breathless gasps. The scarred flesh around her belly ached against the frigid mud. But her eyes watched another vehicle lurch down the road, engine roaring like an untamed beast. Soon the noise dimmed to the ringing in her ears.

"Give it a minute," Nadie whispered, teeth chattering. She was violently trembling, rippling the muck around them. "They scurry in numbers like rats."

Celeste grunted her reply, eyes peeled to the dim light of the street—but her thoughts flitted like a startled bird. How cruel and cold Celeste's soul had become, Melina doubtlessly dwelled, to reach such fury with her actions. More blood that stained her scarred fingers. Melina had grown to accept her flaws, her wrongdoings, her admissions of guilt over who she had killed—and loved her fiercely despite it all. So why couldn't Celeste find it within herself to return the sentiment? Was she doomed to condemn all she loved to a fate bathed in the blood-red of death? Her heart fluttered and ached, a painful lament for Melina's warmth, the soothing, sweet taste of her lips—

"Commander?"

Her eyes snapped closed, stinging. "Right," she said, then blinked quickly. "We move now."

"It's this this way."

They peeled from the muck like old Band-Aids from a scab, dripping with foul waste. Celeste huffed and pumped her legs through the mud but paused just before the street. Quick glances in either direction revealed eerie, derelict sights; foundations of most buildings sank or collapsed, causing the structures to shift and slant over the streets like wilting weeds. Each window was filled with a dark, unending void, complete blackness. Abandoned and left to rot as a remnant of what once was. She felt a certain sense of contentment for burning her former home into ash that spread back into the wild—if only she would have burned her other sentiments, now lost along her harrowing journey to find her uncle.

"This city is a goddamn maze," Celeste remarked, oddly impressed by the immensity. "The bandits didn't expand beyond the neighborhood near the wall entrance."

Nadie made a strange sound, a loud snort of contempt for such a small woman. "I don't think they realized just how entrenched the military was here. Before the fighting began between bandit camps and renegade forces, the entire west coast was under their authority."

Except that was Vega's plan. Concentrate the forces in one area—bury them in an icy tomb.

But now I have the switch.

"How do you know about this area?" Celeste asked without a second thought or care for her blunt approach. "It seems our unit doesn't have much rank. If any."

Nadie's eyes darted to her then swept through the empty streets. Another strange snort of laughter from her. She waved her through.

"I wasn't always in this unit, you know," she said with a small smile, as if drawn away to a distant memory. "My skills had me climbing the ranks even as a young girl. I used to work for the general, mostly as a tech. But"—she gave her sculpted eyebrows a playful wiggle—"demotion is what happens to those with sticky fingers. It could have been worse, but my S-O vouched for me and ta-da! Here I am in Joke Unit with all my wonderful *friends*."

Celeste choked on a laugh. She followed Nadie down the crumbled path, casting nervous glances over her shoulders. There was a prickle along the back of her neck, like watchful eyes trailing her every movement.

"Let me guess," she asked, "stealing movies?"

"Some asshole used *Training Day* as a goddamn coaster!"

Her eyes rolled. "Should I even ask?"

"Only one of the best movies ever made."

"I used to read a lot of books."

Nadie eased her pace and cautiously watched the street ahead before answering. "I never could understand what the big deal was with reading. I just can't see anything in my head, not like I can with watching a movie, anyway."

"Maybe you haven't found the right book." Celeste shrugged off the chill of her damp clothes. "Sometimes it just takes one good story."

"Well, maybe all it takes is one good movie to change *your* mind, Commander."

"Maybe."

They paused at a split in the road; one way was a steep descent into what appeared to be the ruins of a once-bustling district, with the skeletal remains of skyscrapers and buildings like tall, thin cylinders glinting furiously against the blazing red glow of the setting sun. Billboards with words and images were a swirl of discolouration, faded paint, and grime, almost unintelligible after so many years of battling the elements. The buildings themselves appeared untouched from the siege, merely ravaged by time, weather, and occasional looters. Then she noticed the road was fenced off further down, abruptly ending in a barricade beneath the bridge.

"Is that it?"

"That's the Medical District," explained Nadie in a low, fearful whisper. "I've only heard rumors of what they used to do there."

"Used to?" Disbelief swelled in her throat.

"Before the city fell to the bandits, this is where they kept the creeps."

"For weapons?"

A small shake of her head. "Experiments for a cure, allegedly. But there was talk of what was really going on down there, of all the horrors they were *creating*."

Celeste gazed over the sealed wall; atop the bridge, she spotted another patrol sweeping along the fence, and two others posted near the wall with their weapons drawn. She found it difficult to believe the military had stopped their experimental control, the ability to command the monsters like a trained dog, a vicious and unyielding weapon. She had thought it insane and completely improbable—until she saw their atrocity with her own eyes. Waves of infected had poured through these streets for the glory of victory—but it was Colbat's transformation that truly struck her as strange. It had been of a different caliber. A full transformation so close to death. He should have been like the others she had encountered, half-maddened corpses, what Nadie called creeps, grey skin swirled with black, rotting flesh—but he resembled a hunter, a monster transformed. And it had spoken to her.

No, it had *hissed* at her.

Kill her.

Nadie's firm grip around her forearm snapped her from the waking nightmare.

"Not wise, Commander," she said quietly, nudging her head to the wall. "We've been damn lucky that things have been quiet around here for so long, the patrols are lax near the city. But there'll be guards posted near that district 24/7. There's no chance we're sneaking in for a peek." She added with a slight grumble, "Not that I would want to."

"Well, we can set a charge along these roads and cripple their main route," Celeste decided, grip tightened around her holstered gun. "And then one under their armory."

"Agreed."

Another hesitant sigh. "Can you take me to the general's room?"

"What?" Her comrade sucked in a quick breath, nearly gaping at her reckless determination. "To the Stronghold?"

Celeste only nodded once in response. The air grew icy between them.

"Commander, the plan was to try and map the city to navigate the sewers below," she cautioned. "This is suicide!"

But her resolve was an impervious stone wall. "There must be old blueprints of the city or maps he created. This could be our chance."

And prove what the hell kind of monster's they're trying to create.

To avoid another encounter with a passing patrol meant slipping down into the mudded ditch and pressing flat against the frigid, foul smelling sludge. Boisterous voices carried through the streets like a room full of drunks shouting at each other, then faded to a faint murmur along the night breeze. Another moment crawled by as slow as the slimy-sweat trailing down her cheeks.

"How many times have you been here?" Celeste asked in a harsh whisper. Her voice was broken with her desert-dry tongue. "How fortified is it?"

"The Stronghold itself is just the old city hall, but I know for a fact where the general keeps all the information—I'm a tech-junkie, remember?"

"You set up his electronic storage." Celeste grinned through the mud smeared on her face. She was grateful the muck hid her jagged scars.

Nadie had to smother a small laugh. "Computers, Commander. They're called computers."

"I know that." Her face burned. It had been *far* too long since she'd thought of them at all. "But you can access them, right?"

"I think so," Nadie said, her voice low and tight. Her brown eyes scanned the dimly lit streets. "But I'm not the only person savvy with that kind of tech. He's bound to have someone else tinkering with it."

"We'll have to take that chance."

Nadie made a small motion with her long fingers, curling one at a time as if counting down slowly, then plucked herself from the muck along with Celeste. She hurtled up the mudded edge, boots slick with its rancid runoff.

Celeste fared no better; her boots puddled with sludge, squishing and oozing into her socks. Her clothes permeated with a terrible chill that gripped her by the bones. Her gloved hands plunged deep into the mudded ridge for leverage, muscles strained to hold her weight. Pain flared through her belly, and as she stood, she instinctively reached for her hidden pouch of pills.

No, came strong voice through her muddled thoughts. *Keep your wits sharp.*

Dad?

She shook her head, realizing she'd nearly called for him aloud, chasing old ghosts through her mind.

"...might be in the study," rambled Nadie as she scooped the slimy muck from her jeans. "Or what he refers to as the War Room."

"He's really full of himself."

Nadie scoffed. "You know why he calls his army Red Dawn, right?" She smothered a laugh when Celeste shook her head no. "It's an old ass movie about a group of teenagers who wage guerrilla warfare against the invading Russians. I've heard him quoting the lines as he watched it."

That earned a groan from Celeste, who couldn't be bothered to even clean her boots. She was already frozen. Toes tingled numb. Scars tingled. The heavy evening chill needled her skin with ice.

"His War Room," Celeste said. She resisted the urge to sigh her discontent. She didn't have the breath for it. "Guarded, I presume."

"Somewhat." Nadie quickly wiped the barrel of her machine pistol, smearing mud across the polished black metal. "Near the main entrances. It's for the high-ranking officials only, like your uncle."

Celeste's calves ached from the chill of her jeans. "You really have a way in?"

"Better," said Nadie. "But it's not very pleasant."

"Can't wait," muttered Celeste.

From the ridge she could see all the roads winding into the intersection by the monolithic building, a cascade of glass seeming to spill from the skyline above. It stood as a giant, oval and oblique, the tallest tombstone in the cemetery of skyscrapers, with an inclined entrance as if the front had collapsed in ruin. Instead it was fitted with barred doors like the sealed district behind them. A pale glow beamed from various windows like moonlight. A shimmery, pristine tower, unblemished by the ravages of weather or the fires of a collapsing society. A gleaming beacon of the past.

She could smell the thick, billowy fumes that spewed from the passing vehicles, feel the pinch of the wreckage beneath her feet. They moved quickly—and quietly—advancing in short, intermittent bursts down the descent from their vantage point, halting only to conceal themselves within the shadows at any sign of a patrol or military truck.

The camp layout within and outside of the city was a contrast to how Vega had congested her followers to the outskirts, crammed together like canned sardines in the streets. She had to wonder silently why Vega had refused to seize control of the inner city, especially the Stronghold and Medical District.

"This building looks like a pebble could bring it down," Celeste remarked, slipping through the veil of the dim, empty lot. The darkness was almost smothering, her ears ringing from the eerie silence. "Not exactly a fortified building."

"Only the tip of the iceberg," replied Nadie. There was a short whistle from her nose with every rapid breath. "There's a shelter below that can withstand a direct bomb blast."

Vega wanted no survivors. The grim thought surfaced again, burning like sickness in the back of her throat. *But perhaps she wanted part of the city intact. She could have already plundered the information.*

No, came the cold, chilling part of her mind she had kept buried. *She was killed with the belief her newfound daughter would join the rebellion—not halt it.*

"Where's the armory?" she abruptly asked. So far, her attempts at intel were drawn from her curious journeys through the outer camp. There was no formal barter system like Vega had provided for her people. They were all issued formal weapons but encouraged to secure and maintain their own personal arsenal during missions. She had steadily refused a military-issued firearm in favor of her silver revolver, but now almost regretted the stubborn stance.

"Hell if I know," came the response she had dreaded. "Before the siege, they had a formal armory we could register weapons or secure parts and ammo. But when the bandits came, they took everything that wasn't bolted down. Now everything is likely secured in bunkers and tankers. The big weaponry, well, they're kept with the war machines."

Thunder erupted from her hazy memory, the shockwaves from turret blasts and detonating engines. She cringed as the past raked its red-hot claws into her mind. She shook her head clear of a fog.

"And those are spread out."

"Mostly," said Nadie. A finger jabbed at the jagged skyline beyond the tower of nebulous glass. "A lot of the trucks are kept in the old fire hall."

Thoughts flooded her mind like a burst dam. "There may be a shelter beneath this tower," Celeste said firmly, "but they'll be crippled without their main vehicles."

"What about the others?" asked Nadie, teeth chattering again. "They have patrols along the walls, through the city and outside of camp."

"We set the charges below their strongpoints, and during the confusion, we can get the hell out of here without any worry of pursuit."

"Easier said than done."

Celeste finished with a cold, vicious snarl, "Then we come back and kill the survivors."

She watched as Nadie's eyes rounded with a shimmer. "We could put a *lot* of distance between us and this encampment."

Their gazes leveled to a mirrored glower. "These bastards killed my mom and brother. I'm not letting them get away with it. The river won't flood the whole city."

"I feel that pain," Nadie said. "I really do, Commander. My dad was forced to fight for them, and I never saw him again. But we are severely outgunned here." Celeste felt the strenuous bond between them shatter. "Just stating the obvious. It's a death sentence for us all."

"I've been waiting for this chance." Celeste fell silent, unsettled by the trouble seething through her tangle of thoughts. "The city is damn near empty," she finally continued, "but the military is supposed to be tens of thousands strong. Where the *hell* is everyone?"

"There are other facilities. With how many fell to the bandits, the general has thinned his forces by spreading his reach." She gave a small, disheartened shrug. "They're killing anyone they come across as a show of force."

"Alright," Celeste admitted, bitterly peeling the words from her tongue. "We go with your plan. Blow this camp to hell and then get as far from here as we possibly can."

"If we find the charges."

"*When.*" Celeste felt a sliver of warmth at the thought of Melina and her boundless faith. The corner of her lip quirked into a small smile. "Now show me the way into the general's room."

It was only a quick dash through the lot until they reached a platform near the entrance to the immense tower. There were statues of men in combat gear erected along the smooth, pearly marble, battered from the elements and spattered with slush, draped in a thin veil of rippling shadows. There was a solid metal gate across the marble platform, heavily guarded and teeming with black-garbed soldiers. Dozens. When she gazed to the sky, she could only see the prominence of the glass tower, and the bright, spectral shine of reflected moonlight. She was about to step out of the shroud of darkness when Nadie's grip tightened around her shoulder.

"Wait!"

As if on command, a bright patch of fluorescent light swept through the dais and across the emptied lot. She watched as the streaking light shone brightly in front of them, shards of shattered glass twinkling like stars against the tarry asphalt. Then the glare was gone, blurring across the road and into the darkness pulsing between distant buildings.

Nadie dared breathe again. "The patrols have lessened in recent weeks, but they're still vigilant. This is where the general conducts his business. He says it reminds him of what the old military government building used to be like out east before the sickness spread."

"Right."

The stale rubbery fumes adhered to the back of her throat. Pain radiated from her extremities, gnawed at her muscles and twisted her bones. "How are we getting in?"

"Maintenance hatch," she replied with a gentle whisper. "It's how I gained some old, extra wires I could splice to fix my DVD player."

Celeste smirked at Nadie's ingenuity, then flicked her watchful gaze over to the gated entrance. Another spotlight beamed against the darkness of the city, and more soldiers strolled through the lot ahead of them, weapons poised and trailing the maneuvered light. A few moments passed before they were out of earshot.

"Let's go."

The idea of what they were attempting at last hit her like a bullet; breaking into Vega's personal rooms had been one thing, but the general was fury in flesh. She was a lowly soldier, digging deep into the classified information Red Dawn was so eager to protect. They had set monsters loose through Fort Thompson that slaughtered foe and ally alike. Her persecution likely meant Melina's as well, not to mention her team and anyone else remotely associated with her.

She mulled over that troubled thought while her legs pumped furiously, carrying her across the lot with long, hurtling strides. Nadie nearly outpaced her, slanting their progression toward the gated entrance. At first, Celeste protested, heart *thumping* in her throat. But Nadie insisted and strategically veered them into the path of the sweeping spotlight.

They reached the walkway with little difficulty, remaining perched against the pillared statues—which were now amorphous slanting blots against the castoff glow of the passing spotlight. Shadows slithered and curled around them, ebbing across the smooth marble surface. Nadie pressed a finger against her pursed lips, head cocked to the gated entrance. Fluorescent light spilled across the road and illuminated the sea of fleshy faces, the tense, rigid expressions of soldiers still on duty. There were dozens congregated near the entrance at all times; soldiers passed through the barred doors or rushed back out into the streets on patrol, while others stood with their weapons drawn, inspecting every approaching face for identification. The grinding caterwaul of vehicles rumbled from the rolling hills of the upper city, resounding through the mountains. Through the cacophony, she heard voices pitched low in snickering whispers. A furtive glace over the edge of the marble statue, she spotted two forms blurring through the darkness, rifles shifting noisily against their bulky gear.

Each pass is only a few minutes apart, she surmised, gauging the distance of the soldiers. *We only have moments before the spotlight shines here again.*

This is absolutely insane. She couldn't stop grinning.

"Commander!" hissed Nadie. She gave her another quick wave of her hand. "Move!"

Celeste silently cursed having held such a rigid pose against the statue. Her legs were cramped and awkwardly bent, joints grinding as she scurried against the wall and closer to the gated entrance. Then Nadie vanished from sight. Celeste followed, slowing from apprehension—

—the ground gave out from underneath her.

She smothered a scream when her legs tangled. Pain shocked her hand numb when she smacked it against the wall and clawed for a grip across smooth marble. Her knees smashed into marble stair. She bit down another scream and fell forward, slamming into fleshy resistance. A small grunt escaped Nadie, then a loud *clang* as they both crashed into the wall.

"Shit." She was certain *someone* must have heard their clamorous descent into darkness. "Where are we?"

"Maintenance."

"There should be more guards soon," Celeste said, fingers *drumming* nervously against her revolver. Another glance at Nadie revealed little in the lightless hatch they had fallen into. She discerned nothing through the veil of black but the stairs below her, its marble frigid as ice against her muddy jeans.

"Almost there," she said, voice strained into small, raspy whispers. "These locks are...tricky."

Were those footsteps she heard through the clamor of the crowded entrance? Were they swiftly approaching to their position? Or just her heart hammering against her ribs?

"Come on, Nadie!"

There was a quick, unintelligible curse from the woman, then a drawn-out sigh. "The deadbolt is fully secured," she finally said, defeated. "I rigged the lock so it wouldn't latch properly, and I could slip in and open it from the outside. But someone must have fixed the damn thing."

Celeste grunted her annoyance, hearing nothing but the sharp grinding of her own teeth. "Okay, let me try."

"Commander."

They shifted awkwardly in the small, confined space below cement. Her wet clothes clung to her skin like frost. Celeste felt the woman's pulse when her waist brushed against her thighs. Her hair was scented like the subtle aroma of a daisy, sweet and lingering in the chilly air.

But her mind suddenly ached for Melina.

Slowly, her eyes adjusted to darkness and faint traces of the hatchway blurred into sight. She crouched and ripped into the pouch hidden inside her boot. Her gloved fingers fumbled through the slit in the leather lining.

Never leave the cot without them, she grumbled silently. Pinched between her fingers were two bobby pins, one crooked and twisted, the other bent into a long, thin strip.

"Can you get it open?" Nadie hissed. Her doe eyes were peeled against the gated entrance.

"Maybe." She prodded the cold metal of the deadbolt. *Definitely tricky.*

With the first pin lodged in place and slightly torqued, she dragged the thinner pin through the lock, adjusted again, then proceeded with another attempt. A tumbler *clicked* slightly. Again, she wormed the pin through the lock as carefully as her vibrant nerves would allow.

My skills are rusty.

It had been months since she had done anything but practice her aim and surly expressions. Not only bedridden from pain, but wary of integrating with soldiers her dad had fought so hard to escape from. When she thought of Mengele, the Blonde Man, she knew her life was in his hands, *had* been in his hands—quite literally. A part of her felt her father's resentment for him, the need to bathe the streets 1 his blood—again. Rationale countered that he would hope for her to put as much distance between her and Red Dawn as possible, abandoning the potential to cripple their forces.

*Dad died the day Mom's life was taken by that monster...*Her face burned against the chilly air. *I'll avenge you both. And brother.*

The crooked pin strained against the pressure she applied and then—*snap*—fell to the floor, broken. But with luck seemingly on her side once more, the door *shifted* from the wall, now slightly ajar. A small, sliver of light spilled through the crack.

"It's open!" she quickly said, then wrenched her fingers around the door. She heaved it open, blinded by bursting light. Behind her, Nadie slid a thick, rusted grate over the hatchway, grinding metal against concrete with a *screech*. Celeste froze, still as the marble statues above them, but Nadie barreled into her with more force than such a small woman should possess, and they were both hurled inside.

Through the slivered gap between the metal door and wall, she could see reflected light scatter through the gate. Icy hands clawed into her damp, muddy clothes as Nadie clamored over her, then quickly—but silently—eased the door closed as the light dissolved shadows within the hatchway. She secured the deadbolt, slid down to the floor with small, wheezy gasps, almost as if she couldn't breathe, then burst into a flutteringlaugh.

Celeste couldn't help but laugh as well, giddied from a shot of fear. They sat together, dizzied like young girls sneaking away from their parent's sight. Then the cold chill of reality seeped through their warm laughter, and they fell into bitter silence. Celeste was the first to crawl to her feet, feeling every ache and jolt of pain through her limbs. Her joints *cracked* noisily, like her Dad's old weary limbs once winter approached. Nadie took her extended hand, but Celeste's strength was fleeting, and she was unprepared to brace against a sudden shift in weight. Nadie fought for their balance, then walked on into the heart of the tower of glass.

The air was stale, but humid and thick like a cloud. There was a dull, brazen glow flickering through the cramped corridor. The walls were layered with immense copper pipes that rattled and groaned like old, wailing ghosts. The terrible sound ululated through seemingly endless corridors spanning every direction like a complex maze.

"Where does this all go?" Celeste asked, curiosity welling. "This is *huge*."

Nadie replied, breathless and gasping. "Service tunnels for the shelter, and the tower, I'm sure, but they're rarely used. When I worked for the general, I had to come to this building a lot. It wasn't always pleasant—in fact, it rarely was. More times than I could count, I had to get away from the shit I saw almost every day. This seemed like a better place than any."

"Lead the way."

It was a maze of hazy ruddy light and rusted walls, with overbearing stone arches so low her head glanced off the ceiling with any misstep. The corridors were barely the width of her shoulders, and her elbows grazed against the heated copper pipes. The sultry air was musty from disuse. Sweat made the grime on her skin gritty and mudded.

"Here."

A sharp turn led to a steep, snaking incline. The floors were a grated metal layout like the hidden hatchway, their trail of muck slowly seeping through. The higher they proceeded to climb, the more cramped and confined the corridor became; it was as if her body expanded to the proportions of a giant as she moved, about to burst through the foundation of the building. But it was the ceiling and walls that narrowed and enclosed around her until she had to hunch over on her hands and knees, spine painfully arched, and squeeze herself through. Ahead, the corridor became a small, paltry opening between walls for a band of copper pipes to span through. They halted at a dead end, breathless and anxious. Celeste ran her gloves through her matted hair, throat clenched in disgust. Cobwebs streaked her hair grey. She couldn't determine if the chills crawling across her skin was from her damp clothes or spiders scurrying for a new home. Either way, she shuddered violently and cleared her hair of webbing.

"Okay," Nadie whispered. Her plum lips thinned and paled as

she dwelled on her next thought, palms flat against the boarded ceiling. "If the interior hasn't been changed, we shouldn't be far from the offices he uses. The bastard is an old vet from before the world ended and fancies himself the last authority figure left."

"But he's not great with...computers." Celeste nearly forgot the word again, cheeks tinged red again.

"And he doesn't like anyone but himself knowing secrets," Nadie finished with a bright smile. "We'll use that to our advantage."

"Boots," Celeste quickly said, mind reeling. Her long-numbed fingers refused to bend or move properly, instead tapping furiously against her boot laces. Face scrunched in a dark scowl, she silently cursed the scars and bitter chill that immobilized her hands. Embarrassed, she averted her gaze to the mossy-green spots along the copper pipes above her as Nadie leaned against her leg and untied both boots. Slowly, Celeste plucked her soggy feet from the puddled mud and slime. Chills crept up her legs like terrible aches. Then after setting them aside against the pulsing warmth of the old pipes, she gave Nadie a tense nod.

Then the ceiling cracked open.

With a quick, furtive glance, Nadie peeked through the partial slit in the ceiling. Celeste could hear the woman's heart thundering between unsteady gasps, and soon found her own lungs sweltering as she forced her breathing into a slow and rhythmic pattern. There was a twinge along her scarred fingers when her hand leaned against her revolver. Instinct roiled within her.

But her heart eased its rapid pace at Nadie's signal: All clear and no trouble sighted. Yet. The separated ceiling swung open with a slow and heavy *creak* as rusted hinges protested movement. There was a sudden clatter like objects spilling across the floor. After a tense moment of silence, Nadie heaved herself over the ledge, crouching low with long-bladed knife drawn to her chest. Celeste maneuvered through despite the *groaning* complaints of her knees, aiming her revolver into the blurred surroundings.

The room itself was small, unfurnished and gutted, much like the corridor beneath the tile floor, with the shattered remnants of windows and thick bars across the panes. Cold night air whipped through the broken glass and chilled the room. The was a dim glow ebbing through the door ahead, flicking shadows across the barren walls around them.

Then the door slammed open. The commotion smothered

Nadie's startled gasp, but instinct propelled Celeste into action. Her bare feet slapped loudly against the tile floor with her wild lunge. Her fingers raked across skin and closed around a soft, lumpy throat like crushing talons, snatching her prey back into the darkness. Whoever it had been toppled over her when she fell backward, slamming against the filthy floor.

Slowly, a face below her became visible in the crooked slivers of light. He was gaunt, with sagging skin like it couldn't quite fit over his bones. But with such prominent features, he must have been handsome at some point, long before. His eyes drooped, bloodshot, rapidly darting around to gauge his upturned surroundings. The boy was a skeleton beneath her, just brittle bones and lumpy skin. There was a quick, feeble attempt to struggle against her unyielding grip, before fear settled as a violent, vibrant motion through his limbs with her revolver prodding the base of his throat.

"I'm sorry it has to be this way," Celeste whispered woefully. "Terribly sorry."

But Nadie's grip closed around her wrists. "Commander, stop!"

"We can't—"

But the man's hoarse whisper, a wheezing gasp, forced her silent.

"N-Nadie?"

SEVEN

Give Up the Ghost

CELESTE PULLED her revolver away from the man's throat, easing herself back against the wall. There was a kindness to the man's eyes at the sight of Nadie, a visible relief that washed over him in waves. He fell into her embrace.

"I can't believe you're still alive, Blake."

A semblance of a smile flashed across Blake's gaunt features. "It's nice to see you again, Rook." Excitement cracked his voice. "I've missed you."

"Blake...they said you were killed."

He shrugged off a violent coughing fit with a laugh. "Nearly," he rasped. "Blackwell wanted to deter any other attempt. He keeps me around as a lesson. I hope you don't have sticky fingers still, Rook." His blood-red eyes nervously twitched over Celeste. "New girlfriend?"

"Oh, hush," said Nadie, throwing her arms around his neck tight and strong. "You never took me on that date, asshole."

His battered features lifted, a small gesture that appeared to cause more pain than comfort.

"But it's okay," she went on, "we can go on one soon."

"I can't leave, Nadie!" Fear constricted his voice to a squeal. He convulsed out of her embrace. "He can't know I'm gone, he can't!"

"Hush, friend. I promise I'm here to help."

"No!" he yelped like a cornered puppy. "He can't!"

"Calm down, Blake."

Something sparked in her mind. "Nadie," she whispered softly. "We need him."

From over her shoulder, Nadie's eye narrowed. Celeste hadn't just crossed a line, she'd vaulted over it. "We're *not* using him."

"He can show us the way."

"He can be killed for helping us."

With a quivering lip, he asked, "What are you planning?" His blood-red eyes flitted between them in silent wondering. "What do you need, Rook?"

Nadie's hesitance gnawed on her nerves, but finally the woman replied, "We need into the general's offices. We need access to his files."

A firm line creased the filth on his cheeks as he clenched his jaw tight. His pallid complexion beamed through the grime on his face, and Celeste almost glimpsed his mind warring with itself. Anguish and love dueled behind his blood-red eyes. After a moment, he slowly nodded his head at them.

"I can get you in," he said quietly. His eyes darted through the room like someone could be eavesdropping from any shadowed crevice or cranny. "He's in the Red Zone, some new excavation, but he'll be back soon."

"So," said Celeste, "we just need to be quick then."

"I can do this," Blake asserted. His voice rose with his strengthened resolve, but still crackled like a spitting fire. His eyes searched Nadie's, and there was a glint behind the reddish haze, a spark of what once was between them that seemed to calm his perturbation. "I know you have something planned. I can sense it. You need into his archives. I can bring you there. I want—no—I *need* to help!"

Without another glance or confirmation from Celeste, Nadie said, "Show us the way," and helped her friend to his feet. Blake struggled to stand, his body jarred and bruised from crashing unexpectedly to the floor. He was hunched over like an old, weathered man leaning on a cane. His spine sharply jutted, and his shoulder-blades protruded from his back like stubby wings. Beyond malnourished, he seemed like a walking corpse, gangrenous and rotted, shuffling with the balance of a drunk. She watched the decrepit, but young man move in excruciating pain and it made her heart stir with guilt. She had nearly killed him, though, by his own admission—it would have been a sweet reprieve. Still, she felt the warmth between Nadie and Blake, the impervious bond of trust in each other.

Her heart fluttered. A cascading wildfire dominated her mind. Melina. The light that had once shone from her green and glimmering eyes shattered like glass when Celeste had risked her life for a simple act of rage. In Celeste's mind, it had been vengeance, a recompense for blood drawn. Melina, however, saw only a lust for chaos, for the cold and bitter chill of death. She was abandoned in a warzone as Celeste gallivanted through the ruins of the city, through waves of soldiers and mutated beasts, all for a chance to take the life of a woman—who only *threatened* to hurt Melina. They could have walked away, fled when Stonem and his men had been freed from the hospital prison. Vega had been psychotic, thrice over, frenzied by a chase, forcing Celeste on a wild hunt through the city like a starving wolf.

But she didn't *have* to.

All this love I say I have for her, Celeste thought, repulsed at herself, *and I can't even think and put her needs before my own anger. Ever. Oh, please let me make it up to you...*

When they stepped out of the barred room, she found the halls to be grander, yet still narrow, more so than the small, confined space they had crawled out of. The floor was sleek and dry, yet dreadfully cold beneath her bare feet. Darkness flowed across the walls like spilled ink. The marble ceiling was clear and pearly white, almost glowing. There was a fluorescent glare from the last room on the left, beaming through a slit in the door. Celeste slowed her pace, hand anchored to her revolver.

"We can trust him," Nadie whispered. "Really."

Celeste lowered her voice to a cautious growl. "He could be leading us right to the general."

"He wouldn't betray me."

"That's a broken man, Nadie," said Celeste, but Nadie only turned away from her again. Celeste grumbled and followed them both into the blinding glare of light.

The room was immense, cavernous, and a dark wooded brown like the guts of the forest were splayed across the walls and floor. Curtains and paintings the size of large tapestries, portraits depicting strangers with drab expressions in uniform all draped the windows and trapped a stale warmth within the oval enclosure.

There were more stools and chairs than she had seen in any single tent within camp. The furnishings were laced and gaudy, with stitched floret patterns. The wooden floor rippled upward into stacks near the wall—it was a desk, nearly the height of her, and made of the same dark oak as the walls around them. Scattered atop the gleaming surface were crumpled papers, pens, mismatched batteries, trigger springs, sights, sheets scrawled with looped and curved writing she couldn't read, dozens more items she wasn't particularly interested in. Behind the desk, however, pressed firmly against the wall, were rows and stacks of metal cases, each the height of her waist and the width of her shoulders. Faint letters were etched into the handle of each small compartment.

Nadie was the first to break her stunned and wondering gaze from the oval room. Her plump lips thinned into tight, white lines as she turned to Blake.

"Thank you, friend," she whispered softly. Blake twitched at the sudden sound of her voice, however gentle, and remained perched near the doorway. "You can leave if you need to."

But the man shook his head, eyes shimmery through the filth on his sunken face. "Please, just find what you are looking for—if he catches you here, you're both dead." There was a violent, involuntary shudder that nearly crippled the pitiful boy.

"Blake, you can come with us…"

"No!" He screeched. "You don't understand what he does to those who cross him. I couldn't live knowing that happened to you, too."

Nadie paled in the waning light, and nodded. Celeste caught the faint twinkle in her eye, like a star blinking out into darkness. She needed little urging; she crossed the oak floor in a long, purposeful stride, eyes scanning the items scattered across the desk. Papers were quickly rifled through, upturned and tossed to the other side of the desk with little care. Wires were snatched, studied for a moment in the faint light of the room, then thrown aside in favor of other black, tangled cords.

"It's not here. He moved the damn computers." Her brow wrinkled. "He keeps *every* bit of information on those hard drives."

"Nadie—"

"I can't come all this way," she went on, tears spilling against the gleaming oak surface. "I can't do this just to fail. It's been *so* long since I've felt the need to fight back, to escape this nightmare we've all been trapped in. You showed me a fire that had died in my heart long ago...and now this...I shouldn't have brought you here without more info. I'm so sorry, Commander."

"Nadie," Celeste repeated softly. "The archives."

The locks on each metal container were neither sophisticated nor complex, but infuriatingly small compared to her crooked and bent bobby pins. It took her a few minutes longer than she'd hoped to squirm through the first lock. Finally, the metal drawer shifted and parted from the wall with a sharp, grating screech.

"What is this?" Nadie thumbed through the stacked folders, glancing over the quick scrawls and numbered files with a curious eye. "Photos, medical records, ration debt, surveillance notes—shit, Commander, this cabinet likely has information on every registered soldier in the military."

Icy fear caressed the back of her neck. *More than likely ourselves as well.*

Celeste, heart drumming loudly in her ears, traced a finger along the metallic ridges of the cabinet. She had never disclosed her last name, but perhaps, she thought, it had been placed under her uncle's—Cavarly.

"Nadie, what's your last name?"

"Dunn."

Perfect.

After another long moment, and an impatient *tap-tap-tap* from Blake's filthy fingers drumming against the doorframe behind, she wrenched the twisted pin and propped another open another lock. As she eased the drawer open, careful not to grind metal, Nadie's disheartened gaze drifted back to Blake, who stood hunched over like his brittle bones would crumble under the weight of his own fear.

"Look," Celeste began, stumbling over her thoughts. "I know it must be hard..."

"Commander." Nadie's voice broke as she spoke. "He took the fall for me. I should be the one in here. I should be suffering. Not him. We *have* to get him out."

Blake's clawed fingers raked across the solid oak of the doorframe, and his head lolled in a broken cackle. It was a strange and maddening sound, the remnants of his sanity drifting into a thousand echoes. He stumbled into the room toward them.

"He rounded up nearly everyone, Rook," he hissed, red eyes narrowing. "All the commanding officers in our unit. They were going to search high and low for those missing components, and if they had, where would they have found them? Hm? When I—when I gave them my name, I had *no* idea they would take the others with me. They"—his voice cracked, and his eyes wept dirty tears—"made me listen as Blackwell extracted his blood toll for punishment."

"Blake—"

"You don't know what he does!"

Celeste clenched her jaw tight. "Be quiet."

"You don't know!" he hollered, his face ragged and red with fury. "I tried to escape! I tried! Through the tunnels you told me about. The hatchway. I barely made it a meter down there before I h-heard it—that goddamn scream won't leave my mind! Stop! Stop!"

"Blake!"

"He *flayed* them," he hissed, "inch by inch, every drop of blood, until they were *dead*. I-I wanted to leave, but I can hear them still, I *always* hear them—and they didn't know anything, they didn't know."

Celeste bit her tongue, disturbed, and Nadie stammered through her tears. "Blake, we can help you—"

"No!" Fear engulfed his features. "If I disobey him, he'll take my skin! No! The last man...the last man screamed for a week."

"He's losing it," Celeste warned like a wolf growling over threatened territory.

"I'll show you *losing it!*"

But he was stunned to silence by a distant, but chilling command, a raucous voice that stalked the corridors for its cowering quarry. Fear rounded his red eyes like pooling blood, and his torn lips parted in a breathless gape. He knew what was coming, had likely heard and dreaded the very approach every day of his imprisoned life. For a moment, she felt a sympathetic pang in her heart—until the surly tone of General Blackwell reached her ears.

"He's here!" He almost cackled madly, then lunged for the doorway. "He knows—!"

His words were muffled by a sharp slap of Nadie's hand. Blake staggered, unbalanced by the sudden jarring motion. Before he could scream again, she wrenched her fingers over his mouth. Her other arm slipped around his neck, tightening around his throat like a fleshy noose. She whispered to him—an inaudible string of words. Celeste heard the bootsteps increasing in volume, but her nerve-dead fingers flicked through the archived files with awkward, clumsy twitches. Finally, she plucked a folder from the stack, retracted the heavy, grinding drawer, and then shoved the documents into her coat.

Voices, at least three of them, slowly rising in pitch. One burst into a guffawing fit like her father over a bottle of wine. Shadows danced and curled around the open door, flickering like ebbing light.

"Commander?"

Nadie's voice was barely a squeak. Another small, strangled sound escaped her, and rapid, shuddery breaths. Celeste's gaze swept across the room, searching through the shadows looming in the hallway. She could hear the general's gritty tone, the commands he barked during his approach—she heard him shouting Blake's name, crowing over his perfected servant. In Nadie's grasp, Blake suddenly flailed his gangly limbs, but he was emaciated and weak. He was locked in her arms, shuddering violently at the sound of his name. Fear loomed over him. Celeste felt it, too; they were about to be caught in the lion's den.

"Commander!"

She was drawn to a commotion on her left. She watched a small panel in the chestnut-brown wall lift and swing open like a hidden trapdoor. An assortment of items seemed to bulge from the interior; knotted and braided ropes as thick as her thighs, metal chains dappled with the odd speckle of crimson, mops with broken handles and stained sponges, all cluttered the paltry crawlspace like a neglected closet. Nadie shoved Blake inside first, who resisted with listless strength, then she pressed herself flat against him. Celeste moved quickly, bare feet peeling from the glossy, wooden floor, and threw herself against them. *Clunk.* Splintered wood fell to the floor and over her feet, but Nadie managed to slip her arms around Celeste's waist to grip the edges of the panel door. It wouldn't click shut over their entangled limbs, leaving an inch-wide slit between the wall and panel. A slanted beam of light illuminated Blake's gaunt features. Before his lips parted, Celeste slapped her hand over his mouth and crushed it closed. She felt her friend's arms tremble against her waist, muscles straining to keep the panel from swinging open. The warmth made her stomach tingle—which was quickly replaced with a nauseating chill at the sound of General Blackwell's gritty tone.

"...you know why bitches like bangin' with the lights off, right?"

There was a slight snicker. "No, sir."

The old man's voice crackled. "They can't *stand* to see a man have a good time!"

The raucous sound of their laughter grated her nerves, and Blake flinched and convulsed at every syllable Blackwell muttered, shoving against Nadie and Celeste. The panel door trembled slightly.

"Good one, sir."

Heavy footsteps bounced against the wooded walls and became a faint echo to her ears, muffled from the wild, gasping breaths from them all. The clutter rattled and clanged beneath them as Blake struggled to loosen Celeste's grip. The air between them quickly became a wall of foul warmth. The salty-sour scent burned her nose like sulfur. Worse, cobwebs clung to her bangs and cheek. She tried not to gag, and strained to hear the general's stern commands.

"...when you find him, bring him to me," Blackwell hissed over the sounds of shuffled paper. "I want to know how the hell someone managed to steal a sample from under Mengele's nose."

There was another low, but gruff response, words she couldn't discern over their loud, rapid breaths.

"Sir?"

She recognized the next voice, the soft, yet firm and commanding tone without the arrogance of Blackwell—her uncle.

"Is my niece exonerated now?"

It was a timid query, one the general could only grunt at. "She proved herself an asset. Now, how she'll lead that team is another nightmare, but we'll make a *soldier* out of her, Cavarly, have no worry."

"I would prefer to train her—"

"Let us not forget the last disaster your family caused, Lieutenant."

After a strangled gasp, her uncle replied, "She is not her mother."

"And you are not your brother," Blackwell stated softly. "You have been loyal, fighting for the cause, but I also know how much family meant to you, how despondent you became after they abandoned you. Because *they* didn't understand the work we are attempting to accomplish, the change we bring to this new world! But *you* do!"

"Sir."

Blackwell continued after a gruff chuckle. "That is why I grant you the luxury of having your relative remain within these ranks. Which is *why* I didn't kill the snarky brat when she confronted me in front of my men! For all I knew she has been conditioned by her father to think of us only as enemies! That, and I enjoyed hearing you beg for her life. But she has smarts, that girl, and bigger balls than the boy I keep around here! Speaking of that little shit–Blake! Get in here, we have guests!" A long, weary sigh. "I tell you, Cavarly, you give a little taste of freedom, and they turn on you like starving dogs."

Warmth spattered against her wrist as Blake writhed and desperately sucked air through the cracks in her fingers. He bucked like an agitated bull, and Nadie's shoulder jabbed painfully into her ribs. She felt her spine bounce off the panel with a quiet *thud*. Her chest swelled in fear, and she refused to breathe; but there was no commotion on the other side of the panel, no recognition in their tones as the general guffawed at another unheard perversion. After the raucous, the general's arrogant and raspy tone reached her ears.

"...swept out below?"

"No, sir," was her uncle's response. "Dispatching a covert team of operatives as we speak."

"I'm eager for a progress report–Blake!"

Blake jerked from her grip and kicked the bucket of slop near her feet. Bloody saliva oozed through her fingers. His scrawny limbs pushed against her in a feeble attempt to escape, but she had felt more strength from her wolf when he had been no bigger than a pup. She thought the general would hear Blake thrash her grip every time the sound of his name tore through the room like thunder.

"...an eye on your niece, Cavarly."

"Yes, *sir*." Uncle's voice smoldered. The clapping of his footsteps waned. She felt Nadie's weight suddenly shift against her— and heard the sharp *creak* of the panel door. Celeste pushed to her tiptoes, pressing flat into the clutter. Salty sweat dripped from her brow and clung to her lashes. Her lungs burned for air she refused to inhale.

"...transformation was successful despite the near-death condition of the subject," the general muttered, voice cracked from amusement. "Fascinating report...Mengele wants...is wonderful news...exceptions...for her head."

The conversation fragmented as Blake sank his teeth into her finger. She clenched her jaw against the sharp pain and burst of blood that soaked her glove.

"Yes," the general continued. "I understand that complications arise...if it weren't for that damned wolf, you say, Colbat had a clear shot...Enough, soldier, I will have no ill...of Cavarly...invaluable since the outbreak, and by my side ever since. I have seen him take on more than you will ever imagine...so out of respect, I will have his niece taken out quietly—and discreetly. The deal that was made still holds; her life for cooperation against...If there's blowback, it'll be *your* head along with hers. Flush her out."

Her toes slipped through the slime like it were ice. Her spine jabbed into the panel door, and she felt Nadie's grip falter. She caught herself, hand slapping the wall for balance, just as Blake wrenched his head free. Her other hand released his wrist and *smacked* over his crooked mouth.

"... want you...infiltrating her team, and...father passed on any information...sided with."

A faint murmur in response, words she couldn't discern over the grunts from Blake as he struggled like a pig on its way to the slaughterhouse.

"Oh, and one other thing." Another raspy chuckle left the general. "If that brat finds out, she won't hesitate to kill you—and I'll let her. So, *don't fail.*"

Footsteps amplified—then fell into a clattering echo. She let her rage simmer. Even if she managed to kill them both, the building was surrounded and teeming with soldiers loyal to Blackwell. Out of fear or lunacy, it didn't matter. It only steeled her resolve to blow the place to hell and back. Once she made sure Melina and Nadie were *far* from chaos.

"Well, I'll be damned." Blackwell seethed. "Give that boy the freedom to skulk through the building...*thanks* I get for...Blake! You have one more chance to get your ass in here!"

Silence. Then she swore she felt the ground tremble in fear from the heavy stomp of a boot against the floor.

"Give an inch and they take a mile. If that boy didn't wish he were dead before—well, I'll make sure he can't take his own life now. Shackle him to my desk and make his muscles weak and tender like veal before I peel them from his bones."

Whatever repugnancy the general had seared into Blake's soul, the horrors and torture, the endless days of pain, seemed to spark a final light in the boy's hazy, bloodshot eyes. His atrophied muscles tensed. Before she could react, he prodded her belt, fingers fumbling over the cracked leather. She jerked back, careful not to bash against the wooded panel—but the motion only managed to free her knife, and her mouth slowly parted in a pleading gasp as the steel blade glinted in the faint ebbing light. He was going to stab her.

Except as she braced against the expected blow, he drove the blade into his own throat with a quick and forceful thrust. There was a quiet *thump* as flesh buried steel, and the slight pitter-patter of blood against the floor. He slumped beneath Nadie, spasming violently, blood spurting past the blade with a hot and coppery scent. Nadie recoiled and choked down a sob, burying her face in Celeste's chest. Her fingers slipped across the wooded panel when his convulsions battered his limbs against her. The panel shuddered. Their toes were slick with oozing slime, and slipped as the boy's limp body rolled into her legs. The river of blood splashed across the floor, flowing with the final shudder of his limbs. At any moment, Celeste knew it would flood through the slits in the panel and coat the floor in a slick patch of death.

"Blake!" He was growing impatient—and they were running out of time. Then she heard the general sigh, and imagined the noxious smoke fumes billowing from his nose. "Screw it. I'll clean this shit up myself—where the hell does that boy keep the mop and bucket?"

A terrible, sickening sensation prickled her stomach. She gazed around her, apprehensive, almost fearful to what she might discover by her feet—though she already knew. The mop bucket had splashed her legs with foul brown water, and the jagged handle from the mop was stabbing her ribs. Her heart echoed in her ears. White pulsing clouds dotted her vision. The revolver was deadweight in her palm, an anchor slowing her movements to crawling pace.

Thud. Thud. Thud.

The heavy footsteps grew nearer, smothering the low ramblings of his malice. She was caught in Blake's ghostly stare, the ruddy mess lit by the faint glow creeping through the slit. His eyes were hollowed and dimmed. His blood was on her hands—*oozing* through her toes.

THUD. THUD. THUD.

She was convulsing as Blake had with every heavy stomp of the general's boots. It was like a ticking clock, counting down the seconds until the cannonade and spilling blood, the last stand against tyranny.

Melina, forgive me.

"General Blackwell!" A voice gripped with a sense of panic.

"General Blackwell!"

"Yes, yes, I heard you the first time!"

The response boomed through her ears like rolling thunder.

He was inches from the crawlspace. She scented acrid smoke and bitter cologne.

"Sir!"

"Christ, spit it out already!" Impatience seethed from his tone like venom. His boot squealed across the wooded floor as he rounded on the newcomer in the doorway. Blood would touch his boots at any moment.

"There's something you need to see right away."

A gruff, uninterested reply. "Cavarly can deal with it." Shadows flickered around the gap under the door.

"Cavarly sent me, sir," the timid soldier stated, almost hesitant to speak. "He says it is imperative you oversee this matter immediately. He could not stress that enough."

"Very well," Blackwell stated with a long and wearied sigh. "Brief me as we walk."

"As you know, sir, the patrols have been active in the zones as requested. It also seems your suspicions were correct: It wasn't the only one..."

The oval room fell to a tense and bitter silence for moments that seemed to stretch endlessly, the burning in her lungs was now a fierce wildfire that radiated through her body. Her legs were crooked and tangled with Nadie, her feet slipping through the sticky goop across the floor. Then she felt the panel slip from Nadie's grip, and the door slammed open. The blood-slickened floor was like ice, and they both tumbled from the crawlspace, gasping loudly and retching from the foul stench of death. Her knees clunked against the wooden floor, painfully, and she hunched over on her forearms and coughed until she cleared the vomit from her throat. Nadie was sprawled near the open panel door, her chest heaving in choking sobs. Tears glistened her rounded cheeks, her eyes as red as the blood along the floor. She was clinging to Blake's arm, cradling his bloody hand against her neck.

When she finally spoke, she wasn't sure if her words were intelligible or if they came across as ragged grunts. "Nadie...Nadie, we have to go."

"I-I know," Nadie stammered through her spilling tears. "I know."

Celeste's balance wavered as she stood. Her chest still ached; her lungs sucked in air with short breaths. She was dizzied, but the adrenaline had faded to a dull throb in her head. Bright spots sparkled across her vision. Nadie slowly rose to her feet, refusing

Celeste's extended hand, then turned away from her and the pooling red mess.

Celeste lamented someone she didn't know, and realized then and there, within the throes of mortal heartache, that most who crossed her path met a swift and cruel end. It was a curse—she was certain of it, one that relentlessly chased her down a path of sorrow and lamentation.

There was only a small comfort she could offer. "Nadie," she whispered. "This is my fault, I'm sorry, we didn't find what we needed, and he paid the price for my mistake. We can take his body away from here, find a secluded spot in the woods for a grave—"

"No."

Nadie's cold response was a gust of winter winds, a chill that gripped the bones. She stood straight, stiffened, then marched across the oval room and circled the large, folded desk like vulture over carrion. Some of the files were rifled through until she found one of interest, tugged at the stack of papers within, then shoved the crumpled heap into her coat. When she neared Celeste and the pool of blood, her eyes were a drab grey, jaw clenched and sinking her round cheeks.

"This," began Nadie, voice broken when her eyes fell to the crimsoned floor. "*This* isn't for nothing. I have the files on the recent experiments, and just what the hell happened to Colbat."

Celeste chewed the scar on her lip. "We still haven't found a map to the sewers or city." Her eyes fell to the floor. "Blake..."

Tears shimmered through her adamantine resolve. "The general will discover his body, and with any luck, believe that it was suicide. By that time, we'll be ready to blow this place to hell."

"I can't leave my knife here, they'll know."

"I have Blake's knife..." Her eyes clenched tightly shut, wrinkling her skin. She seemed to have aged years in only a few harrowing moments. "Well, one he gave me as a gift. Unregistered."

Before Celeste protested, however, Nadie was already edging toward the crawlspace. When she reached out, Nadie recoiled from her touch, reeling, her mouth crooked and pursed. It seemed an involuntary reaction, but still she retreated against the wall, shuddering.

"It can still be done, Commander," Nadie continued, speaking harshly through clenched teeth. "We have the detonator. We found the charge near the dam and it was still intact. If we can locate and move the others, we can decimate their forces. And then we can get as far from here as possible. Just like Blake wanted."

When she pulled the knife from her belt, a small black blade folded into the handle, her sorrow simmered with vengeance. Tears splashed against her coat, and the knife nearly slipped from her tremulous grasp.

"Nadie," Celeste whispered. "Let me."

Nadie sobbed soundlessly as Celeste's hand curled around hers. When Celeste took the knife, she attempted to shield the bloodied mess along the floor from view. She leaned into the crawlspace and propped her hip against the open panel, careful not to step in the pooling blood. Blood had smeared like macabre paint across the wooden floor. Blake's body was slumped over the bucket, a cascade of red down his throat. She pulled her own knife from its fleshy hold. Her belly lurched at the sound of separating flesh. *Splat-splat.* She wrenched Nadie's knife into his neck and propped his own fingers around the handle, gave a last, sorrowful look to the broken soul, then turned to find Nadie pushing the panel door shut.

"He was a good friend," Nadie whispered, pressing her palm against the closed panel door. Blood seeped out between the slits. "He died for me, more than once it seems. I'll never know how to repay him. I'll never get to."

"Survive," Celeste said, tears stinging her eyes at the thought of her father. "You survive."

As they processed the reality of their grave situation, they quickly wiped the blood from their feet and hands, smearing any prints they may have left around the panel. It was a shoddy attempt, but Celeste could do little more. They had to leave—now.

The halls echoed with the distant clamor of voices and footsteps, an indistinguishable cacophony. They moved quietly, flat against the walls, leaning around each corner with her revolver drawn and cocked. The room was to their left—she scented the filthy air. They followed it and managed to locate the hidden latch for the trapdoor.

There was an utter lack of warmth in the corridor below the glass skyscraper that had little to do with the damp chill of the underground maze. Celeste stopped under the flickering glow of the service lights, perched against the wall, feet plopped into their soggy boots. As she bent her knees and leaned, she felt a slight jab to her waist.

Files.

She peeled a bloodied glove from her hand, keeping her fingers nervously clenched to conceal the deep ragged scars that were as black as tar on her skin. The files were bent and partially torn, shredded by her hastily drawn zipper. The file with her name had strange marks scrawled along the borders, but whatever was written was no longer decipherable. The other file was old, cracked and crinkled, with a familiar name etched beneath the gashes in the brittle paper.

"Dunn."

With a tentative frown, Nadie stared at the small stack in Celeste's hand. Her eyes, red as the blood stained to their hands, flitted across the files bearing her family name. When she dared reach for them, her cheeks were sunken, her teeth gritted. She flipped through the pages, tanned skin flickering as if a pallor came and went, rocking her nauseous like sudden seasickness.

Celeste reeled and staggered as she gazed through her own files. It was like the fear she felt in her chest slowly clawed its way up her throat and out of her mouth as a shuddery gasp. She retched at the sight of Mengele's scribbled notes, signed and stamped—her medical records.

"Shit," she cursed in a gritty whisper, then crumpled the files into her coat. *Gene therapy? What the hell is that?*

"My dad wasn't killed on duty." The papers shook in Nadie's hands, crinkling under her arched fingers. "They—they imprisoned him, forced the sickness directly into his blood and studied the transformation. It's all here. The medical files, trials, everything, like they were trying to replicate a perfect transformation."

There was a glint of realization in her deep, brown eyes. The crumpled edges of the stolen files from Blackwell's desk were smoothed out by her trembling hands. There, in faint letters scrawled with a lazy hand, barely legible under the dim, reddish glow of the service lights, were the notes and details of their excursion into the woods. Even the attempt on her life. But it was the medical notes on Colbat that forced an icy rush of fear through them both: Blood/virus transfusions—Celeste shuddered—with a newly developed strain to control, delayed transformation, and heightened cognitive functionality...

"Holy hell." Celeste nearly reeled. Her head felt as if it were filled with lead instead of a squishy brain. Fear crept across her skin as a tingling numbness. "They're creating creatures they can directly control, and won't even transform until they're needed."

Nadie's mouth rounded in a small gasp. "Meaning we can *all* be infected at any time."

"Or already are." The words were a bitter realization. "This explains the Colbat-creature's altered state and speech. And its determination to kill me."

"Wait—he spoke after becoming one of those creatures?"

Kill...her! The creature's screech pierced her mind again.

Celeste cleared her parched throat. "Somewhat."

Nadie leaned her head to one side. "But why would they want to have you killed? That is what I don't understand...just who did they make this deal with?"

"My uncle said the Disfigured were a myth, that they are just bandits avenging the loss of their kind."

"Yeah, but *who* are they?"

Celeste could only shrug in response, her guts unsettled by a fierce ache. The floor tilted beneath her—or maybe her vision merely slanted as she staggered—and she fell into the wall, slamming against the old copper pipes. It was like her chest caved inward around her erratic heart and squeezed; her lungs burned for air but only filled with dust, eyes stung with tears she swore would never fall again.

"This is too much."

"That's why we end it," Nadie promised with a wolfish snarl. Her lip curled over her bright, white teeth. "You're right. We come back when they're weak, and we take out the rest."

"We're severely outnumbered," warned Celeste, despite grinning like a madwoman. "Even if we place the charges in the right places, and it all goes off without a hitch, we're still looking at impossible odds."

"We kill them, Commander." Her eyes were moon-wide and just as bright. "We have to, or we will never escape this cycle of chaos. More will die, and soon, it will be us. I've sat by for too long while they slaughtered for the greater cause. I thought I owed them, but I really owe *you*. After all these years, I can finally make my father proud again."

"Then we do this right," Celeste said, firmly. "We map the sewers ourselves and devise a course of action from there. No sloppy moves or unnecessary risks. We have plenty of time." Her throat burned from her upturned stomach. "I'll fall in line and play along with the general until then."

After a quick and awkward embrace, one Celeste found difficult to part from, they embarked down the slanted path into the maze of connected corridors and hatches. Nadie moved with purpose, a nimble stride. Celeste struggled to match pace, and not to stiffen her back under the low arching ceiling, but pain flared from her bones and into her muscles like the blistering heat from a wildfire. It needled her skin, clawed through her guts. It pierced her mind like a hammer striking a set of nails through her eyes. She could almost hear her father, his gruff disappointment in her actions and the consequences they led to, rebuking her yet again for the folly of youth. She had always been naïve, perhaps, and all she had ever known was family. By blindly seeking out her uncle, a man her father had disavowed and spoke little of, she had successfully rendered herself a captive among the military, the same organization that had tried to kill her father—that had succeeded in killing her mother and brother. The same bastards that had experimented on her little brother and tore her family apart. She was in their clutches again. The horrors she had witnessed, the friends she had lost. The people she had killed in a remorseless, sadistic venture with a madman. Their voices, pleading; it all wormed into her dreams and purged her of tranquility, the residual presence of ghosts,. Blood she could never scrub from her hands. The sour scent of death stuck inside her nostrils, filling her lungs with a heavy, poisonous regret.

It only took a moment for Nadie to secure the door behind them, and lift the thick metal grate from the ground above. Celeste scanned the surroundings, but it was a swirling spatter of black and distant glimmering lights. The ache in her stomach was now a shock of pain throughout her abdomen, a debilitating twist to her innards.

At Nadie's signal, she heaved herself up the ledge with a smothered grunt. Nadie followed her ascent, then eased the grate shut. A few more paces and they reached marble statues with indistinguishable features, casting crooked pillars of shadows across the road. There was no patrol in view, and the spotlight remained fixed to the north. Nadie bolted across the road and Celeste followed in a feverish daze, boots skidding as her muscles cramped and seized. No matter how vigorously she pumped, it was as though she waded waist-deep through swampy muck.

But as they neared the outer city, climbing the steep, winding roads of the rolling hills, they were nearly discovered by a patrol, at least a dozen on-duty soldiers slowly progressing the twisting descent into the city's center. They slid into the ditch, buried themselves in mud, and remained motionless as voices broke through the sound of their muffled gasps for air.

"...shot dead, couldn't fight back!" a deep, but strident voice boasted over the uproar of laughter. "So, by the general's own rule, I got all his shit, kid included."

A low grumbled response, "You're just gonna waste her, might as well give her up to one of us."

"Screw that, Trev. She'd be dead in a week. She's a maid now, cleans what I tell her."

"I better find something. Got us going below for some wild goose chase. I don't want to spend my nights freezing my ass off."

Another gravelly voice retorted, "Don't know why we have to. Those bandits couldn't tell their own asses apart, let alone devise..."

After exchanging nervous glances, they remained in the mud until the soldiers were far from earshot and sight, then climbed the rutted ledge onto the asphalt. The soldiers were gone in another direction, a sharp incline that curved around the last hilltop and into another ruined sector of the city. They followed, tentatively, creeping through the deep shadows of debilitated structures or slipping into the ditches when another group of soldiers passed in bulky armored gear that limited movement to a crawling pace, voices loud and hoarse from too much to drink. Bits and fragments of conversation drifted through the chilling night air.

Celeste felt her heart plummet into the pit of her roiling belly.

It was there, perched near the tangled branches of a long-dead berry bush, that she heard the slight *cluck* of teeth chattering, and a short, strangled laugh. A strangely familiar tone rasped from the darkness behind her.

"Ah, the Little Wolf is still prowling about. But what is she hunting this time?"

She spun on her heels, revolver gripped tight, whipping her arm through the snarled bush. Brittle branches splintered as she took aim at the paled face peering at her from the darkness like an apparition. Her finger twitched and arched over the trigger.

"Or rather, I should say, who?"

The man before her was pallid as moonlight, with idiosyncratic slants in in his skull like flesh sunk over portions of missing bone. His cheeks, though fleshy and plump, were scarred and dimpled with pockmarks. Wrinkles ravaged his face like ruts in a mudded road. He was still slightly gaunt, a skeletal figure in the smothering black of night. But his eyes shone like a bright patch of blue sky between the gloom of storm clouds.

"Stonem," she whispered, "you're looking...well."

His hoarse laughter was a brief, but grating sputter. "As well as can be expected after months of starvation and torment. Part of the reason you see me in these splendid rags."

His bony fingers flicked the buttons of his woolen coat. It was a speckled grey, like an old, shag carpet, unfolding past his wobbly knees. The old soldier shrugged at her.

"I'm a nobody now."

Nadie asked, still hesitant, "Just who the hell are—*shit*, you're our former—"

"It's fine," Celeste said, staring down the sight of her gun. "He's an old, dare I say, *friend*. But if he moves, I'll shoot him."

"I catch you skulking around in the dark," he said with a ragged voice, "and you're the one to threaten me for it?" He gave a sudden grin, flashing his scummy teeth. "That's why I liked you, girl. A firecracker, you are."

"So why is a military man such as yourself *skulking* around in the dark as well?" Celeste cocked her brow at him.

"Military man? My days of service were finished the moment I was locked in that dungeon." His eyes glazed over like frost. "My sanity is no longer trusted by the general, and there were certain *repercussions* for helping you and your friend to escape, despite your valiant fight against the Bandit Queen and her rogues. So, I've been relegated to the bottom tier, shoveling the soldiers' shit, so to say. I can't even leave the goddamn city. Not allowed past the front gate! And there I was before, a lieutenant—what a shit show!"

"Tough times all around," Celeste replied, but gave him a deep nod.

"And as for skulking?" He grinned again, wheezing gently. "Well, that's quite simple! I was doing exactly what *you* were doing: Spying on the commotion that has drawn even the general's fleeting attention. I don't know about you, Little Wolf, but I don't want to be in this city when the trouble starts again—and trust me, it *will*— this may be my only chance to get the hell out of here!"

She asked slowly "Stonem, what's going on, what do you know about what will happen?"

"This place will be blown to the sky, girl—boom!" A sudden, flailing gesture startled both women. "They found bombs below the city, and from what I heard, could be a mess of 'em. It'll take weeks to thoroughly search the bloody sewers. No telling what sort of booby-traps and horrors those bandits left..."

The warmth drained from her face.

"Stonem," she managed to croak through her disbelief. "I know life has been in the gutter since the dungeon, but I freed you from that imprisonment. You owe me one."

"I watched over your precious girl," he countered with another wry grin. He flicked his eyes over Nadie's long and slender legs. "Heard you even got a team of your own. Seems like we're even."

She couldn't help grinding her teeth. "Then how about a proposition: You help me, and I can guarantee we will be far from here before night is over."

"Commander." A sense of urgency tensed Nadie's usual soft tone. "What are you saying?"

"We put the plan into motion tonight," Celeste declared with chilling uncertainty. "We have to. Or we'll be hunted like dogs."

"Oh," gasped Stonem, "they'll never let you go without a fight."

"This will never work—"

But Celeste interjected, "We know a way to dismantle the military, at least momentarily. Long enough to escape and put a vast amount of distance between us and them. But if we're going to pull this off tonight and stay ahead of every soldier here, we need your help and expertise. *You* know how they operate. The soldiers, you commanded them once. You said it yourself: you want out before it all goes to hell." Her blunt tone mirrored the gruff demeanor of her late father. "Well, I'm your only ticket out of here."

"Oh, oh, I'd like that *very* much," he whispered. For a moment, there was a glint in his eyes, a fire sparked from a vengeful heart. He met her rigid gaze with a predacious glare of his own. "So, who do we hunt?"

EIGHT

Troubled Waters

Inside the drainage pipe seemed a smothering, unending black.

They couldn't see much beyond the weak bluish glow of her flashlight. The archway had long crumbled to fragments of stone and dust, eroded from the sludge cascading through the cracks in its foundation. Sewage seeped through the fallen debris like a bursting dam, flowing past their feet in an ever-widening river of waste. A putridly warm scent pressed against them, a contrast to the bitter, chilling winds of the city hilltop. Still, at her whistled command, they proceeded into the narrow opening and crossed the grime-streaked rubble.

Shadows ebbed and scurried across the walls, slithered through the rifts in metal. Other pipes protruded through the splits and cracks in the arched ceiling like entrails spilling from a wounded belly, raining thick globs of slime into puddles along the floor. The gentle pitter-patter of leaking filth echoed through the pipe like a babbling brook.

The assault on her senses was an expected, but unwelcomed repugnance. Every breath burned the back of her throat like vomit. The deeper she ventured into darkness, the more the floor slanted and curved beneath her feet as if the walls closed in on them and narrowed to a pinpoint. She hunched, shoulders dragging against the curving walls of the drainage pipe. Dried, discolored biofilm flaked against her coat and sprinkled around the beam of blue light like shimmery dust. Soon she was forced low to the ground, hands plunged into the frothy filth for balance. Slime spattered her neck and face as the wolf tangled with her limbs, flicking his snout through the trickling waste. Disgruntled murmurs echoed through the pipe, but she ignored them; just as she thought they would be forced to crawl and worm their way through, she spotted the abrupt shift in darkness ahead, where the lip of the pipe abruptly ended into a vast and empty black space.

"This is it," Celeste whispered over her hunched shoulder.

She heard Nadie's small, calculated tone echo through the pipe behind her. "We've only gone hundred feet or so."

A blue tint spilled over the lip, faintly illuminating the dark, frothy swamp below. The pipe opened into a narrow chamber, with a river of stagnant sludge flowing down the slanted floor. There were ledges and small platforms, rusted railings and service ladders, and cracked stone walls that glistened with scummy slime. Darkness flickered across the chamber as she exhaled a shaky breath and dropped from the pipe.

She crashed against the platform, but the metal floor *groaned* and shifted with a violent twisting motion. The support beneath the thin, narrow strip of metal snapped, tilting the platform into the flowing sludge at a sharp angle. Her hip bashed against the railing. The rattling metal thundered through the pipes.

"Commander?"

"I'm fine," she gasped. She scrunched her face against the dull throb in her hip. "Pretty much."

She fumbled for the light that was strapped to her chest. A bluish haze swept across the flooded chamber, chased by furling shadows. Thin beams of light spilled through the grates of the slanted floor. Rust had eroded the metal support, weakening the entire platform. She shifted her weight, tentatively, but the platform was wedged against the floor in the scum-pond below.

"Alright, come on down—but watch your step, it's tilted."

"Get moving, *moniyaw!*"

A pale face emerged from the pipe. Bright blue eyes darted through the darkness, then winced against the glare of light. Slowly, Clark swung his legs over the lip of the pipe, blindly kicking his foot for any leverage. With a long, exasperated sigh, Celeste strapped the light to the railing and climbed the slight ascent to remedy her deadweight.

One by one, her team slung from the pipe and shook the platform with a forceful landing. Nadie forced Clark along, rolling her eyes as he stumbled and gasped. Stonem shuffled past with his nose scrunched at the fetid odor of the chamber, disgusted. Celeste thought his own scent wasn't all too pleasant either. Then Melina's fingers intertwined with hers, and as the redhead hopped over the ledge, Celeste curled an arm around her hips. A tangle of red locks caressed her cheek softly as Melina turned, slipping her fingertips along hers.

Aurous whined his discontent behind her, nipping at her ear with his filthy teeth. No longer gaunt and sinewy, he had grown and amassed more muscle over recent months—yet still believed himself no bigger than the pup she had brought home to piss all over the floor of her cabin. She opened her arms to a welcoming embrace, and the wolf sprang from the edge and crashed into her, tongue slathering her face with gritty warmth. She stumbled against his weight, twisted, and then dropped him down the slanted platform. Her legs wobbled, and a deep, red-hot pain shot through her thighs and waist. It boiled her guts. Aurous brushed up against her, still playfully nipping at her fingers.

"Alright," said Celeste, clearing her throat. "We're in. Remember the plan?"

A small grunt from beyond the glow of light. Clark spat, "I don't know why you're dragging us into this."

"Shut up," hissed Nadie. "It's over a klick until the battle ruins, and then many, many of tunnels to search after that—all with soldiers canvassing the area as well. Any further and we risk getting lost."

"This is stupid," Clark whined.

Celeste ignored him. "We need all the time we can get then, so lead the way."

"They'll be down in groups," Stonem rasped through his blackened teeth. "Units like yours. And if they get wind that it's an inside job, well, then we have a round-up, and we'll be the missing pieces to their kaboom puzzle."

Clark moaned loudly, "We'll be killed if we're found down here!"

"Christ, boy," griped Stonem. "These ladies have bigger balls than you. Try and grow a pair, yeah?"

But Nadie persisted, ever a voice of reason. "We could easily detonate it now and seal the sewers under a layer of rubble. The dam will flood a portion of the city."

The tantalizing prospect hung between them like meat surrounded by starving wolves. Through the meager spread of light, Celeste met their piercing gazes, her lips thinned to tight crooked lines.

"No," she finally stated. "Like Stonem said, if they catch wind this was an inside job we'll never escape. The city has been largely uninhabited since the siege, and that's a problem. If we hope for the best and manage to only destroy an empty section of the city, it would be for nothing. We need to cripple their response. So we find the remaining charges, place them below their strongpoints, and then get the hell out of here before they can even react."

"Easier said than done," remarked Nadie with a small shake of her head. "They already know—remember the debacle at the tower."

"We were ill-prepared," Celeste countered flatly. "And reckless." Her dark gaze swiveled to Stonem, whose ghostly hue reflected against the haze of the chamber. "But now we have an insider, someone familiar with every tactic. So, how long before they evacuate?"

His gaunt face crinkled like stiff, folded paper when he grinned at her. "If they believe the charges an inactive trap left by the bandits, likely not at all. They'll simply scour the sewers and city until they find them all."

Celeste chewed her lip, brow furled in thought. "Then we either make a move or miss our only opportunity."

"I vote we go back," mumbled Clark.

"Celeste," said Nadie, "I don't believe in the military or its ranks, but I believe in you. I'll voice my opposition, but in the end, the decision is yours. Commander."

A soft, melodious voice drifted through the ensuing silence. "She's saved my life, I owe her everything," Melina said. Green eyes glimmered through a curtain of red curls. "I have faith in her. Even if I disagree."

"Aye," agreed Stonem through a tarry smile. "This whelp has done the impossible, from the frying pan and into the fire, then again, and *again*. Besides, I don't want to be a casualty. I'm in, Little Wolf."

"What the *hell* am I doing here then?" Clark all but stomped his foot with his childish outburst.

"Because, Clark, I saved your life and now you owe me,"

Celeste growled back at him, thrusting a finger in his face. He flinched at her sudden approach and whimpered like a disobedient pup. "You endangered your team, so you're here to repay that service. This time, there's no helping hands—you either help and fight, or you surrender and die."

"I-I'll fight," he sniveled and smeared snot along his coat sleeve. "I don't want to die."

"Then shut up and move." There was a sharp hiss of torn fabric when she hauled the morose boy to his feet by his coat collar. "Nadie, lead the way and map the direction. We want to get to the battle ruins, but we also need to remember where the rest of the city is."

"Commander."

"Stonem, on our six, I want no surprises."

"Aye," he affirmed.

"Melina," Celeste started.

"I'll stick with you."

"Alright, let's move out quickly—and quietly."

Blue light flickered across the grime-stained walls, cutting through the unending darkness of the chamber. Clark held the flashlight in his trembling hands, shuffling along beside Nadie as she scoured over the details of her hand drawn map. Then her eyes wandered to the ceiling, fixated on jagged cracks and the muck seeping through as muddy rain, as if her gaze could somehow pierce through stone and perceive the streets above them.

"This way," Nadie said with waning confidence. "It should lead us straight there."

A small bridge stretched across the frothy swamp. Bent rebar and twisted pipes poked through the stone walls like bones through flesh in the broken corpse of the city, raining slime down the slick metallic surface. Dust crumbled from the slanted wall, spilling out of the cracks. The stone was warped and bulged like a bubble, and soon they discovered why. The remaining wall had collapsed and buried the other platform in a mountain of impenetrable rubble.

"We have to go around," said Nadie, dismayed. "But find a way back under the direction of the main road."

"Right," agreed Celeste. She didn't hide the disappointment in her voice.

A long sigh left her when her boots *plopped* down into the muck, and she sank up to her knees . The sludge was tepid like recently melted snow, and a greasy, muddy brown as it spattered against her jeans from the wolf's ungraceful descent from the bridge.

The tunnels were a twisting maze of narrow pipes and passageways, split and broken, clogged with rancid waste or fallen debris. Rubble buried maintenance chambers and stairwells, crushed under the collapsing ruins of the city. Moss crawled from the cracks and crevices, spreading across the walls in furry green streaks. They hiked through the muck at a steady pace, down one storm drain through to another tunnel, impeded by barricades of debris and rubble, taking turns which seemed random. Tunnels, tunnels, and more tunnels; an endless revolting labyrinth.

"I wish I didn't wear my nice boots," Melina remarked, ruby lips pursed at the muck puddled around their legs. "And I wish you would tell me *why* you're going through with this."

"You've read what they've done," Celeste began. It was like lead filling her heart, the dredging of an old argument.

But Melina shook her head, scowling as she trudged alongside her through the swampy muck. "I get it, I really do." She seemed to shudder. "The things I've seen at the hospital. But, Celeste, what about your uncle?"

She'd refused to dwell on that thought. She knew how her father once felt about him, the rage that had seethed with the very mention of the atrocities committed by the military. Although her uncle had ensured her survival within the camp, and against General Blackwell's despotic rule, she found it difficult to believe he was blind to the countless experiments and malicious creations. How long until they were all monsters, ravenous for flesh and blood, roaming the land for the living?

"He's done so much to help us, this just feels *wrong*," Melina continued. Her soft tone drowned under the sloshing sound of sewage. "Like we should be helping him, too, the way he helped us."

"I know," she admitted with bitter reluctance. Trudging through the muck agitated the tender patches of healing flesh around her belly, and a numbing-shock gripped her chest.

"Look," Melina said, "I love you. I know you'll do what's right, so I'll go along with whatever you decide. You're still a good person, Celeste, and the reason I'm alive. Try to remember you still have your soul."

A sudden flutter of her heart dispelled the tingling chill of guilt. Breathless, the world seemed to dim and blur into shadowed streaks, with only a brief flicker of fiery red.

"Celeste?"

But as her vision unblurred, she could only laugh in response. The pain in her belly worsened and spread through her limbs like fire raging through tinder.

"I'm fine," said Celeste with an involuntary smile. "I just never thought I would hear you say it in front of everyone."

The redhead's face burned brightly like her fiery hair until every freckle faded. She cleared her throat slowly, then said, "I'm sure I've mentioned it before—"

"I love you, too." Celeste felt the heat radiate from her cheeks. "So, let's make it out of here and finally start our lives."

The swoon of bliss quickly faded to an eerie chill in her chest. When they neared a bend in the tunnel, light blinked into darkness and plunged them into cold sightlessness. After a shaky breath, she called out to the others, fingers curled around the worn grip of her revolver. Warmth pressed against her hip with a small shudder. Celeste shielded Melina from the deep darkness ahead. There was a small hiss, like a whisper or a weary sigh. Then, light flickered back on across the curved walls of the pipe, and her vision filled with bright glowing amber. The wolf stared up at her, tongue lolled over his pink gums, head tilted at her hesitance. His fur was streaked grey with crusted grime and mud. She wrinkled her nose at the foul scent; she would be scrubbing the odor from his fur for weeks.

"Commander, you might want to see this."

After an impatient sigh, she rounded the bend and discovered another wall that had long ago collapsed and buried part of the tunnel in a tomb of jagged stone and busted pipes. Rubble shifted and shook loose from the wall when she traced her finger along the stone. Strings of moss clung to her gloves. The only open passage forked in the opposite direction. One misplaced stone and the rubble could collapse and flood the pipe, crushing them all instantly.

"Yet another detour," mumbled Clark. The boy's nervous and wild gesture of his arms swirled the hazy blue light through the tunnel like an upturned lantern. His voice was brittle and low as he whispered, "This just gets better and better."

"Shut up," Nadie said. She held him still, swearing at him in her own dialect. "But he's right, we won't cover any distance if we have to backtrack the entire way."

Celeste wouldn't hear it. "Then we push through."

"Aye," Stonem rasped from the darkness behind her. "We keep

going."

"This is absolutely ridiculous," Clark muttered. "Not only are you a betrayer, you're going to get us killed."

"Enough!" snapped Celeste. Her voice blasted off the walls and shook the pipes. She pressed forward, hand curled into a shaking fist when she felt Melina's gentle grip around her waist, drawing her away from the fear-stricken boy. As paltry light spilled through his clenched fingers, illuminating his sweat-drenched face and pallor, she caught the twinkling of his rounded eyes. "You think *I'm* the betrayer?"

"Celeste!" Melina gasped. Celeste snarled and clawed for the boy like a ravened wolf snapping its jaws at meat.

"You son of a bitch!" she spat. Aurous growled threateningly beside her, teeth flashing through the ebbing darkness. "You endanger the entire unit, put all our lives at risk, and think you have the balls to call *me* the betrayer? I should have scrambled your brains on the spot!"

He flinched at her words as if each syllable were barbed and pierced his skin. He clenched his jaw tight and asked, "And just what the hell have you been doing, *Commander?*"

Celeste bit her tongue, snarling, and glanced into the darkness down the direction they came from. Her face warmed despite the damp chill of the sewer.

"All right, ladies, safe to say we either keep going or turn around and look for another way." He shrugged. His pale face was shadowed by the lack of light. "Looks to me like we can blow this place to smithereens either way, so let's get on with it."

"Well, I'm not following a *shadow spawn.*"

Before Celeste could react with a vicious remark of her own, Melina's open hand blurred through the dim light and struck the boy across his jaw. She smacked his mouth shut, and the sound of his teeth clacking echoed down the long winding pipe. The boy recoiled with a wild spasm, shrieking as blood dribbled from his quivering lip. Light swept across the walls in bright blurry streaks as the device dropped from his hands and shattered against the rubble. A chilling darkness engulfed the chamber.

Something crashed into her from behind, nearly sweeping her legs out from under her. A muffled scream, and another force pressed against her waist. Aurous growled, snapping his jaws. She was slammed into the slanted wall, pinned against the rubble. Her fingers clawed at darkness for balance, raking through compacted debris.

A piercing light stabbed the darkness and flooded the tunnel a bright blood-red. The rippling glow sizzled and hissed, sparking like burning tinder. Smoky wisps smeared the air a hazy grey.

"How *dare* you!" Melina's voice rose to a shrill pitch, her eyes narrowed to thin slits as she glared at the boy cowering in the corner of the tunnel. "There is absolutely nothing wrong with her! It's time you gave her the same respect she would give you! At least you better—before she knocks your teeth out!"

"Easy, Red," Stonem said as he stepped between them. Red light burned from the flare in his hand, his pale face awash in its bloodied glow. "But she's right, ya little shit. Get up and show your commander exactly what you're made of, because like it or not, you're with us now. That's the price we pay for another chance at life." His eyes sparkled like icy waters under the setting sun. "Isn't that right, Commander?"

Celeste cleared the tickle in her throat, then spat out dirt..

"How far are we from the ruins?" she asked, fingers pressed against the throb in her temples. Pain spanned across her scalp, burned out every nerve, and thudded around her skull. With every passing second she became more acutely aware of the bulge in her coat pocket that pressed against her breast. The last of her pain meds.

"At least another klick, maybe less," Nadie muttered. She squinted at her crinkled map, the ink bleeding across the page in thick splotches, and chewed on her lip. "We should be close...this is just another detour we can't afford."

"Which is why we should all turn back before she gets us killed," whispered Clark, far off in the shadows across from Celeste. "I want to go home."

"Christ," gasped Stonem. "This kid never shuts up."

"He's scared," Nadie said. "Cut him some slack and at least let him get to his feet." She held out her hand to the trembling boy.

"I don't need your help!" he cried out, voice crackling with fear. Another spasm and he was sprawled across the floor, desperately clambering through the rubble to get on his feet. "I need out of here!"

The gash in the wall widened and filled their ears with a sharp splitting howl. Fragments rained into the puddled gunk around their boots as the wall sagged and crumbled like stale bread. It was as if she was snapped from a bowstring when she launched into an ungraceful dive across the tunnel. She slammed into Melina with enough force to sweep both of them off their feet. Then it was like the deafening crash of thunder, blasting the tunnel with roaring winds of waste, broken stone, and sharp fragments of metal pipe. She twisted through the air, certain the sudden vertigo would make her retch. The back of her skull cushioned the fall, blurring her sight. Then, again, her head smacked painfully against stone as Melina tumbled over her and pinned her in the muck.

Everything was streaked white with dazzling, colored pinpoints that danced across her vision. She attempted to call out to someone, anyone, but only debris scoured her lungs. The involuntary gasp dried her tongue to desert sand. No longer was there an isolation of pain, her entire body screamed as it thundered through flesh and into bone.

It took another few moments for cognition to flicker through the fog in her mind. The white smear across her field of sight was a cloud of chalky dust billowing through the tunnel. The flashing pinpoints were the others, her team, as they scrambled through the wreckage of the fallen wall.

"Damn it!"

The next string of curses were smothered by a fit of ragged coughs and heaves, expelling the grime and dust from their throats. Her coat sagged around her shoulders and dripped muck. Her hair was slick and flat against her cheeks. Mud smothered her tongue and stuck in her teeth.

"You alright, Red?"

Stonem was a silhouette in the rippling glow of the flare, but his eyes seemed to pierce through the haze. Melina stirred at the sound of his voice. Her tangled red hair shimmered with dust.

"I-I'm okay," she affirmed with a small, shaky voice. "Really."

"Commander?"

"Breathing," Celeste muttered through the sharp pain pulsing in her head.

Aurous!

As her heart lurched into her gut, a cold slab of ice pressed against her cheek. Then slobbery warmth. Aurous stared back at her with his bright tawny eyes, tongue lolled, legs trembling with anticipation. *It's all a big game to you, isn't it?* Her fingers curled into his musty fur.

"Well, that was too close for comfort," Stonem remarked with a loud, but nervous chuckle. Another flare ignited and burned away the shadows. Melina took his extended hand and slowly climbed to her feet.

"Thanks," she said. "Celeste?"

It was only then Celeste became aware she was crying out when she moved, agitating the old wounds in her guts. The others looked down at her, concerned, ghostly silhouettes in the blood-red light of the flare. She shook her head slowly, but ran her fingers over the small bulge in her coat. Grinding her teeth, she pulled herself up and let out another shaky breath. It appeared only Clark had escaped the cave-in without a scratch.

"So," she croaked, gaze falling over the collapsed wall. The passageway they had wandered through was now sealed off like a coffin. It would take ages to dig through to the other side—if they ever could. "It seems like we only have one option now."

A peculiar sound echoed through the tunnel, like the rising *hiss* of static. With a deep, rumbling growl, the wolf crept into the darkness, fangs bared and ears flat against his head. His dark fur bristled and melted into the shadows until he vanished from her sight. She pressed after him, boots pounding as loudly against the sculpted stone.

"...be a cave-in of some sort," she heard a voice mutter through the rapid *thudding* of her boots. "This death trap is coming down around us. First section eighteen, and now twenty. Can't piss without—what the hell?"

A looming shadow deepened the darkness ahead of her, and only then did her eyes adjust to the sliver of light ahead. A vicious snarl filled her ears, then a piercing, uneven shriek. Pale light darted across the curved tunnel walls from a falling flashlight.

A white blinding flash, thunder that reverberated through her chest, an endless ringing in her ears. She bolted for them, snarling. Someone shot Aurous, or at least tried to, as the wolf furiously snapped his fangs at an exposed throat. A man flailed his arm in another attempt to aim, but Aurous was a flurry of ripping teeth until the man brought the weapon down on the wolf's skull as if he were splitting firewood.

She saw the man tense when he sighted her, wary, and even through darkness she glimpsed the color drain from his face. Perhaps breathless, or rigid from another surge of fear, his reactions were uncoordinated and lacked the vigor of a veteran. Within the short span of a moment, she was on him with the ferocity of her wolf. She buried her blade deep in his soft belly, right under his ballistic armor, and twisted it into his guts. His sputtering flecked her cheek with blood. The man stumbled, slamming hard against the wall. She leaned into him, but his towering height gave him a slight advantage. He sagged against her, deadweight. When her grip faltered on the blade, he staggered away from the wall, fumbling guts between his fingers.

Even disemboweled, however, he managed to aim his weapon at her.

"S-stupid b-bitch," he sputtered.

Then his head abruptly jerked forward, skull split open like an overripe peach. His eyes dulled to a murky white and fluttered shut. Blood trickled down his forehead in a crooked stream, and he slumped into the mud, dead.

A small, shuddery gasp left Melina as she stood over him, the stock of her rifle dripping crimson. A shimmer of disbelief, then her freckled brow furrowed.

"Celeste!" she exclaimed, shaking her head. "What is wrong with you?"

"I'm fine," Celeste managed to say. "Really."

"Oh, I know you're physically fine," she retorted, her words oddly barbed. "But mentally, oh, I'm not so certain."

"What?" Celeste asked.

Melina pursed her lips. "The way you shoot first and ask questions later, how you rush into everything without thinking or warning anyone around you. I thought we were a team!"

Celeste was certain her face burned as bright red as the flare.

A muffled voice broke through a crackling hiss of static. "*Ral, do you copy? What is the status of the area? Ral, stop screwin' around...Shit, he might be hurt from that cave-in—Ral, don't you move, we're coming for ya, okay bud?*"

"Damn," said Stonem, "that'll be one of the units. We better move before we get cornered."

"Commander?"

Again, she replied weakly, "I'm fine."

"Christ," gasped Stonem with a small shake of his head. His bleached skin gleamed in the ruddy glow. "You're falling apart, woman."

"I said I'm fine." Her tone left a bitter taste in her mouth. "Focus on the mission."

"In case you haven't noticed," Stonem coldly countered, "we're on the verge of being discovered, trapped like rats in a maze. Either we stand and fight or we dig our way out."

"It's always been fight."

A faint smile touched his crooked lips. "Then where is that fiery bitch who cut through two armies on her wild hunt for vengeance?"

Her head bobbed, though she was uncertain if the slight movement was an agreement or from the thundering force of her heartbeat. A chill bit down to her bones. She stared at her scarred fingers through the tattered remains of her glove and recoiled, jarred by the patterns of black scars slithering up her skin like serpents.

"So, it really is true?" Clark asked with a squeak of a whisper. "You saw her take out the Bandit Queen?"

"No," admitted Stonem, "but I watched her stand tall against that monstrosity, against all goddamn odds, and free prisoners she owed nothing to. I wouldn't doubt her abilities."

"We all thought it was bullshit," began Clark.

"You can brown-nose later, kid," said Nadie. "We're wasting time!"

Celeste stiffened at the sound of a faint echo in the distance. "Melina, take Aurous and Clark and fall back. Quickly!"

Melina soothed Aurous as he rose from the muck like a decrepit old man. As they retreated to the darkness, Celeste resolved to carefully examine and care for his wounds when they escaped the sewer.

"I assume you have a plan." Stonem's fingers drummed against his rifle.

Maybe. "How many per unit?"

"That depends on their function," he replied grimly. "Assault units are small but armed with high-caliber weaponry, maybe three or four per unit. Two is optimal in close quarters like these shit pipes. Recon units no bigger than yours."

"Recon team," said Nadie. "They don't think it's an immediate threat."

"Aye."

Celeste nodded. "Then we lure them down here, ambush them. Not all of them will advance to assess the situation, so we need to dispatch them quickly—and quietly. Only knives. You and Nadie will take care of anyone who comes through, and I'll rush those who held back."

"You sure that's wise?" Stonem's eyes flicked over her

trembling hands. "You don't seem up for the task."

"Fine," she grunted. "Stonem. If it looks like there's more than one unit, fall back and we'll reassess."

Carious teeth flashed back at her. "My pleasure."

"And smother that damn flare."

Caught in the icy grip of darkness, she found the absolute silence unnerving, at least until her own heart drummed like machine gun fire in her ears. She leaned flat against the tunnel wall and peeked down the access drain. Her eyes were still adjusting, with only a smear of grey in her sight. Slowly the surroundings dimmed to a deep black, like a starless night, with traces of the eroded path and the murky waste trickling into view. There she waited, knife as cold as a slab of ice against her sweaty palm, her muscles spring-loaded and ready to fire. She steadied her breathing, lungs burning. The pain was spreading, closing around her throat...

Her pulsing fingers felt oddly fat and rigid as she fumbled through her coat pocket. The lid snapped open under her thumb, and a few pills slipped through her fingers. She found one, fished out another from the bottle, and popped both into her watering mouth. She stuffed the bottle back in her coat, winced, and choked down the dry pills. The pain in her throat dulled to a tingling ache. For a moment, she felt normal again.

Whispers of sound drifted to her ears. Startled, the sudden unease tightened her stomach into a cold knot. Another quick glance down the tunnel and she glimpsed light piercing the darkness, sweeping across the slanted walls and over the slumped form in the muck.

"Shit, there he is."

"Hold back," said another. A flashlight beamed across the muck, and the filth shimmered crimson. "He looks incapacitated."

"From what?"

"Hell if I know, Binky," the second voice huffed, annoyed. "Check in with the commander and tell him we're retrieving Ral. It looks like..." Another blinding flash of light crossed the tunnel entrance, spilling past the edges of the wall. "Shit, definitely a cave-in. Hit by falling debris, likely."

"Yes, sir," the first voice whispered sullenly. "I can't wait until I'm not a rookie anymore." He then spoke clearly through crackling static. "Commander, we found him. Hurt bad, it looks like."

A sharp *hiss* was followed by an incomprehensible garble. The first soldier advanced, boots sloshing through the bloodied muck, and then the other; yellow light flashed and flitted across the tunnel.

"The name Bink is stuck with ya," the second voice said through a deep guffaw. "The rookie needs his binky."

"Screw you."

"Looks like this whole section should be sealed off after a quick search." *Slosh. Slosh.* "That idiot just had to wander off. Doesn't matter where you shit because *shit* is everywhere. This is his own damn fault, and I don't want to suffer the same indignity."

"This place is falling down around us," Bink said. "Is he even breathing?"

"I can't tell—shit, there's a *lot* of blood."

The sloshing sounds eased, and the murky waste rippled around her legs. She feared they would hear her heart pounding against her chest like a drum.

"I'll check ahead, you take his pulse," the second voice ordered. The sharp *click* of a firearm echoed over the murmured response.

The beam of yellow light flicked through the tunnel entrance, and she could see the barrel of his gun jut past the edge of the wall.

"Oh, shit!"

The soldier halted. "What?" he barked back at Bink, rounding on his timid comrade. "I swear, boy—"

"What the hell!" Bink shrieked like a butchered pig. "He's been gutted!"

"What are you...uhg..."

The soldier's speech slurred into a wordless sputter as Nadie ran her blade across his throat. Warm, steaming crimson cascaded down his motley-black uniform. While his knees buckled, his trembling fingers clutched at the widening gash as if he could somehow staunch the flow of blood.

At that moment, Celeste sprang past the wall, knife oddly balanced in her palm. She leapt over the bleeding man and collided with Bink, who had scrambled to his feet in a desperate effort to flee his unseen pursuers.

But she was on the hunt; he was her prey.

Her stiff fingers wrenched around his coat collar, and she raised her knife to pierce his throat—until he turned with fearful vigor. Her knife glanced off his drawn weapon, jarring it from her grasp. She stumbled—he slammed her against the wall, crushing the air from her lungs.

The pain was infuriating. Her fingers raked across his face, nails gouging his sockets. Sticky warmth spattered her hands. Again, she was crushed against the wall, and the rookie's cold grip tightened around her throat—

—then slacked when she drove her boot into his groin, crushing and twisting her heel into his tender dangling flesh. A strangled cry escaped him, and she heaved against his staggering form. He fell, thrashing into the muck—then a knife pressed against the base of his throat. Nadie flicked the crimsoned blade against his artery.

"No!" hissed Celeste, knees pinned against the rookie's chest. The boy's head bobbed below the surface of the filthy stream. Bubbles formed around his desperate gasps for air. The moment Stonem was through the tunnel, she shifted her weight, and Bink's pinkish-pale face emerged from the muck.

"Commander?" queried Nadie, brown eyes narrowed with unease.

"Stonem will be fine," whispered Celeste. Her lip curled in a vehement snarl. "But this one is going to tell us all about their operation."

"Fat ch-chance," sputtered Bink. A deep frown, furrowed brow, scrunched nose—but a shimmer in his bright eyes betrayed the icy rush of fear he felt in his heart. She could sense it. *Smell* it. "I will never betray my unit."

"Bullshit," she countered grimly. "You can either answer our questions and live another day, or you can die down here where nobody will find your body."

His face wrinkled in despair and the façade shattered. "And what's stopping you from killing me after?"

"Absolutely nothing."

A nervous scoff. Trembling in the water, he appeared far too young and frightened to be there, like the boy on the highway north of Antler Creek, staring death in the face—staring at her.

"But," she relented with a sigh, "you have my word that I won't kill you. As long as you answer truthfully."

She studied his blanched expression as though her eyes could sift through the thoughts hidden within his mind. Finally, he ventured, "You won't kill me?"

"I won't."

He bit his lip, possibly to keep it from trembling as he gave her a small and subtle nod.

"How many in your unit?"

"F-five," he stammered weakly, almost nauseated. "Counting

me."

"Two left," Celeste said. "Are you the only unit down here?"

Confusion wrinkled his brow, and he stared at her for a moment. "No. We were assigned a few sections and our unit stuck to them. We're in constant radio contact."

The radio along his shoulder crackled, but the words were garbled as muck seeped from the device.

Stonem. "How far?"

"You'll be lucky if they haven't heard."

"*...copy? Terry, Rook–*" The muffled words *cracked* into static.

Bink watched her with tentative eyes. Muck streamed from his stubble and dripped down his exposed throat. "If we don't report back in five-minute intervals, they'll be on guard," he said slowly. "They'll come looking–they're armed."

Her fingers tapped the device strapped to his shoulder. "Check in."

"I-I can't!"

"Now!"

But he stammered weakly, "I-if they find out I said anything–"

"If you don't, you'll die," she finished cruelly. She clutched the radio in her palm, thumb pressed firmly against the button. She placed the mic by his trembling lips. His teeth chattered, from the chill and under the threat of drowning, but he managed to mutter, "Got–got Ral to his feet–heading back now, Commander. A few minutes out."

"*Copy that.*"

Bink sputtered as he sank beneath the brown water, shaking the grime from his face.

Celeste pressed him, "What are you searching for down here?"

"What," he spat. "You don't know?"

"We want to know what *you* know," Nadie whispered, and gently dragged the edge of her blade across his cheek. "How you know."

Startled, he gasped, "Routine maintenance! Christ, it was only an accident!" His voice cracked. "Assessing the damage from the battle against the bandits. Some workers spotted something strange. Another recognized the components and realized what it was–that's it, I swear!"

Shit.

"Look," he muttered, eyes rounded and bright. "They thought it was a trip-mine or on a timer, but they eventually figured out it was remotely detonated. That's why they're sending us down here to retrieve the last-ditch effort by the bandits. Five units, each scouting a few sections of the city at once."

Celeste felt her own voice strain. "How many have they discovered?"

"Two," he replied. "One below the ruins and another below the Glass Tower. They figure there could only be three or four at most."

"That means there's only one left," Nadie cautioned.

Celeste gritted her teeth. She could feel Bink's gaze burn through her with scrutiny. His lips thinned white like he held in the disgust roiling in his belly.

"Bandit," he muttered.

"You're wrong" she countered. Her tone remained cold, ferocious. Uncompromising. "And out of time."

He sputtered through the muck, "Y-you said you wouldn't k-kill me!"

"Oh, but I'm not going to—" she started.

"Celeste."

She stood, leaving the rookie on his back, with only his face bobbing above the muck. Melina's freckles and red hair burned brightly like beacons through the shadows. Even her rebuke was gentle, soft like the curls bouncing along her deeply furrowed brow.

"You're not going to kill him, are you?"

Celeste, hand on her revolver, muttered, "We need to—"

"You told him you wouldn't."

"He thinks we're bandits." A weak counter.

"Well." Melina frowned at her. "Maybe he needs to know we're only doing what needs to be done. Like me."

Though Melina's emerald eyes were shadowed by the dim—*very* dim—lighting of the tunnels, the redhead gazed through into her heart, and Celeste threw up her hands in defeat. She ignored Nadie's wandering gaze and blank impression. There was no reasoning with her tempered rose.

Bink sputtered weakly, no longer forcefully submerged in the running waste, and retreated against the tunnel wall with a sharp spasm. His eyes darted from Celeste to Melina, then to the glinting steel of Nadie's drawn knife. His fingers brushed against his waist, skimming the wastewater, but his weapon was far from reach. A sickening realization drained the color from his scruffy cheeks. Melina dropped to her knees and sank into the swampy river, nose wrinkled at the stench that blew past. The wolf crawled over her like a shield, weakly, fangs bared until Melina itched behind his perked ears. Bink jerked away from them, abrading his elbows against stone.

"Please," he began. But Melina's smile was as bright as the sun, and he slowly picked himself up again, propped against the wall.

"I'm only here to talk," she told him. "We're not bandits, and I certainly don't want you hurt."

Bright eyes glazed over and settled on the bodies sinking into the muck. "My team would beg to differ."

"I'm sorry about your friends, I truly am," she lamented. "I know the feeling of loss."

"They weren't my friends."

"They were still people you knew, were around every day."

He dropped his guard with a small, shaky sigh. "Not well enough. I was the rookie, so really, I was just their errand boy. Hell, they even called me Binky. I'm a no one to them. I was a cook before the military took over our safe zone. I only joined a unit to...well, that's not important. I'm going to die down here. Alone."

"For a girl?" Melina asked, smiling sweetly. When his cheeks burned red, she giggled. "I know what that's like—heart fluttering like butterflies, doing whatever possible for a smile in return. Anticipating your next moment alone—"

Bink interjected suddenly, "Her name is Nellie." A brief smile. "Though she hated that name. I always thought it was pretty."

"It's a lovely name," Melina agreed. "Do you have any faith?"

"What?"

"Do you believe in God?"

He frowned at her. "I've never given it much thought until now."

She returned his puzzling look with another smile. "Faith can do amazing things."

"Has it done anything for you?"

A glint in her emerald eyes was like the twinkle of distant stars. "I never used to believe in anything, not until I met someone who changed my life—for better and for worse."

"That doesn't sound so great."

"You can't appreciate the warmth of the sun without first wandering the rain." Melina's face wrinkled in thought. "I was lost and nearly dead, full of despair and hatred for what became of my friends and family, of my life. I thought I could never forgive, not after what happened, after all the blood that had been spilled. Innocent blood. But something compelled me to go back, to help the person who had saved me. I've known love ever since—and fury, and more despair and worry that follows such boundless devotion. But it was *faith* that brought me there. Faith that God would guide me to where I needed to go, to the people who needed my help. Faith guides me still. Maybe that's what brought me to you."

There was a glimmer of hope in his eyes. "You truly believe that?"

"I believe you don't know what's right and what's wrong anymore," she replied softly. "That you are lost and alone with people who do not give you the time of day. But everyone deserves a little happiness. If she—Nellie—is what may make you happy, then you need to make it back to her, right?"

He gave a slight nod of agreement, but his fear-induced pallor flickered like the glow from his muddy flashlight. Melina smiled under a halo of yellow light.

"If you have faith you will see her, that you *must* see her again, then that will be enough. I know it. Then maybe you both can get far away from here and start a new life, a meaningful life. Full of love. But only if you stay away from what is about to happen and out of our way."

"O-okay," he stammered. "I promise I won't talk. I won't say a word to anyone about this. I just want to see her again. Do what you want—"

THWACK!

The back of his skull rocked off the tunnel wall, and his eyes rolled to a glaring white. Blood smeared across stone as he slumped over a startled Melina, groaning weakly. Then he was out cold, paled and still.

"Celeste!" Melina hissed in reprimand, smoothing the boy's brow. "You didn't have to hit him so hard!"

"I didn't have to keep him alive," she replied curtly, regretting her tone almost immediately. She bit her lip. "I'm sorry, really. It's already a risk. But I'll keep my word to you, and to him. He won't die. Hopefully."

"We're going to leave him here."

She nodded. "Luck will have to be on his side for now. We'll leave him tied up in the rubble, and hopefully he'll be awake and be gone before this place blows. Us, too."

"Faith," Melina whispered, smiling despite herself. "Not luck."

Nadie sheathed her knife. "It won't be long before his unit has to check in. After that, they'll send a search party. No loose ends. Ever."

"So, it's now or forever trapped," said Celeste, loosely binding the boy's wrists. Aurous pawed at him with a worried whine, and she couldn't help but frown; the wolf seemed to care more for the boy's wellbeing than her own. "We have limited time, with one bomb remaining. We better hope Stonem eliminated the commander."

They left the boy lost in the blinding darkness, haunted by the corpses of his former team. Celeste searched the deepest crevices of her heart, hoping to discover a glimmer of hope like she had seen in his eyes. When did benevolence become such a foreign and jarring concept to her? It felt like a compromise to survival. Yet Melina had an infectious warmth, and perceived beauty where Celeste only glimpsed chaos and death. There may have been a moment in her life when she would have relented in her attack, sparing the boy and his team such a gruesome fate—perhaps even at the cost of her own life. Now she spilled blood and reveled in despair. What would her father have done? Perhaps what he had always taught her; the strong must protect the weak. Oh, what he must think of her now.

How could you love a monster like me?

As they ventured deeper into the tangled web of tunnels and corridors, they found more entrances sealed by rubble or barred like prison doors. There was a rising murmur like a distant babbling brook. The rancid air thickened like steam as the tunnel narrowed into a cramped conduit flooded by a churning river of waste. The murky sludge slowly crawled down the channel and emptied through several narrow tubes and drainage pipes. Pools of darkness merged and rippled around the beam of light until a figure was visible through the haze—and the gleam of crimson along the channel ledge. The figure regarded their approach with bright, frosty eyes.

Stonem.

Celeste advanced a few paces—not many, and as she did he drew his weapon, startled by the hissing river. His gaze searched the darkness. Aurous nudged her leg, growling at the scent of death.

"Stonem, what's going on?" she asked, fingers pressed against the cold steel of her revolver. "Are you hurt?"

His hoarse voice was barely a whisper. "It isn't just the military down here."

"What?"

"Viciously gutted, throats slashed," he responded grimly, earning a quick gasp from Melina. "All before I arrived. Blood was flowin' hot."

"So, we have an ally," said Melina, "a guardian angel."

Stonem clucked his tongue at her. "Just because they're killing our enemy doesn't mean they have our interests at heart."

"The enemy of my enemy is my friend," Nadie whispered.

"We need to think of them as the enemy, regardless," countered Stonem. "We could lose our opportunity!"

Their words were soon lost, a distant echo, drifting further out of reach from her senses. Her vision clouded white. Fear sank its cruel claws into her heart until she could scarcely draw a breath. Her eyes fluttered, she staggered past the others as if to retch into the murky river.

There was a shimmer through the encompassing darkness, a glint as golden as the risen sun. Brief, but enough to draw her attention. She stared into nothingness, a strange numbing sensation spreading through her chest.

I told you this would happen, came an icy, disembodied voice. Such a hauntingly familiar tone, the sultry-sweet words of a viper. A ghost from the darkest of nights.

Vega.

With eyes blacker than lightlessness, the ghost stared back at her, almost lovingly. Crimson trickled from the wound in her head in a thin rivulet, running over her lips as she spoke.

I told you this would be your burden, the necessary sacrifice, The phantom woman hummed gently, soothing Celeste's fearful spasms. *The absolution of death. Oh my, how you crumble under adversity, my darling daughter.*

I am not your daughter, Celeste seethed silently, gritting her teeth against the rising darkness. *I was only a supplement for your pain—as you were to mine.*

You're not here. You're not here.

Vega smirked through a crimson cascade. *You're following in my footsteps, finishing what I had only begun—you are the heart of this rebellion, just as I trained you to be.*

No.

Her piercing gaze was unrelenting. *Yes!*

No!

You betray your own family for my cause, all so you can lead and not follow. You kill to protect, yes, but also because you need blood. You want it. Chaos. Just as I craved, just as I deserved. You adore it.

"I am nothing like you!"

"Commander?"

She felt the bite of cold steel along her fingers—the revolver trembled in her grasp, stabbing at nothing in the darkness. Vega's voice was now just a whisper to her ears, a murmuring thought she couldn't quite shake from the back of her mind. She turned, slowly, eyes lowered to the blood gently flowing into the channel. She holstered her weapon, took one shaky breath, then pushed past their exchange of frowns and worried glances.

"We keep going," she said, growling like the wolf at her side. "And we stop anybody in our way. We end Red Dawn tonight."

NINE
Whistle in the Dark

IT WASN'T until they cleared the conduit and surrounding tunnels—and any nearby drainage pipes or shafts the killer could have hid within—that Celeste allowed herself a slight sigh of relief. There was no sign of any malevolence towards them—yet. She slowed her pace to match Stonem. "What do you really think of this mysterious benefactor?" she asked him, nerves still tightly wound. "Friend or foe?"

"All my winnings on against," he muttered back, shaking his bald, pale head at her. "Unless you've made some other friends..."

"No."

He shrugged, sliding his fingers sinuously along the sleek barrel of his rifle. "Then assume it's the enemy, Little Wolf."

Slanted beams of light glared across the bend in the tunnel, and she was momentarily plunged into darkness again. "I was taught there were never coincidences."

"Right," he agreed with a huff. "How right you are."

The tunnel shuddered as a vehicle thundered over the street above the sewers. Muck rippled around their boots. Pieces of pipe rattled loose and rained down razor-sharp shrapnel.

"Commander," Nadie whispered from ahead, face blanched under the glare of her flashlight. "If I'm right—Clark, *shut up*—then we should be nearing the Medical District."

Celeste nodded, scanning their grim expressions through the shadows. "So Stonem, what's in the Medical District now?"

"Forbidden shit," he replied with a slight smirk. "We all know that."

Nadie's usual soft tone was as piercing as arctic winds. "Not all of us had command over the city and the experiments conducted with the sickness."

"Oh, don't preach to me," he countered with a scoff. "Holding back and doing nothing absolves you of no sin."

"I was forced—"

"So was I!" Stonem gritted his carious teeth then muttered, "They *kept* everything there: arsenal, bioweapons...After the raid, they relocated and scattered most supplies to their outposts and strongholds. The only thing Blackwell plays close to his chest is his trump card. That freakshow butcher shop is still open for business."

Apprehension gripped Celeste's throat. "Experiments?"

"You bet your arse," he said. "And they'll use 'em, too, if they ever suspect...us..." His eyes slanted shut from a deeply furrowed brow, head cocked as if lost in a wandering thought.

"Stonem," Celeste asked, echoing her wolf's worried whine. "What is it?"

"We haven't encountered another unit," he replied slowly. "Just the one."

"So?"

"So, we're in *deep* shit, that's what," he growled, finger curled around the trigger of his rifle.

Melina gasped, green eyes glimmering tears. "They would release the infected into the city?"

"As much as can be controlled."

Realization settled in Celeste's guts as a sickness. Her eyes desperately searched the shadows for Nadie. "If they use those enhanced hunters like Colbat, we're already dead," she said unholstering her revolver. "But if we blow the bomb now, it's minimal damage."

Nadie agreed with a shaky sigh. "We'll be torn to shreds in close quarters."

Well," said Stonem, "we best get moving then."

The sinuous tunnels extended into a sprawling labyrinth, crossing at intersections and narrowing into grated conduits and collapsed chambers. Many of the passages Nadie led them through pressed them into a single file, knee-deep in stagnant muck and rotted waste.

"Handprints along the wall," remarked Stonem. "Gloved. They were down here."

"Keep moving," Celeste whispered, though her voice reverberated off the conduit walls. "The last bomb is somewhere below the Medical District—it has to be."

No doubt in my mind. Vega would have wanted this place buried in its own rubble for Caylee's sake. Her lip curled over her teeth as if baring fangs. *It's what I would have wanted in such vengeful fury.*

As they moved, she felt Aurous press against her legs—and a tingling sensation of warmth when her hand brushed against Melina's thigh—and they both met her gaze with a loving intensity that brought a blush to her cheeks. Her smile, however, felt hollow and cold in return.

They deserve so much better.

A sinister, disembodied voice echoed through her ears, louder than before. "Love is a weakness. I taught you that, darling daughter, do you recall?"

You're not there, you're not there—she clenched her eyes tightly shut—*get out of my head!*

Vega's ghostly voice hissed, "I sprayed the floor with my lover's brains—because *you* killed his only son in cold blood."

Kill or be killed. Her heart lurched at the thought of his life pulsing through her fingers, his lips forming the soundless words of a final, desperate plea to live...

"You're going to get them killed—your darling redhead and the mangy wolf—your entire team!"

"Stop!" she abruptly yelled, stunning the others to a slower pace. They stared back at her through waning light, their words lost to the ringing in her ears—

—a piercing wail rang the tunnels like a church bell and cleared her mental fog. She stiffened at the inhuman sound.

"And so it starts," said Stonem grimly. "The hunters are now the hunted."

"Then we move," Celeste ordered. "Nadie, caution to the wind; make your best estimate and get us there—now!"

"With no additional information, I can't—" Nadie nervously started.

"Now!"

Light swept across the grime-soaked walls. Nadie's brown eyes flitted through the intersection of pipes and expanding tunnels. She hesitated for an instant. The color drained from her tanned cheeks when one inhuman shriek became a chorus of bloodthirst rising in pitch and volume.

"I don't—shit, this way!" Nadie declared with a panicked tone they had no choice but to obey. The wails amplified, a paralyzing fear beginning to grip their bones. "Come on!" They moved—as swiftly as knee-deep muck would allow—across the channel and into the dark confines of another narrow tunnel. A sharp turn, and another; the tunnel twisted and looped before draining back into the main channel. More twists and turns, and the next passage led to a sprawling expanse of tunnels that were grated shut or buried by a collapsed wall. Soon they were back where they had started—again.

Nadie hesitated, light flickering across the expanse of tunnels and passages. Aurous growled by her side with fangs bared and black fur bristled like spines. He knew they were being hunted by a predator in the shadows.

"We need to get the hell out of here!" screamed Clark. He staggered into the wall, knees buckling. "Or we're going to die! You killed us, bitch! You killed us!"

"Shut up!" Celeste demanded. "Follow me!"

"Commander—"

Celeste growled, "I'm getting that final bomb—and I'm ending Blackwell's reign! This way!"

Every tunnel seemed to drain into the main channel, sinuously connected like a maze—except one that was a small, cramped passage, a conduit meant for waste and not human movement. It narrowed the further they went, forcing them to crawl through the rising muck on their elbows and knees. Soon her shoulders scraped along the walls, and her head glanced against the bowed ceiling. Her lungs were jarred of air, her face prickled by a cold sweat. She could see nothing but darkness ahead, and the dull flicker of her submerged flashlight.

"Commander," she heard Stonem gasp from the distance, spitting muck from his tongue. "We need to turn around before we get stuck!"

"This is insane," Clark moaned. "Why am I here?"

"We lost, Commander," Nadie said. "I'm sorry."

"We haven't lost yet—"

Stonem gave an impatient *click* of his tongue. "In case you've failed to notice, this has been a shit show since the beginning! They know the bombs are here, so even if we had a chance to move the final one, Blackwell knows it's a possibility—he's likely evacuating the new stronghold as we bicker and frolic in their piss and shit. If we keep going, we're either caught or dead—not to mention this *mutt's* fur in my goddamn face!"

"We either turn back and become food," Celeste warned with another growl, "or we keep going and win our lives back."

"It's not that...simple..."

With the cacophony of howls resounding through the pipe behind them, she flung herself forward and wormed through the muck. She felt the others press against her boots, fingers raking through the flowing muck beside her. Terror flushed through their veins, panicking their movements. Aurous snapped his jaws and growled at the darkness, frenzied by the rising sound of the creature's howls. There was no retreating, the pipe walls narrowed and circled around her body until she thought she'd be spaghettified. She squirmed and sputtered against the muck sloshing into her face, her bared teeth gritty with grime. She twisted around another bend—a dead end. She stopped and spread her palms spread flat against the metal grate that sealed the conduit. Light spilled through the slits, casting long and deep shadows beyond her reach. She saw nothing.

They were trapped.

"Commander!"

"Shit," she whispered. Again, she heaved and awkwardly pressed herself against the metal grate. "Come on!" Her knuckles thudded against the bars. "Come! On!" Her shoulder slammed against the grate and wedged between the narrow slit. Frustration escaped her as a deep bellow, a sound that rivaled the terrible roar that trailed their movements through the tunnels. Defeated, she drilled her fist against the wall, splattering muck up her sleeve. She didn't care. She'd lost.

In an instant, there was the earsplitting shrill of grinding metal, then a loud, resounding *crack!* The conduit shuddered, and she was violently pulled under the muck.

A ferocious pain shocked her limbs, burning beneath her tender, bruised flesh. Darkness splayed across her field of sight. She groaned—certain the conduit had collapsed and entombed them in its rubble—and then she stirred when someone felt for the pulse on her neck. Blinding light seared the darkness from her vision. A trickle of sound echoed beyond the ringing in her ears.

"...must be dead," someone said with a tightened tone. Clark? "Leave her here and we might have a chance at pinning it all on this crazy bitch!"

"She's alive." Melina's red curls danced like flames across her freckled forehead. "The fall must have stunned her. Celeste, can you understand me?"

She croaked back, "Fall? What fall?" Something jagged pierced her belly, shocking her old wounds.

"The pipe we were crawling through collapsed," Stonem rasped from Melina's side, pale face sunken into the shadows as he swept the beam of light to the ceiling. Muck seeped through the ruptured metal. "Lucky, if you ask me. We could have plummeted down a hundred-foot drop—but that *thing* is still on our asses."

"Don't you see?" Clark demanded, flinging his arms, eyes wide with anger. "This is what I was afraid of, why I never wanted to be part of this! She led us to a dead end and trapped us with a monster! I told you, I didn't want a part in your shitty rebellion!"

Stonem raised his wispy eyebrows. "Why *did* you bring him along, Little Wolf? He's certainly no prized soldier."

The wolf's tongue lathered her cheek, smearing blood across her scarred skin. She sputtered and wiped the dribble along her sleeve. A scoff was her only response as she shook the debris from her clothes and pushed to her feet, gaze lowered to avoid her redhead's inquisitive glare.

"So that's it, huh," Stonem said with a raspy chuckle. "He's the bait."

"What?" Clark asked, mouth drooped from shock. "What is he talking about?"

Melina's voice tightened. "Celeste..."

"More like reassurance for our escape." The words were razors in her mouth. Her eyes narrowed at the sight of the boy, trembling and pale, sweat beading his raised brow. "Sacrifice."

"Screw you," Clark spat at her, fingers clenched around his pistol. Her own hand drifted to her holstered revolver. He knew she could draw and shoot before his muscles tensed to pull his own pistol loose. His lip quivered. "I should just kill you now."

The deafening shrill that followed was unlike anything she had ever heard from monster or man. It was like metal grinding against metal, the sharp squeal of two glancing blades.

Fangs flashed through the darkness. Aurous let out a guttural growl. She stared at the rupture in the pipe and saw the swirl of darkness ebbing from the glare of her flashlight. "Commander," Melina started, coldly formal. "What are your orders?"

She almost heard Vega taunting from the back of her mind, *Fight or flight? Sacrifice or love?*

"Fall back!"

As her fingers wrenched the wolf's fur and dragged him away—snarling and snapping his frothy jaws—the broken pipe shifted, again shuddering with the *screech* of grinding metal. A deeper darkness seemed to bend shadows around the rupture.

"Through here!" yelled Nadie, forcing Celeste to break sight with the darkness. There was a doorway across the room, unbarred, at least ten feet from their current position. It was their only escape.

"Aurous, come on!"

She hauled him across the puddled muck, but the sound of its bloodthirsty wail pushed the wolf into a deep, relentless frenzy. She couldn't blame him. Her own blood boiled in her veins. They had both fought these creatures to the brink of death and barely survived before, but *they* were the wolves, the hunters, not some infected corpses. Vengeance burned deep in her heart, as it did in her wolf. She wanted to kill as he did, to sink her fangs in its rotted flesh and squeeze the life from out of its throat.

Darkness rippled and ebbed from a faint glow of crimson. Aurous howled for blood. Light scattered around her, casting shadows across the ruptured pipe. In brief flashes, she glimpsed the creature's true form; twisted, elongated limbs with movements of a spider, a protruded snout with bloody, gnashing fangs. Slender, gaunt, flesh black and scaled like armor.

She drew a quick breath, her chest tight with panic—the stench of rot washed over her, burning her nose with a hot sulfur. Curved claws gripped the edge of the pipe, and long, jagged spines abraded the metallic enclosure as the hunter lowered to its haunch, observing its prey with eyes that burned a bloody crimson.

"It's here!" she called to the others, still struggling as Aurous heaved against her grip. The creature had her unremitting attention. Aurous tensed. The hunter's sinuous muscles flexed.

The next moment, the hunter descended from the ceiling, claws ripping through the walls like a tin can. Shadows coalesced around its gaunt form as she reeled, Aurous still tightly bound to her grip, flicking her only source of light toward the doorway. Her leg smacked painfully against her wolf, and they both staggered. Instincts prickled the back of her neck, and she threw herself forward, tumbling over Aurous. A thrashing force surged over her and crashed against the wall, and bony claws ripped through the floor by her feet. The wolf twisted against her, jaws snapping loudly.

"Celeste!"

Melina wrapped her arms around the wolf as Celeste leapt from the floor. Crimson glared after her from the darkness. She moved quickly with her hand closing around her sheathed machete. A terrible roar thundered against her chest. She drew her blade against its advancement—then slashed at the cluster of pipes that extended across the arched doorway. Sewage spewed from the gash and splattered the hunter, extinguishing its crimson glare. Momentarily blinded, the hellhound slashed wildly and struck the wall. Brick crumbled and fell off in chunks from a cracking archway. She retreated a pace, and raised her blade in a final, defiant strike.

"Get down!" Stonem yelled. She watched him flank from her right, shoulder pressed against the sewer wall. He shifted his stance, rifle aimed on the archway, then opened fire.

She fell back from the peal of thunder, eyes shielded from the blinding flash. Bullets chewed through stone and metal, and the falling debris impeded the hunter's advancement. Its inhuman wail rose above the cacophony of gunfire. They were plunged into momentary darkness as Stonem's rifle *clicked* empty.

Celeste gathered her wits. "Everyone get behind me and Stonem then retreat down the corridor! Find another door, a way out, or a blockade—anything!"

She wasn't certain if the others obeyed her orders or if they had even heard her; she dared not remove her unblinking gaze from the hunter and its erratic movement beneath the rubble. She drew her revolver, and there was a sharp *click-snap* as Stonem replaced his spent. Light scattered through the creature's bony quills and dappled the wall with slanting shadows. Its rotting flesh peeled from bone in bloodied strips. Twisted fangs gnashed eagerly—*split-splat-splat.*

"Light 'em up!" Celeste ordered. Stonem opened fire and forced the hunter back. She turned with a wretched feeling in her guts, revolver drawn to the waning darkness. She found the others huddled together as if fending off the chill of the sewer, weapons nervously drawn—they retreated a few paces backwards, but her wolf howled through the clamor. Then she saw it.

Another hunter.

While what remained of its form rippled with muscle, gristly broken bones jutted from its spine and punctured its rancid slopping skin. It had a snout that hadn't quite mutated from its human counterpart, its lips bulged and split, but gnarled humanlike teeth protruded out like an underbite. The skeletal face was narrow like a slender man, but the flesh a rotted black, dripping from bones like boiled meat. Even its eyes, shimmering blue, echoed the ghost of who it had once been. It hadn't fully mutated. But the similarities ceased thereafter. Its spindly body resembled a charred corpse, oozing muddy blood from various ruptures. Tattered skin slung between its curved bone-claws. It flattened against the ground, limbs sharply angled and bent like a frog about to leap.

Then it did.

Aurous tore from Melina's grip and responded with a snap of his fangs. The hunter wrenched its elongated limbs. Its claws missed the wolf and ripped into the wall, pelting them with fragments of stone and dust. Again, the wolf buried his snout in tattered flesh and minced its spilling entrails. The creature screeched madly. Blood sprayed along the wolf's black fur when the hunter's claws grazed his shoulder. There was no yelp of pain, however, only a guttural growl and another *snap* of his fangs. The hunter writhed and closed its hooked claws over its snarling prey.

Thunder *clapped* out of her revolver. Black blood spattered the tunnel wall, and the hunter recoiled in fury. Mouth crooked and twisted wide, it screeched and fixed its predatory hunger on her.

Another blinding flash and the creature's misshapen head snapped back. Flesh tore from its cheek. It screeched again, infuriated, but Aurous leapt through its flailing claws and closed his fangs around its throat. His paws dug between jutted ribs. The hunter was forced against the wall, and Celeste squeezed the trigger again. A bullet punched another hole through its flesh, but failed to penetrate the skull. She took aim again.

Blood seeped from the wolf's clenched fangs, soaking his snout in mudded red. Then he wrenched his jaws and *snapped* the creature's neck. Its arms fell limp, its malformed body slumped against the wall. Aurous turned, still snarling, gaze fixated on the last hunter—Melina was the first to sharpen her wits, separating from the group in two long strides. Aurous seemed to snap forward, until her arms closed around him, shimmery green eyes buried in his blood-soaked fur. Celeste thought for only a moment that Melina had managed to restrain him, only to sheepishly realize her redhead was terrified and silently weeping to their wolf.

But there was little time for sentiments.

Another bloodcurdling roar reverberated through the tunnel as the gunfire eased to a dull ringing in her ears. Darkness blinded until her eyes quickly adjusted to the waning glow of her flashlight. There was no time. She reached for Melina, and the redhead shot to her feet as the wolf's fur bristled. A deep growl crept from his bloody jaws, and he jerked from Melina's grip again. Celeste reeled, calling after the wolf. She knew their game all too well: he gives chase and she finishes the hunt.

But this hunter was unlike any other they had encountered.

As Stonem struggled with his jammed weapon, the wolf darted past his legs as a flickering shadow. Crimson eyes burned deeply ahead. Bullet fragments glinted from its scaly black flesh. It appeared unharmed as it *screeched* at her wolf, greeting his charge with a vicious swipe of its claws.

Aurous weaved between strikes, fangs a blur of gleaming red, and sawed through the hunter's scales. A thrashing limb struck and battered the wolf into the wall. The hunter's snout snapped shut, making a slick spitting sound, its claws curved across the wolf's neck.

She emptied her revolver into the creature.

Two rounds sank through the hunter's neck in a burst of black blood. The last bullet ricocheted off its bony quills and sparked along the wall. Her revolver *clicked* empty and was quickly holstered. The hunter barely flinched, but ferociously *gnashed* its alligator-like jaws at her. The feral growl was a familiar, yet horrifying sound—this was *its* kill, *its* meat.

Her ears ached after each the concussive blast of Stonem's rifle. The hunter *screeched* again, squirming in retreat from the onslaught of lead. *Ting! Ting! Ting! Ting!* Bullets fragmented against its scaled flesh. Still he squeezed the trigger in quick intervals, pushing the hunter back.

Then he was empty.

Hooked claws raked through stone as the hunter bellowed and lunged through the cramped corridor. She reeled, machete drawn from her belt and buried deep into its neck with one fluid swing. Its unstoppable surging force heaved her from the ground and into the wall. The back of her skull rocked off a solid surface as she tangled with its writhing limbs, a firm grip on her sunken machete. Her vision clouded and tilted, but she wrenched her blade and *felt* more than heard the sickening *crunch* of its bones breaking. Still its jaws gnashed and snagged her sleeve, fangs grazing her skin like razors. Warmth crept through the splits in her coat sleeve. Crushed beneath the hunter, there was nothing more she could do.

She watched helplessly as Melina unsheathed her knife and split the hunter's throat with an upwards thrust. Dark blood gushed and dribbled over her hand, but the hunter bucked the small redhead from his shoulder. She was thrown into the muck, blade skidding into the darkness. The hunter reared in anger, claws mincing the floor as it prepared for another lunge.

But Nadie had crept along the rubble of the wall, machine pistol drawn to the wounds in the hunter's neck. She opened fire in quick bursts and peppered its scaled flesh with more bullets. It roared again, infuriated, but abandoned its focus on Celeste and her wounded wolf. Celeste forced herself to stand through the pain scorching her side, and her wolf brushed against her leg, fangs gleaming blood. As every instinct screamed at her to fight, she pulled her wolf into retreat and flicked her light toward the opposite end of the tunnel. The ghostly pale face of Clark flinched against the sudden glare, his cheeks glistened with tears, and she couldn't be sure whether he obeyed her orders to run or if the sight of her, bloodied, battered and near-death, had flushed him with an overwhelming sense of fear. Melina fell in pace by her side, fingers locked with hers. Stonem jammed another clip into his rifle as he and Nadie retreated from the ensuing darkness. Only crimson burned in their wake; the hunter was giving chase.

"Run!" was all she could think to yell at her team. "Run!"

TEN
Hell's Bells and Buckets of Blood

HER BONES were brittle twigs as she stumbled down the corridor, balanced only by the grace of Melina's support. The wolf was snarling madly, but could only struggle weakly against their combined strength. Nervous glances over her shoulder revealed Nadie quickly closing the gap between them, followed by Stonem. A terrible screech resonated from the darkness.

"Stay with Aurous, keep running," she wheezed to Melina, breathless, fumbling with the flashlight strap. She unfastened it from her coat and shoved it into Melina's hands. "Just keep moving!"

"Celeste," Melina started, voice muffled. Her next words were lost to the pounding of their boots in the muck.

"Just go, please!" Celeste pleaded desperately, then turned away from the only person she loved to face absolute death. *Live, Melina.*

The hunter thrashed through the corridor like a bucking bull, shredding walls and crumbling stone around its jutting spine. Its sudden charge shuddered the floor beneath her. Light scattered across the creature when Nadie turned to face the it, but Celeste reached for her friend's coat. Her fingers snagged around the collar, and she yanked Nadie backwards. Claws ripped through the air inches from her nose. The stone wall was gasped open beside them.

Nadie stumbled into Celeste, but Stonem drew aim on the hunter—three more rounds burst free and drilled into the monster's twisted neck, tattering its stringy flesh.

They ran from the enraged creature, their erratic movements smothering the corridor in a swirl of shadows. The hunter melted into darkness, a surging mass of claws and gnashing fangs. When they reached a bend in the tunnel, her grip on Nadie tightened—she slammed into her, and they both careened to the right and battered themselves across the mucky floor. Stonem dove, arms outstretched, and crashed into the wall. She heard the air rush from his lungs with a loud *whooshing* sound as he rolled and lost his grip on his rifle. He flung himself toward them like a writhing worm as the hunter tore through the muck and chomped its long jaws after his legs. *Snap-snap-snap!* His fingers raked through the filth to retrieve his fallen rifle. The hunter towered with its claws gripping into stone.

She threw herself for Stonem's fallen weapon. Her fingertips grazed the rifle barrel—the hunter descended over him. Before she properly aimed, she squeezed the trigger, and the rifle burst into blinding flashes. Her bones shuddered under the unexpected force—her aim faltered, and the wall exploded into a flurry of stone and sparks. The hunter bellowed, but only glared menacingly at Stonem's escape. As the pulsing pain in her ears lessened, a shrill whistle carried through the tunnel. She shook her head to clear it from her mind, but the strange sound persisted. The hunter seemed perplexed as well, almost placid, with vacant crimson eyes. Then its muscles tensed, jaws *snapping* shut at the sight of their blood-soaked bodies in the darkness.

"Give me that!" Stonem was suddenly by her side, and the rifle wrenched out of her grip. "Now it's time we run!"

As the hunter roared a hunger for their flesh, preparing to lunge after its quarry, she followed Stonem and bolted down the winding tunnel. Nadie was only a few paces ahead—beyond that was only darkness. Light flickered weakly.

"Shit!" Nadie slapped the flashlight into her palm. "Batteries are almost dead!"

"So are we!" Stonem countered.

"Keep going!" Celeste gasped. As they neared another bend, her boots seemed to slip out from under her. She fell, twisted, and bashed her hip against solid stone. She slid across the slick surface, clawing at the muck. "Just run!" she called back to the others, but felt a cold dread as the tunnel plunged into impenetrable black.

They were already gone.

Fear needled her skin. She was utterly blind, lost in unending darkness, and heard nothing beyond her heaving for air. Trembling, her grip was uncontrollable, and she failed to loosen the knife from her belt. She cursed silently, then forced her stiff fingers around the handle. *You can do this. If you do, they'll have time to escape.* She bit her lip. *Damn it. I really am a fool to believe I could end this empire myself. Vengeance for my mother and brother.* She stood in defiance of her aching limbs and unsheathed her knife. *I may have underestimated Blackwell.*

Then she heard the hunter, the grating *screech* of its bony quills across the walls, the snort from its heavy breathing, the gnashing of its twisted teeth. A reddish tint permeated the darkness, and she knew its predacious gaze wallowed in her helplessness. A soured warmth rolled over her, her clothes drenched in the spittle from its snout—it almost seemed to *breathe* in her fear like sustenance, prolonging the joy of its kill. The knife trembled in her firm grasp. *But I'm not dying without a fight—*

—there was a sharp squeal and a searing flash of pain through her mind. Vision spotted. Her head pulsed like a beaten drum. It was maddening. Through the shrill, she heard the hunter snort and snarl, claws *scraping* against stone.

"You are a bloody fool!" someone rasped through the squealing darkness. She tried to speak, but only mumbled and heaved in response. Her blinded world tumbled, tilted and twirled, and suddenly her boots were sloshing through muck. She leaned on something solid, yet comforting, the embrace of someone *living*. She thought of that for a moment, legs tangled, dizzied and nearly retching; she was *alive*...somehow. She still couldn't see—where were they going?

"Getting yourself killed when there's an obvious way out is not valiant so much as it is incredibly stupid," the gruff voice rebuked, and she almost thought the words came from her father. Was that his stern tone she heard from the darkness?

Oh dad, she wanted to say to him, *how I miss you.*

The ringing in her ears eased, and her mind cleared with a sudden, jarring thought: the hunter would never abandon its prey. It would still be after them.

Her body stiffened as the voice spoke again. "The others are still moving." It was Stonem. "We have enough time to prepare an ambush when we catch up with them.”

She broke from his grasp and staggered, then pumped her legs. She still couldn’t see, and when her shoulders grazed the tunnel walls, she turned, only to slam into another solid surface. She was flailing in the darkness, blinded. Stonem, however, urged her along calmly, as if he had already committed the layout to memory.

“What happened back there?” she asked breathlessly, smothering her broken voice with a cough. Her guts pooled with icy water. “How do you—”

“Shut up!” he hissed back. He steered to the left, sharply, nearly throwing her around the bend. Another roar haunted the tunnel depths. She stumbled and lost pace with Stonem, and he had to round on her with impatience seething from his tone. “*Hurry!*”

But she slowed instead, an anchor on his side. “We’re not going a step further until I know where Melina is.”

“Celeste!”

Her knees buckled under the sudden weight, and she fell back against the wall. Curls grazed her cheek as smoothly as spun silk. The warmth of Melina’s jarring embrace dulled the pain like the pills in her hand—

—at which point had she reached for the bottle in her coat? There it was, grasped tightly in her palm.

Where’s my knife?

Did I even bring a knife?

It was when she blinked, perplexed at her surroundings, that a glaring light swept over them. It was like fire in her eye sockets. Nadie.

“You’re alive,” she whispered softly, almost in disbelief. Her doe eyes shimmered. “Thank the Creator.”

“Why are you not still moving?” demanded Stonem, pale face gleaming in the waning light. “We’re sitting ducks!”

“There’s nowhere to go,” Clark mumbled grimly. “It’s a damn dead end!”

“What?” Stonem shook his head. “This muck flows *somewhere.* It can’t just be a dead end!”

“This literal shithole doesn’t really lead anywhere to begin with,” Nadie whispered, eyes shut against the rising clamor of the beast. Aurous growled weakly by her side. “It was an antiquated system when the world worked, and now it’s just a labyrinth of neglected waste and runoff. The city likely started small, with chambers like these dug out for other purposes as well as a sewer system. The deeper we get, the older everything seems, until there's no pipes or tubes, just channels that drain into the rivers and streams. That's why they built new systems around it. We're just at the bottom of the main channel we came through. The end of the line."

"So," Celeste asked slowly. "Where does it lead?"

"Christ," cursed Stonem, earning a rebuking glance from Melina. The rifle clacked noisily under his hands. "I'll watch the entrance while you play Watson to her Sherlock."

"Melina," Celeste began, chilled as they parted from their embrace. Melina scrunched her nose. "I'll stay with Aurous," she responded. Her lips brushed gently along the jagged black scars on Celeste's cheek.

"You best get back, too, Red," Stonem said as another howl thundered through the tunnel. "Little Wolf, find our escape!"

It was only a few more feet until she saw what Nadie had attempted to explain. The tunnel expanded into a cavernous hollow, with cragged walls that seemed crudely chiseled from stone. Grime and muck oozed through the slits in the walls, crawling through the channel into a dark descent. Nadie slowly edged forward, hand up to stop Celeste from following. She reached out, carefully, and shone her light into the void below. The flickering beam dissolved a layer of darkness, but it was deep and unending. Perpetually black. There was a gentle *hiss* of a stream cascading over the edge, but no sound of a spatter below.

"The floor is cracked and crumbling," Nadie said, retreating from the edge of the channel. "Light won't pierce through that darkness. We have no idea how far of a drop. There's no other entrances or drainage pipes. We're screwed, Commander."

"No." Celeste's mind spun in all directions. "We have the advantage."

"What?"

"Fall back!" Celeste suddenly yelled. "We have a way out!"

"Commander!" Nadie exclaimed. "There's *no* way out!"

A dangerous grin flashed across her face. "Exactly."

But she felt the warmth drain from her cheeks when the wailing rose in volume. Revolver drawn, she spun the cylinder open and flicked in the bullets that were pinched between her fingers. Then the cylinder *snapped* shut, her thumb jammed down on the hammer. A small gesture of her hand signaled Nadie to retreat.

"It's here!" Stonem called back to them.

Now!

Dread had a vicelike grip on her chest as she raced up the muddy channel. The bright glare of Melina's flashlight suddenly blinked into nothingness.

"Here!"

Chills pricked her skin at the sight of a deep, crimson glow that bled through the darkness. She heard the *huff* from its snout, the spatter of warmth from its expulsed breath. She gagged on the stench of rot. *There you are!*

She squeezed the trigger twice.

Light flashed like a brief strike of lightning, and thunder *boomed* through the hollow. Ricochets sparked off its scales, and its jaws separated in a furious roar that rivaled the blasts of her gun. She turned and ran back down the channel—claws ripped through the oozing surface by her feet. Muck and fragmented stone rained down on her. She whipped her arm behind her—the revolver flared and blasted the hunter's snapping jaws. It stumbled, crouched on all fours, claws flexing into the flowing muck. Shadows slithered across her vision like a blindfold. Her legs pumped fiercely. Finger twitched against the trigger.

"Commander!"

The sudden cry wrenched her attention forward, and she saw light sweep across the channel floor—which abruptly ended in a gap of impenetrable darkness.

Shit!

She threw herself back into the mucky river and sloshed frantically, but momentum kept her sliding toward the edge. Fingers clawed through mud, and she spun to a halt, leg dangling over the edge of the channel. Stone cracked and shifted beneath her weight—and shuddered from the surging force behind her. The hunter stomped over her. Its twisted fangs snapped down for her neck

A whistle shrilled and split her mind with a blinding pain. Her grip faltered, and she nearly plummeted to the nothingness below. The beast snorted, snarled, scraped its claws along stone like it were sharpening blades.

"Come on!"

Jarred, she released her hold and slipped over the edge—only to fall into a reliably firm grip. Ice crawled to her throat. The whistle still pierced her mind, and words slurred and tumbled incoherently from her tongue as she staggered for balance in the darkness. Light flickered across the hunter, its crimson eyes staring past them in a vacuous trace. Then Stonem's rifle erupted in a single deafening blast. The hunter snarled fervidly—then plummeted over the edge and into the icy darkness below. The monster was finally dead.

The shrilling ceased.

She fell to her knees, retched into the rancid muck, then *plopped* her backside into her own sick. She raised a heavy arm to inspect her revolver—only to fumble with an orange bottle. Her pills rattled around in her palm, her tongue pasty and dry as though she had dissolved another...

"Celeste," she heard a melodious whisper from the darkness. "How many of those have you had today?"

The question seemed irrelevant, almost trivial. Where was her revolver?

"You know the doctor told you to only take three a day, and any more could have serious side effects," Melina explained gently. Or perhaps she was chastising her again, another flaw to be declared and scrutinized. She didn't care. Pills smothered the flaring pain and she needed each one.

"Tell me you haven't taken more."

Stonem *clacked* his teeth. "Been poppin' that shit like candy, Red."

"Jesus Christ," Clark squealed like a frightened pig. "We're being led by a junkie!"

"Watch your tone!" Melina reprimanded.

"He's right," said Stonem, shaking his head. Celeste scoffed quietly and rolled her eyes toward the ceiling. "Much as I hate to say it. She can't lead properly if her head is clouded by happy pills."

"It's for pain management," Melina countered, oddly defensive. Her fiery tone warmed a small section of Celeste's heart. "I'm her nurse, *I'll* deal with it."

Celeste peered deeper into the darkness. Her attention was pulled away from the others by a strange glint. They were distant whispers, the bickering of neighbors through steel walls.

"That's not the issue," Nadie said. "What's troubling, Stonem, is just how you managed to stop that thinf."

"Luck," Stonem rasped, snorting loudly. "Or maybe I'm that much better."

Nadie was persistent. "Bullshit. I heard that strange static, and I watched that demon practically bow at your feet."

"Dominance."

Celeste cocked her head, vision blurred from the shadows…but there was something…

"Hey," she whispered to no one.

"I only saw him shoot the hunter before it could devour Celeste," Melina said. "I didn't hear anything."

"I know what I heard *and* what I saw," Nadie asserted. "He's hiding something."

"Someone," she whispered again, wary of pulling her gaze from the blurred outline above, as if it would vanish once it left her sight. She felt a slab of ice press against her cheek. Aurous nuzzled her, whining gently. "Look at this."

"This is such *bullshit!*" Stonem growled back at them. "I just saved your pretty asses, and now you accuse me of—well, just what are you implying, dear?"

"Don't patronize me."

"Hey," she blurted out, "I found the bomb."

Nadie flicked her flashlight to the ceiling in the direction Celeste was staring. There it was: long and wide, boxlike, a glaring white like freshly fallen snow, a clutter of wires bunched from the sides. It was pinned to the stone directly below the main sewer chamber—below the heart of the Medical District.

How icy of a coffin it could have been. Was the thought hers, or Vega's?

"So, it is," Nadie said with a creeping smile. "It's as big as the one on the dam."

Stonem sputtered as he asked incredulously, "There's another on the dam? The *dam?*"

Nadie ignored him and turned to Celeste. "We made it, Commander," she said. "It may take some time, but we can detach it and find a way out from here—"

"No," Celeste croaked, then stiffened against the chill. "You all got me here safely, now it's time to meet me beyond the gates."

Melina gasped sharply. Her gaze turned as fiery as her crimson curls. "You won't make it anywhere."

Celeste couldn't face her. "I can ensure everyone's escape."

"Oh, such gallantry," Melina retorted. "A martyr, is that it? That secures nothing but your death. An easy way out."

Nadie's voice shuddered as she spoke. "Commander, you said it yourself. The best way to hit them is to move that bomb somewhere it can do the *most* damage. Not take down an empty district."

"The dam will still blow," Celeste explained wearily. "The districts will still flood."

"The camps will be untouched," Nadie countered.

"Blackwell will still die!" Her outburst forced them to an unsettling silence. Beside her, Aurous growled his unease, pawing at her lap.

"I can't help but think your thirst for vengeance is blinding," said Nadie, hesitantly. "It's clouded your judgment."

Clark snorted in contempt. "Goddamn junkie."

"I know what I'm doing," Celeste declared with a snarl. "I'm the commander, everyone follows my orders! I'm going to blow the hell out of his army and flood the city. Nobody will notice your escape."

Nadie wouldn't ease. "We still don't know the detonator's range! You might only blow one bomb!"

"Look, this mission has been a disaster," she admitted. The truth was rancid along her tongue. "I foolishly thought we could safely move the bombs and detonate everything from a distance. But the closer they got, the more desperate I became. Now we're trapped under the sewers with an army of infected crawling through every tunnel searching for us. This is *my* fault. The least I can do is let you all escape with your lives."

Refusing an extended hand from Nadie, she stood and braced against the shock of pain that burned through her belly. She felt warmth seep into her jeans. Blood.

"I'll lure as many of those bastards here and let them know it's me. Blackwell won't resist taking me out himself, I'm sure of it." Celeste nodded to her team, but fear formed a jagged lump in her throat. She couldn't meet Melina's darkening expression. "That should buy you enough time to get far from here."

"That should have been the plan from the start!" Melina cried out, voice cracking. "We should have just left..."

"If the dam doesn't blow, I'll set it off myself," Nadie declared, nodding curtly. Her trembling hands sinuously combed through the contents of her motley green rucksack. "But make it out alive, Commander."

"I will," Celeste croaked. She reached for the device in Nadie's hand and squeezed—a parting handshake to her comrade. A loyal friend. "I need you to take care of them until I can. Make sure they survive."

"Of course."

"Celeste, I..." Melina choked on her own words.

A raspy chuckle rang out over Melina's sobbing. "As touching as this was," Stonem whispered. "Nobody leaves."

Apprehension squeezed the air from her chest as she turned to find Stonem's rifle raised to her own head. She stared down the sleek jet-black barrel, throat clenched tight. Her hand instinctively fell to her waist—and brushed against an empty holster.

Nadie flinched and reached for her strapped weapon, but Stonem jabbed the rifle against the bridge of Celeste's crooked nose. Blood trickled out of one nostril. She didn't flinch.

"Don't you move a bloody inch, girl," he snarled. "I swear you'll scrape her brains from the wall if you do."

"What the *hell* is this, Stonem?" Celeste muttered. A small growl rumbled in her wolf's throat. "Getting desperate?"

"You don't know what I've gone through! What they've done to me! There's nowhere for me, and that means there's nowhere for *you!* Prisoners, we all are! Death is the only escape, and I sure as hell won't die in the gutter like a rabid dog. Like a death sentence from the Bandit Queen beyond the grave."

"Stonem," Melina squeaked, "we're your friends. We're helping each other."

He shook his head feverishly. "Even after the city was ours again, I lost my rank and title, power, my name. Everything. I was broken in his eyes, worthy only for the hunt. He was going to have me become a mindless, infected *husk.*" His lip trembled, but his eyes narrowed with a glint of anger. "I couldn't let that happen. I couldn't be sentenced to another prison. I would do anything. So, he set me on *you.* This was my mission, my only way out."

She fought for composure, but her face blanched under a cold, drenching sweat. "We were going to escape together, Stonem, put this nightmare far behind us. Find a home where rank is just another word in the dictionary."

"He *knew* you were trained by the Bandit Queen," he viciously spat at her. "He *knew* you would attempt to spark a rebellion against him. *It's just what they do!* They gave up so easy, there had to be a counterattack. You were the Queen's second, so only you would know. When they found the bomb—oh, they thought they had stopped an attack, but Blackwell saw it as a wasted opportunity. He needed to catch you in the act. Instead he ordered them to excavate, cause a scene—in order to set you loose. It was pure luck I found you creeping about and, well, here you are, Little Wolf."

She gave a slight shake of her head, hair slicked against her forehead from sweat. "He couldn't have known we were there or what we had planned."

Another wheezy chuckle from Stonem. "Oh, there were plenty of plans for getting rid of you, but you are a tenacious little bitch. I admire that. Hard to kill, and I told him as such. I heard the stories, Wolf, how you gunned down everyone in your path. You're bloodthirsty, ferocious—and tainted. You were marked for death the moment your uncle spared your life. Ironic, isn't it?"

"Put the goddamn gun down," Nadie whispered. "We can figure this out."

"I'm sorry," Stonem replied gravely. "I really am. I liked you lot, and I almost thought for a moment you would pull it off. But Blackwell will never stop, and I'll never get my life back."

"Son of a bitch," Celeste growled. "We can walk out of here right now!"

He arched his neck, and the flesh above his shoulder bulged into rigid lump, as if something were attempting to burst free from his neck. "Every movement is being tracked. I could never escape. But stopping you grants me the freedom I deserve. I'm sorry, but Blackwell is going to win. He always has."

"Maybe," Celeste replied slowly. Her fingers tensed around the detonator. "But unlike you I'm willing to die for my beliefs."

"Oh?"

Her eyes searched the darkness. "I'm sorry, Melina," she whispered, loosening the clasp to the detonator. "I love you." Her lungs burned with a final breath. She flipped the trigger.

Nothing happened.

Another moment crawled by as Stonem glared down the sight of his rifle, a sharp grin cutting up his face. "A flair for the dramatic as always. But I'm afraid it's for nothing."

Disbelief fogged her mind. She flipped the trigger again—nothing. "What the hell?"

Stonem pinched the zipper of his coat and opened the flap. Wired into the sleeve was a small black box, like a handheld radio, with antennae hidden inside the folds of his collar.

"Shit." Nadie hissed. "It's a jammer. Blocks radio signals. The detonator is useless right now with him in range."

"Clever girl," Stonem said. "Points for the effort, but it's the end of the line. The moment you discovered that bomb I turned the jammer on. It's too late, they'll already have our final position even without the tracker properly functioning."

"Just kill the bitch and get it over with," Clark sniveled.

Anger twisted Stonem's pale face as he shot a glance over his shoulder at the trembling boy. "None of you are off the hook—"

With his attention fixed on Clark, she slapped the barrel from her face and quickly closed the gap between them. His jaw *cracked* from the upward force of her fist, and he fell back with a loud grunt. She lunged again, fingers clawing at his rifle. He twisted it from her grasp, then forced the barrel into her chest.

Snarling, the wolf buried his fangs into Stonem's arm and wrenched his jaws. Blood squirted between his teeth and streaked along his snout. The rifle wavered.

Clap-clap-clap!

The barrel erupted in his unstable grip, bullets chewing up the floor beside Celeste. The wolf snarled in pain and fury, and Celeste lunged for Stonem again.

CRACK!

Blood burst from her nose in warm streams, and she collapsed with her vision spinning. The detonator slipped from her grasp and into the muck.

"Get off her!"

Her head felt like an anchor she struggled to keep afloat in choppy water. A terrible pain slanted and blurred her sight. Her lips felt oddly numb.

Amorphous shadows coalesced until a strange blinding light streaked across the channel. Tongues of flame licked at the pressing darkness as her eyes trailed the lambency, enamored by its swirling dance. It reminded her of—

Melina.

Melina jumped to her feet as the wolf was battered to the ground and clubbed across his skull with the stock of Stonem's rifle. Aurous convulsed and sprawled across Nadie. Melina screamed. The rifle raised back to Celeste—Melina furiously battered her small fists against him. The dazed wolf snarled and lunged out of Nadie's lap.

A deafening blast erupted from the rifle.

The bullet missed by mere inches, bursting into sparks by Celeste's legs. Her frenzied wolf crashed into Stonem, fangs bloody and grinding through flesh. The sudden force hurtled them over the edge of the channel—with Melina caught in Stonem's iron grip, dragging her down with him into the deep, dark void.

In an instant, all three of them were gone.

A savage sound tore from Celeste's throat as she dropped near the jagged edge of the channel. She felt Nadie's hands around her shoulders like a restraint, but she didn't care; she jerked away from the gentle hold with an impatient shrug. The sudden, jarring loss of everything she loved swept through her like the fury of a storm. It burned through her veins until she raged and screamed their names into the darkness like a despondent wolf howling the loss of its pack.

Lucidity leaked from her mind like blood from a fatal wound. *Come back, please come back.* Helplessly, she stared into the shadows, feeling the bitter chill of regret around her body like chains. *This is my fault.* She attempted to scream again, to desperately shout their names into the darkness, but it felt like her heart had *thumped* up into her throat. Voices drifted to her ears like distant echoes, wordless hums, bouncing around her skull with no meaning.

Don't die. Tears blurred her sight. *Not like Daddy, please.*

Faint whispers rose to a deafening cacophony of shouted commands and vulgar, threatening tones. Shadows scurried across the walls as a blinding glare swept through the chamber, forcing her eyes shut. A snarling sound rumbled in her throat, reminiscent of her wolf, and her lip curled over clenched teeth. The tension in the air smothered her. She turned, fangs bared, eager for the hunt—

—and stared right into the deep, colorless eyes of General Blackwell.

"Well, if it isn't the Bandit Bitch," he growled at her, as though each muttered word fought to control his explosive temper. "Crawling to the gutter like the rat she is."

"You bastard!" she spat at him. Her gaze drifted from his crooked brow to the detonator submerged in the muck near her boots. Blackwell poisoned the silence with his grating laughter.

"I admire your guts," he remarked with a tight voice, chest filled with sour-scented smoke. "*Literally!* I mean, you took three"—he exhaled a thick grey cloud—"to the stomach and lived to tell the tale. Not only that but you slaughtered anyone who stepped in your path, right or wrong. You never let fear motivate your actions. Only rage. In the Old World, you would have been my most prized soldier."

She cursed at him with a vulgar choice of words and took a step toward him—then halted at the chilling sound of a half-dozen automatic weapons raising to greet her unwarranted movements.

She caught sight of his lapdogs, the soldiers in black that oozed out from the shadows around them. Each barrel returned her flinty glare.

Jets of smoke expulsed from his thinly pursed lips. "That is exactly why you lost tonight: sacrificing all your pieces on the board, exposing your queen. Don't give me such a vacant look, girl. *Never interrupt an enemy when he is making a mistake!* You of all people should know the importance of winning at chess—it keeps the mind sharp and your wits sharper, forces the use of your critical thinking. Teaches patience and calculation, which you seem to lack, dear girl. That is the difference between us."

His dark eyes darted to Clark and Nadie, both kneeling under rifle barrels, faces paled and drenched in sweat. Clark was nearly convulsing, smothering a sob into his hands. Nadie stared up the barrel, eyes narrowed in defiance. Blackwell flashed his stained teeth at them.

"You refuse to sacrifice your pawns to ensure victory," he continued with a raspy chuckle. "I know their true value, how to lure the other pieces to destruction. Stonem may not have been a knight or a bishop. Hell, he wasn't even a rook, but he did lure out the queen. And if I'm being honest, I did *not* expect you to take him out, as I assume you have. I even gave him the key to your new weakness. My failsafe against Mengele's creations. Thought he would be stronger than that, but then again, your team seems a few men short. Did he manage to finally get his way with that fire-crotched bitch?"

"Screw you!" she snarled at him, and instinctively raised her fists—then painfully dropped to her knees, hands clasped over her ears. She screamed. Her thoughts were disrupted and by the strange, shrill whistle. Pressure formed in her head like a buildup of steam in a kettle until it felt like her skull would burst and dribble out her ears like bloody ooze. Then as quickly as it rose in pitch, the piercing sound vanished.

"This bitch still needs to learn her place in the new world!" Blackwell declared. "It's about time someone *really* showed you!"

Her eyes opened to a thrown punch. White flashes crossed her sight when his knuckles thudded hard against her socket. The crushing blow drove her flat against the ground, head bouncing off the jagged edge of the channel. Her fingers fumbled along her belt for a knife—

—the stabbing pain in her mind returned, ears splitting from the shrill sound. She writhed as the pain spread through her muscles. The moment she screamed in utter agony the sound ceased.

"How Stonem could have lost to such a weak, tainted mutt is beyond me," he said with a heavy sigh. "Have your friends figured it out yet, girl? Why this harmless static debilitates you? Or did you honestly believe you were cured? You believed that, didn't you? Deep down, that those disgusting marks on your skin were just carvings from the past. But really, it's a path to your future. So, do they know?"

His fingers raked across her skull, twisted her hair into a tight grip, and jerked her head back to fully expose her throat. She felt the sharp pinch of his blade and the warm rivulet of crimson that trailed the steel's cold bite.

"Not only do you carry the blood of traitors in your veins," he hissed venomously, then flicked her own blood across her swelling cheek. "But you're infected with a controlled variation of the sickness, a living bioweapon just waiting to be unleashed. I'm certain you still recall Colbat. Well, now that's you. It's a work in progress, I admit, but once the infected host begins to die"—she flinched when he *snapped* his fingers—"no more uncontrolled mutation. Mostly. So, once I decide to cut this pretty little throat of yours, you'll be one of them: a freak, a monster, leashed to my will for as long as that mutated corpse can suffer such a fate."

A small sound of disgust escaped Nadie, and Clark whimpered and sputtered a curse toward her. *Shadow spawn.* General Blackwell erupted in a howl of laughter, barking his excitement into the darkness around them.

"This is where it the fun begins!" he told her, flattening the blade against her cheek. She gritted her teeth, glaring at him through her swollen eye. "This is where, despite your valiant efforts otherwise, you become loyal to my whims. That signal inhibits an infected mind so I can exert a certain degree of control on my pets. Once you're a mindless beast, I'll let you devour your friends. The ones that are left, I mean. Isn't that ironic, hm? Killing the people you want to save."

There was a slight *hiss* of ripping fabric as his knife cut under the collar of her coat. As the tip carved into her breast, he pulled the knife away, blood trickling from the steel.

"Well," he said. He licked his flaky lips. "Why don't we bring that creature out of you piece by bloody piece!"

He dropped atop of her and drove his knee into her belly. She retched for air. He locked his bony fingers around her wrist like a shackle and jarred her left arm from its socket. Then he plunged the blade into her hand.

A white-hot burning intensity lanced up her limb as blood spurted and steamed across the blade. She felt steel grinding against bone before—*snap*—her severed fingers plopped into the muck beside her. The terribly slick warmth gushed through her remaining two fingers that were curled tightly under her thumb. Her stunned lungs expanded, and a scream rose to her throat—until the hilt of his blade jarred her silent, splitting her lip and loosening two teeth in her bottom jaw. She groaned weakly, eyes fluttering.

"You're going to die just like your whore of a mother," he spat. He smeared her own blood along her cheek with the edge of the knife. "Like your father should have for the damage he caused! I recall him well—the arrogance of his perceived intelligence, not unlike yourself, the sickening righteous morals. I had to break that, because Cavarly was always blinded by his ties to family.

"That boy has been with me since the beginning. I trained him in the academy, he was the top of his goddamn class. Expert marksmen, hand-to-hand, you name it. When the quarantines fell and the government crumbled, Cavarly was the only soldier who stayed, and we fought a horde of infected to establish the first real safe zone. We recruited survivors and regained power. Our quarantine zones worked. He is the only man I trust to carry the mantle after I am gone. Loyal above all else—but always sentimental, searching for word of his family, of *you*."

Another sharp blow across her face filled her mouth with bitter blood. Roused from a stupor, she choked and sputtered, writhing weakly under Blackwell's crushing hold. The agony pulsing from her partially severed hand was like a hammer striking nails through her bones. A vicious twist of his knife gashed her scarred forearm.

"When your father finally found us, he was much like you—questioning my authority, my methods, my *rule*. He accused me of tampering with the sickness, of spreading it to my own people—I was searching for a cure! Oh, how he needed to be broken, but Cavarly was too soft. I burned that bridge for him. When your father took his family and left, planning to expose *my* research, I found them, stripped him of all he had. You were supposed to die that night, you and your mother. He was lucky some of my men are not as cunning and vile as he was. He burned my facilities to the ground, slaughtered my men, destroyed many *years* of research. Those bandits helped him in his vengeance—he burned two more outposts before vanishing from the face of this scorched earth. Of course, Cavarly was distraught that his brother could betray him for the bandits, but now he could focus on the greater cause. We are *fixing* this world, and you're a distraction to him, a weakness!"

With a snarl, he pressed the edge of the blade against her throat. Warmth trickled down her chest.

"*Victory belongs to the most persevering!*" He licked his lips. "I couldn't kill him—but I get to kill you!"

As she clenched her eyes tightly shut against death, three loud blasts thundered through the chamber.

For a moment, she thought it was the pain pounding in her skull—until she felt a sticky warmth spatter against her face. Air rushed through her lungs when the weight against her gut suddenly lifted, and she gasped wildly. Her eyes snapped open to Blackwell as he fell back, tattered flesh slung from his shoulder in ribbons. Thick streams of blood waterfalled down his chest. Beside her, a soldier slumped in the muck, eyes dimmed and vacant. The soldier who had stood over Clark was now hunched on his knees with his hands clutched around a gaping hole in his abdomen. Entrails slipped through his fingers like slimy sausages. In the initial confusion, Nadie's guard turned his head—which proved a fatal decision. Nadie lunged for his knife, gripped tightly, and then forced the blade between his ribs. There was a slight grunt and a shudder before he collapsed, already dead. She yanked the rifle from his loose grasp.

"Kill them!" Blackwell roared in fury and utter agony. "Kill the traitorous bastards!"

A peal of gunfire erupted through chamber, blinding Celeste as she struggled to her feet. Nadie brandished the rifle and opened fire on two remaining soldiers—who had themselves reeled to fire blindly into the surrounding darkness—bursting both skulls with pinpoint precision.

Celeste let her eyes slowly adjust to the dimming light. *Knife,* was the first coherent thought in her skull. She glimpsed the fallen blade, submerged in her own blood, and quickly retrieved the weapon. Her arm shuddered with pain when she pressed her bleeding stumps against her hip to clot the wounds. She caught a glimmer in the encroaching darkness. *Aurous?* Beneath the rippling strands of gold was a piercing blue, an untouched sky, staring back at her.

"Commander," said a droll, snickering voice. "It seems I'm always saving your ass."

"Snyder?"

Her blonde hair was streaked with mud and slicked against her forehead. Blood soaked through her lavender coat, most of it certainly not hers, leaving dark streaks dripping down her jeans. But as her bright eyes fell over Celeste and her grievous wounds, the sly grin twitched to a frown. The oak-brown Springfield in her hands shook, a slight but noticeable tremble of anger.

"It took me longer than anticipated to shake off those damn hellhounds."

"It was you," Celeste muttered weakly. "You killed those soldiers."

"It was obvious you and the maid were planning something in the forest," Snyder replied, rifle lowered to the general gasping by Celeste's feet. "I decided to see for myself. I figured out quickly what you were up to once word spread about the bombs. This place has done more than piss on my family's name and waste my talent. This asshole has taken everything from me. I wanted a chance to take as many out as I could for my brother—to die as a real soldier like he wanted."

"Bullshit," Nadie muttered, grip tightening on her weapon. "How can we believe that?"

The blonde shrugged. "I just turned the general's chest into minced meat."

"T-traitor!" Blackwell's face was a deep crimson like his spilling blood. "I'm going to gut you personally!"

Snyder's eyes narrowed at him. "Keep reaching for that gun, old man, and I'll scatter your brains into the mud."

"Bitch!"

"I know you experimented on him." She spoke with a low, trembling voice, teeth gritted. "After his leg was paralyzed. His *leg*. He was one of the mutated during the city siege, the poor bastards you slaughtered to turn the tide for your vendetta. Your own loyal soldiers, infected. I found out from his own unit, his *friends*, who drink themselves to a stupor every night because of what you made them do. I almost killed them, goddamn blue falcons, but they were pathetic enough already."

"They knew what they were getting into! They wanted it! You speak of a soldier's death, well, that is one, girl! You could only be so lucky!"

Celeste shuddered from disbelief and setting shock. "You never stopped, did you, General? All these years and you still used your loyal men as lab rats. All of our families suffered under your cruelty."

"I'll kill every last one of you traitors!"

Snyder spat at his gushing wound, then turned to Celeste. "He's all yours, Commander."

Still cradling her bloody stumps, she dropped over Blackwell and crushed his gunshot wounds with her knee. He roared his agony until her fist crushed his windpipe closed. He choked and sputtered on his scream, then clawed at her face with smoke-stained nails. She struck like a viper; her knife sank through the flesh of his raised arm and *thudded* against bone. She wrenched the blade from its hold, then plunged it through the same wound. He choked and rasped in spurts of pain. She pressed the blade, stained with his blood and hers, against the base of his throat.

"Goodbye," she hissed cruelly, licking her bloodied teeth. "*Little Corporal.*"

"Halt!"

The command chilled her to inaction. She sat over a rasping Blackwell, and his mouth gaped in wordless pain. Nadie raised her weapon at the source of the interruption—then quickly lowered it at the sight of dozens more soldiers and the threatening glare of high-caliber rifles. Snyder sneered and dropped her weapon at the sight of a small army emerging from the tunnel. One man stepped forward, unarmed, boots *sloshing* through the spilled brains of his comrades. His crestfallen gaze swam through the ocean of blood around her. Celeste stared back at him, defiantly silent, blade dug into Blackwell's throat. Her uncle slowly raised a hand to signal his men to lower their weapons.

"Celeste," he said quietly, brow furled at the sight of Blackwell's wounds. "Please put the weapon down and we can work this out civilly."

"He's killed our families," she croaked at him, blood drooling down her chin. "He admitted it, he admitted everything! He manipulated you into believing it was for the cure—he's making living weapons! He's taken everything from us! He *needs* to die!"

A slight shake of his head. "We can hold him accountable for any crimes committed." He cleared his throat. "And I will guarantee you and your friends a fair trial for the bloodshed this night. This has been a long time coming"—his eyes narrowed to dark shadows when he met Blackwell's gaze—"*certainly*. But we have protocol to follow."

The wolf inside her howled its appetence for more blood. Her eyes fell to Blackwell, who returned her furious glare with a sharp, viperous grin. She slowly shook her head.

"*Victory belongs to the most persevering.*"

The blade sank through his throat. Blood fountained from the gash in bright red spurts, and his grin twisted to a desperate, soundless gape for mercy. Tears welled in his fluttering eyes. He was dead before she dropped the knife into his own gushing blood.

"Oh Celeste, what have you done?" Her uncle whispered woefully, "I won't be able to protect you now."

The absolution she felt was shockingly numb. There was nothing beyond a faint tingle in her chest, not even pain. Her own eyes rolled into the back of her skull, and she collapsed in the pooling blood. The last thing she recalled as she slipped into the comforting black was her uncle, and how he had abandoned the façade of familiarity for a callous military bark.

"Arrest her entire unit and have them detained until they're ready for transport," he commanded. "Blackwell's assumptions were correct, they're working for the bandits. Dismantle the bomb. We'll forgo a public hearing and commence sentencing. Celeste"—he cleared his throat, choking back his disappointment—"you are hereby sentenced to death for the murder of General Blackwell and countless others. Do you have any last words you wish recorded? Remorse for your actions?"

I'm so sorry, Melina.

"No."

PART II.
PRISON (EARLY AUTUMN)

ELEVEN
Old Sins Cast Long Shadows

A SHARP, slewing motion jarred her awake.

Scattered sunlight stabbed her vision to a painful white blur. She groaned, lips chapped and painfully splitting open. The salty-sour scent of blood clung to her nostrils like slime. Her neck was stiff and rigid, head propped and lightly *thudding* against a pane of thick, blurry glass. Any attempted movement was met with resistance, the walls seemed to close in on her like a coffin. Her wrists were tightly bound above her head, caught in a cold, metallic grip. Her knees were drawn against her chest in the fetal position. A fierce ache shocked her shoulders numb. After a moment of utter confusion a rumbling sound reached her ears, a steady mechanical growl. *Right*, she thought with a sinking gut. *Still in the truck.* Three weeks she'd spent chained to a cot while a surgeon fixed her minced hand with the grace of a butcher, relieving her of all feeling and dexterity, only to be dragged and chained into a truck for another day. At least as far as she could tell it had only been a day.

"I shouldn't be in here!"

A stentorian voice shook the walls around her. She blinked, unblurring her vision.

"I was promised exemption from my crimes!" the voice bellowed. "Blackwell guaranteed it once the Bandit Bitch was apprehended!"

Another stern voice grumbled back, "Blackwell is dead. His successor, Cavarly, has ordered anyone involved with the rebellion to be imprisoned. Be lucky it wasn't death on the spot."

"It might as well be!"

There was a loud crashing noise, and the floor beneath violently lurched and bucked her up into the ceiling. Pain permeated the mental fog, wrenching her mind from the haze. When she slammed back into her seat, sight returned with a nauseating swirl of light.

Where's my team?

Torn bandages wrapped around her hand, crusted with dried blood and flaky pus. Her wrists were shackled so tightly that her flesh bruised purple and swelled like melons over the handcuffs. The metal chains extended from the ceiling, looped through locked bars and left a pitiful inch of slack for maneuvering. A quick glance around her confinement revealed steel wall-like panels—with only three slits, each the width of her face and barred like a gate. Beside her was a window, similarly barred, and thick enough to partially obscure view. Crooked beams of light dappled her with a sunny glow, a stark contrast to her tattered clothes that were stained dark from her blood and the filth of the sewer. She fought the jarring motion of the truck to crane her stiff neck and peer through the slit in the side panel.

"Let me out!" the voice roared again. Dark hair rippled around the glare of sunlight, weaved into knotted patterns down a burly chest. Harn.

What about Nadie? Snyder?

"Either shut up, or we put a bullet where your mouth is," another voice piped in from ahead of her, bitter and raspy. She shifted and pushed against the wall, and arched her neck to peer through the front slit. The dark shade of military armor, and tanned hands spinning along with a steering wheel. She was hurled against the barred window as the truck took a sharp left. "I don't need you whining the whole damn drive."

"This is such bullshit!"

Another twisting pain in her head spotted her sight. She was flung forward and slammed against the enclosure. She couldn't maneuver in her seat without knocking her knees into the walls, and contorting her body only allowed a sliver of sight. Wearied from what little movement she managed, her muscles slacked and eyelids fluttered. A stabbing agony in her hand—or where her fingers used to be—radiated up her arm and forced a pathetic groan from her.

"H-hello," she croaked, voice gritty and broken. Her tongue peeled from the roof of her mouth. "Please..."

"Shut up back there."

"Please," she muttered weakly. "I need to pee."

A scoff in response. "Piss yourself for all I care."

Her head rocked from the jarring turns of the truck, and she only glimpsed the pair of soft brown eyes through the slit in the front panel.

"Cap," the voice whispered, barely audible under the roar of the truck's engine. "It's Cavarly's niece, the girl he told us to take care of."

The gruff voice shot back, "She's going where the rest of 'em are going. Don't necessarily matter how they get there."

"He was mighty particular about treating her fairly..."

The truck abruptly swerved right and lurched to a halt. As she was thrown against the front panel, elbows painfully clacking against metal, she heard the driver bark back, "If you want to deal with some hormonal bitch, be my guest! She stays in chains and keep your goddamn rifle drawn on her *always!* Clear?"

"Clear, sir."

It was another moment before the door to her confinement unlatched with a heavy crashing sound and swung open to a gust of summer wind and the nostalgic scent of pine. It was soothing to her lungs. At first, she had to squint against the glare of sunlight over the mountains. She caught sight of jagged silhouettes in the bright sky, monstrous, looming shadows in the distance. Around her proximity was only a deep, sprawling sea of green bristly pine. The dense coniferous forest echoed the home from her past, but the aroma that danced with the wind caused a terrible ache in her chest, as if her heart were about to burst free from her ribcage. *Melina...Aurous...*

I need you.

The soldier stepped into sight, with his rifle barrel leveled with her chest. He was young, perhaps near her age, skinny even when draped in ballistic armor, with limbs as thick as a sapling's branches. His face was clean shaven, unscarred by any fight or tousle through the dirt. She studied his eyes—bright brown and nervously wide—as he released the lock to the bar and yanked her handcuffed wrists from the ceiling. Unable to brace against the sudden weight, the chains crashed down against her lap. Her wounded hand pulsed with sickening warmth. The pain almost made her retch all over his boots.

"No funny business," the soldier boy said, lips pressed tight as she shuddered and staggered out of her seat. "Take your piss and then we're back on the road."

She gave a slight nod, neck still painfully stiff. Her legs were like tangled rubber bands as she braced against the open door. Blood *thumped* through her legs, then her toes were lost to a creeping numbness. It spread through her calf muscles until she wobbled as she stood, head swirling with nausea.

"You have thirty seconds," he whispered to her, rifle still drawn on her chest.

"There's nowhere to go," she countered, but he shook his head.

"Right where you're standing is fine."

She gave him a sullen glare. With great difficulty, she managed to peel her stiff, musty jeans from scarred thighs. She crouched—more so leaned awkwardly into the door—and relieved the pressure in her side. When she finished, he jabbed her chest with the rifle barrel and ordered her back into the truck, which she had no choice but to obey. Her shackled wrists were locked through the bar and the door latched shut. The bitter chill of her confinement and sour scent of her own blood cleaved through the last of the sun's warmth. She shuddered.

"Hey, you," someone called through the slit behind her, a light, but hoarse voice. "They let you out to piss? *Piss?*"

When she didn't answer, the voice snarled, "You're a stupid bitch—you could have died with dignity, trying to escape! But you cower at their feet like a loyal mutt!"

"Why are you still here then?" she asked cruelly. "Can't eat your own words?"

"We don't have the luxury of being treated as royalty—unlike you, *Bandit Bitch.*"

Celeste fell silent, eyes sagged shut. Nausea roiled in her belly until she felt that each rocking motion of the truck would make her retch her guts over her lap. It wasn't long before her mind reeled back into the comforting embrace of darkness.

Intractable pain burned through her fingers—or at least the two that were missing. Her phantom fingers throbbed with every beat of her heart as if they were only severed in flesh and not from her nerves. There was no response to movement, only an endless burning sensation, a vicious bite that thundered down to her bones. It woke her in intervals, forcing her to cry out for mercy like the voices of the dead howling endlessly through her mind. Often a brilliance of red would flash across her thoughts, and her lips would tingle with the warmth of their last kiss. But she always woke to a lingering chill and wept until the lurching movement of the truck lulled her back into a hellish sleep.

When she opened her eyes again, her tongue felt like sandpaper scraping across the roof of her mouth.

"W-water," she whispered hoarsely. "P-please. Water."

"A sip. Lick up what you can."

Water squirted through the panel and trickled down the metal panel in thin silver rivulets. She dove forward, pressed her cheek against the cold metal, and lapped up the meager dribbles with her tongue. Their laughter burned her face bright red, but she didn't stop. Tears would have to wait.

Hunched forward, she placed her head in the crook of her arched arms and squeezed her eyes shut. The truck heaved like a boat crashing against waves, and through the barred window she caught only fleeting glances of the ascending landscape. The green expanse of pine thinned to clusters among the vibrant burn of autumn. Leaves shimmered with bright colours and swirled like fireflies in the wind. Rolling, wooded hills—just like the forest near father's old cabin. She had to wonder how far she was from the last place she could truly call home.

"Please, I need to pee."

A scoff was her only response. Their muffled voices drifted through the panel, but their words were smothered by the engine's roar. Mocking her, undoubtedly.

"It hurts," she pleaded pitifully, then buried her face in her arms. "Please."

The response she was hoping for. "Aw hell, pull over."

"Are you kidding me?" the driver spat angrily. "Again?"

"Last time until the prison," the boy reasoned, "then we're done with 'em."

"Fine." She was slammed against the panel as the truck screeched to a sudden halt. "Make it quick."

Moments dragged by. She fought for control of her erratic

breathing, but her heart thundered loudly in her chest. The door swung open to another glare of sunlight. She heard her chains rattle as the lock slipped off from the link. She was ready for the shift in weight and cradled her bound hands. She slipped down from the seat and wiggled her jeans past her waist. The boy averted his gaze—

—and that's when she hurled herself at him, chains taut and rigid in her partial grasp. Metal thrashed his face into a burst of red mist—he fell back with a gurgling grunt. He stirred, rifle fumbling in his grip—*crunch*—she drove the heel of her foot into his face. Blood warmed her toes as she stumbled over him, legs bowing like windblown trees. She made a mad dash for the hills.

Then her world spun uncontrollably.

Her knees buckled and momentum flung her forward. A vicious pain tore through her wounded hand when she used her bound limbs to break her fall. Mud caked her tongue when she screamed.

Crack!

Her face bashed against dirt, head fogged and oddly throbbing. Warmth trickled down her neck, and for only a moment she abandoned the horror of the world. *Melina.*

"...bitch, I should put a bullet in your skull for that."

The strangled tone slowly crept through her mental fog, but her sight remained blurred and crooked.

"Don' kill 'er, Theo," said another voice, with a softer, yet strangely pitched tone. "We need 'er alibe."

Her next moments were a nauseating vertigo as she was plucked from the dirt like a weakly writhing worm caught in a bird's beak. Distorted colors played across her sight. Her belly rumbled with sickness. The only thing she remained acutely aware of was the pulsing pain in her hand.

"Shit, Jay, look what she did to your nose!" the rough voice shouted in her ears. "You're going to let some ragged-out bitch do that to you? Break hers!"

A grueling moment of silence. Then the boy replied with his nose pinched between his fingers, "Already ith."

"Break her goddamn teeth then."

"I god' a bedder idea."

Blood smeared a trail of red through the dirt with her shackled arms dragging beneath her. She gritted her teeth against the pain, snarling as her wolf would have done. Let them see her fangs. She growled at them, "You might as well kill me."

He wrenched his grip in her hair like he was attempting to peel back her scalp. The burning pain made her scream. Rocks and dirt carved her dragging limbs with bloody welts and scrapes. Filthy bandages tattered around her shackled hands. The door swung open with a sharp squeal. Then the clatter of chains. She blinked and focused on the others peering back at her through the slits in the panels. They were separated into kennels like stray dogs. They even whined, whimpered, and retreated at their approach. The boy-soldier reached for the first panel, fingers crawling through his ring of keys. When the panel opened, a gaunt, filthy woman with brown matted hair the color of waste flung herself back from the sunlight as if it burned her skin. The boy-soldier glanced back at Celeste with his nose pinched between his fingers. Blood still streamed through his knuckles. His gaze stayed on her, and his other hand slowly drifted toward his holster. The pistol was drawn with a quick, snapping motion and positioned against the prisoner's head.

"Nuddin'," he sputtered with a small shake of his head, then forced the panel shut. There were four more panels alongside the first, and from what she could vaguely see, at least four more opposite of her own narrow kennel. He awkwardly fumbled through his keys to the next lock. The panel unlatched with another rusty squeal. The boy-soldier glared at her past his bloodied fingers.

Jaw clenched tight, lips pursed, she stared into the sky-bright eyes of Snyder. Her blonde hair was like a glimmer of sunlight in the shadows of her confinement, but her skin was smeared with filth, eyes bloodshot and bruised. Celeste dared not glance aside, attempting to remain apathetic—but the boy noticed the slight narrowing of her eyes, the spark of recognition between them, if only for a moment. It was enough.

He raised the pistol to Snyder's head, scoffed—sputtered, mostly—at the blonde's rebellious sneer.

"You'll learn," he muttered, blood drooling over his lips. His finger slipped through the trigger-guard.

"No!" Celeste blurted out, then cursed quietly. "Please, don't kill her. I'll obey, I swear."

"Just shoot the ugly bitch," Theo snarled, tightening his grip around Celeste's throat.

Her heart thrashed inside her chest until the boy-soldier lowered the pistol and heaved the panel shut. "We need 'em."

Theo sighed with impatience. "Yeah, you're right. The more we bring, the more we're paid. Heard they're getting light on test subjects anyway. Their fault, the way they sort 'em out. Two out of every three dead. I'm sure Hellpit will put some sense into these hens."

They chattered like gossiping girls as Theo hauled her alongside the armored truck and shoved her back into the cramped confinement. Her nose stung with the stench that permeated the chill of the vehicle. There would be no escaping now—though she was ambivalent whether that had been her true intention. Only death knew the path to Melina now, only death could take her home again.

"Princess," she heard a voice rasp from behind her. The gaunt woman. "You couldn't do it, huh? You couldn't escape?"

Tears blurred her sight; her chest swelled with poignant regret. "No, I couldn't," she admitted slowly.

"You deserve to die then!" the woman shrieked between intermittent *thumps* against the panel. "Die! Die! Die!"

Her shrill echoed like the ravenous wails of infected as Celeste drifted from one nightmare only to wake in another.

Hours later Celeste shuddered awake, feverish, skin needled by the damp chill of her confinement. She stirred—and cried out in a moment of shocking pain. The ache in her propped arms had long numbed, but her wounded hand had wedged into the chains. She felt the bandages warm with a fresh spurt of bloody pus. Tears misted her eyes again.

Gather your wits, Celeste. She slowly shook her head, blinded by matted strands of her hair. The dark carmine flare had faded to a soot-black from the filth of the sewer and the blood she had spilled. *What would Father think?*

The truck shifted sharply like the ground had been pulled out from beneath the wheels. She was hurled backwards in her seat, shoulders nearly ripping out from their sockets. Apprehension fluttered in her chest as she glimpsed the valley below.

The forest had thinned to sparse clusters of evergreens that dared root in the rocky soil, but even the heartiest of them couldn't cling to the precipitous bluffs the truck ascended at a slow but steady crawl. No longer were the mountains only a comforting sight in the distance; she was plunged under the chilling shadow of their sheer cragged cliffs. Snow-capped spires pierced the sky and faded into the pearly mists of clouds. She was farther from home than she had ever been in her life.

Even with her eyes forced shut, rest was elusive with the throb in her hand. Her skin felt clammy and cold despite a thin sheet of sweat along her brow. Even her toes felt crushed and cramped in the corners of the panels. Time became an intractable blur of pain and lamentation, a perpetual torment. She lost track of how many hours passed since the sun had disappeared beyond the cragged peaks, darkening the mountain walls to sharp silhouettes against the sky. She began to wonder if she would ever have the chance to feel its warmth again.

Her eyes fluttered open when the vehicle screeched to a halt and she was thrown into the front panel. Through the barred window she saw the cliff walls that appeared to close in around them, extending endlessly above her line of sight.

Where am I?

The vehicle shifted and the door abruptly swung open. The glacial mountain wind gripped her with a chill she hadn't felt since the vicious storms of her childhood. It was like blades stabbing her lungs with every short, rapid breath she took. The boy glared at her down the sight of his rifle. His eye was bloodshot, swollen and spotted with a bruise that streaked down the bridge of his now-crooked nose. Dried blood flaked from his lips when he spoke.

"Don't you dare move."

Her brazen attempt at escape had far from intimidated him. Neither was he phased by her cold glare. His brow furled in a flash of anger. The rifle raised to her head. Still, she glowered at him as her father would have.

"If you weren't so damn important to the new general, I would have taken the time to break every one of your bones," the boy-soldier hissed. "But they need all the specimens they can get." His face scrunched in disgust when his eyes slowly wandered over the swirling, jagged scars along her neck and cheek. "But I'm assuming they already had you."

"I should have killed you," she whispered with regret. "Slowly."

"Twisted whore!"

"Get the shackles around her feet and unlock her already," Theo ordered, voice rising over the clatter of chains. "Unless you're afraid she might bite again."

She pressed herself flat against the panel at the boy's advancement. A feeble attempt. Her body shuddered with weakness, an ache that spread from her belly through to her muscles. He reached for her, rifle poised, and snatched at her ankle. He wrenched her leg from under her, and with a helpless scream, she was splayed across the doorway of the vehicle. Her wrists twisted and welted against the handcuffs. She felt the same cold sting of metal around her ankles, tightening until her feet swelled and throbbed like a setting bruise. She cried out, but with her legs anchored by chains, she could barely maneuver under him. He climbed over her and stabbed the barrel into her solar plexus. A chilling fear squeezed her lungs of air.

"You try anything, and I'll break your front teeth," he promised cruelly, then took a single step back, rifle continually trained on her center mass. "Prisoner, slowly move away from the vehicle."

It took a considerable amount of effort to heave herself from the truck with her limbs tightly bound with shackles and chains. She could stand, but found it difficult to maneuver with little slack in the chains around her ankles. She could only separate her feet a shoulder-length apart, which halved her stride and restricted her to a shambling gait. She halted at his command and cast her eyes upwards to the looming cliffs, unable to distinguish the summit from the ever-darkening sky. Even the air seemed thin and crisp, leaving her slightly breathless as she marveled at the surrounding peaks of grey rock.

"Commander?"

Brown eyes shimmered through the misty dark. Nadie. Her face was gashed and crudely stitched back together, her black hair matted and tangled around her shoulders, a set jaw that seemed slightly shifted and bruised black.

"I knew you were still alive," Nadie whispered, then flinched as the boy-soldier shoved his rifle at her.

"No talking!" he barked then rounded the rifle to Celeste. "Remember what happened last time."

She stiffened at the chill of his threat and the frosty winds of the mountain, then grudgingly turned away from Nadie. She heard Theo's gruff voice carry from beyond the vehicle, and the *clink* of metal scraping against the cracked and crumbling pavement. She dared a small glance over her shoulder.

The first prisoner to shuffle forward had the same matted brown hair as the gaunt woman, her squirrel-like eyes flitting between them like she was a mouse under the glare of a starving cat. She was as skeletal and decrepit as a rotting corpse. Behind her a large figure loomed, with long, weaved strands of hair and a dark scowl on his bearded face. Harn shambled forward more slowly than the others and had chains extending from his wrists to his waist that forced his arms flat against his side. He was only missing the bolts in his neck to complete the image of Frankenstein's monster. Behind him there was another flash of gold and piercing blue. Snyder. Another form lurked behind her, sniveling and trembling. Pale, gaunt, Clark seemed as brittle as a branch in a windstorm, trembling against the howling storm. The last prisoner who ambled into view was Twist, as cruelly chained as Harn to restrict even the most basic movements of his thick, tree-trunk arms. Prodded along at gunpoint by Theo, he wore a vacant expression, a simple smile with his tongue pushed between pursed lips. His gaze trailed from the cliff walls with a childlike wonderment, awed by its majestic climb into the dark sky. When his simple stare wandered to the others, and eventually her, his face cheek wrinkled with a sudden grin.

"Commander!" he shouted with sheer glee, beaming as he caught sight of her. "Mission now?"

"Fall back in line, prisoner!" demanded Theo, rifle raised to Twist's head. "I will shoot!"

Twist neither understood the intent nor cared. His brow furled over his beady eyes, and he scowled at the soldier's threatening gesture.

"Puny man," Twist said dully. He stomped a heavy foot into the pavement.

"Twist, stop!" Celeste called out, then recoiled as the rifle swept across the line of prisoners and settled on her. She spoke slowly. "Twist, the mission is to stay quiet and follow the leader. Can you do that, big guy?"

His tongue rolled across his lips. Finally, he replied with a simple "Okay," and abruptly abandoned his frustration with Theo.

"Don't think you're in charge anymore," the boy hissed to her, glaring at her with his blood-streaked eye. "You're nothing here."

"Alright!" Theo barked and trained his rifle on them. "Time to get moving! You will stay in a single file and move until we tell you to stop. If you try to escape, you will be shot. Hell, if you so much as *talk*, you will be shot."

"Follow me," the boy-soldier ordered, voice brittle against the howling winds. He jerked his rifle at Celeste. "Move, Bandit Bitch."

She crossed the windswept road at a crawling pace, arms curled against her chest to trap even a sliver of warmth. There was a small barricade of unfenced gates and debris that impeded any vehicle advancement. Deliberate, she figured, glimpsing a void in the road ahead like a vast chasm in the mountain. There was only a small platform extending from the edge, a narrow bridge that spanned at least a quarter mile into the setting darkness. Then she saw it: a colossal structure carved into the skyline like a deep, impenetrable shadow, a tower jutting far above the snow-capped spires of the mountaintop. It was as immense as the sleek skyscraper of glass in the city, but a stark grey, windowless, a patchwork of concrete and metal. The curving tower extended deep into the chasm like a castle surrounded by a vast moat.

"What the hell is this place?" the gaunt woman gasped, sobering at the sight of what looked like a prison tower. "Where are we?"

"Shut up," the soldier muttered. "Keep moving."

Celeste shuffled on. Her feet painfully peeled from the metallic platform with each step, scabs rubbed raw and bleeding. The silver bridge flexed and shifted beneath her weight, and her heart fluttered in her chest whenever it swayed her off balance. When her elbows grazed against the railing, the boy soldier snapped forward and wrenched his grip around her shoulder. He yanked her away from the edge like a wayward child, but she had caught glimpses of the chasm, the precipitous cliffs of jagged rock that walled in the bridge and tower. Impassable, to say the least—any attempt to scale the cliff would result in impalement on the rocks below.

"Anyone jumps and they'll flatten across the rocks like roadkill," he said with a tone that almost dared them to. Then he lowered his voice so only Celeste would hear his cruel taunt. "Except for you, Bandit Bitch. Orders are to deliver you alive."

He shoved her along and she stumbled at an awkwardly slow pace, feet shocked numb from the biting cold metal. Every few steps the boy soldier chastised their tedious pace, and stabbed the rifle into her spine. But her movements were sluggish as if her bones were made of lead. Her lungs shuddered from the frosty air. The chill seeped through to every molecule in her body.

The tower spiraled into the sky and speared the bleak night atmosphere. There was a faint trickle of light near the base of the tower just above the end of the bridge. The fluorescent glare illuminated the bright blood-red gates, the only discernable entrance to the windowless structure. An inked silhouette of a palisade fenced in the tower's lower base, with barbed wire and razors protruding over the interior, as if to keep the occupants *within.* She had never heard of such a structure existing within the military's control—and from the mystified gasps of everyone else, it appeared to be a well-guarded secret. She felt another paralyzing chill that had little to do with the bitter winds.

"This is Division Charlie," the boy soldier said between the intermittent *hiss* of static. "Delivering a fresh batch."

"*Stand by for authorization.*"

Following a sharp mechanical groan, a burst of light flooded the bridge. The barrel jerked into her spine, and she trudged forward, her line of sight a milky, opaque haze. The red gate parted with a sound as if the gates of hell itself welcomed her.

A warm gust of wind brought the tangy scent of pine to her nose, but it was peculiar, burning the back of her throat.

Disinfectant.

The sudden warmth needled her skin. The flesh along the bottoms of her feet were tender and torn raw, blood squishing between her tingling toes.

Sight slowly returned to a glaring white. The walls were fluorescently bright, nauseatingly so, and barely the width of a small corridor. The others pressed against her as the guards urged them into the small room, crammed like corpses in a mass grave.

"You know, I find it amusing," Theo said over the *thudding* of his boots down the bridge. "Nobody ever chooses to jump."

"They might end up jumping, anyways," the boy soldier replied with a snicker.

"Alright, Division Charlie clear. Close the gate and begin the process."

She heard the *hiss* of shifting gears and pistons like an engine, and then the heavy grind of metal as the gate heaved shut behind them. Then there was a gulfing silence, broken only by the small but rapid breaths they heaved in trepidation. After a moment, a slit appeared in the white wall mere inches above their heads, slowly widening like the gash across Blackwell's throat when she slid the blade into his soft, saggy flesh...

The pungent scent of pine burned her nostrils.

"Cover your eyes!" she called out, weakly raising her bound arms over her face. "And your mouth!"

Harn growled deeply. "I don't take orders from yo—"

A delicate mist drizzled from the opening above them, then intensified into a flood of stinging rain. It frosted her skin, but scorched her open wounds. An involuntary scream tore out from her mouth, and she gagged from the bitter mist. It beaded across her face, gathered around her eyes as caustic tears. She shivered as the icy spray soaked through her tattered clothes.

Her feet slipped through the film along the padded floor, searing her raw flesh. She spat the bitter substance from her lips. Harn expelled the disinfectant from his lungs in a hoarse cough, sputtering incoherently. Slowly, her eyes opened to a stinging blur. A featureless shadow stood in the haze of white, an hourglass figure inches away from where they were deloused.

"Now that you are clean of all that outside filth," the shadow drawled in a squeaky voice, "We can begin the process. Follow me."

The shadow stirred and dimmed from her line of sight. Celeste was hesitant, and her lungs burned from a reluctance to breathe. She had to find a way out.

"Please," the voice called back, impatiently. "Follow me through the doorway, it's not very difficult."

Celeste took a step out of the room and her vision slowly adjusted. The corridor extended and split into several adjacent directions, each hall a bright and nauseating white, unfurnished and featureless. Memories raced through her mind in quick flashes; painful incisions probing her spine; blood warming the back of her neck; vials with tubes snaking into her veins; her bare feet pounding against the cold tile floor in a desperate attempt to escape the hospital.

Another step and the tile pricked her feet with sharp chills. She blinked at the figure in front of her. A woman of small stature, rounded at the lower waist, with a face painted as pale as the drab walls around them. Her prismatically shaded hair was trimmed jaw-length and tightly tucked behind her ears, with bangs that looped into a ringlet over her forehead. Her ruby-red lips pursed with impatience. Shadows seemed to form around her, flowing through the bright hallway like night cutting through the last light of day. Celeste blinked away her dotted-black vision.

"Let me see," the woman started slowly. Her eyes narrowed at their tentative approach and swept past Celeste. "Seven subjects— two less than the order promised, but we shall make do, I suppose."

There was another woman behind them, head lowered to avoid their gazes. She was taller in height, though her hair was similarly cropped and shaded, face paled with powdered makeup. A spatter of red blemished the white of her gown near the collar, like blood, below a pinpoint of white flesh in her neck...

Annie. She recalled the warmth of the nurse's blood when Celeste drove a pen into her soft, supple neck. *Where am I?*

"Take the two big ones to Block A—oh, look at that one cowering—put him in with one of the big boys." The nurse pursed her blood-gleamed lips. "Take the exotic one as well."

Where was I before?

"The rest are for Block D. Take the Bandit Bitch."

Harn gritted his teeth at the plump nurse. "I want to know what the *hell* this place is."

The lady pursed her lip to a pout, hands propped against her protruding hips. "Odd choice of word. This is segregation. You will be escorted to your cells shortly."

"No," he spat. "What is this place?"

"Your new home," she replied. "Welcome to Hellpit."

The thought was as chilling as the tile floor.

"Please," said Annie, as quiet as a whisper. She gestured toward Harn, Twist, Clark and—Nadie. The nurse kept her gaze lowered to the tile. "If you will follow me to your cells."

Twist lumbered forward like a bear, chains clattering around his thick limbs. Nadie peeled her despondent gaze from the others, and Celeste could only flinch at the advancement of two soldiers, their long rifles trained on their hearts. She watched helplessly as her former team fragmented and wandered farther down the curving hall. The nurse named Annie cast a single glance over her shoulder. Celeste felt her blood boil.

I should have killed you when I had the chance.

That anger dissolved as the nurse commanded them forward, and she was forced under the glare of countless rifles. It was still difficult to maneuver in handcuffs and shackles. Instead of a simple stride, she had to edge forward to prevent the metal links from looping around her toes.

The corridor bowed along at a constant curve, which struck her as odd. The hall seemed to circle the interior of the tower, with windowless doors tightly sealed and no discernable handles or locks, only small keypads wired into the adjacent wall. A lock she could never pick.

Not like I have my pins strapped between my toes.

The other doors were a sleek reflective steel, topped with rows of crystalline numbers that blinked intermittently like a slow, steady countdown. There was a perplexing amount of numbers adjoined by lettered combinations she couldn't quite decipher, as if the tower had a myriad of floors spanning every conceivable direction. She had to wonder, with a slight chill along her spine, just how far the tower extended down into the mountain. Perched in the crevice between the wall and ceiling were a trio of small black cameras, *whirring* mechanically as the lenses shifted into focus on the her.

"You son of a bitch!" she yelled at the cameras, stunning the nurse to slow her stride. Rifles raised to greet her vicious spat. She didn't care. "I know you can see me! Stop being a coward and confront me yourself, Mengele!"

"Such barbaric behavior," the nurse scolded between delicate gasps. "An utter lack of etiquette."

"Stand down, prisoner!" one of the soldiers commanded. "Or you will be taken out!"

"Coward!" she screamed, voice cracking. "I know you see me!"

The nurse made a small noise of discomfort. "Please, this is the end of the line. There is no road to redemption from here."

"Mengele, I swear to whatever god you believe in, I will *kill* you!"

"Stand down!" The soldier stomped forward.

"God has long ago abandoned his creations."

The voice was smooth, magniloquent, the haunting sound she heard nearly every night in the clutch of nightmares. The words dripped from his tongue and seeped into her thoughts like an agonizing venom. She turned to lay eyes on the monster from her past and thought she would heave with sickness.

He was near the entrance to the last elevator shaft, standing directly behind them in a button-up coat he was slowly fastening over grime-spattered garments. He smoothed his blonde hair flat against his scalp. His complexion was as pale as ever, skin scarred with intricate patterns like a spider's weaved web. It was as though his flesh had been carved from the bone, and then crudely patched together like an old ripped shirt. His eyes, a dead icy blue, swept over her slowly, as if admiring every fine detail of her body. His features were sharp, almost skeletal, yet as his confident stride brought him within inches of her face, he became a terrifying presence, a monster with the charm of death itself. He leaned forward, grinning like a child tantalized with the prospect of a new toy. A rancid odor cleaved through the lingering disinfectant, and she gagged. It was as though his skin had rotted and crisped in the sun, reeking of death and bodily excretions—

"My, my," he said. "You lack the eloquence of your mother, and the wit of your father."

Her voice trembled. "My father killed you."

"Yet here I am alive and well, as are you." When he brought his face closer to hers, a thick tarry scent lingered on his breath. "Though it seems I'm not the only one who's gained scars."

"No thanks to you!" she shot back. "You're creating weapons for war, not searching for a cure! You're tampering with something that should be destroyed!"

His voice was a threatening growl. "We are curing this world of its sickness, of its weakness—you will see soon enough."

Her face scrunched in disgust. "I'm not your experiment. I am *not* like your infected hounds."

"Like them?" His predatory smile was unnerving. "You are far more significant. And when you're alone and willing to accept your fate—you'll call for me. I'm the only one with a cure to your weakness, the only one who can give you what you truly need—but you have to survive first."

It was her turn to growl at him like a cornered wolf. "I will kill you, Mengele, just like I killed Blackwell."

"Save the ferocity for Hellpit," he replied coldly. "Cavarly has no reign here, even as acting general. This is *my* world." *You'll call for me soon,* his icy eyes promised with a sneer. When he turned to the nurse, a smile curved up his scarred cheek, sagging the skin around his eye like a rubbery mask. "Make sure she can hear her friends plead for their deaths."

He winked at her, turned without a second glance, and she screamed furiously at his retreat. The soldiers remained an overwhelming presence, rifles stabbing at her to move. Her arms were painfully wrenched forward, pinned under their boots. Her severed hand burned with white-hot thundering pain. The metal clasped around her wrists were ripped loose, and her hands fell limp, burning with relief. The chains around her feet were pulled out from beneath her, and she was finally free from that cold, iron grip. But there was little time for comfort. Hauled from the floor, she furiously kicked, bit, screamed, cursing Mengele and his soldiers at the top of her lungs, until her throat shredded raw. The others around her were given the same treatment, thrown to the floor with their shackles forcefully removed. The nurse stood by a row of opened doors, judging her prisoners with silent cruelty. At her nodded command, Celeste and Snyder were dragged into one of the cells.

"Three inmates, one night," the nurse cooed from corridor. "The better genetics will prevail."

The doors closed behind them with a grinding squeal and latched shut.

Her sight blurred in the darkness until she saw only faint shapes and shadows. The walls were thick steel, like the door, with a ceiling so low she could graze the top with her fingertips. The floor was a blood-spattered grey, rough as gravel, and extended only a few meters before abruptly ending in an empty void. As far as she could see, there was no fourth wall—only deep, perpetual black, and the hideous whispers that rose above even her own rapid and uneven breaths.

Hellpit.

"Snyder?" she whispered hesitantly.

Shadows stirred against the void, and she heard another deep guttural sound.

"Commander!" The voice came from behind her, a small shadow pressed into the crevice of two adjoining walls.

"Shit," Celeste cursed quietly, eyes darting toward the other shadow. "Look," she began tentatively, shrinking against the steel door. She cradled her wounded hand against her belly. "We can all figure a way out of here, but only if we work together—do you understand?"

There was another disgusting guttural noise, and a sharp *click* of a tongue. Then a screeching laughter rang from the gaunt woman's throat.

"Die, die, die," the raspy voice chanted, cackling madly. "Die, die, die!"

The gaunt woman lunged at her.

Twelve
Heart of Glass

IT WAS the instinct of prey, a fearsome chill through her heart, that made Celeste fall to the concrete with her arms curled over her face in pathetic defense. The gaunt woman crashed into her, walloping her with long, spindly limbs. Celeste pushed off the wall with her feet and spasmodically lurched from the flurry of fists, peeling from the tarry floor. The uncontrolled slide brought her terrifyingly close to the edge, and with an unwanted glance into the perceived emptiness, she caught a horrendous sight: across the vast gulf of darkness, there was an impossibly large wall of smooth, sculpted stone that curved out toward their room. Her ears rang with the hellish sounds of teeth gnashing flesh and bone.

What the—

The gaunt woman screamed, twisted and hunched forward on bowed limbs like a predator stalking prey, panting heavily from the thrill of the hunt. It was then Celeste realized the strange guttural noises echoed from far below in the darkness—not from the mad prisoner. The woman shrieked and jumped for Celeste—

A thrown punch snapped the woman's jaw shut, cracking her carious teeth. She fell back with a gurgling grunt. When the woman looked up, blood streaked down her chin, eyes wild and bright with the rabid look of a beast. A second punch *crunched* in the woman's nose, spattering Snyder's wispy blonde hair bright red. The woman launched at Snyder with a spasm-like movement, clawing madly for her face.

Celeste gritted her teeth with a snarl; the wolf inside her howled fiercely.

She clambered to her feet, then hurled herself at the gaunt woman. Her teeth sank into the soft, patchy flesh near the back of her neck, and she wrenched her jaws until skin and muscle tissue ripped like fabric, and a pulpy, sour warmth flooded her mouth.

An inhuman screech rang through the hollow construct, and the woman spun Celeste into the wall with a surprising burst of strength. Celeste slammed hard, air crushed from her lungs. Her grip around the woman faltered.

Celeste heaved. Bright pinpoints spotted her vision. She was lost in a mental fog. Pain was only a tingling sensation to her mind, a distant worry she need not bother with—her vision tunneled.

She gasped wildly, sucking in quick breaths of stuffy air—then she was thrown from her feet, sprawled across the slime. Blood trickled down her jawline. Another shriek rang from the gaunt woman. Celeste howled her own fury—then swept the woman's legs out from under her. She crashed against the floor near Celeste and clawed toward her, snarling and gnashing her broken teeth with a grating *clatter*. Celeste felt her own blood boil with rage; she fumbled her good hand around the woman's neck, wrenched her fingers around her throat, then applied enough pressure to nearly crush the delicate trachea. The woman writhed, bent her neck, then plunged her jagged shards of teeth through the bandages around Celeste's hand.

It was an unbearable amount of pain—the woman's teeth were grinding against the broken bones in her stubby fingers. Celeste screamed in both fury and agony, an intense ragged sound that seemed more of a savage creature than a mere girl. She brought her other fist down like a hammer, and bludgeoned until a sharp pain thundered through her bones. The woman's grip around the wound slackened, and her eyes dulled to a glazy white.

The woman shrieked. Her long, jagged nails raked Celeste's thigh, snaring her flesh like hooks. Dragged downward, her bare feet slipped through the layer of slime, and it was like the floor lurched beneath her. Her shoulder cushioned the fall against the concrete. Although dazed, she summoned enough strength to retreat from the woman's wild lashing—until her elbows grazed the rounded edge of the floor.

The woman leaped over Celeste's kicking legs, hands closing around her throat—then clawed desperately at her tattering clothes. Snyder had slammed into her—hard. The woman's feet entangled with Celeste, but her gained momentum sent her plummeting over the edge with a shrill, gurgling screech that sounded like water violently boiling from a pot. The bloodcurdling sound rang off the curving walls of the hollow tower, then—*SPLAT!*

The darkness woke.

It began as a whisper, a distant babbling brook, which then erupted into a howling tempest thundering from otherworldly throats. The ghoulish cacophony intensified, an abhorrence rising from the bowels of hell. With her gaze swimming through a sea of black, she caught a shimmer of movement—shadows undulated through the darkness. Rotted flesh and pulverized bone. The malignance roused at the offering of fresh meat, *gnashing* teeth and howling for blood. Infected corpses—more than she could reliably count, stirring within the depths of the hollow tower.

A deep bellow snared her attention and carried her gaze across the dark expanse. It seemed human, an outburst of agony, pain. The curving wall extended beyond her sight, a smear of hazy grey across her entire field of vision. Shadows slotted the wall directly across from their room, extending like a ring around the interior of the tower—ending at either side of their own containment. The other cells, from all the other blocks.

But how many?

A glance skyward revealed a long, narrowing tunnel that ended in a patch of black, dotted with scintillating pinpoints and a swirling, creamy glow.

Stars?

"Commander?"

The voice seemed smothered, distant, lost in the raucous below.

"Are you okay?"

Celeste closed her stinging eyes. She crawled from the edge, her chest fluttering with warmth at the sight of the blonde's icy stare and thin lips crooked with worry. The apathy drained from Snyder's expression, and she flung her arms around Celeste for an uncharacteristic embrace. A strange, strangled sound escaped her. She was shaking, chilled to her bones, clothes soaked with blood that wasn't hers. For a moment, she sobbed into Celeste's shoulder, then quickly cleared her throat.

Tears stung Celeste's eyes. Her own heart drummed wildly, a torrent of fear and bitter triumph, the intoxicating rush of survival under the reaper's scythe. She trembled, also, unable to muster any comforting words for consolidation, no vindication—

—warmth pressed firmly against her lips, gritty, yet oddly sweetened. She kissed Snyder back. It sparked a delicate tingle along her skin, and she gasped from utter ecstasy, swept into the dizzying throe of emotion.

Melina.

It was an ache so terrible she thought it would cleave her heart in two. She pulled away from Snyder, until a chill crawled between them. Snyder frowned, then her expression steeled—she leaned back, stern gaze drawn to the gutted tower in a grisly assessment of their new abode.

"So," she whispered, "this is the infamous Hole."

Celeste grimaced against the resurgence of pain in her hand, though scoffed quickly to mask her agonized cry. "You knew about this place?"

"Rumors, really," she said with a shrug. She slumped against the wall, regarding the steel walls of their confine. It was scarcely larger than their pitiful compartments within the transport truck.

"Like the Disfigured?"

"I gave it about as much thought as them—and a lot of good that did us."

Celeste grinned, still panting wildly, like a wolf relishing the thrill of a successful hunt.

Her heart twisted up into her throat. *Aurous.*

"I think we're screwed, Commander."

"We were screwed back in the sewers," Celeste admitted. "That's when I stopped being your commander."

"I like to think of myself as an underdog." A sneer narrowed Snyder's icy eyes. "Always underestimated, always coming out on top."

"Alright, I get it—thanks for saving my ass back there, and in the sewers."

"Yeah, I think I've mentioned it once or twice."

Celeste shook her head, mystified at such a callous resolve. "Why did you help me? I mean, truthfully. You could have killed Blackwell anytime, and after the way I treated you, I thought you wanted me dead as well."

"Is that why I wasn't recruited for your mission?"

Celeste cocked a brow at her. The irascible blonde almost seemed, if only for a moment, hurt by an apparent betrayal. Snyder scoffed silently.

"I gave you such a hard time because I thought you were given command due to your blood," she said. A curious shade of crimson burned beneath the grime on her cheeks. "Not that—I mean, family. Your uncle. As you might have noticed, I don't really believe rumors. I thought you were a pampered princess—shit, even the scars didn't convince me of your heroics."

"What did?"

"Watching you handle that revolver." Was there a glint of admiration in her frosty gaze? "How you commanded us in a firefight, never took shit from anyone, even me. But most of all, the way you told Blackwell to basically screw himself. I hated that bastard for what he did to my brother, but I could never get close enough to try and take him out, not alone. He was so careful after the bandits raided our city. Then you came along like a wildfire—and I just wanted his kingdom to burn."

"I'm sorry you didn't get to avenge your brother the way you wanted," Celeste muttered.

"Watching you carve out his throat like a roasted ham was a close second." Snyder grinned. "I consider it a win."

"I don't consider dying here much of a win."

"Then find us a way out so we can finish what we started."

"We're trapped."

Snyder cocked a brow. "Until morning."

The howling had abated to slick, *squishing* sounds like the rending of meat, echoing from the noisome sea of corpses below. A rancid breeze blew through the cells, carrying the stink from the swamp below. Across the expanse, white moonlight slanted across the wall as it spilled down from the top of the tower. The stone walls were smooth, impossible to grasp, and the rooms separated by more than an arms-length between each—an inconceivable climb.

It was useless.

With all other options exhausted, take the foolish route. The flutter from her heart was bittersweet, a gentle nudge from whatever part of her father remained. It was like a kind rebuke of her predicament, and she could practically hear the disappointed, yet grudging resolve that she *must* survive—and may as well put her stupidity to use.

Right, Dad.

Thoughts were discordant. The floor spun—and her along with it. She collapsed, scraped her elbows along the edge, and proceeded to retch yellowish-grey foam.

"Shit, you don't look so hot," Snyder remarked bluntly, then edged closer to inspect her wounded hand.

"I'm fine," Celeste said, pulling away. Her face chilled with sweat. "We only have a few hours to get the hell out of here."

"That looks like a nasty infection—"

A fiendish fire scorched through her last nerves. "I know!" she cried out viciously, almost snarling. "I haven't had my meds in weeks and I feel like a twice-beaten sack of shit! I'm feeling every ounce of pain from the last six months! And now that I know my fate is to...I screwed *everything* up and now I'm stuck in a literal hellhole—shit." Her eyes blurred. "I can't do this without you, I really can't."

She buried her head into her arms and wept and until she fell into a shuddering silence. Snyder seemed hesitant, treading unfamiliar territory when she attempted, quite horribly, to soften her tone in a response to such distress.

"I'm really sorry about your, uh, girl," she said, then cleared her throat with a small grunt. "You seemed to care for her a lot."

"I did." Celeste choked on a sob. "I do."

"You know," Snyder said, "I wanted to be a soldier ever since my brother taught me how to shoot at our former outpost. An old revolver, like yours, and boy, was I terrible. A waste of bullets, he would say. I spent years trying to impress him, fighting for a marksmen position in the Red Dawn military like he had. I wanted to be exactly like him, to *be* him. Exalted by the general. He gave his life to them, and he was *always* better than me.

"When a stray bullet paralyzed his leg, they abandoned him, cut off his rations, forced him to sell any belongings so we could eat. That's how Blackwell reeled him into the program, with promises of luxury and life for those he cared for. But the moment he was gone—I was forgotten. When they told me he died on the frontlines, I knew it was a goddamn lie."

Celeste muttered with disgust, "One man took so much from us all..."

"Not one man—one *army*." Snyder's eyes narrowed dangerously. "And we need vengeance. For my brother—for your girl."

"You won't like the plan."

An intolerable pain thundered through her mangled hand,

seeping foulness into her blood. But fury stubbornly burned through the chill of sickness. Removing the tattered layer of her shirt was strenuous with her throbbing stumps-for-fingers, with each wiggle ripping open the scabs. Still, she clutched feebly at her shirt, yanked it over her head, and tossed the torn, crumpled heap into Snyder's lap. As Snyder peeled her own soggy sweater from her shoulders, Celeste told her the plan—excruciatingly slow, as her words often slurred into an unintelligible garble like a drunk. Waves of pain violently crashed through her, throat scorched dry from vomit, and every spasm brought on another reluctant mouthful of the acidic gunk. It felt like someone gripped and twisted her belly, cruelly squeezed until she retched into the darkness once more. Snyder shook her head as she finished.

"So that's it, huh?" the blonde asked with a wry grin. "Descend into Hellpit, cross the *hungry* corpses, and hope to some god that one of our starved comrades will have enough strength to hoist us back up?"

Celeste nodded, sheepishly pulling her undershirt down over her tarry-patched belly. Lip split between her grinding teeth, she tore at the sleeves and frayed the fabric around her shoulders.

"First, we need to fashion a rope with as much length as possible," she said.

Snyder wiggled a brow at her, then unfurled her shirt over her taut belly and swelling chest. Celeste cleared her throat and lowered her gaze, heat rising to her cheeks. There was more definition to Snyder's physique than Celeste had ever amassed during her years of training routines her father had drilled her on. Not only slender, but curvaceous, muscles rigid yet flexing with each subtle movement of her hips. Her jeans were peeled from her thighs, skin beaming like a bright pale light, and then ripped at the crotch. After discarding her clothes into the crumpled heap, she stood with more flesh exposed than modestly appropriate, down to her thin and tattered undergarments.

"That should be enough," Snyder declared. A pink hue tinted Celeste's skin. "You can keep the rest on. It shouldn't be more than twenty feet—at least I hope not."

Celeste was almost hesitant to ask. "And if it is?"

"You heard what happens."

Snyder worked quite rapidly; fabric was ripped between her teeth, swiftly braided and knotted, then lengthened into a coiling rope around her shoulders. Celeste offered to help, but only fumbled with only one hand, pain erupting from the oozing wound. She contented herself with watching the blonde swiftly knot the remaining strips of fabric. When she was done, her blue eyes drifted over the edge and scanned the darkness below.

"Okay, Commander," said Snyder, ignoring any sound of protest. "I know you want to be invincible, but with your infection spreading I think it's safe to presume I'll be lowering you down first. Once down, you will coil the rope around your shoulder, if possible, while I scale the wall as far as I can before—well, dropping."

Celeste shuddered. "Will you make it?"

"Hopefully," the blonde replied with a grim smile. "We'll be fine. Let's hope the others are still alive."

"We're a team," Celeste asserted. "We made a plan—they could have as well."

But Snyder's sneering expression contrasted any sliver of hope. "I think there's a point to this madness, Commander, a reason for the barbaric conditions. They made sure to separate our cells with great lengths, so we're utterly uncoordinated. It's like we're animals to them, so they treat us as such. Animals fight for territory, for food—for survival. We're supposed to turn on each other, and if not, well, there's plenty of bullets for everyone."

Nadie. Adrenaline soaked into her blood. *I promise to get you out of here.*

"We have to try," she said through gritted teeth.

Snyder shrugged, still grinning like a madwoman. "We're dead anyway."

"Ever the optimist."

Snyder's frosted gaze leveled with Celeste, and she held the coiled rope out for her at arms-length.

"Tie one end tightly around your waist," she said slowly. "I'll use the wall for a brace to lower you down."

A disturbing sound echoed distantly from the darkness, a howl of utter agony, excruciating pain—but all too human. As the sound once again gave rise to the hideous cacophony from below, a chilling uncertainty swept between them like a sudden gust of wind. No more words were exchanged as they both carefully lowered to the edge—Snyder leaned against the wall, rope corkscrewed around her forearm, while Celeste swung her legs into the glacial-cold gap and rolled to her belly. Her elbows painfully pressed against the concrete floor, and her wounded hand pulsed with a ferocious pain at every slight movement. Still, she persistently wiggled her hips over the edge until the rope strained against her dropping weight. Snyder gasped, grunted, cursed, her fingers swelled bright red under the tightly drawn rope, and her feet slid through the filth spread across the floor. She dug her heel into the crevice of the wall, and slowly—*carefully*—unfurled the rope, lowering Celeste into void.

Celeste leaned back into the contusing grip around her waist. Her toes scraped against the sheer wall, twisting her into an uncontrolled spin. Crushing her hand, she screamed in bitter agony—then quickly smothered her involuntary outburst. Pain shocked her arm like a knife cruelly carving through her flesh. A faint murmuring carried through the tower. The darkness stirred.

"Are you okay?" Snyder's voice was barely a whisper, a disembodied worry from above. "S-shit, I can't hold this much longer—"

"I'm fine, keep going," Celeste replied, cautiously quiet against the growing dissonance below her. The rope quivered then slacked, and she felt her heart plummet into her belly. Her feet pressed against the wall, and she strained to see Snyder in the darkness of the cell—spotting nothing but a sliver of a gap between the ascending walls. The glittery starlight above seemed unfathomably far, merely a blurry swirl of milk up a long straw. Darkness reigned below, and her sight blurred and slowly adjusted, but perceived only faint ripples through the veil. It was as if whatever surface lay below the hollow tower warped and tilted like a funhouse floor. Distorted shapes and shadows, a terribly rancid odor—*It's like this whole place is—*

—a mechanical *whirring* noise shattered the uneasy silence. The discord rang through the tower, splitting her mind with a vicious, stabbing pain.

What the—

Chills needled her gut.

Oh, shit!

"Commander!" Snyder hissed through the rising tumult. "The door is opening! We have *no* time!"

Celeste gave a furtive glance into the darkness. Fear only strengthened its grip around her heart. "I'm only halfway!"

The blonde cursed with more vulgarity than Celeste's father had ever managed. "I'm sorry, Commander!" she yelled over the grinding *screech* of metal. "Brace yourself!"

Before Celeste uttered another word, the rope twisted and slacked—as Snyder leapt over the edge after her. Cold air *snapped* its chilling jaws around her flesh, and her body contorted and painfully slammed off the wall.

They both plummeted into hellish darkness.

Thirteen
Foolish Beyond Measure

THERE WAS a strange ululation creeping through the pain in her ears.

Her eyes snapped opened to a blur of darkness, a suffocating fog. Her limbs were oddly stiff and contorted, disjointedly sprawled. A wheezy groan escaped her when she stirred and raised her head. Something sharp pinched her shoulder, gouging the tender flesh below her collarbone. Blinking, her senses slowly adjusted to looming shadows and rotting stench. When she pushed herself up, her elbows sank into a swampy substance, skin grazed by floating debris. She wiggled through the muck, spitting the gritty warmth from her lips.

Snap-snap-snap!

The gnashing clatter reached her ears as the thick pool of filth rippled and disturbed the swampy water. Something jagged twisted further into her flesh—a broken bone, with gristle and stringy ribbons of flesh, protruded from the filth and into her shoulder like a sharp blade. The bone shuddered along with a horrifying sound.

A corpse snapped its teeth at her.

Black, bloated flesh oozed around greyish bone, weeping between gnashing teeth. Dull, glazy eyes stared back at her, voraciously wide. Its face slanted inward at a sharp angle like its nose had collapsed in on itself. Its jaw hung from a few strands of discolored tissue. Clumps of curly brown hair seemed to be all that remained of its former humanity. It was pinned in the rotting swamp of its own tattering flesh, coagulated blood, and other foul substances that made her belly quiver, just one of countless in a field of bony stakes. The surrounding shadows were mounds and piles of corpses that stirred to any sound or scent in the rancid depths. Excrement, blood, and other foul viscous fluids seeped through the trashy debris and congealed into a thick, swampy stew. It was as if the tower's base was a trash heap for their corpses and failed experiments, a hole to bury the infected and other biohazard waste. It was a sewer clogged with the dead.

Shit!

"Snyder!" she whispered hoarsely, and almost retched. She peeled herself from the filth. Her joints were grinding through pain, her flesh spongy and numb. She felt like a walking contusion. Even the throb in her hand became a distant memory compared the shrieking agony throughout her body. Had her bones been pulverized to smithereens from the fall?

"Snyder!" she hissed, binding the soggy rope around her waist.

"Present," came a droll response that masked a small grunt of pain. "I think, anyway." She groaned. "Is this literal Hell?"

Panic strained Celeste's voice as she recoiled from another stirring corpse, its teeth dangerously close to snapping at her remaining set of fingers. "Are you hurt? Cut? Did anything get in your eyes or mouth?"

"No, *Mother*." The blonde's irritability returned, though her voice was lowered to a small whisper and broke. "You broke my fall with that bony body of yours. I checked. Over and over."

That's why I feel like a truck hit me. "Be careful where you step—this is a pit alright, where they dump the infected experiments"—her nose wrinkled from the stench that pressed against her like a rotten tropic wind—"and other waste, I'm sure."

Waves rippled through the inky filth, and a terrible, rasping resounded from depths. Fresh blood had been scented.

Snyder's voice was hollow, shaken. "I don't think we have to worry about that." *Plop-plop.* Her feet shifted through the filth, and her balance wavered. "My leg is pretty screwed up from that fall. I'm not getting far." The inhuman wailing intensified around them. "Not now, anyway."

Celeste gritted her teeth. Her heart was heavy as a stone and sinking to her guts. "I'm not leaving you!"

"I'll only slow you down," Snyder protested, "but I can buy you time..."

"Shut up!" snarled Celeste. She wrenched a tight grip around the blonde's arm. "We're getting out of here—so keep your mouth shut!"

The distant sounds howled over them like tempestuous winds. The swamp bubbled and frothed as if something clawed its way up to the sludgy surface. The sound of their legs *sloshing* through the muck agitated the precipitous wall of shadows—until the darkness writhed loose, crashed and roiled down the slopes behind them in storming waves. Skulls with rotted, peeling flesh that had bloated to a spongy-black, chattered against the surface of the swamp, hissing and sputtering ravenously. Though the corpses were essentially immobilized beneath the debris or withered from decaying muscle and tissue, the rotting masses unfurled like waves and gave chase as one. Bony fingers wiggled up from the filth and crawled over her feet. Snyder dragged behind with an arm twisted in Celeste's unrelenting grip. Snyder limped, throwing Celeste off balance— *PLOP!*—her favored leg buckled and she sank into the murky waste. Celeste hauled her up with all the strength she could summon beyond the wall of fatigue—but the sediment sagged and plunged her belly-deep into the tarry pit. Rancid smelling steam rolled across the inky surface and suffocated her. Chills clawed at her flesh, dragging her beneath the churning waves of sludge. Darkness swelled and surged behind them.

"Go!" Snyder yelled over the howling cacophony.

Celeste cast one last desperate glance at the boggy pit ahead, then rolled her eyes to the mounds of mangled corpses and oozing trash.

Survive!

Without proper footing in the sinking sediment, she fought against the current, swinging her arm around Snyder for a tenuous hold—a vicious wave of pain thundered from her ghostly appendages. Her other hand reached forward and gripped a soggy clump of flesh—blood *squished* between her fingers. It was like digging through slop. Finally, her fingers closed around something solid. She dug her nails into gristle and gripped tight the split ribcage of a corpse. She hauled with fleeting strength, strenuously plucking herself and Snyder from the adhering grip of the swamp. They collapsed on the slope as the sludge lapped against their feet.

Celeste clawed forward, Snyder's weight supported on her shoulder, and they both scrambled for the peak. Oozing flesh rippled or sank under their weight and exposed a clattering echo of skulls. The sticky mass of decay and tar stirred beneath; teeth gnashing, bony fingers clawing for their bare flesh. Crushed into waste, the skulls shifted slightly, or sank into the layers of torn limbs and strewn guts. Snyder scrambled, half-limping and staggering in Celeste's grip—which sent a shocking sensation through her wounded hand. Pain pierced her sides like blades, slowly carving through her ribs and deep into her heart. Her lungs, ribboning under the phantom pain, refused air.

As the filth below eased to a murmuring trickle, another terrible *splitting* noise amplified around them. Curving grey claws ripped open the tarry surface of the mound, mincing through the mass of rotting waste. Teeth *snapped* and sprayed frothy old blood. A rotting face emerged, twisted and malformed. Wisps of stringy black flesh clung to the gristle around its jaw. It writhed to the surface like a worm from the dirt, its body rotted to gleaming bone and withering tissue. It trampled forward on bowed limbs, barely mobile, its innards trailing through the waste in long, discolored strands.

Creep!

Celeste reeled, spinning Snyder off-balance—the blonde staggered from Celeste's grip as the monster barreled between them, thrashing its long, rickety limbs. Finger claws scythed through the mound, shattering bones like glass. It turned, convulsed, jaws separated in a *clicking* howl. Flesh around its throat dribbled down over its concaved chest. It lunged at her, clawing with wild spasms. She retreated a pace—a layer of bones *snapped* beneath her misplaced step, plunging her leg deep into the sticky mound of rot. Her leg buckled, and she brought her arms against her face as the creature thrashed her with terrifying might.

Thwack! Thwack!

Its gangly limbs bludgeoned her until the flesh of its arms spattered and rained down against the mound, its muscles fraying and utterly useless. It sputtered in an attempted shriek. Its jaws twisted until its teeth jutted outward at a sharp angle. *Snap-snap!* Pulpy saliva slopped against her face as it leaned over her, teeth chattering for her flesh. Pressed into the muck, she shoved both hands against its gnarled spine as a feeble restraint from the creature snapping its jutting teeth. Her leg kicked wildly, but the other remained wedged inside the tarry mound. Her strength waned as the creature's jaws neared her flesh—

—there was a heavy *crunch,* and a warm drizzle of slime. The creature convulsed and slumped into her, completely limp. Wedged deep through the eye socket was a thin curving bone, stained with filth and remnants of greying flesh. Snyder stood over her, the same filth dripping from her slender fingers.

"Don't touch it!" Celeste gasped as she heaved the deadweight off her. "Make sure there's no cuts on your hands—and don't touch your face!"

"I think that point is a little moot," was the blonde's snarky reply. "We're surrounded by the sickness in case you haven't noticed by now."

"Hell, humor me for once and obey a command," Celeste growled. With a surge of strength, she flung the ragged corpse over the side of the mound. It spun down the slope with a wild cartwheeling motion, then *smacked* loudly into the swamp. Darkness surged around the disturbance.

"Move," Celeste whispered, then braced to support Snyder's weight on her shoulder. "Quietly—and watch your step."

With each step, she stubbed her toes against bone, heard the sharp *snaps* of buried teeth eager for her flesh—but she didn't care. She pressed forward with Snyder limping slowly alongside her. The blonde leaned into her, huffing warmly in her ear and spreading a slight tingle down the back of her neck. Each step was a wary gamble, a sinking pit of tar or a stained pair of fangs gnashing for her toes.

"We're almost there," Celeste huffed, eyes peeled into the darkness ahead. Moonlight gleamed against the curving wall of the tower in long, slanted beams, illuminating the smooth stone between elongated gaps of seemingly impenetrable black.

"We don't even know which ones they were placed in!"

"Block A!" Celeste hissed through gritted teeth, almost growling. "They led them in the opposite direction—it has to be one of these rooms!"

Their feet slipped through swamp when the mound abruptly slanted. They sank into the depression, slammed against the tar, and were wrenched from each other's grip. Celeste heaved. Her vision tilted, blurred, and she almost screamed with the sudden sensation of plummeting. She shook her head as if to clear the fever's grip on her mind.

Didn't I warn you that they would die by your hand?

"What?" Celeste asked, incredulous. Darkness hazed her sight. "I didn't kill th—I didn't mean to!"

Yes, you did, the disembodied voice purred, haughty with delight. Vega had her ghostly claws deep in her thoughts. *You knew what you were doing, deep down, you knew those you loved would perish for the cause.*

"Not them!"

Vega purred threateningly, *It's not easy being the Phantom Woman, is it? The undying monster—but this is what you wanted, what you sought when you came after me, bloodthirsty and hungry for revenge for all the wrongs committed against you and your precious family. All that sorrow and pain bottled up over time will become a tempest of violence.*

"Shut up!" Celeste exploded. She jolted awake with a sharp spasm and retched into the swamp.

"Commander!"

She blinked twice before Snyder's icy blue eyes shimmered through the hazy veil around her sight. The slender blonde jutted her chin with worry, but Celeste waved her away and retched again.

"You're shaking like the last leaf on the branch," whispered Snyder, slowly shaking her head. "That means your infection is worse than we thought—or your withdrawals."

Celeste narrowed her gaze into a sneer that surely paled in comparison to what the blonde could manage. "I'm fine—but *we* won't be soon."

The wailing reverberated through the tower like rolling thunder. Inhuman forms rose from the bubbling surface and slowly clawed up the mound. The cacophony of corpses scented their blood.

Running was no longer an option. They were both weary to the brink of exhaustion, but Snyder's limp fared worse without Celeste's strength to compensate. Their balance wavered, and their feet slipped uncontrollably through the thick slime. Predatory roars chased them from the awoken darkness. Shadows slithered from the swamp to feast on fresh meat and warm blood.

"We're not close enough!" Snyder cried out, halting at the edge of the mound. It was a steep drop into the swamp below, and yet another sheer wall of waste across the tarry stream. A nervous glance over her shoulder unraveled a string of curses from her tongue.

Celeste, grinding her teeth slowly, focused on the steep descent. The ooze pulsated from the mound like blood from a wound, spewing down the slope in thick, sludgy streams. They had to cross—quickly.

It was at that moment her weight shifted against the slope, and her feet slipped through the sludge like it were ice. They both tumbled forward, limbs interlocked, and painfully *smacked* against the tarry mound. Snyder reeled into an ungraceful glissade, and Celeste clawed at the muck to slow her summersaulted descent, but only spun wildly into the soupy filth.

SPLOOSH!

She flailed helplessly in her disorientation, sinking herself into the sediment. Panic shocked her immobile and her lungs withered from the lack of air. The swamp would be her coffin, and no thought had frightened her more.

She was plucked out of the coagulating sludge, gasping and sputtering, shaking the gunk from her face. Snyder had waded into the muck, heaved her up from the sinking sediment, and proceeded to drag her through the swamp as the slopes behind them shuddered and rolled toward them.

Cognition returned with an agonizing pulse in her head. Her vision slowly adjusted, and her legs scrambled to keep pace in the thick mire. Snyder turned, grip tight around Celeste's waist—

—something thrashed along the surface of the swamp, and the murky waters rippled into monstrous waves as corpses clawed and writhed to the surface, howling and sputtering their hunger.

"Come on!" Snyder yelled. She threw Celeste from the waste and climbed out after her. They collapsed against the slope, breathless and utterly exhausted. Snyder recoiled from the *snapping* of jaws in the swamp beneath them. Pinpoints danced across Celeste's vision. There was little time to nurse her sickness, or stem the flow of blood from her hand. They ascended the slope slowly, eyes nervously cast toward the frothing swamp below.

Corpses stirred within the mire.

"Shit!"

"We're here!" Celeste gasped incredulously. Each step was a struggle to regain balance—but a few paces ahead, she saw the looming tower wall encompassing her entire field of view, spanning far above her until the starry sky shone through a mere pinpoint. She staggered into the wall and pressed her palms flat against the cold stone.

"Hey!" Snyder called out, raising her voice above the tumult from the swamp below. The rotting darkness flooded the mound like a rising sea tide. "Anyone alive?"

"Nadie!" Celeste's voice was ragged and brittle. *Please be alive!* "Nadie! We need your help!"

Snyder huffed in annoyance. "I doubt she could lift either of us—"

"Nadie!"

"We can try another," Snyder began, another nervous glance over her shoulder.

"The mound ends a few feet on either side," Celeste croaked. "We'd have to cross the swamp again."

Huffing from her nose, Snyder narrowed her eyes toward the clambering corpses. "Then we cross that goddamn swamp."

We'll die either way.

Then she heard it: distant, nearly imperceptible through the screaming symphony of the dead—the faint sound seized her attention with an iron grip. Her body froze, as if the chill spread from her heart through to her veins. Then she heard it again.

"Commander?" The voice was small, dulled, almost a whisper. "Are you there?"

"Twist! Twist, is that you?"

She stared up the sheer stone, then dissolved into a fit of giggles when she glimpsed his small head jut out from the gap in the wall. She could make out his simple, scrunched complexion, as if deep in the beginning of a thought he would never complete, and his beady eyes that stared down at her in childish wonder. Relief flooded her veins like a strong wine—until the *hissing* of roaming corpses intensified around them.

"I've never been so happy to see a man," Snyder remarked with a wry grin. She jutted her narrow chin in amusement. "Well, maybe seeing one leave."

"Commander!" Twist called out to her, waving a hand over the edge. "Hi!"

"Twist! We need your help, okay?" She peeled the braided rope from around her hips, wringing out the muck between her functioning fingers.

He pursed his lips in thought, another expression that seemed to stretch into eternity before he simply replied, "I'll come down there?" and then flopped his rotund torso against the edge in a careless effort to climb down the sheer vertical wall like a ladder.

"No!" she exclaimed, alarmed that the simple man had no concept of height. "Stay up there, I want you to stay where you are!"

He slowed his movements, and his brow wrinkled as he mulled over the significance of her words. "Then how can I help?"

"We'll throw you a rope," she explained, enunciating each word slowly. "You catch it, hold one end really tight and then drop the other end to us, got it?"

But he cocked his head at her, oblivious. "But how will you get up if I throw the rope back down?"

Celeste cursed quietly through gritted teeth. *I don't have time for this!*

Snyder quickly cleared her throat. "It's like training, remember that? Climbing the rope wall? You're going to help us climb!"

His tongue stuck out. "Oh! I get it!"

The blonde grinned, snatching the rope from Celeste. Her eyes scanned the wall's edge, and she leaned back—then flung the rope like a baseball.

Splat!

The soggy fabric clung to the wall like paste, then slowly peeled away—Twist, seemingly nimbler than his wide, meaty frame would otherwise suggest, practically dove over the edge with his arms extended as far as he could reach, then *clapped.* He caught the fabric in his large hands, the impact wringing it dry and spattering gunk down the wall in dark streaks. He slowly unfurled the rope in his hands. His face scrunched up—he was utterly pleased with himself.

"Got it!" he exclaimed proudly, then cocked his head at darkness. "What's that noise?"

The rasping increased to thunderous howls. The infected clawed and clambered up the slope from the murky depths of the swamp, their bodies were decayed or bloated to near-immobility. Their persistence only woke the sunken dead, until screeches and rippling moans carried through the hollow tower, and the darkness converged on the swamp water below. Rotted filth emerged from the mire, crawling toward the scent of meat.

"Bad things," Celeste whispered.

"Okay," Snyder called out. "Now I need you to let one end down—slowly. Can you do that, big guy?"

"Sure," Twist replied with a grin and a slight shrug of his massive shoulders. "Like rope climbing in training."

"Yes," said Snyder, with more patience than Celeste could have ever imagined possible. "Just like training! You need to hold your end of the rope nice and tight, okay?"

"Okay."

Snyder braced against the wall, then leapt for the dangling end of rope like a fish for a baited hook. Snatching it, she made a small motion to hand off the rope, but Celeste shook her head in refusal.

"You're going first," she said slowly. "Your leg is messed up. You can barely stand. If one of those *things* manages to draw blood you might get infected. I'm—just go!"

"Don't make me climb back down to save your ass again," Snyder sneered playfully, though her carving grin slowly faded as she secured the rope around her waist. "Commander."

Her heart briefly fluttered with warmth, then she rolled her eyes skyward. "Twist! Time to pull her up!"

"Right!" he called out. His prevailing dull tone was now tight with rising excitement. It was all a game to the simple man. He retreated from sight with a deep grunt as he hauled on the rope—the fabric *snapped* straight and rigid, and Snyder was jerked against the wall, quickly hoisted up from her feet. She twisted with the rope, attempting to keep pace with Twist's long, heavy heaves.

Celeste watched her, tentatively, shadows stirring along the periphery of her sight, crawling over the sloping mound. The moment Snyder's legs swung over the edge and she was safely out of sight, Celeste allowed herself a slight sigh of relief—

—until a strangely familiar scream was nearly lost to the tumult around her, a faint sound that was unmistakably human.

Nadie!

"Get off me!"

Her voice heavy with a sense of panic unlike any she had ever heard since—*Caden.* She heard a snarl that may as well have been from a starving corpse beside her—someone else was smothering Nadie. Their shadows flickered along the edge of the cell next to Twist's.

"Let her go, you son of a bitch!"

The third voice was a fearful squeak. A loud and heavy *smack* echoed from above, then a loud grunt. Somebody screamed, and the sharply pitched sound rang through the tower as an immense blurred form plunged into the frothing swamp.

Shit!

After a nervous glance up the tower wall, she abandoned her stable footing on the mound and slipped down through the oozing filth. She neared the figure, now slumped in the muck and barely stirring, only a few feet away from the rising sea of corpses. She slowed her descent through the muck to a cautious approach. There was a gurgling sound—then a small, weak whimper. Long, brown hair shimmered faintly in the dim haze of moonlight.

"Nadie!" Celeste hissed, extending an arm to her. Any closer and she risked slipping into the clawing clutches of the dead. "Nadie!"

"C-commander?" Her voice heavy with disbelief, and she only stared back at the gesture in absolute shock. "Is that you?"

"No time!" Celeste ordered. "Take my hand!"

But her friend seemed disorientated, mystified at her darkened surroundings. "Where am I?"

"Take my *goddamn* hand!"

Nadie sobered at the vicious tone. Her brown eyes flitted through the surging darkness. She lunged forward, hand clasping around the pustular wound—a shocking jolt of pain raced through Celeste's arm, thundered through her bones—and she hauled Nadie out from the tar and they both scrambled for the wall.

Except something closed around her ankle with an crushing grip. Celeste slipped into the waste, clawing desperately at the slick surface.

"Y-you bitches!" they sputtered, nearly crushed into a depression in the slope. The hulking form shifted, then roared with agony. "Help me!"

"Harn," Celeste hissed through clenched teeth. "I hope you rot here."

"Bitch!" He tightened his vicelike grip, but then recoiled at the sight of the corpses clawing at his tattered clothes. "You can't leave me!"

With primal rage like her wolf, she leaned down and pried his fingers from her leg with a vicious *snap* of her fangs. Blood spritzed across her cheek and flooded her mouth with sour warmth—Harn bellowed with in a fury of pain. She wrenched her leg from his grip, desperately clawing up the peak of the mound.

"Bitch!" Harn yelled again. His voice was soon smothered by the wailing of the woken dead. She spared him no second glance.

Another voice broke through the clamor. "Commander!"

"I'm here!" she yelled with a strangled voice. She clambered up the slope with the grace of a walking corpse, slipping two paces backward for every misplaced step. When Nadie's grip seized her outstretched fingers, she was hauled up against the cold stone of the wall, heaving the warm, rotten air.

"Hurry up!" came a sneering demand from above. The braided

rope unfurled against the wall with a moist *splat*. With wide, wondering eyes, Nadie watched Celeste twist the rope around her waist. As she looped the knot, however, she narrowed her eyes at the sight of her friend's leggings torn by the crotch, her dark skin a blistering red.

"This is how you escaped?" Nadie asked with a cautiously soft voice. "You rappelled down here?"

Celeste replied grudgingly, "Sort of."

"Will it hold?"

A slight nod before she called up to Twist. Nadie clenched the taut rope, bent her knees, pressed her feet flat against the wall in a rappelling position. Her despondent gaze was drawn upward, but Celeste still saw the dark patches of flesh puff out below her eyes, like a setting bruise, and the faintest trickle of blood from her lip. Her shirt was torn over her breast, with red gashes clawed into her smooth skin.

As Nadie ascended out of sight, a deep and ragged bellow wrenched her attention to the swamp below.

Harn.

The hulking man writhed against the dead throng, swinging his massive fists as blunt weaponry. Bones shattered and crumbled like drywall, raining mangled corpses into the swamp. A heavy stomp crushed a corpse into the tar, yet it persistently flailed its limbs in a blinded attempt to claw after flesh. More infected forms crawled from the mire, ghoulish and rotting, their disintegrated throats erupted with rippling screeches and crackling croaks. He leaned forward and charged up the slope, his broad shoulders like battering rams through the rising dead.

The son of a bitch is going to make it.

"Commander!"

She seized the frayed edges of the rope in dismay: the braid was unraveling, untwisting in long, wrinkled strands. With vibrating nerves, she hastily knotted the rope around her waist and called out for Twist. The sudden force jerked her against the wall, and she nearly flipped over backward, and twisted further into the rope. With increasing difficulty, she managed to pace her steps with the wall, abandoning the rotting quarry and the desperate bellows of her former comrade.

It was at least twenty feet, perhaps more, but the strain against her body stretched those moments into an agonizing eternity. When she finally reached the edge, strength fled every muscle, and she collapsed into warm, nursing hands. She gazed up, sight bleary and tilted, expecting to glimpse Nadie's gentle smile and warm assurances—but she stared into the frosted blue eyes of Snyder, who carefully probed her postulating wound.

"It's bleeding again," the blonde remarked with her crooked nose wrinkled in disgust. "Whoever stitched this wound is an absolute butcher."

"Did I do good?" His thick brow furled in apparent thought. "Helped?"

A slight grin touched Snyder's lips. "You did good, big guy."

Celeste's eyes fluttered closed—but a furious howl from the depths of the tower sharpened her cognition. She bolted upright with her eyes snapped open. Abandoning caution, she flung herself near the edge, gaze swimming through the tumultuous sea of black. Her hand fumbled with the rope's knot around her waist, and when she finally unslung the fraying fabric, she dangled the loose end over the edge like a fishing line.

"What are you doing?" Nadie's voice was tight like she spoke through a clenched throat. "You left him down there to die."

"Yet, he's still alive," Celeste said. The words left a foul taste in her mouth. "We need all the strength we can get if any of us want to escape this place."

And I need answers.

Nadie narrowed her eyes, casting her sullen gaze to the floor. She remained bitterly silent.

"Got it!" Twist declared triumphantly, clutching the end of the rope between his pudgy fingers.

Harn managed to ascend the slope, and retreated until his back glanced off the tower wall. With another bellow, he stomped the first corpse to claw at his feet and crushed its skull into the tarry mound. He reeled, hand twisting around the rope—

—a corpse lunged at him, gnashing and ribboning flesh between its teeth. A thick stream of blood gushed from his thigh, barely an inch above his knee. His fist bludgeoned the skull until its features were concave, its body movements limited to spastic jerks against the wall.

"Too...heavy..." Twist grunted. The portly man slipped through the blood-stained floor, fat toes wiggling over the edge. Celeste leapt at him and snatched at the unwinding rope. She burned through her remaining strength, but she pulled, hard—her grip faltered, and Snyder pressed against her for support.

Harn swung across the wall like a pendulum, fraying the rope along the edge. It forced him into an uncontrolled spin, and he dangled helplessly, feet brushing against the swarm of infected corpses. The rope slacked.

Nadie sprang into action. She dove between them, slamming her hip against the floor. The rope was unraveling like a spool of yarn in their clutches, but she held tight and kicked her legs across the floor for leverage—her feet came dangerously close to slipping past the edge. The rope creaked and strained against Harn's weight, and finally slacked when he hauled his hulking body past the lip and splayed himself across the floor.

Harn's crooked grin twisted his thick, braided beard. Sweat pasted his long hair to his face, but bright red marks across his cheek gleamed through the black, greasy strands. He huffed in amusement, intoxicated by the thrill of survival.

Until Nadie hammered his nose flat against his face, staining her knuckles crimson. Blood burst across his lips as he howled in fury, hands clasped over the mushy, purpling flesh of his nose.

"I'll kill you for that!" he roared. He rolled to his knees, and staggered, blood dripping into the slime from the gaping hole in his thigh. He roared in both fury and agony. Celeste leaned over him, face twisted with a scowl that would have frightened even her own father, then plunged her foot into his minced thigh. He writhed, but she only dug deeper into his torn flesh, blood oozing between her toes. He swung for her, roaring like an agitated bear, but her cruelty was boundless. She twisted her foot, and more steaming blood shot up her leg.

"I saved your life, so you tell me the truth," Celeste asked, scraping her nails through torn flesh. "What did you do to her?"

Harn hissed at her, his teeth stained a bright red. "Only what was necessary to live!"

"Bullshit," Nadie whispered quietly, her eyes drawn to the floor.

His eyes were glazed with pain, his filthy black beard spattered with blood—he still grinned at her, licking the blood from his lips.

"If I would have known you wanted a second round, girl, I would have gone a lot har—"

His disparaging remarks slurred into a wordless shriek, and he writhed under the crushing pressure of Celeste's weight. Crimson poured from the chewed meat in his wound. She stepped back, lungs filled with the heavy aroma of blood, and smeared red footprints across the sticky floor. With a small nod of her head, she gestured to the soggy fabric unraveled at their feet.

"Bind that wound, follow my command," she said coldly, "and you may live long enough to die a free man before the sickness claims you."

He reached for the fabric, slowly, his dark eyes level with hers. Anger smothered the pain until even her phantom fingers were a mere ache, an itch that could never be scratched.

"Touch her or any of my friends again and I'll kill you horrifically slow."

Harn's lip twitched into a snarl, but he turned to the gushing wound in his leg and wrapped the rope around his upper thigh as a tourniquet.

"Well," said Snyder, eyeing the pooling blood. "What now, Commander?"

The floor rumbled gently beneath her feet, and the walls shuddered under the sound of grinding metal—an ear-splitting screech that rang through the tower and roiled the darkness in the depths below.

"They're opening the cell doors," Snyder remarked, simmering her excitement. "Starting with the one beside us. Looks like we're trapped again."

Nadie lowered her gaze. "Clark..."

"It's time we get the hell out of here," Celeste declared proudly. She grinned, baring her fangs. "They won't be able to take us all down."

FOURTEEN
Wolves

DESPITE THE furious ache in her bones, and her labored breathing, Celeste remained on her feet, giddied from another wave of adrenaline. Her heart was a thundering drum in her ears. She was flat against the wall, keeping the cell gate in her line of sight. Snyder pressed against her back, her rapid breaths tickling the back of her neck. Harn knelt beside them, a mountain of massive muscle, nearly their height even on his knees. Nadie crouched in the corner of the adjoining walls, wary of Harn's looming presence. Twist, however, was positioned in full view near the cliff into Hellpit, plopped into the bloody goop strewn across the floor—all that remained of his former cellmates. His beady, vacant eyes fixed on the gate, and his lips pursed out thoughtfully.

Then the gate shifted, separating from the wall with a grinding wail. Sparks hissed against the cold, slimy concrete. The walls rattled, the floor lurched, and the gate slammed open.

A sharp, indifferent voice cut through the tense silence. "I see the dull-witted one survived—not like the older gent was much when we found him," Annie remarked, pen scratching into her notepad. "Miss Kay will be pleased to have such a large specimen."

"Old man hit me," Twist said slowly, slapping his palm flat against the pool of blood. "But I hit back."

"I see that," she replied, mimicking his thick, dulled tone. "Why don't you step away from the edge and come with us. You don't want the guard to come in there."

His beady eyes narrowed to thin little slits. "I can't go anywhere."

"Are you hurt?"

"No."

Impatience trickled through. "Too stupid?"

"Not supposed to."

"Oh, Christ—get in there and get him to his feet!"

Boots pounded along the floor in heavy thuds. "Yes ma'am."

"*Alive*, please," she sang.

An oblong shadow extended across the floor, and in that moment, she spotted the gun barrel stab past the gate. She drummed her fingers on Harn's shoulders, and he lunged forward with explosive speed. The guard took a single step beyond the gate before he caught sight of the mountain's charge. Harn slammed him off his feet with the force of a speeding train, one massive hand clutched around the guard's facemask. With a wet, sickening *crunch* sound, the guard was crushed between Harn's monstrous grip and the stone wall, his skull cracking open like an eggshell. As the body spasmed and jerked, a shrieking command from the corridor rang against the barren cell walls. More boots *thudded* in approach.

The next soldier crossed the threshold, rifle raised to Harn.

A feral, predatory instinct fueled her sprint across the room before the second soldier drew another breath. He turned, hesitantly, almost suspended in disbelief, granting ample opportunity for her to close the gap between them. She thrashed against his body armor, forcing him to retreat against the wall. He stumbled over the slumping, bloody mess of his comrade. He clumsily raised the assault rifle to her—but Harn's hand wrenched around his throat and squeezed until blood bubbled through his fingers. The soldier gasped and clutched feebly at his crushed throat.

Celeste slipped across the blood-slicked floor, ripping the rifle from the dead soldier's grip. She spun into a peal of gunfire. Bullets peppered and charred the concrete. She tossed the weapon into far more capable hands—Snyder raised the rifle to her shoulder and took aim.

There was a blinding flash, a thundering pressure inside her ears, and the soldier's face exploded into a red streak across the wall.

"Close the gate! Protect the prisoner!" Another shriek from the nurse, stricken with panic at the violent sloshing of blood. "Close that damn gate!"

Celeste barely breathed during the brief exchange of gunfire. Snyder advanced at her signal, peering down the narrow sight of the rifle. Bullets sparked by her feet, ricocheting into the tower's depths. Snyder didn't dare flinch.

Celeste lurched into the corpse and clambered over it with bullets *whizzing* sharply overhead. She fumbled her fingers across the biting-cold grip of a pistol.

Snyder's forward pace faltered; blood spritzed across the concrete. Crimson cascaded from the gash across her thigh. As the blonde staggered, Celeste whipped her arm forward, a familiar and comfortable weight clenched inside her palm. Her finger slipped against the trigger.

But the violent recoil forced her aim into a wild, upwards swing. The first bullet struck the approaching soldier in his knee, buckling his leg. Armor absorbed the shock of the second shot—but his throat ruptured from the third, and he collapsed with blood on his lips.

"Now!" Celeste commanded. She clambered to her feet, and within two long strides, she reached the gate with her pistol still drawn. Snyder eased against the wall, peering past the cement's bloody edge. She pivoted and raised the rifle to the ceiling in one fast, fluid movement, and another shot rang out. Glass shattered, circuitry sparked and sizzled—the camera scattered across the floor in smoking pieces.

The cannonade erupted.

Concrete exploded from the walls, blinding her with thick plumes of dust. Another soldier fell beyond the gate, limp, eyes vacantly wide and staring at her. Another soldier retreated a single pace, opening fire on Snyder's advancement. With no cover in the narrow confines of the corridor, she was forced to press the issue; a thin red streak ran across her shoulder from a graze, but her calculated shot struck the soldier between his eyes. He slumped forward, instantly dead.

The mechanics within the gate whirred, thundered, and then sparks sprayed from the metal door grinding shut.

Celeste took aim at the remaining soldier—his rifle discharged first. Bullets ripped through the wall, showering her with chalky concrete.

Zing! Zing!

Ricochets whistled past, dangerously close to her head. Her pulse pounded wildly, but her movements were sluggish and feeble. She stumbled, choking on the dust clouding her vision. Through the deep ringing in her ears she caught the shrill sounds of the nurse.

"Kill them!"

Thwap-thwap-thwap-thwap!

She flinched from the pressure that pounded against her chest in quick, rapid succession. She opened her eyes to settling dust, and rivers of steamy blood gushing from another soldier—who was now dead and sprawled across the floor. Someone slumped near the corpse, perilously close to the outburst of bullets, and trembled as the peal of gunfire faded to a ringing echo. Bruises swelled his eyes shut, but he peeked through the slits as they gathered around him. His sunken cheek was scraped and scabbed, oozing a foul discoloration. At the sight of her standing over him with a rifle, the lingering scent of spent gunpowder, Clark was mortified. His pallor was as ghostly as the stark white walls.

"Thanks," she barely breathed, glancing to the looming figure beside her—then clenched her jaw tight. Her eyes rolled to find Harn's contemptuously proud expression. Anger stormed behind his eyes.

Then where's Nadie?

The gate slammed shut, clanked loudly, and sealed against the wall. Twist bumbled toward them, contently led by the hand like a wayward child. Nadie released his hand, eyes lowered to avoid any gaze, and crossed the corridor toward Clark. Her features softened, if only for a moment, as she knelt beside him in the blood.

"I did as I was told," Twist said proudly, dimpling his pudgy cheeks. Celeste grinned back at him, relieved by his ignorance. *Can't forget he takes every order in the literal sense.*

"That you did, big guy," she said. Turning to Harn, she muttered, "Kill anyone who walks into this corridor."

No exchange of words or pleasantries, just a stiff nod then he was gone, limping out of sight behind them.

"Commander," Snyder said. "We have a survivor."

She heard a whimper squeak out after each shuddering breath, a faint *tap-tap-tap* as pedicured nails nervously flicked over a keypad.

"I'd stop if I were you," growled Celeste, "and turn around slowly."

The short, plump woman froze from the threat, her shoulders

hunching as she began to sob and tremble. Her hand fell in defeat. She shuffled awkwardly to face Celeste, wobbling on her slanted heels. Blood speckled her stark-white gown. Tears ran down her cheeks and smeared the painted sheen to a clown's expression.

"Hello, Annie."

"P-please don't kill me," she pleaded.

Her arm trembled from the weight in her hand, but Celeste kept the pistol drawn on the nurse's heart. "Elevator, now."

"I-I can't," she began.

"*Now.*" Celeste bared her teeth and took a single pace forward. Her finger slipped through the trigger-guard. "And I let you live. Again."

Annie bit her trembling lip, smoothing her spastic movements with an exaggerated bow. "O-okay," she said. "This way."

There were several thick steel-plated doors with no discernable handle, only small rectangular keypads the width and length of her hand. Celeste flicked the pistol at Annie, and the nurse flinched and shuffled to the elevators, high heels striking the floor in quick, sharp claps. She cleared her throat, smoothed the crinkles in her blood-spattered gown, and then curled her fingers over the bright numbered keys. She took a step away from the doors.

"Come on, bitch!" Harn called from down the corridor. "We got company!"

"Stop stalling!" Celeste hissed.

"I'm not, I swear!"

Annie took another step away from the door. The nurse drew a quick breath—and took another step back. Celeste raised her pistol. The elevator doors shifted and slowly crept open—her finger twitched against the trigger—

Beneath the glaring fluorescence, two figures stood, armored in black and rifles drawn and aimed at center mass. *Pop! Pop!* Blood blotted their faces, soaking through the masks. They fell back, and simultaneously struck the elevator floor. She turned to Annie, growling, "Get in."

The sobbing woman edged past the lifeless bodies and rising crimson pools.

Thwap-thwap-thwap-thwap!

Gunfire pounded against her ears. Down the corridor, another group of soldiers pressed through Harn's suppressive fire, callously stepping over their wounded or dying comrades, rifles trained on those who remained in sight.

"Time to go!" Harn bellowed over his shoulder, falling back as his weapon fell empty.

"Move!" Celeste turned to Twist. "You too, big guy. Inside."

The simple man nodded happily, rippling his pudgy cheeks, then lumbered into elevator. "Shiny."

Nadie eased Clark to his feet and dragged him to the elevator. "Snyder! Fall back!

The blonde exchanged another quick burst of gunfire, ducking as the wall above her was shredded and showed debris over her. They reeled and dashed for the shifting doors. Celeste fired blindly until her pistol emptied. They reached the doors, and Celeste pivoted, slamming into Snyder as the concrete ripped apart by their feet. Snyder was hurled through, sloshing through the blood and limp limbs. Celeste dove after her, smacking her shoulder against the closing doors. She rolled to a stop over the corpses, pressed against the legs of the other occupants.

Wearied, bloody, nauseous from the sickly warm scent of death, Celeste struggled to her feet, nursing the oozing wound on her left hand. She swayed as she stood, pressed tightly against the others shoulder-to-shoulder, while her mind whirled and vision blurred to dull, grey streaks.

Boots thundered down the corridor.

"Commander?"

"Ah, hell," Harn growled with a deep sigh. "We should have fought to an honorable death instead of trapping ourselves in a tin can for slaughter."

Celeste spoke through a tight throat. "Annie." The nurse flinched at the mention of her name, shrinking into the corner of the panel and wall. "Take us to the closest exit."

The nurse's curled hair bobbed as she trembled and sobbed. "Y-you can't just walk out—"

"*Now!*"

Annie gulped, plumping her rouge lips. With a sideways glance, she flicked her fingers over the panel, brightening a set of numbers and letters in a sinuous pattern. The machinery whirred from the inputted command. She felt the sickening sensation of plummeting as the elevator lurched downward. The thin walls wailed with a violent shudder, as if the metal would fragment and strip from the compartment during its wild descent. It nearly made Celeste retch all over their feet.

"Commander," said Snyder, relinquishing one of the weapons

she had retrieved from the dead guards. "Take this."

It was a hunting knife, with a long, thin, almost delicate blade, curving slightly near the serrated point. Her fingers barely gripped the monstrously large handle, and it felt more like an anvil in her palm than a weapon to thrust and slash with. Snyder gave her a curt nod, then reloaded the mag. Harn searched the bodies and found a spare clip.

"Why is *he* still alive?"

Clark's voice was strained and small, but disgust oozed from his question like poison. He slouched against the wall, his stubbly-short hair crusted with grime and blood. The bruises around his eyes swelled to the size of baseballs, until what stared back at Harn seemed entirely alien, a malformation not of this world. Hatred clung to his twisted expression.

"He forced himself on Nadie the moment those doors locked," Clark muttered. "I-I tried to stop him, and he beat me until he thought I was dead. Then he went right back to her..." His voice cracked and he trailed into a bitter silence.

An icy-hot rage flushed through her chest, and Celeste shuddered, squeezing the grip of her machete. *He's just like Caden,* she knew, a phantom pain pulsing between her legs. *He needs to die.*

"He lives," she found herself blurting out to them. "He can help us escape." Her wandering gaze found Nadie, though the woman was quick to glance aside, throwing her attention to Clark's wounds. "We're a team." But the words rang out as hollow as the tower. Clark only scoffed at her, slouched against the rattling wall.

"Come on, boy," Harn growled dangerously. "Don't tell me you've *finally* grown some balls—"

Nadie suddenly snarled, "You son of a bitch!"

"I should have killed you both," Harn replied coldly. "Survival of the fittest, ya know? And look at you—a coward and a weak *bitch.*"

Nadie wedged herself between Celeste and Snyder, clawing frantically for Harn's smug grin. His rifle was trained on her spastic lunge, as if he were ready to club a seal, daring her to cross the threshold of her team.

Enough of this.

Celeste corkscrewed her leg around Nadie's, shifting the girl off balance with a gentle nudge. Then Celeste reeled, knife blade slashing upwards through the elevator. The razor tip carved across the metal wall with a streak of spitting sparks. His rifle raised at the sudden commotion, but her blade came to a stop only an inch or so from his throat. His eyes grew wide at the sight of the blade tip millimeters away from his larynx. His fingers, however, *tapped* his finger against the trigger-guard of his rifle—and the barrel jabbed into her chest.

"Your move, *Commander*."

Snyder's cavalier tone broke the tension. "I can't be the only one to figure this out."

The blade wavered in her hand. Slowly, she turned to Snyder. "What?"

The blonde smirked. "We keep going down—so how is there an exit in the middle of a mountain?"

Shit.

"That's not all," Celeste muttered, mind racing. It was starting to make sense; their simple escape, small units engaging in firefights but never flanking. "We haven't triggered any alarms." Her blade lowered, slowly, as she shot a daring glance at the nurse cowering against the panel. Sweat beaded her pallidly painted skin, lips pursed so tightly as if she were about to burst. "Because no one ever escapes. Do they, Annie?"

"So," Snyder said, "where is our little nurse bringing us?"

The crook of Annie's mouth curved into a trembling smirk. "I'm keeping my promise and bringing you to the exit."

The compartment lurched, *screeching* madly, slowing its erratic descent.

"You'll die without us," Annie seethed. "Without our strength, you're nothing! You're right where you should be, traitors! We are going to save this wo...uhhg..."

With a flick of her wrist, Celeste had carved a thin rivulet across the nurse's throat with her blade. The gash opened to a spurt of blood that rapidly pumped down her milky skin. She choked on her words, disbelief prying her eyes wide, then crumpled as the elevator compartment rocked to a jarring halt.

"Shit," Harn muttered. "Some plan this was."

Nadie stepped over the nurse's body, never sparing a glance at her ghostly open eyes, and punched in keys to the control panel. She swore, hammering it with her fist. The controls seized and locked.

"We're screwed."

"No," Celeste said, gripping her knife tight. "We get ready to fight our way to freedom."

The elevator doors shifted and slowly retracted. Rifles raised,

Snyder and Harn flanked the doors. Celeste bent her knees, angling the knife parallel with her thigh. Nadie shrank behind Clark, who had his frail arm around her like a shield. He stood at Celeste's command, eyes burning bright, fist clenched and tucked against his chest. He gave Celeste a small nod.

"Don't move!"

"Hold still assholes!"

Oblong beams of light flashed and flickered, glaring like spotlights through the compartment. Three soldiers had formed a complete blockade of the elevator, weapons drawn on Celeste and her pathetic knife, faces obscured by black masks.

She hesitated, whether out of fear or despondency, she couldn't know. Her muscles were stone, stiff and unyielding to movement. Her heart thrummed in mad rhythm. Her lungs shuddered with her final, icy breath.

The farthest of the three soldiers lowered his rifle as the others boomed their commands, his gaze lowering to his stock. Then his eyes darted between his comrades, grip tensing around his weapon. His next movements were a steady blur; he drove the stock of his rifle into the side of the first soldier's head with enough force to crumple the metal helmet like aluminum, then whipped the rifle like a baseball bat and struck the second soldier as he looked over at his slumping friend, shocked. The blunt force of the rifle stock broke some of his teeth when it hit him. His eyes glazed, and he collapsed against the floor with a grunt. The remaining guard allowed the rifle to dangle by his hip, propping the stock into the dirt as he tugged and loosened the mask around his face.

"Wait," Celeste barely breathed, sensing Snyder's tension. Her finger twitched over the trigger. Celeste recognized the soldier's freshly shaven face that was pink from the chill, and eyes that were sky-bright. It was the same boy from the sewers.

"Bink?" Celeste asked hesitantly.

"You," he replied, then cleared the phlegm from his throat. "I never thought I'd see you alive again."

Disbelief tangled her tongue. "I-I...I don't...Why?"

"Who the hell is this creep?" Harn demanded, huffing through his nose like an agitated boar. "And give me one good reason why I shouldn't paint the ground with your brains?"

"Well, he *did* just save our lives. Unless your train of thought has yet to catch up with the rest of the group." Snyder's contempt burned through each word.

"Go to hell."

"Anywhere with you *is* hell, big fella."

Bink suddenly spoke. "She's right. I did save your lives, but I didn't do it because I think highly of you all." His bright eyes almost dimmed. "I did so to return a favor—where is Melina?"

A bitter chill began creeping through her throat. "She's gone." There was a finality to those words; bitter ash along her tongue.

He was silent a moment longer. "I'm sorry," he said. "She was...something else."

She found herself responding with a slight smirk, then quickly blinked the away tears that stubbornly clung to her lashes.

"She gave me my life, I owed her everything," he went on, and his eyes narrowed at her troubled expression. "She saved me from dying in those sewers."

Clark scoffed. "Seems our beloved commander has made a habit of trying to kill us all."

Celeste buried her bitter response and the twisting feeling of her heart.

"Regardless," Bink said, "I owed her this much."

Harn growled his impatience. "This reunion tickles me pink an' all, but we need to get the *hell* out of here before they send more soldiers after our asses—few bullets, glorified knives. We're outgunned."

"It won't be soldiers you need to worry about," warned Bink, his face awash in an amber flicker. "Not with the alarms triggered. Those elevators are on lockdown—nothing goes up or down, unfortunately."

"Annie led us down here for a reason. No one escapes, remember?" Celeste grimaced at the thought.

"So, we're trapped inside a goddamn mountain."

"Not exactly." Bink stiffened as he turned from them, adjusting his rifle so the flashlight beamed and cut through the surrounding darkness. "But we will be if we don't get moving."

Clark grumbled, "How can we trust him?"

Celeste found herself smirking an oddly humorless smile.

"Faith," she simply said, and stepped into the darkness after Bink.

FIFTEEN

Hunt

THOUGH IT had only been minutes since she was forced to quicken her pace through the tunnels, her muscles burned with a white-hot intensity, and her skin as well, as if her blood boiled beneath. Her holstered pistol, taken from one of the unconscious soldiers, chafed her waist with each step, but could only be adjusted so it hung loosely from her hip bone. She was too skinny now. She cradled her wounded hand against her belly, but wave after wave of nauseating agony crashed against her with every jarring movement. The periphery of her vision blurred; she needed a distraction from the crushing pain.

"So," she said between gasps for air. She staggered, no longer capable of hiding her pronounced limp. She was slowing. "What is this place exactly?"

Bink huffed, flicking his flashlight and splaying a pale glow across the subterranean walls. The moss-furred rock was not the smooth and sculpted stone of the tower or sewer tunnels, but cragged and cracked with beetling ridges and stalactites that gleamed like icicles extending down from the narrow ceiling. It was a somber serpentine passage, littered with rocky debris and brittle twigs that crunched noisily under her feet. A puzzled glance revealed not twigs, but broken bones and crushed skulls partially buried into the gravel like a path to some macabre cemetery.

"Another feeding ground?" she asked. She stopped, breathless, with the warmth draining from her face. She brushed the chalky bone fragments from her scabbed toes. "We just escaped their dumping ground."

"Hellpit?" A sharp whistle undulated through the tunnel. "Hard to believe you all survived that. It used to be a condo for the wealthy, I'm told, a place away from civilization but with all the luxuries of, whatever that means. There was a fallout shelter built into the mountain, but these tunnels are now used for...well, let's just say it's nothing pleasant. We won't have to find out if we hurry."

"Real talk," Snyder said, clear and dangerous. "Why are you helping us escape?"

"For two weeks since being stationed here, I've seen countless horrors I thought was just shit talk from the others," he said, wiping the sheet of sweat from his brow. "Experiments, prisoners forced to slaughter each other for a chance to live as some creature. I didn't even want to be here. They gave me a position in *Paradise*, they called it, because of my bravery in the sewers. You all left me alive, but my team was dead. They thought I fought bravely."

Celeste stumbled, smothered by a wave of nausea.

"I turned it down," he continued, steadying rapid breaths. "At least until my...until Nellie went missing on a recon mission. An excursion to map the plains, her superiors said. Bullshit. No one is allowed in the Red Zone. Well, the report states that hours into the operation they were ambushed and taken by the surviving bandits. Red Dawn won't listen to any of their demands and have effectively sentenced their own soldiers to die."

"Well, I suppose chivalry hasn't died after all," Snyder mused. "You're going to defy the military's orders and search for her."

"This tower is in the Rocky Mountains—the Red Zone is its backyard." He cursed suddenly, pivoting and reeling as the passageway angled sinuously.

Harn grunted, clutching at his leg to brace against his colossal weight as he limped down the tunnel. "Makes sense the bandits are once more moving against the new general."

Uncle. A numbing shock spread through her mind, upheaving all her thoughts. *Wait a minute.*

She slowed her pace, casting a curious glance over her shoulder. Harn's face was pocketed by shadows, but she could feel the intensity of his glare as she flexed her grip around the machete handle.

"What do you mean *that makes sense?*" she asked slowly. "You son of a bitch. It was *you.* The asshole who sold me out on the mission. God*damnit,* I thought it was Stonem."

"Blackwell wanted you gone," Harn replied, insidiously hollow. "He gave the order and that was good enough for me. The casualties are of little importance. You should know that, Bandit Bitch."

"You infiltrated our unit," Nadie accused.

Harn snorted his contempt. "Joke Unit? Your band of misfits was intended to be the fleshy shield for our tented city while we rebuilt. Nothing more. It was all for show to string this little princess along."

Celeste clenched her jaw. Anger boiled in her belly like a sickness, burning her throat as she spoke. "What was the mission?"

"Don't act so naïve. The Disfigured and Blackwell had a cease-fire agreement until the bandits received the Queen Slayer alive, and only then would they aid his cause."

"Why would they care about Vega?"

"She was their leader," he growled, "practically worshipped the damn ground that bitch walked on. They wanted retribution, and Blackwell wanted a stain on his legacy wiped clean."

"Shit," breathed Celeste. "An army, maybe?"

But for what? To fight who?

"You were right," Snyder remarked. An icy-blue eye winked playfully in the shadows. "Someone was trying to have you killed."

"And I thought you were a piece of work, Commander," seethed Clark as he leaned against Nadie. "This guy deserved to be left in Hellpit."

Harn spat at him, "I followed orders like a true soldier. Like *you* should have done instead of cowering during your first mission!"

Clark blanched, lip trembling, and fell silent under Harn's menacing presence.

"Wise words coming from a double agent," Snyder remarked. "What should we do with this blue falcon, Commander?"

"Bullshit!" Harn bellowed. His grip tensed around the rifle. "You'll willingly follow a traitor, yet doubt me?"

"You tried to kill us," Nadie hissed through clenched teeth. "You—"

"I did what I had to, so I could survive!" His dark eyes were desperately wide. "Only one survivor, or do you not remember the goddamn rules! I wanted to live. As did all of you!"

"We worked together," said Snyder. "We got ourselves to you."

"You left me to die!"

"After you nearly killed my friends," Celeste coldly countered.

"I think it's time we get moving." Bink's voice was tight. The glow from his flashlight darted around the tunnel in nervous jerks and ticks.

"High and righteous, are we?" Harn's guffawing was as loud as a revving engine. "Fitting when it comes from a girl determined to blow up a city. Just how many people were you willing to sacrifice for your cause?"

"That was different—"

"It is not, and you know it!"

"Enough!"

The command stunned them to silence. Celeste stared down the dimly lit tunnel as the beam of light swept past her and chased shadows into the jagged crevices of the walls like a scattering of roaches. Then she heard it through the thundering of her own heart: a haunting sound that rang up the tunnel walls like the shrill of sirens. The screeching symphony intensified, rising in pitch, almost as if whatever foul creatures that were down the tunnel had already scented their blood.

Bink swore and his voice constricted to a tight squeak. "And *that* is why we need to go."

"They're releasing infected," Celeste barely breathed. "They'd risk spreading the sickness just for a few prisoners?"

"The tower and the mountains themselves are essentially impregnable." Bink had already left them in the icy clutches of darkness. He was whispering, but his voice was still a shrieking alarm in the confines of the tunnel. Celeste struggled to maintain a steady pace. "But beyond is the Red Zone. Everything is...well, dead or dying. The bandits are said to hold those lands and assault the military—so the military created a barricade of infected."

"Shit," said Snyder, huffing. "While they tinker with the sickness, they release the successful experiments into the Red Zone and render the lands a complete hazard."

"More than it already is, yeah, essentially."

"But why keep the Disfigured a secret?"

Harn's voice cracked when he spoke up again. "After defeating the Vega's army, no soldier from Red Dawn wanted to shake hands with a bandit. Blackwell wanted their cooperation, and they wanted your head. Nobody truly survived an encounter with them, they're like phantoms—" Celeste shuddered "—myths generated by the paranoid to explain the disappearances around camp."

Celeste huffed breathlessly. Exhaustion crept through her like a slow poison. Her pace slowed to a crawl.

Bink shrugged back at him. "That's what anyone with rank told us."

"But you knew better," Celeste said to Bink. "Because of me. I brought validation to the rumors with accusations against Blackwell. The germ of truth."

"It was enough to lead me here." Pale light swept across the moss-imbued walls as he adjusted his rifle. "The rest I found out once I stepped into this hellhole." He shot her a thoughtful look. "No pun intended, I suppose."

There was a scoff from Nadie as she raised her voice above Twist's toneless humming. "I still don't understand why they sent a unit into the Red Zone."

"Isn't it obvious?"

"It was for me," breathed Celeste. Her tongue dried to an old prune in her mouth. "Either to eliminate the leader or...negotiate a new deal."

"The pampered niece has all her problems dealt with...expense of others...rich..."

Their voices slipped beyond focus, fading to dull, wordless tones. Her sight was reduced to pinpoints of light. Movement sluggish and delayed. An odd sensation pressed against her shoulder, then a painful rap on her knee. It was a faint tingle through the creeping numbness in her body, but a lucid spark for her mind to latch to. *Wall.* Her thoughts reeled and sight whirled back into nauseating focus. Light scattered through the tunnel, flickering between the amorphous silhouettes of the others. She had fallen behind, slouched against the wall, heaving deep, ragged breaths like she couldn't suck up enough air to fill her lungs.

Behind you!

The viperous thought twisted her spine with a shiver. Vega's presence probed her thoughts and her heart lurched into overdrive.

She leapt from the wall, drawing her knife with a fumbling, awkward swing. The sultry scent of rot rolled over her as thick as smog, burning her nostrils and sticking to the back of her throat. She hacked her blade through the ripple of shadows, and a warm mist gingerly soaked between her fingers.

Blood.

A ferocious howl tore loose from some unholy throat. She wrenched her blade free from its shoulder with a sickening *crunch*, and again slashed madly at the unseen terror. Steel struck the cavern wall with a ringing clatter and burst of white sparks. A numbing shock thundered up the bones in her arm. But through the flashing sparks, she caught a glimpse of the malevolence: A small, attenuated figure, flesh a sludgy black and rotted, limbs bowed and jutted at inhuman angles. Its claws were gnarled over its palm like a pretzel as it mindlessly swung at her retreat. But its face was an echo of something entirely human. Its features were soft, cheeks pudgy, almost unblemished by the ravages of rotting black skin. Its eyes bright like a patch of blue sky, not the rapacious crimson glare of the infected husks she was accustomed to. It had a peculiarly childlike expression—but its mouth spiraled open below the cleft where its nose should have been, revealing rows of jutting, craggy teeth like the fearsome maw of a shark. Another shriek erupted from the monstrosity.

Hellhound.

She slashed at it, stumbling forward from her overreach. The creature twisted its small body and launched from the wall like it were spring-loaded.

Thwap-thwap-thwap-thwap! Lightning flashed through the tunnel, thunder pummeled and crushed the air from her chest. Bits and pieces of the creature's face burst into a fine black mist, spraying her with disgusting warmth. Its body sagged and fell into the gravel by her feet. Bowed limbs wriggled, crooked claws snipped through the loose stone by her feet like scissors through construction paper. Its remaining humanlike eye eerily rolled in its socket, and found her despondent gaze, and grew wide with what she perceived as pain. Knife raised for the killing strike, she hesitated—and its mouth split into another ear-splitting screech.

She heaved the blade through its neck, ripping through flesh and *snapping* its spine in half. Blood splattered and slopped around its limp form. It was finally dead.

But the screeching didn't stop, the discordance carried through the tunnels, rising in pitch and volume, howling like the winds of an impending storm.

"It's called for others!" Bink warned with a nervous chuckle, releading the spent mag.. Darkness rippled around the flickering flashlight. "We have to go now! The exit shouldn't be far ahead!"

"Everyone," Celeste muttered. "Move out—quickly!"

She reeled into a velvet fog.

Her burning muscles pumped with vigor she thought long exhausted. Darkness swirled across her vision like ink spilling across a page. Cold, brisk air whipped against her face. Her vision was hazy with blurry streaks of light. There was a cold, sharp pinch like the twist of a blade into her skin. She pushed away from the irritant, stumbling like the ground was pulled from beneath her feet. Blinded and nauseous, her heart dropped like an anvil into her gut.

"Commander!"

Her eyes snapped open to a blinding glare. Vision slowly adjusting, she caught swirling glimpses of the deep, sprawling valley. Long brown stalks poked out from the dust, charred and lifeless under a sweltering sun. The mountain air thinned and chilled, but soothed her burning chest. Her heart fluttered at the sight of steep cliff and descent of jagged rocks that protruded from the sheer wall of rock like spikes. Her toes curled around the edge—she'd nearly plummeted into the valley below.

Her ears rang with shrieking from the tunnels. She carefully retreated from the cliffs edge—until she was thrown from her feet with a force of a moving truck. Whatever it was had slammed into her, crushed her against the ground, and shocked her limbs to immobility. All she saw was a Tilt-A-Whirl of black and milky-white and the blur of slashing claws as she rolled across the gravel, a hair's breadth away from the cliff's edge. The peal of gunfire seemed like distant *pops* as the ground slipped out and spun beneath her. The air *whooshed* from her lungs on impact. Claws scythed through the rock by her feet, and another screech rang across the valley as one of hellhounds flailed its crooked limbs, and plummeted over the edge, cartwheeling down the cliffside. Darkness surged around her like black waves crashing up the shoreline. Gunfire erupted, muffling voices to a distant wordless whisper. Jagged teeth flashed for her flesh.

Pinned to the ground, she writhed madly, her throat and nose clogged with dirt and blood. Her blade flashed through the air in clumsy chops. Shadows danced in the dust, wolves circling each other over a kill. The next swing of her knife sank its blade into flesh, ripping muscle and chipping bone. She swung again, skidding the sharpened edge across the gravel. Another mad screech. Hot saliva showed her. The final strike crunched a portion of the hellhound's face, splitting the jaw from its skull. Carious teeth shattered. Blood drooled across her blade. Still, the hellhound pressed against her, slashing at her with its inverted claws. She heaved against it, snarling as it sputtered over her, and wrenched her blade through its misshapen skull. Black blood spurted like a geyser, and the hellhound went limp against her. She crawled forward, feet dangling over the edge of the slope. The cacophony of snarls and shrieks amplified, claws carved and grinded through dirt, eager to thrash her flesh. Someone forced her to her feet, plucking her from the dirt like a battered flower, one arm tucked securely around her waist. Her vision tilted but she regained her footing—the very moment another disjointed creature slammed into her with the force of a speeding truck.

They were all flung over the cliffside.

The back of her head impacted with the rocky slope, then she was hurled onto her stomach. She tumbled onward, colliding with rock and the flesh of another falling body, while her ears rang with the sputtering screech of a twisted hellhound. Its hammering blows hit her body in uneven swings, thumping against her ribs and the side of her head as she descended the cliff in a flailing cartwheel. She hit the ground, unable to draw a breath. Her limbs were aching and unresponsive. A flashing array of lights crossed her spinning vision. She groaned, forcing herself up on rickety limbs.

Everything hurt. Pain was the only pervasive thought in her mind. Her skin burned with abrasions that were gritty with dirt and rock. Her ratty clothes were torn and hanging loosely off her thin frame, but felt heavy as lead on her shoulders. Her phantom fingers flared with an unbearable hammering pain, and she had to clench her teeth tight to stifle the scream rising in her throat. Her balance wavered. Air gently pushed through to her reluctant lungs.

She heard an utterly human scream rise in pitch. Gathering her wits, she shook her head clear of a fog, and turned to find the half-rotted creature pummeling soft, pink skin to a bloody welt. The hellhound was a shadow of stringy flesh clinging to inhumanly twisted bone, and burning-red eyes. Someone curled below the creature, hugging his legs in the fetal position as death roared over him.

Clark!

She stalled, staring at his cowering form. Her heart skipped a beat between every lash that rained down on him from the hellhound. Seconds dragged by while her brain plotted escape.

No!

Celeste lunged at the bow-legged creature, slamming into it with the same force that had hurled them over the edge of the cliff. The creature fell off Clark, but clubbed her with its curled claws. She stumbled like a drunk into the desert-dry dirt. Adrenaline, and a spike of terror, fueled Clark's movements as he leapt over the hellhound and pinned it to the ground, hands wrenched around its twisting neck. Its doll-like face contorted. Its mouth spiraled open to a maw of fangs, widening over Clark's fleshy arms. It would taste his blood at any moment.

Celeste reacted with speed she did not know she possessed. In an instant, she flung herself beside them, both hands—*painfully*—gripped a jagged stone, and raised it far above her head—then brought it down with as much force as she could muster. The stone crushed the hellhound's small skull like a roach under her boot.

Clark recoiled from the oozing blood, collapsing into the ash with a loud sigh of relief. He was trembling, his breaths rapid, shaky, uneven. Dirt and blood caked his pocked face to a tan. He shook his head at Celeste as she pulled herself up from the corpse.

"You could have left me to die," he said, huffing after each word. "But you saved me."

"You saved me up there," she managed to say. "Twice, I presume."

He laughed. It was a strange sound considering all he had done before was moan and curse her presence. "You nearly leapt over the edge like a madwoman."

"I couldn't see."

"Open your goddamn eyes then."

A sloppy grin inched across her face. "I can see now." She straightened herself, stepping awkwardly to her feet. "I can also see that what I thought of you before was...a mistake."

"What do you mean?"

"I mean—"

Another inhuman screech cut down her words, forcing her to choke on them. She studied her newfound surroundings, finding hills that rolled into the jagged slant of rock they had tumbled down from the tunnel exit and the mountains that blocked out the sky. Downhill to that there was a sea of dead black trees poking out of the barren dirt like headless pikes. There was a path of cracked asphalt only a few paces to her right, winding alongside the cliff and up toward the tunnels. It was there the strange wails intensified to howling winds.

"Commander!" Snyder called out. Blonde hair whipped through the trees as she bolted down the asphalt road. "You're alive!"

"Move!" A deep rumbling sound shook the dirt beneath her feet like an earthquake, and she heard Harn bark more commands as he limped after Snyder, blindly firing his rifle behind him. Far to his left, Twist, the simple man, ambled through the trees. His spiky hair gleamed with greasy sweat. Nadie was beside him, carefully leading him away from the wild spray of Harn's rifle.

The ground kept rumbling.

She saw Humvees swerving down the road from the mountain, wheels chewing through dirt and crumbled asphalt, engines roaring like a pack of foul beasts.

"Run!" Celeste called out, hauling Clark to his feet. The movement unbalanced her, and she stumbled into an awkward sprint. But the first Humvee swerved by, tires squealing across the broken asphalt. The spinning wheels missed them by inches. She pulled Clark into the treeline, uncertain if the others would follow. The Humvees crashed through the dead trees like they were twigs, forcing her back to the road.

We're being corralled.

The Humvees—Celeste counted five—circled them like a pack of starving wolves. She searched the scattering of trees for any opening—but they were effectively trapped. The dead trees were too sparse and few between to mask their escape no matter which direction they bolted for.

Shit.

The Humvees rolled and sputtered to a stop, sunlight glinting off the tinted windows. Each vehicle was a motley of brown and black—just another streak of wasteland. She waited, hesitant, fingers on her good hand gently tapping the holstered pistol on her side. She had few bullets for so many soldiers.

One of the Humvee doors swung open.

"I'll be damned...just goddamned."

The words twisted from a caricature grin like some comic book villain. The man propped himself against the Humvee frame, gloved fingers drumming almost impatiently against the tinted windshield. His face was lean and angled sharply, pallid skin stretching thinly over his cheekbones like a corpse crisping from the day's heat. He raised his middle finger, directing the rude gesture over his shoulder.

"I bet them assholes, *there,* you whelps wouldn't make it through the tunnels!" His gritty voice rose to a gravely roar. "But the Bandit Bitch just *had* to survive, huh?"

Breathless, Celeste bit her tongue, swaying, as her vision slanted and danced with bright stars.

"Well," he went on, "I find myself almost admiring your tenacity! They yak and yak about how your family was made up of savages, wolves of the wild, but its goddamn great to see you in action." A small chuckle rumbled from his throat. "Those creatures should have ripped you to shreds. I tell 'em, I do, to let me and my boys deal with the prisoners." With his hand slowly drifting to the side, his narrow eyes flicked to her fingers resting against her holstered pistol. His maniac grin widened. "We can sort out the tough from the weak, piece by piece."

Before the pistol cleared from her waist, she was staring down the deathly glare of a revolver—a gleaming silver like her father's—hammer *snapping* back under his thumb. He had drawn his weapon quicker than the blink of her eye.

He gently shook his head. "*Tsk.* You mustn't give me any trouble. The man who believes himself in charge like he was General *freakin'* Blackwell, wants you alive—as *he* does. Give me any fuss and I'll shoot one of your pathetic friends."

"I can't go back," Clark whispered with a small, cracking voice. "They'll make us...one of those things."

Celeste gritted her teeth and held her tongue. "So," the man said, exaggerating his impatience with a sigh. "Are we ready to comply? No? Oh well—who should I blast first? The exotic one...the goddamn *traitor*...the blonde?"

Snyder glared as sharply as the revolver drawing aim on her head. "Try me, asshole."

"No," Celeste whispered, choking on a sob. The revolver's deadly gaze swept through the huddled group—

—black-red blood and pallid flesh exploded across the windshield and slopped over the hood of the Humvee. The man's jaw was gone, the remnants of his lower face raining blood and stringy shredded meat down his black uniform. Barely a moment later, a gunshot echoed through the dead trees, ringing loudly from a distance. The man convulsed backwards and slammed against the barren field, now motionless in a rising cloud of dust.

"Captain!" someone yelled from the inside of the man's

crimson-painted Humvee.

Zing!

The passenger-side window shattered in a flurry of broken glass and brain matter.

"Sniper!" one of the emerging soldiers yelled. "Get the g-*urg*!" His voice trailed into a gurgle as blood bubbled from the hole in his throat. He stared at Celeste in disbelief as he fell. She fired another two shots—but with her vision twisting and tilting, she missed the soldier approaching her, his rifle drawn to her and Clark.

Shadows streaked across her vision, closing in around the faceless man and his threatening weapon. Flashes erupted, and her ears rang from the thunder. The surging darkness roiled, roared, and devoured the man. Flecks of gold glowed with the thrill of its hunt.

Aurous?

The wolf snarled, fangs splashing with blood, jaws twisting the man's neck to fleshy pulp. Blood soaked into his shadowy fur, gleaming, drooling from the threatening curl of his lips. He stood over her, protecting a defenseless cub, a growl rumbling in his throat at the mechanical predators roaring into action. The soldiers were attempting to flee, like prey should, but the wolf's fur only bristled from excitement of the hunt.

Aurous!

"Oh, my boy," she choked out. A loving warmth swept through her. She felt like a corpse stirring to life, no longer cruelly bound by the chains of death. "Oh, how I've missed you!"

"Get up, ya fool!"

The strangled cry was a whisper beyond the peal of erupting gunfire. Another shadow flickered over her, but he wasn't a wolf, he wasn't pack; a pale face gleamed through the haze like a ghost, his scarred, gaunt features nearly skeletal, bald head prickling along his receding hairline. He even had patchy growths on his neck and cheeks in uneven swirls.

Stonem.

"Get up, Little Wolf," he croaked out as a growl, extending a hand to her. "Or are you prey?"

"Shut up," she muttered, and weakly shoved her pistol into his mid-section. "I should...kill you."

He snorted. "Condition you're in, you'd likely miss from an inch away. Get up, before these rats have a chance to coordinate!"

Hesitation kept her pistol to his liver as she slowly rose and staggered to her feet. She glimpsed movement. The closest Humvee had bullet holes peppered across the hood, smoke belching from the engine, and someone's jaw streaked across the windshield. Both tires were shot out of the next one, bodies littered around the open doors. The few soldiers who remained scrambled for cover from the sniper fire. A third Humvee was screaming to life as its windows shattered, the driver now missing a portion of his head. The Humvee lurched forward and rammed the fleeing soldiers, crashing through dead trees. The others drove back up the winding asphalt road to the mountain.

Stonem fired at their red taillights, bullets sparking against the Humvee, waving Celeste and her team to their feet.

"Get up, idiots! Get up!" he yelled, retreating through a cluster of lifeless trees. "Go to the east while we have cover fire!"

She staggered forward and sprinted after him, heart vaulting into her throat. Pain abandoned her pumping limbs, but she was breathless, exhausted—but nearly growling, moving soundlessly through the dirt beside Aurous, bewitched by the blood they scented in the stale air.

It must be.

Celeste and Aurous weaved through the windswept pine, bark charred to an ashy-black, jutting out at an angle like pikes. She was starved, her movements clumsy and sluggish, but Aurous was lean, swift, nipping at the air as if still tasting the fresh, salty-warm flow of blood. His gaze, glowing gold, found hers, and he yipped and snapped his teeth at the space between them as they escaped the volley of gunfire.

"Up here," Stonem told her, remaining a few paces ahead. She still had her gun drawn on him, and he eyed her like a cat eyeing a mouse hole as they ran.

But then she saw it; curling flames, the warming glow of a rising sun. She moved almost expertly through the trees, swiftly and silently as a wolf, and likely just as deadly now.

She's a survivor, Celeste thought, her heart threatening to beat its way out of her chest. *We always were.*

"Celeste!"

She was close enough to see the freckles on Melina's nose, the glimmer of her emerald eyes, her rosy lips that twisted with worry. She slung the large rifle over her shoulder, tugged at the strap, then swung her arms tight around Celeste when she approached her. Aurous pawed at their feet in excitement.

"I knew you were alive!"

Warmth spread through her, soothing every injury, every worry, quieting every ghost in her head with the melody of her voice.

"I'm sorry," Celeste whispered, falling into her embrace, too weak to move any farther. "I couldn't save you."

"Hush," the redhead purred, pulling her close. "I saved myself, don't you worry about that. I'm here, now."

Stonem huffed. "Hate to break the cute reunion, but we have to get the hell out of here."

Celeste jabbed the pistol into his heart. "I should *kill* you."

"No," Melina said. "I wouldn't have survived without him...though, he wouldn't have survived without me, either. We were coming to break you out. He thought he owed you that much."

Snyder sneered at him. "Blue falcon."

"Go to hell," Stonem rasped back. He nervously scanned the burnt-out landscape. "Take your opinion of me down there with you."

"Too tired," Twist muttered to no one, yawning and scratching his bloody shirt. "Too bored."

Nadie snorted. "*Some* of us should find shelter."

"Not going anywhere, all right?" Harn spat at her. "But you're free to try and make me."

"Commander?" Nadie started.

Celeste scoffed loudly. Her body vibrated with another crippling wave of nausea. "Not anymore."

Melina squeezed her waist, drawing her close and resting her freckled forehead against hers. Bright, glinting green warmed the bitter chill that had so long gripped her heart. The redhead leaned back, clearing her throat. "For now, we all fall back into the woods. We can find something beyond the military's reach. Everyone has wounds that need to be tended."

Even with Melina under her arm and Aurous whining with excitement as he dashed around them, she was chilled by the sullen expression Snyder wore, her eyes a piercing white-blue like icicles as the blonde straightened her posture and marched forward like the soldier she always was.

PART III.
HINTERLANDS (MID-AUTUMN)

SIXTEEN
Bay for Blood

THE FIRE crackled and spat with promised warmth. They reluctantly circled the small pit, trapping the heat in their tattered clothes, drying what was slick or soaking with blood, mud, and other foul and gut-wrenching substances. It wasn't much, there was no game to hunt, no food to be shared. Only a small fire and few bullets.

Celeste shivered. Even through the burning grip of heat, she was overcome with an uncontrollable tremble. Her face misted and paled with sweat. Melina had changed the bandages to her wound, noting the possible infection, and attempted to lance it clean with a red-hot strip of metal. Celeste had spent most of the night stifling a scream into Melina's sweater, soothed only by the redhead's lingering scent; a hint of wildflowers blooming in the springtime rain. With her wounds now bandaged again, she offered to take first watch—they all declined rest, for now, despite the desperate need. She understood. After what they had just endured, the nightmares would torment through sleep.

"So, how did you survive?" Snyder asked, avoiding Celeste's gaze over the dull flicker of fire. Withdrawn and irascible once more, the blonde said little, and obeyed any given command with a sullen demeanor. Once again, just another soldier.

Melina cleared her throat, almost reluctant to share. "It was like hitting pavement, really, I think I was out for at least a few minutes."

"Ten, I reckon," Stonem muttered. "I was awake the whole damn time."

"Five," her redhead corrected, a small grin tugging at her rosy lips. "It was an ocean down there. Garbage, filth, corpses, creepy crawlies, you name it. That wasn't all, there was something else as well. I heard it *snapping* its jaws—and it wasn't you, was it boy?" she trailed off, scratching Aurous behind his perked ears, giggling slightly. Celeste thought there was no melody quite as beautiful.

"Bloody hell," Stonem rasped. "This is no campfire tale. The goddamn beast was in that swampy shit with us. Managed to kill it *while* holding off your damn crazy mutt."

"Being modest?" Melina chirped. "He dragged me up from drowning in the filth, held Aurous off, and got us away from the half-dead hunter. Once I was able to calm Aurous, Stonem killed it. We heard gunshots, but there was nothing we could do. And quite honestly, we were waiting for the entire sewer to collapse once you blew the bomb. But it never did. So, we swam through the filth until we found a passage that wasn't flooded."

Snyder smirked at her, turning her piercing glare on each of them at the fire.

"I can't be the only one to think it," she muttered with cold certainty. "He's probably still feeding our location to the military."

Melina's smile only deepened, and Celeste felt her heart flutter at the lovely crooked curves of her face. Stonem only rasped out a gritty laugh, rolling his knuckles into his palm until the joints *popped* loudly.

"Ship has sailed, sweetie, I promise." He tore the collar to his scratchy wool coat and revealed a jutting collar bone. A zigzag shaped gash had scabbed in dark, purpling welts along his shoulder. "Recent surgery, no anesthetic. Just some heated metal. The goddamn top to a can 'o beans, sharpened razor-thin, and balls as big as boulders."

"How did you know we were at Hellpit?"

Stonem shrugged. "Truth be told, it was only a guess. I managed to sneak back into the city, heard a few rumors. The Little Wolf's uncle, the new general, has tightened security at every checkpoint. Whatever you did to 'em, you scared 'em. We heard of the wolf running a knife through Blackwell's throat. Some say she even drank the blood as it flowed from the wound...like a wolf. Okay, ha! I may have given life to that one...I wouldn't have lost two fingers, though!"

Harn scoffed loudly, then only muttered under the silence, "Cocky prick."

"Watch yourself," Stonem growled back.

Nadie spat into the dying fire. "You're the one that betrayed us, don't forget. You shouldn't be here." Her gaze flicked from him to Harn. "*You* shouldn't be here."

"I thought we moved past that, girlie," Harn huffed, nursing an empty rifle in his grip like a wooden club. After weeks of starvation, even his face appeared gaunt. His braided beard greyed and frazzled, eyes sunken, his skin saggy and loose as his body ate away the muscle in desperation. He was still big, but not as threatening as he once was.

None of them were.

Celeste's clothes barely clung to her skeletal body. Melina had given her a jacket, which smelled sweetly of her, and Celeste had wrapped herself in its treasured warmth. It was all she had over her underwear. Still, the cold clawed through her, and it was more than the biting wind of night; she was haunted by the deathly ambience, the shadows that stalked the desolation, the bleeding silence. She felt like prey, hunted and fearful at every turn and every dancing shadow.

Stonem growled again, "Last time I ever save you mangy whelps."

"Piss off," Snyder snorted, curling her arms around her knees. "You were handing us over to them."

"We *all* would have died if you trusted Little Wolf!"

"Enough," Celeste commanded, with more strength than intended. Her voice boomed over the crackle of rising flames. She whispered, "What's done is done."

"Commander," Clark said, sounding oddly formal. "With all due respect—"

Celeste cut in with a tone as cold as the bitter mountain winds. "I'm *not* your commander. I'm not a commander anymore."

He frowned at her, his face swollen-black and crusted with his own blood, but Nadie gave him a subtle nudge with her leg and pressed her thigh tightly against his. He retreated into silence, and withdrew his gaze to the winding flames.

"You are the commander," Melina whispered lovingly.

Celeste broke the embrace, the chill of nightfall cleaving them further apart. A sharp ache pounded fiercely behind her eyes, and she was sick of forcing them open. She needed sleep, to hell with the nightmares.

I'm not listening to this nonsense anymore.

"Yes, you are," Stonem said slowly. "If you decided to kill me right this moment...I'd still respect you as my commander. I owe you that much, and more. I was never one for such shit, apologies or whatever. We're your soldiers."

"Speak for yourself," Harn grunted.

"You got us out of Hellpit," said Nadie. "You fought back even after we all gave up."

Celeste hissed through her grinding teeth, "It was just blind luck and bullets."

"Blind luck that saved our asses."

"I endangered everyone."

"Look," Snyder interrupted, arms crossed over her exposed chest. "We'll head out before the sun rises, cover as much ground as we can while it's warm. Scavenge for food—we may need to outrun the military again. We need to be prepared." Icy blue eyes cut through their puzzled glances. "Well," she muttered. "If the *shadow spawn* doesn't want to play commander, I will."

Those words hung heavy between them, each syllable like a knife twisting into her heart over and over. Celeste turned from them all, pride stinging, and ambled from the fire to find a quiet place to rest.

To hell with you all.

Those crimson curls were like the touch of silk against her thighs, raising bumps along her damp, scarred skin. Warmth tingled and rushed through her in waves, and she shivered, biting her lip to stifle a sudden gasp. "Stop," she whispered breathlessly, fingers twisted into the collar of Melina's sweater. But she didn't; the redhead gripped her inner thigh, squeezing playfully. Celeste's heart nearly burst at the sight of those crimson curls.

Better get it while you can. The disembodied voice rang out, seemingly from everywhere, every lingering shadow, every burnt-out hollow. The unmistakable sound of the dead. *You don't have much longer.*

What? She muffled a small moan into the sweater.

You heard me, whispered Vega. Celeste couldn't see her, but she *felt* those dark, dead eyes scrutinizing every detail of her battered condition. *You're dying, child.*

Jesus Christ. She bit her lip again, this time drawing blood. *You're not real, get the hell out of my head.*

As real as your own mother, the woman purred. *Like you were as real as my own daughter. Me and you. An unbreakable bond.*

You're as psychotic in my subconscious as you were in life.

She laughed, a sound resembling a hissing snake. *How do you plan to lead a fractured army, my careless daughter?*

Snyder can lead them.

A snort of contempt from her, scolding the stubborn response of a child. *A fighter, but arrogant.*

She's...ready.

Is that what you honestly believe? Vega purred. *Or perhaps that is your ailment...lovesick for another? Is that who you see with your eyes shut?*

Can you just die already?

I'll die when you die, Vega purred from every shadow. *And you're dying quickly.*

"Go...away..." she muttered back.

"Celeste!"

Her eyes peeled open, and she was suddenly painfully aware of the chill sweeping through the wasteland. Her heart thrashed in her chest, face flushed hot, her muscles tensed, locked, loaded.

Am I dying?

"Celeste?"

Celeste nodded. "I-I'm okay."

Melina pressed her fingers along her brow, gasping slightly. "Rising in temperature. Here I thought you felt better since the lancing. We need antibiotics, but those are harder to find than bullets."

"I've never come across any." Celeste tugged the jacket around herself. "Doubt we will out here."

"Probably not."

Celeste sighed. "I've got a plan—"

"Why did you say her name?"

"I don't remember—"

"Don't play dumb with me."

The silence strangled her, the words falling like daggers from her tongue. "She kissed me, I suppose, back in the prison. But it was just that and nothing more—"

"I see." The emerald of her eyes dulled slightly. "But you

thought I was dead, right?"

"Yes."

Melina smoothed her scratchy sweater, cleared her throat. "Get some rest, okay?"

"Wait—"

"I'm not mad." But her light voice bled disappointment; her gaze was hidden under her curling red rings. "I just want you to get better. You need more rest than anyone...this nurse has other patients as well. Sleep tight, my love."

Aurous whined as Melina rose to her feet and swept past them without scratching his ears, his tawny eyes glimmering, watching with worry. Celeste sat up, reached out to tug at his fur, and the wolf pawed her hand and lightly nipped at her fingers. She ran her fingers through his thick black fur, then gently brushed against the swelling near the base of her neck and flinched from a jolting pain.

She wept until her tears ran dry.

The hours dragged by in suffocating silence.

She had remained alone in the shadows, near a burnt-out hollow far from the fire's captivating dance with the crushing presence of darkness. Sweat had soaked through the coat around her shoulders until every breeze that rolled through the wasteland was like ice needling her scarred skin. Despite her exhaustion, every muscle was wound tight and rigid as if she prepared to give chase to prey at any given moment. Aurous was similarly tense by her side. His curly-black fur bristled, and his crimson-stained teeth flashed menacingly from the shadows.

She had to plan their next move, she knew, but lucidity slipped from her mental grasp as if she were intoxicated. Her thoughts were smothered by a carousel of ghostly voices she could neither distinguish nor discern meaning from, each beckoning her or screaming endlessly through her mind. It felt like someone was splitting her skull with a hammer, all the while yelling slurred words in her ears as loud as a foghorn. She swore she felt her severed fingers twitch, somewhere far below in the depths of sewers...

Her uneven breaths hissed steam into the cold and stale wasteland air. She had stared at the fire until it burned the logs to charred stubs, not even realizing time passed in quick lurches. Chills snapped her spine straight, and her eyes barely focused on the dim glow of embers beyond the thicket of denuded black trees. The crooked limbs flexed and extended like outstretched claws from some corrupted being. She paused as her ringing ears caught the delicate sound of her redhead's breathing, like a soft breeze rustling leaves in the forest. Celeste knew she wasn't far, but it felt as if there were a dark and impassable chasm between them. With a drawn-out sigh, fingers locked with the wolf's coarse fur, she rolled into the fierce ache in her hip and pushed to her feet. Joints *popped* and *creaked* in painful protest, and she gasped out breathlessly, not wanting to wake Melina. Aurous whined but stood rigid beneath her wavering balance. The wolf held his strength, belly round and teeth stained with flesh of his last kill. She shuddered at the thought of it being human, but then recalled the spine-twisting terrors of Hellpit.

To hell with them.

"Aurous," she whispered, her voice cracking from her desert-dry throat. "Go to Melina and keep her warm."

Only his tawny eyes shone brightly back at her through the gloom of the wasteland, wandering over her battered state with what she almost perceived as worry. A foolish thought, she mused silently, then nudged him with her foot. He nipped at her fingers gingerly as he shambled past her, and she stood there until she heard a deep sigh of contentment as he settled into the dirt against her redhead. Her lips twitched, almost smiling. He would watch over her and keep her safe.

The rift she had sensed in her former team only deepened with nightfall. Most had chosen to forgo the warmth and comfort of the fire to be as far from the other as possible, while still remaining in sight of them. She couldn't see them, but heard their breaths, their tossing in the dirt as horror stalked them into sleep. She noted their positions, nearly stumbling over the giant hams Twist called fists as he sprawled in the dirt and snorted so loudly she thought for a moment thunder rumbled overhead.

Damn.

Chills had plagued her for over an hour, but the moment she pulled herself to the dying fire, sweat beaded along her brows and splashed her cheeks. She blinked, wiping her face and smearing ash across her scars. It was already entirely too hot.

"You look like you've seen better days."

She stared across the crackling embers to the silhouette beyond its faint glow. Ice crept up her throat. Phantoms must have slipped through the cracks in her sanity, materializing from the shadows to haunt her through every waking moment.

"Vega..." she whispered breathlessly, nearly choking on the name.

"Commander?"

The voice crackled with worry. The shadow peered over a tiny flame that stubbornly clung to life on a charred log. A scream clawed up her throat—until she recognized the features of the shadow through the faint flicker. Purple welts dotted his skin like boils, eyes nearly swollen shut and as dark as the night around them, blood dried to cracked, crusted scabs. Clark limped over to the last flame that twisted through the ashy remains of the log, tossed another bundle of charred sticks and dead pine, and gave the fire one last breathless wheeze. Flame greedily devoured the tinder and blasted her clammy skin with more warmth.

"It's still my watch," Clark said, then clutched at his ribs. His chest heaved heavily, as if he had trouble drawing a proper breath.

"You need rest," he finished. He cleared his throat and collected his assortment of torn clothing from the edge of the firepit. There were more welts and gashes across his shoulders and chest, his rib bones distorted and swollen. Though, she noted, he did not appear battered and broken—only someone who did not back down from the fight.

Celeste grumbled back, "Speak for yourself."

He chuckled quietly, and she suddenly couldn't recall if she had ever heard him laugh before Hellpit. She was almost certain she had.

"Okay," she whispered, her gaze drawn to the rising column of flame. The heat was suffocating, but welcoming. "I need plenty. I could sleep for a damn week."

She heard him scoff, but still couldn't meet his eyes.

"We're alive, at least," he finally said. "Thanks to you."

It was her turn to scoff with disbelief. "I put us there in the first place."

"Yeah...doing what was right."

She dared meet his gaze through the rippling wall of smoke, breathless from the cold indifference in his eyes. Something had changed. Even bruised and bloody, he held himself proper, almost emulating Snyder's rigid posture. His face, beaten and mashed to a pulp, betrayed no hint of fear or emotion as he sat across from her, spine held straight, and hands balled into fists across his lap. He sat there, not as a friend or acquaintance, but a soldier under her command awaiting his next orders.

Now he held the appearance of a true military brat.

"You were taking down a tyrant," he said, "a madman no one had the balls to stand up to. We all thought we were fighting to make this world a better place...but after everything I've seen in Hellpit and whatever the hell those things were in the tunnels..." He shuddered violently, drawing closer to the fire. "They're goddamn evil."

A sob was caught in her throat. "I'm evil," she croaked through gritted teeth. "I've done so many terrible things and I am sick of feeling like a monster."

She felt his stare burn hotter than the pressing heat of the fire. Each passing moment was an eternal torment until her blood ran cold and her gaze slowly met his.

"I'm sorry," she whispered, though the words felt as ashen across her tongue as the dirt at her feet. Had her decisions, so justifiable to her in those chaotic moments, poisoned her with regret? Was she truly so abhorrent and capable of sacrificing one life over her own?

"Yeah." He cleared his throat again, flecking his lip with blood. "What you had planned for me was terrible."

"I shouldn't have—"

"I was an idiot, it's true," he admitted with a sigh that whistled and wheezed from his bruised throat. "I had never shot a gun outside of target practice."

He nudged one of the split logs with his foot, and the embers flared and whipped with the newfound breeze. The firelight chased eerie shadows across his ruptured and swollen features. Her tongue faltered, feeling more like a slab of ice in her mouth than a means of communication. He shook his head, then winced as he grinned madly and distorted the bruise on his cheekbone.

"I always put up this goddamn front like I knew what I was doing. Maybe it was the soldiers I was around, you know? They took me in, let me live, trained me...but training is vastly different than real combat. I saw them go on mission after mission without batting an eye, even when their comrades and friends died. They just continued fighting.

"We believed we were fighting for a cause," he went on, "something righteous, a way to fix the world. I just wanted to be a goddamn soldier. But the moment shit hit the fan, I was broken." His eyes, hard and cold as steel, found hers again with a fierce intensity. "Even in the sewers, where you brought me to die, I was broken with fear."

"I'm sorry," was all she could whisper.

His voice rose over hers. "But something changed that night in the sewers. I watched you, battered and beaten, broken beyond all hope, and you still fought like a ravaged wolf avoiding captivity. You attempted an escape you knew was foolhardy and impossible, and saved one of your friends when it came down to it. We should have all died or turned to one of those monstrosities in those cells...they forced us to turn on each other, to kill for a chance at a fate worse than death...but *you* forced us to work together, to place trust in one another so we could all escape. And we *did* escape."

"But..."

"You did that." His voice rose with the twisting flames. "*You.* And that is what I want to be, Commander. I want to be a fighter."

No, you don't...

"Look," he said, lips drooling bloody saliva. "You made me into something I could have never been with the military. You made me human." His eyes, though cold and frosty like Snyder's sneer, shimmered as he gazed into hers. "The bad does not diminish any good you've done. You may not have my friendship, Commander, but you have my respect."

"The good doesn't diminish the bad, either."

"Hm." Clark stood. "Maybe the world isn't black and white. Only shades of ugly grey."

The chill ate at her bones long before the fire succumbed to its hunger and faded to a dull glow beneath the ash. Long before Clark had staggered from the barren pit with a curt nod of respect she still felt she would never deserve.

She sat and tentatively watched the darkness, weeping silently into the remnants of her redhead's coat.

It still smelled of wildflowers.

The salty-hot scent of death bewitched her senses.

Her nose twitched, snout rising high into the moonlit forest, searching the vibrations in the air....

A faint snap echoed through the trees, soft as the wind's breath—but as loud to her ears as hooves stampeding across the forest floor. Her ears perked toward the strange sound that crashed through the trees, every misplaced step another beacon for her hunger to pursue. Claws raked through the dirt, fur bristled, muscles wound tight, bewitched by the swirling scents of fear, blood, meat.

She exploded forth through the trees in pursuit of scented death.

Paws sunk into the soil with the broken branches and splintered bark, muffling the sound of her swift approach through the trees that stood tall even in death. They scented not of meat, however, and held no interest for her beyond a fleeting peculiarity. Winding along the trail of decay, she heard the other; it crashed through the forest with the sound of grey skies that would gather above and howl back at her during long and restless nights. Those times she would dread; but this other made her blood run hot with rage, forcing her fangs to flash with a menacing snarl.

My kill! she growled at it.

But the other was impetuous, matching her pace through the winding trail. It wailed and screamed its fury, eyes a bloody streak through the dark. The thrill of the hunt was lost on her; the scent was not meat to eat, it was tainted and foul with rot. It was meat to be killed lest it corrupt the ever-giving land.

She leapt at the other.

The cold snapped at her clammy skin like fangs, twisting her spine straight. She was slouched near the cold firepit, having craved the fading warmth as sleep dragged her mind into the depths of a darkness she couldn't escape. She shuddered, eyelids furiously batting away the sticky mess of sleep.

Darkness waned, stars faded and smudged. A crimson glow spilled across the skies like a fresh flow of blood. Shadows slithered and slunk between the dead trees like silhouettes of claws and fangs from ravenous, stalking beasts. She blinked and focused her sight. Morning had crept over the black hills to the east, illuminating their feeble attempts at a camp without proper supplies or amity. Her vision spotted and danced like static. Amorphous shadows took shape. She recognized the silky brown hair Nadie twisted into a simple braid, shimmering in the vibrant hues of morning light. Curled up against her chest like a kitten was Clark, his bruises and contusions darkening his features with the shadows around him. She could hear the crackling wheeze of his shallow and unsteady breaths. A few yards away was Twist, even bigger than Nadie and Clark huddled tightly together. His snoring was still thunder that crashed through the skies with each loud snore, snort, and smack of his lips. Her gaze wandered through the maze of crooked black trees. Snyder sat with her back flat against the base of a burnt hollow, hands folded neatly over the rifle in her lap. She almost appeared at-attention—but her chin was tucked against her chest, head slightly cocked to the side. She dozed. Harn was slumped in an awkward position that favored his shredded leg; his face was a contortion of agony, but she felt little sympathy for the blue falcon.

Blue falcons, she corrected, rolling her eyes over the ragged Stonem, who had sprawled out closest to the dying fire. She swore she could smell his stink over the rest of her old team—combined. A creek or even a puddle of scum would suffice to clean the scent of rot from his pocked skin—or drown him in.

She smirked at that thought.

Something gripped her chest tight as her severed digits pulsed with another wave of crippling pain. Her stomach curdled and turned, emptied of all but its own acidic brew, which scorched its way up her throat. She spewed the foul foam into the dirt, smothering the sound with a coughing fit. Each breath burned her throat. The ashen air was thick like smog, grating her lungs with each unsteady breath.

No one appeared to take notice. They had succumbed to their exhaustion, as unmoving in the abating darkness as rotting corpses. They almost were. Her eyes wandered and searched for her redhead; pawprint impressions meandered through the trees and trailed off over the distant hills of black ash.

Aurous has gone hunting. Her belly groaned and twisted, dulling the stabbing pain in her severed fingers. *Hope he has more luck than us...*

A sudden chill pinpricked her exposed skin. A shadow was missing from the burnt-out land. Her heart hammered furiously beneath her ribs. She stared at the barren ash beneath the familiar crook of a dead tree.

There was no one. Melina was gone.

Calm down, was the only thought she focused on. Dread pooled in her guts. Her limbs felt full of cement as she crept through the trees with the grace of wounded prey. The soft soil broke her stride, and she crashed into the hollow where sleep had eluded her hours before. She paused, breathless. She carefully scanned the shadowed paths between the trees for any other careless footprints, silently cursing her doubled vision.

"Melina?" she whispered into the dead woods, almost fearing another trip down the rabbit hole. *Am I going crazy or is she really gone?*

Did she follow Aurous? Do I wake the others?

Vega?

Silence. Unease gnawed her nerves for every second that dragged by without sight of those fiery curls. She slowly drew the long blade from her belt in an awkward, fumbling grip. It was uncharacteristically heavy and unbalanced, an oblong stone in her hand, but the weight brought on the thrill of the hunt. She could almost taste the blood, breathe deep the coppery-hot scent as it spilled at her feet, feel the tingling warmth as it slicked her fingers scarlet.

She would hunt for her redhead.

The moment she shifted balance to leap through the trees after Melina, she heard it; a soft voice crackling with fear, a shaky whisper from the darkness. A sound that made her skin crawl with more chills, but her blood run hot with fury.

"C-Celeste…"

Snarling, Celeste stalked the shadows between burnt trees. Another delicate whisper echoed with the wild thrum of her heart.

"Celeste—ugh—listen!" Melina's soft whisper was now bursting with panic, and Celeste effortlessly trailed the rise in pitch.

The hunt began.

"Run!"

Melina's sharply pitched scream carried through the trees like the howling dead from Hellpit prison. Celeste launched like a bullet fired from the chamber, a growl rising from her throat as a blood-lusting roar. Brittle branches and charred bits of bark *snapped, crunched* loudly from her reckless charge through the thicket, but she focused her failing sight and fury on the form taking shape from the shadows. She caught a glimpse of those curls, the flicker of fire in the distance—

"Stop or the bitch is dead!"

—she stumbled to a halt, but momentum nearly heaved her into the clawed embrace of a dead hollow. The blade in her grip was heavier than before, almost unbearably so. She glared at her prey. It wasn't the monster she had expected, just a man in black, with only his pale, fear-stricken face exposed from the bulky attire. His ever-bulging eyes darted every direction until she was certain he was having a seizure. His thin lips quivered and gaped, as if on the cusp of speaking but unable to form the words—his chin sank into those bouncing red curls. Prone against a tree to support his stance, he held Melina between them like a shield, her throat gripped tight in the crook of his arm. Melina clawed at his grip as if she fought for air, her rosy lips a deeper red than Celeste recalled. Blood trickled from the corners of her mouth. None of that had forced Celeste to a halt, however. What had was the muzzle of a gun pressed into the redhead's temple, and the finger that trembled over the trigger.

"Don't you dare m-move," the soldier mumbled, clearing his throat with a nervous grunt. "I-I'll blow her pretty brains all over the dirt."

"You have my attention," Celeste snarled through clenched teeth.

"What the hell is going on?"

Clark stumbled through the trees, and she heard other hushed tones through the trees.

"Stop!" the soldier yelled. "I'll shoot, I-I swear!"

"Commander!"

"I'm going to shoot!"

"Everyone, halt!"

Celeste's voice thundered over the growing silence, until all she could hear was the wild drumming of her own heart. The soldier trembled, his prey-like gaze darting from her, to the direction of her old teammates, to the shadows of the trees, and back to her again.

"I said you had my attention," Celeste growled. "I know that's what you wanted—or else you wouldn't have kept her alive. Speak."

"I don't want sh-shit," the man muttered back. He gulped nervously, teeth clenched to stop the clattering, and eyes squeezed shut. "Boss! I got her!"

She heard the *slop* of dirt from a heavy stomp, the *snapping* of branches and charred splinters. Shadows slithered and scurried around the strange form that shambled through the trees like a man on the cusp of death. The shadow was another black uniform, slick with a cascade of blood that sloshed into the dirt. Desiccated skin stretched taut over the protruding facial bones, a disturbing shade of milky grey. It was the man who bore a striking resemblance to a corpse—increasingly so, now.

His oddly grey skin was shredded to meaty ribbons from his cheeks down to his throat. Twisting streams of black ran through the splits in his flesh. He broke his shuffling stride and braced against a dead hollow, adjacent to the soldier with a pistol still snug against Melina's temple. She heard the redhead's fearful whimper, saw her bright green eyes bulge as she recognized the monstrosity before her.

Where his jaw should have been, in the shredded mess of meat that clung to exposed bone, was a strange black protrusion that writhed like two worms in the mud. Blood spritzed and squirted like a severed vein. The protrusion hung from the ribboning flesh, almost like lips—

—it *was* a mouth, slowly widening to a maw of gnarled teeth. A groan gurgled in the back of his throat. Teeth *snapped* shut, grinding loudly like nails down a chalkboard. She swore she saw his malformed lips curl into a vicious grin.

"*You're difficult to track.*"

She nearly choked on the cold lump forming in her throat. "W-what the hell are you?"

"*Pride,*" he crudely hissed with an unhuman snout.

She stared at the rambling, upright corpse, the man who had had his face blown to fleshy bits by a sniper shot, the man who resembled a man no longer. Blood ran in deep crimson spirals down his arm as his fingers raked through the remaining skin on his face, peeling flesh and meat off like clumps of soggy napkins. *Slop-slop-slop.* Whatever unholy being that was hidden beneath now clawed its way to the surface.

Black, rippled skin tore from loose flesh, and his human body sagged around his feet like an old Halloween costume. He fell forward on spindly limbs like a wild beast, and a wolfish snout *snapping* fervently. His attenuated extremities were hooked with dozens of jointed segments until they bowed like spider's legs. His body was disproportioned and bulbous, resembling a corpse bloating in the river. Tattered skin exposed the mesh of twisting bone in its chest, like coiled barbwire. His face was another horror; the snout was wolfish and long, with powerful jaws and fearsome twisting fangs. His eyes were a glaring azure, not the haunting crimson glow of the dead she was accustomed to.

Her belly twisted from the unbearable stench of rot.

"*You're coming home to your family. I'll kill all who stand in my way.*" he hissed at her, his eerily human eyes rolling to meet her stunned gaze. "*It's time to come back to the Brood.*"

SEVENTEEN
Creature Feature

HIS CRIMSON tongue slithered across fangs, drizzling blood from his snout. Old flesh slopped from his twisting face where the bullet had torn through portions of his skull, but humanlike eyes stared right through her.

She heard the startled gasps and disgusted whispers of her former team behind her, the rage-inducing sound of Melina's fear as the soldier jammed the gun into her red curls—but she couldn't turn away from the unimaginable horror. He regarded her with thought, a vast difference to the traits of infected creeps, hellhounds or any hunter she'd previously faced.

Kill her, came the haunting memory of Colbat's final words after his transformation.

The knife trembled in her hand.

"There are six or seven in the back, boss," the soldier stated with newfound nerve. "Some have visible weapons."

The monstrosity twisted his lips and curled them in what might be considered a smile or predacious intent. Celeste refused to even blink.

"*She surrenders quietly, or the girl dies,*" Pride hissed. "*Do we have a deal, Sister?*"

"Commander—"

"I am not like you," Celeste whispered. "I am not a monster."

A furious, screeching howl erupted from Pride as he hunched forward and raked his claws through the dirt. The stench rot warmed the air between them.

"*Choose wisely.*" His snaking tongue lathered its lips. "*Doctor will be pleased to have you back.*"

"Mengele can go to hell!" she yelled fiercely, with more fury than she felt. "And you can, too!"

Come on...where are you?

She clenched her teeth tight. "Release her, and I'll go quietly."

"This isn't a negotiation!" the soldier spat at her.

"*Shut up, fool,*" Pride hissed eagerly, shifting balance on crooked limbs. "*I'll kill them all and bring you in if that's what it takes. You have no other options.*"

"I see why they call you Pride."

Damn...

He *snapped* his jaws at her, misting her with rancid drool. "*You have sealed the fate of your friends.*"

Her blood ran hot as it always had in those rapid moments before a furious battle. She saw as much as *sensed* Pride's muscles wind tight like a predator that stalked its prey. His cracked lips curled and opened a twisting maw of fangs—

—she caught the glint of gold, as bright of a sight to her eyes as the sun shining through the gloom of the dead valley. The glow swam through the shadows.

Melina choked on another sob as the soldier shoved the gun into her tangled mess of red curls—

The wolf ripped around the tree with a wild snapping of fangs. Aurous growled gutturally as blood soaked his snout with a burst of crimson—then came a throat-shredding scream from the soldier, an unsettling pitch of pain and utter confusion. His calf was nearly torn through to the bone, grinding noisily between the wolf's fangs. When it registered to the soldier to react, he moved the gun from Melina's head and shoved it into the wolf's blood-drenched snout, stumbling from his rigid pose against the tree.

It was the opening she had hoped for.

Behind her came the loud *clap* of thunder. Someone, she guessed Stonem, had discharged the high-powered rifle. A red splotch soaked through the fabric around the soldier's arm, and the grip around his pistol faltered. Another bellow tore his throat ragged—Melina's elbow swiftly connected with his chin, his scream ending in a gurgle and a grunt. He slumped behind her, and she broke free from his hold.

Pride only glared at her, a wretched grin warping his horrific features like a reflection from a funhouse mirror.

"I'll kill her myself!"

The wolf's fur bristled as chills pricked her skin. Pride whipped his hooked claws like blades, and the wolf abandoned the soldier's shredded calf. Celeste leapt at the rotting monstrosity, and Aurous snapped his fangs around Melina's wrist, yanking the her into the barren dirt with him. The burnt hollow splintered under the force of Pride's strike.

With fury pulsing in her veins, Celeste reached Pride before the monster could sink his claws into their retreating backs. She threw herself into a vicious swing from her blade.

Pride's terrifying roar rattled her ears as those claws blurred to stall her strike. His drooping body spun, snout widening like a crocodile's jaws over her blade arm. The wolf struck first; his fangs sank into the creature's chest and *crunched* the knot of exposed bone. Celeste retreated, yelling for Aurous—

—her voice was smothered by another blast of a rifle, ringing her ears like a bell. The bullet punched through Pride's corkscrewed neck, but the horror only *snapped* terrifying jaws at them.

"Commander!"

But she was already leaping bounds across the loose dirt, past the writhing form of Pride as he suffered another discharge from Stonem's rifle. She heard the monster shriek, the *slash* of claws, the blasts ripping through the sky. Pride's gaze rolled with her movements, studying her, muscles flexed tight through the rot of his body. Pride gleefully tore his claws from to dirt to squash such an insolent insect as herself.

She dove under the strike, but felt those menacing claws *ripping* through the air. It was an ungraceful tumble through the dirt, but she desperately bucked her legs to kick up a cloud of dust between them.

"Melina!"

THUD!

The ground shuddered, chunks of dirt whipped against her face. Pride's claws punched through the ground by her torso, nearly ripping through her hip.

There was a tight grip around the tattering collar of her jacket, and she was suddenly hauled to her feet, unbalanced. She leaned into a comforting embrace, gathered her wits, inhaled the sharp scent of wildflowers...

"Celeste!"

She blinked, opening her eyes to a spreading fire. Melina's red curls bounced gently against her clammy-white skin. She braced her weight, and they hobbled away from the shrieking terror. A glance thrown over her shoulder revealed the true horror of Pride; his limbs flicked forward and scurried like a half-stomped spider through the trees, his body flapping about behind like a plastic bag in the wind. He wailed and moaned, a grating sound that was almost laughter, the hissing of a cat toying with mice.

"We can't outrun it!" Celeste cried. Her muscles seized. Her chest was gripped tight in a breathless knot. The edges of her vision burned white. She stumbled into Melina and rocked the redhead off balance—then shoved her through the gnarled branches of two twining dead trees. Melina squealed, plummeting into the shadowed thicket with a loud *SNAP!* The wolf *yipped* and howled excitedly, bursting through after her.

"Alright, you sick piece of—" she spun on her heels, throwing her momentum at the charging creature. Through her exhaustion, she swung her blade with vicious precision, eager to hack through a neck.

It was like her blade struck brick wall. Sparks spat from between Pride's spiraling set of fangs, the blade grinding to a halt, caught in his snapping jaws. Warm snot and drool drizzled against her forearm. She wrestled to keep her grip on the handle, but Pride only hissed at her, lips curling in a chillingly human smile.

Pride wrenched his neck and ripped the blade from her grasp, yanking her forward into its razorlike claws like meat on a skewer. The blade cracked and *snapped* under the crushing force of his jaws. A flurry of razor shards whipped against her, puncturing skin and slicing dirt. Celeste stumbled, then felt, and saw, her world spin into nauseating agony.

The ground came up suddenly, and violently, and with enough force to rattle her bones from their meaty hold. She hit hard, the brunt of the impact crushing her wounded hand into her chest. The air *whooshed* from her lungs, grit plugged her nose and tickled her throat. Her eyes furiously blinked away the cloud of upturned dirt.

Then came a terrible cackle, shrieking through the trees like storm winds. Celeste flailed her limbs and desperately wormed backwards through the dirt. The screeching intensified.

"*I told you,*" Pride hissed from everywhere at once, relishing her fear with an eager *smack* of his snout. "*Everyone will die, and it's your fault.*"

Celeste's sight blurred, stung, slowly focused to the absolute horror overtop of her. His decrepit body sagged, leaking strings of hot, decaying flesh over her. She gagged on the sultry stench of rot, kicking her legs to maneuver from under his spindly spiderlike limbs—

—but Pride wasn't hunting her.

He leapt over her, another shriek erupting from his malformed snout like a siren. She screamed at him, but already sensed a hunter's resolve. Prey needed to be eaten.

He dove after Melina.

A pale figure launched through the trees with almost inhuman speed. It thrashed against Pride, disrupting the predator's charge and flinging both their bodies through the cluster of hollows. Branches snapped and splintered as the pale figure rolled to a halt in a cloud of dust, blood trickling from the lacerations to his bald head.

Stonem.

Pride crashed through the trees, uprooting and crushing them into fine bits of sawdust as he *stomped* back on its crooked claws. A menacing shriek rang through the wasteland.

Celeste began the painful climb to her feet as Stonem yelled at them all to run. His desperate plea fell on deaf ears, however, as Snyder sprang past her with a knife rolling dangerously in her palm. She reached Stonem in a few long strides, flicked her knife and loosed it like an arrow from a bow. Pride shrieked, hunched over Stonem, claws ripping through the coat around his abdomen. The loosed knife blurred between them, sinking deep into Pride's humanlike eye with a meaty *thump*. Another shriek rose in pitch through the forest, but this was one of agony, the terror of prey.

Snyder slid through the dirt, grip tight around Stonem's collar, then effortlessly flowed back to her feet, hauling the battered man along with her. Celeste could only admire her in those few moments, watching with newfound glee as Pride clawed the knife from the bloody hole where his eye once was. The sight of it boiled her blood; she wanted to kill him.

"Run!" was all she managed to yell. And they ran.

She glimpsed Melina staggering ahead of Stonem and Snyder, each leaning heavily into the other, with her wolf pacing alongside the redhead. Twist lumbered into view, distraught at the screeching noise whipping through the trees. Nadie evened her stride with Clark's, and Bink emptied the last of his mag into Pride as he retreated behind them. Harn was the slowest, almost crying out with every limp, his leg a torn and shredded mess at the knee. She didn't care; let him be bait.

"Split up!"

The command came from Snyder, and nearly all obeyed without hesitation. Only Celeste's grip around Clark's waist stopped him from maneuvering from the path. She called out to the others to fall back as a unit but received no affirmation, and soon heard their thumping footsteps fade into the silence of the dead woods. Nadie cursed, Clark nervously scanned the spiraling shadows beneath the branches of the hollows. It wasn't panic that widened his eyes, but inquiry, as he gazed over the snaggle of branches and burnt shrubs. Celeste shook her head, then eagerly nodded to the right. Melina had scattered into the dead wood, and Celeste would follow that direction until she found her redhead again. They set off together, keeping an awkward but steady pace through the dreaded silence of the wood.

"We can't hide," mumbled Clark. Branches pinched and snagged their skin and clothes, tattering Celeste's shirt into ragged strips. Celeste heaved, caught between throwing up and gasping for a breath. Sweat drenched her face, the damp biting her to the bone.

"Commander," Nadie started.

"I'm f-fine," Celeste said firmly through chattering teeth. She shook her head to clear the daze and venomous whispers from her mind. "I'm fine."

"Yeah," said Clark, eyeing her with worry. "I heard you the first dozen times."

"What?"

"Quiet!"

The barren land trembled under a violent rampage. Branches and bark ripped from the hollows in a flurry of splinters. Fright pushed them deeper into the brush, but the creature raged through the dead wood like a storm. Claws scythed and sawed through brittle trees, toppling the hollows and stripping branches from dead oaks. Celeste dared another glance over her shoulder as she stumbled alongside Clark.

Pride was toying with them.

His snout snapped shut dangerously close to their heels as they scrambled through dead brush, but his claws were well within reach of disemboweling them where they ran, and they would leave a slime of entrails oozing behind them before they even realized what happened. The only reason Pride had yet to gut them was...

That's it!

She broke from Clark's protective hold, nearly stumbling into her forward momentum. She slowed—then launched herself backwards. Her meager weight crashed into Pride, but did little to slow his predacious charge. Instead, she buckled under the impact and hit the ground spinning. Her bucking legs kicked Pride off balance, hurling the monstrosity through the dead thicket.

Flung into the dirt, she struggled to make sense of her orientation. Her head was still spinning, her limbs aching with pain she had never experienced before. She'd hurl if her stomach had more than its own acid in it. She pushed against what she thought was the grainy soil of the ground—rigid bark pinched her fingers and pricked her throbbing wound. She fell backwards, again, flopping against the ground like a fish out of water.

Get up!

Was that her own thought that rang endlessly through her mind, or was it Vega's, the phantom woman trapped in Celeste's soul? She grimaced and pushed to her feet as pain bludgeoned every fiber of her being. She stood, breathless and broken, with no weapon or means of escape, as Pride stalked her from the shadows. Crimson splashed from the puncture in its face, but its other eye rolled over her with a dangerous glare. Saliva and blood drooled from its gaping fangs.

"*Insolent bitch!*" he hissed, rising in height above her on his spiderlike limbs. "*You thought some meager runts could take down Pride? I am your reckoning, Sister.*"

Celeste spat, "I am *not* your kin."

Pride's unhuman face was a contortion of pent-up fury and dominance. "*I'll catch every one of your friends and make you watch as I—slowly—peel the flesh from their bones. You cannot stop me!*"

"You're absolutely right," Celeste whispered eagerly. "But I can stall your dumbass, though."

Pride's wounded gaze flicked past her and along the trail of broken branches and kicked-up dirt. In those few moments of hesitation, Celeste had plenty of time to respond; she threw herself at his sagging, attenuated body, prepared to fight tooth and nail—literally.

Pride whipped his claws and *smacked* her away like a mere insect. Her battered body was flung through the crooked branches and brittle hollows. The splintering wood cradled her awkward descent to the ashy soil. She hit—rolled—*thwacked* her skull off solid oak—rolled again. Her senses were a nauseous blur of pain and dirt. The air was successfully forced from her lungs twice. Everything beneath her spongy flesh felt pulverized to smithereens, protesting with sharp aches and burning agony at every movement. She pulled herself to her feet, however, gasping for breath, vision tilting and twirling like she continuously cartwheeled through the valley.

"Didn't...hurt," she muttered between gasps. She raised a finger and flicked an obscenity at Pride, who smugly sauntered from the shadows like a predator to its cornered prey.

"*You'd be dead if you weren't useful alive,*" Pride said in an ugly, raspy tone. The grating sound rippled the oozing flesh around its throat. "*But your friends will be so—*"

A thick, burnt bough from an oak tree was swung from the shadows like a baseball bat, exploding into splinters upon impact with Pride's head. The creature was thrown from his spiderlike legs, crashing into the dirt like the ragdoll Celeste had been moments before. Twist stood in Pride's place, dusting his hands of soot and sticking his tongue out through pursed lips at her. She only gaped at his sudden appearance, the strength of his swing, and the general pleasantness of his greeting. He was a child on a battlefield.

And in that moment, she decided she adored him. She gave him a thumbs-up, and quietly told him to find the others, but when he casually grinned and pointed past her, she felt her heart sink deep into her stomach.

She turned to see her former team, defiant and armed with whatever they could manage: knives, rifles and pistols as clubs, sticks, rocks, fists. Her face twisted in a scowl, but a smile tugged at the corners of her mouth. She wasn't going to die alone, at least.

She sure as hell wasn't going with Pride.

"I was giving you all time to get away," she muttered. "Pride won't kill me."

"Aye," spat Stonem, breathless, "but he sure as hell can maim ya. More than usual, I mean."

"Screw off."

He grinned like a madman preparing to die. "There's the feisty bitch I came to know and love."

She was about to curse his very existence when she felt the

brush of warmth against her neck. It dulled the pain to a slight throb, and she straightened her posture and stared after the shadows shifting beneath the trees. Melina breathed softly at her side, and a furious growl rumbled in her wolf's throat. He paced at her feet as the others approached, makeshift weapons drawn. They positioned themselves beside her.

"Besides," said Snyder, "it doesn't matter if we run away separately or as a group. That psycho will pick us off one by one, or all at once."

Clark nodded to Celeste, squinting through the bruises around his eyes. "At least we have a better chance at taking that thing down as a group."

Harn scoffed loudly but had little to say. His flesh had gone cadaverous, with a sickly, leathery appearance. Though, even he stood with them, a rock the size of her head gripped firmly in one hand, bracing for the oncoming monstrosity.

"Well, Joke Unit," Snyder sneered at them, arms crossed, and blade drawn forward like a flashing fang. Celeste felt a flush of pride at the mockery. "We started as nothings, but we go out as goddamn legends."

Bink chuckled nervously, whispering so lightly Celeste almost missed the words, "Love you, Nellie," under the grating screech from a furious Pride.

"Let's kill this motherfu—"

The meandering shadows dissolved around Pride as he hooked his limbs through the charred branches of the hollows and rose to a towering height. His fearsome screech was a downpour of saliva and torn sections of a tattering throat.

Crimson exploded from his face, like his cheek was a bursting paint-filled balloon. Pride screeched, this time in pain, and his hold on the boughs and trunks of the hollows became tenuous at best. Another phantom shot punched through the lower section of his mandible. Pride let loose another screech before plummeting from the treetops.

Celeste heard footsteps before Aurous howled let loose a deep howl. The wolf yipped and yapped, rolling through the dirt by her feet, a trail of red soaking the ashy dirt. He was on his side, body wrenched with his jaws tight around the protrusion in his hip. It wasn't deep, likely clipping the bone, but Celeste recognized the cragged shaft and deadly precision.

Disfigured!

She threw herself over Aurous the moment a staggering blow connected with the back of her skull. Her vision burned an intense white, her thoughts drowned in static. She felt a comforting warmth beneath her; above her was a thundering cacophony.

Footsteps? Voices? Pride disemboweling my friends...

Blood bubbled in her throat, and she retched into the course fuzz of the carpet. She blinked stupidly.

Carpet?

Sight came rushing back in searing flashes. Something made a whining sound beneath her. It was Aurous, she felt his fur, not a carpet she had retched onto. She feebly reached for the arrow shaft that protruded from his hip when thunder struck. Her senses recovered, and horror peeled her eyes wide—

—Pride thrashed across the ground, flesh bursting and bubbling with rancid blood. Arrows hailed down in shadowy blots, striking trees, dirt, and flesh with impunity. Pride sagged, hooked limbs staked into the ground like a tent, but his torn snout still *snapped* dangerously.

"*The...nerve...*"

Celeste dared a glance around her after the volley of arrows struck their intended target. A wall of feet and legs surrounded her, wrapped in a fur-trimmed leather and strips of dyed cloth. She didn't look further. The groan of a drawn bowstring chilled her spine. Then another, and another; they were surrounded by dozens of cloaked figures, all surrounding a wounded Pride.

"Yes," purred a sultry familiar voice, the *hiss* of a serpent from her nightmares. "The nerve of me."

Pride was furious. "*I will kill you all!*"

"Hm," the voice purred again.

Celeste watched, eyes peeled wide and unblinking, as one of the figures strode forward through the soil without sound like a phantom. Delicately gliding across the dirt without leaving any impression in its wake. Confidence oozed from the figure like blood, pride larger than any creature to call itself such. The figure was cloaked and hooded, but Celeste saw the shimmer of olive skin, the fanglike teeth that flashed in the menacing style of a cat eyeing its new toy.

It can't be. She couldn't form the words on her tangled tongue.

Her friends were pinned to the dirt as she was, under the threatening glare of at least a dozen drawn bows. Each shivered in the grasps of the bowmen, and Celeste knew from experience that one small shift meant a puncture—or punch *through*—any one of them. They were completely at their mercy.

But so was Pride.

"*You're going to regret this, bandit,*" Pride cursed, wheezing blood from his torn snout. "*You will all die.*"

The figure strode forward through the drawn bows. Shadows with silvery wisps flowed from beneath the hood, like death itself stalked the wounded creature. Celeste could only stare in horror as the hood fell to the figure's shoulders, and revealed scarred olive skin, nebulous eyes, the small, but slightly shifted nose. The chin was wider, shoulders squarer, but it was her, it had to be her—but Celeste couldn't be certain.

Vega, the phantom woman.

"*You,*" Pride hissed, seething rage. "*I should have known you of all would survive a visit from my brother.*"

The phantom scoffed, and thin, blood-coloured lips twisted into a grin. Three scabbed gashes ran across the length of their neck down to her right shoulder, as if they had been clawed with a pitchfork. "Barely."

"*You will not survive me.*"

"Am I feared?"

Pride was taken aback, squirming under the countless arrows that had punctured and mangled his flesh. "*I fear nothing.*"

Another scoff. "No. Does your master fear me?"

Pride hissed and raked his claws through the dirt. "*The Doctor fears no human.*"

"Mengele was human once," the phantom tartly replied. "As we all once were."

"*You are still human,*" Pride spat. "*Bandit Queen.*"

Those familiar, nebulous eyes were suddenly as bright as a wildfire. The figure crossed between their archers and Pride, only stopping once well within reach of its cragged claws. Pride was unflinchingtheir bold at approach, but his remaining eye eagerly rolled over them.

"*My brother should have killed you,*" Pride rasped. "*Since he cannot—I will.*"

"Developed quite the taste for Ode, and promised to return for her," she replied. "Don't worry, she's eager to return the favor for the damage to our camp."

"*Insolent—*"

"What are you doing in the Dead Wood?" the bandit queen

calmly asked, stunning Pride into a lapse in thought. Part of his snout dangled in meaty strings, and he snapped his teeth shut and remained silent—but his remaining eye flicked toward Celeste, an involuntary and quickly corrected reaction. A smirk tugged at the corners of the queen's mouth.

"Your kind will soon be a horror of the past."

Pride staggered and writhed, but his legs flicked uselessly and crumpled under any weight.

"*Bitch, I will—*" Pride froze in horrified silence as the queen's fist rose a few inches above her shoulder, and watched as both flanks of archers moved in unison, withdrawing their aim on the captives and igniting the tips of their oil-soaked arrows. Black smoke churned up from the flaming rags, gagging Celeste, and even some of the archers, but they swiftly drew aim on the wounded Pride.

"*No—!*"

"Burn."

The queen's fist dropped like an anchor, and Celeste was breathless at the *snap* of each bow. A volley of flames streaked through the air like a rolling wave of wildfire. Pride shrieked in a way she had never heard from him before; instead of fury or dominance, the creature thrashed and crisped beneath column of rising, twisting flames, screaming and pleading for mercy. Flesh peeled and shriveled like old jerky, bones charred ashen, devoured by the flames that danced without rhythm. The fire's rapacious roar drowned out the gurgling groans of agony from Pride, and the creature collapsed into red-hot embers, black smoke belching through the trees like noxious fumes from truck exhaust.

"Well," the queen breathed out a gentle sigh and rounded on them, nebulous eyes flicking over the archers in her command. Within seconds, they had their arrows drawn and aimed on Celeste on her team. The creaks and groans of each flexing bow chilled her to the bone more than the crackling corpse of Mengele's twisted experiment. The queen approached, as silent as the ghost she resembled, the "mother" Celeste had killed in cold blood.

The queen who wore Vega's features like a carefully molded mask of flesh carefully flicked their finger through Celeste's matted hair, parting her tangles and revealing the deep and jagged black scars over half her face.

"You seem to have caught the interest of their so-called master," the familiar stranger purred with the same deep and sultry voice as Vega had. "Doctor Cruel. I want to know what makes you so special. But you were the cause of our downfall, and *all* will swing for your crimes."

No...please.

"Vega...mother...your daughter has returned," was all Celeste muttered as she crashed face-first into the dirt, and into a deep, unending darkness.

Eighteen
The Hangman's Halter

THE WORLD blinked dark, then a blinding white. Odd, tiny sensations pricked her spine like a scurrying spider, as she fell into the clutches of darkness once more.

"Again."

It was a cold, wet slap that woke her, stung her flesh, crawled down her face and neck and splashed into her lap. She drew in quick, shaky breaths, and opened her eyes to a swirling grey. She writhed and threw herself forward—an iron grip tightened and burned into her throat, crushing the scream from her windpipe. Her mouth gaped soundlessly, as if all the oxygen had been sucked out of the air around her. Her legs bucked backwards, useless, and her arms were unresponsive and anchored to her hips. Her knees sank into the soil as she shifted her weight, snapping her spine straight. The strangling grip relaxed, and she sputtered and drooled blood.

What happened? She blinked again and cleared the burning haze from her sight. *The last thing I remember is—*

"You're awake."

Celeste dared lift her gaze.

"I am *not* Vega."

Yet the voice was poisoned with the same subtle ferocity, the sultry-sweet melody of a killer. Their hair was as dark as the shadows slinking through the forest, ribboning down a pockmarked neck and flowing over a ragged mustard-coloured cloak. Those familiar eyes, the gloomy colours of an overcast sky. It appeared to be Vega...but as Celeste ran her gaze over the stranger, who stood over her like a master to a disobedient pup, she discerned the stark differences. The shoulders were broader, more powerful, chest thic, but supple, with a curving waist and thin, slender legs. Those blood-coloured lips twitched into a ghastly grin.

"I am *not* my sister, the Bandit Queen," sneered the stranger in that same sly, cutting tone. "As your kind regarded her so."

Her heart nearly burst free from her chest. A delicate strangled cry. Melina. Celeste writhed again, this time purposefully towards the source of the sound—and froze as her blood iced in her veins.

A haunting melody sang with the wind, a sharp sound like the rusted hinges of a door. Rows of thickly braided rope twined skyward, high into the twisting branches of black pine. The ropes sung an eerie melody in the breeze. Eyes as green as a pasture, and peeled wide enough to see the reds of her sockets, stared back at her. Melina's face was so pale that her freckles faded like stars on a sunny day. Lined up behind her were the others, all forced to kneel in the barren dirt, eyes as wide as Melina's and staring up at her. Each rope was gripped tightly around their necks. Snyder, Nadie, Bink, Clark, the big man, Twist. The traitors, Harn and Stonem. Even the soldier with the shredded leg, curtesy of a wolf's greeting, trembled and whimpered under a noose.

Aurous!

Her pulse pounded loudly in her ears, and she gritted her teeth. She flung herself backwards to Melina—the crushing grip around her throat snapped tight. The noose groaned against her shifted weight. Her lungs burned for air. The edges of her vision blackened.

A firm grip twisted the rope and hauled her upright, and air slammed back into her lungs. There was nothing in her belly, but she retched into the dirt anyway, gagging on acidic spew. Her eyes slowly trailed up the frayed stitching of the a woolly mustard-colored coat, and into those deep nebulous eyes.

"Are you finished, doll?"

Celeste's throat burned raw, and she choked and coughed on any choice words she harbored.

"As I was saying. I am *not* Vega. I am not the salvation of our people. I am what fate has forced me to be, and that is avenger." The stranger took a single pace backwards, rolling their gaze over the jungle of swaying ropes. "I am Theta the Hangman."

Shit, that means–

"I may be her *sister*," Theta continued coldly, a smile tugging at the corners of her mouth. "But I know her faith got her killed. She thought herself immortal, a god, the one chosen to lead our world into a new and peaceful era. She was wrong."

"She was right," Celeste choked out before she could force her mouth shut. A cold sensation crawled down her spine as those deep, hazy eyes bore into hers.

"Was she?" Theta mocked loudly. "Is she here right now to lead our slaughtered people into glory? She brought our warriors into the city to die, got herself captured and then killed. Now we have no *army* to push against the military's rule."

"We're still fighting–"

Her voice became a blistering cold blizzard: "We had a goddamn *deal*. The head of the Queen Slayer, and we would dissolve our clan into the military. General Blackwell gave me his word."

"Well, girlie," said Stonem, "'if that's what ya wanna be. I hate to be the bearer of shitty news, but Blackwell was going to slaughter you all in the end."

"Next person to talk *will* swing."

The sincerity of Theta's tone strangled them into silence. Like the ropes cinched around their throats.

"We had a deal," she repeated softly, almost singing. "I am no fool, I knew of his traitorous ways. It was simple, really. He wanted complete surrender; I wanted the head of my sister's killer."

Celeste's tongue tangled in knots. She only raised her gaze to meet Theta's, unnerved by the swirling black of her eyes.

"Now," Theta purred. She traced a finger along the jagged outline of Celeste's scar. "You are not Caylee, therefor you are not my sister's brat. Ahh, but that's just it, is it not? I see it now! The spitting image—oh, if only she had lived. If only she had been *stronger*."

Theta had drawn closer to her, inches away from her face. Celeste could smell the musty scent of her old coat, the sour note to her breath that was almost like her father's after a night of drinking. She tasted the filth that adhered to her sun-kissed skin. Theta gave her a small and wicked grin.

"You were my sister's little pet, weren't you?" Another laugh like the hiss of a viper. "She lost her mind when Caylee was killed. She always managed to find a replacement...none ever seemed to survive her treatment. Except...well, you, of course."

That wicked grin spread into a chillingly wide smile. "So, you killed my sister for Blackwell. Why? That old prick was ready to sell your head."

Celeste nearly bit her tongue. "I slit his throat myself." The cold absolution of those words shook her to the bone. She swore the vicious smile on Theta's face grew wider, like a predator baring its fangs. It was almost unnatural.

"So my little birds have sung," she said playfully, flicking her tongue across her lips like a serpent. Then as storm clouds can smother the sky in an instant, her demeanor grew grey and dark. "He was *my* kill. You seem to kill with impunity and struggle with loyalty. Who are you fighting for, little one?"

Celeste chose her words carefully, slowly wiggling her wrists from the binds.

"I fight for my friends," she said with her voice strangled raw. "For those I love."

Theta cocked her head over her shoulder, a cold glint in her otherwise stormy eyes. "How dreadfully sentimental. But! I know you must be valuable, pet, otherwise those beasts wouldn't be clawing their way through my Dead Wood searching for you. Blackwell may be dead and gone, and with it, our chance at salvation. But as I said, little one, I am an *avenger*. Not a leader."

As she rose to her feet, whipping the mustard coat around her waist, her eyes flicked over Celeste's loosened binds. A grin as wickedly sharp as a blade spread across her face.

"You may be valuable to the military yet," Theta announced, "but your friends, however, are not!" The storm raged on in her eyes. "For the crime of killing my sister, you should face the same lonely end! But I will settle for the death of those you love, a fate you have already sentenced *me* to!"

Vega, Celeste begged silently, pleading to her shattered mentality. *Help me. Please. How do I deal with your sister? How do I stop her?*

The disembodied voice purred through her ears, *You know what to do, daughter. Monster to monster.*

"I am not a monster," Celeste muttered.

Theta almost squeaked with amusement. "But I am, pet. *I am.*"

"No, please—"

"You shut up." Theta hissed. "Did my sister beg for her life? Or did she even see the reaper coming when it was wearing your face?"

Celeste peeled her chapped and bloody lips apart to speak, but Vega's phantom demands forced her to a grudging silence. She studied Theta's similar features, the androgynous shape of her figure, the muscles that seemed more like Bink's and Clark's than her own or even Snyder's fit physique. Her tongue jabbed at her swollen cheek, and she winced at the sudden flush of pain and blood from the split in flesh. It focused her diminishing sanity, if only for a moment.

She looks like Vega. Incredibly so. But her demeanor is drastically different, barely even comparable. Vega adored theatrics—images flashed across her mind of dead bodies and blood-dappled snow, the color of the polka-dot dress Vega had once given her as a gift, one of many she never wore—*forcing those to believe she really was the Phantom Woman. But not on this level of psychotic...not this hangman's alley. She was swift and brutal, not sadistic.*

"You have caused us all to lose this war," Theta continued. "You singlehandedly condemned us all to a rule worse than Red Dawn. For that, and the death of my beloved sister, you shall pay the hangman's price."

Exhaustion seized the edges of her mind. Her eyes fluttered, and the pain rocking through her body dulled to a distant, tingling sensation she couldn't make sense of. *Think, Celeste,* she pleaded with herself. *Think!*

"I hereby sentence you, Queen Slayer, to watch your friends die. One. By. One."

No! she wanted to scream, but Theta was gazing past her, oblivious to the anguish that played across her bruised and battered face.

"I think we'll start with..." Theta's eyes swept through the jungle of strung rope with cold, calculating certainty. "You, sweetie."

"N-n-no, p-please!"

Celeste nearly twisted her own neck around like a perched owl as she tracked the direction of Theta's wiggling forefinger. At the wrong end of madwoman's decision was the bound soldier that had pursued them with the horror named Pride. With his balaclava-like mask crumpled down around his chin, she saw his pallid skin glisten greasy sweat. His voice trailed into grunts and groans, lips trembled, spewing spit with every wordless sputter. A dark patch around the camouflaged lining of his pants slowly spread from his crotch and down his thighs, then puddled around his knees. His mouth opened once more, pleading with words that would not properly form, when the thick coil of rope around his neck abruptly tightened and crumpled his trachea like wet cardboard. With a jerking motion, he was yanked from the dirt like a plucked weed. His screams were trapped in his throat as grunts, nearly drowned out by the awful *groan* of the shifting noose. His body swayed like a pendulum, legs bucking wildly. His eyes bulged like balloons on the verge of bursting, the veins around his neck swollen and snaking up his cheeks and forehead. Skin no longer pallid, but a bright blood-red. When his eyes locked with Celeste's, he was hoisted higher into the branches of the hollow. She couldn't tear her gaze from the grisly sight. She felt no sympathy for the man who had wanted her dead, but she knew now that this was the fate awaiting those she loved.

And it took far too long for the soldier to die.

She had watched her father kill out of necessity, and cruelty, as she had done herself. Twice, now, she had put a bullet through the heads of those who were unarmed, and bullets into those who had attempted to take her life. She had viciously carved through throats and hearts, left the wounded to die alone or be ravaged by the infected. Nothing had prepared her for such savagery. She had known of hanging by the neck until dead. Many tales her father once told her of outlaws and lawmen routinely ended with the outlaw swinging from a noose like a pendant. While the thought of a bullet to the head is more humane to her, her father had once explained the mechanisms of a noose. How it was the drop from the platform or a certain height that severed the spine in a quick, forceful *snap*. But there was no drop or neck severing. It had taken many long, agonizing minutes for the soldier to stop struggling against the impossibility of his binds, and even longer for his body to cease convulsing after his eyes rolled back into his skull. Then he was limp, slumped into the crushing grip of the noose, swaying with the gentle, haunting whisper of a breeze. The noose groaned like a wailing ghost, while the others smothered their sobs and sputters. Celeste knew what they were all dreading—just who would be next to swing.

"Well." Theta breathed out the word as a long sigh of release, tongue flicking across her blood-colored lips. A shiver bolted down

Celeste's spine as the phantom features played across the madwoman's face. "That was *so* lovely. I need more military brats to decorate my Dead Wood."

"Please," Celeste dared whisper, raising her gaze to meet Theta's piercingly cold glare. "Please don't do this."

She could almost feel Vega's disappointment radiate through her at such a desperate attempt. A shadow danced across Theta's face until only her curving grin shone through that terrible darkness like the Cheshire Cat. She wiggled her fingers again.

"That one," Theta whispered chillingly, gaze still burned into Celeste. "He'll do."

Shit!

Celeste gave a sweeping glace over the group, heart lurching into her throat at the sight of Clark with his head bowed and eyes squeezed shut. Then she heard the dreaded *snap*—Harn almost gave one last defiant roar before the noose squeezed his throat like a garrote. He was hauled from the dirt by his neck, and there was a frailty to him she had never witnessed before. Infection had ravaged the wound on his leg to a putrid black, necrosing the flesh and spreading poison through his system. He was bound to turn any moment, but she had to watch as his eyes bulged impossibly wide like the soldier's had, the same darkness that scarred her skin now flushing through his veins as he dangled from the branches of a hollow.

He squirmed and thrashed far longer than the soldier had, and he continued to writhe until Theta gave a slight nod to her archer, a small, skinny girl with hair the color of a ripe plum, and an arrow was loosed into his skull.

He was bound to turn. He was going to turn...

It was all she could do to stop from retching over Theta's boots.

Theta rolled her knuckles into her palm. "That was...*uneventful,*" she said. Her eyes drifted skyward. "Swing the redhead."

The stranglehold around Celeste's throat was nothing compared to the icy-hot grip around her heart. Her mouth opened into a wordless scream, a purely primal urge to protect her pack. It was almost a wolfish snarl.

Almost.

"Please!" she choked out between howling sobs. *You know how to deal with her. Monster to Monster.* "Please! I'll do anything, I swear by it, on her life and my friends, and my own goddamn throat! I'll take out the new general, I'll bring you his head, I'll topple his army! Just tell me who to kill and I'll kill them! Please, *please,* spare her life, spare *their* lives!"

It felt like an eternity, the anticipation of the bone-chilling *snap* that never came. Celeste still held her breath like it was her last, heart beating against her ribs like a battering ram. She studied Theta's face for any sign of acceptance, whether she had piqued her curiosity—any-goddamned-thing.

The corners of her mouth twitched. "Alright!" she declared proudly, almost purring her content. "You heard the girl. She is sworn to me as she was to my sister—only I will keep a *much* shorter leash on this wolf in sheep's clothing!"

There was the silence Celeste had dreaded. "But?" she questioned slowly, hesitant of the thought of bodies slung throughout the trees above her.

"But," Theta echoed venomously, "I still deserve retribution for my sister's death. Since you swore fealty to me, that means another must die. Oh, don't give me such a sullen look, pet! I know those last two weren't kin...at least not anymore."

Shit. I bargained for the lesser of two devils.

An awful grin spread across Theta's face, and in the haunting light of dawn, it gave her the chilling expression of a jack-o'-lantern.

"You, my pet, will do this for me," she purred playfully. "You will be my hangman."

Her blood chilled colder than ice. "What?"

"I am owed one life, and that life shall be repaid with one of yours—at your own command." The utter amusement in her voice roiled Celeste's belly with sickness.

"I can't—"

"Cut her loose," Theta ordered with that ghastly grin still splayed across her face. "And put an arrow through her leg if she tries anything."

"Right," said the short girl with plum-colored hair, and rich-brown eyes as wide and watchful as a cat. The bow limbs flexed menacingly when she docked a fletched arrow. Celeste studied the weapon carefully as bands of rope were cut loose from her neck, noting with a sharp twist in her heart that the flaked red paint had an eerie similarity to the bow she had lost along that treacherous stretch of highway. There were at least four or five paces between her and the girl, and even with the bow only slightly drawn, Celeste knew there was little chance of closing the gap between them before an arrow punched through her thigh. When the binds around her wrists were loose, and the blood hammered back down through her swollen fingers, she lifted her wary gaze to Theta. The madwoman had cautiously retreated from her reach, remaining vigilant.

There was nothing else Celeste could do.

Rising to her feet was a challenge; her lower legs had long numbed, and upon standing upright, the sensation of feeling returned as pins and needles through her spongy flesh. A furtive glance through the Dead Wood and she discerned dozens, if not more, Disfigured lurking and spectating from the shadows, faceless and vague like ghosts.

There is no other way.

Her heart hammered away at her ribcage, and she was certain Theta could sense that very fear, and relished the agony. Celeste breathed deep and slow, shifting her feet slowly to face the others.

They all looked so terribly young and frightened.

The first step nearly toppled her into Snyder, who was still bound by the throat, but even nearly tumbling into the blonde's lap didn't coax so much as a glance from her. She was a few paces from Clark when he looked up with hollow eyes. He stared at her for only a moment, attempted a nod, then bowed his head as if he knew at any moment he would swing like Harn and the soldier. A sharp pang of guilt; she had far too many demons to conquer.

Twist didn't notice her approach. His beady eyes were entranced by the coiled rope, and the haunting melody of swaying bodies that echoed through the Dead Wood—so loud it was that Celeste wondered if he even comprehended they were about to join that symphony of death. Nadie held her gaze for more than a moment, but her doe eyes were so wide and full of fear, spilling tears down her round cheeks. Bink was only a few paces beyond her, face scrunched up almost as if in thought, gaze burning into the dirt. She knew who dominated what he believed to be his final thoughts.

As she drifted past her friends, wave after wave of shame and fury crashed through her like a violent storm. *Monster to monster.* There was nothing she could do now. She had thrown those she cared for into a maelstrom, and now they had to pay her price. She tried to mouth *I'm sorry* to Melina as she drifted by, but the redhead only stared skyward, green eyes shimmering brightly like scattered sunshine over a valley.

Her wildflower knew.

"So," a terribly raspy voice choked out, "you chose after all, Little Wolf."

Stonem cocked his head at her, and with his bald, scarred, and misshapen skull, he appeared more alien than human. She had never glanced at his scars for more than a moment, but now she found herself studying the ridged and crumpled skin around the crater in the top of his skull, like a butcher had stitched the wound closed without replacing the section of bone that was lost.

"I-I'm sorry," Celeste croaked, uncertain of what to say. *There must be a way out...*

Stonem spat a glob of snot at her feet. "Stuff the empty apologies, ya selfish twat," he hissed. "Thinking with one general under the belt, suddenly ya can play the hero? Really? Like there aren't more factions and assholes struggling for power. Ye've done *nothing*. Ye're a puppet now, Wolf Bitch, and it's bloody pathetic. Leashed and caged, trained to do tricks for treats."

Her vision rippled from the flood of tears, but she saw his mouth form words her ears were deaf to: *So be free, Little Wolf.*

"H-him," she sobbed.

"Swing the bald one!" Theta announced excitedly. "His final breath will be my sister's justice."

"Your sister was a bloody cun—!"

The rope collapsed his windpipe, heaving him up from his knees until only the tips of his toes scraped across the dirt. He didn't flail in panic, or twist the rope in a desperate attempt to breathe. Instead, he gave one last rueful grin, and a small wink to Melina. The redhead still had her eyes skyward, but there was a fresh flow of tears, and Celeste knew she had caught his farewell. It all happened in one swift, bittersweet moment. Then he was hauled high into the canopy of dead trees, face swollen red and eyes squeezed shut, but it took a few moments for him to begin struggling instinctively, convulsing as the lack of oxygen began shutting down the cognitive regions of his brain. She sobbed gently into her drawn fist when his mouth opened as if he could taste the fresh air one last time—and then he slumped further into the strangling rope, chillingly still.

There was a sudden sharp, rhythmic clap. "Now," said Theta, inhaling sharply as if she could smell the sudden release of death. "That was the final breath I had hoped for—the one he could never have."

"I did your bidding," Celeste muttered coldly, the words as heavy as stones in her mouth. "I proved my loyalty. I hope you uphold your end of the bargain."

"I'm satisfied." The madwoman scarcely made a sound as she sauntered through the rows of her noosed prisoners. She stood by Celeste, nearly shoulder-to-shoulder, flicking her long and sable hair from her face. There was a smug glint in her otherwise stormy eyes.

Celeste wanted to carve both out of her skull.

Monster to monster.

Theta breathed out a gentle sigh. "You did well, pet," she said proudly, then lowered her voice to a dangerous whisper, "But if you think I'm giving you free rein, you're mistaken. You'll swing just as easily as the rest if I do not trust you."

Celeste shuddered under another crippling wave of fear, or nausea—or both. She just couldn't be bothered to know the difference any longer.

"I understand," she replied.

"Good." Theta *snapped* her fingers, and the sharp sound sent another shiver crawling down Celeste's spine. "Free the ones who are still alive, they're no longer our prisoners. For now. Pet, you come with me. We're going to need you and your team in better shape if you all want to survive this mission."

The mustard-colored coat whipped as she turned and sauntered back through her scattered team, fingers idly flicking the ropes still noosed around their necks. The others, as nervous and battered as they were, all seemed flushed with relief—except one.

Melina kept her eyes on the dappled skylight, the greens of her irises only a slight shimmer. The silence between them was an uncrossable chasm, broken only by the ghostly groans of nooses twisting with the gently blowing breeze.

NINETEEN
The Devil's Due

"HOW DOES it fit?"

Celeste wiggled and squeezed her three remaining fingers into the tight confines of the leather glove. Inspecting the glove, she felt the sharp pinch against her properly-stitched wound. She was still attempting to twitch the fingers that were no longer there. Theta only grinned at her.

"You'll get used to it."

Celeste grunted. "I suppose you've lost fingers before?"

"No," Theta said, "but I have seen those with no arms or legs continue to fight. Count yourself lucky you only lost two fingers."

"I'm running out of body to scar."

Theta snorted and cackled like a madwoman. "You can always lose a limb, pet. Or your entire head if you're not careful."

The hidden camp Theta had brought them to did not appear to be a permanent residence. Military-grade canvas tents and deer skin yurts dotted the wooded hills, with stocks of high-caliber weapons with no ammunition, stacks of drying grey meat from wasteland hunts, steam baths and community hearths. It held the appearance of the military camp outside of the city ruins—only the bandits shared resources and jobs as a community rather than hierarchy. They weren't soldiers, but they could all very well draw a bow or rifle. Celeste quickly gathered the bandit group had been a hunting excursion, food cache, and reconnaissance. She recalled what Bink had told them about the tunnels leading out of Hellpit, and the twisted experiments that had given chase. There were no grown men, those who would be expected to fight in a war.

Where the military had doctors and modern supplies scavenged from hospitals, the bandits had healers and medicine men, with natural remedies and knowledge of their ancestors in the Old World. A salve of honey and herbs and been generously applied before and after stitching up her butcher's wound, and in the days since, the swelling had receded, fever cooled, her stomach calmed—though it was nearly bursting with smoked meat and steamy broth. The others grudgingly had their wounds tended to and bandaged in adjoining tents, but Theta had separated them almost immediately after forcing Celeste to choose...

So be free, Little Wolf.

A swampy warmth drooled down her arm. When she smiled and reached down, she felt the coarse and tangled fur of her wolf, snagging it between her remaining fingers.

"You like it, too?" Celeste asked with a smirk, flicking his cold nose with her fingers. His tawny eyes were like rays of sunshine to her, but his body was, to his dismay and annoyance, bandaged in cloth like her. He was prone to prodding the arrow wound with his tongue, so she had layered the bandage around his chest thicker than his own coat. Theta had told her the sole reason she had the wolf saved was how he had fought against Pride—her scouts had reported the conflict with such detail that Celeste was now certain if Pride hadn't hunted them down, Theta would have. Celeste knew better than to point out Aurous had only been injured on her order. She had grown incredibly wary of the madwoman's explosive and highly unpredictable temper. He was alive, that was enough.

For now.

"I'll take that as a yes," Celeste muttered, fumbling her grip on her belt. It slipped off her hip, and the tanned-leather holster thumped around her ankles. "Damn."

"What makes you so special, pet?"

The cold calculation to her tone unnerved Celeste. She looked up to find Theta eyeing her like a wolf over a piece of meat, tongue pressed between her bared teeth. Celeste shook her head, choking on her response. The wolf's fur raised like the bumps across her own skin.

Theta clicked her teeth together. "I only ask because of those lovely scars," she whispered sweetly. "Is there something you're not sharing with everyone? You seem to be connected to the Doctor and his awful Brood."

"No," Celeste impulsively responded. "Not a chance."

"Do not lie to me, pet."

The storm in her mind had eased, but her thoughts were still scattered and lost. "I'm not lying," she said. "I don't know what they want from me. We escaped Hellpit, I assume it's because we were next on the list of experiments."

Another predacious smile. "*You* survived Hellpit?"

"We *all* did."

Theta snorted. "Barbaric. They have unlocked the genetic code to determine the perfect candidates for experimentation, yet still subject them to torture and a gladiator's fate."

"It doesn't make sense."

"Of course it doesn't. Decisions of a mad mind are inscrutable to the sane. Doctor Cruel believes that not only the genetic code unlocks the potential for evolution, but *strength.* Physical *and* from within. That is why he makes them fight; only the strong will survive."

Celeste's belly quivered with unease. The madwoman seemed to know much of what she had gleaned from the documents stolen from Blackwell. "Those experiments...what the hell was that thing? It called itself Pride?"

"The Brood," Theta whispered. "And they're the next line in evolution, if you ask their master."

"Mengele."

"Familiar with him, are you?"

Celeste's heart twisted in her chest. "Something like that."

"They're creating an army," Theta said, shrugging off the weight of her own words. "Living, breathing, controllable weapons. Deadly, and spreading death and destruction. The sickness infects everybody differently, rotting their bodies and minds, or distorting their bodies, transforming them into deadly beasts. That wasn't the intention of the bioweapon...but you know that already, don't you?"

Celeste answered grudgingly. "They've been developing strains that only alter the genetic code of a few, those who will mutate—evolve—into an actual weapon and not a mindless creep. You're right, they're creating an army. So, this was the reason the world became a hellscape? A bioweapon that grew out of control?"

"I sent my own team into Hellpit to gather intelligence. Contagion levels and dispersion methods, files on the Brood and what their purpose is."

"And?"

Theta's gaze darkened. "They never made it out."

"Then what do we do?"

The playful, catty grin returned. "There's a third player on our gameboard. A man known as Deacon, and an army of followers who he calls his Children of the Last Light. They've never been much more than a dangerous cult on the edge of our radar, but in recent years, the old man has made some bold moves to secure power."

"I've never heard of these people," Celeste muttered, wondering how many more factions existed in the world. It couldn't be *that* big, could it? Everything appeared infinitesimal on all her old maps and atlases.

"They've been raiding the military outposts, killing soldiers, but keeping the engineers and technicians alive. Blackwell was waging war against our kind, believing we were responsible. We wanted him dead, yes, but we had no use for people who cannot fight. No one has ever been to this church and made it out alive, so we have little intelligence on the weapon he is building. But my scout says their last victim was one of Blackwell's most trusted engineers. We need him if we want to know any information on Deacon's weapon."

"What kind of weapon?" Celeste wiggled her fingers through the wolf's fur. His eyes fluttered, and his head shifted against her knee. She leveled with Theta's glare, and there was a dangerous darkness to her eyes.

"The kind that will destroy all life in this land, the way they believe God intended it. They're being led by a self-proclaimed prophet, and they believe they are a cleansing flood to this world."

Celeste nearly burst out laughing. For the first time in weeks, she was beginning to feel like her old self—at least, what constituted normalcy since burning her father's cabin to ashes.

"So, that's it?" she said with a creeping grin. "That was the deal with Blackwell: My head, for your people's cooperation in the war against this...Deacon. You had information to trade."

Theta was anything but amused. "The joy of slitting his throat belonged to me."

Celeste wanted to say she still felt no absolution in his death.

Only a cold, empty space where there was once warmth, and she feared Melina could sense that. Even now, separated as they were across camp. She bit her tongue.

"Yes," Theta confirmed with a mocking sigh. "The weapon may be something that not even monsters can defeat."

"And you think I can?"

Theta cocked her head back, rippling strands of sable hair down her broad shoulders. "I think you have a habit of avoiding death. No one gets away from them—but we are easily discernable." She nearly ripped the collar of her coat away from her neck, and Celeste saw scars that were as bold and dark as her own. They were pockmarks, but like craters of flesh carved from her neck in no discernable pattern, and flecks of green pigmentation. "We're marked, you know. Not only by the land we are forced into, but the food we eat and the water we drink. This is a prison the military has locked us into. We're known as DOS—dead on sight."

Celeste groaned as Theta's smile broadened. With a sharp whistle, a section of her tent folded open to the ashy winds of Dead Wood. The girl with plum-colored hair poked her head in, scowling at Celeste like she were a stain that wouldn't scrub clean. Theta only gave her a small nod, and the girl vanished almost immediately. Within moments, however, the section folded open once more and a sea of familiar faces flooded through.

"Nadie! Clark!" Celeste gasped, flushed with a strange warmth at the sight of them still so close to one another. "You both look better."

Clark grinned, his face now an assortment of yellowing bruises and dried honey-salve. "You only look like a twice-beaten sack of shit."

Nadie managed a smile, but her eyes were dark and haunted. Behind her, Snyder cautiously strolled through with her hands balled into fists and drawn tight against her thighs. She seemed eager to explode at any moment, gaze jumping from one person to the next.

"Celeste," she muttered. She nudged past Clark and toward the center of the tent. It wasn't a large space, yet Snyder seemed to want the world between her and the others.

"Snyder," Celeste responded with the same indifference.

"Christ, that was close," said a strained, but perky voice. Bink popped his head through the flap, whistling at the crafted leather. "Hell of a tent, though."

"You're unusually cheery," Celeste remarked.

Bink shrugged. "Resolution, perhaps."

Nellie.

"Commander!"

Twist was like a giant squeezing through a mousehole. With a scrunched-up face, he went to crush Celeste in his arms—only to stick out his hand out in greeting after a sharp rebuking look from Nadie. Celeste grinned at them both.

"Twist," she said breathlessly, almost too excited at their presence to care about the watchful gaze of the viper in the corner. "Glad you're here, big guy."

"Yup," he replied gleefully, sticking his tongue out at her.

Celeste returned to sentiment, then caught the glimmer of firelight from the corner of her eye. She turned to catch Melina wander into the tent, casting suspicious glances at every shadowed nook and crevice. Her red ringlets were no longer matted and snarled like a windswept rosebush, but bouncing with each cautious step into the confining tent. But that sweeping, hollow gaze was unnerving, and Celeste's stomach twisted when she subtly avoided contact by pushing past her to greet a slobbering Aurous. Celeste cleared her throat and kept her back turned to the others until the heat in her cheeks and neck cooled.

"Are we all present and accounted for?" Theta purred out the question rhetorically, but Celeste could still hear the *smack* of her lips when she spoke as if she referred to a slab of meat she could feast on.

"Those who weren't killed by you," Snyder pointed out.

Celeste cleared her throat again before Theta responded to what she would only perceive as insubordination. *How are you going to react to us, madwoman?*

"Okay," she said quietly, but firmly. "We live under the condition that we succeed in this mission. We *all* walk away." She turned to Theta, twisting up her face like her father when he would glare at her procrastination. She hoped the expression appeared menacing enough—and not that of a cub snarling to a grown wolf. "Agreed?"

"Agreed," Theta echoed. "Get to the church, find the engineer and the weapon—then lower their defenses so my people can ambush the fanatics."

"What the hell!" Snyder began. The shocked and surly looks from the others mirrored her outburst.

Celeste broke in, "*Lower their defenses?* What the hell is right!"

Theta only grinned at her, swirling her thumb along the brim of an old, chipped glass mug. "They have a system of turrets that cut down any living creature in sight, or so my best scout Ode tells me. She'll be joining you, as she led the latest expedition into their lands. Our fighters will trail a few days or so behind, so when you shut down the turrets from within, fire the flare to signal the siege."

"Christ, Celeste," Snyder spat. "You are *terrible* at negotiations."

"Shut up."

"You're all mine now!" Theta snapped at them. Her eyes always stormed like looming rainclouds. "This is *not* a negotiation! I am *telling* you brats what you are doing for *me!*"

Snyder nearly responded. Celeste watched her tense and clench her fists even tighter. She bit back her words, though, and narrowed her icy glare to Celeste as she settled into a stubborn silence. Theta's abrupt shift in mood unbalanced the others, but Celeste was already wary for the next.

"Well," Theta breathed. She *sloshed* around the briny liquid in her mug. "Now that we have that nasty business settled, let me brief you on the mission. I told your valiant *leader* here the gist of it, but just to be sure you all comprehend..." Her eyes rolled up to meet Twist's like she was staring up a skyscraper. She spared him a viperous smile. "You will find the church, blend in with the worshippers, save the engineer, and lower the defense systems for my people. Then we end this war."

"Easy as cake," muttered Snyder. "This is ridiculous. Why not just kill them instead of infiltrate?"

"Even if you made it to their gates, you'd never get a chance at their leader. His people believe him a prophet of the church. We need to know the weapon's capability, if there is more than one, and where it is being stored. We need that engineer."

"A church?" Melina said almost as a squeak. "You're going to kill people of faith?"

Theta watched her from across the tent with those dangerous, cat-like eyes. "I believe you are confusing faith with fanaticism and lies. Those who believe a twisted interpretation of their so-called prophets. We're dealing with those who want to cleanse this land of all life, as they believe God truly wanted when the sickness spread, and they're going to unleash hell upon us all to do their Lord's will—or rather, what they interpret it as."

Melina stared past Celeste almost fondly. "*For behold, I will bring a flood of waters upon the earth to destroy all flesh in which is the breath of life under heaven. Everything that is on the earth shall die.*"

"Scripture," Theta snorted. "But these fools aren't as loving as you, sweetie. They're vicious and they want *all* life to die. My people, yours, the Red Dawn. You. Whatever weapon they're developing, it has power like we haven't seen since the world fell. Don't underestimate their ferocity because of their supposed faith. They'll kill you if they think you're a threat."

"We're used to it," Snyder countered coldly. "We'll get it done. But that doesn't mean I trust you."

Celeste muttered her agreement. "Is everyone ready?"

"One last thing," Theta purred with a growing smile. The unease in Celeste's belly twisted into tight knots as the madwoman hummed each word. "Half of the team is staying in the Dead Wood with me. I need reassurance the mission will be top priority."

Snyder snarled back, "Like hell you're splitting us up!"

The blonde barely had a moment to shield her face before the mug was hurled at her from across the tent, shattering against her drawn elbows and spattering everyone with the tingling scent of salty wine. Celeste had ducked as well, instinctively, and now realized with a bright burning shame in her cheeks that she was nearly flat against the floor.

She still slipped a broken shard of the mug into the fold of her sock.

"Whoa!"

Snyder launched across the tent at Theta. It took Bink *and* Clark's combined strength to hold her back from swinging her fists. Theta only watched her, wild-eyed and twitching with excitement, like a cat eager to pounce. The girl named Odine was between the two women, dead center of the tent, with a sharp, twisted dagger drawn inches from Snyder's throat. Odine was a small, skinny girl with shimmery purple hair, but her eyes were a bright blazing brown like a forest fire, and the dagger was perfectly balanced in her grip.

"You don't have to split us all up," Celeste said. She took a quick step into the blade's deadly range. "You can take me, and the others can finish the mission. They work better as a team."

And Snyder can be the leader she's always wanted to be.

"No," Theta said flatly. "It's more than just a reassurance. These fanatics kill on sight, and they only give help to those they perceive as...*weak.* Better odds if split."

Nadie snorted. "You mean *women*."

"Yes, I do."

"That means we're staying," Clark said, scowling at Celeste. "I don't like it, Commander."

I'm not your bloody commander. "You and Bink can keep an eye on Theta for me."

The madwoman was clearly amused by the choice of words. "The big one stays, too. Twirl, was his name?"

"*Twist*," Celeste corrected, ignoring the big man's queries at the sound of his name. "And he's coming with us. That's the only way someone we don't trust follows us into chaos. I need people I know will watch my back."

Theta's grin was a ghostly reminder of who Celeste was truly bartering with. *Monster to monster.*

"All right," the madwoman said. "He does come across as *harmless*. Those two remain with me. Ode, arm them, will you? Knives and one bow only, we need to keep up the appearance of harmless hunters in search of salvation...it's delightful one of you can speak scripture."

Melina kept her tongue and was the first to follow Odine from the tent, with the wolf trailing behind her with a lolling tongue. Whether to select a knife or to be as far from them as she could, Celeste began to believe it didn't matter. The cold pit in her chest where her heart had fallen into only grew deeper, and colder.

"Rendezvous outside in five," Snyder commanded. She scoffed at the sight of Nadie gently kissing Clark on his scarring chin. Celeste smiled, flushed red once more, and turned to avoid Theta's catlike gaze.

"I suppose it's good I'll be staying."

Bink appeared anything but hopeful. His face was unusually pale, his expression as crestfallen as when his neck was tightly gripped by a noose. She knew what he felt deep inside his heart, but words failed her. They always had. Instead, she reached out to him and drew him close to her, relishing the small amount of warmth shared between them, if only for a moment. She knew it was more comfort to her than him, but still she held on—long enough to slip the jagged shard of glass into his jacket. Before he could pull away from her, she whispered into his ear, "Escape and find us when you can," then kissed his cheek and broke the embrace.

"I was wrong," Bink said with a ghost of a smile. "Melina isn't the only one with warmth. You're the leader everyone needs."

Shame burned through her face. "I don't know why everyone keeps saying that. I'm not fit to lead anyone."

"You care," Theta whispered with a creeping laugh like nails against a chalkboard. "You have a big heart, and it's going to get you killed. That cold feeling in your chest? Embrace it, let it consume your heart."

Celeste turned without another glance at her, silently cursing the icy sensation crawling up her throat.

Monster to monster.

"*Sweetie,*" Theta sang. "*Don't get yourself killed.*"

"I'm so sick of these dead goddamn trees," Snyder complained, unbearably loud. She shouldered her machete. The blade was more of a butcher's cleaver, warped by years of unforgiving use. She still carried it proudly like a soldier's weapon, but hacked and cleaved her way through twisting snarls and leafless boughs.

It had only been ten nights since Celeste had bargained for their lives in that hangman's alley. Each long and sweltering day since had been spent in the scattered shade of thickets, chasing what little rest they could. By night, they wandered cautiously through Dead Wood with limited sight, with no sense of how deep into the uncharted land they were. She had never seen a city marked SAFE on her old maps or any from the military encampment. Her team had been tense, and under Snyder's forced command, they grew increasingly irate. She suspected the bandit girl to betray them at any moment—Celeste knew better, had seen how desperate the madwoman had been. She studied Ode and searched her steel glare for any chink in her armor. She had no trust for her new companion—neither was the girl warming to them. Ode continued caring for Celeste's wound, but had otherwise been as cold and demeaning as Theta.

"Don't call me Ode," she tartly replied one morning while undressing Celeste's soiled bandages. "Only my family can. It's Odine to anyone else."

That had been their proper introduction, and Celeste knew there was nothing to pursue beyond their bandaging ritual each morning.

"We have no idea where we are even going," Snyder muttered again, and Celeste thought it must have been the hundredth time. "*She* could be leading us in circles."

Odine scoffed. "I know this land."

"Yet you've never found the church."

"We know the direction," Odine shot back. "I've watched friends die trying to breach the turret perimeter."

"Yeah," Snyder said. "That's the problem. This is a suicide mission. You know it, I know it. You're okay with that?"

Odine stared back at her with the same scowl she wore throughout the journey; eyes sharply narrowed, nose scrunched up as if in disgust, plum-bright hair ribboning over her high-arching cheekbones. "I don't care what happens. I want inside, and I want Deacon's head."

That coaxed a smirk from the stubborn blonde. "Thought this wasn't an assassination attempt?"

Odine trudged on, fur-trimmed leather shoes sinking into the ashy soil. "You have a mission, and I have my own."

"Maybe we should try and reason with them," Melina said. Her voice was like music to Celeste's ears—a melody she rarely heard now. "After all, if they follow the teachings of Christ, they have to believe in morality. We can help them see our way as well."

"For the last time," spat Snyder, "that is a fever-dream and we're not reasoning with killers."

"*Peacemakers who sow in peace reap a harvest of righteousness.*"

"To hell with that," Snyder muttered.

Melina's gaze flickered over Celeste for only a moment, but it was enough. That cold, accusing glare was a blade plunged into her heart, hacking, carving, twisting. The redhead slowed her pace and fell behind Nadie and Twist, and as the wolf limped alongside her, Celeste felt another sharp sting of abandonment.

It was the right thing to do.

Those words had played across her thoughts ever since Stonem's lips had quivered for a final gasp of air as he swung from the branches of an old, burnt-out pine. It was an endless loop of vindication, but as the days dragged on, that thought became resoundingly hollow. The guilt that shackled in her heart was the prison she rightly deserved for becoming an executioner at the madwoman's request.

My own life was too high of a price to bargain with, she would have killed them one by one. Broke me. Made me hers, like Vega wanted...like Vega did.

"Commander?"

Nadie's voice was pitched unusually high, and Celeste wondered how long her friend had been calling for her as she wandered through the dense thicket in an oblivious haze. She sighed, pulling the fraying edges of the stiff, tanned leather coat around her chest to chase the chills from her bones. Her amputation no longer festered and fouled, though even with the salve and herbal tea, healing sapped the dregs of her strength. The chills clawed through her, even near the warmth of a roaring fire. Her thoughts were a tangled web she couldn't free her mind from.

Melina...

"Commander?"

"What is it?" Celeste sighed, feeling her voice crack from disuse. "And I'm not your commander."

She ignored her, as she had done for days. Without Clark as an anchor, Nadie remained distant from the others—and seemed exceptionally averse to Celeste. "It's important," she said. "We only have enough rations to last another two days."

"Cut the rations in half then," she suggested dully. "Right, Snyder?"

The blonde only scoffed at her.

Nadie wasn't amused. "We can't cut rations anymore and expect not to starve all the same. I haven't seen any birds, or rabbits, or deer. We can't scout for provisions in what is essentially a dead desert. We *need* to turn back."

"There has to be something," sneered Snyder. "These forest dwellers gave us dried meat and fruit, and they hunted and farmed it from somewhere."

Odine snickered, turning. "We're not savages. We have villages, homes, families. Your people forced war on us and drove us into the wastelands. Now it is ours." Her bright hair dangled like ribbons over her dark eyes. "But this is far deeper into the Dead Wood than we have ever charted—or survived to tell of. This is Exalted territory."

"Great," Snyder grumbled. "The wide-open unknown—"

She fell into silence, blade raised, eyes searching the trees. Celeste halted at her abrupt command, fingers drumming against the comfort of her sheathed knife. Her own gaze swept through the thinning clusters of charred and crumbled hollows, ashen soil, and a deep, crushing darkness in the distance.

"What the hell, *Commander?*" Nadie mocked, glaring. The motley bruises on her dark skin twisted her expression into the darkness. "Every night with this, and it's always nothing."

"I heard it."

"Sure."

Twist hummed gently. "Birds."

"What?" Nadie muttered absently. "There are no birds, dear."

"Birds," Twist insisted, proud of his thought. "Birds, birds, birds, birds!"

Odine scoffed, unslinging the blemished bow. "I'll scout ahead for a deer trail if you're feeling *peckish.*"

"So you can target us from the cover of darkness?" Snyder cocked her head, machete dangerously poised by her hip. "Is that your plan, Ode?"

"*Odine*"

"Oh, you mean we're *not* friends?"

"We never will be," Odine spat. "You're military at heart."

"And what about starving? Are you okay with that?"

"*If ye be willing and obedient,*" Melina hummed gently, "*ye shall eat the good of the land.*"

Snyder smoldered. "What did I tell you about those goddamn scriptures?"

"*If ye be willing and obedient...*"

"Mel," Celeste interrupted as Snyder rounded on her. "We need to keep moving. Maybe now isn't the time."

She reached out tentatively, but Melina was a cornered wolf snarling at any who dared approach. She shuddered from her touch, distancing herself from the others. Aurous whined, pawed at her feet, a shimmering worry in his tawny eyes.

"It *is* the time," Melina said, scoffing. "When isn't it the time? You keep wondering why these terrible things happen, why the fighting and bloodshed never stops...but it's you, it has *always* been you! Instead of life, you choose death. Instead of peace, you choose violence. That is why we are here in this wasteland! You can't let vengeance die, so it consumes you to the point where you throw yourself into any conflict just to quell that anger inside. God reaches out to you and gives you a way to peace, and you choose to sin."

Celeste felt her muscles tighten and tense, her breath catch in her throat. "Really?" she asked, incredulously. "I'm a sinner? That's all you think of me now?"

Melina's eyes were green steel. "You killed Stonem after he saved me and Aurous, after he cared for us, hunted for us, *saved you!*"

That boiled her blood. "After he betrayed us to Blackwell. After he was ready to watch us gutted so he can reclaim his rank."

"Because *you* couldn't follow orders!" Melina's voice shrilled with anger like Celeste had never heard. "Your uncle gave you everything and you threw it all away! You always spoke of your family, Celeste, like they were the only love you had ever felt in this world. You finally found someone who had known and been a part of that family, and you turned on him in a thirst for vengeance that had *nothing* to do with you! That was Vega's mess, and you inherited it. But that was what she wanted, right? Manipulated a lost little killer to finish a war she knew she'd never live through. You need salvation, Celeste. Your soul is in the Devil's grip."

Celeste cared little for her face burning brightly in the shadows as the others shifted gazes, cleared throats, and played as if they never heard. Fury shook her to the bone.

"Everything I have done was out of love," Celeste growled dangerously. "I only wanted to protect you because I love you, and I wanted a better life than what I saw at that compound. I went after Vega. I didn't follow her orders! I saw the corruption in the military, saw the butcher that had my family killed *still alive!* We just escaped his barbaric laboratory, waded through a swamp of his experiments, and discovered more horrors that Red Dawn is personally responsible for!"

"Their wrongs do not absolve your sins!"

Celeste clenched her fists tight, trembling. "I don't regret killing Blackwell, and I sure as hell don't regret killing a traitor like Stonem."

"*If thou dost not speak to warn the wicked from his way,*" Melina began as a whispered prayer.

"Enough!" Celeste exploded, stomping forward even as other voices thundered wordlessly in her ears. Aurous growled and viciously bared his teeth—but at her, not the others. Her gaze wandered from the snarling wolf, to Melina, who retreated several paces from her reach. Celeste couldn't bring herself to care anymore.

"God did not put me on this path," she said, smothering her anger. "I did. I gave myself these scars. *I* did. I fought when I had to, as my father taught me, not because I'm consumed by an evil entity. *I'm not an experiment!*"

Melina was unflinching in her response. "Stonem was right, Celeste. You're a puppet now, hiding her sins from God like Cain."

"You killed," Celeste accused, but the words were hollow and cold. "When you thought my life was in danger, you murdered those soldiers."

It was the first time in days those bright green eyes shimmered with tears. "And I have to ask God for His forgiveness every day. Do you, Celeste? Have you felt a sliver of remorse for the blood on your hands?"

"Birds," Twist muttered absently. "Birds, birds, birds."

"Hush, dear," Nadie whispered. "There are no birds at night."

Snyder said quietly, "I think everyone needs to shut up."

"I hear them," Celeste whispered through chattering teeth. Her bones were cruelly gripped by the bitter chill of night. "I hear them in my dreams. I see their faces when I shut my eyes. I feel that cold dread in my chest even when I'm happy with you, lying in our bed."

"That's why you need to ask for His forgiveness."

"No!" Her blood over-boiled. Aurous snarled and snapped at the air between them, frothy spit slowly drooling from his bared fangs. "I'll never forgive *Him!* He took my mother, my brother...my father! I was abandoned to vagrants and murderers, forced to kill or be killed, starve, freeze, watch people I cared for die!"

"Birds," Twist hummed.

"Screw praying," Celeste cursed, trembling. "Piss on forgiveness, and to Hell with your so-called God."

"Goddamn!" Snyder hissed, lowering her stance. "Would you two kindly shut up?"

"Birds."

Birds?

Nadie groaned and rolled her eyes. "For the last time there's no one he—"

"Twist," Celeste interrupted, nearly shouting. An old memory of their first excursion as a team danced through her mind. "What about the birds?"

Twist shrugged, but grinned. "I hear them chirp. Then fly away. Then chirp again but over there." He jabbed a fat finger first to his left, then his right. "Sing a song!" he pleaded to the birds with a toothy smile.

But Celeste felt her boiling blood immediately run cold. "We're being surrounded!"

Snyder exploded into action, leaping past Celeste and running her blade through an amorphous shadow to her left. She gutted the shadow like a trout. The eerie silence of the Dead Wood was shattered by a long wail of agony that carried through the piney hollows like a tortured spirit. The gutted victim staggered and fell, kneeling in their own entrails. Celeste sprang forward, slid her knife into his throat and silenced him. Warm blood squirted through her fingers, and her heart thundered as the sensation crawled along her skin. The wolf was at her side, snarling and snapping at the darkness.

It was time to hunt.

Aurous yipped and twirled, a thin sheen of crimson along the crook of his brow. Unseeing, Celeste plunged her knife into empty air, scraping her elbow off the charred bark of a hollow—she missed—the wolf ripped into the unseen attacker, wrenching his jaws into the fabric of their clothes. She swung again and plunged the knife between someone's ribs. Fangs sank through meat. Her blade dripped with warm crimson. She was thrilled with the hunt.

A primal roar erupted from Snyder as she danced between the gleam of a blade, bringing her own down on an unseen attacker like a hammer strike. Odine flowed like a featureless shadow, silently nocking and loosing arrows in such quick succession that Celeste could only hear the impact of them against a hollow or the loud *thud* of the occasional body against the ground. Twist was shielding Nadie as a returning arrow grazed the rippling fat of his belly. Celeste growled, knife in hand, and threw herself forward—

—all she saw were streaks of lightning. She was sightless, disorientated. She fell and ate dirt.

She blinked, spat and sputtered, blinked again. Running her tongue across her split lip she wondered why her mouth was full of dirt.

Even in the shroud of darkness she knew her team was forced into retreat. Blood crawled down Snyder's fingers as she paced from the advancing shadows, unarmed. Odine nocked another arrow, then reeled and shoved the undrawn bow into the path of a slashing blade. The wooden bow cracked and splintered in her grip, but she jumped back, reached for the knife along her belt—

—and before Celeste could shout in warning, Odine was struck again. Blood burst from her lips like popped balloons. As she stumbled, the stock of a firearm bashed her face again, shifting her nose with a meaty *thwack*. The bright-haired girl fell, grunted, then spat blood at her attacker's feet. Melina was on her knees already, knife thrown out of reach. Nadie did as well, tugging at Twist's arm to have him mirror her movement.

"Get down!" someone shouted with a deep, raspy voice—she shivered as if Stonem's ghost called out to her at that very moment.

"Get down, now!"

"Where is that goddamn dog?"

A glimmer of gold streaked between a thicket of hollows. *Go, she breathed to him. Run.* Days after gaining her freedom once again, she was at the mercy of another blade.

"Is this all they got?"

The raspy voice cursed so loudly Celeste thought her eardrums would burst. Raspy-voice kicked a fallen blade in her tantrum, cursing again.

"Some bloody beef jerky and rotten fruit?"

Someone else grunted, "That's all. We lost five trying to secure 'em. Three more took enough arrows to fill a quiver."

Raspy-voice almost chortled with delight. "Oh, we're going to carve them up and throw them over a fire tonight. Weeks wandering this bloody wasteland and no goddamn paradise!"

"Knew it was too good to be true."

"Take what you want, but let us go," Snyder began until a boot stomped her into silence.

"Shut up!" yelled Raspy-voice. She stood over Celeste, her face but a shadow with bright empty eyes. "You're first, bitch!"

Celeste flinched, grimacing against the warm spatter. But she felt no pain. It wasn't her own blood that rained down on her in thick globs. Raspy-voice sputtered and choked, spewing another mouthful of blood like vomit. Fletching shimmered in the starlit night; an arrow was buried deep into Raspy-voice's throat, right below her jaw. She hit the ground, still shivering as the life drained from her open throat.

"Heathens!"

Fury hammered down from all directions; arrows thudded flesh, blades drew fountains of blood. The screams of those in agony were drowned out by thunderous war cries. The attackers fell into a flurry of steel.

"Kill all heathens!" someone thundered, thrusting a lengthy spear through the throat of a fallen man, killing him instantly. "Slay any with a weapon in their possession!"

A fearful, but sturdy tone carried through the Dead Wood like a bright melody. Melina stood in the chaos, eyes shut, speckled with blood, and no weapon in her hands. *"Walk in obedience to all that the Lord your God has commanded you, so that you may live and prosper and prolong your days in the land that you will possess."*

The thundering man halted. The point of his spear was

dangerously close to gashing Snyder's throat. "So," he said loudly, almost chuckling. "You seek His guidance?"

With only a moment's hesitation Melina whispered softly, "Always."

"You lie. There are many dead at your feet."

"I do not lie." There was a nervous twitch of her eyes towards Celeste. "We were searching for sanctuary when we were attacked and forced to defend ourselves. We search for understanding, for salvation...to *save* our souls, not lose them before accepting our Lord."

The man stepped forward and the faint glow of the night sky danced hauntingly across his rigid features. His leathery skin was so heavily scarred and gashed that it gave him the appearance of an aging man. His eyes were as cold and grey as steel, hair a blast of winter white. As he drew near, she saw the gashes were intricately designed shapes. Scarred lines from his forehead to the crease of his jaw intersected perpendicular to those from his bulbous nose and lumpy ears, the symbol she recognized from Melina's belongings. A cross.

It's them...

A steady boom erupted from the thundering man: "All those who follow His will shall be spared! Those of a peaceful nature are welcome on these lands!"

With the razor-points of his spear driven into the dirt, he gave a slight bow and flicked his fingers to urge them to their feet.

"You have found sanctuary from evil, my friends," he said quite proudly. "Follow us to our safe haven, and to the man chosen by the Almighty to cleanse this wicked word of sin."

Dread pooled like ice-water in her guts. *Aurous, please stay hidden. Please.*

"Come and meet Deacon."

Part IV.
Promised Land (Autumn)

Twenty
Deacon of the Dark

THE CHURCH was no larger than a hill, camouflaged against the stark landscape with its faded, flaking paint, and resembled a skyscraper toppled onto its side. The walls were windowless towers, and the roof a great curve of rust that projected into the bare branches of the hollows. It was largely featureless, except an ornate row of stained-glass crucifixes, polished to a slight sheen, raised over the only archway into the giant building. Extending across the perimeter were rows of sharpened razor wire, thin and nearly invisible to the naked eye, coiling from hollow to hollow, looping through branches and the sections of a brittle and rusted chain-link fence like some metallic spider's web. It was only as Celeste neared the structure did she realize that what she thought of as giant oaks were instead towering titans of steel, painted black and blending into the charred scenery of the wasteland.

Turret towers.

What the hell is this place?

They were marched through a vestibule, under bright, curving, pitted walls splashed with the red-hot glow of thousands of mounted candles. A plume of dust rose under their feet as they walked over a tattered, torn, musty old rug, revealing old tapestries of a man in robes the color of sand, his feet inches over a body of water, and woven patterns of holy crosses, men adorned in armor and a crucifix that towered over them—with the same man in a sand-colored robe and sandals weaved through flowing patches of crimson.

Through the chamber doors there was an eruption of cheers, shouts, chants, and the thundering rhythm of applause, all at a steadily rising pitch, beating against her chest like a shockwave. The chamber they entered must have been the length of the entire building, like a giant's hallway, overflowing with a massive congregation, an endless ocean of featureless faces.

Those nearest to Celeste were incredibly pale, eyes inhumanly wide and unblinking as if they had no eyelids, pouring sweat like leaky faucets, transfixed on the figure that elevated far above the crowd on an old altar in desperate need of repair. The portly man hobbled across the derelict altar almost with a limp, clutching at his bloated gut. When he opened his mouth to speak, silence strangled the crowd like all the air had been sucked out of the room. Soon all she heard was the speeding drum of her own heart.

Deacon.

"The devout!" Deacon's voice carried through the building with the howling force of storm winds. "Warriors of light! For many years God has deemed us unworthy of the world He had given us! Where He once washed humanity of its sins in a flood, He now brings raging fires! The sins of man are now being judged! It began all those years ago with the sickness, do some of you recall as I do? Playing God they called it...yes! The moment they declared themselves a false idol, we were all doomed! God let the sickness spread to cleanse humanity of its sins! And as the sinners who worshiped a false idol fell, we, too, shall fall for our deceit and debauchery, our lust for the wicked! *There was a great earthquake! The sun turned black like sackcloth made of goat hair, the whole moon turned blood red, and the stars in the sky fell to earth, as figs drop from a fig tree when shaken by a strong wind! The heavens receded like a scroll being rolled up, and every mountain and island was removed from its place!*"

Excitement shot through the crowd as a buzzing cacophony. Deacon shuffled closer to the edge, the wood of the altar groaning loudly and bowing under his weight. He scrutinized all who stared up at him in absolute awe with dark, beady eyes.

"We have been faithful to His word! Faithful to His teachings! He has told me of the need to cleanse the world, a need we shall fulfill! It is our guiding light into paradise! As we unfold the final seal, we are His light, those chosen to be His righteous sword against the army of darkness! *Then the kings of the earth, the princes, the generals, the rich, the mighty, and everyone else, both slave and free, hid in caves and among the rocks of the mountains. They called to the mountains and the rocks, Fall on us and hide us from the face of him who sits on the throne and from the wrath of the Lamb! For the great day of their wrath has come, and who can withstand it?"* His fist shot into the air, clenched tight and trembling. "None shall withstand it! None!"

The congregate exploded into roaring applause. The ground shook, it rattled her bones, numbed her flesh. The air was electrified.

"This is a madhouse," she muttered under her breath—

A delicate whisper broke through the uproar. "*Neither repented they of their murders, nor of their sorceries, nor of their fornication, nor of their thefts...*"

Those dazzling green eyes were drawn high to the altar, wide with a glimmer of wonder. Melina was bewitched by the crowd's wordless chants, swaying with the thundering rhythm. Her red curls were dancing flames when she nodded her head along with Deacon, clutching at the front of her shirt so tightly her knuckles were milk white.

The thundering crowd eased to a gentle hum as the Deacon spoke once more. "So blessed we are by the Almighty...all who seek our church discover redemption. It is not coincidence, but His will!" A terribly cold sensation rooted in her belly as the Deacon's eyes swept across the crowd and halted on them. His voice rumbled with amusement. "And I see we have more who seek the comfort of His embrace. Omega, who have you brought before His judgement?"

Their escort, the spearman, cleared his throat and struck the floor with the end of his long pole weapon. The crowd withdrew from his line of sight and exposed Celeste and the others, another spectacle for the wide-eyed and curious to feast on. The whispers and hushed voices flowed through the crowd like the *whoosh* of a rushing river.

"These here are the victims of the evil that plagues our land," Omega declared over the dying whispers of the congregate. "They claim to be seeking salvation."

"Ah! Welcome to the Church of the Last Light!" Deacon declared to another eruption of rumbling applause and roaring cheers. She wanted to run, but her body seized like an old engine, trapped under the Deacon's rapt gaze. The darkness in his eyes was deep and unending like the pitch-black of night, hollow and just as cold. He was a short, but powerful looking man, with broad shoulders and a sagging stomach, buzzed-short grey hair and long grey whiskers like an old cat, cresting his thinly pursed lips and thinning to patchy stubble around his bulgy neck. Muscle bunched in his shoulders and arms, clearly visible even through the droop of his stark white robe. He raised a boulder-sized fist and stepped toward the edge of the stage, limping and leaning heavily on a cane so slender she thought it would splinter under his weight. His eyes searched hers, skulking through her thoughts, like he could read them as plainly as if inked to paper.

Shit.

Sweat beaded her brow. She nearly choked on the deep thump of her own heart.

He knows it's a lie—he knows we're sinners.

Moments dragged into long, agonizing minutes. She felt the entire congregate had followed Deacon's penetrating gaze across the hall, their eyes peeled wide with ravening curiosity, circling and shifting as if they struggled to focus. At long last, Deacon's foghorn voice shattered the tenuous silence. "God smiles upon those who wish to cleanse their souls in His name! Come forward, young ones, and show your devotion to Him!"

With a slight turn of his head, Omega's stern stare urged them to step forward. For a few moments none dared move. Melina, glowing like a blooming rose, was the first to wander toward the stage, still clutching the dingy gold crucifix tightly in her fist. Celeste attempted to clear the lump that had formed in her throat, adjusted the glove that pinched her wounded fingers—then stepped into the splitting crowd.

The nave was hazy and dark, dimly lit by firelight that gently pulsed an eerie ethereal beauty through the dazzling stained-glass walls. hebligjt bathed the altar and the enigmatic Deacon in a mosaic of orange-red. There were portraits on the glass walls, depictions of robed saints who reached up to a figure with arms spread wide and blood draining from a hole inches below the ribs. Near the wound, a spear dripping with blood, and a roman soldier with his eyes as hollow black spots.

Despite the seemingly frail appearance of the elderly Deacon, he reached for Melina and plucked her from the crowd as tenderly as a flower, pulling her to the stage with a fluid swing of his arms.

When her redhead nervously cast a glance to the crowd below, she clutched at her necklace again, but Deacon drummed his fingers on her knuckles and gave her a creeping smile. As Celeste reached the stage, Melina relented and dangled the intricately designed crucifix between her fingers. The glimmer of its gold reflected from the Deacon's eyes.

"You are already a follower of His divine will?" Deacon asked with a gentler tone, never offering a hand to Celeste as she hauled herself up the edge of the stage. She never heard Melina's response as she turned, breathless, extended a hand for Nadie—who promptly refused and proceeded to climb over the edge as she had. Snyder followed, as well as Odine, and then Twist, who simply rolled over the lip of the stage and nearly bowled into Celeste. As her nervous gaze drifted over the crowd, now nothing but impossibly wide eyes staring up at her in scrutiny, she felt her skin heat to a red-hot glow. Her scars were a blinding beacon to the congregate, and she was made even more aware of the chilling distance between her and Melina. She felt stripped naked in front of the crowd as they probed and prodded the tarry-black, jagged, scabby patches of skin that ravaged half her face, neck, shoulder, swirling abstractly down her arm like a grotesque tattoo, and even around the severed stumps of her lost fingers. Her breast, ribs, waist, thighs, all scarred black like a long-festering wound. She knew those unrelenting gazes only saw a portion of shadowed marks, but she felt their eyes burn into her with judgement. Her heart was caught in her throat as she turned her back to the followers.

"My dear girl," the Deacon whispered ruefully, almost mockingly so. "With such a warm and gentle spirit, I see now why He has blessed you with my presence. I sense what you have spoken to be the truth, and I wish to grant you sanctuary against the world." His voice rose, his small, dark eyes rolled over the others—then curiously stalled on Celeste's scars. "We welcome all who take in the word of God! All who pledge their souls to His will...and mine! No matter the colour of their skin, gender, or age, we welcome all who show devotion to our cause!"

Another wave of cheers rang out. When Deacon shifted his gaze back to Melina, the coldness in his eyes softened to a twinkling curiosity. He said to her kindly, "Be a dear and step forth, denounce the wicked of the land and rejoice in the light."

Melina faced the crowd and took a single step forward, a nervous smile tugging at her mouth. Deacon hobbled beside her and gestured to one of his followers. A young boy, dressed in drab grey robes that dragged in tatters across the floor like a mop, carried a large cloth sack tightly bundled with rope in his arms. His wide eyes were almost unseeing as he stared up at Deacon, utterly enraptured by his presence. He lifted the sack high like a trophy. Deacon smiled, nodded, tugged at the knot and unraveled the rope. The child held his arms out straight with a disciplined lack of motion as the contents nearly spilled over the slacking edges. Stacks of cookie wafers, broken into pieces the size of her knuckles. Her mouth involuntarily watered at the scent of its sweetness, however stale. With one pinched between his fat fingers, he beamed over his rejoicing congregate.

The atmosphere underwent a terrible transformation. Discordance reigned. Those to the rear of the hall rushed forward like a rogue wave in an ocean of people. The unification shattered—for a moment. As the crowd fell in on each other, clambering, writhing, flailing for the edge of the dais, Omega struck the floor with his spear, splintering the old wooden panels beneath. The dais trembled under their feet, but the frenzied crowd did not simmer until a roaring declaration broke through the chaos.

"The body of Christ!" Deacon's booming voice was enough to halt all in place. They were desperate for every word like drowning men were for air. "He died for our sins, so we may find redemption in the next life! We must accept His sacrifice...but only if we too sacrifice for him. Those who need His blessing, and those who strive to maintain it! If He is so willing as to accept our new pledges to the light, then those who have serviced our savior may bring forward the fruits of their endeavors and receive the holy presence with the body of Christ!"

Through the rising roar of the crowd, he whispered to Melina, "Step forward, sweet girl, allow His presence within you."

Melina stepped forward, and Deacon crumbled the wafer between his fingers, lifting his hand slightly above her bouncy red curls. For a moment, she hesitated, eyes rolling upward—then a bright smile played across her face, her mouth opened, and Deacon sprinkled the wafer over her tongue. Within a heartbeat, another young boy in the same drab-grey bathrobes as the other boy, took impossibly long strides across the dais with another leather sack bulging under a tiny arm. She could hear the contents *slosh* loudly like a waterskin. The boy presented the leather sack on one knee like a pledge to a king, and Deacon gave him a slight, but gentle smile as he reached for it. There was no rope wrapped like a ribbon around a prize, only a long nozzle Deacon uncapped with a flick of his thumb. Almost immediately there was a bitterly sweet scent in the air, like fruit spoiling under her nose. It tickled her throat. Her belly rumbled. The stench was achingly familiar. Lifting the ballooning wineskin to Melina's mouth, he spilled red over her chin like a fresh burst of blood. She gulped two mouthfuls, giggling, eyes wide and shimmering like starlight. When she stepped back, her complexion waned, her impossibly-wide eyes dulled—only a sliver of green ringed her dilating pupils—her lips trembled, gaping.

Celeste felt her heart catch in her throat.

But Melina suddenly gasped, clutching at her chest. She was smiling, catching her breath, eyes drawn to the ceiling of painted crosses, bright stained-glass depictions of saints and worshippers. Sweat beaded her forehead, clung to her brow, dripped over her bulgy cheeks. She looked utterly blissful.

Something is wrong.

"My dear girl," Deacon began, hushing the increasingly anxious crowd. The followers were pacing, bound by Deacon's words yet salivating like starving dogs at their master's feet. "Do you feel Him? Do you feel His holy presence?"

Melina's lips quivered, gaping like a fish out of water. Her eyes were spinning like wheels in their sockets. "I do," she whispered. "I feel Him."

In her captivation, Melina twirled beneath the shimmering stained-glass crosses, dancing in the reflection of splendid pointillist patterns. Her skin flushed and darkened like one giant freckle. Her lips stretched thin across her face like a cartoonish smile.

"I feel Him!"

When her arms raised above her head, Deacon bellowed his approval to the congregate, and nearly all who had gathered before the dais exploded into resounding praise. The thunder pounded against her chest, thrashed her ears, painfully squeezed her brain. With a simple gesture of his hand, the crowd abruptly fell into another grudgingly held silence, eyes peeled eerily wide and spinning in their sockets, saliva drooling from gaping lips.

"We welcome those wandering the land in search of virtue!" Deacon roared proudly. "We welcome those with open arms. We welcome those who stand against the false prophet and his demons! We welcome all who have fought, those who are"—he stared right at Celeste—"*scarred* and soulless, for with the love of the Almighty, *your soul will be returned when you accept Him!"*

Deacon rapped his cane against the bowed edge of the dais until silence gripped the feverish crowd.

"He has sent us a guiding light to bring glory to his creation! Our faith in Him is sharper than any blade, swifter than any bullet! We are the Children of the Last Light!"

With a smile glowing as brightly as the rising sun, Melina twirled her coattails, spinning on her heels.

"Next child." The delicate whisper still hammered chills into her bones. "We welcome you to the light."

Wide, brown, doleful eyes met Celeste's for scarcely a moment before the crowd roiled with another frenzied wave of excitement. Nadie's dark complexion was pallid beneath the glinting, garish light of the fiery crosses. Her fingers were locked tightly across her belly. Her knees wobbled. While Nadie slowly paced toward Deacon, Celeste felt his gaze hang over her like some impending doom. His dark, spec-like eyes seemed capable of reading every tumultuous thought from her mind as plain as the features on her face. His gaze spread to consume Nadie with the same burning intensity. Fat fingers rummaged through the burlap sack, pinched a crumbling wafer, then dangled those crumbs above her head like the only lifeline from starvation.

"Allow His blessing to cleanse and save your soul."

An uneasy silence had fallen among the crowd, though they were wide-eyed with teeth bared like wolves at the scent of blood. Celeste felt the high-voltage rush of their hunger vibrate down to her bones. The crushing excitement spread like a contagion, and at any moment she thought the rickety scaffold would collapse in a splintering mess from their riotous advance.

It was only brief, but like stalking predators they sensed Nadie's hesitance. A quiver of her lips was all it took, and Deacon crumbled the wafer between his pinched fingers. She nearly sputtered, dragging her tongue across her lips. Her brown eyes peeled, and her pupils rounded nearly as wide. A terribly small gasp escaped her, lips trembling. Barely a moment passed before Deacon tipped the wineskin over her.

"I feel Him," she choked out, splashing discolored spew into her sleeve. She heaved, and her pallor flickered and waned—then burned bright with warmth. Trembling slightly, she whispered again, "I feel Him."

"Yes, you do," replied Deacon, though his eyes were anywhere but Nadie. Those menacing dots scorched Celeste like miniature black suns. "Next child."

Aversion twisted her bones, pooled in her guts like a slab of ice. Each cautious step to the front of the scaffold was like she was paraded before the mindlessly ravenous, to trust her fate to the crumbs of a colorless cookie. To hide from those impossibly black, all-knowing eyes.

Deacon was not a tall man by any means, standing a few feet shorter than her father had, yet he loomed over her as if his presence were gargantuan, to be revered and worshipped and praised. She was caught in that enigmatic gaze, shivers creeping down her spine like the slow, rhythmic twirls of a dancer.

"Allow His presence to cleanse you, child," he whispered eagerly through gritted teeth. His pinched fingers hovered over her gaping mouth. "Feel His holy spirit."

The crumbs dusted her tongue, sandy dry but thick like flour. A bitter flavor needled her taste buds, nearly causing her to choke and sputter and scream—but her throat clenched shut, and her chest burned like her heart had just burst into a pulpy mess beneath her ribs. Her eyes fluttered impossibly wide.

"Do you feel..."

His voice faded down what sounded like a narrow tube, echoing gently into the harsh clanging in her ears that only seemed to increase in pitch. Her thoughts exploded from her mind like water bursting from a dam, drowning her under waves of incoherence. Shock-white streaked across her vision with every heavy thump of her increasingly rising heartrate. Her flesh prickled and bumped, ashen and cold, then flushed red-hot like running blood. Her chest heaved, lungs quivered for air, lips rounded in a breathless gape.

Is this God?

The thought whizzed though her mind like a bullet.

The holy presence?

The warmth was a mother's loving touch, an embrace capable of more warmth and comfort than the crackling flames of a fire through a long, dark night.

Is God real?

This is anything but God!

The disembodied voice hammered every thought to a standstill amidst that exhilarating fog of confusion. It came not from Deacon, not from the crowd; her surroundings were lost to blinding streaks of white. Somehow, though, those nebulous eyes shimmered through the fog of her vision, and she saw Vega's bloodstained lips part to a viciously pointed set of yellow wolf fangs.

This is not God, daughter of mine, nor faith. The Phantom Woman's tone was as sharp as a serpent's hiss. *You know what this is. You know the feeling; strange, yet familiar. Remember it. Know it. Feel it.*

"I-I..."

Feel it.

Celeste's voice clawed up her clenched throat. "I-I...don't..."

Feel it.

The sensation was like broken glass stabbing her belly. The warmth drained from her and ice gripped her bones. Her blood ran hot, her eyes flushed with grief as thoughts of Stonem swinging in the dead pine flooded her mind, her hands balled into awkward fists as the wolf inside growled a forewarning of death.

Feel it!

The ghostly voice howled like a violent mountain winds, lifting the thoughts from the clutches of that confusing fog. The world rushed into focus.

"Do you feel Him?" Deacon's voice barely penetrated the whirling screech in her ears. "Do you feel His holy presence?"

"I-I can't..." she began, her tongue involuntarily unraveling.

There was a sound of crashing thunder, and when she turned her attention across the altar, she caught sight of a ghost.

Briefly, she believed so. It was a boy no older than her, with a pale, pocked complexion and irises as bright and blue as the sky. A crooked brow, and thin, upward-curving lips. His nose was a nub of flesh, like most of it had been torn from the cartilage. The sandy hair slicked back over the uneven bumps of his skull. He was almost a portrait of the boy she had gutted in the hospital basement, flesh snagged by the skeletal fingers of Stonem and his imprisoned unit. Michael's son.

Chills kissed her warming skin.

It's not him, it's not him.

The crushing feeling in her throat rose through her skull until she thought the pressure would *pop* her eyeballs out of their sockets. The boy sauntered through the chamber doors with his pimpled face twisted from an overarching grin. The congregation, Deacon as well, fell silent as the boy approached. No shabby grey robe flowed around him. Thick cracked leather was strapped and loosely stitched or patched into the clothing over his vital points like plates of armor. Leisurely propped against his shoulder was another polearm weapon similar to Omega's deadly spear, and although the staff was half the pike's length, it still stood roughly the height of the boy's shoulders, and ended in a crescent blade, a star-shaped spearpoint, and a thorn like an eagle's ripping beak. The halberd, still stained with a thin sheen of crimson, was displayed for the congregation like a trophy. The crowd split like they had for Omega, though it appeared more of a grudging retreat. There were four that marched a slow but steady progression behind him, all young like the halberd boy, in torn clothes soiled to discoloration, skin sullied with a weeks' layer of dirt.

"You're late," Omega growled.

Deacon was piqued by the interruption. "Alpha," he greeted formally, though his eyes were a storm of blackness behind his rounded spectacles. "Alive and well."

"Deacon," Alpha squeaked back, splitting the crowd. "I bring more for salvation."

"The ceremony has already begun."

"I found them dying in the Scorch." His voice rose over the silence of the crowd, pride oozing from his tone like slime. "I promised salvation."

Deacon was a stone wall. "They shall have to wait."

"All shall be brought before Him to be judged—"

"And I said they shall have to wait."

There was a fracture in Alpha's prideful tone when he stammered over the silence, but after a simple, listless wave of Deacon's hand, the halberd boy abruptly fell quiet as well. He stood within the split of the crowd, rolling his eyes over Celeste.

Was that disgust she caught shadowing his piercing blue eyes? His gaze rose not to meet hers, but to scrutinize every jagged, black scar that besmirched her milky skin. Or was he looking past her, at the others? She dared not blink.

Her heart hammered wildly against her chest; she thought the entire chamber reverberated with its thundering beat.

Flesh prickled and chilled.

Lungs ached.

She wondered why she held her breath.

"Deacon," Omega whispered over Celeste, whose attention vaulted from the ghostly echo of Abbot, to Deacon and his stormy glare. "Perhaps we should consider. The boy has been absent for some time and reaches for redemption. They may be worthy of communion. Or sacrificial rite." A slight bow of his head, and blizzard-white hair clumped over his brow like frost. "The Almighty would be appeased after such a long while...and for the boy..."

"Yes," Deacon abruptly finished, almost like a conceding sigh. "And bearing such a striking resemblance." Then that deep, rumbling voice broke over the congregation like a storm. "We gain more children seeking the warmth of the light! With open arms, we welcome those who accept purification, to join the ranks of His army against the invading darkness! Step up, my children, and feel His holy presence!"

Alpha guided his followers with a threatening motion of his halberd, herding them like sickly cattle to the dais. They were marched past Celeste and Omega, their ghostly gazes drawn to the splintering floor, never rising to meet theirs, or Deacon's. Alpha, however, sneered as he sauntered past, eyes like blades ribboning her heart.

The gut-ripping sensation clawed into her throat.

Her tongue was dry and shriveled like salted meat.

Jaw clenched, grinding.

Sweat pooled across her brow, misted her lashes and stung her eyes, dribbled down her red-hot cheeks like freshly flowing tears.

She was holding her breath again.

Wait.

An echo of her father, a faint whisper of the past, almost as though he was guiding her heart from far beyond her own reach. It seized her like a strangling grip, robbed her lungs of air, snagged her fleeting gaze to the irregular movement of Alpha's flock of followers. They straggled warily, with their gazes drawn to the slight movements of their own feet—all but one. The third follower, with the sunken features of a decomposing corpse, shoved to the front to meet Deacon's risen hand, arms tensely tucked against hips. She saw the eager shine in his otherworldly wide eyes; they were unlike the members of the congregation, ravenously bright like the spread of flames. The follower's eyes were steeled and dark, smoldering with an intense determination that was far too familiar. A feeling she was once drunk with. Celeste flinched.

He's going to–!

A dangerous glint of steel, reflecting the pulsing light of the crosses. Those smoldering eyes ignited with a vicious, blood-lusting desire. Steel was driven with an unexpected burst of speed, plunging into Deacon's protruding mid-section.

The blade's edge tore the grubby-grey robe with a sharp *hiss*, exposing Deacon's rounded bare belly, and left a thin graze of red across his skin. Steel blurred for Deacon's throat.

The blade was abruptly stuck midair, his wrists caught by the crushing grip of Deacon's mallet-sized fist. The follower's forearm snapped, *crunching* loudly like brittle branches under a boot. The butcher knife fell. A helpless, terrified scream tore through the chamber. Snot bubbled and tears fell like rain over the fallen blade. The boy's last words were lost in a wailing incoherency.

Blood burst and slopped over the floor like broken water pipe, misting the air with a sultry-sweet scent. Omega had the silent, blurring movements of a ghost, the steel spear raining down on the follower before the boy's gaze could track the movements. The frail boy gurgled on his last breath, ribcage bursting open in a slurry of red, and the spearpoint twisted through and out of the spine to be driven through the wooden floor. When Omega took a single pace back and admired his art, the dead boy was skewered on the upright spear like a piece of meat.

Celeste had barely processed the mayhem when the crowd erupted into a vicious, growling chant at the spillage of blood. Alpha hesitated for only a moment, then lunged for the next follower he had just paraded through the congregation. He lacked the graceful fluid movements of Omega, and the thundering godlike force, however. An awkward slash opened the second follower's neck but missed the carotid artery by an inch. The boy fell in shock, crying out, "You promised!" to Alpha before the thorn ripped out through his throat with more precise aim.

Despite the advances in age, Omega reacted with the grace of a seasoned warrior. Leaving the spear driven into the bloodied floor, he seized another of Alpha's followers and unceremoniously opened the boy's throat with a dagger. Steamy blood fountained, and before the boy's knees clapped against the floorboards and splashed in his own blood, Omega had gashed the throat of the final follower. Hair tangled in his unyielding grip, Omega held the dying boy over the rising raucous of the crowd, reveling in the fog of blood.

"This is what happens to those who betray the sanctity of His name!" Deacon's voice rose over the palpable excitement of the crowd. "A sacrifice of blood, a sacrifice of life! The Almighty has chosen the symbol of desecration, for those who relish sin rather than eternal glory! I am blessed, and those with hearts of sin cannot lay their hands on His divine warrior!"

The gathering blood meandered past Celeste's feet in dark, scarlet streams. Although her eyes were steeled against the violence she had witnessed, and once perpetuated, her heart hammered as fast as a rapid-fire rifle, flushing her vibrating body with gut-wrenching fear.

Vega's venomous influence seeped through the cracks of her rationale, whispering even beyond death for her daughter to bare fangs against those who threaten the pack. However, it was her father's soulful counsel she adhered to, the gentle rebuke to fortify her mind against the poison crawling through her veins, to calculate her surroundings.

Survive.

She held her ground against the advancing killers. Omega was wielding a dagger that gleamed with a sticky smear of red and Alpha rounded on her with an awkward, but deadly grip on his halberd. The hair on the back of her neck bristled like wolf fur. A scream clawed up her throat.

She bit her tongue.

"I ask you this only once, child," Deacon growled at her, beady eyes burning with a darkness she couldn't escape; it consumed her every thought. "Are you worthy of His mercy?"

"Yes," she blurted, teeth chattering as she spoke. *Melina.* "I am worthy. I seek forgiveness in His eyes. I-I seek redemption for the wrong I have done. I want to make things right. I want my soul back."

Her heart withered under his smoldering glare. "You are His children now." Turning his back to her, he hobbled over to the edge of the dais, bloody footprints soaked into the wood. "The blood rites shall commence!"

The congregate exploded into a furious, raving madness, howling a propensity for blood that rattled to her bones. Even with his back turned to her, she felt his scorching glare linger over her, sifting through the lies and remorseful façade with cold calculation.

He knows.

The chilling thought drifted endlessly along the fringes of her mind. He knew, she was certain, that there were rats in his vipers nest. He knew there was nothing those rats could do but become his next meal.

Without sparing a second glance at her, Deacon turned to Omega with a droll whisper, "Show His new children to their sleeping quarters." A sardonic grin sliced through greying whiskers. "I'm sure they'll find the arrangement quite comfortable."

TWENTY-ONE
O Ye, of Little Faith

OMEGA OBSERVED Celeste's frantically wandering gaze absorb every detail of the desecrated building with those grey-as-steel eyes of his as they were shepherded out of the blood-soaked chamber. Paint and shabby wallpaper from the old times peeled in thin strips like fraying fabric, faded to a dull and filthy discoloration that gave the corridors the hauntingly lonely and forgotten appearance. Cobwebs slung in every crevice and corner were long abandoned to a thick layer of dust.

There was still an unbearable stench of death that seemed to shadow her every movement.

"Our day begins precisely at first light and ends in full darkness," Omega explained with a hint sympathy. Celeste found his faint expression of remorse still gave her chills. "There are chores to be accomplished; the farm plots need tending and water irrigated and collected from rain barrels; extra hands are always welcome for communion cooking; there is plenty of wash, the latrines must be scrubbed and rinsed daily; the grounds must be patrolled at all times. Grace will only be earned with work, and only a Watcher may offer Grace. What is yours is ours. That means you must provide anything you scavenge and discover. As it is the Almighty's before it is yours, and you shall be blessed accordingly for your sacrifice with the body and blood of Christ. There are no weapons permitted within the church grounds..."

His voice was a passing whisper beneath the thundering of her heart. Focus fleeted within moments, thoughts zinged like bullets, teeth grinded to powder. Vega's presence slithered along the fringe of her mind, hissing and spitting venom like the viper she had once been. There were other ghosts who wailed stronger than mountain winds, drowning her in contrition as she marched down the cold halls of the church

"I have experience with gizmos, gadgets, anything electronic really, if I can take it apart I can put it back together. I can possibly help wire these old light fixtures and outlets," Nadie rambled on, distracting Celeste from her bombardment of thoughts. "If the system relies on a generator, I may be able—"

"Quiet," Alpha sneered over his shoulder. "Only those truly blessed by the Almighty may have the privilege to serve directly. You'll do as your told, when your told—there is always a need for sacrificial rites."

"Alpha." Omega's voice was almost a low rumbling growl. "I pray you did not orchestrate such blasphemy."

"I did nothing but offer His mercy to those who are lost to sin." Alpha's response was calculating and candid.

"You must remember what she once taught you."

There was a slight break in Alpha's tone. "But *she* is no longer here, and I need remember nothing but the glory of the Almighty." His bright eyes frosted. "It is Deacon who must remember what he once taught."

"Deacon is a prophet of the Almighty."

A showering flash of sparks when Alpha rapped the end of the halberd against the cement floor. "If Deacon had moved against the heathens—"

"Boy, you had best recall your place," warned Omega, "and who gave you the honor to wield Morning Light."

Alpha regarded his bloodstained axehead with a motherly fondness, leaving Celeste to struggle with her own barrage of thoughts, and stumble along at their awkwardly slow pace. They hadn't wandered far from the congregation; the rhythmic bass of their chanting and stampeding against the dais beat like a steady drum against her chest until even her heartrate thumped alongside the reverberating madness.

"...restricted to the commons for the duration of nightfall

unless otherwise directed by one of the Watchers or Deacon himself."

Alpha snorted over Omega. "Sacrificial rites await those who betray His mercy."

Celeste caught the glimmer of ice in Snyder's gaze. "We'll be good," the blonde said, lightening her voice to a faint squeak, and revealing that amiable facet cleverly buried beneath a stonewall of irritability. "Once we eat and get a good night's rest—"

"Eat?" scoffed Alpha. "Dinner *is* grace if there is an accepted offer."

"Alpha." Omega whispered his name in a threatening growl. "The theatrics of your sacrificial rites interrupted grace. Child, there will be porridge served to all within His grace when the sun rises."

They neared a sharp incline and were placidly marched through another steel gate, bladed with curving razor steel with flaking rust and grime. The hall split into several expanding chambers hazily lit with the intermittent flicker of a buzzing fluorescent light and mounted overhead lamplights. The mouldy scent of sweat rolled off the walls like a damp, noxious chill. There was a creeping cold that plummeted from her lungs and down into her roiling guts. Led through the final chamber, Celeste laid eyes on a vast sea of mottled-brown wool spread in every direction over the worn floorboards. There were sections of musty articles of clothing piled in rows along the makeshift woolen carpet, along with patchy and fraying blankets and lumpy pillows, a scattered assortment of belongings such as dirty, chipping plates, cracked cups and mugs, squeezed-dry bottles, and ratty footwear. With only a foot or so of length between each blanketed section and no discernable pathway, they had to cautiously place each step as they entered the humid chamber. It resembled a shantytown. And they weren't alone.

There were two of them, men as old as Omega in appearance but with frail figures and bowing limbs from the ravages of age. Their hair had been neglectfully sheared, scraggily clinging to their chins like fraying fabric. Wide eyes greeted them, but there was no hint of madness, only confusion, like a deer caught in headlights.

"O-Omega," one of the older men nervously choked out. The pouch in his bony grasp was clutched tightly to his chest like a child told to relinquish a favorite toy. "We weren't expecting—"

Alpha interrupted with a cold whisper, "Why are you both absent from communion?"

The first man swallowed his words nervously, while the second chimed in with a slithering response, "We were just scouting for stragglers and any clandestine activity."

Omega drew the massively long spear to his chest, thrusting the bladed point between them. The lancing weapon dwarfed them in height. "You are in the selection for a new Watcher, correct?" he gravely asked, pacing a single step toward them. "Why is it you are not present with an offering for the Almighty?"

"But it is as I—"

"You will not lie in the presence of a Watcher!" Alpha shouted, but it was Omega who intervened when he abruptly rounded on the second man, asking intently, "Where did you obtain that pouch?"

"I-I...It is mine, sir," the man rasped slowly between his unsteadily heaving breaths.

"What are its contents?"

The man stammered, "W-w-what?"

"Name the contents of the pouch," Omega commanded. "Then empty the contents along the ground."

The second man's bones nearly clattered out from under his skin he was so visibly shaken from the demand. His bony fingers slowly and carefully raked across the pouch firmly in his grasp, palpating the leather like a wound beneath the flesh. *Foolish.* She was certain Omega's watchdog gaze trailed the subtly sinuous movement of his fingers as she did.

"It is...well...that would be..." The old man was confounded by the unraveling of his own lie and suffocated in a terrifying silence. Celeste swore she could hear his heartbeat accelerate to a pace that echoed her own. With tears in his eyes, the man turned to his companion and whispered, "Mark..."

"Sacrificial rites," Alpha said eagerly.

Omega disagreed, to Alpha's dismay. "No," he said quietly, but relinquished a sigh at Alpha's disappointment. "He is to have his purification instead."

The old man clutching the pouch to his chest stared at his companion, Mark, trembling like a tree whipping in the wind.

A bloodthirsty grin brightened Alpha's face like some jack-o'-lantern sculpted from flesh. He looked at the first man, tongue sinisterly slithering across his lips. "Another subordinate."

"P-please, no! I will put it back!" The old man pleaded, but tears fell as swiftly as the cascade of steaming scarlet around his feet. A forward thrust from the lengthy bladed spear ran through his throat, bursting blood across the polished wooden pole. A sobbing choke, clicking gurgle, and the old man shuddered and crashed to the woolen spread in his own blood. With a shriek and a mist of sticky red, Mark staggered aside and muttered slurs that would have made her father blush.

"You are to be brought forward to Deacon," ordered Omega, gently swaying the bloody spear to the other man's throat. "You are to be sentenced, officially, for betraying the cross and your word you put forward for the position of Watcher."

The wailing man was marched through his companion's blood. His feet *squished* the sodden wool spread.

"The doors will be barred after communion," Omega said, and turned his back on the stunned group. "Locate an empty bedroll and be ready for chores at first light. The Almighty deserves our upmost devotion."

"And know this punishment befalls those who tempt the mercy of the church," Alpha sneered over his shoulder. "The Lord takes His offering and then graces your devotion—if you are deemed worthy."

The sharp whistle was a disturbingly somber melody from the dying man's ruptured throat. It was his last attempted breath, and he died under the intensely perturbed gazes of complete strangers, tears still falling as blood flowing from the gash slowed to a faint trickle.

"This is *not* good," Snyder hissed through clenched teeth once the Watchers were out of earshot. "We're disarmed and drastically outnumbered. We need a plan to get out *now*."

Odine glared through ratted strands of her vibrantly colored hair. "We're hens in the wolf den," she said, grinning slyly. "They won't expect us."

"They need food," Twist chimed in his disappointment.

Nadie hushed him, gaze wandering between Celeste and Snyder as if each woman held a blade to her throat and demanded loyalty. "We still need to assess what sort of power grid they've assembled for those—"

Melina hummed distractedly, "These are believers, the devout; they seek salvation in His name. We should be heeding Deacon's words."

Celeste's chapped lips painfully peeled apart like the sticky side of tape, but her teeth chattered loudly whenever she spoke. She bit her tongue, halting the aching grind of her jaw. It felt like her eyes rolled around in their sockets, shifting, nearly vibrating out of her skull. Her eyesight waned to a blurry smear of white.

"...e...ste..."

Repeated blinks snapped her vision into focus. She stared at the others, and felt like her stomach was up in her throat; the souring stench of blood was absolutely strangling.

"What?" she croaked, voice shattering. She cleared her throat with a quick cough. "What is it?"

"W-what did he feed us?" Nadie asked. "What was that?"

"Damn," Snyder cursed. "You two seem off." Then she lowered her voice to a cautious whisper, "Red needs to be left out of the loop for now. She's enamored with all this church shit."

Celeste swallowed past her heart thumping in her throat. "Deacon can see through it all. He knows. He must know. Didn't you feel it?"

Snyder scoffed. "Well, you've all finally lost it. More reason to get the hell out of here."

"Follow through with your orders," Odine warned. "We have a few days before Theta arrives."

"Why isn't there any *food*," muttered Twist, ignoring Nadie's soothing response.

"Look," Snyder said, "your leader's brilliant plan isn't going to work. I am not going to be her pawn. We're leaving."

Nadie hissed her annoyance, teeth chattering. "Did none of you see those towers on the way in? Those are turrets, likely with sensors that detect and track any movement. Nothing is getting in or out until *we* shut them down—until *I* shut them down."

"Jesus Christ," Snyder cursed, a bladed glare thrown at Melina. The redhead was as brightly flushed as she had been during the communion, shimmery green eyes drawn to the ceiling as they spun in their sockets like wheels, thin red lips crooked with a bewitched grin. Snyder slowly nodded to her, whispering icily, "We can't rely on *everyone* to watch our six."

Odine watched her intently, bug-eyed. "There was something in that food and drink."

"Celeste?" Nadie echoed hesitantly. "You don't look so well. I don't feel so well. Do I look well?"

Celeste became achingly aware of her clenched jaw when she spoke, "I-I'm trying to think."

Snyder clicked her tongue. "Think quickly."

Shit. She tripped over a tangled tongue.

"We need to *go*."

"No," Celeste choked out. She gave her head a small shake but felt like her brain painfully sloshed around inside her skull. "I just...I need..."

An impatient snort. "We don't have time, *shadow spawn*."

"I can't focus," she admitted impatiently, smothering a frustrated scream in her throat. "Odine is right. Something was in that food, something familiar—sort of. It doesn't feel the same as my pain killers, but somehow, similar—if that makes any goddamn sense. I don't know. My heart just won't slow down."

"Neither will your mouth," Snyder said, rolling her frosty eyes. She snorted on laughter, clacked her teeth. "Shit. Stimulants, why didn't I think of it before. Blackwell would dope the soldiers up during long excursions and city sieges. Amphetamines, mostly, though my brother once said the soldiers scavenged any medical facilities and houses for anything. Stands to reason that this Deacon prick can do the same. If he controls the east like Theta believes, who knows how far he's looted and scavenged for supplies."

Nadie stared at Celeste for a moment, then Melina, who had taken to wandering through the sectional rows of blankets and belongings. "That's how he's controlling them." Disappointment tightened her voice to slight whisper. "Shit, that's how he's trying to control *us*. I swear I felt it. I swear."

Vega's ghostly warning tore through Celeste's mind like a fired bullet, *This is anything but God!*

"Shit," she cursed with a single, shuddering breath. "Snyder is right. We were drugged. It's ripping my guts apart." She found herself leering at Melina, who was now kneeling far from them and consumed in a muttering prayer. Those words of fervor rang like a shrill scream in Celeste's ears. "Hearing Deacon speak was dangerously alluring. If he captivates these people like..." She struggled to utter her redhead's name.

Snyder finished pointedly, "Then he has a massive and *loyal* army. So, let me reiterate; we need to get out of here while we still can."

"If we can find their terminals, I can force a backdoor in," Nadie whispered, oak-brown eyes rounding. "Shut down the turret system long enough for us to escape—and Theta can do whatever it is she pleases."

Odine snorted with contempt, flicking her plum-bright hair from her slender face. "Theta will burn this place to the hell it belongs to."

With a series of sweeping glances, Nadie said, "I'll work on locating—"

"No," Celeste interrupted breathlessly. Her lungs shuddered from a gripping chill. "We do nothing for now. It's too dangerous."

Incredulity shadowed Snyder's eyes. "You can't seriously believe in this suicide mission."

"We do nothing."

A threatening growl. "You're not our *commander*, remember?"

A paralyzing silence gripped her throat as the floor trembled beneath their feet. It was like a storm brewing over the distant mountains, rumbling down from the heavens themselves. Hundreds of voices carried like a babbling brook as the worshippers flowed into the chamber as a torrent of flesh, pooling across the woolen spread into a dizzying sea of unfamiliar faces.

"We need to keep quiet," Nadie whispered, withdrawing her gaze from the oncoming throng. "We can't talk here. Whisper, whisper."

"Blend in," Snyder ordered with a quick snap of her fingers. She stared to each of them, jaw unhinged, lip curling in a wolfish snarl until Celeste nodded, cleared her throat, and turned away from the corpse and its freshly warm pooling blood.

An icy breath was stuck in her throat.

The legion of worshippers were shabbily robed and hooded, with a myriad of glaring eyes that burned into her until even her bones broiled under their intense condemnation. They marched through the chamber like ants, buzzing with a palpable excitement, hissing whispers to one another with their gazes drawn to the slumping dead body and the bedrolls soaking in a crimson pool.

Holy shit. Celeste choked on the sour-scent of so many unwashed bodies. *There must be hundreds between us and the only exit.*

Another peculiarity caught in the web her rapid-firing senses—there were more men than women, and more younger boys than girls. It was a frighteningly disparaging difference. The men were further along in age, hair receding and ashy-grey, skin milky or dark but craggy and pockmarked. There were older women, too. Though smooth-faced with brightly burning eyes, though they lacked the familiarity of the women she had grown accustomed to even within the military's ranks. Their features were gaunt and sallow, callous and deadpan, hair cropped to a soldier's trim barely a finger's width, bodies attenuated yet strangely sinewy and firmly tight like Snyder's thin, wiry frame.

The corpse on the floor, sprawled over fraying blankets and a meager pile of stained clothing, was scarcely spared a second glance from the worshippers as they spread out around them.

"Shit," Snyder cursed. Sweat slicked the fringes of her blonde hair, dripped over her lashes. "Stick together, move slowly."

"Excuse me?"

The scratchy voice belonged to a woman far older than Celeste, with her sheared hair just a shimmer of bright gold along her scarred scalp, and eyes crinkled and silvery. Her gaze held a glimmer of curiosity and not the predacious glare of the other worshippers. The throng fragmented around them, and she cautiously approached with her fingers tightly locked across her drooping belly. None made a gesture to greet her.

"You are the newly Exalted, yes?" the woman asked softly. As her gaze wandered between them, Celeste caught the iridescence speckled around her brow, similarly designed like the designs etched into Omega's skin. "Welcome to the Church of the Last Light." Her smile was faint, tugging stubbornly at the corners of her pursed rosy lips. She paused for a moment, then said quickly, "If you will follow me, I can show you all to a vacancy."

Nadie nervously shifted her stance and against Twist. "What about...him?"

With a shrug of her small shoulders, the woman said, "Someone will deal with that in due time. Come along."

She didn't bother to wait for a response. Moments crawled by, the woman was flickering out of sight, and Celeste stumbled into the crowd after her.

The stench of blood was far too heavy in the air.

The others followed at a grudging pace, even Melina, whose meadow-green eyes were perfectly rounded and captivated by the shanty community. The worshippers hung back, retreated slightly at their approach, intently fixed on the newcomers and the blood that dappled their fresh faces. It was predacious, Celeste thought, how their eyes wandered over them like fresh meat. Like the infected, like the hunters and hellhounds and creepers she had fought through the city and sewers.

The woman paused momentarily, regarded the empty spread before her, then gestured to them with the slightest nod of her shaved head. Her brow was raised, ink glimmering around her left eye. Her face was sun-kissed, features narrow and tapered to a pointed chin, her bulbous nose shifted to the left as if recently broken.

"Exceptional amount," she said after another passing glance over them. "Brought in by Omega, no doubt. He has a soft spot for the Almighty's lost children."

"Right," Snyder said softly. Her wary eyes were peeled wide against the other worshippers who muttered and whispered as they passed with curious glances.

The woman smiled faintly. "I'm Azazel," she said. "Just Aza is sufficient. You'll find everything you'll need for the night provided for you here. There is a shortage of workers for the gardens, that is where you all shall start at dawn. Whatever you collect is for the church. Meals are provided when communion begins but only if you have earned grace."

Snyder clicked her tongue but remained hidden beneath her docile façade. "What about clothes? Weapons for when we scavenge beyond the grounds?"

"There are seamstresses you may seek out, either for their handywork or to apprentice." Azazel arched her brow and smothered an attempted grin. "But *only* those who serve a Watcher directly may venture beyond the grounds."

"We're prisoners." Snyder's jovial mask began to crumble, but Azazel only shot another curious glance at her, silver eyes as sharp and glinting as a polished blade.

"You are not prisoners, no," she replied. "But there is a high risk when leaving the safety of these grounds. Infected roam free, a blight under God's eye, and it is His will that you have not caught that terrible sickness while lost out in the Scorch already. For your safety as well as the rest of His children, you must only travel with a Watcher."

Quite simply, we're prisoners.

Celeste cleared her throat, face red-hot under Azazel's studious gaze. "You're a Watcher, yes?"

Only the corner of Azazel's mouth twisted, but her steel-silver eyes narrowed slightly. "Yes," she said slowly, rolling her tongue. "And you look like you've survived a few fights. Those are the scars of a warrior, not a damsel."

"A few," Celeste blurted, then tied her unraveling tongue. "B-but I only seek His forgiveness now."

The silver of Azazel's eyes shone as her prying gaze lingered on Celeste a moment longer. "Be risen at dawn, and eager for a day's work in His name."

"Miss Azazel," Melina sang. "What will happen to the gentleman who broke his faith?"

There was something dark in Azazel's impassive expression. For another moment she stared at the redhead like a predator gauges the weakest in the herd.

"Well," she finally said, gesturing to the corpse across the chamber, whose clothes had already been ransacked, leaving him bare and bloody as three others heaved him from the floor. "If death was not immediately warranted then he has a chance for His forgiveness."

"Purification?"

A hollow smile. "Faith in the Almighty will uproot the sin deep in his soul. He must only accept His glory."

Melina's freckles faded when her face flushed red. "He is all forgiving."

Another hollow smile and Azazel turned her back. "Morning, be ready."

The gathering had long fragmented and scattered throughout the room, but it was still unbearably crowded, almost shoulder-to-shoulder as everyone settled and filled every available blanket. Even if they wanted to leave, they wouldn't be able to walk without tripping over limbs.

The air grew hot and stale, and the stench of a hundred sweaty bodies clung to the back of her throat. She slowly sank into the blanket that grated her skin like sandpaper. Snyder sat across from her, and her mouth hung in disgust at the sullied state of her sheets. Celeste could feel the uneven wooden boards of the floor painfully jab her through the blankets, and judging by the twisting expressions of the others, they found little comfort in their new bedding. Lying on his back, Twist was nearly spread out across two bedrolls, leaving Nadie to cling to the tattering edges of her blanket. The poor woman trembled and heaved, her mind endlessly circling. She seemed so broken.

Celeste was familiar with those demons. Caden's blood had become a frozen splotch of crimson buried in a blizzard, butchered and long dead, yet she still felt his icy fingers worm across her flesh, plucking at her exposed skin, ramming his rancidity against her for days, for weeks, for months. She still felt the chilling slither of his tongue on her neck.

Odine was as withdrawn as Nadie, hovering along the fringe of the team she was forced to join. Twisted strands of her plum-colored hair shadowed her gaze, but Celeste knew the bandit girl kept her senses sharpened and attuned to any looming threat—she had seen her in blood-spilling action.

Melina bowed her head and muttered to herself, eyes clenched, red curls bouncing with each nod of her head. She wouldn't even look in her direction. The chasm between them seemed deep and unending, impossible to cross. After a moment, Celeste breathed out a defeated sigh and slunk deeper into the firm embrace of the floor.

There would no love from her wildflower.

Sleep mocked her every attempt. She thrashed about as wild as her heartrate. The blankets were scratchy thorn bushes. She was sweating one minute and shivering with chills the next. She sat upright, hearing the sound of whispers as a distant babbling brook. She felt the air thicken with that same raving madness from the communion, saw the eyes around her grow wildly round, heard his name whispered eerily from their lips like a beloved hymn.

Deacon.

His round face beamed a rosy shade of delight. A forming smile twisted his scraggily whispers that thinned to a point under a bulgy chin. His eyes were like beady shadows, sweeping through the crowd with adoration. Robed as modestly as the rest, patched with irregular seams and contrasting colors to the drab grey. She saw the age that folded his skin, the awkward amble on his oak-carved cane, his hunched shoulders and sagging paunch. A frail old man in appearance, but beneath she sensed the vigor that coursed through him like the narcotic in her own veins, the raw horsepower he had displayed when snapping a bone like an old, brittle branch. He was an imposing man, like Blackwell had been, only Deacon radiated an intensity she had only felt in brief flashes from her father when he had fought for survival. Blackwell had been cruel, sadistic, but Deacon seemed to believe himself a god.

She wasn't sure which was ultimately worse.

Deacon wobbled through the gathering stragglers, nodding his praise and commending the order of their sleeping arrangements. He stepped lightly, tapping his cane as he went, shadowed by his deadly Watchers. Omega was a pace behind and to Deacon's left, dwarfed by the bladed spear against his shoulder. A sneering face shadowed Deacon's right, axehead spinning into a blur of blood-red steel. Alpha's eyes were a brightly burning wildfire, consuming all in his sight. There was nearly a skip to his step.

There was another familiar face slowly trailing behind them.

He was a shambling drunk, teetering off balance with every misplaced step. He hunched forward like he was about to somersault, head cocked over his bony shoulder. Blood dried to a flaking crust across his crinkled forehead. Milky-white eyes gazed far but saw little, only following the sharp clicks of Alpha's tongue like a loyal mutt. The old man they had briefly encountered on their arrival to the room was only a shell of his former self.

"Deacon!"

"It's Deacon!"

"Why is he here?"

"Join us for prayers, Deacon!"

"Deacon!"

A small gasp escaped Melina, eyes bursting with green and bulging wide. She sat upright, turning a shoulder to Celeste, red curls a fiery beacon in the churning sea of pale flesh. His name brushed against her lips, her delicately small voice rising to join the haunting chant. Deacon stood over her, and she stared up at him like he were the glorious warmth of the sun kissing her skin for the first time. Only Celeste felt the immeasurable chill behind the darkness of his eyes; she could only wonder how stained his hands were from the blood of innocence. She found herself staring down at her own trembling hands. Crimson specked in the fine ridges of her prints. It gathered, dripping like wax around a burning flame, trickling from her wrists, pooling as a sticky mass of tar in her lap.

An involuntary scream was smothered in her throat, and she coughed quietly, furiously blinking away the hallucination of blood. Her gloved fingers flexed, constricting the tight leather around her severed stumps. Was she going mad?

"Hello, child."

Deacon leaned over the crook of his cane, eyes peeking over the droopy pudge of his cheeks. His smile was broad and bright, but shadows danced through his eyes.

"Deacon," Melina breathed with a smile so wide Celeste thought it would stretch off her face. "I am gracious for your hospitality and kindness."

Those perpetually dark eyes narrowed slightly. "And I am gracious to the Almighty to guide only the most devout to these holy grounds." When his gaze flicked over Celeste, she swore she caught the gleam of bloodlust she recognized all too well. "We are grateful for *all* His children."

"He is all-giving," Melina whispered softly, almost trance-like. "On behalf of us all I would like to extend a prayer to Him."

Celeste caught Snyder's involuntarily fidget from her peripheral, and the crinkle of her brow. She felt her own heart lurch into a nervously swifter pace. What did Deacon want?

She could already hear Vega's poisonous purr, chastising her muddled mind. *He's a predator, we're his prey; he's gauging for weaknesses.*

His cheeks rippled from another broad smile. The whites of his teeth gleamed. His beady eyes were enthusiastically bright.

No. Strength.

"A prayer would be most welcome," he pleasantly agreed and drew his face closer to hers. "We may do so, if you would care to join myself and the Watchers for some dandelion tea? It is a delight during the nightly chill."

Melina nearly burst with joy. "I would love to!" She was on her feet before the words excitedly leapt from her tongue.

"The tea is plenty sweet this year, we have had a blessed harvest," Deacon said, sweeping the redhead under the ballooning flesh of his arm. The flexing wood of his cane woefully groaned under his corpulence.

It was like a sharp blade twisting into her heart.

"Melina," she breathed.

"Perhaps another time," Omega whispered, frowning. As he turned to leave, Alpha shoved past the oddly complacent old man and sneered back, "Invitation only, *cur*." With a snorting snicker he added to the old man, "You can stay here as a warning to our new friends."

Her redhead was abruptly gone.

But the old man shuffled his bare and bloody feet to steady his balance, though he made little effort to notice he was being left behind. His eyes were as cloudy white as curdling milk, irregular blotches of crimson flaked from his cheeks to his chin, and ripples of skin twisted in the center of his forehead. Swaying where he stood, knees slightly bent, he lurched and clumsily slammed down to his backside. He sat across from Celeste, milky eyes lost to the scrutiny of her own glare.

"What the hell is wrong with him?" Snyder hissed.

Only Celeste saw the blood that ejected from his forehead like spittle, the fleshy murky-grey chucks that dribbled from what she thought were wrinkles; the flesh had peeled in strings like wood shavings around a bullet-sized gap in his forehead, like his skull had been drilled into. Spurts of minced brain matter and blood splashed down over his vacant expression.

"Holy shit."

A sickening dread wrung her stomach like a wet rag, and Celeste gagged and retched between her lap. Nadie choked on a sob, while Twist offered a tree-trunk for an arm as comfort. Snyder turned aside, scoffing her disgust. A frown sank Odine's sharp features, and her glinting hazel eyes glared at the dead man through the strands of her bright hair.

Celeste crawled to her side, nauseated, and cradled the sharp twinge she felt burrowed deep within her neck.

TWENTY-TWO
Sheep's Clothing

IT FELT like her skull had been pulverized with a claw hammer.

Her mouth was a desert of discomfort, her belly impossibly knotted. The numbing flesh of her fingers felt like stiff rubber, swelled inside the confines of the glove. With a thumping ache behind her eyes, she woke to Melina's empty blankets, and felt the heat rise to her cheeks. Groggily, she groaned and shifted her creaking limbs. Every muscle felt seized, her spine disjointed and crooked, neck kinked and throbbing. Whatever that substance had been, coursing through her veins for the night's entirety, fire crawled under her skin at the thought of more.

Get a grip, you've only just cleared your mind.

Her stomach throbbed.

"I'm starving, and I doubt they have catered breakfast," Snyder quipped over the *crackling* of her flexing joints. "I can't wait to work my ass off today."

Shut up, Celeste wanted to say, but she couldn't bring herself to speak through the mind-rattling pain inside her skull. Even with her eyes tightly shut, the thump of her heartbeat shocked her vision white. Wave after wave of agony crippled her thoughts. Another moment crawled past, and she fought the urge to snicker at her misfortune. The torment would never cease. She might as well wake.

Nadie was seated with Twist, flicking woolen fuzz from the giant man's thick neck. Her hair was a tangled nest of soot-black curly hair, and her face pallid and slick with sweat. Twist was beginning to look less of a gargantuan child and more like the hulking man that he was beneath such simple innocence. His face was patchy with wiry stubble, his mohawk now a furling wave down the side of his head.

Ever the army brat, Snyder sat over her perfectly folded sheets with edges of her patchy blanket tucked neatly under her. Hands folded, spine rigidly straight, lengthy blonde hair slicked into a tail, eyes narrowed to icy pinpoints. Scrutinizing every face that passed, every glance cast in her direction, every movement caught in her peripheral sight. Her flitting gaze studied the strangers innocuously gathered near her.

The room was sprawling and uncomfortably large, but crammed to the point of claustrophobia. The air was humid and thick like a sightless fog. Celeste unwillingly breathed in the air expelled from every stranger's lungs in the room. She was unsure if it was hunger that gnashed her belly or the putrid stench of unwashed flesh. She cringed, shivering. The old man had long succumbed to the excavation of his brain, his skin as milky white as his vacantly open eyes. Blood settled and bloated the carcass to a ticking time-bomb of rot.

So much for forgiveness.

Celeste felt the back of her neck warm, and she glanced over her shoulder to Odine's petulant glare, those bug-eyes studying her as if she could read every thought in Celeste's head. Celeste held her tongue, and the bandit woman clung to the silence like command. The pugnacious attitude roiling beneath such a taut look, the utter defiance in her glare. It was clear what dominated her thoughts; either Celeste would act first, or Odine would, and Celeste was certain the would-be assassin was swiftly losing patience like blood from a severed artery.

"Well, isn't this a disappointment."

Aza's deadpanned voice nearly drowned in the murmur of the waking crowd. Her mouth was crooked in both corners when she smiled, almost like a sneer, scrunching her wide nose. Her eyes flicked to the cold-grey corpse a few feet from them.

"It seems He has spoken," Snyder cooed with precisely recited words that may as well have fallen from Melina's tongue. The blonde even adopted similar mannerisms; a distressingly alien smile deformed her usual grimace. "Forgiveness is not a reward for the unfaithful."

"A peculiar truth," Aza snorted, giving the blonde a listless glance. "To think all he had to accomplish was acceptance of fate. That hole in his earthly vessel wouldn't have been of any importance."

As Celeste mulled over those odd words, Aza's voice rose to command. "You will be escorted to the garden grounds, and from then until communion you will dig, plant, harvest, whatever there is to do. If you earn enough, you are entitled to His Grace under my order. If not, there is always tomorrow."

"And if we starve, Miss Aza?" Snyder asked, slick with mockery even through her carefully calculated restraint.

It wasn't lost on Aza, who responded tartly, "Feast on your faith."

The grounds extended far from sight and deep into the uncharted Dead Wood, or the Scorch as the Watchers called it, canopied by crooked black branches weaved like wicker baskets. Charred thickets fenced the length of the property and were a densely tangled and an impenetrable jungle of thorn, carved to sharp points like pikes, with razor-wire strung throughout the knotted branches.

The gardens were an uneven terrain of rolling mounds that were more like sandy dunes than soil to be tilled and seeded. Wilting weeds clung to the slopes, brittle and dried to a crisp like tinder by the scattered sunshine filtered by the branched canopy. Celeste saw the patches of vibrantly green life winding through the dead desert. Beanstalks snaked through wooden mesh, plucked clean and trimmed; bladed leaves and twisted vines with blood-red and grass-green tomatoes that were splitting with ripeness; twiggy bushes with withering raspberries; scrawny purple plum trees stood barely the same height as her. There were carrots, cucumbers, potatoes, but they were clustered in small patches, dying of thirst and mud-brown, webbed by insects and other buzzing pests. The soil a dry unyielding desert, crops crippled with blight. They were haphazardly tended by few worshippers, while others milled about nearby as if they assessed the boundaries of the grounds or gathered in prayer around the withering weeds as if seeded purely on their faith. Celeste couldn't help but subtly admire their tenacity, no matter how much of a wasted effort she knew it to be.

"Tools must be repaired if broken, and cleaned after each use. If there is none to your liking, you may construct one of your own," Aza explained, though Celeste's attention was lulled away by a distant trumpeting crow. Was it as her father had told her all those years ago in the mountains? She had to wonder. Was that his soul, intact and irascible as he could ever be, squawking his rebuke at her from beyond the dense thicket? Aza's voice was drowned out as she concentrated, ears perked to hear if anyone else cawed their disappointment.

She mused with an uncontrollable twitch of a smirk, *I was brash and imprudent, hard-headed and believing I had known the workings of the world from a goddamn mountaintop.*

"...fashion a weapon and conspire to harm a member of this church, you will be excommunicated," Aza went on with a playful flick of her tongue. "Hell has plenty of room for unbelievers."

"There are so many of us," Odine said pointedly. "How is it you keep the order?"

Another half-smile. "We are Watchers, we see all."

"Still, it must be difficult."

"So is tilling the soil," Aza snarked, "though you have yet to start."

It was near impossible to mark the progression of time with the sky blotted by a black thicket of dead, gnarled branches. They had discovered, quite unfortunately, the lack of any tools or means to immediately craft exactly what they needed. Nadie observed a few of the dedicated using nothing but their fingers to claw through the soil like a well-worn trowel. Gathering discarded or fallen sticks splintered from the overhead snarl, Snyder handed the bundle between them, shrugging her shoulders at the dismal looks she received. "Better then dirtying your nails, right?" she mocked, glowering. "Plant the goddamn seeds."

Aza, true to her title, watched with the intensity of a wolf scenting blood from a wound. Snyder chose a mound and struck dirt. Grudgingly, Celeste put only a few paces between herself and the intractable blonde. A gentle and patient Nadie explained the repetition to Twist, who hobbled down to one knee with a breathless wheeze, twisted his melon-sized fist around the browning stalks, and crunched them to a leafy dust.

While Odine appeared immodest, sinking her knees into the dirt and tilling by hand, she had swiftly cleared an arm's length of weeds and tangled snarl, flattened several depressions in the slope, prepared the sticks and splintered bark to divide the sections. Snyder's was uneven and choppy, but the blonde seemed more intent on slashing at the earth like a blade hacking flesh rather than dirt to be tilled and rowed.

Whether it had been minutes or hours, Celeste was unsure, but after she was drenched in pasty sweat, hair sticking out in every direction like a tumbleweed, Melina was escorted through the barren gardens by two Watchers she had not seen on the premises before. They were unusual in height with long lanky limbs like some hairless albino chimp, spackle-black bowler hats tipped forward to shadow the whites of their eyes, faces slender and tapered to narrowing chins, ink vibrantly designed and intersecting across their necks. They were nearly identical, clothed in creased suits as grey as their taut grey skin.

For a moment Celeste's heart lurched and painfully skipped a beat. Those red curls were slicked straight and greasy, the luster of a smoldering fire. Eyes bursting wide with only a sliver of green, skin as white as her exposed sockets. She strode calmly between the elongated twins, a strangely crooked smile stretching thinly across her face, fingers tightly clasped and raised against her chest as if she squeezed her own beating heart. Her gaze wandered over the sparsely clustered stalks and leafy vines, and as if in some silent appraisal, cooed gently to the diggers, tenders, harvesters, and even the wanderers who had withdrawn to the stubbornly green verdure nearest the walls of thorn. It wasn't mocking their work or the stingy piles of half-rotted, fly-swarmed fruits and vegetables, but rather admiration for what *could* be accomplished in His glory. The sentiment was not lost on the worshippers, many of whom regarded the redhead with gestures of embrace and prayers. Celeste saw the kindling spark to a roaring fire in her redhead's eyes. It would do them well, she must have thought, God had welcomed her with open arms.

Celeste withdrew her gaze and idle hands to the task before her. The dirt was as coarse as sand, but digging deeper revealed a rich vein of moist clay-soil, which was compact and solid, and splintered most of the hollow twigs and branches Snyder had collected, until she simply resigned to clawing through the mixture with her fingers. Her father had long ago taught her the importance of mixing minerals in barren soil, so she crumbled thick clay, slivered the broken branches, churned the mulch like butter, and sat back with a breathless huff. Melina was watching her, the green of her irises still only a sliver. Her smile was genuinely bright but scattered like the sunshine through the snarl, her heart beating elsewhere.

"You look peaceful, Celeste, with her hands dirty from a garden instead of blood."

"My dad taught me how to plant," Celeste said. "I miss those simple days with him."

It was the first time Melina had spoken to her since their capture in the Dead Wood. The Watchers drifted alongside her like phantoms, their eyes unnervingly shadowed so Celeste was unsure of where their gazes truly haunted. They stood idly for a moment longer, signaled to leave only by a sweetly courteous smile from Melina. Shaded pale and slinking away, they resembled ghosts even more, and their presence had unnerved the others as well.

"You know what I mean," Melina said, jaw shifting. "You're happy here."

Celeste ignored the sting to her pride. "We haven't really had a chance to garden."

"You could have with the military."

"I was too busy fighting their war," Celeste muttered, but smiled bitterly. "I'm done facing them head on."

Melina chewed on her chapped lip, drowning in a silence that had become far too familiar to them. She lowered herself to her knees, content with squeezing the mulch into an even mix. They worked in tandem, tilling rows, spreading mulch, shifting soil. She had been right, Celeste thought, it was more than peaceful. Celeste was warmed by her presence.

But it wasn't to last.

How much of the day had progressed was lost on her, but the exertion whittled away at her stamina, twisted her belly in a vicelike grip. She leaned back, steadied her rapid breathing, and couldn't stop her skin from crawling with chills. There was a sliver of her that craved whatever communion had been, the feeling of bliss that had numbed her from such bodily agony. There was a stabbing ache that radiated through the severed portion of her hand, a pain that made her acutely aware of the jagged spongy flesh stretched over her stumpy knuckles in a crude attempt to seal the old wound. She was exhausted from the constant throbbing discomfort.

"We should stay," Melina finally said, delicately quiet. "We could make a home here"

Celeste peeled her shriveled-dry tongue from the roof of her mouth. "We have friends being held by Theta," she said. "We can't just leave them."

"Of course not," she said, dismissing her worry with a broader smile. It was almost unnerving. "We would help them. It's wonderful to see you care for others, truly...but this is an opportunity given to us by God. This is just like how He had our paths cross for many reasons. I believe this is one of them."

Ice-cold guilt was a harrowing and sobering reality. Celeste had always been a magnet for chaos with a developed penchant for blood, yet Melina had absolved her of all that was foul and filth in her soul with an open declaration of love. No matter the atrocities committed, the ensuing mayhem, the bloodshed, Melina held only love for her. Celeste could, at the very least, let her wildflower bloom.

But for how long?

"Okay," Celeste said, clearing the word from her throat like an irritating cough. Her redhead's eyes danced like firelight. "Okay," she said again. "We give this place a fair chance. We try and make a life here."

"Promise?"

She felt the blistering cold sting of the shackles around her heart. "I promise, Melina."

Her heart was in her throat when Melina leaned closer, warming her skin with a gentle but shaky breath. The days of silence had made them hesitant, but Celeste breathed in that aromatic scent that sent shivers crawling down her spine. A delicate brush of their lips, the taste of honey that lingered for a few sobering moments. Celeste whispered her aching love, then giggled when the redhead flicked her with dirt.

How she had missed her blooming wildflower.

Days were spent in the arid gardens while under the scrutiny of Aza. The barren ground was cleared, tilled, rowed, dug into sectional rows, filled with rich mulch mixture. The other tenders had taken notice, watching intently from afar or approaching with a hesitance that made Celeste aware of how wary they still were of outsiders. Within the span of a few days, they had warmed to Melina exceptionally, fervently embracing her kind and gentle preaching like they had Deacon's. She would often stand over the nearest and highest mound of untouched dirt, gesturing and declaring a bountiful harvest, and praising honest work that wiped a sinner's hands clean. It struck a poignant cord with the followers; they fell alongside Celeste and the others, working shoulder-to-shoulder in the dirt, and eventually began conversing lightly with those they had once considered outsiders. They spared few details of their lives before the church, as if they had blotted out every memory of the past, but that was another way Deacon exerted his fanatical control over the members to his church. The narcotic dangled for those who devoted themselves to the Almighty, whose words came only to the messiah-like Deacon, and were nothing more than shackles around their necks. He was an anchor to the way they believed the world was supposed to be under God, and they were tethered to him with the drug. The relationship was purely parasitical. The Watchers were even worse, however, as they killed with little discretion for any who rejected the faith. It was peculiar, but even the military had its fanatics and zealots stalking the fringes of their ranks. But the sociopathic Watchers had steadily risen in rank within the Church of the Last Light, second in strength only to the ruthless Deacon, and remained ever true to their bestowed title. Scarcely a moment passed without their owl-like eyes sweeping over every inch of the premises with gazes that held little beyond the terrifying gleam of death. They were the reaper's scythe poised over all their necks like a guillotine.

A bell rung when the sky smoldered to dusk, echoed by a symphony of shrieking crows; Communion, when worshippers diligently flocked back into the church in raving, chanting droves, and they were whisked away into the rushing rapids of madness. Flickering fire animated the stained-glass walls with shifting mosaics of light, and their scintillating patterns wandered over the derelict altar and enigmatic Deacon as his booming words coursed through the blood of every parishioner in the nave. Only those who contributed to the church offertory under their Watcher were summoned to the alter to kneel before Deacon and the young practitioners, and were offered a blessing of the host and consecrated wine.

Aware of the narcotic's harrowing effects, Celeste and her reluctant team committed only to a half day's work each day, cautious of Aza and her hawkish sight. It had taken days to pry those viciously hypnotic hooks from her mind and smother the sharp stabbing ache in her gut. It had fogged her mind until all she saw were the shadows cast by her old sins. So similar to the seductive lure of the painkillers she had indulged in like sweets. Nadie had gagged and retched while she slept, sallow and sweat-soaked, and Celeste swore she could hear the woman's bones rattling beneath her flesh as she shivered and convulsed for two nights straight. Celeste, as well. The craving roiled her guts and shoved her beating heart up into her throat.

The blooming gardens were the consequence of Melina's preaching, but Celeste saw little harm to the distraction. It allowed the rest of them the freedom to mill about while the parishioners began working tirelessly for the offertory. Though Celeste feigned admiration of the Deacon's heavenly words, she was cautious to limit any interaction with the clandestine leader and his loyal Watchers. Melina, however, was enraptured by her newfound life. It became a nightly ritual for the Deacon and the elongated Watcher twins to stroll through his congregation while his worshippers bowed and reached out for him like he were a crowned king meeting peasant folk, extending a hand to join him for an indulgence of consecrated food and drink. Her redhead would always accept with a glowing smile and abandon her bedding for the night, only returning to the gardens when the sun had long chased the chill that lingered in the grounds.

While Celeste and the others spurned true devotion to the Almighty, Odine simulated a rising devotion to the faith. The bandit soaked up the gospel Melina radiantly preached from the garden hilltops, recited scripture with an airy tone that often stunned Celeste to silence, and reported to Aza and the offertory. Her shrilly voice rose with the chanting gospel of communion. Deacon was eerily blind to her devotion, and Aza the Watcher never spoke more than a quickly issued command. Celeste was certain they scented rats. Odine could never get close enough to Deacon without the scrutiny of his Watchers.

As the days wore on in a slogging routine, the team slowly found themselves fragmented until the madness of Communion, with Deacon's powerful words drowning their thoughts in a great flood, and dozens of strange faces Celeste couldn't discern from others she hadn't bothered committing to memory. It began with Nadie one morning while she was withdrawn from Melina's gospel, observing Twist and his fascination with the birds *cawing* and flitting through the snarl of dead branches. Aza had approached with a lopsided grin and directed Nadie to follow her to another mandatory work detail. Irrigation, apparently, had an increasing shortage of workers. Stricken at the thought of being alone she had begged Aza for Twist as company, and shockingly, the Watcher cooperated with the plea. That very night upon their return to their blankets, Nadie was back, filthy and spitting mud. "Not a working shovel in sight," she grumbled. "Broken trawls. It was a mess, Commander. They said we were digging irrigation channels to soak the church gardens...these channels were as wide and deep as the church halls."

Celeste pressed her for more details and began sketching a mental map of the church grounds.

Snyder was next to be grudgingly led to another section of the church. According to the surly blonde, she was under the command of a gigantic man who dwarfed even Twist, with the brightly dappled skin of a starry night sky and the voice of a revving engine, and unusually black irises and bright cherry-red sclera. White pointillism patterns were inked perpendicular to his wide-set mouth and ran far into a receding hairline, splotched into crescent shapes under his eyes. He was imposing and had clearly unnerved her. She had been escorted from the building and marched towards a staircase spiraling skyward against the external wall, years of neglect giving the gnarled metal a flaking orange coat. From there she was joined by other members she had not met, faces sunken and sallow, hair crudely cropped to the length of their ears. Elevated across the roof were dozens of rows of rusting steel-framed black panels the length and width of twin beds. Heat wriggled from them like the sun beating against asphalt. It was as sweltering as a sauna, Snyder said, being forced to meticulously scrub the panels of any accumulating filth, even with the brisk chill of autumn snapping with the wind. Snyder had described the Watcher with more frightening detail than the grounds she had covered, which was unsettling for Celeste also, but she managed to wring enough information from the intractable blonde to glean a clearer image of the holy grounds. The northern sector was mentally mapped.

"How long until they sculpt us into faceless silhouettes in the crowd?" Snyder questioned bitterly, to which Celeste dismissed with a silence far more sullen than her father could have managed.

With the team fragmented during the day, and Melina swept into the throes of devotion with her fellow parishioners, Celeste was left with Odine for a heavily silent and grudging comradery in the growing garden throng. The bandit was becoming increasingly anxious that Deacon was never seen without a flock of his devoutly followers, never caught with his dark beady eyes unaware, never without the terrifying presence of his Watchers. They fell under scrutinizing eyes from the moment they were escorted into the gardens, the sleeping hall, and through the labyrinth of corridors between communion. Any attempt to leave the confines of the sleeping hall was met with confrontation. Celeste knew she had to keep a watchful eye on Odine and her simmering temper. The bandit was thirsting for Deacon's blood. She had to act or run the risk of Odine exposing their true motives. Theta, undoubtedly, would be positioning to strike at any moment, awaiting the signal to ignite.

Which Celeste knew had to be soon.

As Communion waned and the hall flooded with wave after wave of neurotic worshippers still echoing the blessed words of Deacon, Celeste watched intently as Deacon strolled away with Melina, her eyes blood red and skin a pasty milk white. They ambled through the crowd and under the envious gazes of the other worshippers. While her team was on the brink of exhaustion, she surreptitiously slipped from her blankets and cut through the crowd clustering in Deacon's wake. With a patchy hood pulled over her eyes, she vanished into the sea of grey, keeping Melina's bouncing curls in sight. She shadowed them, sight drawn to her immediate left; the post Aza stood at nightly with her sweeping owlish gaze was empty, and had been since Communion ended. An oddity since their arrival. She had observed them posted throughout the auditorium-like room, patrolling the barred-shut doors, eerily ghosting the sectional rows like prison guards conducting a headcount in twenty minute intervals. It was almost too convenient, but with Odine's bloodlust nearing the boiling point and Snyder recklessly taking the reins of their team, she had to leap at any advantage that presented itself.

Even if it *was* cheese to bait a rat.

She moved swiftly, pivoted, and squeezed through the pressing crowd. Jabbing elbows were like punches to her ribs and belly, her arms pinched tightly together. The stench of filthy clothes and sweat burned her nostrils and tickled her throat, though by the third night her eyes had stopped stinging to tears from the sultry air. The Watchers trailed the portly Deacon by a few shuffling paces, weapons the length of their elongated limbs, twin steel leather-wrapped shafts mounted with metal balls and spiky flanges that were the size of her own head. Velvet black bowler hats bobbed above like ducks on a pond, and she propelled after them, gliding beneath the surface of flesh like a swimming shark. The murmur of the crowd buzzed loudly in her ears. Her beating heart clenched tight in her throat. Her breaths were shaky, rapidly uneven. The guard posts near the chamber doors that fed into the many corridors and locked rooms had been abandoned, with the nearest Watcher sweeping through the clusters of praying parishioners far from earshot, but that ice-cold dread knotted her belly. It felt like Deacon would turn at any moment, shadows burning in his eyes, marking her movements through the crowd. It was unnatural, prey stalking predator. He would scent her, she knew it.

Monster to monster.

The twin Watchers gave another sweeping glare over the enamored worshippers, then followed the portly leader and Melina through the open doors. Celeste cut through to her right, shadowing her face with a shabby wool hood. Slowing her pace to a crawl, she peeked through the fraying strings of wool, steadied her breaths as a countdown. Deacon was the first to hobble from view, then Melina with the collar of her rose-coloured shirt clutched in a tiny freckled fist—but the elongated Watchers stalled at the door, peeling their hellish gazes from each other like a reflection in the mirror, casting it over the few worshippers still chanting Deacon's name like a melody. It was a warning, but the parishioners were like sheep herded into the safety of the pen, or horses loosely hitched; they dared not pass the chamber doors, either out of fear or vacuous devotion for Deacon's demands. The Watchers were satisfied, lurching forward with the grace of stiff corpses, and again she hesitated with bated breath. Enamored chants rang through the crowd, his name, excitement palpable as their self-proclaimed prophet vanished into the unending dark of the corridor. She waited for the last smile to recede, the last furtive glance, and then she slipped into the darkness after Deacon and Melina.

The lights had been dimmed down to a faint flicker. She dragged her fingertips across the corridor walls, peeling corners of the cardboard plaster as she followed the gentle *rapping* echo of shoes against the tile floor. A melody of giggles raised bumps along the back of her neck, and she knew she had neared Melina. She cautiously slowed, eager not to have her brains pulverized into mush; the Watchers were not far behind their prophet. Slowly, blurry shapes danced across her sight. She passed the gargantuan Communion hall, empty, and she swore she caught the faint rotten scent of wine. The corridor extended beyond the room, splitting into a labyrinth of halls, walkways and solid-oak doors that were barred or chained shut. She wandered past them, ears perked against the ringing silence, sight strained blurry and narrowed. Her phantom-fingers painfully twitched and throbbed her stitched wound. A searing light forced her eyes shut, and in a panic, her muscles seized to immobility. She stood frozen.

Shit!

The brightness waned to a fuzzy sliver of light cast perpendicular to the floor, thin like the width of a blade, slicing through the cracks of a closing door. The bass of their voices rumbled through the wall, barely audible.

"...dear girl, there has been...for our souls...eternity..."

Deacon's deep voice was faint, but still carried a chill to her bones as bitter as winter wind. A growl rose in her throat, lunged past her clenched teeth.

Closer.

Closer.

Closer.

She placed each inching step carefully as if the tile were a thin sheet of ice hesitantly cracking under her weight. With her ear cupped in her hand and pressed firmly against the wall, she waited for Deacon to speak.

"*And night will be no more. They will need no light of lamp or sun, for the Lord God will be their light, and they will reign forever and ever.* Do you see, my child? Our heavenly path to absolution?"

Melina's voice was confidently high pitched. "I believe I do, Your Holiness. A paradise is destined for those who follow His light."

"Precisely, child," Deacon answered. "The gates of the Garden of Eden will open once we cast the sin from this land."

"Revelations?"

"It is as the Almighty commands. The Church of the Last Light is His sword and shield, all that is holy, and as the Almighty had once cleansed the Earth of sin with a great flood, so shall we."

Melina sang, "He would bestow us with such an honor?"

"He has," Deacon assured. "When we cleanse our souls, the land is purged of its sin."

"The sickness."

"Yes, we will rid the world of the wicked. I promise, child, you will be welcomed into the Garden of Eden...but only if your faith is all that you follow."

Even through the thickly paneled wall Celeste felt the bitter chill of his words as if the temperature abruptly dropped.

"My faith can never be questioned," Melina said. "The church is my home...our home."

"It is a home to all that are faithful. And our faith *will* be tested."

"How soon?"

There was an amused grunt, and the sharp sound of his cane as it *rapped* against the floor. "This is why we have gathered here tonight. The cleansing is nearly upon us. My Watchers are chosen by the Almighty, they are to impose the law of His will. Your name, my child, has been whispered many times."

Tension tightened her chest, shuddered her lungs of air. *This can't be happening!*

"Where is Alpha and Azazel?" Deacon barked loudly, a loud *thud* from his cane. "If that boy has brought more of his unfaithful..."

"Your Holiness." Omega's voice was strict with formality, tense and gruff. "Alpha has paid for sins that were not his."

She heard Deacon's amusement rumble deeply through the walls. "I am hard on the boy, yes, but his mother has left him mighty large shoes to fill. I wish to see his true potential."

"I am certain Alpha is tending to the newly Exalted."

More amusement hummed. "Perhaps. Omega, Beshnaal. Please locate our lost friends. Revelations will soon begin, and we must catch our lovely little Melina up with our scripture."

The door shifted, rusted hinges sharply *squealing*. Light blossomed across the walls in blindingly bright spots. With her heart thumping into her throat, Celeste reeled, legs tangled, and stumbled against the wall. The first door she tried was locked, chains rattling against the splintering wooden frame. The second as well. There was no third, only a split in the corridor. She scrambled past the edge as light glared off the walls, slinking through the shadows like a scurrying rat. Flattened against the opposite wall, jagged splinters digging into her heels, she sucked in a last icy breath and hoped no one could hear the thrashing beat of her heart. Gruff voices rose in volume, the bright light of a lantern flicking through the corridor. Even when the light faded and blinked into darkness, their voices a faint whisper in the distance, she dared not move or breathe.

Revelations? A swirling blizzard of thoughts stormed her mind. *Oh, Father, why did religion have to be such a joke to you?*

"...cautious, or else we may find ourselves in for purification."

A shrill whisper, rising in pitch with each word. Shadows swam through the pressing blackness. So terribly close, she scented the tangy stench of their breaths.

She was within arm's reach.

"There is someone here!" The voice was constricted to a panicked screech. "Aza!"

RUN!

The air shifted with a chill. There was a bloodthirsty glint visible even in the smothering black of the corridor. The hair on the back of her neck stood stiff like a wolf with bristling fur, and she threw herself to the side, thrashing the corner of her eye socket against the wall with an achingly loud *thud.* She spun on her heel, flattened her palms against the wall—a sliver of a chill glided across the base of her neck, and for a moment she thought her throat had been slit open. It may as well have been. The razor edge of a blade kissed her skin; a tickling warmth ran down her throat.

"Don't you *dare* move."

The voice was a hoarse whisper, as chilling as the blade against her throat. She recognized the deadly tone.

Aza.

"It's one of the Exalted." The condescending tone of a ghost. Alpha. "Sticking her nose where it doesn't belong."

"I see that," Aza drawled. "What are Watchers without sight?"

A quiet, nervous scoff. "Kill the heathen and let us be done with it. Deacon has sent others to search for us by now."

Celeste felt the warmth drain from her face. A gulp of air throbbed past the knife pressing into her throat. An involuntary shiver twisted her spine. She was already dead.

But Aza only breathed her response quietly, blade trembling in her grip. "Go. Inform Deacon there was a breach in the northern sector that was immediately repaired. Blame it on the faun, they've been spotted near the grounds again, hunted by some wolf."

"Aza, if he knows we tampered with the system he will just—"

Aza gave the boy a menacing hiss, "Shut up!"

"—reboot—just kill the bitch!"

"And hide the body where, exactly?" Aza rounded on him, digging the blade into Celeste's skin. Warmth blossomed around the cold pressing steel. "If we are to succeed, you need to report to

Deacon immediately! A dead body near Deacon's chambers would raise more suspicions than our absence today!"

"But the bitch—"

"She'll keep her scarred little mouth shut," Aza promised with deadly sincerity. "Or I'll carve that pretty little redhead's heart out." Her eyes widened until the whites of her sockets were bright spotlights in the darkness. "Ah yes, darling, I see the way your eyes wander over her, undressing that supple thing in your mind. You speak of this and I'll not only cut her heart out, I'll feed it to you while it still *beats*."

No words crept past the razor-sharp edge. Celeste gave a slight tremble of her head, and felt the stinging kiss of the blade slice deeper into her scarred skin.

"Aza, we should cleanse her with Purification," Alpha warned, *cracking* the joints in his fingers. "The heathen would be sentenced if she were to be found sniffing around Deacon's quarters."

Aza growled dangerously, as much of a threat to him as the blade to Celeste's throat. "You are a fool, boy," she hissed. "Whether she is caught dead or alive here, it only complicates matters more. Report the breach and containment in the northern sector. *Now!*"

"She is not worthy to live."

"No, she is not."

When his footsteps faded to a subtle *tap-tap-tap* down the corridor, Aza withdrew the blade, sheathing it in her sleeve with a fluid flick of her wrist.

"Follow me."

Without the cold pinch of the blade against her throat, Celeste gulped down air. A cold sweat drenched her forehead, misting her eyes.

"Do not make me tell you twice."

Aza retreated from the corridor that forked into Deacon's quarters, vanishing into the unending black with Celeste hesitantly at her heels. With her vision adjusting to the dark, she shadowed Aza as the Watcher moved in a graceful and deadly silence, door-to-door, never pausing more than a moment to gauge the silence. They passed through empty halls and rooms filled with a dizzying array of scents she recognized from the military compound. *Some sort of fuel.*

Only amorphous shadows danced across her field of vision, indiscernible shapes and nonsensical patterns. The next room was dimly lit. Humid air, the *whirring* of machinery, tentacles of hanging wires, stacked screens blinking into a blizzard of static. Celeste lingered a moment longer, slowing her pace to fall behind Aza. Lines of static cascaded down the screens but images blurred beneath the artificial snow. It was faint and difficult to discern, but for a moment she thought she caught a glitch—

—the collar of her shirt twisted like a noose around her neck. She panicked, thrashing backwards, but Aza had a firm and unrelenting grip around her wrung shirt.

"Take any longer and I'll think twice about *not* taking your head."

When Aza turned on her heels, she dragged Celeste alongside her like a disobedient pup, making certain to limit her view of the screens that blinked with intermittent static. Celeste begrudged her the privacy, but her mind flickered with a series of grainy images; dusk falling on the garden dunes, the sprouting beanstalks shivering in the breeze; the emptied stadium-sized nave and ornate stained-glass walls casting a haunting tessellating glow, patterns shifting and flickering into ghostly apparitions across the altar; silhouettes of gnarled branches twisting across the main gates to the southeast entrance of the church; a grainy darkness broken by scattering of pale light from the exterior of Deacon's quarters, focused squarely on the flimsy door; blips of featureless faces like a storm of static; moonlight sheening the smooth surface of the rooftop panels; the smothering black of many corridors extending through the church.

Celeste only caught fleeting glances, but two peculiarities immediately struck. The intricate placement of cameras allowed Deacon an almost omnipresence, his hypervigilant gaze looming over every inch of the premises, and every member of the church, like some unscrupulous god. From the garden dunes, to the rooftop panels and turbines, to rooms where access had been barred and bolted from her view like the doors to her prison cell in Hellpit. Within one of those rooms, she caught the wary glance of another prisoner hiding in the shadowy corner.

The exterior of the church, where they slept, ate, relieved themselves, all was meticulously monitored by mechanical eyes. Every door, gate, pathway, bedroll, chamber, corridor, room.

All but one.

Celeste focused on that blank screen. The narrowing path that led through the northern sector and the surrounding snarl was notably absent, and Celeste conjectured it was more than a glitch in their system. It gnawed at her guts, probed at her thoughts. *How many more pieces to the puzzle am I missing?*

"Why did you keep me alive?" Celeste asked.

Aza grunted, disarming the bolt to another door. "Easier to have you walk than to drape your cold corpse over my shoulder."

"With two people it's a secret," Celeste said. "With three it becomes the truth."

A grin as wickedly sharp as a blade carved through her heart-shaped face. "Once another soul knows, it is a secret no longer. Two, three, or more, it matters not."

The chilling effect of her words bit to the bone. The door swung open, grinding through rust, with Aza throwing her weight against the frame to ease the sharp squeal of metal on metal. They had circled the confined corridors of the building to the altar swirling in flickering gaslight. Another spreading grin revealed Aza's yellowing fang-like teeth.

"Follow my every step and stick to the shadows," she warned. "Or you may find yourself the victim of purification."

"Victim?" echoed Celeste, slinking into the darkness like a rat. *Perhaps I am. Running from those mechanical eyes.* Aza slipped through the shadows with the confidence of a woman who had committed to memory a route beyond the omnipresent eyes. She was short, broad-hipped and stocky, but as athletically toned as Snyder, zigzagging along the edge of the altar and through to the Communion Hall. Celeste kept pace, but breathlessly, her wary gaze shifting from Aza to the rafters, where the mechanical eye *whirred* in the darkness, all-knowing.

"Victim of disbelief." Aza clicked her tongue. "If it is the Almighty's will..."

"Is Revelations part of the Almighty's will or Deacon's?"

"Tell me, are you faithful?" The sliver of her eyes glinted like a drawn blade. "Or a wolf in sheep's wool?"

"We all must dress our part," Celeste said, stepping through to the corridor. Gaslight glow flickered eerily across the rotted plywood walls. A smothering silence grew between them like the charge before a storm.

"Revelations will fall to those who believe and don't all the same," said Aza, as Celeste inched past her into the common room. "What you fight for, and who, is entirely your decision. Make peace with your faith...last light will arrive shortly."

"Who do you fight for?"

Aza never responded, instead retreating into the shadowy

crevices of the corridor. The Watcher was gone, leaving her in the commons, the scattered and restless crowd still explosive with excitement.

Celeste knew the moment she reached her blankets that her capture was looming along the horizon. Snyder had grown increasingly anxious at her absence, which Celeste managed to explain away with an urge to piss anywhere other than the slop buckets in the corners of the room. Snyder didn't buy it.

"You and that little redhead have been sneaking around since we got here," she sneered, slicking her blonde hair from her eyes. "Is there a change of heart we should be aware of?"

"Shut up," grumbled Celeste. "My loyalty is to family, and these people are anything but."

"Sleeping," Twist muttered into the nook of his bulging arm. "You sleep, too."

Snyder ignored the gentle rebuke that caused Nadie to stir upright. "Well," the blonde remarked. "Who *is* your family now?"

Nadie whispered, "Snyder, can this wait until morning? She's back, that's what matters." Her doe-eyes fluttered as she peeked over Twist's slumping shoulder. "Celeste, we thought you had been taken below."

An itch her nails couldn't scratch. "Below?"

Twist poked his head up, his one eye twitching open. "Man hit other man for throwing dirt. Hit him hard. With shovel." With awkward writhing that made him appear like a turtle on its shell, he motioned three successful swings of his arm. "Thump, thump, thump. Ghost-men take him, but he says he doesn't want to go below."

"Purification," Celeste breathed, vision blurring.

Below.

A blizzard of distortion, flickering grey and white.

Below.

Four walls, the width of a man and the length of a small cot, barred and closing in like the prison.

Below.

A wary, bespectacled glance from the shadows.

"Below."

"That doesn't help us," Snyder scoffed. "You're compromised. You have been since you bowed to Theta and acted as her executioner."

Celeste spat, "Ironic, truly, from someone who couldn't bloody her own hands against Blackwell."

"Screw you, Shadow Spawn."

"You first, sweetheart," Celeste said. "Go to sleep. For once, don't stick your nose into everything."

Snyder snorted. "You act as if you have a plan."

"I do." *Somewhat.*

"I call bullshit. You've been bottle-deep into pills since Blackwell, barely functioning at best when you made a deal with the devil, and now you let that redheaded tart parade around with the church like we're meant to worship here for the rest of our lives, however *short* that may be now."

Snyder's irritation carried her voice through the room like a siren, alarming Celeste with the attention it drew to them. Snyder didn't seem to care.

"Well?" she went on. "Is your plan to get us thrown into a prison again? Maybe the hangman's noose? You keep telling us you have one, but so far all you've managed is to get us killed one by one. You're no leader, Celeste, you're barely part of the team."

"Whatever you thought was going to happen, it won't. You've failed long ago." The cold determination in Odine's voice was loud enough to reach their ears only. "If you thought you could squirm from Theta's grasp, you were wrong. We do her bidding, we fight until we die, we take *his* head. That is all we can hope for."

Snyder's glare frosted the air between them. "See what you've accomplished, Celeste? You brought us into a suicide mission. Either we fight for the bandits or we fight for the church. Which death would be preferable to our fearless leader? The bandit here is fine with either."

Another contemptuous snort. "I know my part in this mission," Odine snarled. "Do you?"

"Yes," Snyder said. "I have to decide how to get us out of here alive." Uncrossing her legs, she shot upright, almost standing at attention, chin jutted out as if she looked down on the gathering faithful. Countless curious gazes were drawn to her sudden outburst.

"You're running out of time to shut down the weapons and signal Theta." Odie was grinning. "I suggest you sort out your differences quickly."

Snyder spat. "We're ending this now. Nadie?"

"Y-yeah?"

"If you had access to their terminals could you disarm their weapons system?"

A tentative response, brown eyes rounding with worry. "Maybe, depends on how secure it is. Th-theoretically."

"Stand down." Celeste balled hands into fists. Snyder rounded on her, standing at least half a foot taller, her slender frame now lanky and gaunt. Still, she seemed wiry and explosive. Her thin lips twisted into a checkmark-shaped grin.

"*No.*"

Celeste was grinding her teeth. "Stand down, Snyder."

"You're not our commander, remember?"

I need more time, give me more time!

"Hey, enough," Nadie warned. "We have an audience."

It wasn't only the worshippers drawn to the commotion. The Watchers, Alpha and Omega, were perched like vultures over the main entrance. Through the darkness of the corridor, red curls glowed like candlelight. Melina skipped out from the darkness with Deacon hobbling along after her on his warping cane.

"Well, is this your doing?" Snyder scoffed. "Is Red gracing you with an invitation to dine with Deacon while the rest of us get a bowl of gruel in the morning?"

Shit, think!

"You're going to get the rest of us killed."

"Shut up," Celeste hissed. "You don't know how to follow orders, let alone lead an actual team. You're the one who wandered into a trap with the scavengers, remember?"

"I *knew* we were being watched, while *you* herded us right to them!"

"You know one thing, and that's military rule. You're still nothing but a soldier, so follow orders and *stand down.*"

"Go to hell, Bandit Bitch."

Their antagonism reached its boiling point. Snyder, once athletically built and sinuously toned, was still quick, but Celeste proved quicker. She landed a pulverizing blow against the side of the blonde's face, shifting her jaw, loosening a few teeth. Their blankets wrapped around her feet, throwing her balance, and Celeste pummeled her with another fist. Two more solid blows connected before Snyder found the footing to throw a punch of her own. White spots danced across Celeste's vision as she pulled back, fists up.

Snyder spat blood, running her knuckles red across her chin.

Celeste rammed Snyder like she was shouldering open a door,

hurling the blonde from her feet.

They both thrashed across the floor, writhing madly, clawing for the other's throat. An iron grip closed around Celeste's neck, but she rolled into the awkward motion, throwing Snyder to her back. It took three heavy hits to crush the cartilage in Snyder's nose to breadcrumbs. The grip around her throat slacked, and Celeste bloodied her knuckles again.

"Your faith means nothing to me!" Celeste spat. "Your God is not mine!"

"W-what?" Snyder sputtered. Another thrown punch crimsoned her teeth.

"Keep your faith! You feel him, but I don't! I don't!"

The next few moments were an incomprehensible blur of events. Someone had torn her from Snyder, her knuckles dripping a syrupy red, still raving about the faith that eluded her. Whether she had been apprehended by a member of her own team, or one of the many Watchers that had flocked to the entrance, she remained uncertain. She was quickly hauled from her knees, arms firmly clasped against her spine, still smoldering with pent-up fury. Forcefully marched in front of Deacon, she barely heard his voice storming with gravitas, sentencing her to cleanse her soul of sin, to fall with the unfaithful, to be imprisoned below.

Below.

But the shimmering green of Melina's eyes, a sun-kissed meadow after rainfall, was all she saw, the melody of her name delicately whispered from rosy lips all she heard, as she was marched away from the prying eyes of the faithful, and down far below into the abyss.

TWENTY-THREE
Revelation to John

IT WAS a filthy, primitive accommodation, if one even dared call it that. Dank and narrow, it was a closet of concrete, even the enormously thick door, with a dim flicker of light stabbing the jet-black darkness from a single panel the width of her fist. It was the only window to the world, and after the Watcher had retreated from sight, there was nothing else to be seen but another concrete wall grotesquely slopped with blood like some macabre paintjob, its pungency a pervasive sickness to the stale air. The chilly concrete slabs of her confines leached her warmth and gnawed her bones to icy bits.

"Well, here I am at last." Her voice cut through the deafening silence like a knife. "Below."

Below.

She flattened her hands against the biting cold concrete and traced the length of her cell, slowly dragging her fingers across the surface of each wall. It was smooth and icy-cold, except near the corner of the door, where the concrete had been crudely carved. *Tally marks,* she thought, counting a dozen faintly etched into the slab.

"Focus," she breathed slowly. "Remember why you're here. Strong like Father, fearless like Mother."

Faint candlelight pulsed gently, rippling shadows, spilling through the slit in a narrow beam. She couldn't see much outside of her cell. Not even with her face pressed up against the concrete.

"H-hello?"

Bruises burned and throbbed around her throat, lips jaggedly split, stiff, and bloodied. Flesh was spongy and swollen around her eye, forcing a squint. Coagulated globs of blood clung to her chin. *The blonde bitch can still hit hard.* Celeste was grinning at the thought.

I hit harder.

"Hello?"

Again, there was only the shrill reverberation of her own voice. She called out twice more, thumping her forehead against one wall, then leaned back and knocked the thumped the back of her head on the opposite. The weight of her actions was now a tightening knot in her chest.

I need more time, that's all. Somehow.

"I just need more time," she whispered to no one.

Which is why her skin crawled when she got a chilling response.

"Time is a luxury you can no longer afford."

She launched toward the panel as if she could squeeze herself out inch by inch.

"Hello?" A slight pause. "I know someone is there."

Nothing more. Distaste bubbled and burned the back of her throat raw. Whoever it had been was right, however, the seconds were slipping from her fingers with alarming speed. With Theta and her army camped in Dead Wood and surrounding the church, Deacon preparing his worshippers for Revelations—whatever that was—and her team fragmented and simmering fury, she was risking not only their lives with her last gamble, but their deaths as well.

Just give me more time before...

"Revelations," she whispered with a careful breath. "It begins."

The response was a whimper. "Oh, it does?"

"Tomorrow, yes."

Another pause, but she swore she heard them hyperventilating. The air thickened with fear. She bit her tongue, bating her breath, and slowly the voice carried as silently as a whisper not meant for her ears.

"If what you speak is true, then I'm afraid time is no longer a luxury for either of us."

"What does Revelations mean?"

There was another troubling pause. "It means the end for us all."

"You're the engineer, aren't you?" Celeste asked.

The voice increased in pitch, but it was strained and hoarse like someone gasped after a coughing fit. As if he had not spoken for quite some time, and if he did, it was brief and only initiated by another. She could barely hear the echo of a grating voice, but she knew it was close, likely in the next cell. She had spied a few on her prisoner's march through below. Blood soaked floors, smeared red walls, swarms of buzzing flies. Tables, benches, floors, walls, all tarped or bundled tightly in sheets. Chambers for slaughter.

"Engineer?" the voice rasped. "Perhaps, though that is an unbearably broad term. And I have a name. Well, I *had* a name. Oppenheim."

"How long have you been here?"

"It's difficult to say. A year or two?" An uncomfortable sound squeaked from his throat. "Maybe more? Time has no meaning here. I think I lost track of it when the city was under siege."

That sparked a wildfire of interest. "Fort Thompson?"

"Yes..." Then, brimming with excitement, "Are you Red Dawn?"

Her tongue knotted. Who was she, truly? Her father's naïve daughter; a puppet for Red Dawn; a leashed hound for Theta and the Disfigured; an abdicated leader. There were no more masks to hide the ugliness of her scars.

"Once," she admitted.

"Me, as well," Oppenheim replied. "The siege..."

"Fort Thompson is under military control again, but that was months ago, not years."

Relief rippled the engineer's voice. "Truly? Honestly? I had always hoped for a home to go back to. Someday. With..."

Her heart stirred. "Is there someone waiting for you at Fort Thompson?"

"There used to be, but I doubt anyone thinks I'm still alive."

"Love will always wait," she said, cheeks burning. Vibrant green, milky skin dappled with freckles, brightly burning hair. *Melina.* "Always."

"Love, soulmates, destiny. It is all a fallacy we cling to, a fabrication that we will not die alone."

"Love is stronger than that."

Oppenheim choked on a laugh, or perhaps it had been a gentle sob. She wasn't certain. She offered few words of comfort. In this hell, in the confines of darkness, there was only oneself and the ghosts of one's old sins. The desolation was strangling.

"I'm a long way from anywhere I'd call home," she muttered, not caring if he listened or not. Whether or not her words were heard, she no longer cared. "In fact, Fort Thompson is not my home, and never was. I-uh"—she choked on the sob lumping in her throat—"I grew up somewhere in the mountains to the west, in a cabin my father had built after my mother and brother caught the sickness. So far from anyone, in fact, my nearest neighbors were wolves, and they ended up killing my father out of starvation. So, alone I was, venturing into a broken world I was entirely unprepared for. I've done things I shouldn't have when I was a kid, but I did it out of survival. I killed. More than once. But...the more I fought for my life, pushed against all odds, the more my blood boiled for that conflict, life seeping from one quick stroke of a blade. I chose a side, in the end, like we all do. Red Dawn.

"But I chose that side for the sake of someone I loved. I took everything from her. *Everything.* No amount of love I have for her will ever bring her family back. But I still love her. I fight for her. I spill blood for her. I've killed for her. I'm rotting in this tomb for *her.* The only reason I'm alive, the only reason I'm even breathing, is because she's all I see. Every dream, every waking moment. It's only her. I *will* survive to find her again. Will you survive to find those you love?"

A deafening moment of silence, her ears thundering with the rapid beat of her heart.

"I want to," Oppenheim finally said, voice trembling. "Levin is his name. My husband of nearly thirty years. We were...high school sweethearts at a time when it wasn't socially acceptable to be. It was before this catastrophe, this sickness. When it was first spreading, my ingenuity secured our positions in the new world. Red Dawn had only just formed as a response to the government's falling to disorder, and my knowledge was indispensable to them. Levin was admitted to the military ranks, and by some grace of luck, we made it to middle age together. Maybe it was as you said, about love. Maybe it was love that kept us alive, made sure we found each other at the end of the day. You know, Levin always said my brain was going to get me in trouble some day.

"All those years I honestly believed I was making the world a better place. I passed on my knowledge and expertise, but I also engineered morally questionable weapons, conducted research that would drive the sanity from a normal mind, put countless innocent people through unmitigated horror. I should have been with him when the city fell! I should have been there to take care of him, not in that wretched hellhole! It was my fault, and Deacon must be right, I'm paying for those sins now!" Oppenheim dissolved into sobs as violent as her rupturing heart.

"You built weapons for General Blackwell? You tampered with the sickness?" Then, with ice forming on her tongue, she spat, "You worked for Mengele."

The Blonde Man.

"I'm not like him!" But fear shriveled his voice. "I'm not like Doctor Cruel!"

"You helped him."

"I did what I had to for love!"

"For love," Celeste repeated in a soothing whisper. "You did what you were ordered to do, or you would have been separated from Levin. Blackwell had no use for weakness or disobedience."

"Yes, I—wait, what do you mean *had?*"

Tongue pressed against her teeth, she held her silence a moment more. "There was an attempted coup. He didn't make it."

There was another ugly pause, then a hissing whisper, "*Good.*"

"Red Dawn lives on," she said slowly, dangling more bait. "Which is why I'm trying to find out about Revelations. I know you were taken, and while the stories blame the Disfigured, it was Deacon and the faithful."

"Doesn't sound like much of a question," Oppenheim whispered pointedly. "Yes. When the bandits took Fort Thompson, Levin contacted me to say they were marching to take it back. I knew I had to be there for him, but I was under strict orders not to leave. I should have waited, perhaps, but as the days went by, and I had no word from him...I-I panicked..."

"You left without an escort."

His snorting laugh dissolved into a hoarse cough. Then, slowly, "I figured I'd be safe with a gun. Levin taught me to shoot, though I could barely hit a bottle from a few meters. A human body is bigger than a bottle, right?"—another snort—"I thought I could make it, I knew the roads, I had enough gasoline...it was fine for a day, but the moment I pulled over to rest was when I was ambushed. I don't remember much apart from being clubbed like a baby seal. This...has been my home ever since. I-I can't bring myself to end it and meet Levin again, I can't be with him, so I do what I do best. It's all that I have left. I was promised a peaceful end if I did."

But why...

An icy chill gripped her bones. "You're working on Revelations."

Oppenheim's voice was a shuddering, shrilly squeak. "He kills everyone who disobeys, everyone who refuses to cooperate! I don't want to die, but I don't want to live without Levin!"

"Hope." Warmth blossomed from her chest. "You have hope in those you love. If he's out there, he's coming to find you, and he'll cross the wasteland to get you. I would do anything for the woman I love, and I know she would for me. I *know* it."

"I would do anything for Levin."

"Then tell me what Revelations is and how to stop it."

"What's the point? We're already buried alive."

She steadied her breaths. "I'll make sure you see Levin again. You will be together again, I promise."

She drowned in silence. When he finally breathed out a long sigh, she heard and felt a concussive *thump-thump-thump* reverberating through the cement. Then he spoke, carefully, his whispers a faint, grating echo as he recounted one of the unmitigated horrors her father had refused to speak of.

"I am—*was*—a nuclear physicist, one of the key members to a project known as *The Last Titans*. We were tasked with engineering a series of nuclear warheads that would not only destroy a city, but it would 'scrub' the air clean of any particulates—the sickness can survive in moisture. When it became apparent that it was spreading uncontrollably and rapidly overseas, two titans were launched; parts of Europe were vaporized, Russia. South America was reported as completely compromised. The repercussions were not instant, but we had long ago calculated the damage it would case. It would be three years of winter, the sky a dismal grey. So we asked, back then, what would happen if we launched them all? Because that was the dilemma we began to face. The sickness kept spreading.

"When our own facility was compromised, it was evident our government had failed its quarantine. And soon people weren't just dying...they were...*changing*. Everyone panicked. Those who ran first, died first. But it was weeks before the realization that there would be no rescue, likely ever, and those who couldn't tolerate that prospect, ended it quickly. Levin and I, we were never the outdoorsy type. I had never even left the city, let alone been camping. I was scared and wanted to stay. Levin wanted to go. The others had accepted this glorified belief that they were humanity's last defense and wanted to launch the remaining titans to completely eradicate the sickness and any carrying host.

"By then, all but four of us had fallen ill. Shit...I don't even remember their names now, but by the time the sickness showed in them, Levin forced us to leave—Gabe! That's one of the names, I remember him. It showed in Gabe, and he was a proponent for eliminating the sickness completely. When the third titan was launched, he died before he finished the sequence, and it detonated in its silo. That is, I believe, the Scorch. We were far by then, but I remember the blinding flash, the violently pulsating wind that followed minutes later. A colossal cloud of ash mushrooming over the horizon. Months of scavenging and barely surviving across the countryside, our homes both gone, families gone. That's when Blackwell found us."

"Your expertise made you indispensable to Blackwell." Celeste choked as each word dripped from her tongue like slime. "He needed you as much as you needed him. That's how you survived. You and Levin, together."

"Yes," he admitted shakily. "He kept us alive, kept us fed, made sure we weren't ripped apart and eaten by those *things*. He helped us survive...in exchange for..."

"Knowledge," she finished. "But why abandon the remaining titans?"

Oppenheim grunted. "Red Dawn was barely a unit of soldiers, let alone an army. Blackwell's efforts were primarily on liberating the people of sickness. Once he had the strength to mobilize an effort to uncover the remaining titan silos, there were bandit clans waging battles against him, the Church of the Last Light rising to power. War was beginning to brew. Unfortunately, not everyone agreed with Blackwell, and information is currency in the new world. Once it was known about *Last Titans* and who I was, it was only a matter of time before I was in somebody's crosshairs."

Blackwell wanted to sell me for information on the titans. She knew he would have craved nothing more than to control the remaining silos, and would have done anything, even feed his lieutenant's niece to the bloodlust of bandits, to dominate the remaining world. Theta would ally with Blackwell, and together, strike at Deacon. With control of the silos, Blackwell could have risen from the ashes of the old world as an unchallenged emperor.

I liberated Fort Thompson for you, asshole.

"Not every titan was completed," Oppenheim prattled on as if he couldn't stop, tangling his tongue with a rapid flow of words. "But over the years, students and colleagues began vanishing from the camp, research facilities, outposts, cities. All taken, abducted by those fanatics, given the choice of a grim death or servitude...they hid among the Disfigured. I envy those who refused, I really do...but those who didn't were forced to assemble components to a titan. I-I've been finishing what I started, what I should have done years ago."

The realization hit her like a bullet.

"This isn't a church," she said with a lurch of her belly. "This is a silo."

Oppenheim made a strange squeaking sound as if the air were slowly squeezed from his lungs. "You wanted to know what Revelations was!" he choked out between loud, bleating sobs. "It means a titan will launch, and it means Deacon has won! He *always* wins!"

"He hasn't won yet!"

"Y-yes he has!"

"I can stop him! I can stop Revelations—if you *help* me! I can get us out of here, Oppenheim, I can get you to Levin, I promise!"

"Levin is..."

She snarled at his crumbling indifferent façade. "You speak of your love for Levin, you mourn his loss when he could be out there searching for you or waiting for you to come home. What if he is, Oppenheim?"

A tentative response: "He's not."

"But what if he is? He could be searching for you, never knowing where you were but still not giving up hope! Wherever that missile hits, it has a chance to hurt Levin! How could you live with yourself, Oppenheim, even knowing there was a chance you killed him?"

But her words crumbled to ash on her tongue. *Melina, I love you.*

"I appreciate the therapy session," said Oppenheim, his grainy voice as steady and loud as a beating drum. "But a purification is the only way you're getting out of that cell."

Her heart swelled. "Unlike you," she growled, "I don't lose hope in the ones I love. I *never* will. You shouldn't either. We can stop this madness. I can get you out of here."

There was a strange chirping sound that rang off the cement walls. It was the first time Celeste had heard the man known as Oppenheim genuinely fall into laughter.

"It was pleasant to speak to you," Oppenheim said. "Maybe I needed to unburden my conscience, but you have not been the only one to approach me. I have not lost hope, no, what I do now"—his voice was growing increasingly somber and tenuous as he went on—"I do now for Levin, to atone for all the sins I have done. To see him again and free myself of this prison. If I can fix some of my mistakes, Levin can find peace. There will be a Revelations, but it will be my own."

No matter how much more she screamed his name, silence gripped Oppenheim's tongue, and soon the only sound was her crackling voice ringing off the cement walls. The final pieces to the puzzle clipped, twisted, and snapped into a clear image of her war looming on their horizon. She called out again—

A searing flash of sparks jetted through the panel, and a sharp clanging sound echoed off the cement like a tolling bell. A curving gleam of steel, its razor-edge chipped and stained brown like an old teacup, grinded to a halt against the panel an inch from where her nose had just been. She flung herself backwards, elbows thudding painfully across the floor.

"I knew you were the Devil's offspring the moment I laid eyes upon your ugly marks."

Wrenching and grinding the axe blade loose, those ghoulishly familiar eyes, deep blue like a corpse bloating in water, leered at her through with panel with the same wretched contempt as Abbot had nearly a year prior. She had gutted him, though, and she would gut this ghost of a boy as well. The calming rush of his warm, spilling blood would be all the sanctification she would need.

When the boy's ghostly eyes slipped from view, her boiling blood ran cold. For a heart-wrenching moment, she felt the intensity of her wolfish ferocity as Melina would, the shuddering fear it ripped apart her heart with. Was that the barbaric penchant for blood that her rose had grown so wary of?

It was a moment that nearly proved fatal.

While lost in her melancholic stupor, the deadlatch to her confine *clinked* and shifted, then the heavy cement-bound door swung open with a grating screech that sounded like the terrified cries of some dying animal. Alpha stood as a shroud of shadows. The axe blade of his halberd, Morning Light, was a menacing silhouette against the flicker of ghoulish light.

"*Demon.*" The word dripped from his tongue like poison. "I saw that malevolence hiding in your heart. You're a disgusting creature, a stain from the bowels of Hell. I'm here to bring justice to the Almighty's name."

It happened before the blink of an eye; his eyes sharpened, the air constricted between them, his muscles flexed as Morning Light gleamed and swung. She jumped to her feet, snarling like the demon he thought she was—but Alpha brought the halberd crashing down against her skull. Her head exploded with an immense amount of pain.

And then there was nothing.

***

Nauseous, groggy.

A blistering ache hammered the front of her skull.

Vision a bleary, tilting pinpoint.

Cold cement dragged across her, snapping at her flesh.

Battered by darkness, she struggled to keep her mind above those violently crashing waves, thoughts a cacophony of what sounded like foreign voices, each yelling and screaming over the other to be heard. She peeled her eyes open to swirling grey and long sinuous smears of crimson. A groan died in her throat, smothered by a detonating pain in her shifted jaw. It hurt to even be hurt.

Her cognitive faculties flickered with clarity. Her arms were slung above her head, her left leg awkwardly angled against the wall, the back of her skull repeatedly bouncing off the floor. She was being dragged from her cell by her foot like a fresh kill, the cement scraping her skin raw and bloody. She could see the thick cement door, which was more of a wall, to her cell open and blocking the narrow passage behind her. The cell next to hers was sealed shut, door flush with the wall, the only discernable opening a small, fist-sized panel. She caught a glimpse of blood-red bespectacled eyes, then blinked, and they were gone just as quickly. Perhaps Oppenheim didn't wish to see her die. She didn't blame him, but she yelled his name as loud as she possibly could anyway.

It took only a second longer for panic to fuel a sudden burst of strength; she struggled in Alpha's grip, but the passageway was as narrow as her cell, barely the width of her shoulders, and writhing only brought her into glancing blows against the walls. It felt like she struggled to free herself from inside her own coffin. Alpha cared little, her skin pinched and twisted in his crushing hold. Her nails were like claws raking into his flesh, but he only grunted his disgust at her, cursing her depravity under each huffing breath. She clawed at his grip, prying each finger from her leg like nails from wood. For a fleeting moment when his grip slacked, and her leg slipped loose, she thought herself freed, but he towered over her and hacked at her with the blunt face of the axe head. It felt as though her skull cracked open like an egg, blood slopping over the side of her face like runny yolk. Her brain thudded inside her skull, and that calm, creeping darkness smothered her once more.

The pain was agony, burning up her limbs like a fever. Tightly cinched ligatures dug furrows into the flesh around her wrists and ankles, binding her to a crinkling opaque tarpaulin. Writhing involuntarily, she was only able to raise her chest a few inches against the binds before collapsing. Panic rose in her throat as a wolfish whine, smothered by the sound of Alpha's sneering cackle.

"We'll cleanse that darkness from your soul, demon." His hissing whisper was pungently warm against her neck, like the winds carrying the fresh stench of a corpse. "You won't stain my faith much longer."

Celeste spat at him. "Coming from a traitor's tongue."

That riled his blood. A tightly clenched jaw creased and sunk his cheeks. Each constricted movement against her binds twisted and pulled the corners of his mouth into a lecherous smile as crooked as cracking ice.

"You have lost the way, and so has Deacon," he growled with contempt. "I'm here to show you all the path of the faithful, the true divine, as my mother had once been. I'm here to finish what she started, what Deacon fears to do, what Aza fears to do, what you all"—he hammered a fist into her face, bloodied his knuckles across her lips—"fear to accomplish! I inherited Alpha, I am the beginning of God and His reckoning!"

The dreary grey world spun around her. Alpha's ravenous murmurs faded to a droning hum in her ears. His fingers tangled with her hair and yanked her head forward, chin pinned to her chest, until the pain was so excruciating she feared her scalp would peel away from her skull. Another cinch strapped around her forehead like a belt, pulled crushingly tight until even her eyes were forced moon-wide. Tighter, tighter, tighter he pulled, until her head thumped painfully with each furious beat of her heart, until she was sure she heard the bones in her head crack and split under the immense pressure, even beyond the ghostly wails of her own torment.

"You will finally see Him!" Alpha praised. "You will *have* to see Him and all His glory! This world shall see fire and brimstone like never before, and it is by His will!"

"Screw you!" she screamed.

A tick of the corner of his mouth, and he leaned into her, squeezing her lungs of air. He jerked the cinch, twisted her neck, and bashed the back of her skull against the tarpaulin. With one hand gripped around the cinch, he produced a long corkscrew-shaped rod with the other. Crimson globs crusted the twisting steel.

A deep shame burned through her at the thought of her own throat slit open as wide as Blackwell's had been, granting her a swift, prey-like death. It was a foolish thought, she knew, because Alpha had no intention of giving her the peaceful end. She recalled with vivid horror the man with hole in his head, viscous brain matter gushing and slopping to the floor until he was no more than a greying corpse with an invalid's smile. That was to be her fate.

I hope I've spared you all an end like this. Please, Snyder, get them out of here. Read between the lines, you stubborn bitch.

It was the only light afloat in a drowning sea of darkness that she could cling to.

"I refuse to give in to the temptation of flesh, unlike you," he snarled, lips slathered in drool. "Azazel is not the only Watcher with a keen line of sight, *whore*. The way your eyes undress that red tart's skirts, I bet you dream of sticking your tongue where it doesn't belong!"

"G-greedy asshole," she sputtered through bloody lips. "You only want to be Deacon."

Fury reddened his face like a spreading fire. "Wench! You and Deacon are both abominations, false to the word of the Almighty! I know his true intentions, his arrogance, his lust to control the world! That is why *I*"—the corkscrew's steel gleamed through the thick splotches of blood when he held it over her eyes—"will lead our faithful followers to salvation, to the glory of Heaven and all that was promised! The world belongs as ashes, like it was in the Great Flood, like the sickness"—he jammed the corkscrew against her forehead, the razor point digging a bloody welt into her skin—"was supposed to do! Cleanse the evil of this world, the wicked and the tormented...that is the power of the divine! Do you"—skin

peeled in painful, bloody strips as metal scraped against her skull—
"not see the path to godliness? You will, demon, you"—grinding,
grinding, grinding through skin and bone, her screams not enough
to drown out Alpha's errant words—"will see all His glory and all
His might, before you are back into the Hell you crawled out from!"

I love you, Melina. Aurous, my boy, so much.

I'm so sorry, Nadie. Clark. Twist. Bink. Hell, Odine.

Snyder...

I thought I could win.

I thought I could—

"Alpha!"

The pain *thudded* to an agonizing halt, blood trickling in thin,
warm streams over her eyes. She shuddered violently, crinkling the
tarpaulin, thrashing against her binds. Her heart thundered like a
rapid-fire machine gun, cracking her ribs. Alpha leered at her, jaw
shifting, and spoke to the figure in the doorway.

"You know what she's seen, the risk she poses to our plan," he
seethed through gritted teeth. "That traitorous Oppenheim is next.
He was about to tell her *everything. Everything.* She is the Judas of this
church, and she needs to be cleansed."

"Alpha, this is not the time," growled Aza. "Deacon is on his
way to sentence the unbeliever, though the redhead called for
counsel on her behalf. We have minutes, Alpha, until he is here.
We have a limited window of opportunity, do not waste it on her."

There was a shift in his gaze, a glinting spark in his icy eyes, but
reason was lost to the spreading darkness. "She is a *demon!*"

"Deacon can let a wolf into his flock, that is not our problem!"

Melina. Her heart swelled with a tender warmth that eased the
agony that racked her body. *You're always fighting for me. I love you. I
promise I do.*

But he was completely unhinged, from his slithering smile to
his knitted brow, it was morbidly clear the infliction of pain was to
be thoroughly savored and enjoyed, a craving that could no longer
be ignored. His icy eyes now smoldered with the same savage
intensity she undoubtedly wore when blood was steaming from
corpses at her feet. She stared into the eyes of her own bloodlust.

"She's going to be cleansed of her sin," he declared proudly.
"Her sins, the sins of her demon friends—"

"Alpha," whispered Aza.

"—and then, most deservedly, *Deacon,* and any false prophets
who follow! Aza, the time has come for the righteous to cleanse the

world with fire! You said it yourself! We are the rightful heirs!"

"You have lost the way, Alpha."

Alpha snarled, his trembling grip on the corkscrew a painful shuddering through her skull. "You promised me revenge against that heathen, you swore his blood would stain Morning Light! He sent her to die...he sent her to die...tied to a tree like Judas."

"Alpha. We are *out* of time."

"I will cleanse all, I will be the Almighty's fury against the sin that runs rampant in this wretched world! You will help me, Aza, you swore your life to His cause! You swore you would help me bring the false prophet to his knees! You do, or you die, like the rest of the unbelievers! This is our time! You will not turn your back on the Almighty as he has! We have come too far! Deacon will know the pain he has infli—!"

Celeste never saw it coming, and neither did Alpha. Blood, brain, skin, bone exploded through the room as a syrupy splatter, misting her white skin with a fine sheen of crimson. Alpha was thrown against the wall, his own halberd splitting his skull like firewood. The axe blade struck with enough force to wedge it firmly into the wall. Alpha slumped motionlessly, knees buckled and twisted against the floor, spine bent and hunching him forward as if he was about to leap at Celeste with the same vehemence in death as in life. Half his scalp dangled like loose meat over the axe blade. The boy was dead before the last word fell from his tongue.

"My apologies, Kara," Aza whispered somberly, to no one, both hands trembling around the long handle of the halberd. Her smooth, black leather-plated clothes were now dappled and smeared with running red. "Your boy was lost without your guidance, blinded by his faith, and fueled by revenge. I gave him a cleaner death than Deacon ever would have."

"S-shit," Celeste cursed, retching.

Aza's narrowing almond-shaped eyes glimmered with some sense of urgency, rolling over Celeste and the ligatures binding her to the tarpaulin. An eerie and deathly silence consumed them both, broken only by the concussive rhythm of her pounding heart and the remnants of Alpha's brains and blood *slopping* to the floor. Her crooked mouth twitched, not quite a smile, not quite a scowl. She looked as if she were about to hurl her belly over the slaughterhouse mess.

"I was supposed to protect him," she whispered, but not to Celeste, even staring into her eyes as dead as the hacked corpse pinned to the wall. "He was going to get himself tortured by Deacon."

Celeste nodded once. Aza turned, her wrinkled eyes a hazy silver. She lost her grip on the halberd, fingers slipping from the blood-soaked handle, and stood very still at the edge of the tarpaulin table. Celeste hesitantly bit her tongue, hoping her silence was reassuring.

"I tried to help him, but if he were caught...there would be no world to escape to. I had to, Kara, I had to." Her fingers fumbled along the blood-slicked cinch around her forehead. "I'll make sure Deacon pays for it all...someday."

Celeste felt her tongue wiggle free. "I want to help take Deacon down."

Aza's eyes widened, almost in shock, as if she had forgotten Celeste was bound to the table below her. She regarded her almost thoughtfully a moment longer, then unfastened the cinch from her swollen wrists.

"Alpha saw a demon in you," Aza said. "I only see a tamed wolf. A glorified lapdog."

"I don't fight on anyone's orders," Celeste growled.

"Only yourself?"

Celeste countered, "Only for freedom, as you do."

"Yourself," Aza assured, but Celeste launched herself against the snapping hold of her bindings. "Please!" she cried, "if you can't help me, take my friends with you! My family! They're not like the others, they're not blindly devoted!"

"What has Oppenheim revealed?"

"Revelations begins at dawn."

Silence dominated her once more. Aza slowly and absently loosened the ligatures around her limbs. Feeling *thumped* back through Celeste's limbs in painful jolts. Aza's silver-fringed eyes never wandered from her own, even when Celeste struggled to her feet, the woman retreated through the slop and positioned herself within arm's reach of Morning Light.

Aza resigned herself to a troubled sigh. "I cannot grant you a swift death," she said sorrowfully. "I will see what I can do about your friends. Some. But if you have any final words you wish to be pass—"

If Aza had said more, it went unheard as the corridor erupted with long, bloodcurdling shrieks that chilled them both to inaction.

"Please! I told you who! No—ugh! Az...a...er...Le..."

Oppenheim?

But when Celeste took a single, unsteady pace forward, Morning Light was wrenched from the wall and torn loose from the boy's split skull, his limp body smacking against the floor. Aza slashed at Celeste, missing her nose by a mere inch, though she was acutely aware the Watcher could have hacked through her skull as effortlessly as Alpha's. She threateningly balanced Morning Light parallel with her shoulders, and even in the narrow confines of the chamber and adjacent corridor, she could mercilessly slash and dismember her before Celeste managed to leap within arm's length of attacking. There was an ugly pause between them, one raised finger gently pressed against Aza's pursed lips. She retreated—slowly—and gestured for Celeste to follow with a menacing wave of the axe. With the silver of her eyes gleaming like the bloody blade in her grip, she peeked through the drawn tarpaulin curtain, crooked lip curled over her pointed teeth in a snarl. Whoever she saw wasn't Oppenheim.

"Come along," she ordered with a sterner tone, clearing her throat. "It's over, *heathen*."

Shit.

A hesitant step forward. "Please, Aza," Celeste pleaded. "Make sure they get *far* from here."

"Another word and I cut your tongue out."

Celeste found her threat more than credible. She knew who stood on the other side of the tarpaulin, the only one to strike hesitation into Aza's heart. She knew she had already lost.

Deacon.

His paunchy gut bulged the width of the corridor, as did his massive shoulders, though he was hunched far forward as if his spine folded neatly in half. His cane was raised from the ground, significantly shorter and tapering to a fine, bladed point. An ominous drip of blood splatted the floor by his feet, and his whiskers were flecked with crimson. His bullfrog throat rippled with each deep breath he took, and his burning eyes found her despondent look, wide nostrils flaring like a warthog about to charge. He was in the doorway of Oppenheim's unlocked cell, standing like a wilting weed over the blood slowly creeping from the confine. When he laid eyes on them, his face betrayed no emotion, only stone-cold determination.

"Azazel," he wheezed, sliding the blood-soaked blade from his cane into the separated half like a sheath. "I see some harm may have befallen our dear Alpha."

Celeste caught the slight hesitance in Aza's response. Was it as palpable to Deacon?

"Alpha attempted Purification on his own," Aza said. "It seems the heathen overpowered and attacked him with Morning Light. He is no longer with us."

Deacon was nonplussed. "It seems there are foxes in our henhouse, Azazel. I found our beloved Oppenheim disemboweled in his chamber."

"W-why," Celeste stammered.

Deacon shifted sideways, leaning heavily on his cane until the end was profoundly warped under his weight, and wobbly gut scraped off the cement wall. Behind him, with her arms bound tightly to her spine as Celeste's had been, the bandit girl Odine was forced to kneel in the spreading pool of blood. Her ratty clothes were dappled red, the side of her jaw a swollen mess of contusions and crusting blood, right eye a black puffy blob of flesh. Severely beaten, long plum-bright hair twisted like a braid into the paled grip of a Watcher twin, she growled and denied Deacon's charge by spitting a glob of blood at his feet. The Watcher wrenched his grip, twisting Odine's neck like he was trying to wring her spine of all fluid.

"It seems my throat was the next to be cut," Deacon proudly declared, his unblemished neck wobbling like Jell-O. "She came to free her leader, found Oppenheim and tortured information from him before he tried to escape...he was gutted quite cruelly after he spilled *every little detail*. I stumbled upon her, and without Elizio, I would undoubtedly be dead as well. My Watchers rarely fail me, and when they do"—his priggishly small eyes raged like a thundering cloud and stormed past Celeste and Aza—"they suffer a heathen's death. God whispers in my ear, about all, of all. Always. I am the beginning and the end."

Celeste swore she heard Aza's heart beat in tandem with the rapid rhythm of her own. After an uncomfortable moment under Deacon's intense scrutiny, Aza prodded Celeste with the sticky axe blade and nudged her forward.

"Elizio, would you fetch our dear Melina?"

The Watcher dipped his black bowler hat over his eyes in compliance.

"No," Celeste whispered, a surging fear clawing up her throat. "Leave her out of this!"

"Hush, child."

The Watcher's footsteps receded, and Celeste fought every urge jolting through her body to leap at Deacon and tear into his throat with her bared fangs. His thick fingers drummed against his bowing cane, and again, she wondered how much damage she could inflict before that hidden blade punctured her heart. If he dared harm a single red hair on Melina's head—

Those wild, blazing curls lapped through the darkness. Melina appeared, her freckled face taut and pale, thinned rosy lips pursed, chin drawn high as she sauntered through the puddled blood to stand by Deacon's side. She had to crane her neck to see past his protruding belly, but her terribly cold eyes wandered over the gore, the blood on Celeste's clothes and face, and the bloody, stringy scalp still clinging to Morning Light's blade. The bursting green of her eyes had dimmed to a serpent's gleam.

Melina was in no more danger than Deacon had been.

"You were right, my child," Deacon praised, his voice rumbling like thunder in the dismally cold corridor. "*For all have sinned and fall short of the glory of God.*"

"*And then many will fall away and betray one another and hate one another,*" Melina echoed his contemptuous tone.

A massive hand fell to her shoulder, nearly encompassing her entire breast in his grip. "The Almighty smiles upon you, child, for all the good you have done this night. The Promised Land belongs to the faithful—"

"—never the heathenistic," the Watcher Elizio, and Melina hauntingly harmonized.

Celeste reeled from a feverish burn. Her lungs were heavy with the rot of death, her tongue a dry, swollen prune. It was the frost in Melina's glare, however, that turned her belly and iced a glacier over her heart.

Her rose had betrayed them to Deacon.

Melina scrunched her freckled nose and whispered, "You lied when you said we would make this our home. *You* betrayed us and everything we fought for, and I won't let you destroy *our* faith."

TWENTY-FOUR
Leader of the Pack

IT WASN'T lust that violently crashed through her, or even any semblance of jealousy, only a chilling, hollow despair she hadn't felt since torching her father's cabin to ashes. She was deathly sick of secrets. They seemed to unravel all around her and seep into her blood like parasites, to slowly leech the life from her beating heart. Melina was just another casualty. Whether Celeste's intentions were pure of heart or not, they carried a poison to Melina's soul that was as deadly as the sickness, corrupting her into some incomprehensible form.

Did she even blame her?

Celeste thought she had almost dozed, hands tightly bound and throbbing numb, shuffling like the drunk her father had been on occasion. The spearpoint dug bloody welts in her spine, marching her forward, but it all passed in a painful blur. She and Odine were led out from below to the gaslit altar. The nave was as empty as her heart and just as devoid of warmth. As upon their arrival with Omega, they were paraded to the edge of the altar, forced to their knees in the blood that had dried in the cracks of the wood, in the very location where Deacon and his Watchers had opened the throats of Alpha's prospects. The pallid twins stalked the shadows like hyenas with silently cackling grins, bewitched by the promise of blood, crossing the other in a figure 8 shaped pace. Balanced firmly in their grips were arm-length metal clubs rounded to weighted heads and sculpted with razor-sharp flanges and blunt knobs, a deathly hum resonating from every swing. The demand to bludgeon her skull in was extremely palpable.

Drawn by Aza's silent scrutiny, Celeste followed her gaze. The mystery had finally come full circle, and the Watcher was playing her cards as dangerously close to her chest as Celeste was. Her silver-rimmed eyes never wandered far from Deacon, who hobbled along the altar, his cane *thudding* ominously slow against the bowing wood. His puritanical words fell on deaf ears, and Celeste had to wonder, as Aza certainly was, how much Deacon had gleaned from Oppenheim before running his hidden blade through his guts.

It was a long while before Melina returned.

When she did, she was in the presence of the man Snyder had described with frightening detail. Towering over the redhead at more than twice her height was a prodigious presence, with skin as dark as infected blood, a scrawling white etch in the distinct shape of a holy cross that covered a wide, flat face. With a head like a cinder block, oak barrels for shoulders and sledgehammers for fists, he was a walking mountain, and dwarfed even the enormous Twist. He was the only Watcher to be fashioned in similar robes as the worshippers, a motley of grey and dried blood. Following as closely as their shadows were the others from her former team. Snyder, sun-bright hair now a rat's nest of crimson and her slender face mottled black with deep-setting bruises. She had her hands tightly bound from her wrists to nearly her elbows. Nadie was beside her, similarly bound, a vibrant fear in her bronze eyes. She was unblemished, except for red flecking her oak-brown skin. Twist, by comparison to Snyder's biblical Goliath seemed of average stature, and waddled after them sulking. His face was like an overblown balloon of meat near bursting. Blood crusted the fuzz on his chin and neck, splotched the front of his ratty old shirt and fanned brightly from his dimpled knuckles to his ham-sized forearms. While his hands and wrists had been heavily bound with rope and stripped fabric, the simple man had the body of a giant tree trunk and was likely just as flexible, so the ligatures loosened and frayed around his separated forearms.

"Commander!" the simple man piped up as he waddled past, face a motley of bruises that deformed his smile. "They hurt. I want to go. Hurt them back?"

"Not now, Twist," she pleaded with shaky breaths. "Just listen to the man. I'll tell you when it's time to go, okay? I promise. I'll say when it's time to go."

Pouting, he replied, "Okay, Commander."

A creeping grin touched her lips; she had to wonder how many blows it took just to subdue Twist. Hopefully, a few faces were caved into the back of skulls like fleshy sinkholes.

As Melina led the prisoners through the hollow nave, Celeste devoured her every movement. Her hair no longer bounced along her shoulders, but had been pulled tight into a blazing comet's tail. Her skin had the sallow complexion of curdled milk, her brows firmly knitted, the green of her eyes now a smoldering grassfire, button nose wrinkled at the sight of Celeste as if she could scent the sins that bloodied her hands. Melina's gait was methodically rigid and composed, almost like a soldier—or a Watcher—though given the weeks recovering and training under Stonem's guidance, and an aptitude for a long-range specialist, Celeste was hardly surprised of her fortitude. No. She was alarmed by Melina's furious obstinacy, the declaration of God through the blood she swore against.

"Deacon," her voice rang out like a choir. "I have brought the remaining sinners to face judgement."

"Bitch," Snyder muttered through split, puffy lips, but Melina spared little attention as her fuming gaze spanned the ruddy altar and luridly stained-glass walls. "Where are the others?"

Deacon paused, leaning over his cane with a huff. The altar, or his bowing cane, groaned sharply under his weight. Deacon limped across the altar with elephantine thuds, bowing the wood beneath their knees.

"There has been a slight change of plan."

As his words struck the nave like rolling thunder, Celeste swore she felt the chilling effect of Aza's blood running cold. There was a fearful glint to her silver eyes. Celeste had to wonder if she could wedge herself in the cracks of the Watcher's obedience.

Tick tock. She wrestled with a smile.

"Oh?" That furious gaze of Melina's followed the shifting pattern of distorted firelight, the wrinkles in her brow smoothing. Roseate light shone with ethereal beauty, wandering across her vacuous expression, inviting her thoughts to wander as well. Sheets of glass from the leaded walls were intricately carved and shaped into the plight and salvation of their beliefs, and for once, Celeste saw the whole picture as it was meant to be witnessed. Across the nave, near the castle-like iron gates, the walls were blown and cast into the same Georgian-style glass, a sprawling crystalline mosaic of blue. Nonsensical, she had thought, until she saw the waves of a churning ocean, splitting and rising over the gate. The blue shifted into a floral composition, spreading parallel across each wall. The faces weaved into the patterns were unfamiliar, but shining bright in silver armor under a heavenly glow. Hanging like chandeliers from the vaulted ceiling, spinning and twinkling like a drunk under a starry night sky, massive crosses hung over her as judgement from above. Distorted patterns of crimson lit the glass wall encompassing the altar. The last prismed portrait was detailed with ribboning robes of beige, a man with a wispy brown beard like Deacon. A crown distorted his features with twisting thorns and a shimmering cascade of burning red. His arms were grotesquely slung perpendicular to his spine in a cruel crucifixion, dwarfed by the gargantuan cross that burned like a beacon behind him.

A warming smile touched Melina's rosy lips. "Will it still be so?"

"Revelations cannot be stopped," Deacon preached as if the congregation had gathered. "It is the frightening inevitability of His will."

"What the hell is this nonsense, Shadow Spawn?" But Snyder was like a yowling kitten. "What has this bitch done?"

Melina was a tempest, a fierce howling wind. "The will of the Almighty is not nonsense! Revelations is His final word! You will listen to the prophet of God, the all-knowing, the all-seer!"

Snyder clicked her tongue. "You've lost your marbles."

"And your sins will *never* be forgiven!"

"Goddamned blue falcon!"

A sulky sigh blew through the cacophony. "Commander," Twist huffed. "I want to go."

"Bitch!"

Celeste breathed out slowly.

"Snyder, enough," she said. "Please."

The blonde's lip curled into a vehement snarl, but Melina's melodious giggle drowned them into bone-chilling silence.

"I loved you, Celeste," Melina whispered. There was something maddening to her tone. "But that love was of sin, of torment, of death. You loved only blood. You made deals with the Devil, and you say it was for me, but I had God by my side. *We* were by your side. You had no use for either of us. Everyone around you dies, or suffers the consequence of it. Revelations was never a moment you or Theta could stop because it isn't one moment in time, or the meager plans of mortals. It is the Almighty's will, and we are purveyors of His salvation."

A response died in Celeste's throat, bitter and caustic. Vision bleary, stinging. Cheeks warming. Was her redhead truly so far lost to the throes of their heartache?

Melina went on, voice strangled, but that eerily warming smile never left her lips. "I only wish you could witness it yourself, Celeste. I'd hoped you would accept His love into your soul and ask forgiveness for all the wrongs you held so dearly. But you're corrupted and foul, and you need to pay for the sins you've committed." The green in her eyes brightened to a storming iridescence. "You and the heathens you dare call friends."

"Let them go," Celeste whispered weakly, her eyes searching those crackling green irises for any sliver of the woman she knew. Melina's tender features were gaunt and stiff, cheekbones stabbing out from her face, lips pursed to a beak shape. There was a shadow dancing across her sullen expression.

"Like you let Stonem go?" Ice crept through her tone. "Like you let him die?"

Deacon spoke next. "Only through the name of God should life be taken. Only through Him should blood be spilled. You will answer for your crimes, here and in the depths of Hell. By the name of the Almighty and His glory, you will never witness the Promised Land. You will be ash like the rest of the world. Like the Almighty intended, a flood of fire and brimstone to cleanse the sin of sickness, the sin of violence and bloodshed. A Promised Land for the faithful."

Melina's eyes greyed. "We could have made this our home, Celeste. You betrayed *us.*"

"My child," said Deacon, *thumping* his way to the edge of the altar. "Your duty to the faith has pleased our Lord."

"I am happy to serve Him."

A creeping smile wrung the last shred of humanity from his face. "There is no greater satisfaction," he agreed proudly. "However, my child, you will serve him in more ways than just prayer. The whispers of His will declare you reborn."

No...

The Deacon's cane struck the alter like a gavel's final judgement. "Abandon the sinfulness of old, shed the darkness of your past. You are Melina no longer; you are a Watcher, the eyes of God, a shield against sin."

"No!" Celeste snarled, baring her teeth as fangs.

"You are now Magdalene."

"No! You're Melina! You've always been Melina!"

"God Himself whispers into Deacon's ear," she declared. "Melina died with your sins, Celeste. I am Magdalene now, and always will be. It is His will, and He has spoken."

Amused by Celeste's wordless savagery, Deacon boasted, "And how loud He has spoken to His prophet! Though, alike the Son of God, a Judas at our table was to be known, a betrayer of His will!"

Melina the Magdalene let her green eyes simmer with contempt. "The unfaithful disguised as a prayer."

"But unlike the Son of God! The sins of the Judas shall *not* be forgiven!" Deacon's smile was a twisting serpent that slithered across his pudgy features. "An army of heathens, led by Celeste of the Bandits, has been preparing to lay siege to the faithful who find refuge in His church! These wolves were led to our doorstep, but a child blessed of His will was reborn and freed of her sin! You have done well, Magdalene the Watcher, and in His name, you shall be praised!"

Magdalene spared no glance for Celeste, but swept her fuming eyes over the others, sparking a furious sneer at the bandit. "Revelations *must* persist!"

"As it is told by the Almighty!"

Deacon roared on, commanding the presence of every Watcher in his sight. The twins ghosted from the shadows, the mountainous man Beshnaal slowly paced towards the alter with earth-shattering stomps. Amusement played across Melina the Magdalene's chalky face. Even Aza hung on the edge of every booming word.

"We have come to an impasse with the unfaithful! While they seek to destroy our faith and corrupt the land of life, we seek to bring balance the way God intended! With fire and brimstone!"

Deacon rapped the edge of the altar, his smile like a bright beacon of light over Melina. "Tell me, my Magdalene," he whispered. "How were the heathens to lay siege on our home of worship?"

Magdalene abandoned all the hesitance of her former self, cheeks burning with fury. "After dealing with the engineer they were to shut down the defenses and signal Theta's army to advance and burn the faithful out."

"How shall we deal with these heathens at our doorstep, Magdalene?" Deacon's small eyes were scorched black with fearsome ferocity. "The Promised Land is within our reach."

"Since the traitors want war, Your Holiness, and with the defenses compromised," Magdalene replied with an inching smile. "I would fire the flare that's meant to alert Theta's army and allow them to approach the church. They will hear the warnings of God and accept His word—and their sin will be scorched from this wretched land with Revelations."

Celeste stared at her former love, feeling her heart sag in her chest like a deflating balloon. A stranger stood before her in slicked red hair, and a dismally grey robe that flowed around her waist like a bloated corpse. Melina was no more, the ashes of her former self scattering with the ghosts of old sins. No longer was there the woman Celeste had survived with along the highway, had grown to care for in the city, whose loving touch had shown her a rush of ecstasy rivaled only by the thrill of spilling blood. The ghost of who she was faded into the darkness of the church. There was only the other now.

The Magdalene.

"There is much you will accomplish in His name, my Magdalene," Deacon replied, chewing on every word and spitting them like venom at Celeste. "Abel. I believe it is time to signal the heathens to advance on the church. Lower the defenses and let the attack commence—when the time is right, when the heathens refuse the one true faith—God will strike with a fury that will not be matched. Eli—alert Omega and have him secure passage through the eastern tunnels. Those who cannot fight will bring His word to the other congregations. The rest—gather and smite the unbelievers as God Himself intended."

"Your Holiness," the Watcher twins harmonized, hissing with snake-like tongues. They departed as silently as the ghosts they looked like, pallid skin gleaming like beacons in the shadows.

Snarling and foaming at the mouth like some rabid cur, Odine's eyes burst into a furious wildfire of emotion. Even with her arms tightly bound, she wrenched her slender body, swinging her fists like a club. She was sprawled across the alter before she could sweep out Deacon's stumpy legs, and instead found her skull *cracking* loudly against the warped end of his oak-carved cane. Blood fanned across the splintering floor, spurting from her cracked lips. Amusement crept into Deacon's tone.

"Though I admire such tenacity"—he swung his cane like a golf club and *thwacked* her skull with another hammering blow—"in one so young and strong-willed, you and your people worship pagan gods that are as vile as demons. There is no place in the Promised Land for heathens. Your kind brought wolves to our doorstep before, and those wolves were slaughtered for meat. Were they"—THWACK!—"kin of yours, perhaps? Hm? The unfaithful who never returned? They were as unsuccessful as you are. They pleaded for salvation"—*THWACK!*—"as they sat and ate Communion with those of true faith, and then they turned to give thanks with blades. They deserved heathen deaths, as you do, as you *all* do."

Magdalene's voice cut like a knife through the creeping silence.

"Deacon is all-seeing, all-knowing," she praised. "The Almighty blesses him with sight. No Judas may hide among our congregation."

"Speaking of a Judas."

There was an audible noise caught in Aza's throat when she was thrown under Deacon's menacing glare. His scorching eyes beat down on her like miniature suns, beads of sweat dripping from her deeply ridged brow. Her silver eyes shifted and gleamed like spinning sawblades, flicking from the moving mountain Beshnaal, Magdalene, to Deacon's enigmatic grin.

"Azazel, I am disappointed."

Her hesitance was a moment too long. "Deacon."

"While the wolves howled at our doorstep," Deacon said, "a fox roamed the henhouse."

Magdalene hissed, "A *snake* in our Eden."

Deacon slowly hobbled along the altar edge. *Thud. Thud. Thud. Thud.*

"Oppenheim, a man blessed with the knowledge from above, but cursed by enemies at all fronts, was led astray of his sworn duty to the faith and forced to sabotage the Almighty's will. When preparations were to begin at first light for Revelations, the fire from above would have scorched the church, and Azazel and the unbelievers would seek to claim the untouched Promised Land as their own.

"But God himself would never allow such a travesty to befall those of true faith. His whispers of your betrayal even reached the ears of your fellow Watchers, snaring the young and impressionable Alpha onto a sinful path. Would his mother be proud of her sister, hm? Would she be pleased to have his blood on your hands? You led him astray, as the Devil led you astray."

The green of Melina's eyes shimmered like slithering snakes. "Revelations would have welcomed the faithful, Azazel, the Promised Land would have been ours."

Aza knitted her brow. Her mouth twitched into a crooked smile. "You're a naïve fool to believe this false prophet. Revelations is not the work of some god, and this station is not the only silo to deliver his fire and brimstone."

While Melina was briefly puzzled by Aza's words, a struggle of reason and irrevocable belief played across her face in a twisting sneer. Celeste sucked in an icy breath. Her chest was ready to burst from the hammering pace of her heart. How far gone was her wild rose?

"Oh, my dear Azazel," he said carefully, cane *thumping* furiously. "The most you have accomplished is delaying Revelations. You will still suffer the cleansing fire from above. Beshnaal, please. Apprehend our traitorous Watcher."

"With pleasure, Your Holiness." The mountain man's voice was the rumbling of a storm.

"Watch out for her weapon," Deacon warned with a wag of his fat finger. "Reaper's Claw."

The mountain-on-legs Beshnaal glanced at the blur of stained steel spinning in her grip.

"There is no firewood here, Azazel," he coyly observed. "It is time to put down the child's toy—"

With the last of her nerves short-fused, Celeste threw her head back, a sharp cackle snapping out from her manically wide smile. The cracking sound halted Beshnaal in place, while drawing Deacon's ire and Magdalene's intense fury. Her fit of laughter brought a stabbing ache to her abdomen. Blood dried to a thick paste along her tongue. Tears warmed her icy cheeks.

When she finally found her bearings, mouth mangled into a smile that nearly twisted off her face, she found Magdalene glaring, her face as furiously red as her hair.

"This is *not* a game, Celeste," Magdalene warned. "The Almighty demands retribution for your sins."

Celeste fought the urge to burst into another fit of laughter. A wild shake of her head whipped her sweat-slicked hair across her face.

"Please, Melina—" Celeste began, despondence strangling her voice to a whisper.

"Magdalene," she corrected with a sneer. "You had your chance to absolve your wrongs, but you chose blood. So, blood you shall have. I want you to know, Celeste, that Melina would never want this—but Magdalene *does*."

"You truly are lost," Celeste snarled. "And so is Revelations. It is not only Theta's army that draws near. I've drawn a target on this false prophet."

Magdalene flinched. "What are you talking about?"

"Stonem may be swinging in Dead Wood," Celeste spat cruelly, "but his dirty tactics live on through me."

She wrenched her neck and exposed the fist-sized lump that ran from the base of her throat down to her clavicle bone. Magdalene studied the sinuously sutured flesh with bright, rounding eyes. Celeste smothered another laugh. "Just like with Stonem, Red Dawn has been tracking every movement I made. They know the coordinates of Theta's camp. They know where this church is. If you think they'll leave any survivors—well, where do you think my penchant for violence is from, *Magdalene?*"

Magdalene's rosy lips gaped. "You bluff."

"What is the meaning of this, my Magdalene?" *Thump. Thump. Thump.* "There is no use for conversing with these heathens."

"After Blackwell was killed at my hand, Uncle had only one use for me." A smile played at the corners of Celeste's eyes. "My head for Theta's allegiance. At first, I thought he spared my life over some struggle with morality—I *am* his only niece—but I was wrong. He orchestrated every event that led us into Dead Wood and right into Theta's grasp. Either I died in Hellpit, at Theta's hand—or I'd lead them right to Deacon's doorstep."

Words were lost to Magdalene as her eyes furiously wandered over the sutured slab of flesh. The threads of all their machinations unraveled around them. Denial was at the edge of her pursed lips, but her eyes were moon-wide; she had removed the same device from a similar wound on Stonem's neck.

Deacon struck the altar with his cane. "What does this heathen speak of?"

"I-it can't be."

"Magdalene!" *THUMP!*

With her teeth bared in a menacing smile, Celeste counseled herself to patience. The Watchers and Deacon floundered along the edges of her peripheral sight. She ached to kill them all, and knew there was nothing more dangerous than a survivor hellbent on revenge.

"She's not bluffing." A long, uneven pause. "We have to leave!"

"Nonsense, Magdalene," said Deacon, drawing the blade from his cane. "We will deal with these heathens now. Beshnaal, proceed. There is plenty of time before first light to initiate blood rites."

"No, we must go now!"

It happened within the span of a few seconds. Deacon was perturbed by Magdalene's stricken face, his piggish eyes squinting with worry. A heavy stomp forward and Beshnaal began to close the gap between his sledgehammer fists and the halberd in Aza's grip. The simple Twist fidgeted with his binds, tongue stabbing past his lips in thought.

Celeste sprang on the moment.

She plunged over the edge of the altar, shouldering into the floor with a bone-shuddering *THUD*. White-hot pain flared through her ribs as the air whistled from her lungs. Deacon's barked orders were lost to the thundering of her own heart. Magdalene shrieked. Celeste didn't care. She pushed off the floor with one knee, yelled hoarsely, "Twist, go!" and threw herself to her feet. Beshnaal took his eyes off Aza, craggy face contorted into a sneer, and rose like a mountain into the sky to challenge Celeste.

A near fatal mistake.

The axe hit the floor like a spinning sawblade, chopping dangerously close at Celeste's feet. Fury erupted like a lion's roar from Beshnaal. Celeste dove for the axe blade. Aza drew a leather-bound hilt from her waist with a deadly glint of rolling steel. It was like the tip of a sword had curled and rolled neatly into the hilt, and with one smooth motion, the folded steel unfurled like a scroll and fractured into five long, thin strips of razor-wire that *snapped* at the floor like cracking whips. Before Beshnaal could react, Aza threw her arm back, razor-wire twirling around her body like a dancer's flowing ribbon. A whistling blur of steel whipped and slashed at Beshnaal, clawing deep crimson gashes across his craggy face. Blood misted and smeared his tattooed skin, his minced lips bursting with a furious bellow of fleshy spittle.

Celeste dragged the binds across the axe blade, fraying and unraveling the knotted rope. Her arms snapped loose.

As her hands fell across Morning Light, she heard the furious roar of a bear provoked from its slumber. Twist had managed to free himself, ripping his binds into strips, and threw his tree-trunk arms around Nadie as a red rivulet gleamed across the back of his neck. Deacon lunged again, blade skewering Twist's shoulder blade. Another slash—but Odine launched into him and clubbed the blade from his grip. They were thrown off balance, sprawling across the altar. Deacon floundered, winded, while Snyder reeled and scrambled to her feet—then caught a swift blow across her jaw, slamming her head back into the altar floor. Magdalene shrieked and rained fists down on her that landed with loud, meaty *thumps*.

Celeste grinned. It was the war-like pandemonium that boiled her blood.

Beshnaal retreated a few paces, keeping Aza's whipping blades in sight, when Celeste raised the axe blade against him. He yelled, "For the Almighty!" and unsheathed a deadly long blade as curved and thick as a crescent moon. He swung at her.

Morning Light was an odd balance in her grip, counteracting the muscle memory patterned from her old machete. All her life she had split firewood as a near-nightly chore for her father, but Morning Light was top-heavy and more than the length of her arm, with an axe blade the size of her head, a jutting spear, and a razor-sharp hook like a reaper's scythe. It was a strain on her arms, painfully shredding muscles and *popping* joints, but she held firm against the flashing strike of Beshnaal's scimitar blade. The hammering blow rattled her bones, shocked her arms numb, threw her from her feet. Her knee slammed against the floor, bracing for the second strike. Blood smeared down his face from the gashes, pulsating as fury contorted his stony features.

It was like a discharge of lightning crackling through air. Razor-wire snapped and struck with whistling lashes. Beshnaal swung his scimitar, blade sparking against the hissing metallic vipers. Celeste spun the axe and plunged its razor talon into Beshnaal's calf muscle, ripping into sinewy muscle like a vulture on a carcass.

It was a short-lived victory.

Fingers like boulders closed around her throat, crushing her airway shut, and plucked her off her feet like a child's doll. The halberd crashed to the floor. Nails raked bloody gashes into his steel-hard fist, but her strength waned. Her head was about to burst like a balloon. Beshnaal was reeling, shifting his stance, when he circumvented two whipping slashes of razor-wire, a third in a spray of sparks. Celeste was heaved from her feet, strangled like Stonem in the branches of Dead Wood. Her vision pounded white, circling to pinpoints. She vaguely saw Odine behind the mountain of muscle, binds hacked to ribbons around her feet, the warped end of Deacon's cane balanced her hands like a fencing sword. A flashy lunge and slash aimed for Deacon's neck, but the portly old man caught her arm and twisted her elbow to an inhuman angle. The bandit was undeterred by the pain. With the cane wrenched from her grip, she landed three separate blows to Deacon's face before the bladed edge was gliding toward her belly.

With a pounding war cry, Snyder barreled into Deacon. The altar heaved and rattled loose, snapping and splintering under Deacon's crushing weight as he rolled and thrashed with the blonde across the edge. The cane-blade clattered away from his grip. Snyder raised her bound fists and hammered his face, but he was powerfully stout, and enraged like a warthog. After another heavy *thump* of her fists, blood spurting across his greying whiskers, he slammed his rock-like knuckles into her chin. Snyder went limp, for a moment, skull bouncing off the altar like a basketball.

Celeste gaped breathlessly, her vision dimmed and foggy, thudding her fists against Beshnaal's vise-grip.

Razor-wire slithered and sharply slapped against Beshnaal's scimitar. Beshnaal sidestepped the strike, wires whipping against the floor.

The edges of her vision pounded black.

Another shriek rang from the altar. Deacon stood triumphant over Snyder, his boot crushing her bloodied face into the wood. Odine was on her feet, eyes darting from the fallen cane-blade a few paces to her right, to Deacon, who stood with his hunched back toward her—but it was Magdalene's zealous rage that was bloodcurdling. She stormed across the altar, face a bloody mess, an unrecognizable sound of fury erupting from her. Odine had only a moment to decide, Celeste saw, whether to snatch the blade and spear Magdalene's heart, or save Snyder from having her skull pulverized under his boot—but not both.

Celeste clawed at Beshnaal's grip, pried loose his boulder-like fingers, gulped desperately for a meager flow of air before her throat was constricted and cinched shut. Her heart thundered between scorched lungs, igniting into a fury of pain that radiated through her limbs. Her sight dimmed to a hazy black.

The last few moments played out like a dream amid a waking fog. Blood thumped to a painful halt in her throat, throbbing against Beshnaal's viselike grip. Numbness radiated through her limbs. Over the mountainous peak of Beshnaal's shoulder, she saw

Odine blur into a forward charge across the altar, Magdalene snapping fervently at her heels.

Odine dove for Snyder, sweeping Deacon's stumpy legs.

Magdalene snatched the fallen cane, shoving its blade past Deacon.

Deacon toppled into the altar and ruptured the wood in a rippling shockwave. Snyder was thrown from the edge. Odine reeled—the blade ran through her left eye in a slurry of viscous fluid. Odine fell from the altar and crashed to the floor in a bloody heap. Magdalene held the crimson-sheened blade high into the prismatic glow of the altar, Deacon leaning into her for support as he hobbled to his feet.

Vision blinked black. She gasped, squeaking a whisper of air into her lungs. An amorphous shadow blotted her fading sight, slowly taking shape as a blur of rippling flesh. Swooping arms closed around Beshnaal's cinderblock head, sandwiching his skull, then ruthlessly twisted his neck until his spinal column *snapped* like bubble wrap. Beshnaal went limp instantaneously, Celeste falling from his viselike grip, and his knees buckled and noodled under his tremendous weight. The impact violently shook the floor like an earthquake.

"Hn—ugh!"

Celeste sputtered and retched over Beshnaal, vision still pounding black. Air wheezed into her aching lungs. Feeling crept back through her extremities as a pulsing pain. Her bleary eyes wandered up a wall of fleshy muscle, finding Twist's simple smile stretching his disproportionately swollen face. Tongue pushed from his pursed lips, he nudged Beshnaal with his foot and sneered in a childish sulk, then happily reported, "Stopped the mean one!" squinting from between baseball-sized lumps around his eyes. "Nadie say 'save her, save her', so I save you."

"Y-yes," Celeste rasped. "Thank you, big guy."

Melina!

It took considerable effort to climb to her feet, and even more not to retch what little content clung to her guts.

"M-Melina!" she yelled, wrenching a sturdy grip around Twist's tree-trunk arm.

But Melina—Magdalene—was gone.

The beams beneath the altar bowed and splintered, tilting its blood-splotched floor at a steep downward angle. Her own vision twirled, head throbbing with a pain she never thought possible to feel. Below the crumbling wood of the altar, Snyder's blonde hair glimmered under gaslight. She leaned over a plume of bright hair, searching Nadie's bronzing eyes with panic.

"It's okay," Nadie hushed, more for Snyder's frantic outburst than Odine's silent, writhing agony. Blood slopped over her jutting cheekbone, dripping from Nadie's cupped hand. "You're going to make it."

"Purple girl is hurt," Twist mumbled through mashed lips. "She can't see."

"Shit," Celeste breathed, limping into Twist.

Nadie was remarkably composed given the situation. She directed Snyder's bound hands over an eye socket flooding with blood, pinching flesh shut with the pressure of her weight. There was a sharp hiss of ripping fabric as Nadie tore her shirt into long, thin strips, balled some of it, and bated her breath. After a swift countdown, Snyder removed the pressure for only a moment—blood spritzed and flecked their faces crimson—and Nadie plugged the skewered socket with bandage. Red pulsed and soaked the fabric. She twisted and tied the remaining strips through Odine's bright plum-coloured hair like laces through a boot, tying the bandage tight enough to dig furrows into her forehead. Palpating the edges of the bandage, Nadie inched a grin across her face and whispered, "Told you, it's just a flesh wound," and dabbed the flecks of blood from her face. Odine nodded curtly, mouth crooked, one wild eye darting across the dilapidated altar.

"Where'd that bitch go?" Snyder snarled.

Celeste opened her mouth to respond, but there was a chilling response beneath the sharp *snapping* of steel.

"Deacon and his pet have long escaped."

Shadows slithered around Aza, her eyes as glinting grey as the razor-wire claw. She approached slowly, a single pace at a time, thin blades coiling like a rope into the hilt. Diluted blood beaded her forehead, dripping with sweat, but despite the advancement of her age she moved effortlessly, and seemed as if she could whip and slash them all to ribbons without losing another breath.

"There are labyrinths of tunnels that lead far from here," she continued. "Paths for the Faithful to tread. Deacon will have abandoned the church. Those who remain will fight tooth and nail against invaders."

Snyder growled dangerously, "She can't stop *all* of us."

Celeste vehemently disagreed, and from the smile tugging at

Aza's eyes, she did also.

"The Titan will never launch," she warned. "These holy grounds will be razed, but not by some vengeful god. For weeks, we've had Oppenheim developing a bug in the launch system, with the promise of freedom from this world—which I had intended to keep until your leader exposed our plan."

"Why should we trust anything you tell us, *Watcher*?"

A brief shrug, then Aza responded, "I still saved your leader's life."

Glowering, Snyder clicked her tongue and fell into a string of obscenities that would have made Celeste's own father blush.

"Leader?" she gawked at Celeste, her eyes an icy blizzard. "Was it your plan to lead us from one deathtrap into the jaws of another? There was nobody for you to lead, Celeste, we weren't a team! You kept *everyone* in the dark! Who the *hell* are you, really, and who the *hell* do you fight for?"

Celeste bit her tongue for a moment, a sealed vault of the few secrets she still held close to her heart. Though, the moment her tongue unraveled like rolling yarn, relief flooded her veins like Deacon's drug, soothing her short-circuited nerves.

She told them how it began with cutting Blackwell's throat.

"It had taken me days to regain any form of consciousness," she said, "and by then, my wounds had been medically tended to by who I can only describe as a butcher. Fragments of bone had been clipped, flesh hacked away, sutured and stapled shut. There were no machines that monitored vitals, no drugs to dull the pain. Not even a blanket. Only the cold irons that shackled my wrists and feet to the bedframe.

"It all seemed to be one waking blur of teeth-grinding pain. Twice, my uncle had called on me and demanded my loyalty, and twice, I refused him. Uncle's terms were short and simple: swear to Red Dawn and execute my team for igniting the rebellion, and my life would be spared. After the second refusal, he couldn't even meet my gaze when he sentenced me to die in Hellpit. The last thing I recalled"—terror constricted her voice to a whisper—"was Mengele, the Blonde Man—or Doctor Cruel, as he was known throughout Red Dawn—and the needle that pinched the artery in my throat.

"When I woke, with butcher's wounds and a fever, I started piecing together the intricacies of the puzzle.

"Blackwell had wanted me alive as a bargaining chip for the

Disfigured. I had executed Vega, the harbinger of war, and the Disfigured demanded retribution. They had something Blackwell needed. Peace was unlikely; Blackwell would never forgive their insurgence against Fort Thompson. An alliance, perhaps, against an enemy far too threatening to fight alone. I couldn't be certain. I didn't even want to be a soldier. Hell, I wanted nothing to do with Blackwell's new order or his vendettas against the bandits. And he wanted me dead. But with his throat gashed, the Disfigured lost their advantage. Uncle is fervently against them, willing to scorch the landscape in retribution for Fort Thompson and whatever my father had done in their name, so there would be no exchange with the sworn enemy to Red Dawn—not even for a treasonous general killer. How could he hunt the sheep and herd them into his pen?

"Send a wolf to sniff them out.

"But the wolf needed training, had to be muzzled and leashed, taught when to snap fangs and when to slink back to the cage. Uncle knew I was as intractable as my father and would do just as he had done when he was exposed to the barbaric tactics of the military—run like hell and never look back. Hellpit would take my friends and shape them into grotesque, bloodthirsty creatures. I only had one direction to flee: east.

"If I died attempting to escape, it was a traitor's death. And if Theta hanged me in the branches of Dead Wood, Uncle could destroy the last bandit encampment.

"It became evident that General Blackwell was not the powerful mind that orchestrated Stonem's treachery. Uncle had fought for my exoneration, gave me command of a unit as protection against the prejudice of Red Dawn, warned me of Blackwell's upcoming trials of allegiance. Blackwell would have sooner cut my throat and fed me to the bandits if not for my uncle's intervening hand. But despite all his love, or sympathy, his loyalty would always be to Red Dawn. He alone saw the value of a long game. Blackwell would have ordered the execution of our entire unit—it was *my* uncle's plot to flush the rats out, the blue falcons in his midst, and snare the bandits in their own trap. When I was exposed, he had a final card to play; a trial run had already proven a success with Stonem. It didn't take long for me to suspect the device. The swelling, putrid flesh was a strong indicator of a stubborn infection—my body rejecting a foreign substance."

She spilled every thought she'd had, every lingering suspicion of how Blackwell and her uncle operated in the shadows. She had wanted to spare them the horror of it all, shoving them far from the danger, but she revealed her secrets to the wide-eyed bunch, even Aza, who hovered on the fringes with her silver eyes whirring in wonder. Those secrets had kept her anchored alone in the darkness far too long, and she felt the weight of its burden lift from her chest. She could finally breathe.

All that remained, however, was a slithering tendril of darkness, strung to her heart and around her very being.

That terrible secret, for now, was a poison meant only for her.

"Shit," whispered Snyder.

"Commander..."

"Why didn't you tell us?"

Celeste choked on her words. "I-I couldn't know who to trust," she managed. "If I had even told Melina..."

Snyder bit her tongue, but Nadie whispered the cold, uncomforting thought that plagued them all, "We would have been dead long ago."

Tears stung her burning eyes, though, whether from her broken body or broken heart, not even she was certain. Melina—*Magdalene*—was a thought that consumed her until she was hollow and torn, a feeling that only intensified with the absence of her wolf. Was he as lost as her wild rose, she wondered, caught in the storm of a war he had no care for? Perhaps he was doing exactly what he was meant to do, as she was once meant to do alongside him: hunting the woods and fishing the streams, sun beating him into a warm slumber, dozing off in the shade with a belly nearly bursting. Far from the worries of her complicated human world.

She could only hope.

"Yeah," she echoed with a voice as heavy as lead. "A long time ago."

"So," said Snyder, "you had this planned since carving Blackwell's throat?"

More or less, she wanted to say, but instead only nodded. Shame broiled her skin red. *It wasn't that simple, was it, killing your way to an endgame?*

Melina.

I told you, daughter, Vega purred from the back of her mind, *you would be the death of that girl.*

Red hair curled into lapping flames, spreading from the embers of her broken thoughts. Her vendetta against Red Dawn had severed the only love she had ever known beyond the fading grip of her father's, and the love of a mother she could only recall as a lingering scent of flowers after rainfall.

Melina.

Sandy freckles across gleaming, milky skin, rosy lips as sweet as the taste of honey.

One down, one to go, came another thought cloaked in Vega's hissing tongue. *Only the Magdalene remains.*

With a slow, steady breath, one by one, her eyes rolled over the fragments of her former team.

"It was to start with me, and end with me. I see now that I was wrong, wholeheartedly. Melina..." Words died in her throat. She blinked away her tears. "My father spent his whole life sheltering me from how cruel this world was. The lies he told, the secrets he held, it all killed him. He had his family, he had me, and he couldn't share the burden or blame, he shouldered it alone. That's what I did, I shrouded myself in those lies and told myself I was protecting Melina. I was protecting all of you.

"That isn't how this world works. We survive by banding together, we survive by becoming family. We survive as a pack." Their gazes followed hers, blazing with the same intensity that spurred her into action. She knew, as well as they, that survival depended entirely on the other. "We survive as one. I can no longer do this alone, and I am no longer forcing you to my side. I fight for the freedom of all. So, I'm leaving the choice to each of you. Follow me and fight for our freedom or live your life however you choose. I will *not* stop you."

One by one, there was a slight nod from them, with Twist stabbing his tongue far between his lips and declaring, "Commander!" as loudly as he could bellow through the empty nave. While his voice clapped like thunder, a grin melted Snyder's icy features.

"If you're going to take out Red Dawn, I'm in," the sneering blonde said, eyes glimmering like a calm ocean. "To hell with them and this church. It's good to see you back, *Commander.*"

Nadie nodded, tilting her head. Twist bellowed again, shrugging as she gently hushed him. Celeste gave them a curt nod, heart swelling. Scorching eyes fell on Odine, the bandit girl sprawled in Snyder's lap, her angled face splotchy with blood. Her one eye rolled to meet Celeste's fiery gaze.

"Odine." Celeste said with a dangerous edge to her tone. "You have ties to the Disfigured, whether by kin or obligation, I don't care. I don't want your hesitation. I don't want your treachery. If you want to leave and join Theta's side, I will not stop you, and neither will anyone here. You are free to choose your own path. But if you join us"—the bandit's eye rippled with shadows—"then I promise you that Deacon's head is yours to take."

The fury written on the bandit's face was plain, the corners of her mouth crooking in smile. She clambered to her feet, almost bowing to Celeste, then spat a glob of blood at the splintered altar.

"Give me his goddamn head," she whispered coldly, "and I'll follow your every order until I die."

Snyder clicked her tongue. "What about *her?*"

Aza was a haunting silhouette against the shifting patterns of gaslight, watching them as intently as a hawk over field mice. The corners of her eyes wrinkled, muscles taut and tensed, but Celeste exhaled slowly, calming the snarling wolf inside.

"She's going to get us out of here."

That caused the former Watcher to unexpectedly flinch. "Oh?" she purred. "And why would I do that?" She gauged them all with a quick glance, eyes shimmering at the odds. She almost appeared eager to spill more blood, as if the duel with Beshnaal had been an interrupted warm-up. A small sound of amusement escaped her pursing lips. "I suppose the same offer of freedom does not extend to me, regardless of how I spared your life—twice."

Her threatening reminder left chills scurrying across Celeste's skin. Her black scars stung like fresh wounds. Celeste studied her face, but Aza was as enigmatic as Deacon had been, revealing nothing with her lurid eyes but danger, like the glow of a predator's gaze in the shadows.

Vega slunk from the edges of her mind, reminding her with a hissing whisper that she was to lead, not follow, to rise from the ashes of the old world, not fall with another to its smoldering grave. She was the leader of the pack, not the Disfigured, not Red Dawn or the Children of the Last Light. Theta. Uncle. Deacon. They were all tyrants and despots, heralds of war and harbingers of death, spreading pestilence and plague wherever they warred. Deacon scorched a path with fire and brimstone, sacrificing his followers to an errant god. Uncle imposed a militaristic rule on the land and its people, unleashing Doctor Cruel and his twisted experiments into the world. Theta was a madwoman determined to avenge her sister's death by any and all sacrifice, including the people she claimed to protect. Vega had been no different than the grievous General

Blackwell. Imperialistic, murderous, pugnacious. Razing cities to overthrow the other in a twisted game of cat and mouse. Was Celeste to be as Vega intended, molded into a blade who can strike at the heart of the military and its rising empire? What would that make her? A weapon for Vega, wielded by a phantom from beyond the grave? Another despot in a race for ultimate control? Did she want the world to tremble and fall to its knees before her, demanding mercy for the love it tore away from her?

No.

She had to be different, she had to be her father, her mother. End the cycle of violence, at least begin to. Fight for what Father would die for.

Is that what you have been secretly fighting for as well, Aza?

"Because we fight for the same cause," she replied in earnest. "Freedom. I do not seek your allegiance, Aza, or your devotion. If either of us want to survive, we do it together. Whatever you decide after we gain our freedom is up to you and the few who follow."

That crooked grin spread as wide as the Cheshire Cat's. Gears grinding in her head, Aza flicked her gaze over them like she was only a moment away from pouncing with her claws extended.

"I knew there was more to you than the naked eye perceives," Aza said coyly. "You are cunning, resourceful, ruthlessly intelligent. You are more alike to Deacon than you wish to admit, but he lost himself to his own fanaticism. Will you as well when you wage a war over your woman?"

Celeste had never observed a shred of humanity in Deacon, only a dangerous charisma that scented and pounced on any weakness. Though, given his advancement in age, he appeared far older than her father had been at the end of his years. He was a relic of the old world, before the sickness, before the lines between life and death were irrevocably blurred. Had he been a father once, as well, holding a daughter like Celeste in his arms as the world fell to unimaginable chaos? Did he whisper his love to her as the sickness ravaged her small, fragile body into a blood lusting creature of hell?

Perhaps.

"I don't know," Celeste found herself saying. The lies exhausted her, she saw no point in their futility. The thought of Melina was the spark that could consume her life like it were kindling. "I've lost everything. I *keep* losing everything...this world has robbed me of my soul. This is more than me, more than us. It's our future, the future of those we love. We can fight ourselves, or we can lose our souls like...like Melina."

Se met each of their gazes again.

"So, I can't promise that I will never be blinded by love," she admitted. "But I can promise that we will never stop fighting for what we believe in, as a family, as a pack. We don't abandon our family, no matter what, even if they lose the way. So, Aza, you can decide. Die for nothing, or die for a cause."

Aza let the silence carve a giant chasm between them, but Nadie rose to her feet, determination scowling her face. Her smooth, honeyed skin was bloody and bruised, but shone under the shifting columns of light. Bumps raised on the back of her neck. She stood as she hadn't before, eyes down and chin held up, that mischievous grin inching through her heart-shaped face.

"For Melina," whispered Nadie, eyes glinting dangerously. "For the life she should have lived. I'm...I'm sorry, Commander."

Slowly, Snyder rose to her feet, extending a bloodstained hand to the former bandit, and gave Celeste a curt nod as she steadied Odine's balance.

"For Melina," Snyder scoffed. "She saved our asses with one hell of a shot. To hell with *Magdalene*."

"Commander!" Twist erupted in a singsong bellow, a hammy fist pumping into the air. "Commander!"

Celeste was reeling. Her heart had been gruesomely carved away, piece by agonizing piece, leaving only a corpse of who she was. Though, in that moment, she felt the wolf inside her growl its satisfaction, warning the phantoms of her mind that she and it were not prey. They were hunters.

It was time to hunt.

"You certainly inspire and embolden," Aza praised with a disturbing frown. "However, words won't win this war. Can you fight as well as you can speak?"

A small sigh escaped Nadie. "Turrets," she said. Unease strained her voice. "Those turrets will slaughter *us* as well. Unless..."

Without hesitation, Celeste ordered, "We need to hold the northern sector and bottleneck the armies from both sides. Theta and her people will be slaughtered by those turrets, and she's going to be pissed when she breaks through the north gate. We engage both, then use the distraction to cut our way through to Theta's camp, free Clark and Bink, and get the *hell* out of here before that missile launches."

Aza almost winked. "The turrets won't activate. That army will overrun the church."

"Yes they will," Celeste said. "Nadie will make certain that *all* systems are activated. Everywhere."—she swore Aza winked at her— "except the northern section. When the Watchers notice the army breaking through their gates, they'll have no choice but to face them head-on or give them control of the church. We'll use that advantage and pit them against each other."

Snyder huffed, "Are you going to be okay with that, Odine, fighting your former family?"

"I only want Deacon's head." A flicker of darkness crossed her features. "Theta is not our chosen leader."

"Fair enough." Snyder shrugged. "Is this your new plan to get us killed, Commander? We'll be sitting ducks out there, surrounded by armies who likely have weapons, and who knows what else on our heels."

"Trenches."

That grabbed their attention. Amusement lingered in Aza's tone, and Celeste couldn't help but grin. She knew the Watcher had a few tricks remaining up her sleeve. The northern section had been cut off from the video feed for a reason.

"There are trenches dug through the parameters of the church," she said with a maddening grin as sinuously sharp as her razor-wire. "They can't breach the north gate without going through the trenches. We could fend off an army or two for quite some time."

"Guerrilla warfare," Celeste stated with chilling certainty. "We only need to create a distraction to slip through. Once Red Dawn descends on these grounds, it will be pandemonium, and we won't stand much of a chance on our own."

Aza licked her crooked lips, eyeing them with unnerving anticipation.

"Well, what are we waiting for?" she asked. "Let's hunt."

TWENTY-FIVE
Discordia

RECENT RAINFALL had sopped the grounds to a congealing stew of mud, threatening to sink them deeper beneath the gritty, icy surface. Ribbons of shadows unfurled from beneath the church, jagging obliquely, with interlinking lines that crossed under the snarl and splintered into the darkness of the surrounding Dead Wood. The trenches were dug grave-deep and nearly as narrow, flooded with stagnant muck that was dank and cold like the sewer system snaking beneath the asphalt of Fort Thompson. Visibility was limited to rippling mire and tall, smothering shadows. Celeste had to smile; so much for the irrigation channels Nadie had dug for the gardens. They moved slowly, like wading through a swamp, on Celeste's silent command, and positioned themselves between the church and the north gate. A hundred meters of no man's land unfolded into a blinding fog in both directions. Any furtive glance over the slopping embankment revealed a swirling white mist creeping forward from Dead Wood, threatening a blinding encroach of the grounds. The tall, dead giants twisted into slithering patterns across the charcoal horizon, and crimson glimmered through the snarl like blood-red stars. Celeste heard a quick intake of breath from behind her. Aza paused at the ominous glow, but Celeste pushed forward with a quick *snap* of her fingers. It was no warning from God; the flares had been fired.

The Disfigured were advancing the line.

It was as if the funereal night bated its breath, awaiting a maddening descent into chaos. The silence consumed them, with Celeste locking her gaze with Snyder, who flanked her to the left of the trench. Steel sheened in the blonde's trembling hands, a hunting knife with a blade as serrated as wolf teeth, pulled from the belt of the dead Watcher, Beshnaal. The knife wasn't ideal, but time was a literal ticking bomb, they had to adapt and survive. Odine took point a few paces from Snyder, a splintered pole from the altar carved to a spear, and jagged pieces of glass tied with torn strips of her sleeves. Nadie was shrouded and unseen in the far reaches of the winding trench, her gifted blade *flicking* in and out from the handle. Twist was undoubtedly somewhere beside her, Beshnaal's curving scimitar like a kitchen knife in his meaty grip, a blade he had proudly—and aptly—named Bendy. Aza was directly to her right. Tension sharply *creaked* the coiled razor-wires like stabbing violin strings. There were three others in her charge, as well, whose names had fallen on deaf ears to Celeste. Former Watchers. Blue falcons to their own kind. Could they—should they—be trusted not to bury a blade in their backs? Aza was an enigma shrouded by shadows, and their desires fell in line with hers, or they wouldn't have abandoned the church. *No matter*, came the cold, calculating thought. *I'll be waiting with a blade of their own.*

Morning Light still felt odd as she played with its balance in her grip. Weighted like a sledgehammer, and as awkward to swing, she shouldered the halberd and slicked her fingers in the blood meandering across the leather handle. Alpha's brains, undoubtedly, or meat from Beshnaal's torn hamstrings. The thought repulsed her, wringing her belly, and she was certain if there any contents left to retch, she would have. Nadie had. Twice. A thoughtful pat on the back from Twist had nearly spiraled the poor girl into the trench muck.

While their nerves short-circuited from anxiety, Celeste wore a chillingly flippant smile, unable to shake the rotating thoughts from her head. When *was* the last time she ate? Breakfast? The morning before? She couldn't be sure. It tasted like grit and was still stuck between her bloody teeth. Thoughts of Nadie circled her mind. During a brief exchange with her, out of earshot of the others, Celeste had wondered aloud if she were walking the right path, or merely retreading old sins.

"That's up to you to decide," Nadie had whispered, running her fingers through a tangle of shimmery-black hair. "What you want us all to become." Celeste had barely registered a response before Nadie grinned, a shadow of mischief playing at her doe-wide eyes, and whispered, "But for what it's worth, the name fits, and I think you're badass enough to pull it off."

Thanks, she wanted to say, but Celeste allowed a curt nod only, eyes stinging. When she turned, however, Nadie's hand fell into hers with a gentle, but firm warmth.

"I'm sorry, Commander," she said, "I really am, and I know you did what was best for us...or what you thought was best...and Harn..."

The pain would always be a fresh, bleeding wound, Celeste ached to explain. She couldn't.

"Is it wrong to feel joy at the thought of someone suffering so much?"

It had been difficult to separate their embrace.

Once the echo of those words ceased rattling in her skull, her mind was a blank slate. There was nothing in that void but the smothered sounds of rapid, uneven breaths, the thundering storm of her own heart, and the *squeal* of her fingers slipping across the blood-soaked halberd. Another furtive glance to Snyder, but the blonde's gaze was attentive and alert to the shadows that loomed over them like phantoms. Celeste steadied her next breath; they all knew their roles and the only outcome beyond death.

It wouldn't be long now.

The blood-red stars blinked into ashen snow, the white mists rolled over the grounds like sea-churning waves, the sky was a spreading plume of darkness.

It began.

Death chilled the air with a loathsome symphony. Shockwaves cracked the silence and rippled from the trees like a tempest. Rapid bursts of light, like the flicker of a distant campfires, streaked through the blinding mists. Artillery shells were cutting through wood and flesh alike, splintering branches and rending limbs in an unfettered fury, ripping through organs and trees and thudding into the earth. Blood would be soaking the barren soil, crushed under the boots of those next to advance. Dead men walking. The echo of gunfire rang out over the grounds with their inevitable screams.

When those bright flashes waned in the pearly white mist, and the cacophony of death to an echo ringing over the hills, she sucked in one last, soothing breath. Death no longer howled like the winds. It was the calm before the storm.

Seconds stretched into minutes, and minutes into gnawing doubt. Would they blunder through the north gate, she wondered, or retreat into the safety of Dead Wood? Is it remotely possible Theta would abandon the assault for the safety of her people? Would Celeste, with a fury only quenched by blood, choose to a retreat or march into certain death? Foolish thoughts rotated in her head. She would fling flesh at any barricade for vengeance. She had torn through lives, soldiers and infected, blade bloody against all who stood between her and the Phantom Woman. Her violent crusade through Fort Thompson had filled those streets with rivers of scarlet. All for one madwoman's head. Is that why Melina abandoned her? Was she as indistinguishable from the other monsters whetting their appetites? Perhaps. The thought was a sharp pang in her chest.

Monster to monster.

The storm raged on.

Pressed against the embankment, she saw shadows blot the swirling white and muddy-green grounds, heard boots sopping through muck, and sharp whistles ringing out from the lifeless trees like the shrill warnings of birds. Celeste waited longer, stealing one last glance at Snyder's oceanic eyes, and then shouldered the halberd with a smile nearly as long as the weapon itself. So it began.

Just as she predicated.

The trenches were crudely constructed ditches, sopping wet with mud and runoff, and at best, a shield from the prying eye of a scope. By nightfall, however, they were carefully constructed traps for prey to wander across, and Celeste and the others nested like spiders at a trapdoor.

The first victim fell to their fangs.

He may have never noticed the gap in the muddy-green field. His boots slipped through the muck, hurling him face-first down the embankment. A surprised grunt was caught in his throat as he *plopped* into the icy mud. He did not hear Celeste grunt herself, axe swinging down from her shoulder, and never knew the sickening sound of his own skull *crunching* under one heavy, hammering blow. He would never know he was their first victim, but not the last. Never the last.

The war fell at their feet.

Flesh rained and flooded the trench. Each swing brought the

axe blade through vital points in a vicious bloodlust, skewering hearts, throats, bellies. They fell into the muck, dying or dead, glazed eyes only a ghostly reminder of whoever they had been, and filled the trench like a mass grave. Celeste was forced to retreat, losing sight of Snyder of the others, tangled in hacked limbs and spilling entrails, thrown shoulder-to-shoulder with Aza. Boots pounded above the trench, flinging muck into the air like a muddy fog, hurtling over the piling corpses or the gaps in the field. In the sheer confusion, the advancing line continued to stumble into the trap, and Celeste, Aza, and the former Watchers clambered over the dying and dead, bodies squirming under their feet. Whistles rang out in coded signals, between sharply-pitched barks like prairie dogs—as Odine had warned, they'd grown wary of the traps. It mattered little, however, as Celeste *thudded* the axe blade against bone, arteries bursting like broken water pipes. She was counting on it.

The trenches ran hot with noisome steam. Each pace backwards piled another body up like a barricade—or flesh to bridge the gap—and soon the bandits crossed the trench, abandoning the folly of the fallen. Her team struck as phantoms in the darkness of the trench, unseen, gliding through the dead, flanking the bandits.

Pounding bellows joined the furious cacophony, rising and falling from every direction. A blur of grey swelled from the church and rushed over the faltering line. The bandits were swept into a violent, bladed current. They were forced back over the trench that overflowed with their own dead, and those who fell were trampled and crushed into the corpses by the retreating line. It was a ploy, and even Celeste saw through the flimsy façade. The worshippers charging over the trench, however, did not. The bandits rose in waves, crashing against the shores of the church. Dozens of them, blades whipping in glints of steel and crimson, charged into the faithful. Sharp squeals of steel striking steel, screams strangled to wordless fury and pain, bodies *thudding* as they hit the earth. The worshippers outnumbered them ten-to-one, the whites of their eyes peeled manically wide, and proceeded to cut through the bandits like a butcher blade through meat. The worshippers not only pushed back against the bandits, they attempted to outflank them as well—just as Celeste and her team were—and splintered their charge through the trench.

"Rear!"

It was Aza who had noticed *they* were flanked while Celeste buried the spearpoint into a fallen bandit, then unwound Reaper's Claw with a flick of her wrist. It was one of her teammates who had fallen to a blade, shoulder torn into by steel. The worshippers were on them in seconds, but Aza was more agile than a woman half as young; she vaulted over corpses, Reaper's Claw *snapping* like hissing serpents, and sent those blades slashing through the trench as a whirlwind of whipping steel. The first dead worshipper fell to a slurry of muddy red, and her teammate clambered to his feet.

"Judas!"

Thunder boomed through the trenches, a furious howl for blood. Shock-white hair, peppered crimson and slicked flat, crowned a craggy, blood-red face. Eyes danced like shadows rippling around firelight.

Omega.

"The Almighty scorns unbelievers!"

The spear extended meters across the trench and closed the gap in a matter of moments. Before their teammate found his balance, the spear punctured his chest, *cracking* bones, and burst through his spine until he was completely skewered to the weapon like a slab of meat. Omega didn't stop there; his rage carried him further, dangling the dead man's feet, and launched the bladed spear to another throat.

Aza was a blur of steel. She whipped her arm, razor-wire ribboning from the hilt, and yelled, "Gav!" a moment before she *snapped* the sinuous blades against the spear in a bright burst of sparks. The spear ripped through dirt, missing Gav's throat by an inch. He fell backwards, grimacing, and kicked at the muck in a panic. Omega abandoned his spear, his face contorted and bloodred with fury, and charged the fallen man with thunder in his voice.

"You killed my boy!" he raged. "You killed him!"

As Celeste fell back against waves of worshippers, and the bodies piling the trench like a mountain of flesh, she heard Aza scream, "Kara wanted *you* dead!" as Reaper's Claw *cracked* like whips against his leather armor. Deep gashes pulsed a bright red; steel had bitten through to flesh. Omega was unfettered, shrugging off wounds with a bloodthirsty roar, and when he reached Gav, he was about to crush the man's skull into the mud. Aza sprang, whipping— Omega's hands snapped closed around her throat and brutally crushed her windpipe. She had fallen for his trap, and by the sadistic smile crinkling his hatchet-face, he enjoyed squeezing her throat like a noose. He wanted to see the life creep from her eyes.

Celeste was too far, axe blade sheathed in a bandit's chest; Gav was on his knees, fumbling in the muck for his knife. A young girl, with cropped, muddy-blonde hair, stuck her blade through a belly, leapt past Aza with a strangled cry, and plunged that knife between Omega's ribs. Celeste heard the blade clip bone, and the girl's grip was jarred loose. Omega drove his elbow into her face, *crunching* a button nose into mush, and she was thrown into the trench wall. Celeste held her ground, but her axe was a heavy anchor in her arms, and glimpsed the turmoil above soil. The worshippers had pummeled the bandit line and were closing in on both sides of the trench. Their white, hawkish eyes scanned the bloody descent, blazed at the sight of Celeste, and then hurtled down the ravine of flesh after her. She yelled, "Fall back!" to anyone within earshot, reeled and drew the halberd to her chest. Then she charged the thundering man.

It was these moments she recalled the most; the mire creeping up her leggings like tiny icy claws, the coppery scent of blood sweltering her lungs, muscles primed with vigor from an unadulterated, primal fear. She knew the halberd may as well have been a boulder in her hands, her muscles grinding through months of rust, but the death that fell around her was an intoxicating frenzy. Noisome vapor rolling skyward from gutted corpses and severed limbs; it was the streets of Fort Thompson again, soaked in muddy crimson. The wolf inside her howled an appetence for blood. Morning Light speared for Omega's heart.

As worshippers poured through the trench in bladed waves, converging on her team from all sides, Celeste threw herself at Omega. Morning Light glanced off his armor, spearing the dirt wall between him and Aza's limp body. Gav fumbled through the muck by her feet. To her left, there was a terrible scream twisted by infuriation, and a blade slashed dangerously close to her throat. The attacker faltered as the muddy-blonde girl sank another knife through flesh, ripping through shabby grey robes, and threw herself into the wave of worshippers descending into the trench. The small girl was nearly lost to the advancing throng. The axe was wrenched from the wall, spinning in her blood-drenched grip, and the talon snagged the exposed muscle in Omega's shoulder. Simultaneously, Gav produced the knife from the mud, and plunged it hilt-deep into the back of Omega's knee. He staggered with a fearsome roar, grip slacking around Aza's throat, as his leg involuntarily buckled. Aza slipped from his crushing hold. Gav scrambled up the trench wall.

Omega's defenses were shattered.

Celeste dragged the halberd to her chest and speared Omega's throat. A thin, red rivulet ran across his skin, his eyes glittered with the promise of death. Another narrow miss. For a moment, the battle that raged around them was a distant echo; death was ever encroaching, it just seemed unimportant. Omega's grip fell opposite of hers on the halberd, wrenching the weapon in her hands. "I'm going to kill you for what you've done," he promised with fearsome savagery.

Adrenaline soaked her muscles with strength, heightened her senses, stirred the wolf within her heart to growl, *Hunt in the now, lick wounds later.* A cornered wolf would always bite. Omega, however, despite his advanced years, was powerfully built and vigorously seasoned for battle. No matter her strength, it paled against his unbound fury. He was a tower of a man even on his knees. He tossed her, still gripping the halberd, into the trench wall, and it knocked the air from her. Shoving against him was like throwing herself against a brick building and expecting it to topple. He didn't sway an inch. He rose from his knee, lifting the halberd above her head—she bucked at his injured leg and dragged her heel across the wound. Another roar rattled her to the bone, a burst of crimson warmed her face. Someone's knife thudded to a halt between his ribs. When he dropped the halberd and cradled the hilt sticking from his ribcage, she jumped up to shoulder him into the trench wall. A firm grip, she wasn't certain whose, reeled her toward the opposite wall. Her peripheral sight blotted with grey and glinting blades. Omega's fury thundered after them, "Death to the heathens! Death to them all! For Alpha! Alpha!"

Blood stained the muddy trench a bright crimson. The dying were buried by the dead, trampled and crushed into the mud, their anguish as unanswered as their desperate prayers. Celeste stumbled through hacked limbs, losing sight of her team. Surging through the trench ahead of her were the worshippers, so close she could see the bulging whites of their collective eyes. Opposite of her, closing the gap between her and Omega, there were even more of them. She halted, eyes thrown skyward. The fighting raged above ground—or slaughter, as the bandit line had been battered into retreat. She knew, silently cursing herself, the importance of holding the trench wall. The retreat was a feint. The entire bandit front line was a feint.

"Shit." She shouldered Morning Light and clawed up the muddy wall.

Death rotted the air. Even the winds were sultry and bitter. Corpses littered the grounds, scattered like autumn leaves in the breeze. The discord of howls from both the living and the dying soon flowed into harmony, filling the air with the melody of battle. For only a moment, she was bewitched by the silent approval of Vega in the back of her mind. Was this as the Phantom Woman foresaw, the embers of rebellion fanned into the flames of an uncontrollable war? No man's land stretched endlessly into the rolling white mists, and those foggy tendrils slithered around her and encompassed the trench in a blinding haze. With one slow, shuddering exhale, she bolted into the mists, a mad dash for the north gate, with the members of the church fervently snapping at her heels.

The bandits hadn't retreated far—several meters, at most, straggling the north gate like bait dangling over the jaws of predators. The worshippers didn't care; they charged over and out of the trench after them like rabid dogs.

She knew her body was running on fumes already, the acceleration of her heart painfully dangerous, soaking her body in adrenaline. The mist was a cloak she wore as a phantom, gliding unseen across the bloody-green field, leaping over the fallen dead, Morning Light humming gently in her hands as if the cold, hard steel were alive and ravenous. The first bandit she came across was retreating with his back turned to her. The thrill of death impelled her to leap, and with one swing she severed his spine with a loud, meaty *thwack*. Almost instantaneously, his limbs buckled and went limp, crashing him face-first into the dirt. Another came lunging to her right, but she shoved Morning Light past his blade. A jet of sparks burned through the mist, axe blade grinding steel, its vicious talon shredding cloth and flesh. The bandit fell in a slurry of crimson, the axe head snagged in his shroud. The forward momentum hurled them into an ungraceful glissade through the muck. She thrashed through his guard and mounted him, axe pressed like a garrote against his throat, but from the corner of her eye, she caught the glint of his blade. She could crush his windpipe and be gutted in the process, or surrender her advantage and run the risk of getting her throat cut, but not both. Ending her split-second ambivalence, she shifted her weight over the axe and collapsed his trachea. Simultaneously, cold steel bit into her thigh. Muddy crimson steamed from a gash; the knife skittered into the mud. She stood, dazed and bloody, as the worshippers closed in.

It woke the fury of battle inside of her. It ached with every beat of her heart.

She'd kill them all.

With a flashy lunge, she parried a strike and spun on her heels, cleanly hacking through a limb like chopping a vegetable. Ice crept along her shoulder, then burned white-hot. Someone had stabbed her. A ripping slash with the spearpoint opened a belly like a torn rucksack full of grain. They screamed and barked all around her like gunshots. The worshippers were on her in a slew of rising and falling blades, bludgeoning through her defenses, jarring the halberd in her numbing grip. Axes for chopping firewood, butcher knives, sharpened kitchen utensils, spears carved from mops and brooms and fitted with sawblades, coiling barbwire, and studded with bent, rusted nails—they were swinging their improvised weapons with such savage indiscretion that some, if not most, of their blows struck one another and warmed the air with a thick haze of crimson. She swung the halberd, but there was no force to the blow. Another stinging pain warmed from her hip and through the muscles in her back. Blood sprayed from her shoulder. Someone fell to her feet, trampled beneath the swelling throng, and the axe blade plummeted through his skull. Bones were crushed like glass. Gashes pulsed a muddy red across her scarred arm. She heaved the halberd to her waist for a follow-up thrust, but fatigue gnawed at her, movements sluggishly uncoordinated. She fell to their blades, twisting and writhing, axe raised in a final defense.

Shadows poisoned the skyward mists like a dark, thundering cloud.

Arrows hailed down from the sky in thick, whistling blots. Screams gurgled and died in throats. Bodies slammed to the field, blood fountained and stained the green grass a ruddy hue. She inhaled sharply. There was a slight tremble to the ground beneath her, a rapid succession of *thuds*, and arrows buried themselves shaft-deep around her like tentpole stakes, one missing her neck by inches. Two worshippers, the whites of their eyes swallowing any color of their pupils, were fleshy shields against the splintering shadows. Arrows felled them, puncturing through their shoulders and necks at sharp angles, and when they slumped over her, she heard boots stomp in and out of earshot around her. The worshippers, or what remained of them, simply resumed the foolhardy blitz and charged to their deaths.

Celeste groaned. She would have preferred to remain

cocooned by still-warm corpses, not stumbling through a blinding hail of arrows, but she was certain the north gate was only a few more paces—*hell*, she hoped her team made it through without her—and the longer she spent beneath the rotting comfort of the dead, the more she wished to join them. Damn, how everything *hurt*; bone-racking pain pulsed through her arms, every gash, every contusion pounded with the rapid pace of her heart, her head felt like a deflated balloon. Scoffing at herself, she kicked free of those corpses, her whole body burning with anguish. She knew the seconds were limited and ticked away like a time bomb in her lap.

She also knew the sound of a blade whistling death.

The moment she was on her feet, she reeled and swung heavy—perhaps *too* heavy. While the spearhead shoved deep into someone's chest, a knife bit into her hip and clipped bone. The worshipper fell with the halberd planted in his chest like a flag. She rolled, her grip jarred loose, and her face dragged through the icy muck.

She spat grit from her tongue. Heaving, she dragged to her feet and stumbled forward, reached for the axe—

The worshipper wasn't dead.

It raised the hair on the back of her neck to see a man with a spearpoint buried deep in his chest cavity then struggle to his feet, belting out a scream that would have made even the Devil's blood run cold. He stammered something unintelligible, eyes glazing over like he was already dead, then brandished the knife still dripping with her blood. She snapped forward, launched herself at him—he whipped his arm, steel blade glinting dangerously close to her throat.

Once her grip fell to the halberd, she shouldered into him with enough force to spiral them both to the ground, knife narrowly missing her belly. The axe blade was wedged firmly between his splintered ribs and wouldn't budge. Fortuitous, perhaps, because as they tumbled to the field, she wrenched the axe and flung his body over hers as those familiar shadows darkened the mist above like spilling blood. She hit the dirt, screaming from both fury and fear.

Arrows pelted flesh with meaty *thwacks*. The worshipper's final breath wheezed through the deep punctures in his back. White-hot pain ripped through her thigh, burning with a fire's intensity. An involuntary scream rang harmoniously with the anguish of the dying that littered the field around her. Heaving the literal dead weight off her, she rolled to her feet—pain thundered through her flesh, hammered into her bones. Her leg buckled, and she braced against the embedded axe blade, the dead man's ribcage collapsing under her weight. An arrow shaft jutted from her thigh. Crimson pulsed through her leggings.

"Shit," she cursed breathlessly. What was it that Melina had taught her? Her thoughts wandered with a pang in her heart—and her goddamn *thigh*.

Stymie the bleeding, but do not remove any foreign objects, right? Apply pressure. Shit. Thoughts cascaded into discordance. Memories, in the red-hot rage of battle, were the distant echo of a dream. Red, curling hair like the lambent tongues of flame, eyes that glittered like unearthed emeralds; her breath was caught in her throat, cheeks burning against the chill of a silent, blood-drenched battlefield. She muttered quietly, "Thanks, Nurse," grunted as blood drizzled from her thigh, then splintered the shaft with the axe blade so only an inch of jagged wood jutted from her leggings. Crimson rippled out from the wound, a gentle warmth to her skin. *Good enough.* Any pressure and the barbed arrowhead pinched her nerves, grinded through into bone like hacksaw; the awkward gait may as well have been a bright neon sign that emphatically flashed *PREY*. Another breathless curse, and she hobbled on the halberd like Deacon with his cane, biting against the pain thundering through her bones. Time was a luxury she could no longer afford; she had to be through the north gate before the next volley fell. Before the worshippers managed—

She found the abrupt silence disquieting, scanning the skyward mists and ruddy field behind her. Had the worshippers caught on to the ploy? *They would be fools not to. But even bigger fools to yield the trench.* Aza had warned those trenches snaked for miles around the church and through Dead Wood like an unmapped labyrinth. They were dug perpendicular with the woodland edge and the church entrance, obliquely staggered to the east and west as a swift escape beneath the snarled fence line—or fortifications against an impending army. Either direction, Aza warned, splintered into five more trenches that snaked and splintered again into five more, and then again, until Dead Wood was encompassed and gutted. The traverse, the sharp alternating angles of the trenches, were built to blind and hinder progression, and often led to pitted nests of coiling barbed wire at least a meter deep. Some of the unbelievers, she had said with a cold, casual shrug of her shoulders, had been tossed in, flesh peeled to ribbons whenever they moved a hair's breadth through the razor's embrace. They immediately died writhing and squealing like butchered pigs, sinking deeper into the coiling snare. *Lovely.* Most importantly, the trenches crossed extensively under the church, which, Celeste had thought bitterly, explained how the worshippers flanked the trap she had set. Now, however, both sides would be reeling from heavy losses, and she could only imagine how disconnected Theta was becoming with reality. Were Clark and Bink still alive? Panic rose to her throat as a growl, and she strode through a graveyard of the unburied, the halberd Morning Light heavy in her hands.

No one else she loved was going to die. That promise thundered with her heart.

TWENTY-SIX
Greyfang

THE NORTH gate wasn't really a gate in the literal sense. There were no twisting walls of thickets and craggy snarls extending skyward like bony fingers reaching out from the grave. No razor mesh or gates of cannibalized steel. Twin spires jutted from the ground like the crowns of a castle, stabbing the skyline with the dead, slender trees of the woodland. She knew those cameras observed the woodland edge with a bird's eye view but lay as still as the dead around her feet. Whatever Aza had done to disrupt the security systems seemed to still be in play, but for how long, she wasn't certain. With a shrug, she figured she would find out eventually. She always did; luck always favored her enemies. A twinge of a smile touched her puffy lips.

At least *I'm not dead.* The pink scars dotting her belly like buckshot burned freshly anew. *Again.*

With her wide, studious eyes stuck to the skyward spires, she passed beneath the turrets, tentatively striding on the halberd. Fog smothered the woodland edge, which must have been another dozen meters north, and leached the field of any color. Grey mist curled from those monstrously long rotating barrels fixated directly over her path. So engrossed by the fear of those barrels rapidly spinning to a blur, flashing with bright, blinding bursts, thundering with the rage of tempest, that she stumbled blindly into the brume.

Another near-fatal mistake.

There were a dozen or so, visibly injured and as exhausted as she felt, figures smothered by shrouds that were soaked and spattered crimson, with deeply pocked skin around their eyes. The bandit's fractured front line. They each mirrored the other's movements like their limbs were marionetted, raising their machetes, axes, spears, and then boldly bellowed for her blood. "Damnit," she cursed breathlessly, then spun into action.

The axe blade sank through limbs like they were as soft as butter. Its talon tore muscles and meat. Spearhead punctured throats. She was a menacing onslaught, but even a wolf had a limit to how long, and how much it could hunt. She slew another, running the spear through his belly, and then swung for another's neck. But she was sluggish, stumbling. Her movements were sloppy. Red rivulets ran across her cheek, her shoulder, her clavicle, her calve muscle. The sultry scent of her own blood steamed from her scarred skin. The bandits fringed the defense of the axe and began flanking her. One lunged at her. A fresh flow of warmth crept down her thigh, but she reeled and lopped her attacker's arm off at the shoulder with an executioner's swing. As he let out a muffled scream from his cowl, she cleanly separated his head from his neck. Blood fountained, a body collapsed, and a head thudded and rolled, kicked between the throng like a soccer ball. She retreated another pace, with another swing of the halberd, blood flecking their cowls. She was losing ground, again, and her strength rapidly waned. They began taunting her, meekly lunging forward and forcing her to parry, only to bounce from the axe's scything reach. *Come on, Celeste. Quit overreacting.* But fear spiked her heart rate; two more bandits flanked her, and in a panic, she swung wide, heavy, and detrimentally slow. An icy feeling formed beneath her ribs long before it was a stinging warmth that slowly crawled down her waist. A misstep, and she chopped clumsily into the dirt. Lacerations, superficial mostly. Still, it was catching up to her. She cursed loudly, voice twisted with fury, then leapt into a retreat. She spied three more shadows blotting the mist to her right. She was drastically outnumbered and separated from her team. *Shit.* Closing in, circling and jeering like hyenas around slow, staggering prey. She lost count of them, now amorphous silhouettes in the icy fog, but she raised—

A disembodied voice crackled down from the heavens with sinister energy like shrieking, arctic winds. "*Celeste, Celeste,*"

Magdalene shrilled from everywhere, yet nowhere, the melody to her voice now a playing like a sour note. "*Heathens play, and heathens die; this world is His, not yours, nor mine!*"

Mystified eyes searched the churning fog, but Celeste knew, with a sharp pang in her chest, Magdalene's howling mockery came from atop the spires. In her mind's eye there was only glittering green that scorned her from the heavens like the judgement of their Almighty.

"Melina!" Desperation strangled her voice hoarse, and she lowered the halberd, pleading to the speakers in the spires. "Please, come back! I was wrong, I was wrong!"

But Magdalene droned on, voice cracking through the static, as if she didn't, or wouldn't hear those empty words. "*And if she smite him with an instrument of iron, so that he die*"—the clustered barrels slowly rotated, grinding and squealing from disuse—"*she is a murderer: and the murderer*"—spinning into a squealing blur, both barrels idly began scanning the woodland edge with hawkish eyes— "*shall surely be put to death!*"

Celeste was unaware when the bandits halted, perplexed, but her stride carried her back to the spires. "Melina!" she kept calling out, but it was soundless to her wilted rose. "Please, Melina, I love— !"

It came as a blinding shock of white, like bolts of lightning jagging across the sky. The booming thunder strikes tore a rent across the field, a whirlwind of dirt thrown into the air and muddying the mist. Shockwaves rippled outwards and splintered the tall, slender trees. The ground roiled like a storming sea of dirt. Flesh was pummeled into unrecognizable crimson mist. Violent flashes illuminated those twin barrels in a deafening concussion, drowning out her anguished cries, and the rapid-fired projectiles gutted the field and rained hell down on her.

While she was painfully shoved from her feet, a dizzying cloud of grassy dirt belched upwards and engulfed the mist to a starless night, twisting into the air like smoke. The world spun uncontrollably around her. Dirt clogged her nose, mouth, throat, bleared her vision a muddy grey. A sharply pitched squeal cut through the thunder in her ears. Flashing heat hammered against her skin. She hit the ground, shouldered her weight—displacing joints with loud *pops*—and folded from pain exploding throughout her body.

Bright, pounding lights snapped her eyes open.

Heat pulsed like the sun beating down against asphalt. Dirt fell as muddied snow. A groan crept from her lips, lungs scorched from the hazy air, and she peeled herself from the grit of the agitated earth. Sticky warmth crawled from her scalp and meandered down the shift in her nose. She stood on shaky limbs, her hand still numbly wrenched around the muddy halberd, and couldn't quite discern whether it was her body convulsing involuntarily or the ground tilting beneath her feet. She heaved, retched, and spewed the mud from her throat. Her gaze wandered skyward, caught in the spectral shine of slim, silver crescents like twin moons, and for a moment she had to absently wonder what made her vision double. She blinked again, a firm grip closing around her shoulder.

The ground exploded and rained upwards.

She was forced into a bumbling stride, feet tangling in knots, yet somehow, she was propelled through the hailing storm of ripped up earth without losing her balance. How was she moving? The thought came and went as quickly as she blinked. What was she carrying, an anchor? She had half a thought to let it—

"Wake up, you fool!"

A viper's tongue flicked and hissed, dripping venom, and pierced the shrilling ring in her ears.

Vega?

"Fool!"

Shadows fluttered around those whirling, silver eyes, and Aza twisted her grip into Celeste's shirt collar and dragged her to her feet. Her balance rocked back and forth, like a staggering drunk under a helpful friend's arm, and she blew wads of muddy snot from her nostrils. She could barely breathe, choking on the gritty haze, and found Aza's forceful insistence to be more than agitating. Where was the former Watcher taking her?

"Snap out of it or die!"

Her vision crashed into focus.

White, blinding flashes plunged from the sky, stabbing through the ground like knives through flesh. Chunks of ripped up dirt were heaved into the air and flung through the woods, bouncing off the trees like hail hitting a tin roof, and whipped against her face as thousands of tiny missiles. Rapid, successive blasts gouged a chasm in the field. When the chest-pounding firing ceased, and its terrible reverberation cracked across the horizon, putridly black smoke churned from the muddy rubble like a rising, hissing serpent. Projectiles had exploded the treeline to splintered, smoldering debris, its violent trajectory ripping an obliquely charred path half a mile into Dead Wood. When the dirt settled to a low, muddy fog, only bits and pieces of limbs were scattered in the deeply furrowed field. No one was left alive.

A terrible chill clawed up her throat, froze her tongue to a glacier, and crept from her lips like the frosty bite of winter winds: "*Magdalene.*"

Aza wasn't the type of mince her words. "Now you see," she said coldly, "how dangerous Deacon is as the only source of light to the lost, the hopeless, the broken."

"She would never kill," Celeste choked out, almost retching again. "Not in cold blood."

"She did not kill in cold blood, girl, she killed in the name of her Almighty."

Silence gripped her throat like a noose. A growl rumbled in her throat. *I'll kill him.* She raked her nails across the scummy axe. The violent thought reverberated to her bones.

"We must go," Aza whispered, "before the Watchers—"

Celeste froze—a chilling breath of air glided across her cheek, and before she could blink, bark splintered from the tree behind her. A shivering arrow was buried halfway into the wood. Aza flattened herself against the shadows, slithering through the trees like a snake. Celeste, dizzied by an array of exhaustive pain, stumbled to her right.

"You bastards!"

The ragged cry was followed by another loosed arrow.

"I'll kill every last one of ya!"

Another arrow loosed and splintered branches above Celeste's head. She was hunched forward using a tree as thin as her halberd handle for a shield. At least her center-of-mass was *somewhat* protected, though she was aware of the grinding throb in her thigh. She scanned the rutted field through the trees that stood like inky strokes on newspaper, those skyward spires looming on her peripheral sight, and saw the brief blur of a shadow's movement a moment before—

Another arrow thudded into tree.

She dove, elbows painfully slamming against the ground, then shouldered into a roll. Getting to her feet, however, proved challenging; she half leapt, half tripped over her feet, and vaulted forward as if running on all fours like a wolf. A split-second later, however, and she face-planted, *smacking* off the grassy dirt and—

The ground gave way, and she desperately clawed at whatever she could grip—loose dirt and dead, brittle grass—and painfully raked deep gouges in a hardwood surface. When she hit the mud, it was like plunging through river ice and freezing into its motionless current.

"Up!"

She slowly hauled her leaden bones from the mud, climbing up the halberd like a cripple on a crutch, and staggered into the wood paneling. A quick glance, and fear snapped at her disjointed thoughts: muddied wood encased her like a tight, nailed-shut coffin. After a moment of heart-wrenching panic, she caught the bitter scent of blood and felt the icy kiss of wind against her skin. Mists crawled overhead like clouds swelling with rain. Aza shadowed the edge of the traverse. With a quick glance over her shoulder, Celeste caught sight of it; thick metal wires were sinuously slung across the edges of the trench like a spider's spun web. A nest of viperous barbed wire, a few feet from where Celeste had plunged face-first into the mud—

Twisting limbs with flesh shredded to the bone like grated cheese, reached from the razor pit like a zombie from a grave. He hadn't been there long; blood collected in tiny droplets on the tips of his wrenched fingers, spattering the coiling razor-steel. Dread drained the warmth from her face, and she turned to Aza as she disappeared around the traverse. The look in those wide, silvery eyes said it all: Run!

She bolted for the traverse.

"You bast'ids!"

The arrow didn't make a sound as it was loosed into the traverse wall, mere inches from where her head had been, buried fletching-deep in the parapet. Another was drawn in rapid succession, and she knew it was loosed before she heard it *thwack* into the wood an inch from her face. She found cover behind the wall, but highly doubted the archer would stop. He held higher ground, and for all Celeste knew, she would blindly tangle herself into a web of razor steel while attempting to escape his near-precise aim. Maybe that's all he had to do, herd them into the deadly embrace of razors. With ice in her belly, she zigzagged the traverse like a lightning bolt—

An arrow thudded another inch from her neck.

—her feet slid through the muck, shoulder pounding against the jagging traverse. The arrow shaft shivered, splitting the ends of her hair, having nearly punched through the back of her neck. Her stride faltered and legs buckled—

A second arrow struck above her head.

—her knees slopped into the muck, splattering up her coat—

Another struck the trench wall above her head, splintering the wooden parapet.

"Bitch!" the bandit snarled, and she swore she heard the *snap* of the bowstring.

But razor-wire *crackled* against the air, sinuously slashing over her head, and whipped flesh from bone with several, snapping strikes. Losing his footing, the bandit plummeted into the trench— and Celeste was on him in a deadly, snarling frenzy. Before his body slopped into the mud, she heaved the halberd from over her shoulder and threw all her weight behind one heavy, downward swing. It sapped the rest of her strength to wrench the axe blade free.

"Best keep up."

There was a dangerous edge to Aza's tone. Celeste watched her effortlessly vault over the trench wall, and flicked the muddy blood from the halberd. She had to wonder how far her trust for the former Watcher could extend. The harrowing thought churned endlessly in her mind as she followed Aza over the trench wall.

It took considerable effort to climb back to her feet. She felt like a battered corpse grotesquely frozen in place with rigor mortis, sprawled disjointedly in some unmarked grave. How long, she wondered, until her body failed and faltered like her father's had? Exhaustion wrung her muscles dry of any adrenaline like an old dish cloth, and that sweet narcotic-like sustenance could only carry her battered and broken body so far. When Aza was a few paces out of earshot, Celeste quietly retched and staggered through the thin thicket, dragging the halberd like a caveman's club. Where was she? Dead Wood, she knew, or the woodland edge at the very least. Where were those turret spires?

Melina...

A deadly tongue hissed, "Still want to play leader?"

She lost the strength to even growl her response. "I need a moment to rest," she muttered hoarsely. "Maybe a few."

"You'll have eternity to rest if we don't move." Aza grunted her disappointment. "So young and so foolhardy, should be full of piss and vinegar."

Celeste rolled her eyes, breathless, and huffed, "You sound like my father."

"He sounds like a *great* man."

"He was."

"Hm."

She dragged her scabbed lip across her teeth—or what was left of the flesh. Minced, swollen, a fresh burst of syrupy warmth; her lips, and face, were mangled and contused to an unrecognizable lump. Pain shocked through her limbs with every subtle movement, like she was one giant, walking bruise. It was difficult to match pace with Aza, who kept ghosting through the lifeless, windswept trees.

"Where are the others?" she asked. Exhaling the fetid vapor of the dead, she scanned the greying depths of the mist for any sign of where they were headed—or where they even where. Sprawling wooded hills as charred black as a firepit, with mists distending like clouds. She was lost and uncoordinated outside of the church grounds. Aza moved with purpose, as if she adhered to a committed routine, unperturbed by the rising cacophony of clanging blades, gutted screams, and the occasional *pop* of distant gunfire. Celeste followed with caution underfoot, aching fingers clawed around the halberd, and kept her studious gaze fixed on Aza as they trailed a branching arm of the trench deeper into the Dead Wood mists. There was no deception lurking behind those silvery eyes, but Aza was as cold-blooded as a reptile and betrayed as much emotion in her placid, and quite enigmatic response, "Alive," without sparing a second glance to see if Celeste even bothered to follow. Celeste noted the fresh, pulsing red lacerations near the base of the woman's throat, the gashes under her ribs and the shredded armor plating to accompany, and the slight favoring of her right leg. She tucked that tidbit of intel to the back of her mind for now.

It took only a few agonizing minutes of darting tree-to-tree for adrenaline to sweetly hum through her blood, numbing the frailty of her broken body, and for her stride to match the maddening race of her own heart. The axe was a feather in her hands, and her muscles, as weary and overstrung as every strand and fiber felt, pumped vigorously and harmoniously with the anchor-heavy weapon as if the cold, ornately forged metal was another extension of her body. It was becoming a familiar comfort like the old, ruddy bow from her father, now a splintered relic lost to the bitter winter of the highway. *Morning Light.* She matched Aza's zigzagging pace. *Should I give it a more fitting name? Could I? Come to think of it, the practice seemed utterly strange apart from the fantasy novels Father had squirreled away to read to me at bedtime.* But the feeling gripped her to the bones. An odd resonance hummed through her blood-soaked fingers, pulsed rhythmically with the beat of her heart.

Greyfang.

Strangled screams pierced the breathless silence, snatching her attention, and she slowed her zigzagging stride. Aza flattened herself to the elongated shape of a wilting thicket, lowered to her knees, as statuesque as if she were carved from marble, and flashed a bladed glance across the long and rambling trench. Celeste followed her gaze. Tufts of gold glimmered through snagging branches in the distance like bright, scattering sunshine. Plum-colored hair cascaded like an unfurling lilac.

"Shit," Celeste cursed with an uneasy breath.

Broad strokes of blood painted Snyder's milky skin like a tiger's stripes. Bruises blotted and leached Odine's of any color. Injured, Celeste noted, and breathing.

But not alone.

Long pale faces haunted the mists, baying like coyotes at injured prey, and circled another man whose name she would never recall. He had held the trench line with herself and Aza, and barely escaped the ambush, leaving his only allies to be slaughtered in a hole. His knife was curved like a hook, dancing from one hand to the other, viciously spinning like a buzzsaw. He carried himself with the stature of a deadly fighter, striking with deft precision and speed. With a low, angled stance, he swept forward like a dancer, slashing once, twice, three times. Four. Each blurring strike ripped through nothing but air. The twin figures may as well have been apparitions.

It was over an in instant.

He threw himself at one of the pale figures, blade hooking over his shoulder, but it was a feint to draw a counterattack. When one pale figure brandished the metal club with an upwards swing, the man spun on his heels and whipped that blade behind him, aiming for the second twin's throat—or where the twin should have been. The second twin, however, had dissolved moments before into the shadow with slight dip of his bowler hat. Staggering, the man turned his attention to the first twin, eyes fixed on the swinging club. The first twin, with a comically caricature grin, threw himself forward in a twirling lunge. The feint drew the man's counterattack, however, just as it had for him, and he overcompensated the miss by stabbing for an exposed throat.

Nebulous shadows melted around a pale skull like the Grim Reaper, and the man was dead long before he even knew his misstep had been fatal. His head rocked forward, chin-to-chest, and the back of his skull cracked open like an egg. The razor-sharp flanges of the club split bone and shocked the man's eyes a dull, glazy white, and forced him into a spiraling stagger. The twins eerily mirrored the other's movements, swinging their flanged maces like baseball bats, and savagely bludgeoned his body into a form that had lost all humanly shape. Those hollow, lifeless eyes wandered back to Snyder and Odine.

Red-hot rage boiled her blood, and Celeste was on her feet in seconds. Snyder was on her knees, gazing skyward to the greying mists as if lost in prayer. Fresh blood pulsed from her scalp. Disoriented and vacuous, she was unresponsive. Odine, nursing a visible gash along her abdomen, scooped Snyder under arm and heaved. Odine saw, as did Celeste, that there was no escape from the cackling twins. They circled like buzzards over a carcass. With Greyfang in hand, Celeste snarled and leapt—

While Celeste had been watching the performance with avid interest, Aza had positioned herself between her and the trench. Crimson flecked the silver of her irises, and a taunting smile played at the corners of her wide-set eyes. She paused a moment, then whispered, "Wait," and gestured with a curt nod of her head to the horror unfolding across the trench.

In a single glance, Celeste saw the events play out like a movie. The Watchers could have made short work of the women and bludgeoned them with the same apathetic savagery they showed the nameless man. But their attention was drawn elsewhere. Slender and small, the shadow of a field mouse defied the gutting talons of buzzards, leaping out from the surrounding thicket. The muddy-blonde girl. Her abrupt entrance had caught them off-guard. She bounced forward, ducking under the reeling swing of a mace, her hands caught in the dripping-red shawl around her waist. The once-dull silk was embroidered with delicate floral patterns, sinuously weaved around her shoulders to her waist like makeshift armor, and now as emphatically red as blood pulsing from a heart, scarred from the throes from combat. She stood at almost half their height, with bronzing skin and eyes a glossy, shadow-blue like the deep reaches of the ocean. Her oddly light hair curled down her neck in perfectly shaped rings. Her face was plump, her chest and waist boxy and undeveloped, her limbs awkwardly lanky. A few years behind

Celeste, at least. Perhaps more. With her arms curled around herself like a loving embrace, Celeste thought she resembled a flower about to bloom, delicate in sight but thorny to the touch. The Watchers abandoned their jeers and closed the gap. A grin as sharp as a blade sliced up the young girl's cheek.

The first twin launched at her.

The girl had been tentatively keeping both in her peripheral sight, and drew two ugly, battered blades from her shawl with a blurring motion, then turned to meet his attack head-on. The blades were warped in waves and the length of a forearm, a tarry, battered black, and seemed like the brittle metal would explode into dust on contact. Both blades struck against the mace with a resounding *clang*, but the girl's strength waned under the crushing force. The second twin leapt from behind. The girl was about to be bludgeoned.

Aza wetted her lips.

Spitting sparks ignited a furious incandescence. Steel was devoured in a scorching flash, and eager flames twisted, crackled, furled from the edges of her black blades. The Watchers recoiled from the smoldering heat. She guided those blades through the air like streaking comets, excitement blazing her eyes just as bright, and flicked both at the twins like a crook of her finger. There was a sliver of a moment where the twins' gazes flickered to the other in some silent coordination, a wordless language decipherable only to their hollow, glazy eyes, and the girl seized that moment with fervency. Fire rippled, roared, lapped at the first twin's pallid face, but he barely managed to avoid the red-hot blade. She spun on her heels, kicking up loose dirt and grass, and swung tandem at the second twin. It was clearly an unexpected move, and not the feint he had been expecting. Both blades snapped through his meager defense, battered his grip loose from the mace, and very nearly skewered his belly. The first twin swung his mace down on her head like a gavel. When he missed, the second twin hammered her sidestep, fumbling his mace like a football. Her shoulder took the brunt of his attack, but she rolled into it, shawl tattering along the razor-sharp flanges, and burned through his hip with a quick stroke of her blade. He staggered with his guard breached. She prepared the final strike for his throat.

The second twin was absolutely enraged, yowling furiously like a cornered cat. He leapt at her with his face pulsing red, about to bludgeon the back of her skull. But a quick gasp escaped his lips.

She reeled on one foot and shoved her glowing-hot blade deep into his chest, searing between his ribs, and drained the touch of color from his cheeks. He took a single pace more as blood bubbled from his thin, chapped lips. His legs buckled, and his knees slapped against the dirt. The sword was buried hilt-deep and extinguished, with the smoldering black blade jutting out from his spine. He sputtered, "Heathen bastard," as she wrenched the blade into his heart, watched salaciously as his lips quivered with a final breath, and allowed his body to fold boneless by her feet. The small-statured girl stomped his belly and slowly unsheathed the burnt blade from his heart. Her second blade raised to challenge the first twin, fire *crackling* from the molten-hot edges of the steel, and his frost-white features bathed in its red-hot glow. She held his wrathful gaze, head cocked, as if the significance of death were lost on her. "Are you finished as well?" she asked tonelessly, knees bent, stance shifting.

"Brother!" the first twin howled with unbounded fury. Yellow, serpent eyes stabbed through the greying mists, flaring with rage, and narrowed with dangerous intent. "Bastard," he snarled, "your birth was always a blight upon our faith!"

The girl did not flinch at his outburst, or even blink. "If your heart is so tethered to your kin," she said, shrugging, "you may follow him to Hell."

The Watcher choked on his rage. "I am the Almighty's chosen child! You're the spawn of Satan!"

A shrug. "And you're *half* dead."

Blood pooled under the mace, meandered under his gumboots. He took a single pace forward–

Those serpent slits for eyes bugged wide when they caught sight of Aza approaching the trench. Within a second, his demeanor changed. He flinched, retreated into the mists, and threw a sideways glance to Celeste, his snakelike eyes promising blood. Celeste instinctively growled. *Give chase, while prey is wounded,* came a wolfish thought.

Aurous. The sultry-sweet aroma of blood filled the air with dreadful memories. *Would their scent be off as well?*

The Watcher sunk his cheeks. He would not make the same fatal mistake as his brother. Celeste saw the calculation play across his skeletal face. They could cut him down within seconds. He saw it as well, and retreated from them, carefully edging away from the girl with the glowing-hot swords. He dissolved into the mists like a ghost vanishing on sight.

"She let him live," Celeste muttered aloud, a pace behind Aza. "Revenge breeds capable killers."

Celeste could almost hear Aza smirk as the woman purred her response. "As evident by Uriel the Bastard."

Bastard? It hit Celeste like bullets ripping into her guts. "She's Deacon's daughter," she blurted out. "And you trust her completely?"

Aza huffed. "She was considered unblessed, having been born without the privilege of a cock"—she leapt over the gapped trench without breaking her stride—"as have we all, wouldn't you say?"

"I'm doing just fine," Celeste muttered, even as she nearly lost her footing along the parapet. "My father taught me how to survive."

"Where do you think Uriel honed such skill?" Aza asked icily, shifting a narrow, silver eye over her shoulder. "You are not the only one who commands loyalty, dear."

Celeste grimaced, uncertain if the turmoil in her belly was from the thinly-veiled threat or the putrefying corpse that she reluctantly sidestepped. She spied the muddy-blonde haired Uriel from the corner of her eye, expecting ruggedly cut features to match her apathy. But her bronzing skin gleamed, flecked crimson, and her gaze listlessly wandered over Celeste as she rushed to Snyder and Odine.

The bandit's one eye was as bloodshot as the dripping-wet bandage around her wounded socket. She peeked through stiff strands of dirty hair, her mouth drawn tight. She looked like a once-blooming flower stomped into the mud. Celeste only offered a stiff nod, knowing death would be an old, bloodcurdling presence. "Where are the others?" she asked tentatively, almost as if she feared the answer, then *snapped* her fingers at Snyder's glazy eyes. She didn't even blink.

Odine shrugged, but worry crooked the corners of her mouth. "They were to wait until a clear line of sight," she said, shouldering Snyder's staggering weight, "and then escape as you had commanded if separated. Blondeie played distraction." From the bitter edge to her tone, Celeste gathered she had no choice but to play it as well. "She took a nasty hit from that...weapon."

A shudder jolted her spine. "Killing for survival is one thing," Celeste muttered pointedly, "but the Faithful bathe in blood."

"Do you trust them?"

About as much as I trust anyone.

"For now and not a moment longer," she whispered, then, "Signal the others." She bit her tongue, and Odine whistled rhythmically into the snarled bramble. Aza approached with Uriel as swift and silent as her shadow. The girl seemed even smaller with her blades tucked back into her slopping red shawl, even the hilts sheathed from view. She beamed over the lifeless body, cocked her head at the blood that bubbled into the dirt. Celeste shuddered again. It was impossible not to compare her cold, calculating demeanor to that of a robot, hardwired and programmed to kill on command. It seemed so unnatural, unnerving. Was that how Mel—Magdalene—perceived her as, some irredeemable killer without remorse? Where was that line, and how far was she willing to go until she could never cross back over? Those thoughts gnawed at her mind like a wolf on a bone, curdling her blood. Aza was a similarly constructed weapon, and killed with the impunity that Caden had. The former Watchers made the hair on the back of her neck stand on end.

"Well?" Aza asked, brimming with amusement. "Does our fearless leader have a plan?"

"Oh, my god!"

Nadie made a panicked chirp, bouncing from under Twist's arms and out of the bramble thicket. He lumbered after her, whispering with a dopy smile, "Commander!" She was quickly by Snyder's side, prodding the oozing wound to the back of her skull. Snyder winced, then groaned, but Celeste was almost certain she heard her familiar vulgarity. The man named Gav was next to squirrel out from the bony branches. Terror gripped his gaunt, bespectacled face, and he shot a noticeably nervous glance to Aza, then Uriel, before settling his bulgy eyes to the dirt. Celeste studied him a moment longer. His arms were long and weak like a sapling's branches, his back slightly hunched, shoulders narrow and bony. His hands were neatly folded over his belly, free of scars and callouses as if scribbling a pen was the extent of his training. Celeste had to wonder how this hollow shell of a man had been a Watcher, and what his purpose was to Aza. Celeste abandoned the thought; for now, at least, they were stuck with each other.

"She's probably got a concussion," Nadie said. "Saw a lot of them during training. She won't be particularly good in a fight now."

Celeste nodded, but a sigh escaped her lips. Every fiber of her being burned red-hot beneath her flesh. Sweat, grime, and blood glued her hair to her forehead like a soggy napkin. Her eyelids sagged. It felt exhaustive just to breathe.

Uriel's gaze swept over them like an arctic wind. "She will only slow us down."

Celeste's blood roiled. Greyfang was between them like a snarling wolf. Aza recoiled slightly, wrist bent forward into her sleeve, but Uriel only cocked her head like a curious pup. Shadows swam through her deep eyes as they wandered along the shimmery metal of the halberd. "That does not belong to you," she stated plainly, her fingers flicking sinuously against her shawl. Her muscles tensed.

"We don't leave one of our own behind," Celeste warned with a snarl of her own. "*Ever.*"

Uriel shrugged. "Then we die."

"Hey," Nadie muttered, "that's only one possibility."

"*Some* of us die?" Aza asked facetiously.

Celeste lowered Greyfang. Slowly. "None of us."

Twist hammered his hands together, knuckles *cracking* like the sound of chopped firewood. "We kill them!"

It was brief, like the flicker of lightning. Uriel's eyes burned with a pulse-pounding rage, the only gleam of emotion she seemed capable of projecting. Her fingers clawed into her shawl. Greyfang hummed for blood. She stepped forward—

Her flesh bumped and prickled.

The silence was incongruous and smothering. Fog swirled and churned, a grey smoothness broken only by the thin, black strokes of trees and tendrils of bramble, like the blotting paint of watercolours. No discernable shapes or forms, no canopy of tangling branches and fiery autumn foliage for cover, but they were as blind as if their eyelids were sewn shut.

A silently loosed arrow struck and shivered into the dirt, its trajectory an inch from Odine's neck. She barely flinched, cocking her gaze over her shoulder, and quietly warned them to inaction. There was no where to run, she knew better than any, and Celeste could only recall the nightmare-plagued memories of the ambush in the wooded hills beyond Fort Thompson. Her blood scorched with instinctual rage, Greyfang light as air in her shuddering grip. But she exhaled slowly, heart like a jackhammer cracking her ribcage open. Another three arrows volleyed from the mists, and though each missed and buried itself in the dirt, Celeste knew they were just sitting ducks to their archers, and their aim could have been far more precise and deadly.

"What is this?" Aza asked, hissing, but Celeste ordered her to firmly stand down. The older woman gave her a bladed look, retracted her fingers from her sleeve, then whispered, "You best be right, girl, or you're the first one I cut down." Celeste felt her temper simmer just like her father's, and hoped her scowl matched his ferocity. Greyfang lowered and speared the dirt.

They were surrounded.

The Disfigured blotted the mist like leaden skies, materializing in ubiquitous fashion, and fanned out through the fire-swept trees. Bows loosely docked but drawn to their hearts, the vanguard marched towards them. They moved as a phalanx of warriors, crashed through the trees in a solid formation, splintered their files and flooded the parapets.

Celeste struggled with a grin. She counted a few dozen, perhaps less, with most nursing deep, bloody wounds. They reeked of blood and sweat. They were far from the formidable force Theta had promised to raze the church with. She happily estimated over half had been shredded under the turret-guns.

That was for Stonem. Her throat clenched shut. *This is for Clark and Bink.*

Vega's reign ends here.

Her blood ran hot like a snarling wolf. She took a single pace forward, agitating the archers and drawing their aim. Their eyes flickered with familiarity, and she saw that they were all the men, women, and even children from Theta's encampment. It was enough to make her retch. She was playing as deadly of a game as Theta.

No more tyrants.

A slick, disembodied voice shrilled like a siren: "One *fucking* order!" The wall of shielded bandits parted like a mechanized gate. Slick, black hair flicked and curled like the shadow of a flame. Slit-eyes darker than a moonless night. Olive skin exposed, scabrous and pockmarked, but unblemished by blood, grime, and sweat. The leather armor draped over her broadly defined shoulders was old and boiled a corpse-grey, and fitted like loose cotton, fraying and tattering at vital points. Her hands were shoved behind her back, thick cords of rope trailing her imperious stride like slithering serpents. The cords were slung around the necks of her men, Clark and Bink, who shuffled behind her at a broken pace, both hands bound tightly in front of them. Clark's head was a snarled mess of curls, pocked face battered and bruised to a bloody pulp, thinly veiled with a ruddy beard. Bink was in the same condition. His eyes were swollen grapefruits, vision narrowed to thin slits. Every few paces they would stumble into one another, chafing shoulders or tangling their steps, and the rope would tighten and furrow into their throats. Choking, sputtering, crying out wordlessly, they staggered behind her like leashed dogs, beaten and dragged to the slaughter.

Theta the Hangman.

Celeste growled as the hairs raised on the back of her neck. Fury broiled her skin red; she could have killed the bitch right there. She exhaled slowly, carefully. There was a cold, absolute stillness to the night.

Nothing, yet.

"I gave you one, simple order." Theta set her square jaw, lips twisting into a sneer. A violent temper raged beneath her apathy. Celeste bit her tongue, knowing her words were only accelerant to the flame. She needed time. "You were to *shut* down Deacon's defenses, so we could burn this weapon of his to the ground. And my dear Ode was supposed to cut your throat afterwards."

Odine shifted her stance, hands clear of the knife at her belt. "Theta—" she began.

"Was she that important to you?" Theta's gaze wandered over the others like a butcher inspecting cattle. "So entangled with your heart, you would betray the very people who took you in?"

Odine didn't miss a beat. "She was my sister."

Those winding cords of rope *snapped* tight and rigid, wrenching them forward. "Some *bitch* who abandoned us for the faith!"

"She was *my* sister."

"Bitch!" Theta spat. "Odine Blackriver, as a traitor, you are sentenced to death, and you will be hanged by the fucking neck until dead! And if your sister were still alive, still blowing Deacon for salvation, she would swing alongside *all* of you!"

"I was loyal to my sister, and to vengeance," Odine whispered, chin stuck out. "I never betrayed my people."

Rope burned into Bink's throat as Theta shoved a finger at Celeste. "She still breathes." Poison dripped from her accusation. "The weapon still operates. I'd say you betrayed all you've ever known. All for a traitorous bitch."

"You slaughtered any tribe opposed to joining your war," Odine said. "You promised peace while holding a blade to our throats. My sister saw through you, that's why she ran to Deacon and warned him about you. But he was another head to the same serpent. It doesn't end with his." Her voice was as low as a growl. "And that's why I'll take yours next."

Theta's rage boiled over. "You could have had your revenge! We could have taken his head! *You just had to kill this bitch first!*" She took a breath to compose herself, beads of sweat running off her furrowed brow. "And now, my dear Ode, you will die alongside them as a traitor. I should have allowed Lust to feast on your entrails."

Celeste's voice cracked like a gunshot. Theta flinched. "Don't you *get* it, Theta?" she mocked, stomach knotting. She considered her words carefully. "We all see through your façade. Killing Deacon was never your priority. You don't want to stop that weapon, you want control of it, *all* of them. So he had to live, right? You want to wipe the church and Red Dawn off the map, but not for your people. You want power, just like your goddamn sister. Yes, Theta, the *bitch*"—Theta involuntarily flinched again, her face beat red—"that I *shot* in the head. And I would shoot her again, and you along with her, if it meant that all these people under your control could fight for their freedom, and not for vengeance of another usurper."

Tremors ran through Theta's hands as she coiled the ropes around her forearms, forcing Clark and Bink to their knees at her feet. "I was going to free this land," she hissed, "I was going to lift the new world from its ashes. Not Vega, and certainly not her groomed pet." Venom flicked from her tongue. "What makes you any better than us, Queen Slayer?"

A distant reverberance, almost like the low crackling of static, carried through the fog. Celeste tensed at the slight sound, the corners of her mouth tugging into a smile. A break in the stillness. Relief warmed the shivers from her spine and the dread knotting her stomach. She met Theta's gaze with a slow shake of her head.

"Because I'm not trying to rule," she declared, every word pounding like drum. "I'm not trying to fix the world, Theta. I'm just liberating its people."

Theta's eyes were an unending black. "You will die a prisoner"—she snapped the ropes tight, strangling Clark and Bink, who seemed too weak to even stand—"just like your pathetic friends"—their chins lifted, throats clenched shut—"and any who follow in your footsteps!"

Wapwapwapwapwap!

"I gave you one order!" she exploded, chomping her teeth like fangs. "We could have all lived! I gave you one fu–!"

WAPWAPWAPWAPWAP!

Fog dispersed in a slapping gust of wind that howled from above. Branches snapped and whizzed through the air like missiles. Theta snarled, pulled her mustard coat tight from whipping in wind, and shot Celeste a look that promised blood. Celeste grinned.

WAPWAPWAPWAPWAP!

A helicopter swung over them, blades beating the fog into a swirling tornado, its subdued black paint nearly indistinguishable from the bleakly grey skies. It swayed laterally, spinning. Celeste discerned no faces through the opaque bubble window, she didn't have to. She knew who glared down at her, eyes flaring contempt. For a bone-chilling moment, she thought the helicopter would plunge and crash into her out of sheer spite, making certain she was a bloody smear across the forest floor. A bloody smear with *no* problems. She sighed. Wouldn't that be pleasant.

WAPWAPWAPWAPWAP!

The helicopter rotated, swinging upwards, and ascended slowly into the greying skies. Its slapping blades reverberated across the horizon. Then a thundering cacophony beat against the stillness of the night. There were more of them, an immeasurable swarm of helicopters and aircrafts in every direction. The sky grew darker, as if they were blotting out the last of the light. A storm was on the horizon.

"This is *your* doing," Theta accused, banding those thick cords around her arms. She shoved a finger at Celeste, dragging Bink's knees through the dirt, and snarled over her shoulder, "Put an arrow in this bitch's heart!"

But there was a murmuring to the crowd that rivaled the buzzing cacophony along the horizon. Wary glances were exchanged, bloody cowls ripped from gaping mouths. The smallest, likely the youngest, of the vanguard lowered their drawn arrows, their taller bows trembling in their tiny grasps. Theta screamed her orders again, face beating as red as fresh blood. Hesitance poisoned those nearest to her. Weapons dropped or dangled by their sides. Faces were no longer shrouded, fleshy boils and cratered pockmarks as plain as the disgust that twisted their horribly scarred features. Emotions swirled and flowed like rapid currents, and the atmosphere changed in a single breath.

Theta was indifferent. "You *will* do what I order," she shouted, "or you will hang by your necks until dead! You will fight when I tell you to fight, and you will die for our cause, for our name! You will do as I say!"

As the last word spat from her tongue like a spark from a crackling flame, Bink's binds frayed and unraveled around his wrists. Blood slopped from his clenched hand, palm sliced into ribbons from a jagged piece of glass, but he held it as tightly as any knife. He clawed bloody marks into Theta's mustard coat, pulled himself to his feet, and plunged the broken glass into her neck. It ripped deep, nicking her windpipe, and wedged firmly in a furrow of flesh. Blood pulsed over the glass, between Bink's fingers, and Theta's eyes bulged. Her knees buckled. Blood bubbled from the back of her throat. Her hands shot to her belt, and in a blur of steel, slashed at Bink as they both toppled into the dirt—Bink rolled off her, and when she missed, she stuck the knife hilt deep into Clark's belly. When they all hit the dirt, Theta writhed, gurgling and spewing blood. Nadie screamed, "Clark!" and bolted for him, with Twist lumbering in tow, unstrapping Bendy from his waist. The Disfigured retreated a pace from the giant man and his giant curved blade. Hesitance was boiling over to uncertainty, and fear spread through them like a plague. Their formation fractured. The vanguard disbanded and scattered. Bink pulled himself up, standing over Theta and a spreading pool of blood, his own and hers. Her fingers fumbled over the jagged gash in her throat and clotted the wound. She stared up at him, eyes blazing hatred, and sputtered a wordless curse at him. Bink's eyes were nearly swollen shut, slits through puffy flesh, but Celeste saw they were fiercely bright. He delighted in the sight of Theta bleeding out by his feet, alone and bewildered. He drank in every second of her misery. The Disfigured fled through the trees, disillusioned and rife with panic, fleeing like mice as the skies swarmed with birds of prey.

"My brothers, my sisters!"

A few glances fell to Odine as she stepped forward, her one eye sweeping over those who fled in turmoil. She shouted again, her throaty voice rising over the buzzing cacophony of the skies, and a few more slowed and shot her wary looks from the trees.

"We do not have to die here!" Odine raised her blood-soaked hands, almost pleading. "We don't have to fight Theta's war!"

"No," huffed a man nearest to her, "we would just bow to another tyrant." His machete blade dropped to the dirt, and he turned with sagging shoulders, retreating. Others who had heard murmured their agreement, treading after him through the trees. Odine fell silent.

"Then don't bow," Celeste declared, inhaling slowly. Her voice was hoarse and crackling, as if a shout were only a whisper to their ears, but her words carried through the trees like a howl from a wolf. It was enough. "I don't want to rule you, I want you to fight for yourselves, fight for the world *you* want to live in! We are not fighting for control of this land, because this land already belongs to all of us! We are a pack, and we are many, yes, but we are also one! We move as one, we live as one, we die as one!"

Those who heard her words halted their retreat, eyes shadowed with doubt but fixed on her, unmoving. Others despondently held their gazes to the sky as clouds turned black and the winds whipped up into a roaring storm.

"Theta brought you here to fight her war and die in vain," Celeste called out, glancing at the blood running from Theta's throat. Those shadowy eyes danced with malice. "I'm not asking you to sacrifice your lives for me, I'm pleading with you to help each other survive. You may leave, you are all free men. But I will fight for you, and for them, and for every one of us." Her heart drummed excitedly. "We are one! We are pack! We are Mahihkan!"

Odine pumped her fist into the air, knife blade gleaming, and chanted, "Mahihkan! Mahihkan! Mahihkan!"

"Wolf!" Celeste yelled, raising Greyfang in both hands like a guillotine blade. "Mahihkan!"

"Mahihkan!" Nadie rang out, cradling Clark in her lap. He was conscious, grinning through his crimson-flecked beard, and mouthing *Mahihkan* along with Nadie. Twist stood over them, tongue jabbed past his lips as if he were stuck in deep thought, then slowly chanted along with Nadie, sounding out the word, "Mah-hee-kun?"

The air was charged, the excitement palpable and spreading faster than sickness through the scattered line. Some halted and stared. Some returned with their weapons drawn and eyes blazing. Others stood in the trees, uncertainty looming like the swarm of aircrafts buzzing through the skies. Some chose to flee into woods. She didn't blame them.

"Mahihkan! Mahihkan! Mahihkan!" they all chorused, the sound growing in strength to rival the chopping thunder from the helicopters circling above them. Less than half remained, impetuously driven and drunk off rage. She saw it flash through their eyes; this was their land, their right, their lives, and they would take it for themselves, not for a madwoman. It stirred her heart, riled her blood. She joined in, defying the whipping winds, certain she heard the howling of wolves resounding alongside her across the sky. They were pack, they were one.

They were Mahihkan.

Two lancelike rays of light burned brightly across the blacked-out sky, then arced downwards in a shrieking blast of smoke. They struck where the spires rose to meet the skyline, and a flash of blinding light turned night into midday. A second after impact, a shockwave ripped through the trees with hurricane force, and a giant, furling ball of flames belched into the air. A deadly downpour of red-hot shrapnel and embers exploded through the trees. Celeste held her ground, still howling furiously, even as the world erupted into flames around her.

TWENTY-SEVEN
Beast of Gévauden

EDGES OF the sky burned crimson, the color of blood, and ashen snow fell in deep, billowing drifts. Flames rose from the cracked earth, as if belched from the bowels of Hell, and consumed the spires in a blinding incandescence. Another eruption to the east convulsed the earth. A spiraling column of fire climbed through the splintered trees, licking at the iron-wrought gate to the east of the church, curling into the sky. A series of flashes blinked toward the church, and shockwaves rippled outwards through Dead Wood and twisted the land.

Celeste struggled to her feet and shivered, crossing her arms over her chest. *Why am I cold?* Pain lanced from her thigh and to her hip, buckling her leg, and when she staggered, blood gushed hotly over her knee. The embedded arrow was dislodged from the bandage, rupturing the wound, and wrenched into the muscle. She stared at it for a dumbfounded moment.

"Celeste!"

She blinked, dazed. "What?" she asked, swatting the insignificant voice from her ears like a buzzing mosquito. She just wanted rest.

"Don't move." Odine's voice was sharp, distant, but her grip twisting the arrow shaft was another jolt of gut-wrenching pain. The bandage was tight enough to dig deep furrows into her thigh, knotted to the arrow shaft, but a small trickle of blood meandered from the tear. "It'll hold for now," Odine muttered, more to herself, leaning in to inspect her work with a rolling eye. Celeste blinked her bleary sight into focus. The church grounds blazed crimson and illuminated the woods with ghoulish rays of light. Bodies were scattered, charred and smoldering, blown to pieces or crumpled in crudely angled heaps. Greyfang was at her feet, splotched red, the leather-strapped handle frayed and blackened with ash. Blood fanned the dead grass, sunk into the soil, glimmered in flecks across the broken piece of glass. Theta's body was nowhere to be seen, but Celeste knew she wouldn't get far with that wound in her neck. The military would find her, or she'd die slowly from blood loss. Perhaps her own followers would tear her apart like rabid dogs over a rotting carcass. *What an odd comfort.*

"Celeste!"

Déjà vu. "What?"

An exasperated look wrung the color from Odine's cheeks. "She's alive." To which Aza tartly replied, "Effervescently," and feigned disappointment with a sigh. "If she is not ready to lead..." The last words dangled from tongue like tantalizing fruit.

"I'm fine," Celeste muttered, reality seeping into the edges of her mind. Helicopters thundered over the forest and descended intermittently into any clearing or rift in the trees, forming a crescent-shaped pattern that walled them into the church. Trees bowed and snapped, windswept and smoldering, broken branches whipped from every direction. *Shit.* The air was sultry and strangling, thick with black smoke. The ground heaved like a storm-tossed ocean. Still, there were people milling about, scrambling to collect abandoned weapons and leather-plated armor from the dead or dying, and one after the other, their fearful gazes fell to her. She could hear Vega slither along the fringe of her mind, hissing from the depths of her depravity. *This is what you were meant for.*

Odine gauged her with one squinting eye, as if she sensed the struggle within. "Gathering them was the easy part," she warned. "Now you have to lead."

Crimson light radiated across the skyline like a giant, flickering flame. The network of trenches extended through Dead Wood like a spider's web, shadowed by night fall, and were far deadlier to traverse than open terrain. Celeste cursed silently. Helicopters descended in flocks, circling the church like buzzards, and strangled any hope of retreat. There were dozens in the air, and on the ground, and likely along the horizon as well. She cursed again. *I always underestimate their true might.* Thoughts spun in her head as chaotic fragments. She felt as trapped as prey.

"Nadie!" she barked abruptly, clawing Greyfang from the dirt. It felt disproportionately balanced, almost deadweight in her hands.

"It's Clark," Nadie responded absently, the boy's head resting in her lap. His face was a ghostly white, sweat running through the crimson splotched to his beard. "He's hurt, he can't move fast. We can't leave him." But he kept shaking his head, rasping, "I'm fine, Nadie, I'm fine." Blood gushed between Nadie's fingers, firmly clamped around his bandaged belly. "I just need a moment to catch my breath."

We're not all going to make it at this rate. Celeste grimaced as if the thought left a bitter taste on her tongue. She shoved the thought aside. "Snyder as well," she said. "We need to make it to those helicopters, it's our only chance to make it out of here before dawn, so Nadie, I need you to tell me—"

"No, no," Nadie whispered, shaking her head.

"—can you fly one?"

"Shit." Nadie inhaled sharply, brown eyes shimmering and wide. "I-I've trained, a few times. B-Blake ran me through a few simulations."

Celeste felt her jawline tense and ache. "It'll have to do, Nadie."

"In a decommissioned aircraft."

Her father used to growl and curse under his breath that if it hadn't been for bad luck their family would have none. *Oh, how right you were.* She wanted to hug him tightly for always being right. But for passing along his bad luck to her, she'd kick him, too.

"Better than nothing," was all she could say, breathlessly giddy. She turned to Odine, then swept her gaze over the disheveled team. "Alright, we *have* to get to those helicopters. It's our only chance to make it out of here alive."

"There's an army between us and those flying machines," Odine noted. "And an army behind us."

A stammer broke through the scattered crowd. "I-I may know o-of a solution."

The bespectacled face stood out from the crowd of scarred, pocked skin and leather-plated clothing. Adjusting the horn-rimmed glasses that pinched red dots on the bridge of his nose, he nervously cleared his throat, shuffling backwards, as if he immediately regretted the decision to speak.

"Gavin," Aza cooed, "do remember why I kept you alive all these years, because it certainly was not for your prowess in battle. Speak up," she added with a click of her tongue.

Gavin rubbed his fingers into his palm, gulped, then spoke with a tentative voice. "W-well, I believe a simple and"—his gaze fell to Celeste's feet—"if I am not mistaken, military maneuver called overwatch can get us past a larger force if necessary."

That's why you're alive. Celeste chewed her tongue. *Even a basic understanding of military formations would be an advantage to someone like her.* The question now, however, was how extensive his network of knowledge was, and what Aza planned with his mind.

"We run those drills as rookies," Nadie warned, shouldering Clark's weight with a grunt. "Until they feel as natural as breathing."

Gavin fingered the horn-rimmed glasses up the bridge of his nose, stammering, "Well, perhaps they m-may not be expecting such tactics from the church, let alone these he—bandits..." His skeletal face pulsed bright red. If he could have willed himself into inexistence right then and there, Celeste thought he would have. He cleared the nerves from his throat and went on, "We may gain the advantage of surprise with a pincer ambush."

Celeste winced, her belly knotting. "They'll be using a different tactic to take us down," she said slowly, until every pocked face, every wide staring eye burned into her. She inhaled deeply, steadied her fraying nerves. She motioned to Odine, flipped the halberd and speared its ripping point into the ground, sketching a crude map of the trees and military line. "They're going to hit hard and fast. Soldiers first, then the creatures"—distraught murmurs buzzed through the agitated crowd that was gathering around her—"that we call hunters. Some of you may have encountered one. Some. Because most who cross this breed of monster will not live long enough to scream in fear. Infected is bad enough."

"*Umbri,*" Odine whispered fearfully in her native tongue. "The Shadows of Death."

Aza snorted her disgust. "The Soulless."

"We *have* to make it to those helicopters," Celeste continued, raising her voice to a shout, "we have to get through their soldiers *before* those hunters are on us! If we do this, as a team, as Mahihkan, we *will* survive." She rounded on Gavin, and the disheveled man nearly fainted, eyes falling to the weapon in her hand. "So," she said quickly, "pincer ambush?"

While Gavin fumbled his explanation, Celeste etched those details into her map. "We-we will be segmented into three units, creating a U-shaped formation, with the middle unit a-advancing far slower than the points in order to draw in the attacking force, and the two flanking units closing in from the sides. From there, firearms can be sc-scavenged, giving them a distinct advantage over their blades and clubs"—Celeste frowned, reluctantly growing fond of Greyfang—"and from there the units b-become two, with one supressing the attacking force while the second flanks them."

Simple enough. I wonder if we should account for my terrible luck...

Celeste found herself barking orders, and to her amazement, their units were hastily gathered at three checkpoints and scattered uniformly through the trees. Celeste placed Odine and Bink within the right flanking unit, Team A, and Nadie and Clark rounding out the second, Team B. The injured and incapacitated, such as Snyder and Clark, were staggered through each flank to ensure mobility. Celeste chose herself, Aza and Uriel specifically for Team C, the unit that would pull the attacking force into the heart of their flank. Aza had proven to be deadly, and Uriel appeared far more capable of holding her own in a fight. Celeste had to keep one eye on them. Preferably two. Once everyone retreated out of sight to their coordinated positions, there were two alternating chirps through the buzzing in the skies. Celeste caught the gleam in Aza's eyes, and the fire burning behind Uriel's; they relished the spill of blood, fed on the chaos of fighting. She now knew that was the look Melina had feared and then grew to loathe. Celeste shook her head clear of those thoughts. Later. Team A and Team B were cloaked in the long reaching shadows. It was time for them to move. She signaled both teams with a long sharply pitched whistle, and then advanced into the darkness.

Pain stabbed at her body. Everywhere. Like broken glass had been ground into her muscles, shredding the sinewy fibers to a pulpy mess with every movement, but desperation eclipsed exhaustion. She sprinted breathlessly, matching pace with Aza and Uriel, zigzagging through the trees and what little cover they provided. Even as her eyes adjusted for the deep dark, she was still effectively blind and only capable of distinguishing crude, amorphous shadows in her line of sight. Still they crept through the woods like prowling wolves, sniffing for any subtle shift in the air.

Her blood ran hot; she still loved the hunt.

She spotted them.

It was a brief *crackling* of static that gave away their position. They were at least a dozen metres from her, cutting through the trees in a triangular formation. The only other hint of their approach was a soft rustling of their boots through the forest litter. Celeste counted four, maybe five. A small fireteam, but they moved with deadly precision and silent communication, weapons drawn to their line of sights and stabbing forward, their uniforms and ballistic armour as black as the surrounding shadows, as were their eyes—

The soldier reeled, gun sweeping over her position, and she caught the gleam of his weapon's scope. Hackles along her neck raised. She dove as a bright flash erupted through the trees—*popopopopopop!*—and branches above her head splintered. Bullets peppered downwards, ripping charred bits of bark. She scrambled across the dirt, rolled, then shot to her feet. She spied Aza, ducking under a thicket, her eyes bulgy and brimming uncertainty. Another burst of bullets forced her eyes shut, and splintering branches rained down on her. Celeste sucked in an icy breath, then darted through the shadows—bullets tore through the ground where her feet had just been. Her elbows painfully dug into the dirt, halberd spinning from her grasp,. Bootsteps *crunched* the bramble behind her—the rifle raised and drew a bead on her head—

Odine struck hard, and fast, connecting the mace—rescued from the stiff grip of the dead twin—with the soldier's chin in a lunging upswing. Teeth *cracked* together, a wordless grunt and gurgle escaped his bloody lips, and the blow nearly sent him reeling into a backflip. A rapid burst of gunfire sprayed through the trees above Celeste, its white-hot heat pounding against her face and spotting her vision. The soldier spasmed once on his back—the mace crushed his face, killing him instantly.

The second soldier flanked Odine.

Uriel was a viper, flashing in and out of sight, sinking her fangs through flesh with every wild slash of her charred blade. The soldier fired blindly into the thicket, alerting the rest of his team, and Uriel struck from behind—again, and again, and again—until his head rolled from his shoulders and into the smoldering thicket.

The rest of the fireteam tactically closed their ranks, committing each rifle to an alternating sweep of their line of sight. With 360-degree vision, they pinned Celeste and her teams in the paltry cover of the trees. "One every five!" one of them shouted, a single shot ripping through the silence of Dead Wood. There was movement beyond Celeste's line of sight, a shout, and another *crack* resounded through the trees. A body *thudded* limply through the dirt. Another cry rang out, another shot pierced the horizon. *Shit.* Celeste bit her tongue. *I'm not letting you kill anyone else.*

She took a single step into the clearing.

"Tell my uncle that I'm right here!" she shouted, lowering the halberd to her side. "Tell the new general to dirty his own hands!"

"There's the freak," one of them spat over the commander's shoulder, jerking his rifle toward her centre-of-mass. "We can just kill—"

A bone-shattering roar, as if from a starving bear, was quickly followed by a sporadic, uneven burst of gunfire. Twist rose from the darkness like a mountain looming along the horizon, his mallet-sized hands closing around the distracted soldier's throat, his glazy eyes squinting with furious concentration. The soldier was ripped from his feet, the back of his head jerking into his spine with a forceful *snap.* A sudden spasming of his limbs unloaded the rifle into the dirt, disrupting the fireteam's coordination, and in the chaos, they were completely overrun by the bandits. They fell in a flashing brilliance. Gunfire waned, and the soldiers were torn limb-from-limb. "The head!" Celeste was yelling hoarsely, "Kill the head!" But there were only snippets of the humanly forms the soldiers once held, crudely butchered and tossed aside like rotting meat unfit for consumption.

"Quickly!" Celeste barked, stripping the grotesque dead form of its ballistic vest, combat knife, a rifle, and its ammunition. Crimson sheened the armor like dragon's scales. It slipped over her shoulders like a wet rag, slopping heavily against her shirt, still eerily warm with spilled life. Odine ripped armor from the second dead form, misting the air a hazy red. Nadie was next to pluck her gear from the corpse, though Twist, ever the gentleman, smeared giant handprints across the plated vest in a wholehearted attempt to clean it for her. Bink decided to forgo his armor, securing the vest and the combat knife onto Snyder. She was vacuous, her eyes greying like a clouded sky, her movements wooden and uncoordinated. She was like a child, groggy from being woken in the middle of the night. Clark was cradling his gut, stemming the blood from the gash above his belly button, limping forward like he was about to retch. None of the vests would fit Twist, maybe one for each of his tree trunk arms, but his only concern was for his new sword, Bendy. Blood blemished the curving steel, and he wouldn't have that. Not one spot. When she gave the remaining vest to Aza, concern flashed through Odine's gaze, but the former Watcher regarded the ballistic armour with avid interest as if it were a lost family heirloom. "Follow my lead," Celeste growled, keeping Uriel well within her peripheral sight. *Do they smell of wolves?*

Within minutes, the soldiers had been ransacked and their supplies divided up, and then they were left as puddles of flesh in the forest. Two teams would redirect and engage the advancing forces, alternating in offense and defense, leapfrogging their injured and incapacitated along the way. Odine gathered the bandits to her team. There were far more young than old remaining. Celeste grimaced; she had been the catalyst to that tragedy.

"I'm staying with Clark," Nadie insisted. Twist grudgingly nodded, pouted, and refused to look up from his tattering boots. Celeste ordered Aza and Uriel with her. Bink refused to follow the wounded.

"I want to fight, I don't need a damn vest," he insisted stubbornly, eyes blazing through slits in his swollen face. His fingers sinuously flicked over the rifle in his hands, loading the clip with a quick *snap*. She caught Bink's wrist and held his battered gaze.

"What happened to Nellie?"

His throat tightened. "There are slavers to the north, in what they call the Frost Lands," he said, voice cracking. "I begged that *bitch* to tell me what was done with her body...it took her days of beating me stupid just to tell me she was alive when she had traded them for weapons, but she'd be worked to death by now."

"She's a liar," Celeste seethed. "Odine will tell us about the north, and we'll get her back—I promise," she added with a snarl. Bink nodded curtly, a single tear brimming from the corner of his puffy eye. She turned from him with a strange fear gripped tightly around her heart.

I'll save you, too, Melina.

With the rifle slung over her shoulder, and the halberd against her left, she watched Odine and her team dissolve in the shadows, her heart pounding with explosive speed. She ticked off the seconds, strained her ears against the dismal silence of the woods. Shadows danced and haunted the edges of her sight like phantoms. Breaths became shallow and uneven, billowing steam into the icy darkness. She waited. A sense of anticipation electrified the air, palpable and contagious, raising her spirits to giddying heights. Bink sensed it, too, the drum of his own heart shuddering every breath he took. The rifle quivered. "You good?" Celeste asked with barely a whisper. His grip tightened, knuckles white. She nodded, grinding her teeth to stop the incessant chattering. "Heart, or head," she explained slowly, grinning as Twist repeated her words dully. "Kill, or don't try."

The stolen radio *crackled: "Bravo Team is a go."*

Celeste sprang forward, feet slopping through the blood-soaked grass, and bolted blindly through the trees. Every muscle in her arm protested the weight of the halberd. Her gait was no more than an awkward stumble at best, and losing luster by the second. *Come on, come on,* she willed her battered body to perform. But hers was an engine barely sputtering to a start, choking on fumes for the last lick of fuel. Her muscles were seizing, tendons stretched to their limits, bones creaking like thin ice. But her blood was running hotly, her array of senses sharper than a razor, skin prickling at the slightest shift in the air. The wild hunt impelled her through the woods, fangs bared, fur bristled. A howl rumbled in her throat; she could almost hear the night air fill with the chorus of wolves. Her and Aurous.

Where are you, boy?

Pale light flashed with waning tendrils, casting distorted shadows against the trees. She speared the halberd into the dirt and recoiled from a shot that rang out through the woods. Another wailed past her head, and she yelled out sharply, "One every five!"

Her vision narrowed into the scope's line of sight. Her finger flicked against the trigger.

To her eye, the forest was midday and a deep verdant green like it had never been scorched and rendered unearthly black, instead bursting with life and color where a second before it had been indiscernible shadows. *No wonder they were picking us off like chickens in a coop.* She tracked sudden movement and inched the barrel to the right—the muzzle flashed, and the single shot cut through the foggy air. It was an odd comfort, the thump of the stock welting her shoulder, the jolt numbing her fingers, the acrid smoke of a spent casing. Her blood roiled from the thrill. *Three.* She twitched the barrel into the trees. *Four—*

A bullet splintered the bark above her head, and she rolled as another *thudded* into the ground after her. Bink was on his feet in an instant, weaving between trees, and baited the shots away from her. Celeste cursed and brought the scope to her eye, steeling her frayed nerves. Sight dragged over the solider taking aim at Bink—

Steel wire whipped around the soldier's neck like a noose, but tangled around his ballistic armour. His throat had been nicked, however, spraying the trees with a muddy red arterial flow. Reaper's Claw twirled in Aza's cruel grip, and the soldier was hurled into the dirt, spasming, gurgling his own blood. A smile touched Aza's crooked lips.

"No!" Celeste shouted a little too late.

The soldier's paling face contorted, and blackened, and peeled from bone like skin withering in some unseen flame. Aza fell back, uncertainty playing across her rounded face. His body convulsed, then writhed madly, as if something was trying to claw its way *out* of him. Teeth twisted and gnashed feverishly. Human features melted from its face, hanging from meat and bone like a cheap Halloween mask. Flesh split from the tips of its fingers like bony claws. Its limbs were inhumanly angled, spasming and pummeling the dirt, its flesh a splotchy black like charred wood. It clawed upright, snapping its uneven teeth at Aza—then lunged like a snarling beast.

Celeste saw, through the rifle's scope, that Aza was utterly petrified, and the creature was on her in a split second. Two shots *cracked* out in quick succession, hitting the infected's skull like hail against a tin roof. It was enough to throw the creature off balance, but little more than that. Bony fingers raked deep gashes into the tree, ribboning bark, then its jaws snapped wide with an infuriated screech. Hesitation overcame her, and the paltry window of opportunity came and went within a blink of an eye. Celeste ignored the peppering gunfire and steadied another shot. The creature came down on Aza with monstrous blows.

Celeste twitched away from the trigger.

A shadow blurred between Aza and the infected, slashing upright with enough force to lop its arm off at the shoulder. Muddy blood misted the trees. Its slopping-meat face rippled with fury as it *screeched;* Uriel flashed a look equally as grim.

It swung its clawed fingers at her.

Uriel drew the other blade from her shawl.

Black metal sank deep into the infected's chest, sliding smoothly between its malformed ribs. Its limbs spasmed, its charge slowing as it neared the hilt. The blade's tip ripped out of its spine. Its jaws *snapped* inches away from Uriel's bronze skin, spittle raining to the dirt. A wheeze was caught in its throat, its eyes a milky, uneven white. She effortlessly lopped its head off, and it slid off the blade and fell limply to the ground.

"I told you to go for the kill," Celeste chided coldly, sprinting toward the gunfire. "Or leave it to someone who can. Stay away from its blood and don't breathe its scent."

"The infected do not make it this far," Aza said, masking her face with the crook of her arm. "It's been...years since we have encountered them. They seem far more monstrous."

"The sickness is mutating."

"Hm. Are you a scientist as well?"

Celeste left it at that, chewing her lips skinless. It was only a few paces into the trees where they found Bink, crouched over the limp form of a soldier. Limbs were disjointly sprawled, bits and pieces of skull blown across the forest floor. Bink was ripping the straps from the vest when he squinted down the barrel at Celeste's approach, rifle swaying in his one-handed grip. "That bandit girl flanked the last of the fireteam," he informed her with a shake of his head. "I knew this asshole. Jacobson. Remember him? He still had the scar from where I knocked him out. Look." He jabbed a finger into the fractured skull. He paused. He muttered, "Asshole," then ripped the vest from the dead man's shoulders.

"I remember," Celeste began, but a shriek carried through the woods like a raid siren, a long, distressing shrill of panic. It raised the hair on the back of her neck, pumped ice water in her veins. She and Bink exchanged a paling glance. She bolted over the corpse, Bink shoved the vest over his shoulders and matched her pace. *Shit. Shit. Shit.* Her feet pounded the dirt as rapidly as her heart, branches snagged her skin and left bright red welts. The disturbing squeal died, choking and sputtering like an engine running out of gasoline. The air was warm with a rancid odor. She slowed, carving left into the trees—and immediately gagged and retched.

Twist was standing impossibly still, his immense shoulders bunched to his ears. Sweat gleamed from the spider's web pattern of scars along the back of his neck and head. His squinting eyes were drawn downward, like he was stuck with a thought he couldn't quite grasp the meaning of. Bendy, his rescued scimitar blade, trembled in his meaty grasp. Blood slimed the steel a muddy grey. Horrified, Celeste noted the blood not only pooled in thick goblets under his blade, but ran through the forest in wide, gushing streams, splashed up the trees like a rising tideline. Whoever screamed had been eviscerated, their discolored innards strewn through the branches like decorative tinsel. The body fared worse, formless and puddled flesh. Though that wasn't what Twist stared at with perplexing scrutiny—four long gashes ran parallel through the blood trail, and deep into the shadowy, blood-stained thicket. Bink stepped forward, flecking his legs with blood, and leaned over the shapeless mass of flesh and bone. "It's a bandit," he said tersely, casting a wayward eye to the claw marks through the blood.

From the trees came a peculiar murmuring that spread like wildfire through those who had been drawn to the horrendous sound of terror. Faces she couldn't put names to, young who should have been playing war with stick-guns, not fighting in a real battle. The sheer disgust of the scene drove nearly half of them to vomit. Celeste didn't blame them; if there had been any contents left in her belly, it would have been spewed at her feet.

"Hm." Aza pursed her crooked lips. "Did the slow one forget who the enemy was?"

Celeste almost snarled at her. *I sure as hell haven't.* "He didn't do this," she said through gritted teeth.

"Big bad," Twist said with a shrug. He swayed like a wobbly bowling pin, his gaze unusually sharp and pressed into the deepening shadows. One of the bandits stepped forward, ripping cowl from around his mouth. His lips were like minced meat, his nose chewed to a nostril hole in his cratered face. He spat, "Seems like he did! Look at those sword marks!" and traced his gloved fingers across the jagging marks in the bark of a tree. "He killed them!"

Bink scoffed, grip tensing around the rifle. "What, you really believe he made those slash marks?"

"I believe you military cunts always kill when our backs are turned."

"Call me a cunt again," Bink hissed, "you saw what I did to your leader."

Stop, she wanted to scream, but her throat clenched tight. The cold fury of their voices dimmed to an echo in the distance. The air was sultry with rot, billowing from the darkness. The stench, much worse than mere death, chilled her blood. In that instant, she saw it; crimson burned through the blackness like lit beacons, shadows rolled and undulated like a flag in the gentle breeze.

Darkness exploded from the trees.

It melted from the shadows, and struck hard, fast, and with deadly precision. Scythe-like claws ripped past Bink, hurling him to the ground in a flurry of gunfire, and sank through the bandit's chest like a fork piercing roasted meat. His shredded face twisted as blood flecked his silently parting lips. The undulating shadow rose and fell, bisecting the bandit and flinging steamy innards at their feet, and a slanted, alligator-long snout crushed his skull. Crimson slits burned as bright as the gushing streams of blood.

Hunter.

Its body was long and slender like a wolf, nearly two metres in length, a scabrous black and sinewy with muscle, and even hunched on all four of its powerfully built limbs, its sharp shoulders rose to match her in height. Bony plates jutted from its spine like butcher knives, raking into tree bark like nails down a chalkboard. A lash of its spiny tail ripped chunks of dirt into a blinding haze. Blood slopped from its slanting mandibles, shone off its jagged, broken glass-shaped fangs. It slunk over its kill like a jaguar, a roar rumbling from its unholy throat, and its claws minced through the tattering remains of the bandit's corpse.

"Run!"

The rifle pounded in her grip, spitting fire from the muzzle in rapid bursts, but the hunter's powerful limbs launched it at its next victim like a blurring missile of claws and fangs. Bink scrambled to his feet, brought his eye to the scope of his rifle, and let off a single shot into the hunter's snapping snout. The bullet fragmented into sparks across its armoured skin. It flashed a menacing glare at Bink, like the rippling of firelight against the darkness, and snapped its jaws wide with a howl that projected its raw fury through the woods like a shockwave.

Hysteria was a plague quickly spread, and drove their teams to break ranks and scatter into the trees like prey. "Twist, cover me!" she yelled, shouldering the rifle stock—the hunter flexed its enormously ripping claws—

Twist whipped around and clashed steel with claw, spinning as fluidly as a dancer would, and roared with the same brutality as the beast. The scimitar blade, Bendy, sparked and twisted in the hunter's pincerlike grip. Its jaws *snapped* inches from his pursed lips, misting his cheeks a deeper red than ripe tomatoes. His feet were shoved backwards through the blood-drenched dirt. Bony quills raked through the surrounding thicket.

A primal rage thundered from her heart. This world was *hers*, not theirs; this was her territory, her land, her pack.

Her hunt.

The rifle erupted with three bright pulses, rocking in her grip, as she circled and flanked Twist. Each shot sparked across the hunter's scaly skin. Its fire-lit glare fell on her, jagged fangs *gnashing* in a splatter of blood. Twist was thrown backwards, stumbling, and the hunter launched at her—Bink opened fire in the same instant, and a string of bullets ripped through its crescent-shaped eye.

Celeste reeled and lost her footing, claws slashing the air where she had just been, and the hunter, half-blinded, snapped its jaws into the neck of a fleeing bandit, a woman with hair so long it snagged throughout its craggy teeth. Claws gripped the dirt like a balled fist, its eye burning brightly through the darkness.

Bink exchanged a worried glance. "We can't let it pass," he warned with a low, unsteady voice. "Odine can get them to the choppers in the meantime."

Celeste grimaced, then braced as the hunter *roared* and rained fleshy spittle between them. Its eye rolled in its enormous skull, spreading like a flame through tinder, staring fervently past her at its fleeting prey. Its muscles rippled with power.

"Move!"

She raised the rifle, flicked her finger over the trigger—the hunter exploded with speed quicker than her eyes could follow. Her hackles raised, and instinct impelled her to throw herself backwards. Claws slashed above her head, ripped and splintered trees, toppling them like a buzzsaw. She shouldered the dirt, rolling into her halberd—the hunter's talon-like claws *crushed* the stock of her rifle and tore it from her grip, nearly snapping off each of her fingers. It pried apart the metal and crumpled it like a piece of paper. It wrenched its jaws for her neck. She stuck the halberd handle into its fangs, spraying sparks, and rancid saliva sizzled like frypan grease against her face. Each jagged tooth was as long and wide as her fingers. Leather frayed and ribboned from the halberd, grinding into its fangs. Gunfire peppered the hunter's snout and pounded against her eardrums. It let loose a guttural sound at any who dared come near. *My kill!* it was snarling.

Twist, built like three linebackers in a football match, threw his colossal weight into the hunter with the force of a speeding truck, and slammed its malformed body through the trees. Simultaneously, his scimitar, Bendy, rose and fell with the speed of her own thundering heart, a blurring arc of silver that ripped into the hunter's underbelly. Twist's momentum carried such tremendous force, that even when the hunter writhed and rammed its bony spines into his arm like a shield, his scimitar *cracked* its scaly flesh and drew fountains of black blood. The hunter let loose a loathsomely human scream, like the soul of its former self clawed free from the monster's throat, and then *snapped* its long jaws at Twist. He shoved the scimitar between its chattering teeth and wrenched the blade with a violent upswing that cleaved cleanly through its mandible. Then he drove the blade through its throat. The hunter shook, writhing and whining pathetically like a beaten cur, then stilled as the last of its vital fluid squirted through its gaping wounds instead of being carried to its inhuman brain. Twist was breathing heavily, wheezing, and plucking his scimitar from the hunter's torn snout. "Comm...ander...okay?" he asked breathlessly, admiring his blade with a childlike enthusiasm for a new favorite toy.

"I-I'm fine," she choked out, staggering to her feet. "Thanks, big guy."

He flicked the black blood from his blade and gave her a dopey, impish grin. His shoulders bunched and his arms flexed powerfully. She now saw there was more muscle than fat beneath that stoutly brickhouse frame, and a subtle cleverness. He was an overgrown wolf cub.

A spine-tingling sound carried with the rotting winds, bestial and exploding with rage, joined by another, ringing from the opposite direction, and then another; a loathsome chorus of howls broke across the sky as if one had disturbed Cerberus near the gates of the underworld. Bink shot a deeply troubled glance at Celeste, and even his contusions waned to the complexion of a ghost. *We're too late,* they both thought grimly. Ice sunk into her belly. She snatched up the fallen halberd, tightened her grip on it and pushed it forward like a spear—then bolted for the woods.

Towards the howling of hell.

The forest was alive and vibrant to her senses. The desert-dry soil, the tufting grass, the craggy, twisting grooves of bark and the snarled branches of every tree. She felt it all as just another extension of herself; she saw without sight. Her heart echoed every howl of the icy winds. This was her hunt. This was her pack.

She let loose a solitary howl, like a wolf at the moon, and it chorused with another distant echo in the trees. Bink, matching her stride, shot her a crazy look. She could only smile, fangs bared, caught up in the frenzy. Her footfalls were swift, silent, and calculated, like a predator on the hunt; Bink crashed alongside her, stumbling over every upturned root, snagging his skin on every hooking branch like a deer fleeing in terror. Twist, however, rammed through the forest like a derailed train, bursting with speed that easily outpaced Celeste and Bink. Branches bowed and snapped, whipping around him like gale-force winds, and she swore the ground shivered under each stomp. He leapt ahead of them, veering left into the brambly thicket, and brandished his blade like a torch against the pressing darkness.

Crimson burned menacingly through the gloomy dark. Another hunter.

In a flash of daggerlike fangs, the hunter snapped its powerful jaws shut and snagged Twist's shirt collar, and raked a wide gash across his puffed-out chest. Even as Twist wrung the hunter's neck, heaving the creature from the ground, and drove Bendy into its exposed underbelly, it was a whirlwind of razor-claws that ribboned the flesh around Twist's boulder-sized arm. Still, the giant man slammed the hunter through the woods with the destructive force of a tornado. Jagged spines ripped into trees, and the hunter's skull slammed to a halt against the splintering bark. Twist had rammed his sword into its belly with such tremendous force that he had buried the blade up to its hilt, ripped cleanly through and out of the spine—and speared it deep into the tree he had slammed the hunter against, splitting the wood in two like he were chopping firewood. The hunter writhed, shuddered against his stubborn grip, and slashed for his throat.

Celeste closed the gap between her and the hunter with a heavy, two-handed swing of her halberd. Greyfang bit into the hunter's neck, *thudding* against bone, and lopped its head from its shoulders.

Twist stumbled backwards, skin peeling in long, bloody ribbons around his elbow, but disregarded the extend of his injury with a dopy shrug. He turned, however, and offered his unsullied hand to the thicket.

There were three of them, perhaps a few years younger than herself, shrouded in blue-black furred pelts and tanned leather armour, all huddled tightly together in terror. One by one, however, they reached for Twist's hand, emerging from the thicket with fearful eyes cast upward to the monster, its malformity securely pinned to the tree like some grotesque scarecrow. He wobbled down to his knees, pursed his lips at them, and then swung his log-like arms around them. "Safe now," he whispered. He held on for another moment, and Celeste's heart stirred for her father. *There is always more to someone than the naked eye perceives.* The memory of his gruff, heartfelt demeanor was kindling for the warmth that chased the chills from her bones, if only for a moment. But as Twist stood, his eyes darkened to pinpoints, jaw setting and creasing his pudgy face. Bone-chilling screams carried like sirens with the wind.

The hunt was still on.

Twist led the charge with his scimitar. He was an unstoppable force, a one-man stampede of elephants. Celeste struggled to keep him in her line of sight, and maneuver through the untamed thickets with the young matching at her side. She refused to outpace them, and from the worry shimmering in the slits of his eyes, Bink wouldn't leave them either. Twist became an amorphous silhouette in the shadows. Frantic breaths misted the chilly air. *Where is he?* One of the younger ones cried out, a shaky grip around the wood-carved handle of a crooked dagger. "Keep it raised," she warned. The boy did as he was told, steeling his eyes against the rippling shadows. Someone—some*thing*—stirred from the darkness.

Black flesh tattered and peeled from wiggling bony fingers, like claws ripping out of a glove, and slopped and splattered like rainfall around her feet. Its humanlike face melted from the shadows. A skull with white, rolling eyes flung its limbs at her like a blinded boxer, pummeling bark from trees, peeling its own flesh from its deformed bones. Its teeth snapped for her—she drove the halberd's spearpoint up into its throat, clucking its jaws shut, but its rolling momentum threw her from her feet.

She landed and hit her shoulder—hard—and pain lanced through her arm and loosened her grip on Greyfang. The infected fell over her, still writhing and clawing at her flesh. Then—*SPLAT!* A dagger was buried hilt-deep in its eye, and the corpse slumped into a chilling stillness. The boy bandit still held a shaky grip around the handle, his mossy-green eyes shimmering, as she squirmed from underneath the corpse and thanked him breathlessly.

There was another scream, splitting the breathless silence, followed by a terrible roar that could only be described as an agitated bear. Celeste gathered Greyfang, and formed a chain with the young between herself and Bink, and then dashed blindly toward the horrors.

Blood. It was everywhere. Muddying the soil, splattering the trees in bright red streaks, dripping viscously from the branches like spilled honey. Innards and torn flesh were strewn through the thicket like confetti. She paused, choking on the fetid air, and forced the young to turn away. It was a sight that would turn even a butcher's stomach. Another few meters and her feet *sloshed* through puddles of vital fluids, grazed a dismembered femur, and again she found the shapeless form of another kill so mutilated she couldn't discern what the person had been wearing, let alone their dismembered features.

"Help!"

Someone bolted ahead of them, stumbling with uncoordinated footfalls, haunted by a shadow that moved between the trees with unhuman speed. Celeste stopped, opened her mouth to scream—the shadow struck, bisecting the bandit with one sword-like stroke, and warmed the air with a fine, red mist. The bandit's upper body was flung into the trees, and it was almost comical how his legs tangled and leapt forward, as if he were still fleeing in absolute terror, until the hunter snatched them up like a mutt with a bone. It caught Celeste in its glare, then hungrily swept over the young and Bink, who trained his rifle on its face. Its long, lithe body tensed, claws ripped into the dirt, long jaws parting with a steamy *hiss*—then dissolved into the shadows, crimson eyes burning furiously. A guttural sound died in its throat. *Is it retreating?* She shook her head at the foolish thought, grip tightening on Greyfang. *No, it senses easier prey.*

"Follow it!" Celeste ordered. Bink began to protest but she ignored him, snatched the young one's hand, and raced into the icy darkness of the woods.

Branches snagged her hair, welted her skin.

Her footfalls *crashed* over the uneven terrain, snagging on upturned roots and branches, dragged off-balance by the young ones tumbling and clambering in fear.

Darkness abated to near darkness.

Screams bludgeoned her eardrums, from all directions, from everywhere at once. Her feet slid to a stop in an inch-thick stream of blood that meandered through the trees like a scarlet river. Black figures haunted the edges of her sight, clawing through the darkness like skeletons from the grave, *snapping* their teeth fervently, hungrily.

Infected.

Celeste recoiled from writhing corpses, bony fingers inches from her face, as Bink trained his rifle on them and opened fire. One fell to her feet, lifeless, and soon Celeste was cutting, thrusting, hacking through the dead with cold fury. If she had been alone, she most certainly would have fallen. Bink calculated each shot with precision, and even the young ones weaved in-and-out with knife thrusts, or chirped shrill warnings in her ears of more infected. Slowly she cut through the wave, skewering a corpse through the throat, and leaving its bloody, struggling form for one of the others to dispatch. The more ground she gained, the more resistance she threw herself against; it wasn't merely infected soldiers, there were hunters gliding through the shadows, closing in on their prey. "Ahead!" she heard Bink yell, and she had spotted it as well. Glinting steel in a churning sea of blackness.

Aza.

When there was a gap in the infected, she knew it was her only opportunity, as ugly as it seemed. She threw all of her weight into a forward charge, thrusting Greyfang like a spear. The first infected corpse fell, clawing at the steel buried in its chest, and she beheaded the second with a swift upswing. As she struck, she thanked the church (and by proxy, she supposed, God) for the awkward length of the halberd. The metal talon opened another throat, and a corpse fell gurgling at her feet.

Razor-wire *crackled* through the air like bolts of lightning, coiling tight around a corpse's throat. It wasn't enough to kill it. Steel sliced through to the bone like a garrote, but it was distracted enough not to see its own demise. Celeste struck its skull with enough force to split it open like a ripe melon. Its limp form smacked into the trunk of a tree, slumping dead.

"Celes—!"

There was a sudden lancing pain through her ribcage and the tremendous weight of a hot, scaly body thrown against her. She went down hard. There was no way she could bring the halberd in for a killing stroke, so she rammed the pommel into the hunter's neck. Its jaws swung and snapped at her face, its rancid breath blasting her with gnawed bits of flesh and bone. Its sword-long claws raked through the dirt like a closing fist to eviscerate her. She screamed and howled furiously—and caught Aza on the edges of her sight, slowly retreating—and a sharp protest as Uriel shoved past her with one black blade burning orange-red. She was a blur of rapid movement, but each stroke scarcely grazed the hunter's scaly armor. Its claws clashed against steel, *snapping* it like a brittle twig, and it gave off a deep roar of exultation as it turned its attention back toward its dinner.

Guttural growls and sharp snarls, claws clattering against the hard earth, a shimmer of sunlit gold. Shadows took the shape of a wolf and collided with the hunter in a flash of ripping fangs. The hunter was thrown from her, feverishly snapping its jaws—the shadow darted from its reach, claws raking into its soft underbelly. The hunter corrected its momentum, throwing all of its weight at the shadow—a wolfish snarl, muddy-black fangs bared—

Twist flattened the thicket as he crashed through, stampeding like the elephant he was, and hurled himself into the hunter like a battering ram. As he shouldered the infected beast, its jagged spines stabbed and ripped through tender muscle and flesh, clipping against bone. His arm was all but useless, but in his other he held Bendy, and plunged it in-and-out of the hunter's belly and throat with speed her sight had difficulty processing as more than a blur of steel and pulsing black blood. There was a sort of squeal from the hunter, a strange sound of death and fear, and it convulsed and went limp in the dirt.

It wasn't the only one.

Celeste barely made it to her feet as another roar rippled through the forest like storm winds. Screams became a cacophony of howls, both terror and in dying agony. She shot a wary glance at Aza, nodded briefly to Uriel—then set off after Twist, with the wolf at her side, excitedly snipping his fangs. His sharp pants synced with her rapid breaths. Her footfalls fell as silently as his. The forest came alive again beneath their feet, living, breathing, *moving*, as if they were all a single being connected by a beating heart. They sprinted—no, they *flowed* through the trees as smoothly as a river current. Elation chased the gnawing pain from her bones, soaked her muscles in a giddying wave of adrenaline. Her heart felt only half as empty. In her mind's eye, she saw nothing but long, untamed fields of shimmering green. *We never abandon pack.*

When they struck, they struck as one; fangs were grinding against exposed bone as her halberd skewered necks and severed spinal columns. They never broke their stride. Another corpse clawed its way from the dirt, stumbling on all four of its long, spindly limbs, black flesh disintegrating from its twisting skeletal frame. It cried out—in a horribly human voice—as if it were trapped between forms, aching and pleading for death to come. It did, and quite swiftly, when Aurous raked his fangs into its throat, *crushing* its spine between its jaws. They were off again, howling at one another, yipping, barking, like two cubs honing the method of their hunt.

White-hot light pulsed through trees, along with the bellow of thunder. Odine was pressed against a cluster of windswept pine with six or seven of her people, who were all huddled under the snarled thicket like an impenetrable shield, with every blast of her rifle keeping one of the two circling hunters at bay. Celeste knew, better than most, that any hunter would claw through wood like soft butter. Odine kept the rifle on a swivel, firing at one—a blaze of light shimmered across scaly armored skin—and then the other, in rapid succession, and then it *clicked* empty. Without a second thought, Odine abandoned the rifle and drew the mace from her belt, but even that savage weapon paled to the prodigiously ripping claws of the hunter, and its jagged, daggerlike fangs. Celeste and Aurous raced, faster, and faster, willing their overdriven muscles to pump with *just a bit more strength*—they would never make it time.

Twist, however, stampeding through the trees like a strategically-aimed herd of wildebeests, had already reached the first hunter. Bendy was a blur of steel, and Twist swung heavy—and left the hunter with a ruthlessly torn throat. When he shouldered against its tremendous weight, the creature's long, twisting fangs sawed through his bulging belly. Twist reeled, keeping his momentum surging forward, and slashed through a bright, crimson eye. As he stumbled forward, Celeste and Aurous outflanked the fallen hunter. She swung her halberd, he wrenched his fangs. It was simple prey, wounded and dying, and not of the sport they enjoyed. But it had to be done. Twist never slowed his frenetic pace. He launched at the second hunter, bellowing with an unadulterated rage, and struck its skull with enough force to *shatter* the scimitar like glass. As Bendy, now the length of a dagger and ending in a prong of broken steel, was brought down for a final strike, the hunter's jaws *snapped* shut around his arm—but he managed to force the blade through its eye and deep into its mutated brain.

His left arm was nearly shredded to the bone, like a wrung cloth below the elbow. Four deep gashes, cutting clean through his shoulder, pulsed with a fresh spray of blood. Clothes hung in tatters around his bulky frame, drenched in blood or soiled with dirt, and had offered little by means of protection. Dozens of jagged gashes crisscrossed his chest. The wounds to his stomach weren't deep enough to allow his vitals to spill out, but blood flowed freely like a leaking tap, trickling down his legs. When he turned to Odine, however, there was no pain visible on his scrunched face. His lips were pursed, his brow pushed down as if in thought—but his eyes held a bright shimmer of worry. "Nadie?" was all he asked, letting the dead hunter fall to his feet. Odine shook her head, slowly, but it was Clark who mustered what little strength he had left.

"She went after the young," he said weakly. "We were trying to follow when we got cut off by those things...one went after her."

Shit. "Okay," Celeste said, mind racing. "Odine, get our people out of here and secure an aircraft. It's our only way out. I'll get Nadie—no, Clark! You're going with Odine and you're making sure *everyone* gets on!"

Odine hesitated. Uncertainty played across her narrow face, her olive skin spattered with a sticky coat of blood, her one eye sweeping over the paltry number of survivors. She gave Celeste a chilling glare, a look that told her she better finish what was started. She'd better not die.

It all happened quickly. Odine had her back turned to the roiling mass of shadows. Aurous, hackles raised, snarled and *snapped* his fangs. Celeste lunged—with no time to swing, she was forced to raise the halberd defensively, like a jutting spear, and an infected corpse impaled itself when it launched from the shadows. Incapacitated, certainly, but sheer velocity threw it forward and rammed into her with nauseating force. She was thrown backwards, rolling over the corpse, as a flicker of a shadow lunged from the corner of her eye—another corpse lunged—

It was like an arc of lightning, a blur of blonde and pale skin, that struck the second infected. Those eyes were as lambent and blue as burning brimstone. Crashing to the dirt, Snyder and the corpse were locked in a death-grip, knife savagely hacking its face again and again. She finally buried the blade into its eye and brain. Groggily, she sat up, sweaty, waxy and waning, a skeletal shell of her former self. Blood trickled in thin rivulets from her temple, dripping from her chin. "I need to rest," she huffed breathlessly, eyes rolling. "Watch your own ass, Commander."

Celeste scoffed, and a smile reluctantly played across her face. A sharp whistle to Aurous, and the wolf stuck his nose into the air, sniffing at the rot. Any corpses that weren't *just* corpses, he would root out and howl a warning long before her dull human senses. As she struggled to her feet, she heard an unmistakable roar of thunder, fiercer than any mutated beast she had ever encountered, than any storm that had ripped across the sky. It struck fear into her, rattled her bones and gripped her heart. It wasn't her wolf or any infected—it was Twist, his face pulsing as red as his gaping wounds. She followed his fervent, lidless stare, and saw what boiled his blood.

Someone sprinted towards them, unmistakably human in the way they panicked and moved as prey. She knew it to be Nadie, as certainly as Twist did, with three others—a woman, cloaked in a silver-orange pelt, a man in all black like the shadows that pressed around him, and a young girl clutched under Nadie's arm. Celeste saw, with her blood running cold, the horrors that snapped at their heels.

A pack only moved as swiftly as their slowest and meekest member, and the young girl added only a pittance of speed to Nadie's long stride. Hot, scaly shadows snapped at her heel and tremendous claws ripped up the rocky earth. She was losing ground to them, and quickly. The man in all black broke away from Nadie, the whites of his eyes as bright as snow, as one of the hunter's sprang forward, its long jaws swinging wildly. He reached for his knife, fumbling with the sheath. The hunter jumped at him, crushing the man's head with its talonlike claws. The body hit the dirt, rolled and *smacked* against the trees, and the hunter turned and cornered its other prey. Nadie stumbled to a halt, clutching the child to her hip, and then pitifully raised her knife—

Twist sprang into action as fast as a fired bullet. The sounds of his rage filled the forest like a pack of howling wolves. The hunter was snarling at Nadie, fangs wide, when Twist slammed into its scaly body. The broken scimitar, Bendy, was a flash of silver in his grip, punching in and out of the hunter's throat as they both fell. Its limp form hit the ground, dead, as another hunter altered course and lunged for Twist. As it collided with him, forcefully, its claws viciously ripped into his stomach, spilling hot blood to the ground. Twist roared, more out of infuriation than of pain, and shoved the blade, sideways, down its steamy, gaping maw. It died struggling to breathe through its own pooling blood, fangs making minced meat out of Twist's shoulders.

Muscle and flesh were essentially frayed to the bone, ribboning around both of his dangling arms. An unhealthy amount of blood fountained to the dirt. Nadie let out a small scream, clutching the young one—no more than a *child,* Celeste noted with absolute disgust—against her hip to shield her view. Twist struggled through his injuries, shouldering the scaly corpse off him, and managed to wobble to his feet. Nadie was only able to take a single step toward him before he shouted at her, "Stay back! Protect!" and scrunched his face and jutted his tongue toward the every-growing darkness. He saw something they didn't.

There were two more figures, shadowy and indistinct in the haze of night, that slowly approached through the narrow dead trees. One man was unnaturally tall, at least seven or eight feet, enough that tree limbs bowed and *snapped* around his unmoving head while he lurched towards them. His arms were long and spindly, almost reaching past his knees like a lumbering gorilla, but his body was attenuated, skeletal. His skin was waxy and spotted black, lips wrenched into a frown, his nose bulbous and too big for his small head. His eyes glittered white under his wavy, ashen hair. Muscle rippled along his bare chest, but his belly was so thin and cratered it was like his guts were stuck to his spine. A strange, shadowy ooze pulsed from the scarred cracks that covered his grey skin with spiderwebbed patterns.

The second man, as he shifted into a faint ray of silver light, smiled at her—and her blood froze to solid chunks of ice in her veins. It was as if he'd wormed his way from her nightmares, clawing from the depths of her subconscious thoughts, frenzied by her blood like a shark to chum. His whirlpool-blue eyes glittered with a promise of carnage. Stitch-pattern scars intricately ran across his skin in jagged patterns like fleshy puzzle pieces. His hair was slicked flat to his head. His attire was incongruous to the armor the soldier's adorned; a buttoned charcoal suit, almost as black as the shadows that flickered around his ghostly being, long-sleeved and tailored to fit snugly against his thin frame. She saw him whenever her eyes closed, whenever sleep dragged her to the depths of her childhood fears. He who mocked Death with every beat of his foul heart.

The Blonde Man.

They appeared a few feet behind Nadie, prompting a territorial bellow from Twist that would have made any hunter's blood run cold. He kicked forward, wobbling without his arms to pump for balance, and charged with the coordination of a nose-diving plane. A boundless fury erupted from him, a deep burning rage she hadn't seen since her father. He was a few feet away from them, and picking up more and more speed, when the Blonde Man gave a swift nod to the other.

The tall man stepped forward. The skin of his outstretched arm cracked like shattering glass, muddy blood bursting in a fine mist, and his flesh began to peel like it unzipped from the bone. A scaly darkness rippled through the mulching tissue, then exploded sinuously down the entire length of the limb. It came shooting out as a tangling mass of tentacles at Twist, slithering around his throat and squeezing, *squeezing* so very tight—the giant man was dangling a few feet from the ground now, still running through empty air, his face distorted and purpling. One eye, shimmering bright, focused on Nadie. His last whisper was nearly inaudible through the *crunching* of his own skull. "Run," he barely choked out—the wriggling swarm of scaly tentacles, now double the length of the tall man's arm, constricted Twist's upper body with the crushing force of a python. Blood meandered down scaly flesh in hot streams, and as the darkness receded, his limp body slammed into the dirt, barely making a sound when it hit. There was blood *everywhere*, but still, Celeste searched desperately for any sign of life—but his neck was sharply angled, his skull no longer solid or shapely, and the sharp bends in his spine, which had nearly folded over itself, had forcefully *cracked* open his ribcage. The tall man flicked his swarming tentacles, which hungrily writhed like serpents over the mutilated corpse, and his ugly face beamed with rancorous delight— even more so when Nadie screamed hysterically.

The Blonde Man inched around the corpse and pooling blood, as if concerned it would blemish his leather soles, and gave Celeste a faint, almost apologetic smile. A smile as hollow as a jack-o'-lantern.

"Come now," he whispered icily, "it's time you joined your true family."

TWENTY-EIGHT
Luxuria

GRIEF WELLED up inside Celeste with such tremendous force that she nearly lost the purpose to her movements. By the time she had reached Nadie, Aurous viciously snarling and barking from her side, her friend had dissolved into hysterical rage. Celeste grabbed her by the shirt, but Nadie struggled against her shackling embrace. Numbly, she allowed her friend to grieve, her own tears splashing hotly down her face, as Bink snatched the young bandit girl from Nadie's hip. Nadie was screaming for the both of them, voicing the fearsome loss that struck at both their hearts. Her own rage was sharp and focused, simmering beneath a cold demeanor, as she shut her eyes against the grotesquely bloody scene.

Twist. He was truly gone. He had remained by her side for so long she found it impossible to grasp never seeing his pudgy face scrunching in thought or lumbering protectively over Nadie ever again. She only realized, in that heart-wrenching moment, how much she'd come to rely on his presence. She never voiced her thanks or lamentations for how she had dragged him into a war he knew nothing of. Had she ever told him she thought of him as a friend?

"We can't leave him!" Nadie screamed.

Celeste pulled her close, whispering, "He's gone, Nadie." The finality of those words bit her to the bone. "I'm so, so sorry that he's gone. But listen to me, you have to get everyone out of here, okay?"

Nadie turned on her with a fierce expression. "I'm *not* leaving without him!"

"Nadie, that's not what he wanted." Celeste's voice broke. Every word made Nadie flinch as if she'd struck her, and she shook her head, as if it were all nonsensically untrue. "He loved you, so very much, but he wanted you to escape. You have to get out of here."

As her struggles waned in strength, sobbing her anguish into a blood-splattered coat, Celeste pulled her—gently—away from what remained of Twist. She threw her father's best glare at Mengele, the Blonde Man, who smoothed the creases from his charcoal suit then crooked a finger directly at her. Chills gnawed at her bones as if he drew the warmth from her flesh with a single gesture. Celeste clenched her teeth to keep them from chattering out of her skull. She smothered fear with a hot, simmering rage.

"Take her and get out of here," she hissed at Bink, and Aurous voiced her fury with a resounding growl. "Clark will help her."

"Shit." His voice was tight and faint. Nadie clenched onto his blood-soaked shirt, sobbing hoarsely. "And you?"

A sudden faintness welled up inside of her. *Death.* The world spun around her, blurring, and it took a considerable effort to remain on her feet. Wave after wave of nausea and grief washed over her, drowning her, and every cell of her body was racked with an immeasurable pain. Existing *hurt.* Blood squirted hotly down her thigh, steaming into the night air. For a moment she was unable to move or process another thought. Strength flickered inside her like a dying fire. It wasn't enough given the grueling extent of her wounds. She sighed, caught her breath, then lifted Greyfang in a show of confidence she did not feel.

The Blonde Man smiled, looking like a hissing snake, and continued his slow pace forward.

Celeste nodded once to Bink then, softly, called to Nadie.

It was as if her friend didn't hear her words, or couldn't make sense of them. A few seconds after, she stared up from Bink, her eyes puffy and her face sloppy wet from tears. Trembling violently, she sagged against him, then bit her lip and listened to what she had to tell her.

"Bink is going to take you to Clark," Celeste said, "and you're all going to secure an aircraft and prepare to get the *hell* out of here, okay?"

"I can't lose you, too!" Nadie protested, squirming in Bink's gentle grip. "I can't!"

"I'll be right behind you."

"Promise me! Promise!" Nadie sobbed and screamed as Bink—with a gentle urgency—dragged her and the young bandit back to Odine and the others. Celeste steeled her heart and didn't answer. Truthfully, she didn't have one. She turned and faced Mengele and tried not to feel afraid.

"You are, without a doubt, the consequence of my failures," Mengele hissed icily, with a flick of his snakelike tongue. He took another calculated step towards her like a slow dripping poison. The tall man lingered over her friend's corpse another moment, worming his sinuously long, rubberlike limbs through the pooling blood like a mess of feelers. "General Cavarly was tempted to call off the search but I knew our precious little project would survive. Very tenacious blood. However, to my—*our* disappointment"—his creeping smile *peeled* the skin from his cheekbone like piece of sticky tape—"you remain trapped in the flesh of the past, a ghost of this new world. You are reprehensible."

"You know *nothing* of me!" Aurous echoed her growl. Mengele slowed his stride, flashed her another awful smile, and gestured wildly to the bright burning skies, the blood—oh, there was *so* much blood everywhere—and those who were fleeing through the trees under Odine's command like so many scattering birds. That sparked a flicker of interest in the tall man's eyes, and his hollow gaze trailed their movements with the heightened interest of a cat. He made some strange guttural sound, caught between a growl and an agitated bark, and *slathered* his scaly-black tentacled limb in the blood-soaked earth. After a few moments he appeared disquieted from Mengele's lack of interest; his razor teeth were bared, grinding, and viciously hooked inwards like a shark's deadly maw.

"She's...*leaving*..." the tall man seethed through his yellowing teeth, with a thick voice sticky with mucus. He flicked his tongue as if to taste the air.

While Mengele *shushed* him gently, flicking his hand in and out of his charcoal suit, Celeste abruptly froze. *Weapon?* She raised the halberd instinctively like a shield—as if it would somehow stop the deadly trajectory of a bullet. Whatever it was, a glinting black and no larger than the handle of a bladeless knife, was clenched so tightly that his hand formed a proper fist. Celeste bit her tongue, and her heart pounded so loud she had difficulty concentrating on his voice, which was low but simmering anger.

"You will wait your turn," he said and gestured at the tall man with his fisted hand. "Do not disappoint me like your *brother* has"—the coldness in his eyes was unforgiving—"like *she* continuously has." He regarded Celeste with his cold, dead eyes. "Dear girl, he was only attempting to bring you home."

"I didn't kill Pride." Her grip tightened, fingers raking gashes into the banded leather of the halberd. "But I'll kill you both."

The tall man ignored the warning. "You're letting her leave!" Anger rising, his tentacle limb slapped the ground, ripping chunks of dirt into the air. "They're taking her away! I'll kill them all, I'll kill them all!"

Mengele sighed. "I am the father to such wretched children." He ran his thumb along the edges of the black object in his grip. The tall man was exploding with anger, but even he shrunk back from Mengele's subtle gesture. "Did you really believe you could escape what you truly were?"

Her eyes went shock-wide; she suddenly knew what the device was—

She was blasted with a high-pitched and deafening sound she not only heard, but *felt* inside her bones. She was driven to her knees, every thought disrupted, scattered and staticky, with no sense of who or what had been, or what was—like being ripped apart at the atomic level, dissolving, quite painfully, into nothingness. It was unlike any other agony she had ever been subjected to. When, however, the tormenting sound ceased as immediately as it began, her body—now a sensation she was momentarily unfamiliar with—was stiff and violently shaking from some sharp, electrical impulse. Her throat was tight as if squeezed shut by an invisible grip. Her lungs quivered for the slightest blip of air. Her heart was painfully seized in her chest as if disturbed from its natural rhythm.

The tall man was affected by the stressor as well; he shambled forward, fingers raking long black gashes up his hollow cheek, while his tentacle limb writhed in agony like a slug that shriveled up from a dash of salt. When his fingers clawed into his skull, a fistful of ragged-brown mop hair ripped from his scalp in thick bloody bands. He was, for the moment, as immobilized as she had been—but he recovered rapidly, snapping his spine rigidly straight, and thrashed his slithery tentacles through the dirt. His frost white eyes never left her.

No, not me...

He was staring *past* her, his unhuman eyes searching the shadowy network of dead thickets and brambled paths. His chest expanded, ribs rippled and *cracked* like brittle tree limbs. His grey skin split and slopped to the dirt. Black tendrils sinuously flickered from the gashes like a rising flame, interlinking and spreading outwards across his body like a black, mossy growth. Darkness consumed his form until he was a vague silhouette against the night, imposingly tall even at a distance, another lithe giant of the forest, with prodigious claws that belonged to some prehistoric beast. Its amorphous head doubled in size, but it had no discernable features of a face. Only a suggestive blackness where its face should have been, an enormous maw like a wide, gaping frown, and round milky eyes that flickered with an avid hunger.

"*Odine!*"

Mengele shrugged. "You could have spared them." He smiled at her with his dead eyes. "Lust—you may avenge your brother."

Celeste fought her urge to retreat and saw that most, if not all, of the bandits had retreated from sight—except Odine and an ever-stubborn Bink. She cursed loudly, and at the same moment, felt the earth violently wrench under her feet. The tall man, the creature called Lust, propelled at her with explosive speed. He charged, head down like a rhino, stomping his hind claws into the dirt. She raised and swung the halberd—Aurous snapped his fangs at his hot, scaly skin—and both chopped at empty air. She watched, quite helplessly, as Lust regarded her no more than one would an ant under a shoe. She was about to yell when her skin prickled inexplicably. Aurous snarled and viciously barked at that very moment—as Mengele's creeping voice slithered through her ears, "You will watch them die, and you will accept your fate."

For a horrifying moment—what lasted seconds to the world but felt like eternal torment for her—it was all she could do.

Accept her fate.

Lust thrashed through the trees with the force of a thundering gale, leaving their limbs windswept and splintering outwards, his long slithery tentacle *whipping* behind him and dragging deep furrows through the dirt. Despite his imposing height at twelve feet tall, his legs were thick as oak trees and angled inward, with elongated feet that balanced on clawed digits like some biped dinosaur. Each long stride was like leaping a chasm, hurling him forward like a runaway train. A titan of a poltergeist that raged through the dark forest. There was a flicker of panic in Odine's eye—Bink shouldered his rifle and quickly drew aim on the monster's head.

Celeste ached to help, but it was as if she fell under some hypnotic power, petrified and leached of any warmth. Her limbs were frozen in place. Her throat clenched shut, almost violently, her heart pounded rapidly against her ribs like a jackhammer. *No. Dad. Tell me what to do. Please.*

Bink's rifle erupted in white-hot light—but the blood-drenched darkness absorbed its rapid flashes, and Lust struck with a massive, writhing limb. Branches exploded into splinters. Trees violently ripped from roots, flinging a haze of dirt into the air. Bink retreated a few paces from the viciously clawed earth, jerking his rifle downward and opening fire on a slithering python-sized tentacle. One—two—three shots sparked across scabrous scales. Lust towered over him, hunching closer, maw gaping wide. Odine, with an upswing of her mace, bludgeoned the creature's featureless face, lacerating his shadowy flesh. Muddy-red blood crawled from his maw like slime—but his eyes glittered at the sight of her, his head unmoved from the blow as if he never even felt it. The only sound from his gaping maw was the steamy hissing of her name. Tendrils wormed through the flesh of his other arm, curling over his long skeleton fingers like a jaguar's extending claws. His tentacle limb shot outwards over Bink, cast like a fishermen's net—colossal claws struck the mace away in a bright spray of sparks.

"You were a genetic anomaly," Mengele hissed, "the sum to the equation that eluded even the brightest minds of the Old World. Yet, here you are, clinging to some profound sense of humanity as if you belong with them, as if your blood is pristine and your heart just as pure. You assiduously preserved their lives over your own when they are irrelevant, and *you* know it. You've always known it."

"No..." she whispered, "y-you don't know who I am."

She could almost hear the grin slither across his puzzle-piece scarred face. "Your denial is predictable, but have you ever wondered exactly *what* you are?" He smacked his lips at her, his voice creeping ever closer. Fiery light flashed, thunder pounded through the skinny black trees—Lust roared and gave chase to those fleeting shadowy forms. "How often do you tire, Celeste?" he asked, prowling around her like a wolf. "How many were felled by that axe—how many more will meet its vicious bite?"

No. With a sharp whine and guttural bark Aurous pawed at her feet. *I'm not a monster.*

"This battle has, undoubtedly, awoken the alteration that courses through you. Yet, despite my sincerest efforts, you remain irrevocably human as if you still hold some measure of control." His rancorous voice pierced her ear like an icy needle as he brushed up against her rigid form. Aurous paced rapidly in front of her, snarling and swinging his fangs, his tawny-bright eyes narrowing at Mengele. "It is disappointing but not unexpected," he hissed, "because whichever path you chose would have led you, inexorably, to me. You may not see it yet, but behold the sight before you and know"—Lust *roared* with the temperament of a starving bear, splintering thickets in his python grip—"that you are a work of art, an utterly magnificent design of evolution. Those tiny genetic markers separate you from the weak. You could be flawless, perfect—like me."

Celeste fumbled weakly, "I am not like you."

"You are sublime," he insisted, "but your emotions dismantle logic, emotions that are blinding you to the truth of what you could be. When you watch them all die, one by one, you will abandon the fragility of your humanity. It is always a chain reaction, a process born from death." She felt him press against her back with the inhuman chill of a blizzard. "Your assumptions prove correct, however. You are not, as you so adequately stated, like me...*but you will be!*"

A dead-cold sensation pierced her abdomen and ripped inward toward her belly. A faint gasp touched her lips—Aurous snarled and barked, saliva flinging from his snapping fangs, but it was as if he were afraid of her, afraid of *him*—and she shuddered violently as a flash flood of warmth drenched her ballistic armour. Her knees quivered and buckled. She painfully slid down from the hooking grip of the knife in her guts, hitting the dirt with a bright shock of pain. The gaping wound leached the warmth from her body, and it was like blood swirling around a drain. Reality blurred into snippets of nonsensical images. It took her a moment to realize she was crying and furiously blinking away her tears. Glittering gold filled her vision with a brightness that felt like a sliver of morning light against her skin. *Run, boy,* she pleaded silently, begging that he understood her desperate silence.

She felt the thundering reverberance through the forest, and opened her bleary eyes to see the branches of the dying trees stir with a force that was not windborne. Another roar rippled outward from Lust like a shockwave as his tentacles tore trees asunder with hurricane strength. An intermittent pulse of light scattered through the whirlwind of splintering branches and dirt as Bink reloaded his rifle. But the abominable creature rose over him, eyes burning like white-hot flames, his fangs glisteningly unhuman.

Lust stopped.

For another moment he was frozen in place, then his enormous dinosaur head tilted skywards as if scenting some subtle shift in the air. His eyes were smoldering flames, gaze sweeping through the torn trees—and Odine's name erupted from his maw when he sighted her a dozen meters to his left. He abandoned the gristle and gave chase to a meatier dinner.

"Stop wasting your time," Mengele cursed, his voice barely an audible whisper. Celeste caught him from the corner of her eye. He absently paced forward and dragged his thumb over the trigger of the sonic device. "Kill the others, and after you may have the girl for yourself! They are a thinly veiled distraction!"

In that twisted moment of irony, the paralyzing fear shattered, and she struck, and she struck hard and fast. Waves of pain radiated from the stab wound in her abdomen, but she wrenched her hips and brought the halberd down on Mengele's arm like a blacksmith pounding red-hot iron into shape. The axe blade, dulled from battle, still chewed flesh and loudly crunched through bone. The heavy downward swing cleaved his arm off in a burst of black, slushy blood—his arm fell still clutching the device between his rigid dead fingers. Though his eyes were as piercing cold as winter, his brow furrowed and stretched the skin across his forehead as thin as cellophane, almost as if he reached for a thought dangling just out of his mind's reach...

Celeste abandoned her grip on the halberd and lunged for his throat as Aurous snapped his fangs at his belly with a feverish pace. They both collided with him as one hulking beast. She viciously clawed up him, and his charcoal suit tattered around her wolf's fangs. Mengele was thrown to his back, and she fell with him, and they hit the ground with enough force to drive the air from his lungs—but his remaining hand wrenched tightly around her throat, squeezing her of any breath, and used the momentum of their fall to fling her forward. She hit the ground again—*hard*—and a shock of pain impacted her ribcage. Her lungs quivered for air they paradoxically refused.

Mengele was already on his feet by the time she was clambering, quite breathlessly, to hers. Aurous still had his fangs wrenched in the belly of his charcoal suit, ripping the silky fabric with sharp *hisses*, and exposed the jigsaw pattern of murky flesh that rippled like a disturbed pond, as if his organs churned beneath, repositioning, reconstructing. A thin smile carved through his face like a blade. She saw, with sheer horror in her eyes, as the rotten viscous sludge that bled from his severed stump of an arm formed hideous prehensile claws. Like long strips of black bone, curling into the shape of a fist, as razor thin and sharp as Reaper's Claw. Shadowy tendrils curled from the cracks in his jigsaw skin like wisps of smoke.

"Humanity is no longer pertinent, just another fossil in the long line of evolution. The strong have not only survived, dear girl"—his skeletal claw gripped the handle of her halberd with a peculiarly human grip—"we've inherited the Earth!"

He launched the halberd at her with the speed of a loosed arrow. As she recoiled from the blurring steel, it struck the ground only an inch from where she stood, buried a few feet up to its handle. Aurous reacted in the same instant, yowling with a feverish pitch, and lunged at Mengele with ripping fangs. Celeste frantically dove for the halberd—

A loathsome shadow blotted out her entire vision. Pain invaded every bone in her arm, an icy sensation that ribboned her sleeve and carved scarlet furrows into the flesh beneath. His clawed grip wrenched around her arm, his profound strength nearly ripping it from the socket, as he shoved her several feet away through the dirt. Aurous shot at him as a flurry of fangs and claws, but viciously ripped through empty air. Sidestepping, Mengele connected a quick and painful kick to the wolf's underbelly. Celeste heard the air *thump* from his lungs, and the sharp cracking of bones when he hit the dirt. Mengele attacked as fast as an animal gone rabid; his sinuously long claws fell over her like a sky full of arrows. One by one he brought them down, stabbing into the dirt as she rolled to her feet—

The wolf impacted with him as a snarling flash of razor teeth, wrenching his powerful jaws around the clawed hand and—*SNAP!*—crunching bone between his fangs like a brittle piece of wood. While Aurous tore Mengele off balance, Celeste found her footing, quickly, and retreated for the halberd.

As fast as she thought she was, Mengele fell on her like she were unsuspecting prey. Her outstretched fingers were inches from the halberd when he struck, hard, and she was catapulted face-first into the ground. Flung through the dirt like a ragdoll, her head *smacked* as she went like a pebble skipping over a pond. For moments that seemed to stretch eternally, she was unable to summon the strength to move.

"You are no longer bound by mortal constraints," he spat. "Yet you foul your blood with weakness and squander your abilities. A martyr for the marred." His boot steps kicked up a cloud of choking dust in her face. "They are a dead branch on the tree of life, as charred and lifeless as this petrified forest." Bemused laughter dripped from his snakelike tongue. "You are *so* much more—"

It was in that moment she pounced. The pain was a secondary thought to the pounding fury in her blood, though she felt every pulpy bruise, ripping laceration, torn and frayed muscle burning in protest. She slammed into him full force, throwing her weight behind the blow. She felt the shock of it reverberate through her bones, and Mengele barely gave an inch of ground to her assault. Her fingers raked across his exposed belly with desperate determination. His skin was disturbingly frost cold and oily like a waterlogged corpse, bloated, discoloured, and putrid. The fingers of his unchanged hand tangled in her hair and jerked her head back, shocking her to immobility. In a swift snapping motion, the back of her head rocked against the ground, blinding her with pain, and then she was thrust into the air with her feet dangling inches from the ground. "Your loyalty is inexplicable," he hissed at her, ripping her hair out in bloody strands. "But you are the magnificence of natural selection, and I know you see it; you've seen the change for some time, have you not?"

She struck like a cobra, several times, ripping a blade into his arm and out the other side, steel grating against bone—with the same knife he had used to stab her, still crimson with her blood, stolen from the sheath on his belt. Flesh and bloody bits of bone clung to the blade. His grip slacked, and his clawed hand went for her neck—but the tip of her blade found his, gliding through his throat with an upswing, and misted the air with sultry red. He sputtered wordlessly in an attempt to hurl a vile curse at her. She recoiled from his reach as he lashed out needlessly, drawing him into the paltry cover of the trees. He shambled forward as if briefly losing motor function, and instead of a bright red gash across his throat, a black substance as thick as oil crawled down his jigsaw patterned skin. She'd only gone a few paces into the trees when he lunged after her.

She was ready, the wolf inside her snarled viciously.

Steel clashed against claw in a spitting spray of sparks. The thundering force shocked her limbs numb, but she shoved her blade down his shadowy claw, warping the crude steel against his scaly bones. Black blood sprayed up her knuckles—claw painfully bit into her shoulder, ripping through muscle. She yanked her blade, took a single pace backwards—his fist impacted with her solar plexus. Her ribcage shuddered and cracked. Her lungs were robbed of precious air. Blood bubbled past her lips. She stumbled and caught his blurring movements from the peripheral of her sight. When she ducked under his colossal claw, the tree next to her exploded into a flurry of splinters. She weaved around another strike, and another tree met the same splintery fate. She counterattacked. Her blade sank through his belly, rupturing the bloated flesh like an infected wound. Shadowy tendrils spilled from where his entrails should have been, writhing and worming like hatched larvae. Disgust burned the back of her throat, and she nearly heaved from the hot, rolling wave of rot that washed over her. His cold, calculating façade shattered like glass. Infuriated, he screamed for her blood, and he ferociously slashed for her neck. She threw her head back, felt the massive claw clip the tip of her nose, and slammed her spine—and the back of her head—hard against the craggy bark of a tree. She ducked again, and his claw tore through the entire trunk, toppling the pine tree like a chainsaw. Half of it crashed down from the snarled canopy, whipping sharp splinters at her in the whooshing wind of its fall. She lunged between strikes, knife piercing for his throat—his speed was far superior, and he brought his claw down on her like a hammer. Slashing upwards, steel grated claw, and she was forced to her knees and nearly crushed into the dirt. Now defenseless, his other fist found a target, and her nose *crunched* against his knuckles, staining them bright red. She was thrown backwards, losing her upright balance—his enormous claws closed in on her like sword thrusts from every direction. Pain lanced throughout her body. Blood burst from her shoulder, gushed from her ribs, ran in thick rivulets down her scalp. Shielding her face in the crook of her raised arms, those claws pincered tightly, crushing her skull, painfully slicing through her scarred skin and grinding against bone. Screaming only filled her mouth with her own blood. But it wasn't only her.

The forest was a hell of tortured screams, paralyzing and raw. She heard Bink through her own torment, consumed by pain, screaming his fury. She swore she could hear the sharp *snapping* of bones. Gritting her teeth, she struggled against Mengele's crushing grip.

"Do you hear," he asked, "the sounds of the Old World dying under the new?"

Celeste cursed at him with vulgarity that would have made her father blush. And she fought as he would have, fought with all in her heart that wanted to survive as he had taught her to. Her body pounded with pain. Blood drenched every inch of her. Still, she struggled, because she knew to lose consciousness would mean the death of her friends, her wolf. Her Mahihkan. She channeled all her rage and trepidation into prying those piercing claws from her flesh, but it was like tangling up in barbed wire. The more she struggled, the tighter its razor-sharp grip, ribboning her flesh like peeled potato skins.

A vicious snarl and the slopping sound of ripping meat were barely audible through the feverish rhythm of her own thundering fear. The moment those claws unclenched from her flesh, she tore herself loose, screaming with as much fury as pain. Aurous had Mengele's clavicle firmly crushed between his jaws, wrenching him to the ground, his scaly flesh bursting like a bloody balloon.

Soaked in her own blood, trembling violently, she thrust that knife downward and fell over him. She felt the cold steel sink into chest, gliding cleanly between his ribs, and viciously wrenched it deep into his heart. A viscous black slime exploded like a geyser. He shoved his claw into her belly—she rolled off him, shoulder slamming into the dirt, sparks spitting across her ballistic armor. Pain exploded from her hip to the edge of her armor, deep, but only bit down to the muscle. At least she hoped her entrails wouldn't spill out like spaghetti as she stood and felt the sharp twinge and hot spray of blood. A growl rumbled in her wolf's throat as he retreated to her side, black blood sliming from his fangs. His eyes were a blazing gold like an unclouded sun, alive with the thrill of the hunt. She turned to watch Mengele die.

That oozing black substance pulsed from the stab wound, and he rose over her like a churning column of smoke. Steel withered and warped in his clawed grip like forger's flame, and the knife shattered into whipping shrapnel.

"Such insolence," he seethed. The jigsaw splits in his skin were leaking that oily blackness. "If you were to embrace your genetics, you could save them, but as it is you are an utter disappointment. A consequence of my failure all those years ago."

The raw rage that coursed through her dulled the pain better than any narcotic could. "You destroyed my family," she spat through gritted teeth. "You killed my brother!"

His eyes glittered anger. "You speak with such ignorance. *I* saved him—I was saving you!"

"My brother!" she screamed, and Aurous echoed her lamenting howl. "My mother!"

"Your *father* destroyed them!"

Her nails dug bloody welts into her palm as she balled her hands into fists. "I saw him, my brother, after your people had dissected every crevice of his body!" Tears stung her bleary eyes. "In some twisted attempt at a patient zero for your experimental weapons. Better he died in my father's arms than in the hellish pit of your lab."

"After all you have experienced you still believe death remains a finality. The body"—shadows leached the life from his skin, bursting through the jagging splits in his face—"is merely a shell abandoned after transference. You have plunged over the edge yourself. Do they know, perhaps, that your ascension means their deaths? You are already showing a systematic change. It will not go unnoticed. How long, I wonder, until your *wrath* consumes them as well?"

His human skin peeled from his bloody, shadowy skull, crisping as if he stood in an unseen flame. "But I am the first *and* the last, a god creating a new world! It began with me, and it will end long before I do!"

"Pretentious asshole." She spat a glob of blood into the dirt. "You're a contagion that should have been quarantined and eliminated *before* it destroyed my world."

"I didn't do this to myself, and this isn't your world." His decaying form resembled a human only in the way a crudely dissected corpse would, as if his skeleton had clawed free from its fleshy prison. "I've evolved beyond their mortal limitation. As will you, as will all those who pathetically cling to the ways of old—the *Titan* will spread my brood to the ends of this earth!"

With a sharp growl that rumbled through his bared fangs, Aurous was the first to lunge; he ripped into the sinewy shadows that rippled around Mengele's body like muscle and flesh. Black blood fanned the dirt, dripping from his fangs, and Aurous dashed away excitedly. Celeste recognized it immediately—their old game! Mengele's featureless face, teeth chattering noisily, focused solely on Celeste as his colossal, clawed hand raked trenches into the ground. He wasn't taking the bait—he charged her with inhuman speed.

Celeste knew better than to face that nightmarish creature head-on. He was freakishly fast, and with little cover in sight other than dying trees, she had nothing to shield herself with. Zigzagging through the trees, heart syncing to the rapid rhythm of her footfalls, she was absolutely giddied and bestial. She would have thrown her head back and howled excitedly had she not been so utterly breathless and exhausted. Still, her stride carried her inches away from Mengele's viciously clawed grip. *Come on, boy!*

She saw the halberd jutting from the earth several feet from where she was—

Splinters and dirt pelted her like a hailstorm as his claw tore through tree limbs and craggy bark. She tried not to think how near those bladelike claws came to bisecting her as she ran—she felt the cold kiss of wind against her back from every swing—or fear would have frozen her in place. She was slowly giving more ground, but she was almost there—

Come on, boy!

Without warning Aurous struck like a bullet. In a bloody blur of fangs, his jaws *snapped* around Mengele's neck and crushed whatever remained of his windpipe. Aurous wrenched him to the dirt, but momentum flung them forward, and they rolled in a snarling frenzy of fangs and claws. Celeste grinned, almost maniacally, as Aurous pinned him to the ground, *ripping* out his throat. She kept her feverish pace, inches from the halberd—

A high-pitched howl echoed with pain. It drove chills down her spine. One of Mengele's bladelike claws had torn through her wolf's hip, splashing steamy crimson across the dirt. Aurous whined, his hind legs as sturdy as melting rubber. The sight of him wobbling away, blood leaking like a running faucet, sparked a rage inside her that was like a rapid build-up of steam. Her heart pounded like a war drum in her ears, and all she could taste was her wolf's blood in the air. With her fingers clenched around the handle, she screamed furiously, "Get away from him!" and drew the halberd from earth and swung it forward in one fluid motion. It was like a feather in her hand, almost weightless, a bullet flinging from her grip with rapid precision. She launched the halberd at Mengele like a loosed arrow. It speared through the air at soaring speeds, a blur of blood-soaked steel, and only at the last moment did Mengele flick his skeletal head from its path—but the axe blade cleaved through his shoulder with such force that it nearly ripped through what remained of his throat as well. The halberd struck a tree behind him, splitting it in half with a resounding *crack!* Mengele, black blood fountaining from his gaping wound, staggered and reeled, astonishment darkening those dead eyes. She didn't care. He was foolish enough to, even for a moment, take his eyes from her.

Her roar filled the air like a rumbling of thunder. When she struck, she struck with enough force to completely shatter his bony, featureless face like a pane of glass, whipping glisteningly unhuman flesh and bone through the air like hailstones. He flew backwards several feet and slammed hard enough for the ground to visibly tremble under him. As he rose to his feet, darkness swelled from his features like an overcast sky, rippling and churning like smoke. His crescent shaped eyes, no longer a stagnant blue, bled crimson, and glowed like the embers of a dying fire.

She wasn't certain how she responded so quickly, half-feeling, half-sensing, but when he brought those claws down on her like a guillotine, she had already withdrawn from their reach. He tore into the ground and ripped up segments of dirt and rock twice the size of her head that crashed through the trees like meteors.

She struck him again, like a head-on collision, and the force of it shocked her arm completely numb. Something was unmistakably broken. But it didn't matter to her in the moment, only blood did, and as vile and foul scented as his was, she craved to wring every last, putrid drop from his undead bones. The ground heaved under the impact of his landing. He was still human, in general form, though his limbs were grotesquely angulated and broken, bloody vertebrae jutted sharply from his back. His flesh, whatever *had* been human, had disintegrated to a hazy, oily black that coated his form like skin, and congealed like blood. Crimson eyes glowed from a face completely consumed by darkness. "*She has found herself,*" he hissed, "*what was truly meant—*"

Her fist was like a missile, and hit with as much explosive force. She heard, as much as *felt,* the sharp cracking of his bones. Shadowy tendrils writhed and wriggled from every wound, mending the corpse-grey flesh. She felt a strong grip around her arm, claw to wrist, cutting deep for her artery. Blood boiled through her veins. Her near-fingerless hand wrenched his clawed arm, *snapping* every bone in the process, and violently ripped it from the socket like a stubbornly rooted weed in the garden. His unhuman scream beat against her eardrums like a pack of vicious, bloodthirsty hellhounds—until she dropped her foot into his chest like an anchor, crushed his malforming ribs, and brutally stomped his spine into the dirt. Whatever words, along with blood, that he gurgled on, she hoped it was for mercy. Mercy she would *never* show.

No.

What compelled her to abandon her bloodlust, if only for a heartbeat of a moment, was the gut-wrenching sounds of anguish that filled the air like a slaughterhouse. She stopped her assault, fangs gritted, heart pounding in a frenetic rhythm. She even heard Aurous, waning in strength as he was, howling like a siren. *Never abandon pack.*

Never.

Mengele's mutilated form, shapeless and stirring, she left in the darkness of the forest, alone, but not before she'd retrieved the halberd and hacked every limb from his writhing body, then eventually his head. From what Father had told her of his encounters with The Blonde Man, he was unlikely to die even after dismemberment, and she'd have set fire to his bloody remnants if at all possible. As it was, he was in more pieces than if he had cradled a live grenade in his lap. Whatever he was, whatever he had been, she shoved it as far from her mind as she could.

Celeste had grown numb, drenched head-to-toe in crimson, so much so that she couldn't feel her feet pound against the forest floor. But the torment she heard her friends enduring chilled her bones more than the night air and her own blood combined. Aurous was waiting for her, crouched to his haunches, his tawny eyes glittering from the crimson skies. Excitement electrified the air between them. Tongue lolled, he took off ahead of her, blood spurting from his hip, and snipped at the air with his fangs. Injured or not, he was a bolt of lightning through the trees, and Celeste always had to struggle to keep him in sight, even when she had been lean-framed and forest-fed as he was. Now she easily matched his giddying pace. Ahead of them, another loathsome roar shook the trees like a windstorm.

Aurous snapped at her legs, barking, and cut diagonally through the flattened section of trees, splattered with her blood and Mengele's. He stopped, curiously, for only a moment, and retrieved what she thought was a gristly bone until it spasmodically flopped in his jaws like some fish out of water. Then he was off again, growling gutturally as he couldn't yap with a mouthful of corpse-meat. It was a severed arm still fitted in that charcoal suit—clutching the sonic device with deadlocked fingers. His eyes twinkled, and she was unable to hold back the grin inching across her face. She snatched the severed stump and then pried the device, the same sonic emitter that so effortlessly incapacitated her within seconds, from his vicelike grip. It had stopped her dead in her tracks. However, it had stopped Lust as well. She growled with excitement, Aurous *yipped* and *snapped* at her feet—then bolted for the deep bellowing of a beast, howling for her to follow. Their forest, their pack, their hunt. Not his! She sprinted after him, breathlessly, and they ran together as one howling wolf, as if they weren't overtired and worn from battle. They ran as if they hadn't yet tired of hunting the undead through the forest. Celeste knew better. Her endurance appeared endless, as Mengele had warned, but she was scraping the bottom of the barrel. Truly the only reason she hadn't collapsed for a dirt nap was because she had no opportunity to stand still long enough since the fighting began. It took sheer discipline to keep going, leaping over fallen trees and splintered limbs, ripping through thorny overgrowth, bolting across the savagely gutted land that appeared as if a series of earthquakes had struck, but she had one last gamble, one last—she clutched that sonic emitter to her chest—cast of the die. Scenery blurred and ran together like a whirlpool as she pumped her legs harder. She lagged only a pace behind Aurous, his jaws frothed with fury and snout raised to scent the foul creature. He sharply angled left, snarling, and she fought her forward-flinging momentum—

There were two of them, standing side by side, that she spotted immediately. Clark and Bink, who she would have cursed again if not for the gaping wounds to both his legs. Bink was hunched against the base of a tree, teeth gritted and crimson, as he struggled to staunch the blood flow with his own shirt, already drenched red. Clark stood over him, as pale as any corpse she'd seen, with his eye trained down the rifle. Blood oozed from the obsidian-dark armor around his gaunt frame. If he had been lying still, even napping, she might well have mistaken him for another casualty to the fight. She glowed with admiration, then choked down the bitter taste of guilt. *I'm so sorry.*

Then her heart painfully thumped into her throat. *Shit!*

Plum-purple hair shimmered between the trees like faint flicker of a falling star. Odine moved clumsily, stumbling in a panic through the dense trees and thorny undergrowth, skin snagged and welted red, dead limbs raking through her hair like claws. No, Celeste noted with horror, it wasn't panic; the ground was a roiling ocean of dirt.

Lust.

There he was, an imposing tower of a creature, standing on legs that were thicker than tree trunks, and tremendous prehistoric claws, with a tall, elongated body that resembled a human only if they had been stretched to impossible lengths on a torture rack. The scaly tentacle appendages was nearly double the length of *him*, gliding through the trees like hungry snakes on their bellies, hissing after their next meal, writhing with impatience. Lust lagged behind her, but his enormously long stride could have overlapped her at any moment—the trees did little to impede him, bowing under him like dead wilting weeds. He was *playing* with her, some perverted game of cat-and-mouse. Odine knew that. Celeste saw the wary glance she shot at Clark in the split-second before she bolted for the *opposite* direction. The mess of tentacles, as if possessing minds of their own, lunged after her, spreading across the forest floor like a slithering carpet, and tore through everything in their path. Trees toppled and fell as if parting for Lust, crashing against the ground with thunderous force—enough to throw Odine from her feet, hurling her into the pool of wriggling tentacles—

Without warning, a brilliance of light pulsed through the trees. Clark had drawn his rifle on Lust and opened fire. Celeste never stopped running. Shadows danced and flicked against the sporadic muzzle flash, briefly illuminating the densely tangled path, and she shoved thoughts of stray bullets from her mind even as she heard the sharp *zing* of passing shots. The wolf darted ahead of her, snarling wildly, crimson stained to his giant incisors. She stumbled. She wasn't going to make it in time, neither of them was. How near would she have to be for the device to work? Mengele had been several feet from her. *Last gamble. No chances!*

As Odine fell, those slimy, slithering tentacles rose like furling waves in a swamp and began to crash down on her like a battered shoreline. Then, quite suddenly, there was a gaping hole in the tangled knot of tentacles, ripping upwards and splitting as Moses did the Red Sea. The crude steel of a machete blade warped, and Snyder slashed deeper, hacking through the swarming heads of black serpents—a putrid, glisteningly unhuman ooze fountained and flooded the forest floor—like roving through an untamed jungle. The blonde was viciously accurate with her blade, rending and sawing through anything that moved like some manic butcher, and bought Odine a brief moment to pick herself up from the ground, her own blade gleaming against the pressing darkness. Snyder shoved her backwards, recoiling from a viperous lunge—she stuck her blade into a writhing tentacle, but it coiled around the steel and crushed it like an aluminum can.

I'm almost there!

Lust roared and rained meaty spittle over them, his white-hot burning eyes flashing with resentment. His possessive gaze was interrupted by Snyder, shielding Odine from his sight, and it utterly infuriated the behemoth. His tentacles slithered past the crumpled blade, coiled tightly around Snyder's wrist and yanked her to the dirt—she hit with a loud *oof* rushing from her lungs, and was dragged into the writhing mass of serpentine limbs. It snaked up her arm, leached the color from her skin and withered it to a corpse-grey, as if he were draining the life from every cell in her body. Odine frantically clawed at her, but her grip was no match for the slithering mass. Razorlike barbs snagged into flesh like hooks, gripping into flesh and sinew. Snyder screamed, loudly, but more out of anger than fear; she wasn't going to die without a fight.

Distance be damned, Celeste drew her halberd back and yelled fiercely, "I killed Doctor Cruel!" and raised the sonic emitter with her other hand. If Snyder held his attention by interfering with his—*meal*—than Celeste occupied every thought rotating in that rancorous mind. She didn't care. She had his attention, if only for a moment. It was all she needed. She had his amorphous blot of a face at spearpoint, and she hurled the halberd with the last of her rage channeled into the blood-stained steel. It flung from her grip as a blur, ripping skywards for his emberlike eyes, and at the very same moment, tightly squeezed the emitter in her palm.

It started as a sharp squelch that rapidly amplified into a screeching shockwave that tore through her eardrums, seized every muscle in her body, and violently jarred her bones loose. A white-hot, lancing pain shot up her spine, as if each vertebra burst into a splatter of raw, still-functioning nerves. Driven to her knees, the agony radiated like a spreading flame over tinder, engulfing her brittle body in waves and waves of sheer pain. She would have howled if she could, her vision searing white, but stubbornly focused on Lust. It felt like every atom in her body was violently ripping apart. Lust howled with discomfort, eyes dimming, and *smacked* the halberd from midair like some buzzing insect, its jutting spearpoint a hair's breadth from his face. While his stride faltered, his tentacles writhed, shriveled and squirmed, but the razorlike barbs adhered to Snyder's flesh, dragging her further into the slithering serpent pit.

Snyder cursed at the behemoth with her last inhale of air.

Plunging her blade point-first, Odine fell over Snyder.

Aurous, with a frenzied snarl, leapt at Lust with ruddy fangs gleaming.

The next few moments played out in patchy, blurry snippets like the details of some near-forgotten dream. The forest and its shadows swirled like paint running down a canvas, her vision pounding red and black, body ransacked with raw anguish that forced her to the ground. Shock blotted the edges of her sight, a creeping numbness from the back of her skull. It was crippling, and felt as if she was flayed alive, skin carefully peeled from the subcutaneous layer of fat, the fat boiled off in steamy, coagulated chunks, stringy muscles unraveling like spools of yarn, every raw nerve exposed and torched from the caustic air. She glimpsed, with bleary, pinpointed eyesight, the darting shadow that was her wolf rake his forepaws into Lust's long craning neck, and ripped his incisors into the creature's bulbous eyes. Black blood spurted hotly through his wrenching jaws. Simultaneously, below them, as the sticky mess of tendrils violently writhed and withered, Odine sank the blade of her large knife into Snyder's arm and crudely sawed through bone like some blind butcher. The blood was steamy-hot and poured from the forming stump like sticky syrup. In the next instant, she wrenched her arms around Snyder's waist, and scrambled away from the hissing and flicking tendrils that seemed to independently move with minds of their own. Snyder's blue eyes were dull and fluttered closed, like a clear sky now roiling with clouds. A ferocious howling chorus, like the sound of a thousand wolves, filled her mind with a raw viciousness, a pack that had cornered its quarry. Then it all slipped from her mind's grasp.

Blackness, that's all there was, and she couldn't be happier.

TWENTY-NINE
Twelve Feet

COLD. THAT'S what roused her, quite painfully, from a deep and unfeeling slumber. Blood bubbled in the back of her throat when she tried to take a deep gulping breath. She couldn't scream if she wanted to—and she *wanted* to. Pain wasn't what racked every fiber of her being, no, it was whatever vile and nefarious force that came to torment *pain* into oblivion. Pressure pounded inside her skull as if something, her brain perhaps, thrashed needlessly to find a way out. It took another agonizing moment to realize it was her heartbeat. *Just let me die,* she willed her stubbornly pumping muscle. *Shut off and rest.* Then her stomach would stop twisting in on itself. All she scented was death, every gory bit of it smeared through the forest, assaulting every sense simultaneously. The air was putridly hot and rotted, like gases in a bloated corpse. And she was the worst of those assailers. She needed to bathe. Desperately. *Or bury me six feet under. No. Make it twelve, so I don't stink even more when I'm finally dead.*

"Celeste."

The sound was strident and grating, sharply ringing to her ears like steel pounding steel. *Go away.* Her body was seized stiff, like rigor mortis, though she knew it couldn't have possibly set in so quickly. Maybe paralysis. Then she wondered, perhaps hopefully, if she had been lying for hours as another of the dead, a sorrowful casualty of battle. She was already a corpse, she figured, she strongly reeked of one, so she may as well be buried right here and now. She wanted to tell that to whoever yelled in her ears.

Twelve feet, remember.

But as she was dragged into that churning sea of blackness again, a strong grip hauled her up from the thrashing current. The worse-than-pain exploded throughout her body again, a shock of agony, crushing the air from her lungs, every molecule of her being white-hot and scorching. She couldn't see who lifted her corpse-weight to her floppy noodle-strong limbs, her vision was seared to uselessness, but whoever it was became her only anchor to the waking world. Something pricked her skin, another flare of worse-than-pain torching every nerve along the way. Course, stiff. Like a patch of dead grass crisping brown under the sun. But her extremities tingled with warmth. *Home.* She knew it was her wolf that brushed up against her fingers. She could breathe again, and expelled a bloody mucus from her lungs. Her entire body shook as violently as a sapling in a windstorm.

"Almost there."

She spat and blew out the dirt clogging her nostrils. Or was it blood? She drew a slow, deep breath. She stumbled, awkward and heavy-gaited on bloody and bruised feet that were cold, unfeeling slabs of ice. Her eyes opened only slightly, nearly swollen shut, but she discerned a hazy silhouette against her, painfully propping her on feet that wouldn't quite properly work.

"I'm sorry," she muttered, "for everything, for all of this pain."

A bitter silence, with only her dragging footfalls echoing sharply through the trees. Her wolf whined, his snout wrenching the air for any alarming scents, and brushed against her leg as if to reassure them both of each other's presence.

"I'm sorry, Clark," she said again. He stiffened at the faint sound of her sobbing, and replied, if a little coldly, "It's fine." The wolf whined again.

But it wasn't. Not to her. "I dragged you all into this, I nearly buried us all for a vendetta that my father gave his life to shield me from. I...I killed so many people, Clark, so many that I've now forgotten how sick it used to make me"—her feet slipped and tangled through the undergrowth, and Clark had to shoulder most of her weight to keep her from dragging them both down the slight incline—"how their faces, their *eyes*, would linger in my mind like so many ghosts. Now there's nothing, there's"—tears splashed hotly against the blood dried to her cheeks—"only a cold abscess where my heart once was. I lost who I am, who my father raised me to be. I hurt people, inadvertently and with malice, and I've torn apart the only love I've ever known with my deceit. I treated you as a pawn, Clark, but you've proven to be a more valuable piece on the board than I ever was. I'm sorry."

"I told you at the fire," he whispered, "I thought being a soldier for Red Dawn would make me a badass. But I watched an actual badass save us from the jaws of death more than once. We wouldn't be alive without you. Stop"—he shook his head angrily at her protest—"being selfish, Commander. Not every problem in the world belongs to you. Blackwell had to be exposed. I thought...hell, I don't know what I thought, really. I just ate Blackwell's shit with a grin, and believed we were fighting against the sickness. Liberating the world."

"I ruined your life."

"You've done some shitty things," he admitted. "We all have. The bad you've done will never outweigh the good. And the good will never outweigh the bad. As our commander, you have to find a balance. You've earned my respect, even if we never began as friends."

She struggled to find the right thing to say, but the sentiment died in her throat. It felt *wrong*. But she caught the faint slip of a shadow play across his face; he was grinning at her.

"Besides," he said, "I'd rather be on the winning side."

Breathless, and consumed with raw anguish, they both dissolved into a fit of inexplicable laughter. She leaned into him, more for comfort now than support, and reached out for his hand. Hers was slick and dripping with blood, and his were bruised and burned with binding marks, as rough as sun-worn leather, but their fingers interlocked and tightly squeezed. Aurous nuzzled her thigh, a whine dying in his throat. She made certain to scratch behind his ears.

It took a few moments to gather themselves from the giddying laughter, and for a brief time, Celeste gave no thought to the ghosts that sat, ever hungry, on the edges of her mind. She was with pack.

While feeling crept through her extremities and unstiffened her limbs, she lacked dexterity for controlled movement, so she hobbled along with Clark shouldering her like a crutch, and her wolf at her side. Clark had the pallor of a corpse, profusely sweaty, and stubble length hair on both his chin and head stained scarlet like a redhead. Still, there was a fierce determination that shone in his eyes, a flicker of strength she cursed herself for not recognizing before. As they stumbled along the path their pack had traversed, Aurous breathing in their scent, Clark briefed her of the aftermath.

Their battle with Lust had been egregiously one-sided. Whatever she had done to disable him, it worked, and Odine was able to drag Snyder to safety. Her wolf took the behemoth's eyes—she swore she glimpsed Aurous wink at her—and held him back while Clark grabbed her. It was thanks to her, he commended, that Snyder was still alive, for the moment. Distaste formed in her mouth. She didn't share his high regard. The bandits had faced all fears and not only returned to the battle, but offered aid to those who had been trying to kill them only hours before. They whisked Bink away, who had suffered a shattered leg, and staunched the blood flow from Snyder's severed arm as well. They were, Celeste thought without a doubt, the out-and-out heroes. They were pack. The wolf had only withdrawn when they were far from his—and therefor Lust's—predatory sight, and while Clark remained confident it was a crippling blow, Celeste wasn't curious to discover if it was. She wanted as much distance between her and that behemoth as possible. Continents and oceans, preferably.

They were all waiting, as Clark explained, at the edge of a narrow clearing in the trees, and Celeste only glimpsed a flicker of movement slip in and out of the shadows by chance. They were expertly hidden, and utterly elusive, but a sharp whistle from Clark brought them trickling into view. Slowly at first, their eyes inexorably drawn to her, as if she was not who they were expecting to receive. Then they poured from the shadows like a wave, parting around her and the wolf, buzzing with palpable curiosity. Celeste tried not to count how dwindled their numbers were, but as she scanned the crowd, tears stubbornly clung to her lashes but lacked substance to fall. She was already severely dehydrated, and crying only leached her body of its most precious fuel. Her tongue was as shriveled and dry as a prune in the sun. There were so few of them remaining, and grotesquely scarred and malformed as some of their features were, they were as fresh-faced and young as she had been on the journey from her mountain home. And, alarmingly, even younger. With a pang that was almost crippling, she knew those deaths fell on her shoulders alone. Which was why she thought there was a creeping contempt to their collective voices as they whispered and chanted in a strange blend of chirps and twisting vowels. She gulped down icy breaths as Odine edged through the crowd with a grin on her blood-splattered face. She reached for Celeste's hand and drew her close, embracing her tightly.

"They call you Revenant," Odine whispered with a hint of amusement. Their round eyes flickered between fear and wonder. "The Undying." It was then Celeste noticed to eerie gleam of scarlet from her fingers, hands, and forearms; she was splashed head-to-toe in blood. It was fitting, she thought, that she *looked* as well as *felt* like a walking corpse, and that no one could see her blush through the macabre face paint. Nadie was the next to force her way past the circling crowd, and her round eyes shone with elation at the sight of her. She threw her arms around Celeste like she was the only lifeline in the violent currents of grief, and held tight enough to restrict her of air. She didn't care. She sank into the warmth, and her own tears flicked from her fluttering eyelashes. Grief welled up between them both.

"I was so worried," Nadie choked out. "Bink is okay, and Snyder is...breathing. I thought..."

"I'm okay." Celeste held her gaze, heart bursting for her friend. "I'm sorry."

"I hate to interrupt this welcoming party." Aza's husky voice slithered from the shadows. "But time is a commodity we can no longer afford."

Celeste eyed her warily. The former Watcher stalked the edges of the crowd with fluid catlike movements, with Uriel shadowing her every turn. Darkness radiated from Aza's gaze like night devouring the last light of day, and she gauged her possible quarry with the threatening interest of a snake. There was a shimmer of interest in the back of Uriel's eyes, a sharp contrast to Aza's. Recognition? Admiration? Perhaps. But their scent was still *wrong* to her nose. Aurous shared her sentiment; a threatening growl shook her wolf's jaws. They weren't pack. But Aza was right, they had to move.

Celeste saw they were about 100 yards below a ridge, a steep incline of windswept trees, with the only path a thin ribbon of trampled wood winding upwards to where the earth was far too rocky for many trees to take root. After carrying upwards, it hooked out of sight, to where the aircraft had been spotted, and, according to recon, a small and heavily armed unit of soldiers. It may have been a fifteen-minute climb on her own, a little longer with her team, but it would take considerable effort and time to move the injured and incapacitated. They would have to strike hard, and fast.

And that's exactly what they did.

The soldiers were in view clear of any trees, their rifles drawn to their searching beams of light. Shadows shifted and flickered, chased like prey through the few stocky trees, a taunting challenge from Death itself. They flanked the large aircraft that, even from a distance, dominated the trees like it had the sky as it had over the battlefield like a vulture circling carrion. Celeste knew from her own grueling training how prepared and drilled for every contingency they would be. They'd chosen the highest vantage point, spreading out in a wide circle like a slowly radiating shockwave. Any fool vaulting over the ridge would soak up bullets like a sponge. Any attempted ambush would be target practice to their ubiquitous aim. They were prepared for any counterattack.

Except a wolf.

A shadow seemed to move suddenly from between the trees. It caught a soldier's eye a moment too late. The wolf was on him with wrenching jaws, and *snapped* his neck before the fear of death could register in his brain. When the wolf struck again, the next soldier attempted to bring his rifle between him and those viciously sharp incisors as a defense, and his scream sounded like an alarm—then gurgled softly through a punctured throat. Flashlights flicked to the direction the sound, briefly illuminating an obsidian fanged nightmare and the glint of crimson. Haunting yellow eyes shone like streaks of morning light. In a blur of black and gleaming red, he was gone.

It happened in that split-second of confusion, those few hazy moments as the brain processes shock. Celeste and her team, like a starving pack of wolves, stalked and cornered their quarry from the shadows—then confronted them in force. It brought no pleasure to viciously cut their throats, and steam the air with the sultry-sweet scent of blood. It was wasted meat. As fear of the wild hunt dawned on their prey, and they fought back with rifles nervously drawn and thundering, the wolves ran fangs through flesh, rending meat from bone and abandoning their kill for the frenzy of another. When it was over, in a few shocking seconds, the dirt was muddy red with blood. The few who managed to escape their jaws were run down by her wolf. One soldier had tossed his rifle, sprawling in the dirt as if he'd been killed—but he couldn't conceal his beating heart. The wolf sniffed out his pulsing blood, and he died pleading for mercy with his life spurting hotly through those wrenching jaws. It was done. They were all dead.

"They'll hunt us for this," Clark said, and stared after the burning silhouette of the church. "All of them."

Celeste reached out to one of the young bandits, no older than fifteen and drenched in blood that wasn't her own, and hauled her up into the aircraft doorway. She handled her forcefully yet gently, strapping her into a harness that was at least triple the young girl's body size. It would have to do for now, their options were severely limited. They crammed into the aircraft shoulder-to-shoulder, with little room to maneuver, and it gave Celeste the grim certainty of a mass grave. They'd simply saved someone the trouble of piling the bodies themselves. As the engines roared and jetted black smoke, and the blades rapidly chopped the air with the sound of thunder, the aircraft violently jarred and rattled as if the metal hull was ripping apart before it even managed to properly lift from the ground. Celeste gritted her teeth, narrowing her eyes to the church that shone scarlet like some distant beacon in the darkness. She knew it was razed and burning to the ground.

Melina...are you safe?

"They can try and hunt us," Celeste growled, "but prey doesn't give chase to wolves."

Clark struggled to grin through the heavy contusions to his face. It gave him the appearance of a Grim Reaper. "That's the last of us, Commander," he said with a weary exhale of air. Exhaustion cracked his voice. "We're set for takeoff."

Sparks suddenly spat across the reinforced window, and she recoiled slightly, a streaking mark in the glass where her reflection's forehead was. Dead center between the eyes. Pinpoints sparked across the glass again, this time a few inches to her left—close enough to the open door that sparks singed the young girl strapped into the last harness. Celeste growled, turning on her heels, but Clark drew his rifle and took determined aim from the door. He didn't even flinch when a shot rang out from the shadows, bursting into sparks across the metal hull. Another few inches and it would have hit his heart. With a slight twitch of the rifle, he discharged a single shot and exhaled sharply, as if he'd been bating his breath. Even at close range, the sound was nothing more than a distant *pop* under the heavy roar of chopping blades. There was a glinting spray of crimson, and a humanly form that dissolved into the waning shadows of the night.

"Commander?" Clark started as she departed the aircraft with a cold-burning fury. The winds were howling from above like the onslaught of a storm, whipping rocks and dirt outwards in rippling clouds. Her fingers raked the cold steel of a fallen pistol.

"I have to finish this, once and for all," she growled. "For my family."

Clark hesitated. "Time is running out. You know that."

"If I'm not back in ten minutes, Nadie is to lift off and get the hell out of here."

"Commander—"

Her eyes narrowed dangerously. "That's an order, Clark."

"Ten minutes." The corners of his mouth ticked. "Commander."

She nodded slowly, and as chopping winds beat down on her, and thin tendrils of scarlet light wormed across the eastern skyline, she resolved to finish the hunt.

She set off after her uncle.

THIRTY
Sic Semper Tyrannis

LOSS WAS like an old wound, drained of vital fluids and necrosing. Incapable of healing properly. Infected by despair. Celeste knew that better than any.

Morning came. Scarlet stabbed through the sky in glistening streaks like rivers running red with blood, and shadows grudgingly gave way and ebbed between the few trees rooting to the rocky slope. The chill of a cold wind carried acrid smoke into the air, and with it, the tangy fragrance of death. The ground lurched forward with the terrible sound of extended thunder, a heavy rumble of hunger from deep within the earth's belly, and violently tossed around like a roiling ocean of dirt.

She stood at the crest of the path and, over the turbulent earth, was absolutely still. Her fingers traced the fine webwork of grooves engraved along the pistol's mercurial-silver metal. A ceremonious engraving, a symbolism of authority, more ornate than for sheer stopping power. Six rounds in the magazine. The barrel was as stubby and thick as two of her extended fingers, but shone with a meticulously polished gleam. The words *si vis pacem* ran the length of one side of the barrel, as if penned by an elegant hand, and *para bellum* alongside the opposite. She grimaced. It had been *his*. She could almost feel the swell of his pride and cold ghostly grip that shadowed her own around the pistol. Finger flicking over the trigger, she stared down the sheen of silver from the barrel and drew aim on an amorphous silhouette taking form between the trees.

"You're a traitor to the cause." His voice cracked weakly, shuddering with every sharp inhale. "Worse, to your family."

She steeled her heart. "My mother and brother were killed at the hands of Red Dawn. My father died to protect me from the world *you* helped destroy, Uncle."

"You are just like him, so goddamn"—blood spurted hotly from his hip and steamed the air—"stubborn and thick-headed, viewing the world as black and white instead of segments of grey like it truly is. Red Dawn didn't kill you mother, Celeste, or your brother. They were sick, I've seen their files. Don't be so naïve."

"You're a lying piece of *shit*." She took a single pace toward him. "Blackwell groomed you as his successor, he was to be your only family. Mengele wanted my mother and brother, and me as well. My father stood in their way. I know all of this, Uncle, because Father told me what Mengele did, and I have seen it myself. *You* already know the sickness is weaponized, not controlled. Or do you not have clearance to access Hellpit?" Another step. "Don't be so naïve."

"Do you hear yourself? How crazy you sound?"

"Enlighten me."

He staggered backwards into tree, smearing crimson handprints across the peeling white bark. She sought his eyes, and when she found them, they were piercing and unwarm, sterilized of all familiarity. Blood flecked the sharply-defined features of his face—none of it his—and smeared the obsidian-black armor strapped to his midsection in broad clawed strokes. She had to wonder with creeping amusement if Aurous had recognized his scent well enough to consider him the pack's ally. Or perhaps it held similarity to her own.

"Your father—*my* brother—was paranoid, delusional, and utterly destroyed when your mother and brother fell victim to this sickness." He hunched forward, stemming the blood flow from his hip. "There was nothing we could do to save them, and he blamed us for that. We tried, Celeste, believe me when I say that. I was there. When we couldn't save them, we knew we could still learn from them, and possibly save others—such as *yourself*—from fully succumbing to the sickness. Your father refused to believe they were untreatable and violently freed them from quarantine. To stop the sickness from infecting others, Blackwell had to try and stop him.”

She kept her aim on him, teeth gritted, and muttered, “That’s Blackwell’s narrative.”

“No,” he said, sighing. “That’s mine. We gave him a chance to help others, but he had to blame someone, he had to direct his anger somewhere. That’s what he did, you know, he lashed out at everyone and everything, destroying anything in his path. That’s why your mother left him before the world fell. She would have, again, if she didn’t pass away. He was a thorn in our asses, Celeste. I gave him every opportunity to make a difference, and he chose to fight those he blamed for killing his family. Not the sickness. Us. He torched our bases and killed brave men and women who fought to keep this world in order. That was what he truly was. A marauder, a bandit, a murderer.”

Her pace faltered as the ground shook and smoke belched over the prismatically burning church grounds behind Uncle’s back. “You’re lying,” she whispered meekly. “My father told me the truth.”

“Your father told *his* truth,” Uncle persisted, tapping his heart through the blood-splattered armor. “And he wrote it in this journal as if to justify his actions against me. Every goddam detail of his treachery. He’s not the hero.” His eyes glittered menacingly. “But you’ve managed to fill those mighty big shoes of his, huh? Passed along his treacherous blood. You fell prey to those bandits, exactly the way he did. You’re *just* like him, directing your anger at everyone and everything in your path.”

“Mengele is a monster, you have to see that,” she pleaded with her grip tightening around the cold steel. “You have to see he’s mutating the sickness and creating living bioweapons.”

There was a flash of antipathy in his eyes, a glimmer of his former morality. Then shadows flourished once more. “He’s necessary,” he admitted. “He has a complex understanding of the sickness, and is able to control outbreaks with utmost precision. We need him, as he needs our resources to work for a cure. We’ve made progress, Celeste.” Those shadows burned blacker. “You *were* living proof of that.”

Hesitation iced her reflexes. She had glimpsed the slight tremble of his muscles tightening, his fist unclenching from the wound on his hip. Even as he drew and took aim, her finger remained achingly still over the trigger. Seconds dragged by. They stood suspended in time, their eyes frantically searching the other’s for any semblance of accord between them, any thread of connection past the thinly veiled familial bond. She found nothing—only the blinding flash of a discharging gun.

A loud, splitting *crack* shook the tree, inches from her skull, and bark splintered and whipped against her face. The second shot rang out immediately after, renting the air as it passed by her head. Instincts raged. She dove for the dirt, robbing her lungs of air when she landed, and shouldered into a roll. Except it was more of an ungraceful glissade down the roiling mound of dirt and windswept trees, like her wolf clawing for balance on a frozen pond. Rock tumbled loose, sweeping her down the slope.

Zing!

Another bullet ripped by her, striking the dirt where she had been a moment before.

Zing!

With her long-bounding stride gaining on him, Uncle abandoned his aim and staggered into the shadows of the waning night. He slipped from her field of vision, but her senses were electrified and buzzing excitedly. She followed the intangible trail of salty-hot through the towering pine. Her heart raced in a feverish rhythm she knew all too well. The hunt was on.

"I gave you every opportunity"—his disembodied voice rang out as sharply as the bullet that followed his grating words—"just like your bandit father"—splintered bark pelted her from above like hail— "and you pissed it all away for some filthy savages"—the glinting black of his barrel caught her eye as she weaved between two trees no wider than her forearms—"just like your father!"—the tree she slammed her back against shook from the bullet's impact.

She inhaled slowly with the pistol drawn to her thundering heart. "My father trusted you to know right from wrong. And even when you chose Red Dawn over blood, he never hated you. He disagreed with your path, certainly, but he spoke as if he never would have hurt you."

"He never would have had the chance!" he snarled back, but his voice cracked and wavered. "Blackwell fought to liberate this land, and those bandits want to burn anything they can't have for themselves! That's who your father chose!"

"They're just people," Celeste said with an ache in her heart, "trying to survive like us."

"Is that why they wanted your head?" he hissed. "Survival? Were the men and women they slaughtered pertinent for their continued existence?"

She was smothered by an ugly pause. Vega's tendrils of influence slithered in the back of her mind, probing her thoughts for any weaknesses to exploit. *You should have taken my sister's head to their feet*, the ghost of a thought purred. *They'll never allow you to rule for letting a prisoner kill her.*

She steeled her heart and her mind. *I'm not going to rule them. I'm going to fight* with *them.*

"You never sent a team to kill Theta," Celeste whispered back, tears clinging to her lashes. "You sent innocent people to her as tribute."

"To save your life!" His sudden emotional outburst stunned her to another grueling silence. "Blackwell needed that intel on the church. This decade-long war has dwindled our hold on the land and drained our resources. He was trying to build from the ground up while waging a battle on all fronts. With the church gathering power, a deal was struck with the bandit leader, some bitch they called Theta. I did *not* know of the deal to hand you over. I never would have stood for my own *niece*"—she heard the slight tremble to his voice as he said that word—"in the clutches of those savages. They wanted to parade your head around on a pike. If Blackwell gave them you, then we could seize control of the Titans. With"—his voice shuddered between words as he inhaled sharply—"his untimely demise at your hands, I found out his plans for you...I sent fifty men and women into the Exclusion Zone under the pretense of recognizance. Yes, it was like leading sheep into the wolf den. I hate that I did it, Celeste, but I did it for my family. Like I betrayed Blackwell all those years ago to secure your father's life as he fled Red Dawn.

"Theta refused to divulge any intel unless she got her hands on you. Fifty. She took fifty and it *still* wasn't enough blood for payment. That is how much you were worth—to Blackwell *and* Theta. I couldn't hand you over to die, Niece, not ever. But I could give you a fighting chance. I'm positive by now you've figured out you're being tracked."

Celeste clenched her jaw as if rending meat from bone. "I knew immediately." A pasty face she could barely recall haunted her thoughts, his tremulous voice begging her to release the delicate nurse Annie. She wanted to kill him, too. "Your surgeon is a goddamn butcher."

He scoffed loudly, dramatically, masking the faint *clicks* of his discharging magazine. "I knew your father instilled a brutal will to survive in you," he said slowly, breathlessly. He was losing blood. A lot of it. His clumsy footfalls through the smattering of windblown debris were a wailing siren to her ears. "There was little doubt you would secure, indirectly, Theta's location—I thought you would have carved her throat as deep as you did Blackwell's. We nearly descended on her camp when, once again, you were on the move, escaping death by the skin of your teeth. And you led us straight to the Titan and what Mengele and I will use to liberate this world from undeath—just as Blackwell envisioned!"

Splinters ripped from the tree she was leaning against, and a spray of bullets blazed past her head. She hurled forward, a sharp jolt of pain in her shoulder, as if someone had delivered a solid blow to her back. Another round was rapidly fired into the trees and pelted bark like winter hail. She spun on her heels, pistol drawn— and let off two bone-rattling shots in rapid succession that missed his neck by inches. She cursed and tilted her aim as his rifle rose to meet hers. His mouth twisted and formed words she couldn't hear over the deafening drum of her own heartbeat. She didn't care. The wolf in her lunged for the kill. She squeezed the trigger once, twice—white-hot light erupted from his rifle—the third shot grazed his shoulder. Something impacted with her chest at the same moment, with enough pounding force to slam her back against the rocky earth. Uncle flinched, his aim faltered, and his rifle fired a rapid burst skywards. He stumbled behind the cover of a bullet-peppered tree.

Celeste gaped, breathless, and clutched at her chest with swelling panic. Smoldering bullet fragments singed her fingers. Spiderwebbed grooves patterned the scaled armor like broken glass. As her bruising lungs struggled for air, she clambered to her feet. Her pistol shook in an unsteady grip.

"I never intended for you to die, Niece," he huffed, nearly grunting the words out. "Never. I still don't. I'm giving you one last chance to put your weapon down and surrender, face the charges, and find some peace within yourself. We have the Titan. A transmission for a cure and a deterrent of war. Mengele is trying to fix this world, Niece. Like he fixed you."

I'm his pet project, she snarled silently, but only sputtered and retched blood into the dirt. *His pet.*

"Think carefully," he warned, "because that vest won't protect against another bullet."

She sucked in a slip of icy air, drove the pain as far into the back of her mind as she could, and took a single step forward—pistol lowered to her hip.

"A fool may give a wise man council," she said slowly. "And you're no fool, Uncle. If I'm wrong, if you think my father was wrong, you can kill me now. Letting me bleed out in the snow would have made your life simple. Come on"—the pistol dangled loosely from her fingertips—"and finish what Red Dawn started."

Anger flashed through his eyes when he revealed himself, rifle drawn to her, death glinting from the barrel. His finger twitched and jammed against the trigger.

Empty.

Her grip snapped back around the pistol. She stabbed it forward, and a rocking blast thundered through her flesh. Uncle fell back with a sharp yelp, blood fanned the trees with a fine mist and spilled from a thin rivulet across his neck, just above his shoulder. Another inch and it would have nicked his carotid artery and robbed his brain of essential vital fluids within seconds. Stunned, he pressed his fingers tight against the graze, and blood bubbled through his fingers.

Vega's phantom thoughts probed her mind with vicious precision. *No mercy. Eliminate any potential threat.* Howling strong under the spell of a moonlit night, the wolf in her scented the blood of dying prey and urged her to finish the hunt. *No better than me,* Caden's voice slithered to the forefront. *Always kill ya problems, right, girlie?* Desiccated flesh peeled from bone, the skull beneath chattering its teeth without voice, the front of the throat clenched tight against the back of the spine by a thick band of tangled rope. Only the eyes retained any life, but the pupils were pinpoints and rolled so far upwards as to nearly vanish behind the orbital bones. *Little Wolf.*

Survive, came the strongest voice, and chased the shadows that lingered in her mind. *And don't look back.*

I need you, Father. Tears clung to her lashes.

Uncle kicked his legs like the involuntary movements of dying prey, and fumbled to reload his rifle with one hand. His eyes were wide, but unfearful, his lips thinned and pursed as he bit back his contempt. He would die with dignity; it was written plainly on his stoic features. He expected a bullet between the eyes. Just like Vega. As her shadow fell over him, she wondered if he stared up and saw her father's fury burning in her eyes. She hoped so. The pistol trembled in her hand.

"You used me to get your intel," she said through clenched teeth. "And I led you here to spark a war that would end the reign of tyrants. Deacon, however, outsmarted us all. Lured to the Venus flytrap with the promise of shit. You feel the ground moving, Uncle? The earth doesn't tremble beneath the might of Red Dawn. The Titan is attempting to launch."

"My men have taken control of the church. We'll shut it down."

She shook her head. "It won't launch. It's been sabotaged and set to detonate in the hanger. You're too late." She almost smiled despite herself. "Maybe we all are."

"You're lying."

"I'm not," she said. "And I'm not the enemy, Uncle. Mengele is. He's creating an army behind your back, not a cure, and he intends to reshape this world with his own twisted vision. I should know because I am *not* cured." Her grip on the pistol tightened, and the steel crumpled like an aluminum can in her fist.

Shock rounded his eyes. "What—!"

"I don't even know what I am anymore." Shattered pieces of metal fell between her fingers like a fistful of sand. "But I know Mengele is not human. He's something *more*. Maybe he always was. He's parasitical, and spreading. He needs to be stopped. Red Dawn needs to be stopped."

She leaned over him, and he recoiled from her as if she were a snarling beast that snapped her jaws at him. To him, perhaps, she now was. She ripped the armored vest open like a piece of Velcro. His heart pounded with feverish speed she heard it bashing his ribcage to mush. She found it tucked into his jacket, stitched into the lining. Her father's crimson-laced journal. She thumbed the yellowing pages, and cursed her father's absence with a softness to her voice.

"Get your people out of here," she pleaded. "Live. If you see the truth someday, and I know you will, Uncle, then you'll be able to send word for me." She paused for a moment, then turned on her heels. "My mother's gravesite."

He yelled at her back, "I gave you everything! Just like your father! I loved you, Celeste, we're family!"

"My family is waiting for me," she said.

She never looked back.

***

Within the wispy tendrils of clouds, Dead Wood was black ink spilling over a green canvas of land. Vast mountains that once stabbed into the horizon now appeared flat against the surface of the earth. Barren riverbeds snaked through the black terrain, dried up lakes dotted the half-dead forest like so many impact craters. Valleys carved so deep into the scorch that life blossomed in glinting emerald, ensconced by walls of craggy rock and untamed forest. It was like staring at a richly detailed map. Celeste had never seen from such heights before. Often, she wondered if this was the view from the highest mountain peak.

She was mesmerized by the prismatic brilliance of morning light that rushed through the grey skies and chased the gloom to the corners and crevices of the world. Apprehension bubbled in her chest and tingled her throat. A calm before the storm, she knew. This land would soon be as scarred as she was.

She caught her reflection in the bubbled glass of the cockpit. Crimson sheened from her skin like a fresh wound, her eyes sunken and dark like an exposed skull. Scars appeared to churn and pulse, slithering across half her body. She blinked, quickly, and the shadows waned and withered from her skin. A trick of the eye, perhaps. But her scars were unwarming even under the glowing-hot sunrise.

Celeste was ripped from her mental fog by the jarring forward pitch of the helicopter. The rotors whined, the blades chopped heavily and beat against the whipping air. Nadie cursed loudly, seated to Celeste's left, and steadied the cyclic bar against her knee. Her grip on it was shaky at best, and the rotors reacted to every fine movement of it. Sweat beaded her oak-brown skin. She was unnerved, jaw clenched, her eyes rounded and unblinking with intense focus. But there was a light to them that hadn't shone for weeks. She combed over the instrument panel and bank of blinking switches, her fingers sinuously flicking through a rapid sequence of them. This was her element. Engineer by trade, a tinkerer of toys. She craved mental stimulation, and since their team was apprehended in the sewers below Fort Thompson, she'd had little to contain her flitting focus. Only trauma that necrosed and slowly bled, refusing to scar. Her mind had nothing to tinker with but itself. Nadie Dunn, brimming with intellect and ebullience, had become withdrawn and scornful.

"I've been thinking about that thing in your neck," Nadie repeated. It was difficult to be heard through the thunder of chopping blades and roaring rotors. "Maybe we can salvage the tech, make use of it somehow." Doubt shadowed her eyes. "Or at least destroy it."

Celeste bit her lip until blood soured her tongue. She glanced back over her shoulder, and her heart swelled with tingling warmth. Bink was as blood-drenched and battered as she was, and his face grimaced with intense pain from a shattered leg. But the corners of his mouth twitched into a smile, tongue jabbed, and eyes narrowed. A young girl across from him mirrored the twisting facial expression, giggling like the child she should have been. The girl stopped. She drew a blade with a cracking wooden handle, and for a heart-thrashing moment, Celeste almost snarled at the threat—but even her wolf lolled his tongue at the girl, yipped excitedly, and then lowered his head back to the floor as the helicopter pitched forward again. He would never want to fly again. The young girl flashed the knife's blade across her palm and smeared her tanned skin scarlet. Reaching forward, she took his lacerated hand in hers and cradled gently, their blood meandering as a stream down her arm. Bink smiled and shook her hand. Clark refused to sit, and edged through the crowded carrier to hand out what little provisions had been stocked for emergencies. A few sealed bottles of water, enough to wet their tongues, and thick bricks of chocolate flavored energy bars that neither looked nor tasted like chocolate. He crumbled a piece for Odine, who ate without betraying a hint of its desert-dry taste. Snyder's stump of an arm was heavily bandaged on her lap, soaked in blood and pus, and her eyes clenched shut and still rapidly darting back and forth in excruciating, unconscious pain.

"Commander?" asked Nadie.

"Salvage it," Celeste ordered, unsure if she even should. Was that her call to make? *No more tyrants.* "And that sonic device," she said, exhaling sharply. "Find out how it works and replicate it."

Nadie caught her reflection in the bubbled glass of the cockpit, and her eyes glittered knowingly. "Okay, boss."

Celeste shifted. "I'm sorry about Twist. I should have done something sooner."

An ugly silence brewed. Nadie's jawline tensed. Tears welled in her caramel-colored eyes.

"Did anyone ever tell you about those scars on his head?" she asked in a soft voice barely audible over the roaring rotors.

"No." But she recalled in vivid detail the webbed pattern of white scars across the back of his head, as if his skull had been shattered like glass and glued back together with crudely shaped pieces. There was a pang in her heart that wouldn't dull.

"He was part of the retaliation force against the occupied Fort Thompson," she said with a crackling voice. "He liberated the hospital, where Red Dawn soldiers were being held prisoner. He got them all out. Including Stonem. They were nearly to the gates when the mortars hit. Twist was a willing shield." Tears fell from her unblinking eyes. "He saved them all. Every one of them. And how did they repay his valiant effort?" Anger shimmered beneath those tears. "When his body recovered but his mind didn't, he was tossed into Joke Unit with the losers and misfits who had no other place in Red Dawn. He deserved better than to be forgotten."

"He won't be forgotten," Celeste whispered. The words choked her. "I have seen cowards die countless times in the face of fear. But a hero never dies. His name echoes with every beat of our hearts, and always will."

"He's a hero," she repeated, brimming pride. "He is Mahihkan."

Celeste smiled.

Then there was a rapid flashing light as the sky filled with a terrible sound like the atmosphere ripped away and hammered down into the earth's crust. The winds whipped and howled over the thundering rotors, which were now spinning uselessly against the gale. An immense fireball that dwarfed the luminosity of the sun flattened over the land behind the aircraft, and a churning column of smoke mushroomed and blotted out the southern horizon.

"Hold on!" Nadie yelled.

The helicopter pitched violently through the hammering shockwaves like a ship tossed on an ocean storm. The ground seemed to punch upwards into the sky. The helicopter spiraled.

Sirens screamed in warning. Lights flickered emphatically red.

Celeste braced for impact.

End of Book Two

ABOUT THE AUTHOR

Tyler Stewart lives in British Columbia, Canada, with his adoring wife, Omegga, and their two sons, Lachlan and Nico. When he isn't coming up with new ideas, he is either wrestling with his kids to eat dinner or running out of shelf space for his new books.

He writes the majority of his novels while sidelining as a medic, squeezing in sentences between Band-Aids and splints. As he pens the *Wild Hunt*'s conclusion, he's also producing the series for audiobook release.